For Catherine:
   Through the generosity
of your delightful daughter,
Julie. My first sale tonight.
   Nurses are the hope of
the world — All the world
loves a reader — especially
a family saga reader.
   Kindest personal regards,
Theodore Roosevelt Gardner ^··
      11/14/92

# THE PAPER

Allen A. Knoll, Publishers

# DYNASTY

THEODORE
ROOSEVELT
GARDNER II

This book was frankly inspired by a major newspaper and
the unique family that owns it. Some of the actions of the
characters were based on the actions of family members as
well as the members of unrelated press families, but the
story was cut from the whole cloth. So you might say everything in the book is fictitious except the City of Los Angeles
which, given the vagaries of nature, could become fictitious
at any moment.

Second printing  1992

Two gentlemen have, through the years, given generously of their considerable talent, time and advice, with a selflessness way beyond the milk of human kindness; my gratitude shall ever abound to:

Giulio Anfuso
and
Sidney Stebel

Since this book has been in progress about twelve years, it is difficult to remember the names of all who have contributed to it. Wherever they are, living or dead, they have my appreciation.

Here is a partial alphabetical list: Nancy Barnes, Jeanne Burns, Elaine Cappleman, Barbara Coe, Su Conahan, Abby Gardner, Julia Gardner, Melora Gardner, Nicole Kempler, Ann LaFarge, Sandra Lindsey, Jean Preston.

# Olin and Sutler
# Family Tree

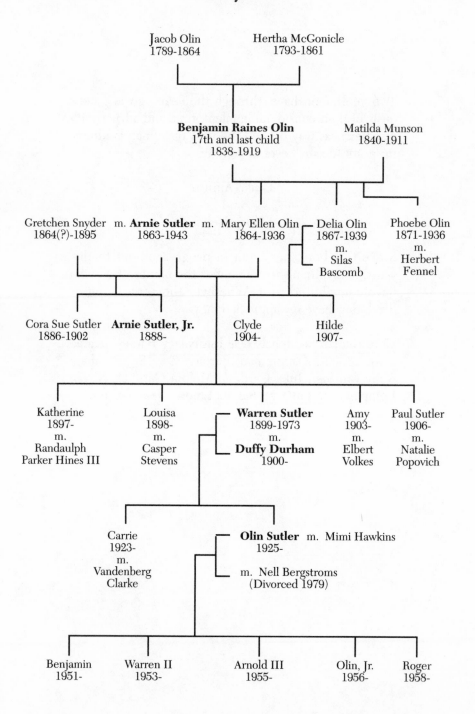

# CONTENTS

# THE PAPER DYNASTY

A history of idiocy highlighted
by a few morons who stand out
as comparative geniuses.

—William S. Burroughs
*The Adding Machine*
Selected Essays

# Prologue

In the beginning God created the heaven and the earth. Many thought His first real competition came when General Olin created Los Angeles.

Benjamin Raines Olin, publisher of the Los Angeles *Tribune*, was always willing to concede God the credit for the heaven and part of the earth, but he conceded to no one the credit for his city.

It wasn't until the final moments of his life that the shriveled shadow of the man lying in the darkened room made his first delirious concession: "Of course God took only seven days. I required longer."

—from the unpublished *Remembrances* of Mary Ellen Olin Sutler, destroyed by her surviving husband Arnie Sutler.

## 1980

Above the junction of the Hollywood and Pasadena freeways, a modest mountain stands guard over downtown Los Angeles. It is a benign lump on the breast of the angels.

On the hill are three reservoirs, a hospital, the Dodger Baseball Stadium, the Police Academy, Elysian Park, and Hilltop High School.

It is not generally known that the Hilltop High School football field was built over a graveyard, and conscientious as those responsible for the move were, a few of the bodies were left behind.

It was to that field that the black Cadillac limousine was headed when it turned off the freeway and made its way like a sleek and intrepid whale up the stream of asphalt.

It was the car you would picture driving up to the Pearly Gates in one of those jokes about God returning from a day on Earth playing newspaper publisher.

Below the hill curves a cement channel amusingly referred to on maps as the Los Angeles River. The mountain is one of many that surround the city trapping in the hydrocarbons that hang there like an off-color movie.

With the gathering traffic behind it, the crawling limousine heeled to the starboard and floated through wrought iron gates onto the grounds of the Hilltop High School.

There it passed among hefty sycamore trees bent with the cares of the day, but still clinging jealously to their yellowing leaves.

The Gothic school building was designed by an architect smitten with medieval cathedrals. The ornate concrete facade was white now, but it could turn gray or beige, depending on the angle of the sun.

A gym class engaged in a football scrimmage paused to watch the endless car go by. It drifted to a stop at the far end of the field, as though it had run out of gas. The bleachers behind the car were deserted today, brittle and gray like the parched bones of a skeleton.

When the back door finally opened, it ricocheted like the ball in one of those ball-to-wall sports. The dove-gray ten-gallon hat came out first. Then the tall, lean figure uncoiled like a relaxing snake and the tan, snaky, three-piece double knit suit followed. It was a wool and polyester blend that he had bought off the rack at some discount outlet, now bankrupt, and it hung on him like the loose flesh of the damned.

"It's a gunslinger," a tight-end chortled.

It was Yank Sutler, and he was no gunslinger. In his hand was a bouquet of daisies, a couple of yellow roses, some statice and baby's breath.

He looked like a praying mantis going about his business as he moved across the twenty-yard line. His steps were not those of a fullback or a wide receiver but more like one of those song-and-dance celebrities who had lent his name to a franchise to teach the unsuspecting the cha-cha-cha.

The kids were laughing at Yank, but he didn't hear them. He had a Lucite plug in each ear, but they only helped him to hear when he turned up the volume. Here his communication was going to be with the dead.

He looked through Coke bottle lenses at the grass, mottled with large brownish patches. The rain, too, had been spotty that season. The air was as dense as chicken gravy and almost the same color.

A third of the way across the field, Yank dropped to his knees and laid the flowers on the dead grass as if placing a blanket on a sleeping baby.

His knees felt the earth tremble from the scrimmages at the other end of the field.

The tears came as they always did, as though he were nothing more than a small rusty part of an automatic sprinkler system.

When he spoke his voice was hoarse, like a referee who had stopped too many fights. He bowed his head and closed his eyes, "It is for you I do this thing, dearest Theresa."

He was only halfway up when he felt the pounding. A young man with a football under his arm had materialized from nowhere to cut around him, while his pursuer took the straighter path. Yank raised his hand in a fist as if it were on a string, and then it dropped as though the string were cut. The pursuer knocked him to the ground to squash the blossoms on Theresa's grave.

Yank bent over and tried to revive the flowers, but they were beyond resurrection.

Sadly he made his way back across the field to the limousine. The strange old man reversed the process to get back in the car, the dove-gray ten-gallon hat disappearing last.

In the driver's seat Miss Henrietta Tober, chauffeur and secretary, eased the Caddy into a turn, and they crept out, retracing their path through the sycamores. A single reluctant leaf parted forever from its tree and fluttered to the ground.

Miss Tober's face was a topo map of time. She had seventy-some winters under her garter belt, seventy-some cold and lonely winters, and her face showed the forbearance of the ages.

She had done the old man's bidding even before he was old, but today the air in the car was thick with tension.

"You are nothing but a cantankerous old goat," she said, breaking the silence. Her pipes were Listerine cooled. She spoke loudly and distinctly through curled lips that showed teeth in want of orthodontia.

Yank was looking out the window at the blurring landscape; the *Tribune* was everywhere—piled on the top of trash cans set out for the semi-weekly pickup, covering the hole in a broken store window, wall-to-wall carpet in a pet shop window. A souvenir store was using it shredded to pack plaster madonnas, and across the street a fishmonger was employing the financial pages to wrap thin red snapper for a plump woman.

It had so many uses.

They entered downtown over a four-tiered freeway. The city was a tribute to the tenacity of the bulldozer.

They drove down Bunker Hill, and Yank could remember when he could see on horseback the top of the tallest building. Now so many of them were out of his sight, and they had sprung up like stalagmites in a big mouthed cave.

When Miss Tober could endure the slight of silence no longer she shouted, "You are making the biggest mistake of your life, you old fool."

His attention engaged, Yank said, "Right some wrongs."

"But you are ninety-two years old."

"I'm not so old I have forgotten my age, Miss Tober." He lapsed into a momentary silence, then added softly, "nor what they have done."

"But you are *family* Mr. Sutler. *Family!*"

"A matter of definition," he muttered. "The sacrifices: my mother, my sister and my sweetie. They gave their lives to the paper."

"It's too late," she said. "They are too big. Too powerful."

"She was the only sweetie I ever had," he grumbled, and the tears were beginning to roll again. "I never had another."

"Not because you couldn't have," she harumphed.

He did not respond. If she was still smarting from some past slight, he couldn't be bothered. Not today.

The big boat was docked at the curb in front of the concrete mass of the *Tribune* Building.

"I come to bury Olin Sutler," he said, "not to praise him."

"Well then," she sighed in resignation, "good luck. We're here."

He opened the door and hoisted himself out. He stood next to a ficus tree which was, like its fellows, surrounded with a four-foot iron fence to protect it from vandals. On the other side of him stood a row of iron maidens cemented into the sidewalk. Their jaws were clamped on their own newspapers as they were anywhere in town where a market existed for local and national news, for dating aids or the purveyance of prurience.

Yank stood shaking the sleep out of one leg, then the other, as if some nippy insects had nested in his pants.

He turned to face the fulsome facade of the concrete *Tribune* Building—a block-long, squat, suntanned fist clenched against the earth with its center tower a big finger rising to the heavens.

The front passenger window glided electronically down and Miss Tober leaned over to plead, "Come on, get in Mr. Sutler. Let's go home."

He had his back to her and was looking up to where he remembered seeing the bold Trajan lettering chiseled in stone:

## THE TRIBUNE

"It's just like a big tombstone, Miss Tober," he croaked, making his first concession to her. "All that's missing is the date of death." The sun beamed on his thick rimless spectacles, forcing his pale eyes shut. In a moment he braved them open.

"Let's put on today's date," he said. "Good as any."

The window slowly closed and the car glided reluctantly from its mooring.

The way he remembered it, the Eastern boarding-school boys called him "Yank," to make fun of the Texas hats he wore even then. He wanted to be called "Tex" so they called him "Yank," and the name stuck for over eighty years. That wasn't the real origin of the nickname, but that's the way he remembered it now.

The *Tribune's* lobby was austere white and mint green marble: a cold and empty rotunda that looked like one of those marble memorials to a dead president. Off to the side reposed a padded red desk of the early cocktail-lounge period. Yank could feel the pretty receptionist smiling when he gave her his name. She didn't believe there *was* an Arnie Sutler Junior. Well, tomorrow she would know.

He pushed the "6" button and rose in the formica box amid the whoosh of hydraulics over the presses that were never idle, printing the multi sections of the *Tribune* and its various editions, along with telephone books and even other newspapers. He rose past the advertising department, production, business affairs, public relations, city room, wire services, syndication, photography, editorial—right to the executive suite on the top floor.

His path was a richly carpeted corridor to two dark teakwood doors. Yank pushed open the door to a gaggle of people in the anteroom of the main auditorium.

He made out Nora Crown, a pleasant-looking short woman with a round open face and dark hair, eyes glistening with friendship, always looking ten or so years younger he thought, or was that his diminished eyesight? That was Duffy Durham Sutler with her. Duffy had been through so much, and the corners of her mouth still betrayed her discomfort.

There was a glare from beyond that made Nora and Duffy look, to Yank, like two madonnas by Botticelli. Undressed, he thought, they would look more Rubens.

They were his partners today.

Yank stood off to the side studying the four men in the gilt-framed oil portraits on the wall. Yank knew them all. He was the only living soul who did.

General Benjamin Raines Olin, in full military regalia, severe and austere with stone-gray sideburns and muttonchops and a drooping mustache, looked like a tuskless walrus. His face was a little too puffy for the artist to minimize, but his eyes were hard and unyielding. An amateurish oil by a man who worked as the town barber and dentist.

The General, as he wanted to be called, was the founder, and none of his successors—each for his own legitimate reason—could have started the dynasty and made such a success of the paper and of the dusty, sleepy cowtown on the western edge of nowhere. It was difficult to tell his age, for at forty he already looked sixty.

Next to the General was the portrait of Arnie Sutler, Yank's father, painted with rosy complexion and hearty eyes to give his face a high class hucksterish glow, but there was no mistaking the unforgiving eyes. Arnie sat for the painting twenty years after his marriage to the General's daughter, Mary Ellen Olin.

The oils were sparingly applied to the canvas by an artist who cut his rate to get the commission, with the assurance that he would get more work. He didn't.

Warren Sutler was next, painted under his mild protest that no one could possibly care to look at a portrait of him. A benign face, kind, friendly, fatherly, with full, generous lips that spoke only kindness. To Yank, he seemed out of place in this pool of barracudas. He would have successfully resisted the portrait and broken the tradition had it not been for his wife, Duffy, who insisted on it, saying she would have one done of herself at the same time. Warren was happy to hang them both together in this reception room, but after he died, their son, Olin, removed the portrait of his mother.

The oil portrait of Warren Sutler showed a surer hand. The artist's price was not quibbled with. The trouble was they didn't know art from Shinola and calling the portrait pedestrian would be charitable.

Olin Sutler, merging both families in his name and his features, sat for his portrait the day after his father made the dramatic announcement at a hasty press conference, passing the helm to his thirty-four-year-old son, Olin, whose response was "Gosh."

Olin fidgeted so impatiently that the artist had to finish the painting from a photograph. But it turned out to be the most artistic rendition of all the portraits. It was frame-filling impressionist work in broad strokes and vivid colors. Olin Sutler looked powerful, like an athlete who specialized in brute strength sports. His face was angular and distinctive, his hair blondish brown. He was the most glorious physical specimen in the family. Yet his face was strangely simple, naive almost, with a touch of his father's gentleness and his mother's tenacity.

It was said if you crossed the General, he would write scathing swipes about you in his paper and possibly hurt your business.

But if you crossed Yank's father, Arnie Sutler, you could pack your bags because you were through in town.

If you crossed Warren Sutler, he would write you a kind letter apologizing for causing you whatever discomfort had made you feel unkindly disposed to him.

If you crossed Olin Sutler, he wouldn't understand it.

Duffy had drifted from Nora to another group of stockholders, and Yank made his way to Nora's side.

"Hello Yank," she said, opening her face to welcome the whole outdoors.

"Is Duffy firm?" he asked Nora, looking after Duffy Sutler with sheep dog eyes.

Nora held up a hand. The fingers were crossed.

The tall teak doors opened and Olin Sutler came bounding in with his retinue of executives that the Eastern snobs said would have been bus drivers in New York. Olin had made a lot of changes. Minorities and ethnic groups abounded now, and, outside of the family, the old line WASPs were as scarce as conservative opinions on the *Tribune's* editorial pages. Nobody could argue the business was not successful. No, the dissidents' gripes went way back, and had nothing to do with the balance sheet.

The tailback was far ahead of his blockers, and he swept into the auditorium as though he were carrying the ball to the winning touchdown. Yank wondered why Olin looked so confident.

"How do you like the portraits?" Nora asked him.

"After the meeting we'll take them all down," he said, his liver-spotted hand sweeping across the staring faces.

She laughed and went into the auditorium.

Yank paused to turn his hearing aid to full volume. He looked at the portraits again:

Benjamin Raines Olin. Dead.

Arnie Sutler. Dead.

Warren Sutler. Dead.

This afternoon maybe Olin Sutler would wish he were dead.

Yank was alive.

He turned to the portrait of General Olin, resplendent with medals and gold epaulets, and saluted it.

"You may have started it, you old goat, but I'm going to end it." And he marched into the meeting.

# BOOK I

## THE POWER OF PERSUASION

# General Benjamin Raines Olin

# THE CREATOR

If the red slayer thinks
he slays,
    Or if the slain think he
is slain,
    They know not well
the subtle ways
    I keep, and pass, and
turn again.

—Ralph Waldo Emerson
*Brahma*

# 1

SITUATION

This newspaper will consider applicants for the position of printer's devil commencing February 18, 1852.

—Notice in the Martin, Ohio, *Gazette*

1852

In those days, if you had two hours and a half sometime and wanted to visit the old Olin place from the closest civilization, you needed a good horse, surefooted and fearless, because the terrain between the town and farm was mean and forbidding. It was not a trip anyone made without some compelling reason.

Legions had scoffed at this acreage, judging it too rough, harsh and uncertain, with a thin, reluctant topsoil that promised only heartbreaks. A wicked wind was drawn up through the hills and blew many less hardy hands to greener pastures.

Jacob Olin crossed the Ohio River with his new bride and built a two-story house of stone on a small rise, adding to it as the family grew until there were enough bedrooms so no one had more than four in a room, or more than two in a bed. The ponderous structure stood as a lonely bulwark against the unfriendly elements.

Too poor for slaves, Jacob and

Hertha Olin had children. Seventeen before the reproductive machinery wore out beyond repair. There were two daughters and four sons left at home to cope with surviving. The girls worked as the house slaves; the boys were the field-niggers.

Three of the squat, sturdy boys—Edgar, Clem and Jeremiah —stood huddled with their picks and shovels against the cold and against their youngest brother, Benjamin, fourteen, who stood on the other side of the obese oak stump, dancing about his crowbar like an impatient pole vaulter.

Planted as a referee between warring enemy factions was Jacob, their father, the dues he'd paid written all over his foreclosed, fur-rowed face. The reins of the horses were in his hands, the fat chain circling the stump attached to the yoke of the team.

The stump cut through the frozen ground like a truncated arm of the devil, reaching in defiance to God and the mustered Olin men. A hundred-odd years it forced its tentacles through the stubborn earth, and it was not yielding this long-fought position without a struggle.

The wicked wind stung their faces. It was the breath of the ice-demon that blew pitilessly through the band of men, chattering the teeth and slowing the blood.

The thick, hairy hooves of the horses slipped on the frozen ground. Benjamin Raines Olin, the youngest, shivered, his skin crawling in the below-zero cold. Angry steam billowed from his mouth and nostrils.

"Spring been a better time for this," he grunted. He moved in faster motions than his resigned brothers and his stolid father, want-ing to get the unpleasantness over with. "Softer ground."

Benjamin kicked his feet at the hard earth, as though he were one of the horses.

Like an old decaying woodcut, the bare skeleton trees veiled the distant hills. The low mounds did nothing to keep out the cold. The ground may have been frozen, Jacob said to his four helping sons, but it was soft potatoes compared to the rocky ground of northern Scotland.

Christmas had passed unnoticed here, and the days were still short—too short for the pleasure of Jacob Olin.

The three boys were working their picks and shovels, fighting the ground around the stump. Benjamin dropped his crowbar to inspect the chain. He thought his hands would fall off from the cold, and kept blowing warm air from deep in his gut through his mouth to warm his nose, extending his lower lip to funnel the scant warmth upward.

"You get away from there," his father had said when Benjamin moved in to inspect the chain on the stump. Couldn't he see the horses were pulling and it was dangerous?

His brothers grunted as one. Benjamin's lips twisted in disgust.

"You got it hooked on wrong...."

Benjamin's voice was gruff with a peculiar erudite edge. And there he was dancing around, like a hedgehog, his roundish head stuck high and his pointy chin sticking out ready to tell you your business, daring you to take a poke at it.

Benjamin was so different. He had a pious look about him and his movements were almost prissy. He was the most damnably opinionated kid Jacob ever had. From the time he was four years old, he would argue with you about things it took you your whole life to learn.

The sun was hiding behind the snowy, ashen hill and sinking faster than the stump was yielding. There was a fierce, deadly slap of reins to rumps, an obsession taking hold of Jacob. The horses gave a lurch, and the stump seemed to twitch for the first time. The thick chain slid to the top and then off, striking its revenge at Benjamin's chest and neck and chin, and slamming him back on the ground.

His dark red blood oozed from the gashes that looked like seams cut by a dull saw. His neck was red and throbbing; he gritted his teeth, clenched his fists, but couldn't get up.

When the brothers carried the gasping, bloody Benjamin into the house, Jacob could not forbear saying, "Next time listen to me, boy."

The pain drew Benjamin's lips taut as though cinched by a drawstring. Benjamin's face mingled pain and sneer. "I told you it was on wrong," he said.

Hertha Olin often wondered what it was all about. You had children to help with the work, and you sacrificed while they were young, banking on a better future. Then you had to work all the harder to take care of all the children you brought into the world—to see that they were all fed and clothed and nursed, and just when they started to be worth something, they left you. Where did it get you besides an indifferent grave? There had to be something wrong with a life that offered nothing to look forward to but the end of it.

She was used to performing all the leftover duties: the cook, cleaning woman, canner, childbearer. Now the commotion at the back door told her they wanted a nurse. It was going to interrupt her dinner preparations.

The boys came in carrying Benjamin, who was bleeding all over her clean pine plank floor. Hertha flushed with anger before she saw it was Benjamin who was down. Her movements quickened. She dropped her paring knife and the potato she was peeling. The girls around her, Abigail and Fiona, scattered squealing while the men carried Benjamin to the fire in the living room. Hertha gave the girls orders for hot water and soft cloths. "And papers," she yelled after them. "Get some papers to catch the blood."

Hertha told the menfolk to stand back, and she worked feverishly over her son, cleansing, probing, soothing.

The smell in the house was of bubble and squeak—the thinly sliced beef they had salted for the winter, fried with cabbage and potatoes—the body sweat of the men and the strong soap the women used to defeat the other odors.

And now you could smell the blood, the fear, the pain.

Hertha told the boys to leave the room. Jacob stood his ground. "I told him a hundred times, if I told him once, to stay away from the stump when the horses were pulling."

"I'm sure you did, Jacob," she said, her chalky lips barely moving.

"He doesn't listen. I hope this knocked some sense into him," he said, looking down at the suffering lump on the floor. "But I don't hold much stock in that."

"Leave us be, Jacob," she said.

He started to say something else, but went out smartly. There was no sense him telling her how her favorite was always gumming up the works. The stump was still in the ground and they had lost precious light playing nurse to him. He'd heard tell of an Eskimo tribe where the mother nursed at her breast the youngest son until he married. Jacob thought Hertha might like that.

Abigail and Fiona came in with the hot water basin and cloths and newspapers and Hertha silently nodded to them and they swooshed out of the room, quiet birds flapping their escape.

In the sparse living room Benjamin clenched his teeth to distract him from the pain as he spoke through them.

"That's it," he hissed. "I'm getting out of here."

His mother gasped, then fell to her knees beside him to wipe his chest with gentle loving strokes of the soft warm cloth. Swabbing the wounds, she watched the red blood crawl from his fought-out body into the darkening fibers of that bloody cloth. She quickly ascertained that the only thing broken was his passionate pride.

"I expect someday you will, Benjamin," she said, unfolding the papers the girls brought and laying them down around him.

"Now," he said.

"Now?"

"Tonight."

She sucked her breath, realizing only Benjamin could be so foolish as to say something so outrageous then hold to it.

Hertha tried to move her son to place newspaper under him to keep his blood off her clean floor, but Benjamin pushed her hand away.

"What are you doing?" his mother asked, her voice a cross caution.

"Haven't read these," he said.

"But there's a ton more of the same out back." There were unsold papers Jacob collected to insulate the underground barrels for winter food storage.

She saw Benjamin turn his head to the paper on the floor, his eyes slanting down to try to read sideways.

Hertha laid the cloths on his face, neck and chest and got up. "Here," she said, "press these tight." She left the room with heavy steps.

She returned with an unsullied copy and thrust it at him.

The paper cast a magical spell over him. He felt its mysterious power. The power of getting others to think like yourself, and those who don't, never argue back. It made his head light, as though it separated from his suffering body and floated on a cool breeze.

While he read the paper with a fanatical devotion, he came upon a small article.

### SITUATION

This newspaper will consider applicants for the position of printer's devil commencing February 18, 1852.

With care and no little pain, he tore the article out and put it in his pocket.

"Can you advance me a few dollars?" Benjamin asked his mother who stood over him with her fists on her hips.

"You know your father keeps the money. What little there is."

Benjamin eyed her with that steady accusative gaze. "I know you put a little away yourself."

She turned to gaze on his prostrate, torn body. "I'm saving that little bit for a rainy day."

"Well, it's pouring today," he said, his face twisting in anguish.

She offered him five dollars, he wanted ten, but she didn't have ten. Even as she was protesting, she knew she would give him anything she had, for she had often dreamed that Benjamin, like Moses, would one day lead them from this desolation; but here he was going off alone.

She would kiss goodbye forever the seven dollars and change she had put away over the years, realizing she would not live long enough to possess such a fortune again.

She looked down at her son who lay by the fire, and, rubbing her hands on the side of her dress, thought, "I will breathe easier with it gone." She had always dreaded the scene if Jacob ever found she had hoarded money.

Overcome with emotion, Hertha left to seek out Jacob in the kitchen, where he stood staring into space across the table worn with the thousands of meals she had put there. His hands were behind him, closer to the fire in the old wood-burning range. He didn't look at Hertha as she spoke, and she was grateful for it.

"Says he's leaving."

He nodded as though he expected it. After a few moments' reflection, Jacob went into the living room where Benjamin lay on the newspapers by the fire. He wanted to say something kind, something loving even. "Well, I suppose you'll be wantin' to hold back a day on your chores."

Benjamin looked up into the furrowed face. "I'm moving out."

"I forbid you to go," Jacob said, his tongue working his lips, searching for understanding.

"Then you better chain me to the floor because I'm going."

Jacob looked down at his seventeenth child. It took something out of you having that many children. At times it was reassuring that you could still bring people into the world, more hands to help out, but it wore thin. Benjamin was more stubborn than any mule he ever had. Jacob ran his hand over his bushy eyebrows and down over his aching lips. "You may try, Benjamin, but you'll fail. The way out of here is too rough. And, you are too headstrong to succeed at anything."

Back in the kitchen, he told his wife, "That one sure got a blowed up opinion of his self."

Hertha took the bubble and squeak off the fire and hoped her husband wouldn't see the tears in her eyes. She hadn't cried since the first time she laid eyes on the land Jacob had picked out for them to settle on, and she had waited then until after he slept that night. Now, as her Bible warned her, the ashes were turning to ashes, and the dust to dust.

She had no cause to trouble herself. Jacob didn't look that closely at her anymore.

In the living room by the fire, Benjamin clenched his teeth and his fists and tried to raise himsef up.

It was only one day before Benjamin raised himself from his newspaper bed on the floor. The pain was still there, but if he had stayed any longer Benjamin feared he might lose his resolve.

While Benjamin was packing the worn out satchel, threadbare and musty from a trip across ocean and land and long idle storage, Hertha went to her room where she took from the top drawer of the chest of drawers she shared with Jacob, the gold watch.

She looked longingly at it, ran her rough fingers over the filigree engraving of her father's initials and recalled the day when she left for the New World and her father had given it to her. It had been his prize possession, given to him on his marriage by his father. It was Hertha's *only* possession.

Her father had not wanted her to leave the security of Scotland for the unknown, but he realized he was powerless to prevent it. Hertha had married and her husband was going and that was that.

She had seen the tears in his eyes when she left him for the last time. And now all she had of him was that watch. The letter from her mother hinted that he had passed of a broken heart. It broke her heart—but there was little time here for self-pity, and the watch had always been her salvation.

She had always wanted Benjamin to have it. It was a beautiful piece of work and would have to belong to someone who would achieve other beautiful things to complement it. The watch was too lonesome with her, Hertha thought. Besides, Benjamin was the only beautiful thing in this house.

She asked her husband if she might not just accómpany Benjamin in the buggy, but Jacob said there was no time for such foolishness.

Jacob went outside to retackle the old oak stump and didn't look up to say goodbye to the boy. If Benjamin was going to be so pig-headed, there wasn't much he could do about it. He suspected the boy would come to his senses and return home.

The boys in the family said perfunctory goodbyes, not betraying their relief at being free of a burr in their socks, and the girls worked up some tears as though it were expected of them.

Hertha shooed them out so she could be alone with her son.

She saw at once his impatience to be on his way, to be free of her.

She did not want to detain him. Hastily she kissed him on the forehead, then took his hand in hers, laid the cold watch in it and closed his fingers over the gold timepiece.

Benjamin looked in his hand to see the watch he had always coveted. He quickly kissed his mother on her lined cheek. It was the first time he had willingly kissed her, and as the tears of joy welled in her eyes, his back was upon her.

She watched him until he was swallowed up by the ghostly trees, his soul merging with spirits of the bleak landscape.

# 2

## Printer's Devil Hired

Mr. J. J. McDonald will fill the post of printer's devil at the Martin *Gazette*. The vacancy was created by the death of Elbert Trinkle who served faithfully for 42 years. Mr. McDonald has experience in Memphis, Tennessee.

—Martin, Ohio, *Gazette*
February 27, 1852

Benjamin Raines Olin marched into town with a name bigger than he was, his scars barely scabbing, tightly clutching the newspaper job announcement of February 15.

But when he paused on the low hill and looked down at the river and the village of Martin, the thrill of his accomplishment pounded in his heart. He set down the carpet satchel containing his worldly goods and gazed at his future.

Ice crystals clung to the bare branches of the somber trees that were skeletons of their lush summer selves.

The air was biting cold, and there was light snow and a wind that bayed like a harmless old coyote. The navy blue cap his mother had knit for him was pulled down over his ears.

Benjamin took from the pocket of his maroon hunting jacket, handed down from a string of brothers too long to remember, the gold watch and popped open the cover. The thin, elegant, arrow-tipped hands pointed to black Roman numerals: it was III after VII in the morning. He had walked for seventeen hours, resting only five hours. He was five minutes ahead of his estimate. The watch had become a companion, and he took great pleasure and comfort in frequently feeling it in his pocket.

The town Benjamin saw was a one-horse town—a wide place in the road with a few store fronts and scattered houses. It was the kind of town you could go through without realizing you had. It was a supply depot for outlying farms, and it was said the weekly newspaper was published more to fill the needs of the publisher than the townspeople.

The *Gazette* gave the news of the church, the sewing circle, the Ohio River activity, along with a touch of gossip, and the excitement of a moored boat or runaway horse. It also offered reprints of articles from the city papers. Nearly everyone who could read English, got the *Gazette*.

Benjamin went right to the ramshackle wood edifice that shielded the *Gazette* from all but the harshest elements. He took off his navy blue wool hat and ran his hand through his pale sandy hair, patting it in place.

The doorknob on the unpainted door was the height of his neck. The simple sign on the door was over his head:

Martin *Gazette*
Henry Sawyer, Prop.

He opened the door as though storming the battlements.

Inside he was faced with a tall, loose-jawed man with azure eyes smiling down on him. The man was hunched over the counter that faced the door, leafing through the crisp gray pages of the big city papers, a pair of scissors in his hand.

In the center of the room, behind the lone man, stood an idle press surrounded by half-empty boxes and sundry trash. Underneath the press a cat lapped laconically at a saucer of milk.

Benjamin sucked a deep draught of the inky air and laid the article on the counter. The clipping was yellow-gray like an oyster too long in the sun.

"I want this job."

The azure eyes rolled over him. "Do, eh?" He paused studying the applicant. "A little on the young side, wouldn't you say?"

"No, sir, I'd say I was just right. It is a *starting* position, isn't it?"

The man spoke with the kindliest tone. "Your ma and pa hereabouts?" he asked.

"No, sir, I'm on my own."

"Mm. Long time?" The man's view was of the top of the straw-blond head and under it, fingers fumbling with the clipping.

"Well, ah—" Benjamin cleared his throat. "No, I'm just setting out. You hire me, sir, I'll promise you won't be sorry. I'm going to work hard and study hard and learn everything I can about newspapers. I will be the best newspaper man you ever saw."

The man smiled and scratched his head. "Boss'll be back in a minute. But I'm 'fraid he's already hired a man for the job."

Benjamin's face fell.

"But you can wait if you like—he's just down by the depot waiting on a part for ole Lizzy here," he threw his thumb over his shoulder at the press.

In a moment, Benjamin saw the man storming toward the shop, kicking up the dust with bitter feet. He was gaunt and brittle, his hair having long since taken flight with his youth. He pushed open the door like a team of dray horses. "Farley," he barked. "Those nitwits don't have it. They don't give a hoot in hell we got a paper to get out."

Farley made sympathetic noises, when suddenly Henry noticed Benjamin sitting in the chair by the door. "Who's the kid?" he asked Farley, jerking his head at the boy.

"Job seeker."

"It's filled," Henry said, waving his flat hand at the air in a stroke of dismissal.

Benjamin jumped as though he had been prodded with an ice pick. He looked square into the drifting eyes of the boss. "I will be better than that man you hired."

Henry shot a glare at the boy as though he had been struck from behind.

Benjamin's fists tightened at his side. He plunged on with the same recitation he had given Farley, but Henry cut him off mid-sentence.

"I don't hire children. The job is filled. Now get out."

"Excuse me, sir," Benjamin said politely without moving. Veins were standing out on the old man's bald head, and Benjamin was fascinated with their urgent pulsing. "I want to help you fix your machine."

"Agh." Henry Sawyer exploded, gave the dead press another

kick, turned on his heels and yelled, "Farley, I'm going to Henley's for a couple boilermakers, calm my nerves. If he's not out of here time I get back, he goes out on his back." And the door slammed behind him, jarring the frame of the wooden shanty.

Farley smiled. "Best not to rile him. He's known for his temper."

"I just offered to fix the machine." Benjamin conceded no ground.

"You reckon you can fix the main-shaft screw, cracked down the middle?"

Benjamin's eyes squinted at the fractured metal.

"I could fetch him another one. The stage isn't getting it."

"Cleveland's about eight to ten days roundtrip. You got a good horse?"

"Could get one."

"Time you get there, the screw'll be here. Now why don't you think 'bout goin' back home?"

"I'm not going home," Benjamin bristled.

Farley scratched his ear. "Heard tell Renny at the stables was lookin' for a hand."

Benjamin waved him off. "I'm going to be a newspaper man," he said.

"Maybe," he said, "but not here. Not so long's Joe Joe McDonald wants the job."

The light of curiosity lit in Benjamin's head. "Where can I find him?"

Farley laughed. "Kid, where'd you ever git that gumption?"

Benjamin thought a moment. "You ever  seen a spider workin'?" he asked.

"Reckon I have," Farley answered.

"I used to watch them on the farm. He goes up and down, up and down, over and across and you can't even see what he's doing, but he doesn't let anything stop him. He just keeps spinning that big old web that's gonna catch him food. A spider is smart and works hard. I'm like that spider."

The two-story alabaster-colored house with the green shutters, broad porch and slanty slate roof stood just back from the main street and far enough from the next house to seem aloof.

In the front yard, below the porch, the sign with white letters on plain board was anchored into the ground with a stake on both ends.

Mrs. Johanson
Boarders Taken

Benjamin knocked at the door. A stoutish woman with clouds of white hair opened it and grinned down at him. "I'd like to see Joe Joe McDonald, please."

"Mr. McDonald isn't in right now," she said, her mothering tones close to suffocating him.

"You wouldn't have a small room to spare would you?"

"Spare," she laughed. "A dollar-fifty a week with full board," she said, "then I'll spare it."

Benjamin swallowed as though clearing his throat of a bothersome burr. The sun was hiding in an unpromising sky. Benjamin rubbed his hands briskly in front of his chest. "You have any chores I could help with to earn that dollar and a half?"

The landlady's eyes smiled at him.

"Well, why don't you come in and we'll talk about it?"

She put him to work on the woodpile out back. There were three fallen trees that needed to be sawed into logs and split with the axe and wedge.

She figured a good day's work if he wasn't a dawdler.

He liked working alone out back, with no one telling him what to do every minute. In a smidgen under four hours he was back standing before Miz Johanson in the kitchen, making a concerted effort to tame his labored breathing.

She was peeling potatoes and looked at him briefly before she went back to watching the paring knife circumnavigate the potato.

"Well, you've been going at it pretty good, kid," she said.

"I'm finished."

"Oh," she raised the eyebrow of surprise. "Quitting, are you? Too hard a job, I suppose, for one so young."

"No, ma'am. I finished the job."

After Miz Johanson had given Benjamin a snack of fried ham, fried potatoes and fried scrapple, she looked at the engaging waif who was so doggone earnest about it all, and allowed as how she might use an extra hand around the place.

Benjamin rose the next morning with the crowing of the roosters, followed by Miz Johanson's poking around the woodpile next to the old horse shed out back. She was gathering the split logs to get the kitchen stove stoked up for the day. It was still pitch dark and there was an awful racket as Miz Johanson clumped into the house with her high-laced boots and threw the logs into the metal belly of the big black stove.

Benjamin sat fully dressed on the edge of his bed. The door was ajar and he was gazing intently at the door across the hall.

Suddenly he felt the whole house tremble on its foundations.

The door across the hall opened. Benjamin sunk into the bed, his mouth agape at the grizzly bear that filled the hall in the smudged coveralls and faded lumberman's flannel shirt. A prolific beard grower, Joe Joe McDonald could hold a shave at four to five hours, but now the dark stubble stood out like bare bramble bushes. He had eyes like a lumberjack who had squinted too long in the sun, a nose broken for some good cause now forgotten, and a Cheshire cat grin.

Benjamin watched Joe Joe unnoticed through the crack in his door as he went downstairs. In a moment Benjamin heard the slamming of the privy door out back, and a few minutes later the house shook again as Joe Joe returned upstairs with the iron basin of steaming water.

Benjamin watched the big bruiser shave with the long straight razor, then open his pants and splash some of the water on his crotch, then touching the water with his right hand, he pushed it through the top of his shirt and patted his left armpit. Removing his hand, he reversed the process.

Benjamin slid off the bed, eased open the door and followed Joe Joe silently down the stairs.

"Mornin' Miz J," Joe Joe sang a guttural song. He pulled up a bentwood chair and threw a beefy leg over it to sit, causing Benjamin to blink in wonderment that the chair didn't collapse.

Benjamin hung back a moment, his eyes taking in the table covered with a pile of flapjacks, syrup, butter, powdered sugar, jam. Miz Johanson was cooking up some ham at the black iron woodburning stove like his ma's. She looked like she was paddling a canoe, her thick, fleshy arms quivering at the task. Benjamin gently pulled the chair next to Joe Joe and slid up into the seat.

Joe Joe looked down at the grim lad. "What's this, Miz J?" he asked.

"New boarder. That's Benjamin."

Joe Joe broke into a wide grin. "Robbing the cradle, are we, me girl? Things come to a pretty pass."

"Small for his age," she allowed, ham fat sizzling all around her.

The muscles of Joe Joe's cheeks worked assiduously, to and fro, like he was secreting some potent fluids. "How old you be, Big Ben?"

"Almost sixteen," he gulped from a glass of milk to cover the lie.

"Was about your age myself when I started out in the world," Joe Joe said. "Course," he added, "I *told* everyone I was almost sixteen, too."

And with that, Joe Joe was off on his life story:

"... so what with the evils of strong spirits, a pestiferous woman and a heartless troop of creditors, I give Memphis my back, but not without I first put my John Hancock to some papers surrendering to usurious garnishee of my wages from the Martin *Gazette*. Well," he said, pushing the insignificant chair back with a protesting scraping sound, "I'm off to make my killing."

Benjamin's question was barely a murmur. "Mind if I tag along?"

"Come ahead," Joe Joe said. "I'd welcome the company."

But when they arrived outside the *Gazette*, Joe Joe said, "See you tonight, pal," and turned to go into the shop—to begin the job Benjamin thought was rightfully his.

# 3

Stupidity's a damn hard
habit to break.

—William Gaddis
*Carpenter's Gothic*

When the night was still dead and
black and the short arrow hand on the
round gold watch was creeping up on V,
Benjamin Olin tumbled out of bed, lit
the kerosene lantern, dressed in the
same heavy clothes he came to town in,
and headed out back for the privy and
the woodpile. Sometimes the snow was
so deep he had to clear a path with the
broad shovel that stood beside the
kitchen door.

Benjamin shoveled the ashes from
the kitchen stove and the parlor stove,
then built a fire in the kitchen (the parlor fire would not be laid and lit until
late afternoon). Then precisely at six-o-
five by his watch, as Joe Joe requested,
Benjamin took the basin of hot water to
the big man's room so Joe Joe could
splash the water on his armpits and
crotch before he got dressed.

By six-ten he was back downstairs
to help Miz Johanson set the table for
breakfast. He always knew, because he
always checked his watch.

After Joe Joe finished his breakfast with the three other men in the boarding house, Benjamin would draw himself up to self-importance, like a preacher in a pulpit about to relieve himself of a Sunday burden, and watch in front of him, announce the time and the number of minutes left before Joe Joe's departure.

Rain or shine, snow or hail, Benjamin was waiting. Joe Joe McDonald could not have had a more faithful dog. In time the snow melted, the street turned to slush, then mud, then the water percolated back underground and here and there a crocus shot up.

One day as the weather turned warm, Henry Sawyer went off to New York State to jaw with his wife's relations. While he was gone, Joe Joe offered to teach the lad the tricks of the trade.

Joe Joe was a good and patient teacher and he showed the boy how to melt the lead, then pour it in the molds for the type; how to read an article with the hen-scratching proof marks and set the type from it; how to lock the type in the big metal frame.

Then he learned to set the pages and hand crank the press, then remove and stack and fold the big paper sheets.

Benjamin begged Joe Joe to let him help when Sawyer returned, but the big grizzly frowned and said, "—He's a funny one, lad—I don't know…"

"The boy works like two men," Farley whispered to Joe Joe one day while Benjamin was working the press at a fevered pitch, "I was you, I'd keep a watch over my shoulder."

Joe Joe laughed, perishing the thought. "I'd trust him with my life."

Sawyer was in good spirits after his trip and said, "Why not? If the kid really doesn't expect wages it's no skin off my nose."

Benjamin lay awake in his small room with the brass bed and the gold watch on the table with the white china washbowl, his carpet valise in the closet and nothing else between him and slow disintegration except his wits. He had an idea, but he wasn't sure what to do with it. The spider was spinning to catch his dinner.

He kept hearing Joe Joe saying to him, "When a man has fifty-seven years behind him, fifty of them a working stiff, he's owed." Benjamin even heard it as he drifted off to sleep that night with the window open, no covers on the bed, perspiring like an overworked horse.

The next evening, after shutting down and cleaning the press, Benjamin sucked up his courage and said, "Joe Joe, we put in a good day's work."

"That we did, Ben."

"How do you like this heat?"

"Gettin' to me, me boy."

"And how would you take it if I offered to show my gratitude to you for teaching me your trade, by standing you to a cool tank of suds?" The boy's black innocent eyes were working; working like a spider.

"Oh, me lad," Joe Joe said, his tongue massaging his parched lips. "Many a day I've thought it would feel all right to sink me nose in some suds."

"Well, we're on then?" Benjamin had worked harder, but perspired less than his mentor.

"Well," Joe Joe said, his tongue making one more round of his dry lips. "So long as you promise absolutely not to let me have more than one. My last bout with the booze laid me low more'n a week."

Benjamin promised.

The heat of the day was a boon to Henley's Saloon trade. Ranchers and merchants bellied up to slake the thirsts of dusty pipes. The room was dark and cooler than the outside.

Jake, the bartender, was hunched over the darkwood varnished bar pretending to listen to a familiar gripe.

Behind Jake, the rows of booze bottles were lined up like glass soldiers. There was a large mirror that reflected them, on which was painted a chubby nude, reclining unnaturally. You had to be out with the cows a long time before you looked at her twice. On the walls were a half-dozen heads of moose and elk. The marbles the taxidermist substituted for the animals' eyes kept a glassy watch on the patrons.

Benjamin fought his way to the bar to buy Joe Joe's beer.

"Gonna down this one nice an' slow, Big Ben," Joe Joe said, taking his place at the bar and forcing Benjamin back to the gallery. "Been a long time."

Joe Joe held the fishbowl-sized schooner in both hands and took the first draught, head back, a stream of the dark amber disappearing under his foam-encrusted nose.

Joe Joe took another swallow, and when he set the fishbowl down, there were only a few fingers of the cool liquid left. Benjamin eyed him like a man trying to work a puzzle.

Two men stood up at a far corner table. Benjamin tugged Joe Joe's sleeve urgently. Joe Joe looked down, "What is it, Ben?"

"Table just opened up. Wanna go over and sit a spell? I'll bring your beer."

"Ah, it's almost done," Joe Joe said, his forehead wrenching unhappily.

"Ah, come on," Benjamin said like he was two feet taller and could look Joe Joe in the eye. "You deserve to rest your dogs." Then he added, "I'll bring the beer, go on an' get it before someone else does."

Joe Joe laid his wide flat hand on the towhead and rubbed it vigorously. "Okay, Ben, you're the host," and he lumbered over to the far corner where he saw the faces of the men leaving the table. It was too late to avoid them. He had been spotted by his boss.

Henry Sawyer was frowning. "What brings you in here, Joe Joe?" he said on seeing Joe Joe backing off. He did not introduce him to Stanley Munson, the flour and feed merchant at his side.

"Oh, hello, boss. Just stopped in to get out of the sunshine."

Henry nodded skeptically. "Thought you said you were off the sauce for good."

"Oh, ah, yes, well…" he sputtered, "I am." He raised his right hand, taking the oath. "Yes, sir, I learned my lesson."

"Well then, take my advice, this is no place to kick the habit. See you in the morning bright and early. We've got our hands full with that special farming edition."

Benjamin had stopped dead in his tracks when he saw the boss and the fancy man leaving, the schooner of beer held between both hands as though it were a sacred chalice. He slid behind a pair of ranchhands, his heart beating wildly. Not until Mr. Sawyer left the barroom did he surface to take his offering to the table where Joe Joe was just flopping into the round back-slatted chair.

Benjamin set the schooner down in front of him. If Joe Joe noticed it was full, he said nothing.

Joe Joe took a gargantuan swallow of suds, smacking his lips and thumping the schooner down on the small table between them. "I ain't touched a drop since I hit this dirty stinking little burg."

"Ah," Benjamin said, drawing himself up in his chair. "Don't pay them any mind. You're a grown man. I reckon you want a schooner now and again, you're entitled."

The big man looked down at his young companion and broke into a big grin.

"Entitled, eh?" He said working the word over on his tongue. "I like that, kid," he announced with a slap of his broad hand on the table, jiggling the schooner of beer to a tidal wave. "Entitled," he said again. "I'm entitled," and he hoisted the glass bowl and drained the beer, finally peering into the empty glass and then holding it upside down overhead, tilting back and opening his mouth to catch the last few drops.

They were silent when he set the empty glass carefully on the table, as though he were afraid of hurting it. He belched loudly and smiled happily.

"Who was that with the boss?" Benjamin asked, his lips puckered thoughtfully.

"That's Stanley Munson."

"Who's he?"

"Just about the richest man hereabouts, maybe in the entire state o' Ohio, all I know," Joe Joe said, looking forlorn at his empty glass.

"What's he doing with Mr. Sawyer?"

"A newspaperman always wants the rich on his side. A paper can make or break a lot of people—put the fear of God in 'em. But you watch, they'll be toadying to the rich right along, because a paper's got to have friends and advertisers—rich and important—or they be left standing alone sometimes."

"But what does the rich man want?"

"Maybe to elect some folk friendly to his business, maybe flattering talk of his wife, maybe a nice piece about his daughter when she gets hitched—it don't matter, it's the same with all papers—big or little."

"I'm going to have a paper someday," Benjamin said with such innocent sincerity that Joe Joe had to keep himself from laughing.

"That so?" he asked.

"Yep." Benjamin nodded, a man with an air of importance. "A big one."

Early in the evening you could still smell the kerosene in the lamps on the wall. As the evening wore on, the smell of beer took over, say by nine or ten, depending on the makeup of the crowd and the heat of the day.

Benjamin knit his brows, considering the next strand of his web, when Joe Joe, who had just downed two beers said, "Tis a pity on a hot day like this a man restricts himself to one beer."

Benjamin looked into his face and saw no argument.

When he put the third schooner in front of Joe Joe, Benjamin began calculating his investment and the probable return.

After the fourth, he asked if Joe Joe would prefer something a mite stronger, just for the sake of variety, and Joe Joe allowed as he might not take unkindly to a shot of whiskey.

Benjamin had the barkeep make it a double.

# 4

To the pure, all things
are pure.

—Morris Ernst

The sun had long since disappeared
over the western hills but the night
brought no relief from the exploding
heat in the half-lit saloon.

"What time's it gettin' to be?" a
sleepy Joe Joe asked the boy.

Benjamin took out the watch,
placed it in his hand atop the table, and
ceremoniously pressed the button to lift
the cover.

"Almost eleven-twenty, sir," he said.

"Hm, gettin' on to bedtime, I suppose."

"Probably hard to sleep in this heat,"
Benjamin said eagerly, eyeing the empty
glass before his insatiable friend.

Benjamin tightened his grip on the
watch as something hard seemed to
catch in his throat. All his money was
gone and Joe Joe was still on his feet.

"Maybe we should go home, Joe
Joe," he said.

"Naw," he said waving his sausage-
sized fingers, "you go on if you want—
I'm going to have another drink." A
thought seemed to enlighten Joe Joe.

"Would you stand me one more of these?"

Joe Joe wavered and his eyes closed for a moment while Benjamin's heart leaped to his throat. He was about to tell Joe Joe he was out of money—that he had nothing left to live on, and had no prospects to earn money—and he would die before he went back to the farm to face his father. Then, his hand closed on the gold watch.

"Wait just a minute," he said, "I'll see if I can raise some more money."

"Bless you, kid," Joe Joe said.

Benjamin fought his way to the bar like a salmon swimming upstream.

He brought out the watch and laid it on the bar.

The barkeep glanced at it, then trained his eyes on the boy.

"Will you lend me money on this?"

The barkeep smiled thinly and scratched his jaw. He took a deep breath, then scratched his ear. It was a striking watch.

"How much you figure on borrowing?"

Benjamin swallowed. "I thought—" Benjamin said, straining his body to see over the lip of the bar, "five dollars—"

The barkeep laughed. "Reckon I could buy a mighty nice new one for that."

"Nicer than this?"

"Hm—maybe not. Want to sell it?"

The keep had the watch in his hand, caressing, weighing and hoisting it to his ear to listen to it ticking.

"Sir—if I could just borrow two dollars on it—" It was an eerie stare the lad fixed on him.

The bartender wished there were something about the kid to make him think he was a child. A dimpled chin, a crooked smile, blinking eyes. Anything. But there was nothing. Made him damned uncomfortable.

The bartender reached in his pocket and spread two coins on the bar.

"One month from today. Two dollars and fifty cents—or the watch is mine." A spider crossed the bar between them. Benjamin's eyes were on it when the formidable thumb of the bartender bore down and squashed it.

"Wait a minute," Benjamin jumped. "I'm only getting two dollars."

"Ever hear of interest, kid?" he said. "You want the deal or not?"

"I want it," he said through the steely eyes "and take another double boilermaker out of it."

After the second boilermaker Benjamin got his first break when Joe Joe, in a moment of extreme mirth, leaned too far back on his chair and fell like an elephant shot through the heart.

Benjamin pulled the little brass gem from its loose moorings in his friend's pocket. As soon as the hand came out of the pocket the hefty Irishman was awake and sitting up before struggling to his feet, Benjamin clutching tightly the key in his fist.

No explanation was called for, just another drink, and Benjamin went to the bartender and asked if he couldn't water down a whiskey for half price.

The keep smiled down and obliged.

When he stood inside the dark printshop, Benjamin realized that while he'd kept to his task like the spinning insect, he had more to think about than which strand to connect next.

When he finished, he dropped Joe Joe's key on the floor. He stopped to survey the havoc he wreaked, and pondered the impression it would make. He caught a sob in his throat and tears stood at the corner of his eyes. He loved Joe Joe, but he wasn't going to starve.

He turned and walked out the back door, leaving it carefully ajar.

He made his way cautiously, hiding behind rain barrels and in the shadow of buildings anytime he heard a noise.

Benjamin lay awake all night waiting for the footsteps on the stairs that would tell him his friend Joe Joe had made it home.

The familiar friendly footsteps never came.

Benjamin walked slowly to the shop.

After hiding for ten minutes in the livery stable across the street, forcing small talk on the stablehand, Benjamin spotted Farley and Henry. After they went into the shop, he counted to sixty, putting one-thousand between each number, so he wouldn't rush, then went out into the sunny street and plunged his hands in his pockets and whistled a tune.

He drifted through the front door of the shop like a bird on the breeze of good fortune. He stopped short and dropped his jaw when he saw the shop. Papers were strewn across the floor, half a jug of ink was spilled, the melting lead was overturned and had hardened in a sky blue pool that looked like refrozen ice. Sawyer's desk was upended and all the contents of the drawers were strewn about, and something seemed wrong with the press.

Henry Sawyer was picking up Joe Joe's key and holding it up in front of his face, turning it back and forth as though he were solving the mystery.

"Somebody break in?" Benjamin asked, his face glowing with innocence.

Farley was on his knees gathering papers and he looked up at Benjamin with that contorted face that told him to be quiet.

Henry spoke with sagging shoulders and a dead, flat voice. "I knew I shouldn'ta hired him," he said. "One time this year we were going to do something special. I guess it wasn't meant to be."

"Aw, boss, don't worry," Benjamin said brightly. "We'll get this place cleaned up in no time."

Henry looked at Benjamin through long-jaded eyes. "Joe Joe won't be back," his voice dull as an old priest giving last rites to an unconscious drifter.

Benjamin gurgled. "Why not?"

"Just saw him sleeping it off outside Henley's, dead to the world." Mr. Sawyer held up the key. "Here's his key—went on another one of his binges. Had a history." Sawyer shook his head sadly.

Benjamin broke into tears. "It's my fault," he sobbed. "My fault."

"What?"

"I shouldn'ta left him alone. I shoulda stayed with him."

It had been so long he couldn't remember when, if ever, Henry Sawyer had felt paternal, but he did now and he put his long octopus arms around Benjamin and hugged him to his bosom, holding his head and rocking him gently.

Benjamin swallowed, startled, when Henry pressed the key in his hand and said, "Take it, the job's yours."

Benjamin pulled away and stood rigid, as though something had terrified him. "Oh no," he said. "Give him one more chance, please," he pleaded, his little eyes growing and growing.

"No chance," he said. "It's two dollars a week. Do you want it or not?"

The eyes suddenly narrowed; the shop went silent, suspicion stirred the air.

"You paid Joe Joe three dollars."

"Joe Joe," the boss said, "was an adult."

Benjamin's tears dried. He thought ruefully, I'm not the only spider in the crowd, and he joined Farley in setting the place right again.

Farley smiled, a knowing smile. "Good goin', kid," he said, full of admiration. "Very, very nicely done."

# 5

We must never look for
discretion in first love.

—Alexander Dumas
*The Three Musketeers*

1857

They met in the Martin Dry Goods
Store. Matilda Munson was buying
material for a dress, and Benjamin was
trying to find a replacement button for
his trousers. He was earnestly pushing
twenty years.

The buttons were in drawers on the
side wall along with the "hardware" section of needles and pins.

Behind Matilda Munson was a
table of thread, their colors splashing
from the refracted light that came in the
high window on the far wall, reminding
Benjamin of the rag rugs his mother
used to make.

Matilda Munson was just home
from Miss Phipp's Finishing School in
Cleveland. She had a fresh look about
her, clean with a crinkly new dress and
pert bonnet perched on her head like a
tipsy bird's nest.

Matilda was pale of face with here
and there a freckle, and a no-nonsense,
sturdy farm stock look about her, yet
giving a feeling of delicacy you would

expect from one who had been sheltered from the harsher realities. Her lips were generous and full of the old nick. She was a high-spirited filly that had been kept in the barn too long.

She had eyes that could not be fooled and they sparkled when she looked at him, like ice crystals on bare black branches.

She wasn't too tall for him like so many girls seemed to be. When he looked at her, it was straight into her eyes. When she looked back, excitement tickled his body.

She wore a long white dress with just a touch of lace around the hem and neck and sleeves, and she seemed so purposeful when she spoke to the clerk across the fabric-strewn table. There was no charming small talk, but she directly dispelled any illusions about who she was and what she wanted. She took up the cloth, said, "Charge it please," with the word "please" carrying no sense of a plea or request. It just hung there, a mechanical dividend of Miss Phipp's Finishing School.

Matilda had been aware of the serious young man in the store, poking in the buttons. Miss Phipp would have chastised him for keeping his derby hat on indoors, but Matilda saw it as non-conformity rather than ignorance. He seemed to be watching her. Perhaps she shouldn't leave the store so quickly. He looked like he needed time to acquire some nerve. She walked closer to him, the cloth in her arms, and seemed to intently inspect the display of thread.

There was an engaging earnestness about him. Something about the way he stood there in his straight-shooter suit, as though he were planted in the ground like a tree with a solid trunk, captured Matilda's fancy. Could he be a little nervous? Surely a lad as old as he was "experienced"? She pegged him at five years older than he was.

Everybody did.

The boy loved to shave, now that it was a necessity. It made him feel manly. He dreamed of silly girls planting moist kisses all over his bare face.

He thought the girls in the town to be rather silly—and he never found any common ground for conversation with them. But when he was alone he had all the girls in wild and outrageous fantasies.

His images of them undressed, passionately pursuing him, were anatomically inaccurate. He just didn't know where anything was.

To Matilda, Benjamin looked severe, like a young man who never laughed. He would have seemed an unlikely suitor in Cleveland, but here in Martin the pickings were slim. She would just have to be the one to get him to laugh. But why, she wondered, did *she* feel so nervous?

She knew her father, Stanley Munson, would not approve of this young man, but this time he couldn't stop her.

Benjamin had mustered his courage to say "Hello," when he heard the hollow-cheeked clerk approach and say, "May I help you with some thread, Miss Munson?"

Benjamin felt a lump the size of an opening oyster clog his throat. Miss *Munson!* Everybody knew they were the richest family for as many miles as anyone had ever been.

"No thank you," she said to the clerk, "I'm just looking."

When the clerk retreated, Matilda laid the bolt of cloth she had been clutching on the edge of the thread counter, balancing it against her body. Then, making a show of reaching to a far edge of the table for a spool of yellow thread, she moved her body so the bolt of fabric spilled to the floor.

Benjamin darted to the floor at Matilda's feet. "Allow me," he said. He gathered the goods in his arms, and stood up, his face red from exertion.

"Excuse me," Benjamin said out on the wooden walk in the shade of the porch roof. "I'm Benjamin Olin, I hope you do not think me presumptuous." He was trying to rewind the bolt but it was too much for him.

"Matilda Munson," she smiled, a smile so friendly Benjamin felt a vast relief wash his rigid body.

"Let me help you with that," she said, and they both took up the task of realigning the fabric.

They asked each other the obligatory questions, and she found him charmingly gruff. He would challenge her Miss Phipp's training.

When she mentioned "Miss Phipp's Finishing School," he asked:

"Did she finish you?"

Matilda laughed, tilting her head back. "I'll let you make that decision, Mr. Olin," she said with the cutest turn of her head.

Swept like a leaf on the brook, Benjamin suggested they meet again.

"I could visit my friend, Julie Eden," she said. "Then you could come and see me—if you wanted to."

Benjamin felt a choking in his throat. A young woman was paying attention to him—on a personal basis. A mighty desirable young woman, at that. And the strangest thing about it was she seemed to actually *like* him.

Matilda had not yet succeeded in making him laugh. But could that be a smile on his lips?

In a handful of years, Benjamin Olin had made his mark on Martin, Ohio, and it should have not been surprising that the two most important men in the area were discussing him with an eye to his future.

"It was good of you to come, Hank."

No one but Stanley Munson called Henry Sawyer "Hank." "Mr. Sawyer," or maybe "Henry"—but no further.

"It is a pleasure to be here," Sawyer answered, sitting on the edge of the plum velvet wing chair, hat in his hands between his knees.

The Munson place was a fearsome spread. The eye could not take it all in, nor, it was said, could the imagination. Stanley Munson was the only man Henry Sawyer knew who could intimidate him.

Sitting here in his study—larger than the entire *Gazette* Building—with stuffed antlered animal heads on the mahogany paneled walls and a glass case of guns in the corner, Henry caught the he-man drift.

Munson, the richest man in memory, had loaned Henry the money to start the unneeded paper. Henry had tried valiantly to pay him on time, but the money was just not in the enterprise. Munson was always extravagantly patient.

Munson never saw his name in the paper in an unfavorable light. No one questioned his profits at what some thought were obscene rates he charged the local farmers—Sawyer's primary subscribers.

Munson was a tough businessman. He could make or break a farmer—and while he made them some money, he made lots for himself.

"Hank," he said, pouring a brandy into a thin glass snifter from the thick cut glass decanter, "I need your advice." He sat behind his desk that was the size of a pool table.

Henry Sawyer nodded as any supplicant would to a deity who couched his commands in the terms of favors.

Stanley Munson's face was chiseled from the finest blemishless white Italian marble, and the sculptor was agile with his tools and the proportions were near perfect. If anything, he cut a tad too much off the nose, for it was narrow and razor sharp at the tip. His lips were thin and pale as icicles and they gave off a fraudulent air of *noblesse oblige*. He had a flair for making people uncomfortable under the guise of putting them at ease.

His eyes always seemed to be looking over your shoulder, even when you were alone with him.

He wore tails and pinstriped pants, broad foulards of the finest silk, but even naked you would take him for a man of substance. He would not be out of place in the U.S. Senate. A lot of people said so. In an earlier time Stanley Munson could have passed for a Caesar.

He sat back in his chair, lounging with one foot up on his desk, nodding to invite his visitor to do the same.

Henry Sawyer knew better.

"My daughter has been seeing your employee with annoying frequency," he said, lighting an odiferous cigar. "Now I don't want to be a dog in the manger or anything, but I would like to know your honest assessment of the boy—is he someone you would want your daughter to marry, Hank?"

Henry coughed, covered it with his hand and shifted his position in his soft velvet chair. Poor Henry Sawyer—even his mother called him "Henry." He was a poor-looking specimen next to Stanley Munson. A rough-hewn man, Henry was whittled from a knotty pine log. His face was a misshapen passel of warts, moles and scars, his chin heavily dimpled and the scant fringes of salt and pepper hair ringing his bald top were infested with dandruff.

"Some good qualities, he has," he began, taking a sip of the brandy to relax.

"Oh?" Munson raised an eyebrow.

"A hard worker—dogged in his determination to get what he wants."

Munson frowned. "Does he get what he wants?"

Sawyer considered. "Usually."

Sawyer set his brandy snifter on the pool table desk between them.

"I'll tell you the kind of boy he is. After work he goes to Pop Peters for lessons in business bookkeeping and that shorthand of Pitman's with the shaded and slanted lines. Then Sunday he goes over to Old Maud Williams who teaches him to write an intelligible English sentence."

"That's sacrilegious, working Sunday."

"Sure it is, but religion's nothing to Benjamin where his success is concerned. He's got a notebook full of big words he is at great pains to use in his articles. Everyday he memorizes a new one—and uses it on me. What was it today? Cacophony. Yesterday was cutaneous." Henry shook his head at the wonder of it all.

"How far do you expect he will go?" Munson seemed prepared to reconsider.

"That," Henry allowed, "is problematic. My own assessment is not very far."

"Why is that?"

"Personality. He has a dead-serious way about him. Not a lad you would want to share brandy and cigars with. He will work like a horse for you, but you can't take any pleasure in his company."

"Hm—I wonder what my daughter sees in him—" Munson mused almost inaudibly.

Henry Sawyer took another sip of his liquor.

"Good brandy, Stanley." Munson had asked him from the first to call him Stanley—but Henry was never comfortable with it.

"I don't like him," Munson snapped, "he's a snake in the grass."

Sawyer settled back in his chair, relaxed and relieved that Munson's purpose with him was not personally threatening. "I don't like him much either, it come to that," he allowed. "Not many as do. But then I'm not a girl and girls I'll never understand."

"Well dammit, I understand them," Munson said, jabbing fitfully the air with his smoldering rolled tobacco. "They are fickle, impressionable, strong-willed and contrary—and I've just begun. Here's what I want you to do."

So that was it—no more soft glove talk about needing advice. Now Henry Sawyer—the fearsome publisher of the Martin *Gazette*—sat quietly and took his instructions.

Benjamin was delighted with the news. Matilda was not. They were behind Renny's Blacksmith Barn, freshly painted red and immaculately kept, in contrast to the ramshackle *Gazette* Building across the street. Matilda's lips were painted as red as the barn. Her father strictly forbid her to wear face paint. That was one reason she wore it.

Matilda couldn't stop kissing Benjamin, transferring the red to his smooth, shaved face, making him look like the victim of some strange elliptical pox. She was making an innocent effort to get him to change his mind. He was trying to duck her assaults.

"You can't leave me, Benjamin." She held tightly to him.

"I'll be back, Matilda," he said, his countenance stern to her zealous pecks. "If I stay here I'll rot with the press before I'll get an opportunity like this. Sawyer said so himself."

"But Lexington is so *far!* I'll never see you again," she wailed.

"I'll write, Matilda. When I make my fortune I'll come for you. We'll get married."

She stopped kissing him and took a step back. Suddenly she dropped her head on his shoulder and cried.

"What's the matter, Matilda?"

"You haven't gone home in five years, and you won't come back here, either."

Benjamin clamped her head in his hands—one over each ear. He looked her right into those teary, soft eyes when he said, "That is a promise. You mean more to me than my family. How did your father say it? I was nothing but the runt in a litter of sheep."

"Oh," she shuddered, "I shouldn't have told you that."

And, she fell to kissing him again with determined, almost angry, pecks that cut off his response.

Benjamin resisted no more. Matilda could feel his excitement against her lower abdomen.

"Let's do it, Benjamin," she blew a hoarse husky whisper in his ear.

"Do what, Matilda?"

"Love, Benjamin," she gasped urgently, "love me...." The repressions of nice girls were losing their hold on her.

"Here? Now?—" His gentlemanly instincts were turning to mush. The demands on his body were magnetic, but his intellect held him back. A pregnant Matilda would end his career.

She coaxed him now with her supple body, fearing she had already waited too long. She had intended to give in, after a ladylike but irresolute refusal, of course. She just wanted to parcel her favors, naturally, to her maximum advantage.

But Benjamin's move to Lexington came on them so suddenly. Matilda feared she had only whetted his appetite and now another girl in Kentucky would reap the harvest.

As Matilda held onto her Benjamin for dear life, she sensed him pulling away from her like a whaling ship pulling out of port for the long hunt.

But somewhere below, almost midships, Matilda felt the stirrings of Benjamin's commitment.

# 6

All men are created
equal and are endowed by
their creator with certain
unalienable rights to life,
liberty and the pursuit of
happiness.

—Thomas Jefferson
Slaveholder and
President of the United States

1859

The buzz of newsroom activity during the day turned to a high-toned hum
just before the deadline at the Lexington *Herald*, then settled to a murmur as
the editorial staff called it a day.

Benjamin stood by the desk of the
man who had given him so many opportunities. A gruff and pompous man,
thick-set and tall with a gently hooked
nose, wire glasses and a thin cigarillo
never far from his lips.

"I wanted to talk to you about your
writing," Horace said looking at a sample
of it in his hands, resting on the desk.

"Yes, sir," Benjamin said brightly,
expecting high praise. He had worked
hard to make his writing stand out from
other reporters'.

"It's god awful."

Benjamin's face sank, and his heart
with it. He gulped down his pride.
"Why is that, sir?"

"Your stilted sentences never end.
You use pretentious words that even I
don't understand, and no one is going to

read a newspaper with a dictionary by his side. Your stuff reads like you sweat blood to write as obscurely as possible and then didn't quite succeed at it."

He looked down at the paper in his hands and began reading aloud.

"An agitated mare contracted a veritable Vesuvius of seasonal ailment and tumbled vehicular conveyer, Edwin Markley, and sent him caterwauling hind end over teacup over the precipice into the gorse bushes in the ravine just east of our fair burgh."

Bellweather drew a breath and looked atop his wire spectacles through an arched brow as the boy twisted his feet.

"The precise notions that infested the cerebellum of this quadruped into the above-mentioned quintessential ecstacies were not gainsayed.

"The landlord of this ruptured conveyance is Mr. Robert Cartwright, whose cart has gone wrong, and he is a local purveyor of protein and dissector of bovine creatures."

Bellweather looked inquiringly at Benjamin over the pool of light.

"I have taken the liberty to put it in more pedestrian prose." He handed Benjamin another paper from his desk.

> A runaway horse, belonging to Mr. Robert Cartwright, local butcher, plunged into the ravine east of town yesterday. Mr. Edwin Markley, the driver, was unhurt. The meat that was being delivered was also unaffected by the accident.

Benjamin sank into the chair beside the desk. The weight of his heart carried him there.

Horace Bellweather was amused but not sorry. He was never sorry to take the wind out of anyone's sails.

"What is it you want out of the newspaper business, kid?" Horace asked, "because if you want to be a writer, I'd look for another trade."

Benjamin sat up. "I want to be part of history," he said, loud enough for the old man to hear. "I want to go to the Republican Convention."

Bellweather chuckled and shook his head. "Maybe you will someday," he said without allowing in his tone any possibility.

"I want to be a publisher someday. I want to go to the Republican

Convention next year."

The old publisher leaned back in his chair. The newsroom was clear of the drones and darkness had settled in. A lone kerosene lamp was lit on Bellweather's cluttered desk and the dull pool of light spread to encompass the publisher's hands, which he lay one atop the other on the desk. Benjamin's hands were quietly twisting in his lap.

"You have a lot of drive, kid, push—but you're not going anywhere for one simple reason, because you don't believe in anything. A publisher is a man of strong convictions with a passion to bring others to his view." He leaned over, putting his arms and the lower half of his face in the light of the kerosene flame. "Now what do you believe in?"

Benjamin slept only fitfully that night. On his nightstand lay the familiar blue envelope with another letter from Matilda in her fine-lined hand. It was unopened. Benjamin just couldn't get his mind on Matilda.

He was up early, pacing the streets of Lexington. If it took a strong belief to get what he wanted, he would get a strong belief. It would not, he finally decided, be detrimental to have his strong beliefs coincide with those of the boss.

So it was when the orange acid ball was high in the sky and frying the back of his neck that he saw in the window of a shack on the main drag, the handbill:

$1500 to $1650!
For Negroes!!
The undersigned wishes to
purchase a large lot of Negroes
for the New Orleans market. I will pay
$1,500 to $1,650 for No. 1 young men,
and $100 to $1,000 for No. 1 young women.
In fact I will pay more for likely
N E G R O E S
than any other trader in Kentucky.

Benjamin wiped his brow with his handkerchief. The ground was hard and hot under his feet. He looked across the street at the Broadway Hotel and the little office next to it where the same poster stood in the window. Working both sides of the street, he thought.

Benjamin had vacillated on the question of slavery. If they'd had slaves on his father's farm, the children might not have been treated like slaves. So he was for it. But they couldn't afford slaves, so he was against it.

He realized the economic system of the southern United States was dependent on slavery and would collapse without it, and so he was for it, but he also realized there was an effective argument that slavery was inhuman, against God's law and against the Declaration of Independence and that stirring phrase written by the old slaveholder, Thomas Jefferson, about all men being created equal. And so he was against it. Sort of.

He took a piece of Mott's candy from his pocket, unwrapped it and put it in his mouth, chewing it carefully. Absently he crumpled the wrapper in his hand.

He wondered how it would feel being a slave.

He knew the argument: slaves were well treated, they were too expensive to mistreat. Why, it would be just like buying an expensive piano and then beating it with a chain. But the Negroes were primitives. They couldn't ever hope for a better life in Africa, and they weren't intelligent enough to function on their own here.

As he was about to drop the candy wrapper on the ground, his instinct to read everything caused him to glance at the printing on the wrapper.

> If slavery comes by color, which God gave, fashion may change, and you become the slave.

Benjamin tilted his head to the sky, oblivious to the burning sun. It was as though the heavens had opened up and the pathway to the stars were under his feet.

He ran as fast as his stumpy legs would carry him back to his desk at the *Herald*, where he reached for a sheath of papers on the neat pile on his desk, took up his quill pen, dipped it in the inkwell and set the tip of the pen on the paper.

He began writing in white heat without laying the pen down until he had finished.

He sat back, let the air that had been pent up with his emotions escape, then slumped in the chair.

"You want strong beliefs," he said to himself, "I'll give you strong beliefs."

Then he picked up the papers and read what he had written.

You are born with a certain skin color, in a far-off continent. You are content with your simple life, you know no other. One day you are descended on, perhaps by a brother with your skin pigment, chained and carted to a huge ship, rocking on an ocean you have probably never seen and instinctively fear.

You are packed away in a sink-hole in the hold of the ship, in total darkness, with nothing but your fears and nightmares and a sea of terrified strangers, who you can't see, for company.

If you are fortunate to be on a ship that subscribes to loose packing of bodies, you will have several inches on all sides of your pallet and you might even be able to sit up without bumping your head on the pallet above. If you are tightly packed instead, you will not be so fortunate. You won't be able to sit up. There will only be one side of you not touching your fellow prisoners, until enough of them die and are thrown overboard, because it is the philosophy of the tight packers that a higher percentage may die in passage when they are tightly packed, and many more arrive disabled, but economically it is sound as the profit is higher because you land with more breathing bodies. The loose packers may be no more humane, but their calculations tell them the return on the investment is greater with the higher survival rate. The real question is how tightly do you pack for optimum profit?

Your sink-hole smells of vomit, disease, body wastes, rancid food, decaying bodies, and after thirty days or so you feel the terrifying rocking motion of your dark hell stop. You are one of the unlucky ones. You have survived.

You are unloaded in chains on a land totally unfamiliar. The people are speaking a peculiar language, the weather is strange, you see structures you have never seen, even the foliage is unfamiliar.

In time you are put up for sale. They look at your teeth, poke your body like you were a horse. If you are a woman you will suffer other indignities which we cannot print in this family paper, but which you can imagine if you remember, gentle women readers, that now you are a slave and strange men are your masters, and their main interest in you is your ability to give birth to as many baby slaves as is humanly possible, to perpetuate the institution for hundreds of years. You can't understand what they are saying, but you can tell by the expressions on their repulsive faces and their lascivious laughter, what is on their minds.

Depending on who buys you, you are put to work, and fed and housed and treated like a favored dog or like a stubborn mule. Of course your own character may affect how you are treated, but you don't speak your master's language or understand it, so you aren't always sure how to please. If you are a young woman you may be paid a personal visit by your master or overseer, usually at night, during which he will attempt to show you how to please him. You may not like it, but the message will be clear.

You will pair off, have children and likely become attached to them. But the economic realities being paramount, your husband or wife and/or children will be sold off to other masters and you will be alone again. Or you may choose the way of the woman written on these pages several weeks ago who on hearing she was to be separated from her baby by one of these sales, threw, instead, her baby down a well and jumped in after him. The master seeing the great financial loss, good money, so to speak, going down the well, organized a rescue party to foil the slave's plans. But that was nothing new. Slaves were never allowed to have plans, dreams, desires. You have no right to your family or loved ones. You have no rights. You can't go anywhere, you can't choose where you live, what you eat, friends, job—nothing. You have become a non-person. You have become an animal.

We all know the arguments for slavery. Economic survival for the South, a better life for the slaves than they had where they came from, forget that they are not given the choice of returning on the offchance that they don't agree.

Have you imagined yourself the slave? The above scene was played out in Lexington, Kentucky, United States of America. Local farmers were captured and taken to Africa, an underdeveloped country that could profit by slave labor. The slaves were white, the masters black.

It couldn't happen, you say? It happened to them. In any event, you would be well advised to keep your backs to the wall, never walk alone, and always look over your shoulder. You never know for certain who might be coming for your mother and father, your sweetheart, or just

You.

Benjamin wanted to run to Horace Bellweather with his piece, but he had sudden doubts, and decided it was safer just to lay it on the copy reader's desk and let it wend its way through the regular channels.

The impact was like an earthquake.

Bellweather stood grinning at the lad at his desk. He waved the sheet of scrawled papers at him. "May have misjudged you, kid," he smiled, his teeth yellowed from all the smoke. "You keep this up, we might make a reporter out of you yet."

After the opus ran, Emerson King, the portly Republican County Chairman, came storming into the *Herald* newsroom waving the folded paper. He appeared agitated and breathless, his face flushed.

"Benjamin Raines Olin," he shouted. "Where is Benjamin Raines Olin?"

Benjamin stood up and moved cautiously across the floor. "I'm Benjamin," he said, fear gripping his stomach. This was the last man he wanted to offend if he was to entertain any hope of going to the Republican Convention.

"Benjamin," he shouted, as though the lad were still on the other side of the noisy room. But now a hush came over the reporters, copy boy and editor at this awesome presence. "This is the best damn thing I ever read. I'm sending a copy to Bill Seward. He should be very pleased."

The huge man turned his broad back and vanished like a star at sunrise.

That afternoon a letter went out:

My Dear Mr. Munson:

Mr. Olin has performed his duties for the Lexington <u>Herald</u> admirably, and I am gratified to inform you that effective the first of next month we will be pleased to begin paying his salary, and I remain.

Yours sincerely,

H. Bellweather

# 7

The responsibility of tolerance lies with those who have the wider vision.

—George Eliot
*The Mill on the Floss*

Phil and Dave Brogger didn't see anything wonderful about Benjamin Olin's article in the *Herald*. They sat at a battered greenish kitchen table in their shack that was bigger but little better than the slave quarters. Their place was just over the rise to the south in a spot where the sun never left them alone.

The poor boys were not as dumb as they looked. That would have been difficult.

One of their drinking buddies at the Tough Times Saloon just off the main drag said the Brogger brothers looked like a pair of shovels...but only when they had their shoes on.

They may have looked like identical twins but they were almost eleven months apart.

Their slaves were fatter than they and had more time to shave. The Broggers attended to their personal hygiene every so often, but always a few days late.

It wasn't easy being the boss. The

slaves did the physical work so they got more food. Besides, that greasy stuff didn't set so good on the Broggers' stomachs no more.

The Brogger boys were scratchers. The only way you could tell them apart was by where they scratched. Dave, the older, scratched his left cheek with his left hand. Phil scratched his crotch, with either hand. And, sometimes both.

They were scratching now like a couple of flea-ridden dogs—scratching and thinking.

"Can't let him get 'way with it," Dave said.

"Can't," Phil agreed, nodding heartily.

The Broggers weren't so stupid they didn't recognize dangerous talk when they heard it. When the talk started they sat down and figured it out and there was just no possible way for them to free the slaves they had this big investment in and pay wages to work the tabaccy.

"We'd never come out ahead," Dave said.

"Couldn't," Phil agreed.

"I mean we work like slaves oursel's." Dave scratched his jaw, "We try'n do right by our families and we got only six lousy slaves."

"Only six." Phil nodded, scratching his crotch in mindless abandon.

They had high hopes when they threw the rock through the window at the *Herald*, but that nigger-lover, Bellweather, didn't cotton. He just put in a new pane and shot off his mouth bigger than before.

There was nothing for it but to fetch the blunderbusses and the rags and the kerosene, two sledgehammers and the long-bladed knife and set out for town.

On the way they gathered those who they knew shared their feelings, and by the time they reached the Lexington *Herald* they had gathered twenty-seven like-minded troops, not overwhelming perhaps, but a respectable mob. They tied their horses and congregated across the street from the lonely *Herald*. In restless foot-shuffling silence they stared at the window and the newly painted gold letters.

Well, there was a score to settle and that's why they were there.

He had blown out the kerosene lamp when he heard them coming. He sat at his desk, looking across the street at their sledgehammers, their pickaxes, their shovels even. Benjamin wondered why a few of them carried shovels. Was it to bury the dead?

They seemed a restless lot, this mob, and yet strangely

becalmed in their torch-lit tableau, like some Roman frieze celebrating agriculture and war by intermingling farmers with their shovels and warriors with their weapons.

Benjamin sat stoically at his desk. He opened the center drawer and carefully took out the derringer and laid it on the desk, closing the drawer quietly as though the mob might hear him.

Looking at the body of malcontents outside, he calculated his chance of prevailing at about one in five hundred.

And yet when he found out from an informant from an outlying saloon that they were coming, he never gave it a second thought, but collected his supplies: the thick black axle grease; the derringer; and the bear traps, those lethal jaw-like horrors with the sharp, pointed teeth.

The Brogger boys were out in front and Dave was yelling something to the mob. His back was to Benjamin, and all that appeared was a pole of a man in a hunting jacket and cap with a sledgehammer over his shoulder, the blunt steel squared head a strange geometry next to Dave's squarish skull.

He thought of Elijah Lovejoy martyred trying to save his press from the mob in Illinois, falling and dying by the same mob who resented his abolitionist views. In a nervous hand, Benjamin scrawled:

Elijah Lovejoy

on the foolscap on his desk. He looked up to see the army cross the street.

Everything was in place, a sweep of Benjamin's eyes accustomed to the darkness told him. He got up and positioned himself in the pressroom on the patch of floor behind the bales of newsprint, the patch he had not "prepared."

He heard the sound of the troops pounding the wooden walk, then the smashing of the front door that led into the editorial room where his desk was. Then the high, nasal, almost girlish voice of Dave Brogger.

"Over here, men," he shouted in his mezzo-soprano. "The presses is through this here door. Follow me."

Benjamin felt like a bear had grabbed his throat. He watched over the bales of newsprint for the hunting cap, the derringer feeling hot and useless in his perspiring hand.

And they came with their sledges and pickaxes, their shovels and hammers, and they came with such enthusiasm that when they hit the area before the presses they went flying as though someone had pulled the rug from under them.

Dave Brogger came to the door to see what the fuss was about—he had not led the charge, not being a man of abundant courage, but rather held back and waved them on like a traffic policeman. And now he heard the clunking sound of the picks and sledges hitting the wood floor instead of the clank clank he expected to hear.

It was while Dave Brogger looked so dumbfounded that the arm whipped out from behind the bales of newsprint and grabbed his wrist and twisted his arm suddenly behind his back. Bringing the derringer's cold nuzzle against his temple, Benjamin said, "Don't move, Brogger."

"What the hell?..." the voice squeaked.

"And keep that sissy mouth shut."

There was more confusion on the floor and among the half-dozen troops who had not yet made it to the pressroom.

"All right," Benjamin barked, surprised at the command in his dry, deep voice. "I got my derringer on Dave's head, don't any of you move, and don't light any lamps or Dave's going where he won't dream anymore."

"You ain't gonna pull that trigger, are you?" Dave squeaked, the terror sending his voice higher to a laughable register, causing some of his gang to shift and cough uneasily.

"You think I won't, you just ask one of your boys to make a move, test me out."

"Don't move, boys!" he shouted. Now Dave was afraid of his leadership. He'd gotten so many men, men he wasn't that sure of. "Oh my God, shoot the slaves," he thought, "I got a wife and little ones."

Benjamin's voice was carrying through the sullen crowd like on a loudspeaker. Many were sitting on the floor, having given up the effort to get to their slippery feet.

"You men have a beef," Benjamin said, "I'd like to hear about it."

No one spoke. He heard uneasy feet and shifting tools.

"Course, I'd have been lots happier you came in daylight and said your piece. Looks to me you had destruction on your minds."

"Put that gun away, Benjamin. We didn't come for no killin'." It was the voice of Phil Brogger, more modulated than Dave's, with a softer quality, like molasses oozing off toast. "We got you twenty-some to one, Benjamin. Don't be foolish. Give me the gun."

"Gun's all I got between me and my maker, Phil."

"You shoot Dave, you won't live two minutes."

"I realize that."

"We don't like what you're stirring up," Phil said. Then added, as though Benjamin might not understand, "'bout the slaves."

"I appreciate that, Phil. I read a lot of things myself that make me mad." He could feel Dave's frightened lung heaving against his chest. He tightened his grip on the twisted arm and Dave gave out a sudden yelp in the darkness.

"But you got to admit," came a voice from the crowd, "you been a little rough."

Benjamin shot back. "So what do you do? You bring your sledgehammers down here and your picks and you want to go to work on the dumb, innocent presses. You want to silence Bellweather, you'll have to kill him, and then you'll have to kill me and everybody else who thinks like us, and that'll be the bloodiest war you ever saw because sooner or later those who think like us are going to start to kill you."

Benjamin stopped and twisted Dave's arm again and got the yelp he wanted to punctuate his message.

"Wouldn't it be a lot simpler just not to read the paper?"

"But you're stirring up trouble. Even if we don't read you, others do."

"Words," Benjamin said. "A few words from a dictionary strung together in a particular order can get you so riled up. You are giving us credit, gentlemen, for more power than we could ever hope to have."

The air smelled of fear and Benjamin knew it wasn't all from Dave.

"Lord God," Benjamin exclaimed. "Here comes the sheriff and his boys and old man Bellweather. Get out the back door while you can and let's start reading the *Chronicle* if you want to have your own opinions petted."

They were already sliding to their feet and scurrying out the back door.

"You stay, Phil." Benjamin commanded.

"Oh yeah, but they're comin'."

"I'm going to let you go, but if there is the slightest hint that you boys are even planning anything, we'll come after you and finish the job."

"We won't." Dave squeaked.

"No, you misunderstand. You are going to be responsible to protect the *Herald* from *all* its enemies."

"How we gonna do that?" Dave yelped.

"You prefer I just pull the trigger and save you the trouble?"

"No. No," he snapped. "We'll do it."

Benjamin was not thanked for his saving the presses until Bellweather had bawled him out for going it alone. "You should have told me," he said.

"I wasn't sure," Benjamin said. "It might have been a false lead."

But he could see his boss was pleased.

A little later, after the shop had been restored and was whirling with activity, people moving like agitated bees, the deadline closing in, Benjamin casually asked what it would have cost to replace three presses.

When Bellweather told him, he said, "What would it cost to send a reporter to Chicago to cover the Republican Convention?"

Bellweather was furious at the kid's audacity. But in spite of himself, he smiled.

# 8

1860

Scorched by the merciless sun that
was quietly cooking Chicago to a frazzle,
and crying for rain, the delegates to the
second Republican Convention in their
sun-soaking black, milled among the
hordes of horses and carriages. The
horses were swishing their tails to fend
off the flies that sucked their sweat.

A few of the delegates, too lazy to
move in the heat, were still inside on
the convention floor. The balcony was
packed with visitors who were afraid to
lose their seats to the enemy camp.

The heat rose mercilessly to that
smoky gallery as it did to the loft in the
barn back home.

The delegates were taking a break
before the first ballot voting.

Benjamin Olin was inside, working.
Benjamin did not take breaks. At two-
and-twenty, he stood as tall as he ever
would, a touch over five and a half feet.
He wore fashionable whiskers and mustaches, his hair was sandy dark and his
face retained the cantaloupe roundness

of babyhood. He had about him a restless determination, like a hound dog chasing flies around its tail.

He had blown into town the night before, the young reporter and delegate bursting with the enthusiasm of youth.

He had taken his gospel to the taverns and saloons, the outlying roadhouses and dank little country hotels that billeted the overflow crowd. He had kept himself pure, as pure as his cause, and when they tried to foist strong drink off on him, he had stoutly declined. And though, by God, he was here to win votes, he would not compromise his principles to do it.

It was only two years after the completion of the Illinois and Michigan Canal and the railroads were already making the canal obsolete. Several lines were finding a hub in Chicago at the nation's central marketplace. Benjamin had ridden part of his journey on a bumpy railroad car and found it exhilarating.

Gordon Hubbard was getting meat packing off the ground, and when the wind was wrong a smell of blood blew over you like death.

But today the delegates were smelling blood of their own.

Inside the huge structure with the endless rows of benches and the balcony covering three sides of the rectangle, the air was hot and sultry and thick with the acrid smoke of green tobacco and the steamy stench of unwashed bodies.

Benjamin moved down the long row of Ohio delegates, hands stiff at his sides, puffing himself up like some warlord, stopping to give his spiel to whoever showed the slightest inclination to listen.

The convention hall, called the Wigwam, began filling up for the first ballot roll call. They were heroes today, these delegates, sought after by every tin-horn leg man, courted, flattered, cajoled, sitting now while the chips fell into place. They had said their piece, stood up and were counted, lending their triumphs and their failures to history. Not until tomorrow would they sink into oblivion, and tomorrow was a long way off.

The results of the first ballot were shouted through the Wigwam.

"Seward, one hundred seventy-three and one-half; Lincoln, one hundred and two; Cameron, fifty and one-half; Chase, forty-nine; Bates, forty-eight;..." The remaining votes spread over seven favorite sons.

Benjamin's cheek twitched with excitement. They were short of the majority, but way ahead. He didn't mind the swelling roar from the gallery when Lincoln's name was mentioned. He knew the gallery didn't vote.

Like flags in some bloody foray, red bandanas appeared

everywhere to dry perspiring faces.

After the second ballot (Lincoln was creeping up), Benjamin was on his way to a man he thought might switch from Chase to Seward when he saw one of his adversaries earnestly bending the ear of an Ohio delegate. It was Jeb Fulton from the Cincinnati *Times*.

Benjamin hadn't meant to eavesdrop. He was just passing by when he heard Jeb say, "I'm very fond of your secretary, Crasner. You have good taste—she is a beautiful girl. Of course I have a soft spot for your wife and children too." Benjamin saw the man squirm under Jeb's broad wink. There was a huddle with four delegates and Benjamin couldn't hear any more.

"There's too much against him." Benjamin had buttonholed a man who was leaning toward Lincoln. "He's hardly been to school. Seward's an educated man. In times like these you need an educated man."

The man nodded without commitment and they both stopped in their tracks as they heard the chairman recognize the delegate from Ohio that Benjamin had seen Jeb Fulton talking to.

"I arise, Mr. Chairman, to announce the change of four Ohio votes from Mr. Chase to Abraham Lincoln."

A great roar rose from the gallery!

The final count from the Ohio delegation was twenty-nine for Lincoln, seventeen for Chase. Benjamin Raines Olin had not succeeded in getting a single vote for Seward. He stood nonplussed, staring accusingly at the man who had changed his vote.

The Ohio delegate was going out of his way to seem relaxed and jovial. His face showed Benjamin nothing so much as a vast relief from a heavy burden.

So this was how history was made. This was the weaving of the fabric of success. Benjamin realized it was a dark and winding road that led him to this hall of iniquity from the days of his father thumping the kitchen table and quoting scriptures.

> Today, (he wrote feverishly) I saw history hatched in the gutter of sin. The ugly, ungainly rail-splitter who lost more elections than the years of Methuselah, riding on the wave of a packed gallery, was nominated by one-half vote with the aid of barefaced blackmail, to run for the highest office in this great land, by the new Republican Party, whose chances for victory now seem slim thanks to the all but sure nomination by the Democrats of Stephen "the little giant" Douglas, who beat Abraham Lincoln for the Senate from Illinois, in the latter's most recent inglorious

defeat. Your scribe witnessed with his own eyes the fatal blackmail by a member of his hallowed profession, a blot on this great nation that brings blush to his cheeks. Numerous backroom deals brought about this strange nomination of the most certified loser ever to run for the nation's highest accolade.

It was no secret in the Ohio delegation that Governor Chase was offered Secretary of Treasury for his support. It was also rumored the Lincoln people were offering anything to anybody for votes, so little hope was there of even having to meet the obligations. It was less than two minutes after the blackmailer did his deed that the gentleman (if indeed he may be termed such) in question switched his vote to the victor and brought along three others he had in his control. It is a sad day for journalism when the power of the press becomes a force for evil coercion. To all loyal Republicans everywhere we can only say, better luck next time!

## BRO

Benjamin was excited when he gave the man at the telegraph office the piece, and watched as he sent it over the wires to Lexington.

He left the telegraph office whistling.

Horace Bellweather, publisher, read the dispatch at his littered desk in the editorial room of the *Herald*. He began making corrections and deletions as he read, his broad black pencil moving with more agitation and striking offensive phrases with increasing force, so that halfway through the opus there were several holes in the paper. Sighing in exasperation, he threw his pencil and the article in the wastebasket.

## 1861

Benjamin Olin stood outside the mail pickup at the General Store with the Philadelphia *Inquirer*, the New York *Times* and the Boston *Globe* under his arm and two letters in his hand. The unopened one was in the weakening hand of his mother; Matilda's he was reading for the second time.

My Dear Mr. Olin:
    We are living life at a hectic pace here. So dull without

your energetic presence. Father says he has a surprise for me for my birthday and the way he said it, I do not think he meant a gift in the usual sense, but time will tell. I have the suspicion it has to do with you, for when I bravely mentioned I missed you, he told me there was to be a surprise that might alleviate that problem. I am hoping against hope he has sent for you, but please do not tell me if he has, I would hate to spoil his surprise. With fond affection I remain

Very truly yours,

Matilda Munson

He read it the third time with deeper confusion, then ambled, preoccupied, back toward the pressroom. The sky was darkening and a bitter wind was kicking small debris at him, stinging his face like tiny pins.

Absently he put the letter from his mother in his pocket unread.

The wind was whipping the dust around him. The sky looked like a good storm was brewing, and Benjamin felt his life was in the vortex of that storm.

He felt stagnated in his job. He was becoming restless and dissatisfied. His boss seemed afraid to give Benjamin his head, tramping down on one story after the other.

The last reporter and copy boy had gone home and the only sounds in the room were from the anxious presses next door. Horace Bellweather, seated at his desk reading the Philadelphia *Inquirer*, searching last week's news for tomorrow's news in his *Herald*, looked out of the corner of his eye and saw Benjamin coming toward him. He could already feel the heat from the fire blowing out of his nostrils.

"Sit down, Benjamin," he said, waving a hand before him at the chair opposite his.

Benjamin sat as though it appeared he were compromising his principles to do it.

Horace Bellweather shifted his body in the chair to get a better perspective of the young reporter.

"My Lincoln article," Benjamin said with that open defiance that was a secret and exclusive weapon of his youth. "Why didn't you run it?"

Bellweather looked at him as though groping for the reply that would cut through the brashness and have some chance to sink into the hard head.

"Benjamin, you're a good reporter," he said and then paused to fumble with some papers on his desk.

"Perhaps," he said, looking up, "it is time to reassess our positions here. I own the paper and I decide what goes in it. That's the system. I don't have to answer to you, you work for me." His tone was benign. "Since I like you, I'll tell you what you already know. You write too harshly. If you think Lincoln is an ape buffoon as you said in your article, that's your privilege, but it is my privilege not to run it in my paper. We are a Republican paper and we support the Republican party."

"But you were a Seward man. *You* got me onto Seward."

"Yes, but he lost. Lincoln won."

"How can you change your principles so fast, like putting on a new pair of shoes?"

Bellweather smiled at Benjamin. "You know, Benjamin, you talk like you write. Like a zealot. An evangelist who is trying to win the world."

Benjamin looked up, the corners of his mouth twisting in shock. "Is there something wrong with that? It was you who criticised me for not having any strong beliefs."

Bellweather sat back and smiled ruefully. "A nice debating point, boy," he said with a touch of admiration. "You've made a big change all right—no taking it away from you—but you went too far. There is a difference between a strong belief and a wall-eyed blind and flaming prejudice," Bellweather said. Lincoln isn't as strong as we would have liked on the slavery thing, but let's give him a chance. He got elected after all.

Benjamin fixed Bellweather in one of his lethal stares, "I will never go soft on my principles."

Horace Bellweather stared back, absorbing the insult and letting it ruminate in his brain. He nodded slowly and muttered, "Perhaps." He was looking for something to bring the kid down to size. His eyes wandered over the dark room, the cluttered desks and empty desk chairs. There was something mausoleum-like about an empty editorial room, he thought. Each night a birth and a death.

And then he found it. Casually, without turning his gaze from the empty room, Bellweather said, "Stanley warned me you were a little bullheaded." He said it as though he were not speaking to anyone in particular.

"Stanley?" Benjamin took the bait right to the sinker.

"Stanley Munson," he said, still offhand.

"You know Stanley Munson?" Benjamin was excited.

The boss nodded. "I should know him, he paid your salary for almost two years." He still spoke as though Benjamin were not in the room with him, but turned to him to savor seeing the boy's jaw drop and his mouth open like a bear trap.

Then suddenly he was sorry. Sorry he had devastated his young reporter.

"I had no idea he had that much confidence in me," Benjamin said, showing a rare bit of teeth.

"Confidence?" Horace Bellweather was perplexed. Was the whippersnapper actually smiling?

"Well obviously," Benjamin said as though his boss were rather thick. "Why else would he subsidize my apprenticeship on a larger paper than we had around Martin?"

Horace Bellweather started to set him straight. "Wasn't there something about a girl?" he said. "His daughter, I believe."

Benjamin was excited. His mind was whirling. He waved him off. "Of course, his daughter is my fianceé. That's why he did it. He must be grooming me for something big." Benjamin jumped up, not noticing his boss's startled face, threw up his arms and let out a yell. "Yeow!" He turned and ran out the door and down the street to his boarding house. If he left now, he would have time to make Matilda's birthday, and have a talk with her father. He had worked hard for this opportunity and he was ready.

That must have been what Matilda's mysterious letter was all about, he thought, his heart leaping to his throat.

# 9

He is not well-bred
who cannot bear ill-
breeding in others.

—Benjamin Franklin

Benjamin was riding his horse,
Steady, like Fury with the Reaper snapping at his heels. He was bent down to
minimize the wind resistance and the
trees at his sides went by so fast they
seemed to be slapping each other.

He had ridden through the night,
with only two hours' rest for the horse.

The letter from Matilda was in his
pocket, the scent of jasmine still strong
on it. He touched it gently through the
cloth of his trousers and thrilled at the
feel of it on his thigh, as though she
were touching him with some secret gift
of her body.

The letter from his mother was on
his small table in Lexington. He had not
had time to open it.

A sudden torrent of rain pelted Benjamin and soon drenched him to the bone.
Mud kicked up from Steady's hooves
and shot backwards like spraying bullets.

He passed the road to his old home-
stead and under different circumstances
he might have detoured. But it would

be over seven miles round trip all told, and he knew a go-getter like Stanley Munson would appreciate his zeal.

Benjamin saw the light of a hundred lanterns before he heard the distant droning sounds from the Munson mansion.

Benjamin went through the pretentious stone pillars and iron gate. The hanging lanterns cast beaming brightness on his face, intermittently blinding him.

The sounds were stronger now: the low grumble of people assembled out of duty. The front of the house was crowded with horses and carriages and Benjamin was reminded of the Republican Convention.

He tied Steady to the ring of a cast iron jockey painted Negro and made his way quietly to the back of the house where the big double French doors from the ballroom opened out to the veranda that smelled like Matilda's perfume.

The rain had stopped but drops of water were still dripping from his chin.

He crouched beside the French doors. Inside they were immaculate in their tails, and they looked so clean and well-bred, like upper class penguins, drifting in lazy reluctance about the fancy floor. He thought of just storming the Bastille, but he had not reckoned with the staged opulence and elegance—the shattering contrast between the clean, tall, half-smiling waltzing man in Matilda's arms, and his mud-splattered self.

Benjamin couldn't take his eyes off the man. His manner and face were so genteel he could have been an Old World count.

He could hear the sophisticated strings floating through the air and he could smell the scent of Matilda's jasmine.

Benjamin's eye traveled to where Stanley Munson was surveying the proceedings, with his patrician eye. Standing next to him his wife, Sarah, resplendent in jewels and in bondage to yards of flowing silk. Her dress looked like a half-raised stage curtain.

Benjamin shifted his position at the French doors to get a better view of Matilda and her dancing man.

He seemed to be getting frisky, and his hands were moving familiarly far down Matilda's back into the hoops of her full, rippling dress. Matilda was not pulling away. Benjamin bolted to his feet. He forgot his dripping skin and soaked muddy clothes, threw out his chest and grasped the brass door lever.

When the butler brought Benjamin to Munson's library, the boy saw a grim face that reminded him of his own father's most disapproving face. Munson moved behind his Louis XIV desk festooned with music boxes and sat, not taking his eyes off Benjamin who was not asked to sit.

Munson looked at the upstart, his eyes flushed with disdain.

"I want to thank you for providing the funds for my apprenticeship," Benjamin began, digging his fingernails into his hands to control his shivering.

The tight eyebrows jumped. "Oh," Munson said, waving his gloved hand. "I knew I couldn't trust Horace Bellweather." He looked away from the soaking ragamuffin. Suffering made him uncomfortable.

"Well, sir, if I may say so, I think it was very generous of you and I appreciate it more than I can say, sir, and your wishing to do it anonymously, to take no credit," (Benjamin was almost breathless with excitement) "well that is just about the most noble thing I ever heard, sir."

'*Sir,*' Stanley Munson thought, he's trying to be ingratiating with all those *sirs* and he doesn't know he's as transparent as a windowpane.

"*Appreciate?*" he said.

"Yes, sir, your generosity is not lost on me, nor will you be sorry. I'll make you a publisher you will be proud of."

"*Publisher?*"

"Yes. The enterprise would be of mutual benefit, of course," Benjamin said expansively. "We are of like minds on politics," he tossed in with a gratuitous twist of his narrow lips which he intended as a smile of conspiracy. "Of course Abraham does not set so easily on my stomach and I fear war, but I stand to do your bidding, to speak with your voice on all matters political."

"How nice," Stanley Munson said, his acerbity touching Benjamin for the first time.

"Well, yes," he said, shifting his weight on his wet shoes, trying to recover. "Since I am about to ask for your daughter's hand in marriage I thought it best if we settled our business first."

Munson stood up slowly as a man preparing to pass by the coffin of an adversary. Benjamin watched, perplexed, his narrow eyes following Munson's movements.

Stanley Munson opened the library door and called out, "Jasper, bring me a kitchen chair." When the old retainer brought the sturdy wooden slab chair, he set it down behind Benjamin and backed out and closed the door.

Munson said, "Sit down, Benjamin."

Benjamin sat gladly, his wet clothes making a squishing sound when they met the chair, feeling triumph rolling with him on the hot, humid air. Munson was standing in his immaculate tails over him, every strand of his flowing platinum hair swept back in its optimum place.

"I'm afraid, Benjamin," he began in earnest, "you have made several faulty assumptions." He paused, looking away from the eager, naive eyes looking up at him. He grasped the back of his Louis XIV chair and sucked in his rightful share of air, "Benjamin, I paid for your apprenticeship, as you call it, not to start you on the road to a brilliant career but rather to get you away from my daughter."

Benjamin's mouth hung slack, he trembled as he felt a cold shiver through him like the wind off the hill. "But—sir—but—why?"

Stanley Munson turned away for a few seconds.

"The Lord has blessed me with but one child, and I am not about to deprive anyone of the hard work, the sweat and misery it takes to build a successful trade. No one handed me any capital, no one handed me a daughter above my station. Rise, by all means, young man, but not at my expense."

Benjamin absorbed the shock. "I shall rapidly prove myself, sir, to be worthy of Matilda's background."

"At that time I may reconsider." His eyelids snapped shut with a deadly finality, then sprung open to find to his disappointment the nervy young man had not disappeared. "The answer is no."

Benjamin blinked back tears. Munson was motioning his dismissal.

Benjamin stood. "I want to see Matilda," he said.

Munson fixed him with the stare of a thousand successes. "Well, you may want to, but you aren't going to."

"I shall marry Matilda," Benjamin announced.

Stanley Munson's face twisted in revulsion.

"When you and Matilda finally understand there will not be one cent coming from me, you might reconsider."

Benjamin glared, then pushed his way past Stanley Munson and ran down the hall.

Benjamin tore through the kitchen and pantry where the candle-light parade of copious food platters had begun with a train of white-coated waiters carrying overhead their silver trays of turkey, ham, beef, shrimp, crab, pork, lamb, assorted salads and steaming vegetables. Between each was a younger servant carrying large candles. The lanterns were doused for the occasion and the effect was spectacular, with enough food being paraded, Benjamin thought, to feed the entire population of Ohio.

Benjamin grabbed a candle from a woman who was lighting them from a kerosene lamp to hand the boys in line. The waiters and bus boys gasped as he joined the procession. Stanley Munson came running out.

"Stop that man!" he shouted from the kitchen.

Stanley Munson pushed ahead of the line to startled looks from his servants and elbowed his way to the ballroom where the assembled awed guests were getting their first look at the spectacle of the candle-lit procession, and of the parody of Benjamin, mudstained and ragged, marching in line with a string of immaculate white coats.

Stanley Munson's first impression was that his guests were laughing at him. He heard his daughter shriek an unholy sound and pronounce "Benjamin" with a vigor he now realized had been lacking all evening.

"Get that man out of here," Munson commanded, and the first waiters who had already set their trays on the long, white tableclothed buffet table festooned with cornucopias of fruit and silver candelabra, came to his rescue.

Benjamin saw only his beloved Matilda in the arms of a stiff penguin who blinked as Matilda deserted him for the filthy spectacle with the candle.

Still holding the candle, Benjamin collided with Matilda and they hugged and whirled around in a tight circle. Matilda's mother, feeling faint at what was being done to Matilda's new dress, began sagging in her own voluminous curtain dress before several women came to her aid with fans and salts.

Stanley Munson was standing next to Benjamin, now glaring at him and saying, "Leave this house at once."

"Yes, sir," Benjamin said, grabbing Matilda by both wrists and hurrying from the parting crowd.

"I'm going with him, Daddy," she shouted, and they were outside in a fresh downpour before Daddy understood.

The guests looked away from Stanley and busied themselves with idle chatter.

Sarah Munson came weakly to Stanley's side.

"Stanley," she pleaded. "What are we going to do?"

Stanley glared at her a moment as though she were an intruding stranger.

By the time they reached the barn, Benjamin and Matilda were both soaked to the skin. Matilda was giggling with delight.

The rain had doused the candle and there was no light in the barn. The smell of the luxurious dry hay and Matilda's subsiding giggles were the only sensory memories he had before the touching of the wet bodies, sliding and slipping and finally warm.

When Matilda and Benjamin returned to the recuperating party holding hands, one dowager remarked to her portly red-nosed companion that they looked like nothing so much as something the cat dragged in. Matilda's stunning dress looked now like she had been wrestling in mud, and her dark hair plastered her head like a dirty wet mop. She stood hand in hand with the ragged Benjamin, swinging their arms back and forth like the old porch swing.

"We're engaged," she giggled.

Then the floodgates let loose and the whole room broke into the most uninhibited laughter.

Benjamin and Matilda were beaming.

Stanley and Sarah were not.

Squaw Harbor, Alaska
October 20, 1867

My dear Matilda,

I would never wish on you or our three lovely daughters a fate similar to this Godforsaken outpost with nothing but ice and seals for company. I am the federal agent to contain seal poaching, and a stranger marriage of task to capability I cannot imagine. I am beginning to wonder if this was Hayes's idea of a joke. This is some reward for my bravery on the battlefields of our glorious Union Army!

How are my girls? I miss you all. I am in receipt of an interesting proposition concerning a California newspaper in a seaside town called Santa Barbara. On my way here I had the good fortune to travel through parts of California, and a fatter land you never did see. It is just waiting there for men of industry and courage. It has given me something to occupy my thoughts these cold nights. Perhaps politics is not my forte. I am aching to get back to the newspaper trade, where a man can control his country's political destiny, rather than vice versa.

Very truly yours,

Colonel Benjamin Raines Olin

# 10

In conformity, therefore, to the clear doctrine of Scripture, we assert that by an eternal and immutable counsel God has once for all determined both whom He would admit to salvation, and whom He would condemn to destruction. We affirm that this counsel, as far as concerns the elect, is founded on His gratuitous mercy, totally irrespective of human merit; ...

—John Calvin
*Christianae Religionis*
*Institutio*

1870

It was a nightmare kind of night. The creepy kind of darkness that stuck to the roof of your mouth when you breathed.

The stingy sliver of a moon was throwing enough light to see two steps in front of you but not much more.

The curtain was drawn on verdant Vermont. The dark air was smelling like lilac and honeysuckle and nightblooming jasmine. The katydids were knocking themselves out in piercing discord.

Seven-year-old Arnie Sutler stepped out of the house in his nightgown, wet grass under his bare feet.

Arnie could feel his heart beat and the breath that rushed in and out of his nostrils with the urgency of the old water pump next to the cold cellar, dredging water from a drying well. The lightning bugs were flashing their tiny gold sparkling light all over.

He was a plain-faced boy, earnest in his innocence. His teeth were tiny forks, brittle and white in their baby purity, and it gave the face a touch of foxiness.

Arnie had thin, wispy muscles and soft cornsilk hair that tickled his eyebrows when he ran. The maple trees were in full, robust leaf. Lamb and boy ran across the furrowed field pungent with cornsilk and tomato plants. Sometimes Arnie would grab a bunch of the silk from the corncob tops and brush the shimmering gold over his nose and kiss it with his lips.

They crossed the grove of white birch trees that looked like skinny ghosts, down to the waterhole where the watercress grew so green and peppery to the tongue.

Lammy Sammy was "it." He was supposed to hunt for Arnie. Arnie could have sworn on a big pile of Bibles that Lammy Sammy understood the game.

Arnie had rolled himself into a tight little ball crouched behind the stone when he heard the piercing bleat that stopped the blood in his veins. He jumped up and saw two blurs under a clump of brush across the meadow.

There was a sudden thrashing. Then a sour spraying of red, and Arnie felt stomach-sick like when Poppa had sliced the hog's throat with the big butcher knife. Poppa had made Arnie watch and said it was part of growing up on a farm.

He started to yell—"Hey you dumb dog get away from my Lammy!" He ran toward the animal and saw Lammy Sammy lying on the ground twisting his neck in gulping agony. He picked up a rock and heaved it, and it struck the wolf who jerked his head, snarling. His seven-year-old adversary picked up every rock and stick he could lay his slim hand on and hurled them at the wolf until the sulking animal finally darted back into the woods.

Arnie gulped the night air as he moved his leaden feet to the fallen lamb. He put his hand on the big black nose and missed the feeling of that gentle air rushing across his fingers—that feeling that showed him he had a friend in the world who wasn't always telling him to grow up.

Arnie sat by his friend and picked up the sticky woolly head and laid it in his lap. All night he kept the vigil—all night he protected his Lammy Sammy without shedding one teardrop. Then all of a sudden when they sat Arnie down to breakfast (after his spanking with the big strap), all the rivers in the world broke from him.

His mother came over to his chair and put her cold hand on the back of his neck. She didn't say anything but Arnie felt, with the touch of her hand, a rare closeness.

"Momma," he gasped, not unlike the lamb's final breath—"why did that old wolf take my Lammy Sammy away from me?"

The only sound in the pristine kitchen was that of the boy gasping for air between sobs that seemed to swallow the whole room.

"Weren't the wolf took him," she allowed the sound to hiss through her stingy lips.

"Was so," Arnie insisted, flailing his arms. "Was *so*—didn't I see it myself?"

She loved her children. Their pain was her pain, no matter her husband didn't want the boys raised as sissies—wouldn't hear of love except in the bedroom after all the lights were out, and then he came on like a lumberjack after a recalcitrant tree, not resting until the job was done to his satisfaction. Whoever thought of satisfying a tree?

"Was God," she said simply.

"Wasn't any God out there I could see. I saw that old wolf with my own eyes." He gulped again, a man sinking in the sea and not caring.

"Turn around," she said. "Look at me."

He turned and looked up into those coal-hard eyes sunk in the parchment.

"We are Calvinists, Arnold. God has preordained our lives. Nothing happens to us—or your lamb—that He doesn't plan before we are born." The tea kettle began to gurgle, then whistle on the old black stove.

The little eyes blinked at her. "You mean," he sniffled one big draught of air, "God *makes* you do *every*thing you do?"

She nodded severely.

"Then it wasn't my fault Lammy Sammy died?"

"No, son."

"Then why did Poppa spank me?"

In spite of herself, a niggardly movement tortured those tight lips into a quarter smile. She muttered about his foolishness and how he'd better get eating so he could do his chores before he was off to school.

She wiped her hands carelessly on her clean apron. That was the thing about the boy. He kept asking questions until you had no answers.

"Everything is preordained," she sighed.

## 1881

Poppa Sutler sat rocking in the parlor, with Momma in her straight chair at his side, looking out the window at the white mounds of snow and the gusty winds swirling the flakes like a cyclone in a featherbed factory.

It was God's plan that the house should have nothing extraneous in the way of furnishing or expressions of the inhabitants' personalities. The chairs were straight unpadded wood, the floors were bare, there were no tables to serve as havens for knicknacks. Momma Sutler had resisted the rocking chair as a frivolous entertainment, certainly not in God's plan for them. But Poppa said he would take his chances. He was secretly relieved that God did not strike him dead after his first good rock in it, and Momma sneaked a rock whenever he was out of sight and she had a minute to sit down.

Eighteen-year old Arnie whirled through the room like a dervish, his gangly limbs fighting air that did not fight back. Poppa said, "You aren't going out in this weather."

Poppa was reading the paper as always with the rimless spectacles pinching his nose and the hunting dog at his feet, the paper folded in the small square of his immediate interest.

"That boy is nothing but trouble," he said, when the door slammed. "You try to tell him anything, he does the opposite."

"God's will."

"Oh, I know all about God's will, but that Arnie sure shows a powerful will of his own. I don't see how any God could put that in him."

"Ezra, you blaspheme."

He grunted and went back to his paper.

The coolish summers in Vermont were paid for in the coin of hellish winters. And on this day, with the temperature somewhere below zero and the wind chilling far below that, cooler heads were keeping their bodies warm anyway they could.

Arnie Sutler was trying to keep warm by getting close to Amanda Savodnic, but Amanda had a sixth sense about not giving her special blessings away lightly.

Arnie was taller than most of his peers, with a spotty crop of pimples on his face and the burden of self-consciousness about him.

A towheaded girl with curls pasted against her forehead, Amanda looked a little ridiculous and had a reputation as an incurable tease, but Arnie was taken with her pretty china doll face and her robust figure, and the challenge of the Main Event.

The way she was bundled up in the long black coat, woollen cap down over her ears and green scarf flapping in the wind, reminded him of the panda bear he had seen in the newspaper as the symbol for some sexual potency elixir promising increased performance.

When he was with her in any weather the air seemed charged with electricity. Those few who bragged of success with her claimed it was like being in the presence of a whirlwind force that took the top right off your head.

Lake Champlain had a respectable coat of ice, but the temperature was so low only a handful of the hardiest sports were out on it.

Arnie kept begging her to go inside and get warm. Her house was, after all, only a block from the lake and her parents were gone on some duty call to a sick relative.

Amanda was bent over strapping her skates to her high-button shoes, saying, "Come on, the ice is perfect."

Arnie was staring at the part of her that was upended, seeing in his mind right through the layers of bulky clothes.

She giggled, that grating, gas-pipe, tittering giggle that should have infuriated him but only made him tingle all over. She skated away from him.

"Please, Amanda." He followed her, but had trouble keeping up. She was a more graceful skater; he was all arms, legs and rubber ankles. His eyes were so earnest. "I love you. I'd do anything for you."

"Oh pshaw." She considered for a moment then shook her head and skated away past two boys who were wrestling.

When Arnie caught up to her, he wrapped his long fingers around her arm.

"I would too," he said.

She giggled, and turned away from his earnest gaze. "If I told you to jump in the lake?"

"Sure."

"Go ahead."

"Well, in summer we'll come out and you just say jump and I'll jump."

"See," she skated away. "You won't do it now." That little pouty turn of those cute lips made her particularly desirable. He stumbled after her again.

"But it's frozen." He choked the words as though someone was strangling him, and his eyes bulged.

"Not in the middle."

"Hey, wait a minute. You trying to kill me?"

She thought a minute. "One more thing," she giggled. "Say 'I love you, Amanda' when you hear the crack." There was that bubbly sound from her throat, that high-pitched gurgle that suggested so much it made him feel like runny pudding. "And yell it so everyone can hear."

"Amanda," he pleaded in a hoarse whisper that sent the steamy ice crystals flooding from his mouth.

The giant lake lay on the map between Vermont and New York like a chubby finger pointed north in foreboding. As he started skating away from the sparse group of skaters near the shore and headed for the thin ice in the middle, Arnie Sutler had a premonition that he was not undertaking the smartest move of his life. But hadn't his mother assured him that God had already planned his every move? And if the Great Man in the Sky wanted him dead now, well there wasn't much he could do about that, was there? And if he didn't die he would find himself in the cushiony arms of sweet Amanda Savodnic.

The air was brutal; the fierce wind came at him like an angry army and numbed his face, but he held his head high, and skated forward, as if in a glorious battle charge.

The ice parted in a sudden taunting sound, and the words, "I love you, Amanda," were more rushed than he had planned, and his thoughts when he hit the water were not of his salvation but if he spoke loudly and clearly enough so that Amanda would not claim default on a technicality.

The ice water enveloped him like a shroud.

Suddenly it came to him that one could only live in this water thirty seconds. He flailed his arms in panic and reached the ice toward the distant shore where he saw three young men skating toward him, one pulling a sled. As he touched the ice, he tried to hoist himself up but it broke away. Another grab yielded the same tragic result. He kept kicking and grabbing. The boys had reached him and had tossed him a scarf. They lay on the ice, one behind the other, each grasping the legs of the boy in front, forming a chain.

They got him on the sled with seconds to spare. They pulled him over the ice to the street between the picturesque longwood houses with the sharp snow-covered roofs like gingerbread houses dripping with sugary icing. He was heard to babble, "Did I do it, Amanda? Did I do it?"

Amanda was giggling with the boys who were pulling the sled. There was a sardonic twist to her luscious lips as she said, "What a stupid thing to do."

She took him to her house, undressed him carefully, wrapped him in blankets, lit the fire and clutched him to the bosom that reminded him so of the bust cream ads in the newspaper.

In his debilitated frozen state there was no question of her having to take her clothes off. It was not her fault the contract could not be consummated.

It was preordained.

The doctor who miraculously saved his life could not cure him of the pneumonia and pleurisy with its wracking cough, and in the alternative, gave his prescription to Arnie's hapless parents in one word:

"California!"

The little shop was tidy but tacky. It smelled darkly of ink and melting metal which kept a pall about the place, as though someone had stirred the pot of cooking type once too often and vaporized the lead.

In the one corner, clanking and clunking in the grating, tedious rhythm, the old dinosaur press fought extinction cranking out the fervent opinions of the proprietor, who stood behind his chest-high writing stand, under the oak-cased clock no one ever caught him looking at.

At forty-three, the Colonel was graying at the temples. He sported a paunch that made him appear more affluent than he was. His body was soft as an overstuffed pillow. The facial hair he lately cultivated—the muttonchop whiskers and drooping mustache—cemented a frown on his face.

Even the three Civil War medals seemed to droop on his white morning coat.

But through all his adversity, Benjamin remained the soldier. His posture was as straight as an exclamation point.

In the back of the shop, the pressman, Elmer Harber, was bent over *his* work like a question mark.

Benjamin winced when he saw his bookkeeper, Agnes Watson, coming toward him with her owl eyes and skin like a wrung-out dish towel.

Agnes was bearing down on Benjamin with that annoying sniffle. He could cope with anything but a whiny woman. He wished for someplace to hide.

He regretted hiring a woman, but she worked cheap, knew her multiplication tables and never asked for a raise. And, she was shorter than he was.

She was shuffling at him, dressed like a schoolgirl in calico and lace and those ridiculous flowers that failed to hide the gray that was leaching the squirrel-brown from her hair.

"Colonel," she began, drawing in air to give her courage, her thin lips parting slightly over malnourished teeth.

He knew what she wanted.

Her feet shifted. "It's about the finances."

Benjamin waved a flaccid hand at her as though brushing a crumb from his frock coat.

Her lips moved, tiny larvae in a tight cocoon. "I can't hold them off any longer." The owl's eyes were damp and useless, but they could pity—pity the broken spirit of the man before her, struggling to be brave.

Benjamin turned away from her. His cheeks worked like there was something bothersome stuck in his teeth.

She spoke again: "It's never gone this long, and for a fact they are many cutting us off. We won't have newsprint beyond the end of the week."

"That will be *all*, Agnes."

"Yes, sir," she sniffled into a lace handkerchief, and retreated to her desk.

He stood up, stretching his arms above his head to purge his body of its pessimism. His arms fell and he threw out his chest, arching his back to put some resolution in his spine.

He began pacing the room. He had tried everything with the *Sun* except tempering the voice of his conscience.

His was a Republican paper in a Democrat town. They had not given him a chance. Every innovation he tried had fallen flat. The society column was immediately picked up by his chief rival, The Santa Barbara *Bugle*, and being part of the society of the town, they spoke with more authority.

He printed fiction—they got better writers. They outdid him at everything.

Most men would have run for it long ago and taken their hide with them. Retreat was foreign to Colonel Benjamin Raines Olin.

The day he took over the *Sun*, one of the old-line establishment met him on the street and proffered him gratuitous welcome: "Well, Colonel, we're right happy to have you here in town—even though we need another newspaper like tits on a boar."

The little house the Olins rented on Gutierrez was up from the big stables where they kept the horses for those exclusive Sunday morning rides on the beach. The Olins were never invited, and their pitiful hints fell on blank-faced socialites who traced their ancestry to the gold rush brothels.

He had looked at his fellows with eyes that still burned on them long after he left. But they had their answers ready for him: "We're so terribly sorry (*and horribly polite*) but we've committed all the funds we can for advertising" (*and we don't cotton to strangers here*). And through it all stood the Colonel with the medals hanging down his breast, and his haughty stare said, *You would be privileged to lick my boots, sir.*

Antietam and Bull Run, three decorations for bravery and as many for wounds.

Santa Barbara was provincial and patrician to Benjamin, bourgeois and boorish. A place with more spleen than heart.

The window now framed a picture that filled Benjamin's stomach with nausea. There, driving a spiffy buckboard, pulled by a gleaming chestnut mare was Frank Stark, and beside him his wife, Nettie, both dressed to the nines, on their way, no doubt, to some exclusive gathering. They were the king and queen of this town.

Benjamin was weary of being a serf.

Tomorrow he would make his move on the Starks.

He snapped his heels to attention, made an about-face, and marched over to the press.

"I'll finish the run, Elmer." Benjamin had a way of treating his employees like children, but now as he spoke to the pressman, there was only sadness.

"I can do it," Elmer said, looking at him, one cheek pulled back inquiringly.

"I wish you would not put me to the embarrassment of seeing you labor on my behalf when I know I will not be able to cover your paycheck."

Elmer looked up into his boss's eyes, the eyes that had so often acted on him like hot coals, the eyes that looked now like dying embers. It was all there in those eyes: the struggle, the faltering, the embarrassment and the failure.

Elmer stepped aside. Benjamin was already bent over the press working feverishly.

"You too, Agnes," Benjamin said, and after a prolonged painful moment, she slipped wordlessly out with Elmer.

"We've been through a lot together, friend," he said to the press as he worked. "Call me pompous, will they?—the Purveyor of Purple Prose; the Little Soldier?"

He patted the press, running his hand down the cold legs as a lover. "We have done our duty together—we must not fear defeat."

The Colonel didn't hear the door open, and he was only dimly aware of the voice.

"Moulie said we'd find you here." It was a cultured voice, well-modulated, unthreatening—but it gave the Colonel a start.

He turned around to face the intruders, his eyes quick with suspicion. The banker explained: "The door was open—we assumed you were open for business. If we were mistaken," he said, bowing slightly from the waist, "we will withdraw with our apologies."

"What business would you be after at this hour, gentlemen?" the Colonel asked, on his guard, his eye cocked under the arched brow taking in his disparate visitors: Prescott Walton, a tall bald man with an erect yet easy carriage and a cherubic face; Moulton C. Farber, "Moulie" to his intimates, politician red. Red of hair, of nose. Everything red but his lips; they were yellow. He was the campaign manager and he made the proposal.

It was not a bribe. Moulie wanted that understood "right now." But Mr. Walton and he were given to understand that Colonel Olin might lean toward Mr. Walton's candidacy for State Senator from Santa Barbara County, and the support of his paper would be appreciated.

In demonstration of their gratitude, Mr. Walton's prosperous bank would happily arrange a long-term, low-interest, easy-payment loan to help ease the Colonel's temporary financial burdens.

"All perfectly legal," Moulie was at pains to protest.

"Gentlemen," Olin pronounced in his stentorian tones. "Your offer is a generous one, and much appreciated." He marched back and forth while the smiling men looked on—the top of Walton's bald head gleaming from the gas lamp on the weathered wall.

Benjamin made several traversings of the small room, then stopped abruptly and faced them, and something on that stern countenance told the two visitors their optimism had been misplaced.

The breeze which had been clearing the room of its fetid smells abruptly ceased.

"I cannot accept your offer."

"But Colonel," Moulie asked with gentle sarcasm, "are you in a position to decline?"

"That, young man, is hardly your affair," Benjamin bristled. "I have my conscience to contend with. I am not opposed to your candidacy, Mr. Walton," he said, looking in the surprised eyes of the silent, bald gentleman. He paused. "But my integrity is not for sale."

A wry smile captured Moulie's cornmeal lips. Walton was annoyed. He didn't like being in this untenable position with this tin-horn, fading publisher. He tugged at his starched shirt collar which seemed to suddenly bind him.

"That's very noble of you, Colonel," Moulie made a short mocking bow. "But I doubt if that sanctimony will save your paper. Mr. Walton will go far in this state. Because we are patient people, I will give you twenty-four hours to think it over."

The visitors left. Perhaps he had been hastily foolish since he was going to support the man anyway. Unless a miracle appeared out of the blue, he would lose the paper. If things went well at the Starks' tomorrow, he told himself, he would reconsider.

# 11

Then thus the chief his dying accents drew:
"Thy rage, implacable! too well I knew:
The Furies that relentless breast have steel'd,
and cursed thee with a heart that cannot yield."

—Homer
*The Iliad,* Book 22.

It was a long time until tomorrow came, and when it did Benjamin swooped down the rutted dirt street like the traveling man late for the stagecoach. In his dark Sunday finest, he tugged behind him his reluctant daughter, Phoebe, barely nine years old, dressed in her white party pinafore, hugging an outsized package that hid the upper half of her body.

"But Poppa," the girl whined, "I don't *want* to go to her dumb old birthday party."

"They *are* this town, dear," he said with forbearance. "We must not give in...."

"But I wasn't even—"

"Hold your tongue," he snapped, pulling her off her feet as she stumbled to keep up.

The sun was burning on the back of Benjamin's neck like a battle wound sustained in his days of glory. But none of the horrors he experienced in the Civil War, none of the scars he brought home with him, seemed as bad as this ordeal.

The large adobe house on the right edge of town stood out in the sunlight like some precious gem in a barnyard. Across the yard was a chestnut mare, holding her head high. She stood behind a low white fence watching Benjamin and his daughter. Benjamin was struck by how easy it would be for the mare to jump over the low fence. But she seemed satisfied, even had a certain pride in her proximity to the sprawling adobe on the right edge of town.

They took their positions on the porch. Benjamin straightened his black coat and black tie, smoothed his white shirt and hoped the perspiration would not begin to show through the coat until his mission was accomplished.

He stood tall, exaggerating his five and a half feet. The neck and shoulders never relaxed.

Benjamin was a man who never let the glories of the military seep from his pores, who never deafened to the clarion call of conflict.

Phoebe stood beside him, sullen in her starched white pinafore, her little patent leather-shod feet picking at the ground.

Her hand was locked in his, barring escape. The big package dwarfed her. It was wrapped in white paper with a gold ribbon and bow, the perfect understatement for the upper class.

Phoebe's white shoes shone like bright new sun-flaked pennies, her blonde hair beribboned like a champion show pig.

The door opened suddenly, as if in anger, and Benjamin and his little daughter behind the huge package faced a slack-faced Mexican woman with buttonhole eyes. Her dress was starched white, an eerie blend with the white door. She glared, waiting for Benjamin to speak. Through the house, they could hear the delighted cries of children as birds flapping in a cool private stream, safe from all predators.

The Colonel introduced himself and his daughter. The Mexican looked from Benjamin down her broad, flat nose at the girl behind the white and gold package. "Was she invited?"

"No, ma'am," the girl answered.

"I'll take the gift then," she said cold as the ice cooling the drinks out back, holding out her chubby arms in smug supplication.

"Phoebe would like to deliver it herself," Benjamin said kindly, giving the woman a wink of conspiratorial savvy.

The Mexican regarded him, her lips thick with suspicion. "One moment please," she said, shutting the white door with a magical, athletic motion, a few inches from Benjamin's face.

Standing there, the sun burning hotter on the back of his neck, Benjamin felt the girl's hand tug away from his. He grasped it firmly without looking down at her. His coat was beginning to bind his armpits and the new shoes pinched his feet, but he kept his eyes steeled forward to meet the eyes of the matron he expected to see on the reopening of the door.

His part had been rehearsed to the last detail. The tip of the hat, the smile—not subservient, not ingratiatingly long, just a pleasant, friendly smile spiced with a twinkle of the eyes. He would not let the humiliation he felt take over his face.

He had told his wife, Matilda, "We'll shame them. You go to the Stark party with Phoebe and a gift."

But Matilda refused. "It's your fault we weren't accepted," she said. "I come from a good family." And he felt the pain again.

The door facing him grew whiter and more intimidating with the interminable wait. Benjamin didn't allow his cast iron gaze to falter lest he be caught off guard when it opened. Phoebe at his side was looking everywhere else.

"Daddy," Phoebe sniffed, "why?..."

Colonel Benjamin Raines Olin squeezed her hand hard as he glanced at his little daughter out of the corner of his eye. He saw fear on her face.

"Ouch!"

Whenever he was afraid, Benjamin would stand as tall as he could, pinch his eyes closed for a second and remember the time in the war between the states—the time his captain was shot. As naturally as getting up in the morning, Benjamin charged up the hill with the volunteers behind him whooping and yelling and scared to death. All fear faded in remembering that terror. He tried it on this porch. It wasn't working.

"You watch, Phoebe, your father is teaching you a lesson today that will stand you in good stead for the rest of your natural days. He is winning them with a kindness they cannot repel. And you watch how Missus Stark melts when she sees my little girl in her party dress holding a present too big for her."

Her father reminded her of the minister on Sunday morning, all serious and holy-looking in his black suit, and talking in riddles she couldn't understand.

A moment later the door opened on the same Mexican presence. Benjamin looked at the clean white uniform and the perfect white door and saw in front of him all the purity of acceptance, the self-confidence that trickled down even to the servants, yea to the old hound dog and the horse across the road.

He knew the moment the door opened on the slack-faced Mexican his case was lost. She eyed him with those case-hardened buttonhole eyes. She was a silent Buddha who had seen pretenders before.

"Missus she say to send her regrets. They places set for twenty-four bambinos an' we just don't have no room for more." She spoke with the air of a woman who had risen far enough above the slings and arrows of prejudice to look down on Benjamin.

My God in heaven, he thought, even the scullery maid is too good for us.

The thick lips pursed in retrenchment. The big round head shook, causing waves in the flaccid, jaundiced skin.

"Missus say to thank you for the gift."

She held out her brown hands to the little girl with the white and gold package, but looked at Benjamin for a sign. Phoebe was trembling as she clutched the package to her thin chest, too proud to release it. Benjamin held the Mexican with his cold eyes until she closed the door on him. Defeat registered with blood flushing his face.

He retreated with the gift and his little daughter back down the dusty road. Tomorrow he would return it to the store for credit.

The chestnut mare had not escaped from her corral. Her head was twitching restlessly in the shadows of a young pepper tree.

Benjamin's daughter in her white dress was still locked in his grip and flapping behind him like a kite on the breeze. He ignored her squealing protests, "You're hurting me, Poppa...." What did she know of pain?

Phoebe Olin noticed her father's step becoming slower as they neared their home. As his business sank further into debt, it became increasingly difficult for Benjamin to return home to his wife, who had given up a life of plenty to throw her bedroll in with him, and had been disowned by her parents in the process.

Standing at the gate to his small home, Benjamin saw Phoebe's sisters, Delia and Mary Ellen, playing in the yard alone. Not a remarkable circumstance for children, but Benjamin saw them now as two gargoyles mocking, in their aloneness, his failures.

Santa Barbara was closed to them. A contingency that had never occurred to him was now a terrifying reality.

Benjamin released his daughter's hand. Relieved to be free of the sweaty grasp, Phoebe went to join her sisters in their indifference.

Benjamin Raines Olin, Colonel, U.S. Army *retired*, stepped

slowly toward the pale timber front door of his bivouac. He was considering retreat for the first time in his life.

But why should he fear facing his wife, Matilda?

It seemed to him as though she had cordoned her life off from his with the yards of silk, the bustles and bunting, the fancy hats piled with crepe and ribbon, grotesque artificial flowers which he felt belittled his place at the pinnacle of the family, while making Matilda taller. The flowing lacy bosoms. Everything about her was foreign to him. And the daughters promised to be more of the same. He could sympathize, he said too often, with Henry the Eighth.

Benjamin slunk into the parlor and his weary body sank into the old oak wicker chair. The children came and went, but he didn't notice. He sat, unflinching, until he became part of that old oak chair, just as surely as if he had been a germinating acorn.

The air was still and a fly was buzzing indifferently around his head. Ordinarily, the Colonel would have pursued the fly to capture and conquest, but now his mind was sinking in a vortex of desperation.

He did not answer the mess call, and when Matilda asked if she might bring him some grub, he rejected it.

At bedtime he still sat, morose, staring blankly at the front window beyond which he could not see in the darkness.

Matilda stopped by on the way to bed. "Are you all right, dear?" she asked.

He was silent as a marble statue. She tiptoed around the chair to face him, the question still on her tilted face. He stared straight ahead through her thickening middle.

She laid a hand on his shoulder—he tried to shrug it off. "What is it, dear? Tell me what's bothering you."

"We are through in this town," he said without shifting his stare.

"Oh, come to bed," she said, brushing a hand on his forehead more seductively than she felt, giving him a shiver of revulsion. "Tomorrow will bring a new outlook."

"You go on," he said, waving a hand of dismissal. "I have some things to sort out."

Matilda didn't realize, he ruminated, the extent of the rebuff. A *servant* brought the news—and a high-toned servant—Mexican. They were flaunting their wealth and position. The servant should be Chinese. It is unseemly to have a Mexican as a domestic. Why they owned this state and the white people were indentured to *them*.

Doubts haunted him. How many men could start over at forty-three?

The light from the cut glass lamp fell on his face, highlighting half a cheek like orange sunlight and shading the other cheek like the devil's darkness.

In Santa Barbara there was no God-given time to pause for reflection on the day's accomplishments or to anticipate the blandishments of the night. In California the sun drowned at the edge of the ocean and you got on with it.

He shifted over his contingency plans. If only there were a good war on someplace. War was his métier.

Well, he would write the letters. The first to appear in his newspaper's next edition—the second would go off to Los Angeles in pursuit of a future.

Benjamin's mind was still turning over the afternoon failures when he wearily climbed the stairs to his bed. He felt helplessly sorry for his daughter and the snubs she and her sisters had to continually endure.

Benjamin crawled under the covers and lay quietly beside his wife. Suddenly his body was wracked with sobs so violent that Matilda awakened.

"Are you all right, dear?" she asked solicitously.

"Of course I'm all right," he said, forcing bravado into his voice.

She was on her elbow. "You seem to be trembling—the bed was shaking."

"Just a sudden coughing spell," he said and coughed wracking, counterfeit coughs to prove it.

# 12

I am come to deliver
them out of the hands of
the Egyptians, and to
bring them out of that
land unto a good land and
a large, unto a land flowing
with milk and honey.

—Exodus 3:8

Isaiah Crown smiled when he read
the letter. He had brought his mail
home to read in the presence of his
wife, Clara, to keep her company while
she lay restricted to her canopied four-
poster bed. Darkness lay with her, a
small kerosene lamp gave a dull glow to
the letter in the studied, careful handwriting.

Clara was sleeping, but she knew
he was with her. He was dead tired and
the letter lay heavy as a stone in his lap.

Dear Mr. Crown:

I have heard tell that Los Angeles
is a wide open town where a man
could reap rewards according to his
gumption, his spit and his mettle. My
abilities have been stifled here in this
provincial, inbred society for nigh on
to five years now and I am sincerely
desirous of a change in my condition.

You have been referred to me as
a man who knows his mind, a man of
fairness and reason who hires according to abilities and energy.

I do not seek, nor would I countenance, any blind faith, or any kindly charitable act, so I shall present myself personally to you, subject to your approval, on Tuesday next, at ten ante meridian, having with mercurial dispatch, wound up my affairs here.

A list of my credentials is enclosed. Although I am not impecunious, I do feel some temporary financial constraints at this point in time, and while I would prefer to be in a position to offer to purchase a share of your newspaper enterprise, I must be satisfied with a temporary supplication for employment, where you think I could be of service to you with my demonstrative talents.

I thank you for your consideration and wish to remain very truly yours,

Colonel Benjamin Raines Olin
Publisher and Editor, Santa Barbara Sun

Rocking gently in the rocker, Isaiah Crown thought, "What an outrageous sounding man." He could write an intelligible English sentence, which was rare enough, but it was all so blessed overblown, and he referred to himself as "Colonel." However, he said he was an editor and publisher and he just might know something about newspapers. Maybe—just maybe—Isaiah could find more time to be with his wife—and, soon, their child. The hypnotic rhythms of the old rocker put him to sleep. The lamp would burn itself out while he slept.

He awoke that morning to birds chirping on his windowsill. The bright yellow eastern sun made a dull glow in the bedroom through the heavy velvet curtains. The doctor said to keep the sunshine out, though Isaiah longed to open them, just to lift Clara's spirits.

He had almost sixty thousand dollars in the old beaten strongbox when he came west from the wilderness of Illinois, and he would gladly give all of it if Clara could have this child.

It was just hard work and savvy that gave him this modest fortune. He started the gas company, laying the lines himself, but after the third miscarriage and his frail wife getting frailer, he piled her and some sentimental belongings in a stage and headed for the land of eternal sunshine. He was twenty-seven years old. She was twenty-nine.

He bought the newspaper after a month's rest. That was three weeks longer than he could stand—he was burning for something to do.

Admittedly, he didn't know much about newspapers, but the

opportunity presented itself through a neighbor who was aching to return to the four seasons.

The *Tribune*'s employees were quick to take to Isaiah's easy manner and they taught him everything he needed to know. It was a happy enterprise.

Isaiah brought his wife, Clara, breakfast on a silver tray with lightly-starched white linen liner and napkin. It was one boiled egg, toast, a cup of warm milk and a glass of prune juice.

She smiled weakly at him. "Oh, I hope I'll be able to eat all that," she said.

"You'd better," he teased, "you're eating for two now."

He laid his hand on top of her hand that lay on the soft mound of her belly—hers was a hand unmarred by labor, but unpretentious and virtuous.

The tender touch of his light fingers barely grazed her thin forehead and the translucent face just below the oak-yellow hair. The dryness of the air seemed to crackle around the indolent fly buzzing overhead. The gold light fighting through the massive velvet curtains cast a glow on the mound on the bed, curved as only God can make a curve. A tiny tear perched in the corner of an eye. He brushed it away from her as if it trespassed on her perfection.

"Happy birthday," she muttered, smiling weakly as though any more exertion would ruin their dream. "I should be doing something...."

"Shh," patting her hand, folding it awkwardly in his. His bones often got in his way when he moved.

The loving husband lifted himself from the scene with muttered signals of understanding. He walked to the door, turning to look at her one more time as though that innocent gesture would ease her burden.

"I've let you down," she said.

"Hush, Clara," he said. "We are only instruments of God's will."

The room smelled like spent rosebuds. He escaped from that dark womb to the teeming industry of life.

He was going to meet with the man from Santa Barbara who had sent him that curious letter, and if things worked out he would have more time to spend with Clara. Perhaps even do some traveling.

Out in the street, Isaiah stopped to give his eyes time to accustom themselves to the bright warm sunlight.

There were cattle in the streets of Los Angeles in 1881. It was a wide-open, rough-and-tumble place—a small and rather insignificant burg by the standards of the day, with about eleven thousand sojourners.

There was nothing here to start with but the sunshine. The sunshine and the brown bare land that you couldn't spit on enough to make anything grow. The river was meager but the air was fresh and sweet and clean, and the sunshine, oh that sunshine warmed the weary bones of the settlers and made them grateful. And if they brought water to Rome, they could bring it here.

It was Small Town, U.S.A., with white picket fences surrounding the houses as Isaiah made his way downtown. Storefront windows on Commercial Street ballyhooed the trade within. The blacksmith did your horse, the tinker your pans, and in most cases the only choice you were given was a number of saloons to belly-up in or churches to kneel and pray in, but there were more of the former than the latter. Times were hard for everyone but bartenders.

A few days before, the wheels of the buggies and wagons had sunk into the adobe mud streets. Now smoky dust swirled about his ankles.

Isaiah missed his Illinois crocuses peeking through the snow, and the glorious blazing reds and yellows streaking the fall landscape, but he had come to California as the last chance on earth to solve Clara's problem; came on the stage through the incredible suffocating dust. There he was, calling it her problem again. He didn't know whose problem it was, it could have been, he supposed, his.

"How's the missus gettin' 'long?" a voice across the dusty street asked, drawing him from his self-pity.

"Fine, thank you, Sam. Any day now."

"We all prayin' for her, Izzy."

"'Preciate it, Sam," and he was on down the street and another well-wisher.

Isaiah stopped as he saw a young woman coming toward him. She had, in one hand, a toddler, and the other was pushing a big black baby buggy.

He did not know the woman, but tipped his hat when she passed. She smiled, but he was looking longingly at the little boy holding her hand—and then at the chubby-cheeked cherub in the buggy.

"You lucky woman," he said to himself and his pulse raced as he watched them glide away—mother and children, as graceful as swans.

The doctor had given him hope. They had followed his instructions to the letter. She had stayed in bed, there were no sudden movements, no opportunities to fall or jar the fetus.

Was it some perverse heredity that had done this to them? He was the only child in seven who had survived infancy, and his wife the only remaining of nine, the second longest-living of which had reached only seven years.

He turned off Commercial Street onto the short side street where stood the little red brick box of a building. The sign out front on the corner was painted wood and precariously lopsided in the dry earth.

## PRINTERS

Someday he must get it redone to say Los Angeles *Tribune*

He stomped his feet on the mat at the door, a meaningless ceremony. Very little of the dust left his shoes and spats.

When he opened the scarred door, loose on its hinges, his senses were bombarded with a great commotion. A tuneless chorus was singing what they must have thought would pass for "Happy Birthday," and the shock blurred his vision and he looked at what seemed to be the pressman, tall and skinny, next to his run-down relic of a press. He was grinning foolishly and holding up a mastheaded front page of the *Tribune* that was just coming into Isaiah's focus. A huge half-page headline:

## HAPPY BIRTHDAY
## IZZY CROWN!!!!

with exclamation points to balance the line.

Felix, the pressman, had set up individual messages from all the staff and advertisers, filling the bottom half of the page, as was the custom of the day, with advertisements—like special birthday messages for the boss. Felix had worked long hours after his normal twelve-hour shift to have it ready for the big day.

"Elsie baked a cake," someone shouted.

There was a man beside the press—the short, graying man with the imposing walrus hair about his lips and chin; a regulation man-about-town black suit and an uncomfortable look about him as though he had stumbled into a house of ill repute, said, "No thank you," with great dignity, when the police burst in. The man's mouth was turned down like the last little crescent sliver of the waning moon.

"Boss, this is Mr. Olin," he heard Elsie say. "Says he has an appointment."

Now the relief of understanding washed him clean. He sneaked a glance at his railroaders' pocket watch and said, "Oh, you are a bit early. I'm sorry. If I had known I wouldn't have kept you waiting."

"Not at all," Benjamin said, advancing to offer his cold hand. "The early bird catches the worm."

"Fisherman, Mr. Olin?" Isaiah said, shaking the hand heartily.

Benjamin Raines Olin stood tall and bristled. A sour note had been struck. "Just a manner of speaking, thank you," he said. His voice was roughhewn, deep and ponderous, farm grown, and he made a manly effort to sound bombastic. "But I prefer to be called 'Colonel' if you don't mind."

"Fine, Colonel," Isaiah said, his tones low and languid, "as long as we don't have to salute."

"Mr. Crown, I don't regard one's service to one's country as a laughing matter."

"Oh dear, forgive me, Mr. ah, Colonel. Will you join us in a piece of Elsie's cake? I can assure you, you will find none finer this side of heaven."

They were gathering around the table where the rectangular cake with the white icing and chocolate lettering stood.

It was the same design as the newspaper masthead:

LOS ANGELES TRIBUNE
H A P P Y   B I R T H D A Y
I Z Z Y   C R O W N ! ! ! !

"Thank you," Benjamin said, "I don't eat cake."

"Let them eat bread, eh, Colonel?"

The cake cut, consumed and cleared, Isaiah Crown invited Benjamin Olin (Colonel) to sit with him at his oak roll-top desk. Crown slumped in his chair, Colonel Olin sat straight as the proudest ramrod the Union Blue ever spawned.

Why was it, Isaiah wondered, that Benjamin Olin gave him the feeling he should be embarrassed by all the birthday sentiment? Was it that sour expression on his face, or the fact that he had not bothered to say happy birthday himself? Or was it just his peculiar stiff manner?

"Let me give you a little of my philosophy of the newspaper business," Isaiah said, "and see if you think you could fit in and be happy here." He paused, stroking his smooth cheek thoughtfully with his hand, the thumb stationary on the one side of the face, the fingers slowly, unconsciously methodical, working the other. "Or adjust," he added as an afterthought.

"I believe the business of a newspaper is news. If you treat it fairly as you see it, and are conscientious, why, the money will take care of itself."

Olin was nodding, but Crown suspected it was in disbelief. "And if it doesn't—if the money doesn't just roll in—and believe me it doesn't always, at least you have the satisfaction of having done right by your customers."

"Little hard to eat satisfactions sometimes, I suppose, Mr. Crown."

"You may call me Izzy."

Olin's face took on the look of an incipient faint.

"Now I expect I have talked enough. May I have your thoughts on working here, if you are still interested?"

"I am indeed interested," the Colonel said, looking around the shop as though still mightily bothered.

"Is something wrong?" Isaiah asked.

"I can promise you, sir, if you do see fit to add me to your employ, you will never have a more conscientious worker or a man more married to the task." The rumbling tones rolled off the floor like heavy artillery. There was never any trouble hearing Colonel Olin above the rumbling press.

"I am, in all frankness, just not used to all this informality. There may indeed be some merit to it, but I've always subscribed to the notion that a taut ship was a happy ship. But I wouldn't presume to tell you how to run your business."

Crown smiled. He knew, of course, that the first chance he got he would *jump* to presume to tell him how to run his business. No matter, Isaiah thought. He knew his mind, he didn't have to fear his employees. He would win him over.

"I suppose I would not be required to fraternize with the ranks?" he asked.

"Well of course fraternization is not part of the job, but you might be happier at it."

"I do not require happiness," he said.

My God, Crown thought. Why am I talking to this apparition? I can't imagine hiring anyone more different than I, and yet...perhaps that would be of some advantage. Might give the old *Tribune* a shot in the arm to have this little soldier on board.

After they had shaken hands, Crown said, "I don't know if you have any housing needs, but I have recently purchased the home of my neighbor near City Park. It is a comfortable house, not pretentious, but close to the office. He was in a bit of a bind and decided to return East. I thought you might be interested. I could rent it to you most reasonably."

"Thank you kindly, sir, but I prefer to buy."

Crown looked down at him blankly. They had stood up and Olin was preparing to depart.

"Well, I would consider selling it to you, of course, on the same price and terms that I paid."

"I'm afraid at the moment I haven't a down payment," Olin said after the terms were described.

"Well, we'll work something out." And Crown agreed to sell him the house, with nothing down, and at payments much below the going rents, saying something in innocent conversation about not being much of a business man, and people always coming before bucks, to which Olin, the recipient of this generosity, blandly replied, "I have heard it said the road to the poorhouse is paved with obliging men."

These last two words were uttered with the barest trace of disdain.

# 13

1882

The old-timers in L.A. always
pegged the beginning of summer to the
Fourth of July. It was when the overcast
cloud layer that enveloped May and
June finally lifted and retreated to the
east, and the sun began to softly simmer
the tar roofs in town. The same sun
kindly warmed the citizenry to the bone,
without the skin-soaking humidity most
of them had experienced back home.

Arnie Sutler, fresh from Vermont,
his health rapidly improving and pimples subsiding, still raw-boned and
eager, stood with a hand on his bicycle
seat and smiled in amusement as he saw
the bearded figure in the Civil War uniform saluting the passing flags like a circus trouper.

Arnie looked across at the young
girls next to the funny old duffer saluting like a wind-up toy. They were
dressed to the nines but looked awkward and ill at ease in the miles of cloth
that must have gone into the overdone
dresses.

The oldest looked about Arnie's age, but she wore a particularly sour expression on the strange arrangement of features on her face—the toucan nose was too close to the coffee eyes, so haughty and forbidding, and the small mean mouth too far from everything. Lord, who would ever want to live with someone like that? he wondered.

His eye traveled further down the line across the street, and landed on a girl so pure and wholesome-looking it stole his breath.

Her lips were generous, not pouting—her brow open, not sullen.

She was laughing and her teeth were flashing pearls, catching the bright sun. They reminded him of the ice he had fallen through for Amanda, the white, gleaming porcelain ice that almost killed him. But it had not been, apparently, preordained.

He pushed his bike through the small line of people ahead of him, and his heart was pounding so heavily he didn't hear the jeers hurled at him for crossing the street during the parade. Arnie was almost knocked down by a horse with a heavy silver saddle. He pulled up, panting excitedly, to see the girl throw her head back and clap her hands once in delight, thrilling him so his voice caught in his throat.

"Enjoying the parade?" he croaked.

The girl turned to him, great whipped blonde hair atop her head waving like wheat in a gentle breeze. "You are talking to me?" she asked, in a voice accented in seductive innocence, the laughter gone from her lips.

"Sure am," Arnie said, grinning foolishly.

She looked him over as if appraising a show pig.

"I live out in the Valley—I got myself a job on a farm there," he said.

She turned and watched the parade, too intently.

"Where do *you* live?" he asked her back.

She rolled her eyes to the sky and turned to her girl friend, who giggled shamelessly.

The girls started to walk off toward the end of the parade route. Arnie pushed his bicycle after them. "Hey, wait a minute," he yelled.

After walking briskly for a half block, the blonde turned in one graceful motion to see if he was following her.

It was all the encouragement he needed.

No matter the sounds of the marching band were hopeless cacophony, they stirred Benjamin's heart as he stood at rigid attention at the side of the dusty street in his full Civil War uniform.

The flag bearers marched past with their somber mien and martyred step. There was just enough breeze to give Old Glory a sassy snap or two as if she were gearing up for a glorious confrontation.

At each passing flag, Colonel Olin saluted smartly.

Some of the boys in the parade sent back to our Colonel mock salutes, some with both hands, twisting their scrawny bodies in contortions of burlesque proportions as they snapped down the saluting arms.

The Colonel paid them no mind. His heart was full of his cause, and nothing could cheapen it. What did they know of valor? Their lives were of indolent ease compared to the bestiality of war, *ergo*, they were not fit to kiss the hem of his uniform.

Most of the marchers were a down-at-the-heel, scruffy bunch, but their enthusiasm carried them along, shouting and waving their arms in engaging abandon. Young boys marched with wooden rifles over their shoulders, swinging their free arms in the raucous rhythms of the march.

The Olin family lined the parade route in front of their home like a flank of artillery. Benjamin stood at attention, the call of battle bugles and the pounding, uncompromising beat of the drums stirring his heart to memories of bravery beyond the ken of these sloppy civilians. The bugle blew to his nostrils the sweet smell of musketry and the glorious traditions of duty, honor and love of his country.

On his heartside stood his wife, Matilda, and their three daughters: Mary Ellen, eighteen; Delia, fifteen; and Phoebe, going on eleven.

Kids were running around and sometimes between them, shooting each other with wooden guns or just their fingers, but it was cowboys and Indians mostly. The Revolutionary War didn't mean much in California.

All around the rigid Olins people sat cross-legged, casually slumped into each other, occasionally looking up to see the passing parade.

No one would have mistaken Matilda for having belonged to anyone other than Benjamin. She shared his barrel shape and girth, was a mite shorter, and both had aged about twenty years with their Santa Barbara experience, as though they had commonly agreed to get their aging over with once and for all.

They looked like plump mannequins stamped from the same mold, outfitted by the same window-dresser.

Matilda was draped in blue crinoline and white lace and crowned with a red bonnet topped with grapes and cherries. It wasn't easy keeping up with Benjamin.

He knew his daughters were bored. He didn't know why he thought of them as birds—perhaps it was the freedom they had that he did not have at their age.

All they seemed to do with their freedom was fight. They were arguing now about Warren Quinn, the banker's son.

Delia insisted Warren was sweet on Sally, the bank bookkeeper, and didn't know Mary Ellen from a common housefly.

"Now you stop that," Mary Ellen shrieked, turning her toucan beak to her canary sister, while Phoebe, the sparrow, stood quietly. "Don't I know he's perfectly civil to me at the bank."

"Ha," the canary sang, "hardly real romance."

Her sisters were infuriating. They refused to give her any credit—they didn't think Warren was interested in her. Well, she would have to show them. There were ways to get men. She knew there were.

Sally was nothing but a plaything that Warren would outgrow. Why, Sally's father was only a butcher in a small shop. Warren might find Sally amusing in some base way, but a girl like that who attracted attention by strutting and showing a simply scandalous amount of her bosom certainly wasn't marriage material.

The parade ended with a whimper. The "in" crowd retreated to Benjamin's lawn for a party.

Every American citizen worth his salt was displaying at least one American flag. Benjamin had three on the street, two more in his front yard, and banners and bunting on all sides of his house. A red, white and blue Fourth of July landscape.

After Benjamin had won the right to host the Fourth of July party that Isaiah Crown had held in his backyard for several years, Benjamin set secretly out to throw a bigger and better party. Isaiah was paying for it.

Benjamin stood still in full military regalia on his side porch surveying the troops. His heart was warmed to see that the gathering had gravitated largely to his yard, as he planned by the strategic placement of what he liked to call the bivouacs to shade the copious food and drink. The party was, of course, supposed to be in both his and Crown's yards, but Clara had been poorly and Benjamin was so thoughtful.

He stepped off his side porch down to the level of his guests.

He moved easily among his phalanx, striding purposefully with military bearing and adulterating it with cordial greetings.

He was gratified to see Isaiah Crown hovering over his wife, Clara, in her wheelchair. It was right courtly of him to pay her so much gallant attention.

When he finally made his way across the lawn and through the opening in the knee-high hedgerow (as if the tension between the families could be cut by a hedgerow) Benjamin went graciously as a victorious general crossing the battlefield to accept surrender.

Isaiah and Clara were stationed alone in the shade of the towering gingerbread house. The Crowns smiled when they saw Benjamin approach. The smile came harder to Clara's lips.

"Well, well," Benjamin said, with a heartiness that could have been taken from his wife's shelf of preserves, "you're looking well, Clara. I'm glad you could come to the party."

Isaiah spoke. "We were mighty lucky to have you take over for us, Colonel."

"Indeed. A pleasure for me to help out."

As if challenged by Mrs. Crown, Benjamin addressed himself to her.

"Lovely day, isn't it, Clara?"

She raised her soft eyes to him with a slanty, curious stare, as if trying to find some answer on those unsmiling lips.

"Yes," she said in a monotone, "it is a lovely day, Benjamin."

Isaiah bent over and whispered gently in her ear, "He prefers to be called Colonel, Clara."

"Of course," she said, without bouncing an eyelash. "The uniform," she muttered, muting the timbre of her voice. "How stupid of me."

"Well, Izzy, why don't you circulate among the troops a bit. I'll stay with Clara."

Isaiah brushed the back of his lean hand against his wife's smooth face and she took his hand and clutched it, frightened, to her face.

"Oh, that's all right, Colonel, we're fine. I appreciate the offer though."

Clara relaxed her grip and her hand fell gratefully to her lap.

Benjamin's eyes traveled across the lawn. He excused himself with a courtly bow.

"Oh, Izzy," Clara took his hand again, that soft and loving hand that wouldn't desert her cheek. "How could you have hired that awful man?" she almost stuttered. "He calls you Izzy, you call him Colonel, it's like you're working for him."

Isaiah laughed easily, dismissing her fear. "I sign the checks."

A small girl, not over four years old, came running toward them, her little fat legs bouncing, her pigtails with the wild cherry ribbons on the air like synchronized kites, her little high-button leather shoes pounded the earth for dear life.

She stopped a moment in front of them and pouted her lips. "I'm sorry your baby died," she said, and she turned to run happily off, the big bow on the back of her dress bouncing against the lacy border of her hem, the end of the message ending the sadness.

Isaiah swallowed hard and Clara's head dropped to her chest and she broke into gasping sobs.

No one seemed to notice.

Benjamin worked his way back up to the porch and stood at his command post, his soldier's hands clutching the rail as though he were about to deliver himself of some weighty warring oration.

He enjoyed looking down on his phalanx, his beloved troops, as if they were passing in review instead of milling listlessly about, drinks and plates of abundant food in hand.

Benjamin's eye fell on that clown dressed up in red, white and blue, complete with a stars and stripes top hat, a goatee, looking just like Uncle Sam, saluting all-comers. The idiot. He owed his livelihood to the papers of the town. He had the distribution contracts. Crown should not have invited him.

Benjamin was angry when his own eyes dropped to the uniform he was wearing and the row of medals over his breast. He knew that Chip in his Uncle Sam suit parodied it.

It occurred to Benjamin while he stood with his fingers splayed on the bunting railing that no one was beating a path to talk to him. In time, the path would be worn dead with supplicants of every stripe.

Chip Jenkins came bounding toward Benjamin. The first person on that path.

"Colonel Olin." He fairly shouted it in a tone so sarcastic it caused Benjamin to shrink. There was a smart salute, "Private Jenkins reporting for duty, sir," with a burlesque laugh, the stilt-like frame quavering.

Satirical Uncle Sam slapped his host on the back. Benjamin pulled back in disgust like a threatened tortoise into its shell.

"Great party," Chip said.

Benjamin fixed him with his most withering stare.

"Thanks for inviting me."

While Benjamin was searching for an opportunity to escape the newspaper distributor, he saw the tall, sardonic shape of Fred Quinn, the banker, standing alone.

"Oh, Quinn," he said, waving his hand as though hailing a servant.

The Colonel marched forward down from his reviewing stand and groped the banker's hand and pumped.

"I'm Colonel Olin," he said smartly.

"Yes," Quinn said, looking over the short man's head—"you're Izzy's new boy, aren't you?"

Hit by a fusillade, the old soldier ricocheted—"Well," he smiled ruefully, "hardly a boy...."

Quinn seemed to look down his thin nose in the direction of the Colonel's white hair, fringing out from the war cap.

"Yes," he said. Quinn touched six feet in height and had an Athenian physique. Ordinarily self-assured, he had a frayed nervousness about him today as his eyes darted about distractedly. Usually Benjamin thought him a snob. He had a belly-full of Quinn's type in Santa Barbara.

"It's a pleasure to have you at my party," Benjamin's voice breathed proprietorial hospitality.

Quinn raised an eyebrow to a fearsome arch, like a cat posing to pounce. "I believe this is Izzy Crown's annual party," he said.

"Ah, yes, we are having it together," he said, loosening his suddenly tight throat. "Since Clara lost the baby, I offered to help out."

Deciding he had been too harsh, Quinn said: "Well, I appreciate you both having me, Mr. Olin," and he smiled as you do when you are careless about showing you don't mean it.

"My friends call me Colonel," Benjamin said, always awkward at affecting friendliness.

"So I've heard," Quinn said. And, he said to himself looking down in the uniformed man's eyes, "The silliest damn affectation."

Benjamin gave his troublesome throat another clearing in an attempt to escape those snobbish eyes.

"Tell me, Quinn," Benjamin said, "Do you make loans?"

"Of course," he said. "I'm a banker."

"How could I get a loan from your bank?"

"For what purpose?"

"Say a business venture—a newspaper, perhaps."

"What collateral would you offer, Mr. Olin?"

The Colonel blinked his disappointment, the blood of anger rising in his neck like a geyser. "My intelligence and ambition, sir."

Quinn was looking over the gold epaulets on the uniformed shoulder, he nodded in distraction. "Board of directors prefer more *tangible* assets," he said. "Do you bank with us, Mr. Olin?"

"Ah," the Colonel straightened his back. For a moment he had lapsed into a subservient posture. "I am meaning to, as soon as I get far enough ahead." And he watched Quinn's eyebrows work again, in concert with that sardonic twist of the mouth.

Benjamin realized he was doing poorly. He leaned toward the man as if to share a naughty confidence—"I understand, Quinn, my eldest daughter, Mary Ellen, has her eyes set on your son—Warren."

The Colonel finally touched a nerve. Quinn took a step back as if to avoid contamination, looked down that damnably thin nose again and said, "Excuse me, Olin," and left, ignoring Benjamin's confidence.

The Colonel felt smaller as he watched the back of banker Quinn slouch with that lackadaisical gait over to the pepper tree where the pretty eyes of Sally, the bookkeeper, watched him approach.

Benjamin's shoulders pulled back when he observed Quinn and the young, comely woman in the low cut dress in a heated exchange, until she walked away from the banker and went into the house. She seemed almost too casual in her movements, as though she were protesting an accusation that was never made.

Banker Fred Quinn, after a decent interval, surreptitiously stalked the same steps.

Timing his move as carefully, the Colonel mounted the bastion as in a stealthy scouting mission. He opened the screen door without making a sound.

At first he heard only urgent whispers. He fixed the source as the parlor where the shades were drawn against the sun, shrouding in an amber haze the room cluttered with bric-a-brac and furnishings, lace doilies and cut glass lamps.

He took his post by the arch that led from the hallway to the parlor, next to the coat stand. The young girl was talking, making less attempt at whispering than the man. "I can add and subtract, you know." Her voice was agitated.

"You're asking too much. If it's money you're after...."

There was a silence where, in spite of the party noise outside,

Benjamin could hear desperate breathing.

"What I want you don't have to steal from the bank."

"It will all be repaid," he whispered hoarsely, his body trembling, "with interest."

Benjamin was startled to hear movement in the room, the swish of her skirts. He looked quickly for some cover.

"No, wait," the sounds of the skirts died in their own wake. "Be reasonable."

She laughed, an engaging, high, musical laugh that Benjamin thought might crack the cut glass lamps. "*You* be reasonable. Warren wants to advance at the bank. You hold all the cards. All he needs is a little encouragement from you."

There was a gulp for air, a drowning man making a last attempt to save himself.

"I'd had such hopes for that boy," he sniffled, soliciting her sympathy.

"I know," she said, "a socialite wife, climbing, always climbing."

In a last plea for understanding, he whined, "I gave you a job when jobs weren't easy to find."

"I suppose I gave you nothing in return?" Her voice was mocking him. "Always a bookkeeper, never a bride makes Sally a dull girl."

In the long silence Benjamin heard the rattling breathing again. Suddenly Benjamin was on the floor of the Lincoln Convention, twenty-two years earlier.

History had been changed by the conversation he overheard there. Ah, the power of persuasion.

The look of death on Fred Quinn's face, the quavering lips begging to form the question, were something Benjamin would never forget.

He put out his hand and took up the reluctant hand of the banker. "Glad you could come," he said, winking at him in fraternal conspiracy. "Mighty glad," he added with too much emphasis.

"Thank you, Mr. Olin." There was a nervous, trembling friendliness about him now.

"Oh, and Quinn."

"Yes, sir?"

"Call me Colonel."

"Yes, Colonel."

You never knew when you could use a banker.

The party thinned out around dusk.

Chip Jenkins was on the street saying goodbye to the haberdasher, his languid body pressed against a buggy tied to the black iron hitching post, when a young buck on a bicycle pulled up and stopped right next to him.

To Chip he looked like an innocent, impish rascal who had grown tall, but not up. The lad's fascinated eyes devoured everything, and when he looked at Chip, with his Uncle Sam suit, his face broke into a grin that said to all the world, "I am your friend."

Arnie got off the bike, his fluid joints allowing him to float through the air like some sleepy bird caught in an updraft.

"Party?" he asked.

Chip nodded and looked at the bicycle, then back at the guileless, smiling face.

Arnie had followed the beautiful blonde girl home without, he was sure, her seeing him.

He was thinking of his cleverness when he heard the man in the Uncle Sam suit talking to him.

"Excuse me?" Arnie begged a repetition.

"I said, nice bike you got there."

"Oh, thanks. Gets me around all right. Isn't new or anything."

"Like to use the bike to earn some spending money?"

"Oh, no thanks," Arnie said, running his big hand through his blown sandy hair, "I got work."

"What doin'?"

And Arnie told him about the farmer in Van Nuys who had taken him in, given him room and board and eighty percent of the take from the crops he harvested and sold to workmen in the Valley.

"Well, what I got in mind wouldn't interfere," Chip said. You'd be finished long before you had to feed the field hands."

"Doin' what?" he asked.

"Delivering the morning papers. Course," he added with a sly look at the young, pimpled face, "you gotta be willing to get up before daylight and work your hind end off for a couple hours, but you willing, you make yourself a nice pot of silver."

And so, Arnie, considering the money and the beautiful blonde girl, arose at four a.m., conquered the rutted dirt roads and open fields, rain or shine, and became the star delivery boy for all the Los Angeles morning papers.

# 14

A mighty will. That's all
there is.

—Henry James

A heavy fog lovingly pressed the
breast of the angels in late November. It
was like the steam from an overcooked
broth, and it oozed between the sparse
houses, covering some and revealing
others like the gap-toothed smile of a
beggar man.

Arnie Sutler rode his bicycle all the
way from the Valley across the worm-
width paths and furrowed fields, and it
took him forever.

When he finally pedaled into town,
the fog was pressing down on the horse
and carriage traffic, and on the horse
drawn trolleys riding the thin tracks
across the dirt-brown streets, and Arnie
had to move at a snail's pace to avoid
hitting them.

Arnie rode out of the mist like a
thief in the night to the entrance of the
Pico House Hotel. He was wearing his
black suit and clutched in his teeth a
single red rose.

It cost Governor Pico eighty-five
thousand dollars to build the hotel, and

it opened in 1870. For years he greeted his guests personally with gracious pride.

It was the golden age of great Mexicans, now remembered chiefly on California street signs: Pico, Sepulveda, Vallejo, Micheltorena, Figueroa.

The son of a warrior, Governor Pio Pico was a hefty man with thick nose and lips, fleshy and flashy with his plaid vests and dandy ties.

He had two terms as governor of California: one three weeks, one sixteen months.

In his later term he made the Northerners mad as the devil when he moved the Capitol to Los Angeles.

Then he gave away the land to keep it out of the hands of the invading Yankees.

Hordes of Yankee immigrants were pouring into California to clear farmland, fell lumber, build flour mills.

The industry of these immigrants astounded Governor Pico. "Whatever this astonishing people will next undertake I cannot say," he said, "but on whatever enterprise they embark they will be sure to be successful."

They were so successful they shoved him out of town.

Los Angeles, thanks in no small measure to Pico, was outgrowing its cowtown image. Business was taking hold. Businessmen were entitled to a luxury hotel.

And Pico returned to give them luxury. It was the first three-story building in town, and there were bathtubs and commodes on every floor, and running tap water too.

In the courtyard a caged songbird sang to exotic tropical plants.

Outside, it was a square wedding cake after the bride and groom dolls had been lifted from the top, ripe and ready for slicing and putting under pillows in the hope of making fate contagious.

The cake had three tiers with dozens of identical arches on the sidewalk. Over eighty rooms with gas lights in every one.

The uniformed doorman asked Arnie to park his bike at the service entrance if he was going to be hanging around the dining room again.

Arnie tried to argue, but the doorman, not much older than himself, flaunted his position. "Got to keep the front clear for the carriages be arriving before long."

With the hard driving energy of youth seething from all pores, Arnie pushed the bike around to the back and gave one of the dishwashers a dime to keep his eye on it. Arnie wasn't afraid it would be stolen, he wanted someone to tell Gretchen Snyder how generous he was.

On the lonely nights in Van Nuys, Arnie thought of little else than Gretchen Snyder. And he woke up thinking of her and delivered his papers with his brain bursting with visions of her loveliness. He returned to the farm by ten and took care of his fruit picking and feeding the local hands. Then he worked another two hours before cleaning up and riding his bike back over washboard paths to see Gretchen at the Pico House where she worked as a waitress.

The bantam cock maitre d' had asked him to stop coming because it disrupted the help—and he couldn't tie up a table that long while Arnie ate all that bread, butter, jam, celery, those carrots and radishes and only bought a cup of coffee.

Last night he was presented a bill for twenty cents for the bread and relish tray.

Tonight he would wait for pretty Gretchen on the sidewalk in front of the hotel. He was angry it was so foggy. Now he would not have the luxury of seeing her walk toward him from the distance with that devastatingly liquid gait of a nymph effortlessly treading water.

Three blocks to the north, in a structure indistinguishable from some better-off folks' tool shed, Aunt Suff watched the girl bathing.

The tiny shoebox of a house had only four rooms: a small living room, bedroom, a narrow kitchen and pantry across the back.

Aunt Suff sat at her sewing table off to the side of her narrow bed. As soon as she was sure her husband wouldn't be back (and some said she had made that decision much too early) she traded the old double bed for a narrow, chaste cot. "You couldn't hardly walk in the room with that big bed," she had said.

She was trying to concentrate on letting out the seams of the minister's black worsted wool pants spread across her lap. She thought he must be eating and drinking a lot more than Jesus did.

Two things distracted her: The arthritis in her fingers flaring up in sharp-stabbing pain when she tried to grasp the needle, and the naked girl standing before her without even the modesty or plain good sense to close the door.

Looking at the nubile body glistening with droplets of water the girl had fetched from the pump and heated on the wood burning stove, Aunt Suff thought, "My God in heaven, she has reached the full flower of womanhood and she's barely sixteen."

Suff had decided there was nothing for it but to have it out with her, once and for all.

Oh, she wouldn't relish talking the facts of life. She found them distasteful, but she couldn't shirk her responsibility. They had dumped the child on her unfairly, but that was no call to have the girl live in ignorance.

She looked at the creamy young skin as soft as moonlight. Suff noticed now to her shame the young nipples that seemed unselfconsciously upturned to match the little innocent nose. Was she washing herself so laboriously to make herself clean for that aggressive boy, or was she scrubbing her sins away?

She cleared her throat and called, "Gretchen," sternly, her voice rough and reedy as an oboe on the lips of a beginner.

"Yes, Aunt Suff?"

"I want to talk to you before you go," her breathy sounds rapped across the tiny room.

"I'll be right out." The music in Gretchen's voice was genuine, like one born to sing.

She began toweling herself with fluid gestures that seemed pagan to Aunt Suff. Did she really linger down there with an innocent animal sensuality, or was it her imagination?

Suff looked up from the lifeless black trousers on her lap into the eyes of the girl and thought she saw the same mocking silence there she had seen ten years earlier.

The girl was fresh and clean and pretty and young, and the only one of those Suff had ever been was clean. She resented the beauty of the girl, just as she had always resented the good looks of her sister. But what had good looks gotten her sister? Running off to Germany with a sailor and a fornication induced death.

"You want me to take the seam out for you, Aunt Suff?" Gretchen broke the silence.

"I can do it," she said, as if startled to find the girl there. She moved the trousers from her lap to the table, straightened her back and smoothed the lap of her pewter dress and pursed her bloodless lips as one about to embark on a matter of great moment.

As the girl looked expectantly down on her, Suff looked to the pantry where the girl's bed was wedged diagonally because the tiny room would not hold it any other way.

Gretchen looked through the pantry window to a stubble of dusty-brown doomed grasses, and a sparse, dehydrated lemon tree that had steadfastly refused to die. Gretchen had always thought her Aunt Suff was all lemony sour like that old tree. Why even the wart on her left cheek puckered out to look like the butt end of a dry lemon.

Aunt Suff was tall and spare, there was no frivolous fat on her self-righteous bones. She had skin, yes, and enough fat to keep out death, though she wasn't sure why, and the bones were as brittle as the dried old branches of the lemon tree.

Suff folded her hands, prayer-like, in her lap. Her eyes were on the girl's hips now, the sensual swell of flesh and muscle, so close in the small room. The towel hung indifferently on her shoulder. Suff blushed because her niece made no attempt to cover her things that should have been private.

"I want to talk to you about that boy."

"Aunt Suff," her eyes pleaded for mercy, "I wrote the letter."

"What's his name again?"

"Arnie Sutler."

"Oh yes." Her lips drew inward. "Sounds Jewish...."

"Well he's not."

"Oh well, Arnold, I was only thinking, well," she floundered, her mind at sea without a chart. "Well...."

Suff frowned. It did not promise to be easy.

"Well, I'm gonna talk plain to you, girl, and I don't want you taking offense or giggling. You know," the voice, harsher now, trembled, "about copulation?"

"What's that?"

"People, men and women...copulating, fornication." Suff's face turned blue.

"You want some water, Aunt Suff?"

"No," she fanned herself with her open hand, the arthritic bumps on her bones jutting in all directions like warts on a frog. "I'm all right." There was a long silence as Aunt Suff swayed with vertigo. "Get dressed, child," she said. She needed the break.

While Gretchen put on her waitress uniform, the black dress and pert white apron, Suff blurted, "There's diseases you can catch and they bring sickness and death and a plague on your generations."

Gretchen's eyes grew at the horrors foretold. She left for work confused and afraid at the face her aunt painted on the Great Mystery of Life.

The cold, foggy evening air sent needles dancing on her skin and she felt her heart pounding faster than it ought.

She grew curious about boys as her body changed from an awkward girl's to a woman's, and as men began looking at her. Then this

boy had talked to her at the Fourth of July parade and she didn't
know what to do. Her instinct told her to be standoffish, but he was
making her feel like a fast ride in a horse buggy, and maybe she had
smiled at him once or twice when she hadn't meant to.

She had always obeyed her aunt. But now that she was working
the dining room at the Pico House the boy would come and sit for
hours and just watch her. Then he would leave her a note telling her
how beautiful she was and asking couldn't she just smile once more
at him.

Her body trembled when she saw him through the fog.

With nervous fingers she reached into her pocket for the letter
she had watched Aunt Suff seal in the envelope. She thrust it at
Arnie with a jerking motion, then ran into the hotel without looking
back.

Arnie took the letter with a proprietorial jealousy to the window
where the dull light from the dining room gas lamps shone yellow
like the haze of a penumbral sun.

Hunched over to shield its magic contents from a casual eaves-
dropper he read:

Dear Mr. Sutler,

    Your attentions to me are annoying my aunt. She does
not think it proper for a young man to carry on so.
    She wants you to stop writing to me and seeing me.

Very truly yours,

Miss Gretchen Snyder

Arnie stuffed the letter in his pocket and pushed through the
brass and glass door to the lobby of the Pico House and sailed like an
armed frigate through the side door into the dining room. The light
of the gas lamps dotting the walls flickered like fireflies in a mating
dance. It cast a jaundiced pall over the handful of people already
seated at tables and the attendant waitresses.

The maitre d', known to the gentry as Roscoe, exhibited his
habitual reflex on seeing Arnie breathlessly scanning the room for his
beloved.

"Not you again." Roscoe's lips congealed.

Arnie looked at the rose in his hand, then reached into his pocket
and passed a quarter to Roscoe.

Roscoe pocketed the quarter with the unobtrusive wave of his hand.

He shook his head, looking up and down at Arnie's threadbare black suit as he did every time he saw him.

The suit had been bought for Arnie on the occasion of his grandmother's funeral. It was used again for an uncle, his grandfather, a neighbor's child, and polished the Presbyterian pews every Sunday while the pinkish preacher pounded home predestination.

The suit was bought with plenty of room to grow and it had been let out in the pant legs and sleeves three times. The marks were as clear as the depth markings on a beached ship.

Gretchen appeared through the kitchen door, carrying a tray of salads. Arnie dashed toward his beloved.

Roscoe followed him with faultless dignity.

"Gretchen!" Arnie tugged at her arm, "you mean it was that old prune all along?"

Without showing him her teary eyes, she nodded.

Roscoe's ministerial tones were upon him. "Mr. Sutler, please," he said, taking him by the arm.

Arnie shook himself loose, handed Roscoe the rose, and ran out, knocking over one of the elegant crocheted chairs.

He ran down Main Street, forgetting his bicycle, passed a haberdasher's without looking at the brand new black suit laid out on display, and passed the new seventy-foot-high single street lamp that had been installed—as if to light the heavens and protect it from the most daring vandals.

It was one long pole with a small platform on the top and another long pole on top of that with a big plate at the top to reflect the light to the street.

After Arnie left, Gretchen brought the man who ordered pork, the pot roast; and the woman who asked for beef steak, the pork.

Arnie's first thoughtful knock on the door of the shoebox was ignored, as was his second considerate one. It wasn't until he pounded the door as an infuriated tympanist that he got action.

"Who is it?" the flat oboe called out from inside.

"Arnie Sutler."

There followed a silence as dark as death.

"Open the door or I'll kick it in."

He heard a tentative rustling sound inside.

She opened the door with a wry mocking smile on her anemic lips, the slow, almost tortuous movement of her limbs were like the arms of a conductor leading a languid funeral march.

"My, my," she said looking up into his eyes without flinching, "we are persistent, aren't we?"

"I want to come in."

"I don't want you to come in."

"What I have to say cannot be said out on this stoop," he said politely but firmly, pushing his way into the startled woman's parlor.

"See here, young man!"

"Why don't you let me talk to Gretchen?"

"Don't sass me, you whippersnapper!" The breath wheezed out of her like a neglected bellows. "What are your intentions, young man? What are your prospects?"

"Well, my intentions were to get to know Gretch—Miss Snyder. My prospects—well, my prospects of that don't seem too good right now."

She made a major effort, slightly raising the corners of her mouth. She invited him to sit down.

Aunt Suff was so stern-looking, ugly actually, with the taut skin and the protruding wart on her cheek.

"I want to get to know the girl," he insisted, sitting on the parlor couch.

"To what end?"

"End? You mean marriage?…well, I suppose that's the normal result isn't it?"

It gave Suff the opening she sought. It was the crafty old fox and the reckless young lion in the arena together.

"I raised that girl from a pup—and I didn't ask for it neither." She sat straight in the chair across from him.

Her eyes misted. "I'll never forget the day Gretchen Snyder arrived here sitting on the keg of nails on the back of that wagon." She was rubbing the bumps on her fingers, reliving the fateful day.

"Weren't nothing but a tag hung round her neck with her name and destination. Wanted no chance of her being sent back. I don't even know how old she is exactly. She's a girl without a birthday. It weren't for twenty-three days I got the letter saying my sister Agnes died and this was my legacy."

She shook her head and waved a bony arm at her fate.

"'Gutentag,' the little snot said to me—all smiles, in her little pigtails that must have bounced all over hell's half acre comin' here." Suff sighed, "Gutentag. The little snot spoke not a word of English. I had to have a German house painter in the congregation translate the letter." She snorted exasperated breath from her lungs. "They think all Americans are rich. Sending her to the land of opportunity," she chortled, clicking her tongue on her yellow teeth.

"I'll never forget that stupid face grinning up at me and neither of us understanding a word."

"How did you manage?" Arnie asked.

"God knows. Sign language—I hated that kid—I hated my sister from the time she was born—and I don't expect to escape my due punishment for it. She was a loose-liver—ran off with a German sailor. I never thought of her but as a harlot—and when she died and left me this child I couldn't even talk to—that was the end. I would have gladly sacrificed myself to hell just to be sure Agnes was there suffering too.

"Oh, I know they laugh about my name—say how right it is for me because I'm always suffering—but it hasn't been easy." Then she added, muttering, as though it might compromise her dignity by explaining, "My name's Sophia.

"But you know something? I got to like the little snot nose. We made out all right. I needed help—she gave it—cheerful—always cheerful." She looked at Arnie with a sharp eye. "You take her from me," she admonished, "I'll miss her. I never admitted that before. Said I'd be glad to get rid of her—more trouble than she's worth—but now," she paused to taste her lips, "now I'm old—and I'm bent up with the rheumatism and not able to work. The girl has just started to bring money in. If she goes, I see nothing for it for me but starvation."

So that was it, Arnie thought, just boiled right down to the almighty dollar.

Suff looked to Arnie like a chicken startled to see its feathers had been plucked. He gave her all kinds of groveling assurances that he would see personally to it that she did not go hungry, and he even exaggerated his wealth just a tad to reassure her, and after she bought his line of goods they settled back to discuss the formality of a proper courtship.

It wasn't until he left the shoebox house and went back to get his bicycle at the Pico House that he realized that he had not only agreed to marry a girl he had barely spoken to, but had contracted to support her aunt for the rest of her life.

# 15

The greatest nuisance
to mankind is men.

—Alexander Pope

Isaiah Crown was awakened at
seven in the morning by a timid knock on
his front door. Answering in his indigo
cotton robe, he found Jake Maybury,
the hardware merchant, on his porch,
woebegone, twisting nervously the hat
in his hands.

According to Jake, it was all innu-
endos and funny looks from Benjamin
Olin, and oblique references to the
French ladies in the Merced Theater
boxes, and what they did to the men
while the show was going on. Then Benjamin showed up at the saloon Saturday
night and gave him the fish eye and
asked after his wife *and* his pretty stock
clerk. Then Monday morning he wondered if Jake wouldn't like to increase
his advertising with the *Tribune*. Jake
said he reckoned he had all he needed,
thanks.

"Well, if you ever change your
mind," Benjamin had said, "just remember you'll get a better press."

Isaiah threw on his clothes, kissed

Clara goodbye and left without breakfast.

His head was bent down and his ears were back like a hound chasing a fox—his heels were kicking up the dust in cloudy explosions.

The only other time he had stalked like this was back in Springfield, Illinois, where he was laying the gas line and a rich merchant had cheated one of his workmen.

In his ears were clashing cymbals and blatant brass, and he was marching in the Army of the Lord.

Oh, he had to admit he'd had some suspicions. There was something sneaky about the lips of the new man when he spoke to him. But he was always pleased with the results—advertising was up, circulation was up, so he didn't ask questions.

So *this* was the way he got more advertising.

He passed without seeing Chan, the vegetable man, with his high-collar coat, long pigtail and his wooden vegetable cart on two big wheels.

Chan was bowing at the waist and beaming at his favorite customer. Yesterday Chan had been glum over a downturn in his business and Isaiah had given him fifty cents to surprise Clara with vegetables. Now, Isaiah was so angry, Chan was afraid the vegetables had displeased him. Today he would give twice as many—free.

Isaiah was so preoccupied with Benjamin buzzing in his mind that he turned one street late and wound up behind the two-story red brick building instead of in front.

Without realizing why, he looked in the back window before going to the front door. He saw Benjamin seated at the desk that belonged to Isaiah, poring feverishly over the big leather-bound ledger of *Tribune* accounts. He was copying things down on another sheet of paper.

Every few minutes, Benjamin would interrupt his copious note-taking and lean out the front window and look up the street.

Isaiah turned to the front of the red brick building, past the crooked sign on the corner of the lot that said:

PRINTERS

He burst suddenly in the front door. Benjamin jumped out of his seat and slammed the ledger closed in one action, and then turned his eyes sharply on his boss.

His accusative tone shot like a cracked whip, "You startled me!"

"Oh, I'm sorry," Isaiah said.

"Just going over the books," Benjamin said, without apology.

"So I see."

"Been meaning to speak to you about a few things."

"Have you?" The blood was rising in Isaiah's throat.

"Yes," Benjamin said, still fixing him with those relentless eyes, turning adversity to advantage, "when you have time..." He let the sentence dangle as a dare.

"I have time." Isaiah returned the gaze. Yesterday his eyes would have been softer, with perhaps a touch of amusement on the lashes.

"Well then," Benjamin said waving his hand in proprietorial generosity, "won't you sit down?" Benjamin sank reflexively back into the chair at Isaiah's roll-top desk.

Isaiah remained standing and looked down at Benjamin's unchanging eyes.

"Would you mind if I sat at my desk?"

Benjamin looked at the desk as though he didn't recognize it.

"Why certainly," he said, the chair scraping on the splintered floor as he pushed it back hurriedly. "If that would please you." He stood slowly. "I didn't realize it was that important to you," he said, looking up at Isaiah, who to maximize the distance between them, drew himself to his full height, a head above Benjamin.

"Please sit down, Colonel," Isaiah said.

"I don't mind standing, sir—"

"Please."

The Colonel recognized the voice of command from a temporary superior officer. They both sat, Benjamin on the simple wooden arm chair and Isaiah at the comfortable mess of his desk which Benjamin had taken the liberty of straightening to place the ledgers in the center.

"Now, Colonel, what are you doing in my ledgers?"

"Well, sir," he began, struggling to form words of what had been building inside him. "As you know, I am used to running my own newspaper—" He waited for a response, but Isaiah merely smiled with an indulgence he would use on a naughty child.

"I consider my devotion to duty at our shop second to none." He paused again, frowning. "Since you snuck up on me, I have not had time to marshal my thoughts."

"You don't have to write a speech to communicate with me," Isaiah said, "just say what's on your mind."

Benjamin tugged at the lapels of his jacket like a man whose clothes fit too tightly. "Thank you, sir," he said. "As I was saying," he cleared his throat like a man embarrassed to cough at a ladies' tea, "I have the interest of this paper at heart. I have taken the liberty to peruse the figures and to offer you the benefit of the not inconsiderable expertise I have accumulated over the years."

He paused, rubbing his hands together briskly, as though they were cold.

"I, ah, that is, it would seem to me that the business end of this newspaper could be more profitable. At least twenty percent more. Naturally I'm interested in my future, and solvency is, of course, a requisite to a sound future."

Benjamin laid out his suggestions, including reducing all salaries ten percent (Isaiah was paying fifteen percent more than the competition anyway), laying off Elsie (Benjamin's wife, Matilda, could do the work in one-quarter the time for one-quarter the pay), increasing advertising prices, selling more advertising with more aggressive salesmanship. (Isaiah thought he had just seen the result of that aggressiveness with Jake Maybury.)

Isaiah leaned back in his seat and hoisted his heavy leg up on the desk.

"I'm just a simple man," Crown said, "with the good intentions that we're told pave the road to hell, but I am a little baffled at you helping yourself to my records."

"I will in all candor admit that not all my actions were motivated by altruism."

"I'm relieved to hear that."

They were like mismatched sparring fighters, one tall, lean and spare, light on his feet—a good Sunday puncher, but with a weak defense. The other was short, pudgy and scrappy—unyielding, too short to do any damage above the heart. But the heart was what he was after.

Benjamin punched on, oblivious to the sardonic jabs. "In due course, when I felt the time augured an auspiciousness I must frankly admit I do not feel now, I was going to request your permission to purchase a share of the paper. Naturally, I wanted to be in a position to make an intelligent and educated offer."

Isaiah had a bemused smile on his lips. He spoke without moving. "How much were you considering investing, Colonel?"

Benjamin's fingers stopped drumming. His hand lifted to his forehead and brushed down across his face to his dark beard, tiny flecks of snowy worry showing here and there as his hand went underneath and fluffed the beard upward.

"I am at the moment unfortunately relatively impecunious, but I was thinking along the lines of our purchase agreement on the house where, for a consideration of a small ownership percentage, say ten or fifteen percent, you deduct a relative amount from my paycheck. I would of course like you to consider in your deliberations on the matter the fact that I have been instrumental in increasing your advertising revenue, as well as my general devotion to my duty here, and in that spirit you might see fit to increase my salary commensurate with the payment I would be required to make."

The smile on Crown's open face broadened. "Let me see if I understand you correctly, Colonel. After six months in my employ you are asking for a percentage of the business?"

Benjamin started to speak but Crown talked over him. "You further suggest financing your purchase by my giving you an increase in pay while cutting everyone else's pay ten percent, and firing Elsie, who has served me well from the beginning. Well, Colonel, I must say your idea does not light a fire in my heart. Yours is a proposition anyone should welcome."

The manicured fingernails drummed on the chair, the eyes held their peace. The tight lips were silent. Suddenly Benjamin jumped up and strutted the small floor, his hands clasped behind his back.

"I hope you will forgive me, sir, for having to make my proposal elsewhere in town. It is not my first choice—that would be the *Tribune*. But I am not a young man like you are, and if I must wait until I accumulate capital, it may well be too late. I must, for the sake of my family, look out for my best interests."

Isaiah was so shocked by Benjamin's brazen proposal that he neglected to confront him with Jake Maybury's story.

He didn't have to.

Later that evening, as the paper was being put to bed, Aaron Birnbaum, the compositor, brought to Isaiah an article written in Benjamin's strict hand.

"I don't like to bother you, boss," he said, hanging his head like a hound dog who failed to bring back the quail, "but I thought I ought to ask your approval of this before I set it."

"No bother, Aaron," he said, extending his hand to receive the paper.

*Runaway Horse* was the heading. Always good, Isaiah thought. Piqued the interest, calamaties did, though these were becoming a bit commonplace.

> The skittish horse belonging to local hardware mer-
> chant, Jake Maybury, broke loose its moorings outside the
> home of the comely widow, Ruth Brown, early today. The
> relationship between Mr. Maybury and Mrs. Brown has
> been the cause of much speculation in the community.
> The horse, a large chestnut bay, carried on like he was out
> of his mind with the strong spirits of the devil, a condition
> not foreign to his owner, Jake Maybury.
> The *Tribune* sought to question Mr. Maybury about his
> relationship with the young, attractive Mrs. Brown and the
> reports she received special considerations from the store
> and its proprietor, but Mr. Maybury refused to be inter-
> viewed.
> Mr. Maybury resides with his wife and two children at
> number 6 Green Street.

Isaiah brought his tall frame to its full height, muttered a
"Thank you" to Aaron and stormed over to where Benjamin stood at
the writing stand he preferred.

"Just what is the meaning of this?" Isaiah demanded.

Benjamin looked up as one peeved at a trivial interruption.

"Readers love a bit of gossip," Benjamin lectured his boss,
wearily. "Your circulation should increase, and he might bump up his
advertising." Benjamin turned back to his work.

Isaiah stared, laboring to control his boiling breath. "Colonel, if
this kind of article promised to make me the richest man in the
world, I would reject it." He tore the article and let the small pieces
fall on Benjamin's table like snow.

After Isaiah left Benjamin's desk, Benjamin's eyes traveled to
where Aaron Birnbaum was hunched over the tray of letters. His
nimble fingers were flying like the wind on the hills, setting up type
in the metal trays. Benjamin rose with deliberation, as if to stretch
his legs, and sauntered over to Aaron. When he stood beside him he
muttered in his ear, "You'll be sorry, you sneaky little Jew."

Later that evening Isaiah looked up and was shocked to see
Benjamin standing over him, his eyes misty, his cantaloupe face soft
putty.

The Colonel hesitated, as though he wasn't sure why he was
standing there. "I came to apologize, sir," he said.

Isaiah laid his pencil carefully on his desk.

"I have always felt that the business of newspapers was business.

I think I have gone too far and I apologize for my actions. With your indulgence I will endeavor to do your bidding exclusively, as behooves a junior officer in the ranks."

Isaiah noticed Benjamin was standing at attention, and Isaiah wanted to say "at ease," but it caught in his throat.

# 16

Princes who have set little store by their word, but have known how to overreach men by their cunning, have accomplished great things, and in the end got the better of those who trusted to honest dealing.

—Machiavelli
*The Prince* XVIII

The pepper tree stood between the house of Crown and the house of Olin as an arbitrator of the uneasy peace that recently prevailed between the warring clans.

Tall, proud, and majestically crowned, the tree covered enough of the neighboring house so each family could almost forget the other was there.

On days like today, it cast a welcome shade on the Crown side.

They were on the edge of that shade, Clara and Isaiah Crown, and a salubrious sun sparkled in the sky. It was the kind of sun that made you want to dance.

If you stood back, they seemed an idyllic couple in paradise, their lips moving in considerate conversation. Dressed all in white, Isaiah with his straw boater and suit, Clara in a Mexican wedding dress, they were two stars in an emerald sky.

Watching their lips you could feel the pulse of their contentment.

She was, in her white Mexican wedding dress with the lacy ventilation, a figure fired in porcelain.

With a suddenness that blurred the tableau, Clara jumped up from her white chair, and moving her arms like Icarus in slow motion, she threw them around Isaiah's neck, thrusting her soft cheek down next to his, bumping the white straw boater askew.

He had just told her he had booked first class passage for them on the steamer to Hawaii.

Then suddenly an invisible hand put a rein on her ecstasy, and a frown crossed the white face.

"But what about the paper?" She breathed in waving motions.

Isaiah looked up into the frightened porcelain eyes and a comforting smile touched his lips.

"The Colonel will run the paper," he said.

Clara put her hand to her heart to quell a sudden pain.

"Oh, no." She gasped the summery sunbeams. "No." She shook her head with a force marring the tranquility. "No, Isaiah, I don't want to go. I don't trust him."

He climbed slowly out of the white lawn chair and held his comforting hands out to her, taking her thin white fingers in his.

"Clara," he asked her softly, "what can he do, steal the paper? We will be gone only two months." He looked into her misting eyes, and kissed her pouting lips—"I'd rather see you happy than have a dozen newspapers."

His eyes were so full of love she couldn't argue. "The old Colonel's become a model employee," he said. "Really! Defers to me all the time. So obsequious sometimes, it's downright embarrassing."

On the day before sailing, Clara scurried joyously about checking their steamer trunks and making arrangements for the care of the house.

That evening, Isaiah went back to the office to give his final instructions.

Benjamin was standing hunched over the front counter, the half light of the gas lamps flickering across his putty face like gently brewing storm clouds.

The street outside was quiet, with only the occasional sounds of horse hooves clapping the hardened clay. Inside, the press clanked the steady rhythm that never failed to delight Isaiah. He could feel the dedicated heartbeats of the men working behind the rickety water-driven press. Felix was there, and Aaron and Pete, and the lead was melting in the old pot with the icicle drips on the sides and the paper stack was growing.

It was home.

The reporters and advertising salesmen had their desks upstairs, and part of the second floor was used for storage. Benjamin's desk was up there. Crown liked to stay on the ground floor with the men who sweated for their living.

"I see you have tomorrow's edition well in hand, Colonel," Isaiah said, standing on the customer side of the counter. "I don't believe I've ever seen you relaxing before."

Benjamin shook his head once, then put his hands on the edge of the counter and, inhaling a large draught, said, "I must tender my resignation, sir." His shoulders drooped like an old soldier at his last muster.

Isaiah Crown froze, staring dazed into the cold eyes as if to melt the mystery.

"I thought we had an agreement?"

"I can explain, sir."

Those infernal eyes tore through Isaiah like a steel arrow. His mind was on Clara's disappointment.

"You will remember our discussion some months ago regarding my offer to buy into your paper, which you rejected." Benjamin paused. "I have been made a handsome offer along those same lines."

Isaiah stared with his paling ice-blue eyes, as if hoping the man would disappear. "When did you get this offer?"

Benjamin glanced at Isaiah as though the question were an impertinence. "The last sev-er-al days," he drawled.

"And you waited until the eleventh hour to tell me?"

Benjamin brought his right hand up and smoothed the bottom side of his beard. "I naturally thought to maximize my advantage," he said. "I, of course, prefer to stay with the *Tribune*. I have a lot invested in it."

And Isaiah, the prophet of grace who said to his wife Clara, "I would rather see you happy than own a dozen newspapers," considered his meager options: cancel the trip and break Clara's heart; or let someone else take charge—Elsie, Aaron Birnbaum, Felix the pressman—he knew that much as he loved and respected them, none could take the responsibility to get the paper out. "Well," he said at last, "I don't see how we'd have time to finalize anything."

"If you'll pardon me, sir," Benjamin said, brightening. He was so respectful now; his movements took a foreign grace, his hand emphasized his speech with the rhythms of a diplomat, "I have taken the liberty to have the contract drawn." Then he added, as if awarding himself a prize for magnanimity, "At my expense, of course."

"How efficient."

And they were sparring again, Isaiah with his quiet fury and mock courtliness, Benjamin with the stiff upper lip, the General Robert E. Lee posture, and going for the aorta.

"Thank you, sir."

Benjamin produced the papers like a sleight-of-hand magician.

Isaiah scanned them quickly. He didn't have time to digest the many clauses, like the one that gave each man the first right of refusal on the sale of any part of the other's share.

The Colonel did not meet Isaiah's eyes. "The terms are as before—I will give up ten percent of my salary for ten percent of the ownership—that's the basic thrust. I will also pay you a thousand dollars when I am paid that amount owed me next year from the sale of my Santa Barbara paper."

He glanced at Crown before he added—"A subsidiary clause allows for fifty percent of the amount I increase your net income to go toward my purchase price." The smug taste of victory caressed his tongue.

Crown took the twenty-three page document to his lawyer, Larry Metzler.

Awakened from a sound sleep, the crafty attorney said, "I wouldn't do this for anyone but you, Isaiah." He sat in his living room stuffed chair with the yellowing antimacassars and frowned his way through the legal verbiage. Isaiah paced the room while the smell of the kerosene lamp bitterly forced its way up his nostrils.

When he finished the document, attorney Metzler stared at the last page a minute before laying it carefully in his lap like some fragile object.

"Well?" Isaiah was eager.

"Legal—competent," Metzler said, "only one thing."

"Yes?"

"I can't see you passing any part of your business to that barracuda, Izzy."

Isaiah smiled weakly. "He's a hard worker."

"So's the devil."

The next morning, Colonel and Mrs. Benjamin Raines Olin bade farewell on the train platform as Isaiah and Clara Crown left for the port of San Francisco to sail for Honolulu.

There were counterfeit smiles pasted on all the faces, as though a paperhanger had hung them there temporarily, while waiting for the genuine article to arrive from the manufacturer.

Clara Crown's smile was the most authentic. She understood the least.

Benjamin's smile was of clandestine triumph.

Isaiah's took more bravery than any of Benjamin's battles.

And Matilda's smile was camouflaged by an averted head to cover a guilty look, as uncomfortable as an illicit lover who put on a borrowed wedding band for the occasion.

Benjamin noticed Isaiah was bravely trying to match Clara's enthusiasm, and as the train pulled out of the station, and he and Matilda were on their way back in the buckboard, Matilda reached out and patted his hand.

"Well done," she said, the guilt gone from her grin.

Benjamin smirked in agreement. "You know," he sighed, sucking voraciously the clear morning air, "if I were in his shoes, I never would have gone away for two months and left me in charge."

Suddenly the buggy trembled as though struck by a tornado. Matilda had never laughed so hard in her life.

# 17

Never slap a man in the face if he is chewing tobacco.

—Abe Martin

The sun was pushing its way in the windows behind the *Tribune* press, silhouetting men and machinery in a frenzy of toil like one of those artistic but ambiguous political statements about the workingman's relationship to the machine.

Each worked with his own posture of doubt: Pete, Clint, Felix, rubbery and disjointed; Aaron, Will and Elsie more rigid. They had all heard the rumbling the night before. They had seen their friend Isaiah's face drained of its life's blood. They didn't have the heart to speak to him. They knew this bantam paper colonel was capable of anything.

Benjamin glanced up, then was sorry he had. He had seen faces like that on the road to Appomattox at the end of the war—long after the volunteers could still afford uniforms, making it difficult to tell friend from foe. The faces were frightened and uncertain because they didn't know if the man looking at them would shoot them or share a bite of hardtack.

The disorganized little company in the shop, back-lighted by sunbeams, weighed their chances against the well-organized enemy.

Benjamin's first official act as publisher of the Los Angeles *Tribune* was to fire Elsie, the bookkeeper.

He couldn't stand her. She reminded him of Agnes, his bookkeeper at the Santa Barbara *Sun*. She had baked him a cake to celebrate his interim control of the *Tribune*, and he had to remind the stupid woman he didn't eat cake.

She had the audacity to say that everyone else did.

"This is a newspaper, not a bakery. With what Crown pays you we could open two bakeries. Kindly remove yourself from the premises awaiting further orders. I will pay you to the end of the week if I don't have to set eyes on you again."

Elsie picked up her cake and considered dumping it on the Colonel, but took it home with her instead and ate it alone in one sitting.

The Colonel sat at Isaiah's desk reading his papers. Being in command always felt good to him. Especially today. He cleared his throat with a harumphing cough. "Front and center, troops," he called imperiously.

They assembled haphazardly like raw recruits. His hellfire eyes shifted down the ranks, where they stood, shifting from one foot to the other, folding and unfolding their arms.

Privately they ridiculed the medals on his white jacket. But the sun hit them a funny way and they sparkled, then turned dull. And when he bent over it was the old rooster's wattle again, or, some thought, the flattened udder of a cow drained of its milk.

Benjamin felt as he had in Lexington, when he stood in the dark waiting to take on the mob who had come to smash the presses—frightened but resolute.

They stood silently by as the bantam colonel laid out his plans. There were heavy inhalations of breath, shifting feet, coughing and sniffling, but they let him have his say. None of them could live without a job or the room would have been empty. Benjamin read the resentment on their curling lips, in their compressing eyes, but he held his ground.

"The lifeblood of a paper is its advertisers. We will boost them in the news—I've done a few articles to get the ball rolling.

"Isaiah is a likable man but he ran a sloppy ship....

"My wife, Matilda, will help out with a society column that will feature our advertisers....

"Now to the unpleasant part." He stopped as if hoping to put an extra edge on the promised unpleasantness. Let them sweat. Maybe it won't seem so unpleasant. The commander looked up into the hostile faces of his troops, as scruffy-looking a bunch of volunteers as he had ever laid eyes on.

"As you know, you are all being paid more than those in similar billets across town, from ten to thirty-five percent more according to my reckoning. Now I know Isaiah means well by it, but the fact is it is just not sound business. Beginning today I will be drawing a paycheck in an amount that is ten percent less than my previous checks. I am offering you an opportunity to follow my lead, voluntarily."

No one volunteered.

"Of course I recognize this may not be forthcoming and so I have a contingent plan."

There was a groan from his troops.

"In the absence of your accord on the pay cuts, I will be forced to discharge one of you. We will draw the name out of a hat."

The eyes of their brave leader traveled over the troops for signs of weakness.

There was a long silence, thick with hate, broken only by the squealing of an ungreased wagon going by the shop.

Aaron Birnbaum spoke with a respectability he did not feel.

"Colonel, did you discuss these measures with Isaiah?"

"Fomenting discord again, Hymie?" Benjamin's voice rang out with righteous indignation.

"No, sir, just getting my thoughts together," Aaron said, squarely facing Benjamin. "I will leave voluntarily, Colonel...I won't return," he said at the door, "while you are in charge."

After the door was closed and the agony spread from face to face of the remaining crew, Benjamin said softly, "You can bet your boots on it, soldier."

Felix Liverwright, pressman, hiked his pants with his suspenders and said, "Someone better go after Aaron, we want to put out a paper by morning."

Benjamin hit him with those anthracite eyes. His arm shot reflexively upward as though he meant to give a salute of dismissal. He dropped it and said, "Man your battle stations," through tight, unyielding lips.

The group dispersed with a low mumble, and Knoll and Martin made a hasty exit, pleading news and ad contacts, and Pete Tullis melted in with Felix Liverwright at the press.

Felix muttered, "If I didn't have a sick mother to look after, I'd be outa here so fast your head'd spin."

"Yeah," Pete said. "I'da taken the ten percent cut, I guess. You?"

"We all woulda, it come to that."

The Colonel stalked over to the letter boxes near the presses. "Give me a hand here, boys," he said, thrusting papers with his scrawling hand into Pete's hands. To Felix he gave an edition of the Philadelphia *Times*, dated some two months earlier with the column about a calamitous fire he wanted set for the front page.

In a few hours it was apparent that Benjamin was rusty, and his progress was often interrupted by trivial matters of everyday operation.

Around midnight, the entire staff was setting type, with six people stumbling over each other.

Benjamin felt a sudden fear rise in his throat. The muscles of his thorax were pressing his heart like the tentacles of an octopus. His breath was holding out on him and too much blood was in his face.

He called Clint Knoll over and told him to reset all the ads with double slugs between lines of type and give a half-inch of white space on top and bottom. Perspiration bubbled from his pores, his head shone with the glimmering dampness.

He took the Philadelphia *Times* from Felix and asked how much he had set.

Silently, Felix pointed to where he was. Benjamin read a few more lines and drew a line with his thick black pencil.

"Stop here," he said, thrusting the paper back at him, "and set the words 'continued tomorrow' underneath. We'll make up the space with expanded ads. Clint," he called to the space salesman. "Put a couple extra cuts in the spaces. Another pig for the butcher, another buggy for the livery, couple more barrels for the liquor store."

The only other calamity that night was the press breakdown. Felix took apart the water pipes that brought water from the canal to run the press, extracted the fish that was clogging it, and put it back together.

By five a.m. Clint and Will went home, Felix and Pete were yawning while Felix fed the press and Pete folded and stacked the papers.

Benjamin was hypnotized at Isaiah's desk by the bold box on the front page. He had written it and set the type himself.

TRIBUNE HAS A NEW PUBLISHER

Colonel Benjamin Raines Olin agreed to assume the responsibility of Editor and Publisher as of this edition of the *Tribune*. He pledges to you honesty and fairness and to report all the news in that same manner. He earnestly solicits your cooperation and wishes to personally thank all the businessmen as well as the subscribers for their patronage.

Mr. Isaiah Crown is vacationing with his ailing wife Clara in the Hawaiian Islands.

When the final page was run, Benjamin felt a sweet release. He had put papers to bed before, but never was it so rewarding.

After Felix and Pete had gone home without saying goodbye, Benjamin sat out back on a rung of a ladder propped against the building, looking at the beautiful stacks of papers neatly awaiting the early morning pickup by the distributor.

His bones were weary and his tendons ached like they had been stretched too far, but Benjamin felt a euphoria as the blood found its way back where it belonged, and his heart's pounding slowed in his barrel chest.

He had compromised but not surrendered. He had won his first battle.

Now, it was on to total victory.

He waited for Chip Jenkins to pick up the papers for distribution to all the subscribers who would read about him taking over the paper. In a few hours his name would be on all the lips in town. It was a delicious thought.

Benjamin decided, now that he was in charge of the paper, he should probably attempt some civility with Jenkins, in spite of the mocking he felt from the distributor's "Uncle Sam," at the Fourth of July party. After all, it wouldn't do to have his baby treated carelessly.

Benjamin heard the squealing wheels of a wagon approach. His eyes tightened to slits when he saw the young boy stop the wagon, already laden with competitive papers. Benjamin stood and smoothed his jacket and pants. The boy jumped down and went for the stacks of paper.

"Who are you?" Benjamin asked.

"Oh, I'm Arnie Sutler," the boy said with a cheerfulness that Benjamin found annoying.

"Chip sick?"

"No," Arnie said, loading the papers. "I bought his route. I'll be distributing the papers from now on."

Benjamin's forehead creased. "Looks like you bought a few others," he said, nodding in the direction of the wagon.

"I'm workin'," the boy smiled, finished loading the paper stacks, climbed back in the wooded slat seat and flicked the reins. "So long," he yelled with a strange eagerness, like one embarking on a great adventure, "see you tomorrow."

Benjamin just stared at the boy. He hadn't helped load the papers as he had planned to help Chip Jenkins. He just couldn't bring himself to lend a hand to one so young. Why, he was no older than his daughters.

"I don't like that kid," Benjamin thought. "I don't know why that should be, but I don't."

# 18

Always keep your pants on. It brings the boys back hoping next time you'll take them off

—Ann Corio
Stripper

They sat facing each other in the "parlor" of the cramped cottage, Arnie on the stiff-back chair (the odd survivor of a Baptist's castoff dining set) and Gretchen on the sofa with the pile of laundry that Aunt Suff put there to foreclose the possibility of their sitting together.

Gretchen took a piece of that laundry, not recognizing her white underpants in their unironed, crinkly form, and began twisting it on her lap, a placid motion that barely stirred the air.

Arnie poked at his fingernails and licked his lips, baring his teeth now and then as if the air would do them some good.

Gretchen, with her gold braids wrapped around her head like a crown, seldom took her expectant eyes from Arnie's face. It melted his heart. When she saw his eager grin, she dropped her lids to cool her eyes.

Gretchen could look at him without speaking, with her pert mouth pouting just a hair, and the luminous cheeks, pink and shiny like young apples, and set his heart pounding in his chest like a sledge in the hand of a mighty woodsman.

Her eyes were so large and trusting, hopeful, and frightened of that hope, loving and anxious for that love *he* was so anxious to give.

"You were going to tell me about your voyage," Arnie said, his voice choking timidly.

"Oh," she said softly. "It is nothing interesting." When she spoke, her tones were the halting accents of her guttural German.

"Come on," he coaxed, leaning forward so far she drew back to the limit of the couch, "I want to know everything about you."

She looked out the window on the street where rain was beginning to fall. He couldn't tell if she was trying to remember or forget.

She turned back, the beautiful smile had faded, "I remember much dark. I was in bottom ship, I think. Creaking the boards, all the time creaking—we are many in one room. I was on bottom bed—two more big people on beds on top of me. Many people sick. The boat it rocks back and front, back and front," she swayed on the couch. "One night I am asleep and I wake up to this bad noise and suddenly on my face is vomit. The lady above me was her head hanging down."

"Oh, no! Didn't that scare you to death?"

"I still remember smell. So sour and bitter."

It was not only her unspoiled beauty, as nearly perfect as anyone he'd ever seen, that captivated Arnie, but some simple goodness, a trait of her character he had not been able to understand. Sometimes she seemed as deep and fathomless as the ocean she had crossed, and at other times shallow and pellucid. She was the tides, high and low, advancing and receding.

The following Sunday, Aunt Suff decreed that the couple could walk out alone of the afternoon. Arnie was jumping with excitement, and even Gretchen felt a pleasant buoyancy.

Arm in arm, they headed for Central Park with a blanket Aunt Suff did not know they had.

It was between Fifth and Sixth Streets at Olive and Hill. Sometimes they called it Sixth Street Park, or City Park.

It was surrounded by close-set pickets, and inside the fence junipers were trimmed like cones and looked like sentries guarding the park from intruders. It was the only discernible concession to design— the square block looked like its seeds were planted with a shotgun. The random trees and shrubs gave it the feeling of a sparse forest.

On one side a sandstone church stood, its bell tower set off of the front corner clanging its clarion call to Jesus.

The rest of the surrounding area was made up of residences, wooden boxes with pitched roofs and Eastern windows, as if any day the shutters would have to be closed up against snowstorms.

Gretchen and Arnie strolled past the Newark Mansion at Seventh and Spring—the house that a man named Van Nuys paid an unheard of six thousand five hundred dollars for. Arnie couldn't believe that a man could make that much money.

Inside the park, they roamed the dirt ground seeking privacy among the trees.

Finding a place near the corner of Fifth and Olive, they settled down behind a young, bushy Monterey pine on the blanket Gretchen brought.

They looked at each other with expectant eyes that said "I am you and you are me and we were always meant so to be...."

A hazy sun in the sky settled on the couple, illuminating them with a heart-tingling glow.

"What's your favorite number?" Arnie asked, lying back on his elbows, his long legs off the blanket. Her playful eyes danced off his nose. "Three," she said, "why?"

"You can't ask that 'til I'm finished. Now what's your favorite month?"

She thought awhile, bringing a cute delicate finger to her shining lips. She hunched her shoulders with the thought—like a child she was, he thought, so like a child. "The month I meet you," she giggled. "July."

"Now how old are you?"

She frowned. "Maybe sixteen, maybe seventeen. Could even be eighteen."

He laughed, "Well how old do you feel?"

"Maybe," she wrinkled her nose, "old," she said.

"Well," he insisted, "pick one."

She frowned, closed her eyes and said—"Eighteen!" She opened and clapped her hands. "But why are you asking me these questions?"

"We are going to get you a real birthday."

"How?"

"We just did it—you were born on July 3, and let's see, this is 1882, so less eighteen—you were born in 1864—and next birthday we will have a big celebration and you will be nineteen."

She giggled; her low, guttural laugh shook her light body. Arnie moved closer to rest his head against her arm.

"I wish I could get to know you."

She frowned, those blonde fuzzy eyebrows dropping as her pert little nose tried to rise to greet them. "But you *are* getting to know me. We have met seven Sundays now."

"You counted!" he smiled. "I wish I could...." He looked around quickly and took her by surprise, planting a firm, dry kiss on her cheek.

She pulled away, then giggled. "Are you a naughty boy?"

"Yes I am," he laughed. "And I'd like to be a lot naughtier."

"My Aunt Suff would be a scandal."

"She would."

"She would," Gretchen struggled to finish the sentence. "She would—Suff-er."

They both laughed.

His second attempt on Commercial Street met with stiff resistance. She said, "Aunt Suff may be watching. If not, God watches."

Arnie persisted in later walks and she relaxed her defenses to his amorous attentions. But she treasured her purity.

It was in the park two weeks later that she made her promise. They had lingered past darkness while their kissing had heated with abandoned passion.

Arnie groped. Her resistance withered.

"No, Arnie," she said. "Not now."

"When?"

"Oh, Arnie."

"When?" He held her tightly to him, pressing her breath from her.

"Oh."

"The ice cream sociable," he said.

"Oh, Arnie."

"Yes?"

"Yes, Arnie. Yes."

No sooner had she made the pact, than she regretted it, and wanted to withdraw the offer.

But Arnie thought it was preordained.

Sally Quinn had never seen Gretchen Snyder look lovelier. She looked so radiant the older girl felt compelled to ask her why she seemed so morose.

They were decorating the Central Baptist Church for the cake-walk and ice cream sociable.

The tiny room, optimistically called the Social Hall, was added to the church by some industrious brothers of the congregation for the expressed good purpose of keeping the social intercourse of the flock intramural.

The hems of the girls' plain dresses brushed the floor as they worked.

Sally, the older girl, moved easily with an almost brazen quality since she had married Warren Quinn, the banker's son, while Gretchen, the younger, seemed frightened of something.

At Warren's request Sally was wearing her frocks higher in the neck. She laughed to herself. If Warren Quinn wanted her looking like Colonel Olin's dowdy daughters, it was jake with her.

There had been, she heard rumors, some funny business there with Warren and Mary Ellen, the oldest Olin girl, but Sally brought home the bacon, so to speak. And that was really all she cared about.

Sally and Gretchen were hanging bunting on the rough-sawn wood walls, Sally tacking her end to the board with a tiny hammer.

Sally walked to Gretchen and took her end of the decoration, and tacked it on the wall.

"Well," she said, "I don't care how much you protest, anybody with eyes can see there is *something* wrong."

Gretchen sulked for a minute, and then let it out.

"Arnie's so smart and successful, and I am nothing," Gretchen said, frowning. "He means to buy more paper routes. He says he will one day control the whole town. But he wants to do many other things—with me."

"Listen, lamb," Sally said, "you don't have to tell me. You aren't the only young woman with those feelings. But the trouble is you don't know anything about men."

Gretchen nodded enthusiastic agreement.

"Men are animals. They will do *anything* to get women, but only as much as they have to. If you give in to the eager beavers in the moonlight, they are painfully slow to settle their accounts in sunlight."

Gretchen blushed.

When another wall was draped with festive bunting, Sally turned her attention back to Gretchen.

"Listen, kid, I've been through the mill. I was used plenty 'til it dawned on me—Sally, he wants this a lot more than you. Control him, and you'll have him eating out of your hand."

Gretchen considered for a moment this new idea. "What do I do when he gets all...excited with passion?"

"*Do?*" Sally said. "Do nothing. If we girls weren't so dumb we could rule the world. Look at me—I got Warren. Who was I? Just a bank teller—and he's the boss's son. Now if you'll only listen to me, I'll get you what you want."

That night when Arnie came to the door looking all tall and handsome in his dark, shiny funeral suit, stiff high collar and tie, Gretchen told him she couldn't go to the sociable with him.

"But we've been looking forward to this night for—a long time," he protested.

"Hm," she said with a softness that melted his heart. "You were. I was scared. You wanted me to promise things I cannot until I'm married."

In a simple ceremony the following Sunday at the Central Baptist Church, under the proud, watchful eyes of Aunt Suff, Arnie Sutler and Gretchen Snyder were married.

It was preordained.

# 19

Dear Matilda,

I am in receipt of your offer of a visit. I have remained firm in my conviction that you have thrown your life away on a no-count high-binding gold digger.

Should you find yourself free of this pompous leech at any time in my lifetime, you will, of course, get a welcome here befitting a daughter. Not before.

—Letter from Stanley Munson to his daughter Matilda Munson Olin.

Los Angeles in 1882 was stretching for fourteen thousand folks. San Francisco had two hundred fifty thousand. Sacramento and Oakland had more people than L.A., but if you were run out of a mining camp, the city of the angels was your refuge.

It was the mines that created California's growth. Those who made it stayed in Northern California. Those who didn't, came to Los Angeles. It is an attitude that prevails in San Francisco to this day.

Benjamin sat at Crown's roll-top desk, wearing his white jacket and Civil War medals. Matilda was at Elsie's table. There was an air of royalty about the place whenever the couple occupied their battle stations. "The King and Queen," Felix Liverwright, the pressman, called them. It was the way they held their heads, in that go-to-hell manner.

Twenty years had rounded Matilda's features and taken the edge off her personality. Her skin had hardened like dry cheese, her thighs were like stovepipes. She had turned over to her three children whatever bloom of youth she might have once had.

When Benjamin paused in his writing, he drummed the end of his pencil in ruffles and flourishes on the desk top. He visualized smartly dressed troops parading down the field.

When Matilda stopped writing she chewed the end of her pencil.

The sharp tapping of hesitant heels on the wooden platform outside brought Jake Maybury into the shop.

Benjamin rose, took Jake's hand and pumped it heartily. Jake looked as forlorn as when he paid his early morning visit to Isaiah Crown. He was twisting his hat as though his hands had never stopped torturing it.

"Came to apologize," Jake muttered.

"Apologize," Benjamin's head drew back. "What on earth for?"

"Misjudged you," Jake pursed his lips, his severe head bobbing. Matilda's smiling puff-ball face was on him.

"Them was mighty nice things you said there in your newspaper 'bout me an' my store."

"Meant every word, Jake," Benjamin nodded.

Jake glanced sheepishly at Matilda. "Jenny, my wife, she's right happy 'bout what you said in your new society column, Miz Olin."

"Good," she nodded curtly. The social grace of Miss Phipp's Finishing School had faded with the frontier.

It had been a report on a fancy dress party given by the Merchants' Association and Matilda gave full rein to her imagination:

> Radiant in her mauve velvet and crinoline gown, Jenny Maybury looked up into the clear, righteous eyes of her handsome husband, Jake, and saw there admiring eyes that bespoke his great love for her....

"Seems like my business even picked up," he said, almost as though he were talking to himself.

"Well you will find that this paper will be solidly pro-business under my stewardship," Benjamin said. "Actually, I wanted to run some articles about you before Izzy Crown vetoed them."

Benjamin suddenly jabbed Jake in the ribs conspiratorially with his elbow, and winked. "When the cat's away the mice will play, eh, Jake?"

"Well," Jake said, twisting his sweat-stained hat, "Jenny and I talked it over and I guess we're willing to pay for the extra advertisin' after all."

Benjamin lifted his arm and draped it around Jake's shoulder, like a father proud of a slow son who had pleasantly surprised him.

"There's no extra charge, Jake. Matilda's already made up the bill for the old amount of space."

"But," his eyes were big as moons, "we got the space, we ought to pay."

"Nonsense, Jake, you didn't ask for it. I'm glad you see some results from it."

Jake ducked his head, "Sure misjudged you," he said, his long face baffled.

"Well, I'm glad you came in so I could clear the air. Because I have always felt advertisers were the backbone of this paper. Now Izzy Crown is strongly pro-labor, and I hold no brief against labor, but I have said before and I will say it again, it is the merchants that are the backbone of this community."

"Hear, hear!" Jake said.

After Jake left, Matilda said, "You know, Colonel, I actually think you are becoming liked in this town."

"Yes," he allowed, "and why not? There is nothing so conducive to popularity as the promotion of someone's self-interest."

She closed her eyes to relish his phrasemaking.

Sooner or later they all came in to see the King and Queen; came in with their lickspittle and gratitude, their heads hanging low, their voices catching in their throats.

Benjamin's editorials were so crammed with opinions near and dear to the merchants, that Pete Tullis was heard to comment that the *Tribune* wasn't a newspaper anymore, it was a house organ for the Merchants' Association. Benjamin fired him.

When Benjamin Olin stepped outside the dark and dank printing shop the glare of the sun shocked his black eyes. He was on his way to the Merchants' Association luncheon, his last before Isaiah came home and took his paper away from him. He was walking tall. He felt good. The sun was warm. The air was clear. His hand went unconsciously up to reassure himself his medals were in place, like a woman gently touching her breast from below.

He paused before he entered the Pico House, wondering if he had left any stone unturned. No, he decided, he had buttered them all.

His heels clicked on the wooden porch like the drums of the Fife and Drum Corps. The door opened just as he reached for the handle. On the other side was Fred Quinn, the banker, with a fearful grin of gratitude.

Matilda had outdone herself in her society column on what a fine, upstanding man he was, and the idyllic relationship he had with his lovely wife of twenty-five years—a love that glowed in every glance between them. It was as though Matilda had only one arrow in her quiver, and she shot it at the suckers time after time without ever missing the bull's-eye.

Benjamin would never forget Fred pleading with the comely bookkeeper from his bank at the Fourth of July party. Fred hadn't forgotten either.

Suddenly Benjamin was alert to a rumbling sound. He looked around the room and realized they were all looking at him and applauding—now they were on their feet and the ovation was being led by Fred Quinn.

Benjamin threw his arm around Fred's shoulder and gave him a reassuring pat. Fred was relieved he did not offer to shake his hand. He didn't want Benjamin to feel the clammy perspiration on his palms.

"Izzy Crown doesn't always agree with me, but I have said before and I'll say again," Benjamin said when they quieted down, "it is the businessmen who are the backbone of this community."

"Hear, hear!" they all shouted.

In the corner the two waitresses with the black dresses and white aprons were appraising the gathering.

"I do not like him," the blonde with the braids tight against her fragile head said.

"Who?"

"The windbag they clap for."

"Why not? You don't even know him."

"I don't have to know him," she said with a dark shiver running down her body, "just look in those eyes. Those black eyes are saying 'You are all fools.' He is a scary man. I couldn't throw him further than I could trust."

"Oh, Gretchen Sutler, I swear that's the silliest thing I ever heard. Now come on, let's get these salads out."

# 20

Someday you will come
upon a man who will lay
down in front of you a new
deck of cards with the seal
unbroken and offer to bet
he can make the jack of
spades jump out and
squirt cider in your ear.
Son, do not bet him
because as sure as you do,
you are going to get an
earful of cider.

—Damon Runyon

The table stood between the coat
rack and the ornate brass canister for
holding umbrellas. Colonel Olin liked
the canister as a reminder that one of
the benefits of Southern California was
you so seldom needed umbrellas. The
telegram lay there on the table lifeless
and ignored—yet not thrown out so
they could forget they were ignoring it.

ARRIVE TOMORROW ON 9 AM
TRAIN STOP CLARA AND ISAIAH
STOP

It was nine A.M. when Mary Ellen
Olin started out of the house for the Los
Angeles Business College. The telegram
was still where it had been dropped,
somehow clinging to the edge of the
vestibule table.

All three of the Olin daughters
passed the telegram on their way to
school. Only Mary Ellen stopped to look
at it.

She was a plain young woman, who

had inherited the worst physical characteristics of both parents—she was short like her father, with his small mouth and round head, and with her mother's dangling nose and meager eyes. But she had the wits of both of them. She learned quickly in school, stood far above the dull competition, and did not endear herself to her classmates in doing so. They ridiculed her looks and her father for being a "tin corporal." The boys never gave her a second look. Colonel Benjamin Olin was well-known—he was connected with a newspaper. It was to Mary Ellen's classmates a position of power and influence—they, for the most part, came from humble families, and they hated her for it.

Her sisters, coming later, benefited from the healing effect of time, from their noncompetitive natures, their average schoolwork, and their good looks and gregariousness.

Mary Ellen held the telegram lightly between her fingers. She imagined it was an urgent message sent to her over distant telegraph wires, urging her to come for a clandestine meeting with a handsome lover.

She felt dizzy for a moment, then carefully placed the telegram back on the table. The tall grandfather clock told her it was nine A.M. already. Her phantom lover would wait another day—another year. Perhaps forever.

And, at nine A.M., Isaiah and Clara stepped off the train into the sunshine of home.

They looked around for the Olins.

"Maybe he didn't get the telegram," Clara allowed, her serene face compressed in the question.

"He knew when we were coming," Isaiah squinted in the sunlight, still looking for Benjamin. "The telegram was a reminder."

"Maybe he forgot—" Clara was so happy, she couldn't worry. She had blossomed on the trip from a delicate flower to a sturdy vine.

They went to the newsstand on the corner. "Hi, Izzy," the vendor said. "Welcome home—*everybody* is going to be glad to see *you*," he said, and handed him the paper before he asked for it.

Isaiah put the two cents on the counter. "Thanks, Pat."

The vendor pushed it back. "It's on me."

When Isaiah looked at the new masthead, a jumble of cuts of paddle wheelers, eagles, American flags, he passed it back to Pat.

"You gave me the wrong...."

Pat shook his head. Isaiah looked down again. It *said* the Los Angeles *Tribune*, it just didn't look like it.

Half of the front page was devoted to ads in little boxes, like side-by-side ladders with staggered rungs.

"He certainly sold a lot of ads," Isaiah said. Then he began reading the framed statement in the top left corner.

> This is the last day of my eight-week tenure at the helm of this newspaper. It has long been my ambition to take a mediocre paper and make it great. Your generous encouragement and praise for my innovations have been graciously appreciated. The tenor of your remarks, coupled with the following statistics would bode some success.
> Permit me to crow a mite:
>
> > Advertising revenues UP 32%
> > Costs of operation down 15%
> > Profit for Isaiah Crown UP 74%
>
> I have always preached that a strong newspaper is the backbone of a strong community and that the business of a community is business, just as the business of a newspaper is business.
> I leave to the judgement of history the value of my gains at the *Tribune*, but I vow that now that I have had a taste of the greatness of this community, my thirst will not be quenched until I see it at the top of the country where it belongs.
> I have always stoutly maintained that the lifeblood of the community, and it naturally follows, of the *Tribune*, were the merchants and businessmen. Isaiah Crown's focus has often been elsewhere. We shall all be watching with interest to see down what path he will take the *Tribune* now that success has been handed him—and what he will choose to make of the dramatic gains of my stewardship.
> And so I pass the mantle to him.
>
> *Palman Qui Meriut Ferat*

Isaiah staggered as though he had been hit broadside with a crowbar. He barely made it to the bench on the wall before he collapsed into it. Clara grabbed the paper and read Benjamin's statement.

"Fire him," she said in the moment her delight turned to horror. "I knew we shouldn't have gone, Izzy."

It wasn't Isaiah Crown that stormed the little two-story brick *Tribune* office that morning, it was Orpheus possessed of a demon.

Benjamin didn't look up. He was at Isaiah's desk—holding his head at that go-to-hell level.

Matilda sat at Elsie's table.

Isaiah Crown stood over Benjamin, glaring down at him—the look demanding an explanation.

"You're back," the Colonel said, barely shifting under his boss's gaze.

"Do you want to explain that editorial?"

"It was written in plain English, sir," he said, shrugging his shoulders so slightly.

"And you couldn't be bothered to meet the train?"

"Too busy."

"Really—at nine in the morning?"

"I'm not a hack driver."

"Where is Elsie?" he asked, puzzled at seeing Matilda in her place.

"I've made a few changes," he said.

"A few? Who else?"

"Pete and Aaron."

"What?" A nausea overtook him.

"Your profit is way up."

"But at what cost?"

"No cost. A savings."

"Get out, Benjamin."

"He prefers to be called 'Colonel'," Matilda chimed in with a silly smile camouflaging her face.

"He used to say that himself—didn't you, Benjamin? Now just get out."

"But I'm not going anywhere," the little colonel stood his shaky ground. "Don't you remember our agreement, Izzy, we're partners."

"Yes," Matilda said, with a sustaining nod.

"I wish I could forget your blackmail. I will buy you out."

"No, I will buy *you* out."

Isaiah looked at his ten percent partner and so many things went through his mind, he had difficulty sorting them out.

Before he lost the last shred of his self-control, Isaiah took the past two months' papers home and spent the remainder of the morning reading them. The fawning flattery in the "society" column, the shameless buttering of advertisers, and the slanted news, turned his stomach.

Isaiah returned to the *Tribune* and told Benjamin he had seven days to buy him out and named his price.

"That's a very high price," Benjamin said, when he heard the figure.

"I'll pay it," Crown said.

"You have only to pay ten percent of it. I have to pay ninety."

Isaiah smiled and went back home. Let the little martinet have another day.

Across the yard in the gingerbread house Isaiah had sold so reasonably that people said he gave it to the Olins, Benjamin came home earlier than usual to his house full of bickering daughters and marched triumphantly through the front hall like Grant through Richmond.

He met Matilda in the kitchen where she was scraping carrots over a newspaper open to her society column. She was reading it one more time as she worked.

"That constant cackling is starting to get on my nerves," he said, breaking off a carrot and chomping on it. "Can't you marry them off?"

"I wish I could." Matilda sensed his heart was not in this small talk.

"You should have seen Fred Quinn's face when he saw me coming into his bank," he blurted. "It had the same expression it had when he came out of our parlor on Independence Day with that pretty young teller."

Matilda looked up from her carrots, her eyes and ears eagerly seeking more. Benjamin enjoyed her rapt curiosity.

"He has a lot of influence, Fred Quinn does. So I told him my plight and asked if he would be good enough to speak to his friends in my behalf. And whatever he couldn't raise outside, I let him understand I would look to the bank for."

"What did he say?"

"Oh, he grumbled and said that was an awful lot of money to borrow on such thin collateral, that it was too high a price for the *Tribune*, I'd be better off starting a new paper for less money; *that*, he was sure, he could help me with."

"So?"

"I told him I wanted the *Tribune*; that the day Isaiah walked out for his trip it was my paper and it always will be."

"Did he say he'd get the money?" she asked.

"Well, he listened politely and then said he was sorry, it just wouldn't be good business to make such a high-risk, poorly collateralized loan; and I just nodded my head gravely like I sympathized with him and I didn't say anything, and he'd stop and look at me, and I held my peace, and he'd start up again like he was afraid of the silence."

"Then what?"

"I looked out at the counter and said, 'I see Sally is still working here.' His face flushed and he said, 'Why yes, shouldn't she be?'

"'Oh,' I said so casually, 'after that little tiff in our parlor at my Independence Day party, I wasn't sure, but I'm glad you were able to straighten it out. She sure is a pretty girl. Married your son, I hear. A nice match for her,' I said. Matt, you should have seen his face."

He had taken to calling her "Matt." He had always been more comfortable in the society of men.

"So is he giving you the money?"

"That was the beautiful part. He started to say something but I ignored him and walked out. He'll be here on his knees before the next edition goes to press. Mark my words."

She jumped up and threw her arms around him, pushing him back with the force of her body and almost knocking him over.

"You know, Colonel," she said, standing back as a mother inspecting a child after some particularly good deed, "I think you'll make something of this paper."

"Not only the paper," he rejoindered; "I'll make something of this town."

The next afternoon Fred Quinn called on Benjamin at the paper to tell him he would have the money before the deadline.

Some sixty years later, after the paper was an established force in California, they printed a booklet called simply *The History of the Tribune*.

The foregoing events were covered thusly under the heading *The Coup of Colonel Olin:*

> Colonel Olin took control of the *Tribune* after a series of fallings out with the moneyed Crown.
>
> Mr. Crown had the money, Colonel Olin had the ambition. Mr. Crown said he would sell or buy Colonel Olin's interest, knowing full well Colonel Olin did not have the money and was already deeply in debt. But he had not reckoned with his man.
>
> Colonel Olin, through his fearless conduct of the edi-

torial policies, had made many friends in the financial world.

He greatly surprised Isaiah Crown by planking down the unheard-of purchase price.

The money, Colonel Olin later let it be known privately, had been supplied by a good friend and local banker.

# BOOK II

# THE POWER OF AMBITION

# ARNIE SUTLER

# THE BUILDER

Casualties were not heavy, simply because most of the men who were not on the sick list, were scattered around the neighboring towns and villages, doing business like sutlers.

—Livy
*History of Early Rome*
Book 5

# 21

Nothing is more respon-
sible for the good old days
than a bad memory.

—Franklin Pierce Adams
Newspaperman

1890

The sun rose and cast its invocation
on Arnie and Gretchen's cottage before
it blessed the rest of Los Angeles. Their
little white clapboard house in the eastern commercial district glowed like a
spread of goldenrods.

The man of the house had been up
for hours, but Gretchen was still sleeping, her thin, pale arms affectionately
entwined with her rag doll.

By 1890, Arnie Sutler controlled the
distribution of all the newspapers in Los
Angeles, and every morning he was up
before dawn supervising the men he had
working for him, now numbering seven.

But times were tough. "The Gay
Nineties" is a retrospective expression.
Many who lived in the 1890's, found little
about which to be gay.

The citrus trees which were pro-
ducing one of Southern California's
leading crops faced total destruction.
Australian ladybugs were imported to
eat the scale insects.

Other foreign imports were not as

welcome. President McKinley would raise duties to a new high in the hope of protecting sagging American industry.

Banks would close all over, and as if to take their minds from the economic slump, home-grown troops would massacre two hundred Sioux Indians at Wounded Knee, South Dakota.

The Gay Nineties, indeed.

For almost a decade railway trains had been breaking down the frontiers for the common man.

Colonel Benjamin Raines Olin put his newspapers on those trains when they headed back to the nation's heartland. And those newspapers trumpeted the glories of his town: the salubrious sunshine and its attendant bone-tingling warmth, year-round.

The booster campaign show stopper was the midwinter edition that coincided with a brutal Midwestern cold spell and the transcontinental train price wars that saw the ticket for a ride from Kansas City to Los Angeles plummet to one dollar.

People were sucked into Los Angeles like it was the vortex of a tornado. Then, just as quickly, they were blown away, leaving the town with stretch marks that would not soon be healed.

The little village swelled from fourteen thousand beating hearts to over one hundred thousand in fewer years than you could count on the fingers of one hand.

The new city halved itself when the lame and the halt did not find the instant cures that were, if not promised, at least strongly suggested in the *Tribune*, and too many of the strong were not able to find work.

But still, when the dust had settled and the train fare from Kansas City had risen, the population had increased fourfold in ten years, and over fifty thousand souls had come to roost on the Land of Opportunity.

Most of those who came and went, and those who stayed, remained loyal to the *Tribune*. In it they read news of the city council, local rodeos, balls, overland traffic, with a tilt toward Pasadena and other more affluent areas.

Many who turned back to the frozen East blamed Colonel Olin for misleading them.

Those who profited from the massive influx of consumers, blessed him.

But no one sought to credit anyone else for the phenomenon. Good or bad, right or wrong, it was his.

In *his* new town, four-story buildings of cut stone and brick were not uncommon. They had bay windows, corner turrets, arches on the ground floor.

Uneven storefronts broke out of the limits of the central business district, swallowing up residential neighborhoods. Now with the bloom off the boom, a third of them stood empty.

It all happened so quickly, there had been no time for planning.

Three-quarters of those remaining in Los Angeles in 1890 were newcomers.

One of them, named Doheny, dug a hole and discovered "black gold."

Oil derricks sprang up in front yards, back yards, even inside the houses. A mania for quick, easy wealth took hold. Oil was in demand for heating and for running those newfangled automobiles that were appearing in the streets and scaring the horses to death.

Arnie Sutler watched this new petroleum phenomenon and pondered. Maybe it was his call to riches. But when a neighbor went bust, Arnie decided it was too risky a business. Building your fortune on three-cent newspapers was perhaps a slower, but surer thing.

Colonel Olin was never tempted with easy money. His game was persuasion.

When Arnie Sutler came back in his bedroom to throw off his heavy work shoes in favor of his softer at-home footwear, the sun had just tickled the eastern horizon.

Gretchen was stirring on the lumpy mattress stuffed with straw and God knows what else. They had bought it secondhand.

The room had a bare flavor with a softwood floor and a washstand beside the bed. In the corner, a cupboard held their scant collection of clothes.

An hour later, Arnie Sutler was sitting at the scarred table, once bright with reflecting varnish, going over his route captains' reports. He didn't want to look up at his wife, Gretchen, as she stood over him with that picnic look on her face.

"Gretchen," he said, "would you quiet the kids down, they're driving me nuts."

"Arnie," her voice was soothing as she lay a hand on his shoulder, "six days shalt thou labor and do all thy work—on the seventh day He rested."

"Tell that to my publishers."

There was a baked ham smell about the place. She would put it in the sandwiches, he knew.

She stood tall above him, though she was not tall. There was a nobility about her sadness. She was still slender, almost frail. Her waist after two babies was still hourglass-narrow. Arnie admitted she was still the prettiest woman in Los Angeles.

She would have liked more children, but Arnie had said, "What's the point? We have one of each." Oh, she'd heard the rumors that he wasn't working on those late nights, that he might have been sowing his seed in other pastures, but she didn't care to listen to that kind of talk. It only made her feel inadequate.

Sometimes Gretchen regretted growing up. Arnie had led her to expect unknown happiness. Her body used to tingle with delight in his presence. Now it quaked with fear.

He went to bed early—wasn't interested there where once she found him insatiable—"I have to get up early," he said, in explanation. So she went to bed early too.

But Arnie asked her not to come to bed until after he was asleep—he said she kept him awake.

So Gretchen moved in and out of her husband's orbit like an eclipsed moon.

The truth was, Gretchen was starting to get on his nerves. He just knew she was bent on holding him back. The expressions she gave to her feelings of inferiority which he used to find so charming, now annoyed him. And Aunt Suff had become truly insufferable in her childish demands. He thought of them all as children—Aunt Suff, Gretchen, Arnie Junior and Cora Sue.

He even hated the names Gretchen had chosen for the children. She must have thought she was flattering him, naming his son after him, but he never liked the name Arnold and had always hated being called Benedict Arnold at school. "Arnie" wasn't much better. And Cora Sue was just the most gawd-awful name he had ever heard, but he had been terribly busy acquiring more paper routes when she was born. He could dimly recall Gretchen's asking him if he had any preferences for names, and his staring at her as though she had just asked him to breastfeed his first child.

Arnie had rented the house without Gretchen seeing it. She would have liked to have been consulted, not that she would ever object to anything he wanted to do.

Oh, she might have fancied a place in a less commercial area, but Arnie needed his space and he needed to be near the papers he carried.

The rough plank floors were partially covered with hooked rugs

Gretchen made out of old rags. She told Aunt Suff it was a pity she didn't know of anything she could make out of leftover newspapers, for the more she could furnish the house without spending money the happier Arnie was.

He had furnished most of their home with late-night trips through junkyards, and by keeping an eye on the townspeople's trash piles. One of their chairs had only three of its original legs. The fourth was a rough piece of lumber added by Arnie. Gretchen called the piece "Peg Leg."

The children were as pieces of furniture to ambitious Arnie. There was a table, a chair and Arnie Junior; a stool, a hatrack and Cora Sue.

Most of the time Arnie spent at home he sat dominating the desk at the far end of the dark room. He was, Gretchen told her Aunt, scheming and conniving.

Arnie jerked his shoulder to cast off Gretchen's tender hand. Her eyes snapped shut. She withdrew from him and from herself. Suddenly she turned cold and shivered.

He stood abruptly, filling the room with his hungry presence, like a nervous boxer impatient for the main event.

"The children," she muttered as if embarrassed to mention them. "The children would like you to go on a picnic...."

"Dammit all, Gretchen, I need some peace. This is the biggest moment of my life, and I've got to have quiet so I can think."

Then he began rambling as she backed off into a corner and stood looking up at him and listening, grateful for any attention from him, even if she were only some faceless listening post.

"Things have changed, Gretchen," he explained. "It's not like it was when I carried all the papers myself." His voice was high and cackly, like an old man's. "I'm on the threshold of real success in this town." As he spoke, Gretchen could see his flushed face transform him into the Arnie his pals knew, ever ready to slap 'em on the back with a hale and hearty greeting.

"I finally made a deal for Casey's route and I've got all the paper routes sewed up now. What did it take me? About seven years all told, but I don't care what they tell you about success, it *is* sweet."

Gretchen's eyes shone, her flesh tingled. He got so caught up in things she couldn't help getting caught up too.

Arnie pondered the "God-Bless-Our-Home" needlepoint sampler on the wall opposite Gretchen.

"Now I've got to make up my mind which paper is going to

survive." Arnie spoke through Gretchen, as though to someone more important behind her. "With me as a partner."

Fear clouded her china doll eyes. "You'd put a man out of business?"

Arnie turned to look at his wife for the first time. His twisting lips tasted sour from her inferiority.

"Oh—" he said, "it's too complex to worry yourself about."

"Arnie?" she asked, tugging at her sleeve as if trying to stretch it, "you work so hard, couldn't you take just one afternoon a week to relax? The children need a father. It's such a nice day, couldn't we just go to the park and have a picnic?"

"Naw, you go ahead," he waved her on, "I've got to work this thing out."

"Oh, Arnie," she went to him to plead, putting her arm around his shoulder, "we have plenty of money."

"I'll never have enough money," he said, twisting away from her embrace, his straw-yellow hair flapping over his forehead.

"But you don't spend it on anything."

"Yes I do."

"On what?"

"On making more money."

"Is that all it is, a game?"

He considered the question, but didn't answer it. Instead, he paused to think of the change that had come over him since he was the shy and loving boy who lost his best friend to the wolf.

In this life it is eat or be eaten, he thought, so he didn't have much choice but to side with the wolves.

Anyway, didn't he learn his lesson well at his mother's knee? Hadn't God laid it all out for him before he was born?

So, if he wasn't always the sweet innocent he had once been, it was simply because it was preordained.

# 22

Our youth, of labor
patient, earn their bread;
   Hardly they work, with
frugal diet fed.
   From plows and har-
rows sent to seek renown,
   They fight in fields, and
storm the shaken town.
   No past of life from
toils of war is free,
   No change in age, or
diff'rence in degree.
   We plow and till in
arms; our oxen feel,
   Instead of goods, the
spur and pointed steel;
   Th' inverted lance
makes furrows in the plain.
   Ev'n time, that changes
all, yet changes us in vain:
   The body, not the
mind; nor can control
   Th' immortal vigor, or
abate the soul.

—Virgil
*The Aeneid* Book IX

Colonel Benjamin Raines Olin was fuming.

One of the ad-takers from the first floor lobby had just fled his office, downtown in the heart of things, after delivering the news that the greasy little wop, Tomasino Taravella, was downstairs insisting on seeing him.

What he didn't need today was a carpetbagging labor agitator. Not one who was a half-inch taller than he was.

Downstairs in the reception room, or "Holding Tank," as Tomasino Taravella liked to refer to it, the reception counter could have graced the finest saloon. It had Colonel Olin's favorite eagles on the corners and dog heads in between.

Colonel Olin had always despised the mud-splattered, scarred counter of his first newspaper office, kicked by the cowboys' manure-caked boots. He dreamed of a counter so beautiful no one would dare touch it. When he got it, he manned it with three husky men to protect it.

Mahogany and brass, it looked like a tall bathtub with eagles' talons scratching the floor as if to scare away the rats.

Through the windows Tomasino could see the American flags and pennants that hung everywhere like some real estate swindle was in the offing.

Above the entry, leaded in green stained glass on a blue background, Tomasino saw the backside of the name

ǝnudirT ǝʜT

"Colonel Olin is not available."

Tomasino Taravella looked up.

"When will he be available?"

"Not for a long time."

"I'll wait," he said after foolishly trying to stare down this lofty sentry. The air was charged with all the right kind of ions to make it crackle.

"You might wait for days," the towering ad-taker said, wanting to get the message through to this pip-squeak without hitting him in the face. "Weeks, even."

"That's all right," Tomasino said. "I'll wait."

The tall man leaned over the ornate counter to engage Tomasino in confidence. "Look here, friend, don't you get the drift? He doesn't really want to see you."

Tomasino fixed the evasive eyes with his resolute soul. "I get the drift," he allowed. "I want to see *him*. A man big as he is should do a man small as me the courtesy. All it is—common courtesy for the common man."

The ad-taker let a sigh escape his nostrils, flapping a few hairs of his mustache. He shook his head. "There are no chairs in here," he said.

"I'll stand."

He stood as he had stood on the entire trip from Naples to New York, with the cold sea spray hitting his olive oil face. He came on the ship when he was only five and a half years old. Most of the trip he spent with his father on the bow gazing expectantly into the approaching horizon, looking for a sign of the New World.

"Kiss poverty goodbye forever," his father had said to Tomasino.

And here he stood in the Los Angeles *Tribune* lobby—for two and three-quarter hours.

And it wasn't until it became obvious that the only solution was the unwelcome scene of a physical eviction that the messenger from God brought the note and handed it with the smirk of house policy to Tomasino.

Mr. Taravella:

> When you read this I will have left by the back dock. I believe in industrial freedom. We speak to individuals, not to organization representatives who do no constructive work themselves. If you want to speak to me, apply for a job as a typesetter and we will see what you can do.

> Colonel Benjamin Raines Olin
> Publisher and General Manager

Tomasino read the note twice, then carefully folded it in quarters.

An economical smile tiptoed on Tomasino's lips. He strode over to the bar festooned with eagles and bird dogs. "I'd like to apply for a job as a typesetter."

There was a flush of faces, a twitch of mustaches, a huddled conference, and the proper bureaucrat was sent for. The flabby gent in shirtsleeves and arm garters told Tomasino they did not hire union men. He was terribly sorry, and if Tomasino wanted to give up his membership....

Tomasino grinned at him—a boyish, unthreatening grin.

"Oh well," he said, carefully unfolding and laying the note from Colonel Olin on the counter, "it wasn't my idea anyway."

He tipped his derby and left.

# 23

I buy woodpulp, pro-
cess it, and sell it at a profit.

—Lord Rothermere
English newspaper tycoon

Arnie Sutler was on the streets, and
when he was, it would take a three-alarm
fire or a runaway horse to take your
attention from his dominating stride.

He was like an upright battering
ram in a black suit, and he stepped aside
for no man.

The sun was pale and the air was
still as Arnie cut through it, and the air
fell down dead in his wake.

He was making his way from publisher's office to publisher's office in Los
Angeles, and it wasn't only because of
his size, but the way he moved that
made you think the sea would part and
the mountains crumble under him.

"I'm sorry, Mr. Crown isn't in," the
secretary at his first stop said; and on to
the next:

"Gus isn't here—" and another:

"Mr. Zimmerman will be out for a
few hours."

No one stopped him as he plowed
through the *Tribune* fortress to the
third floor.

He was a man with advancement on his mind. A man with a grip on the world where it hurt the most. Everyone thought he belonged. A mover. A shaker. The kind of guy they looked on with resentment and awe. Resentment because he was pushy; awe because it got him someplace.

The heat rose to the third floor and so the door to the meeting room stood ajar to ventilate the room. Arnie stopped, looked in, and listened.

The five publishers sat as if guarding the sanctity of the mahogany table that imposed itself between them. The room was painted like the inside of Benjamin's Civil War field tent. Old Glory hung limp in the corner. Colonel Benjamin Olin was proud of his flag, and you couldn't get away from it in his headquarters. A troop of lead soldiers, behind little cannons, was lined up on the table facing a larger scrub troop. It was officers and gentlemen against rabble noncoms.

Four of the men wore identical black suits, white boiled shirts with high starched collars and long drooping black bow ties. Isaiah Crown wore gray pants and a red and green plaid shirt with no tie or jacket. The nonconformity of his garb irked Benjamin, and that was one of the reasons Isaiah dressed that way for the meeting.

The Colonel stood and cleared his throat, laying a fist against the germs. Let there be no doubt who was in charge. The door was behind him. Arnie saw his back—broad and solid. The light from the window beside him dramatized his martial stance. Instead of shades, it had two tent flaps which met at the center of the ceiling above the window and flared on a diagonal to the corners of the floor.

To his left, with new spectacles, looking ever the bookkeeper with all the regulation paraphernalia but the green eyeshade, sat Eldon Searles of the *Post*.

Across the table, Freddy Zimmerman, the *Gazette*, a rough-faced broncobuster in his mid-fifties. His fat, smelly cigar was getting on Benjamin's nerves.

Mountainous Gus Unger, the *Chronicle*, his eyelids drooping after a gargantuan meal. A gravy mishap between plate and palate reposed on his white shirt.

Down at the far end of the table by himself, with that maddeningly smug face, sat Isaiah Crown, who had taken Benjamin's money and started the Los Angeles *News*. He wanted to keep the maximum distance between himself and Benjamin. In the eight years since they had gone their separate ways, they had been at each other's throats, editorially. Crown employed word play and sophistry. Olin used sledgehammer invective, calling Crown things like "fleabrain," and "lily-livered wart-face."

The Colonel was in mufti, so only a single medal hung from the breast of his black suit.

The fan was whirring overhead, the big window and the door were open, but the room still felt stuffy.

"I'm caught in a paradox," Isaiah Crown drawled, slouched at the end of the table in that maddening plaid shirt. "Sergeant Olin, here, mentions the immorality of unionism and then proposes a union of publishers to fight it. Now if freedom and individualism," he gestured with his long arms as if a pious pastor giving an invocation, "are sauce for the gander, what about the proverbial goose?"

Colonel Benjamin Raines Olin was staring him down, his big-bellied frame quivering just a mite.

"Now if I may address the twenty percent ploy—as the devil's advocate, of course," Crown said, his eyes wandering insouciantly. "If we are tying in our losses to the labor force, shall we be obliged to divide the profits with them also? They have seen us through times when we have reaped some tidy profits. Did you offer twenty percent increases, Lieutenant?"

The Colonel flinched. He was being promoted by degrees. "My wages have always been more than competitive."

"You have a lovely new building here, Captain. Much grander than any of the rest of us. A real monument to you, complete with a predatory eagle on top, keeping his eye on the troops."

"Yes, a nice mortgage too," Benjamin grumbled through his white goatee.

"Oh, a mortgage eh? Then I suppose you are asking the bank to take a twenty percent cut in their payments, times being so tough and all?" Isaiah Crown leaned over, his hands on the end of the long mahogany table, leering, as if daring him to answer.

"Oh, shut up, Crown," Freddy Zimmerman said. "You sound like a union agitator. I say we put it to a vote. And I vote to hold firm. Twenty percent cuts across the board. Let them work someplace that pays more. I can replace them."

The vote was four to one against Crown, but still it irked Benjamin he had to go to those men he considered clearly his inferiors. He felt compromised.

The Colonel's head jerked, as Arnie Sutler pulled the door full open and barged into the room.

Arnie dwarfed the Colonel, whose face flushed to a red-beet

hue. The young man put his arm around the older man as though he were a schoolboy.

"Gentlemen. I was just coming to see you all. What good luck to find you together."

"Sutler," the Colonel barked, throwing off Arnie's arm in a huff, "you weren't invited here. This meeting doesn't concern you."

"Oh, but it does. I wanted to show you how I could solve *your* problems."

"Just get out, Sutler. I'll thank you to mind your own business."

"But your business *is* my business. I have contacts. I know what is going on in the minds of labor. I have inside information and I'm willing to share it with you."

"Get out, Sutler. I know your tactics. Get out or I shall have you forcibly ejected!"

Arnie looked around the table for a friend. Only Isaiah Crown smiled at him. No one asked him to stay.

After Arnie was gone, Gus Unger spoke. "I don't know if that was so wise, Colonel," he said, his eyes fully open now. "That Sutler lad has all our distribution routes. Whether we like it or not, he controls us all."

"No one controls me," the Colonel snapped.

The sun was high and hot enough to fry sausages as Benjamin came off the steps of the *Tribune* fortress, the dark fibers of his suit soaking up the warmth like dry sand taking on the ocean. His gait was heavy and uncompromising, to compensate for the meager stride of his stumpy legs.

He didn't invite any of his fellow publishers to lunch. There wasn't one whose company he thought would benefit him.

No one asked the Colonel to lunch. None of them liked him that much.

He crossed the street and dug his heels into the dry earth, raising puffs of dust. He drew in the fresh air and sighed four times. He felt some relief having escaped, but he was still so damned mad, he couldn't breathe normally. Suddenly he sensed someone behind him.

The man passed Benjamin and turned around to present himself in his path.

"Colonel?" Tomasino asked, his voice respectful. "May I have a word with you, sir?"

Colonel Olin regarded him as though having come upon a pesky animal who threatened to get under foot.

"I'm in a hurry," the Colonel replied, and tried to move on, finding his way blocked by the short, wily Tomasino Taravella. Though Tomasino was a mite taller, the Colonel seemed an over-whelming presence.

"It would only take a second," Tomasino said, his eyes pleading. "I can walk fast, I understand you want us to take a twenty percent cut."

Benjamin stopped short. "Where did you hear that? That meeting was over less than an hour ago. Sutler—it must have been Arnie Sutler who told you." Benjamin knew he couldn't trust that snake. "Times are not what they used to be—you know that. The population's cut in half. We're in a depression—"

"They will get better. Colonel Olin, you are wealthy, we're poor."

The Colonel bristled. "There's a reason for that." He moved on, pounding more purpose into the street. Tomasino kept the cadence beside him.

"But these men have helped you build your paper. They've helped you get rich. Doesn't that mean anything to you?"

"It means I gave them work." Benjamin Olin was not accus-tomed to answering questions, and he found himself annoyingly on the defensive twice in this one day. "I wrote the paychecks. After you have done that, come back and talk to me."

"I won't meet a payroll. None of us will. We're poor. You're rich."

"I'm becoming mighty tired of hearing you say that, Taravella. I'm over fifty years old. When I began I was poorer than you. I worked long and hard. I fought and saved. If you want to call the shots, start your own business. That's what this country's all about, boy."

As Benjamin grew gruffer, Tomasino's tones softened. "But we none of us have any capital."

"I didn't either. I didn't have two nickels to rub together. When I made thirty cents a day I saved some of it."

"All right, but you just built a big new plant and office building."

"You any idea what that costs?"

"I haven't noticed you having to sell that big fancy house of yours," Tomasino said, and then apologizing, added hastily, "we live in shacks. You have power, you have wealth. These men are nothing individually. I want to see them band together, to speak as the one voice they feel but can't put in words because they are too dumb, or too scared."

"Look here, you young agitator," Benjamin lectured, maneuver-ing their positions so the hot sun was in Tomasino's eyes. But the heat was still under Benjamin's collar. "What you need is a lesson in elementary capitalism. The weak don't dictate to the strong. That's chaos. The strong cannot be so foolhardy as to take orders from those who have benefited from their industry."

"But you exaggerate our ambition. We only ask to negotiate as one work force," Tomasino pleaded, "not to take your business from you, just to improve the lot of the poor." They had reached the corner and the Colonel stopped. Tomasino looked back at the *Tribune* Building. It dominated the block, a cold granite reminder of the publisher's power.

Tomasino looked into the Colonel's eyes. "A man as successful as you should not fear us."

The publisher bristled, his back straightened. "I fear nothing," he said.

As Colonel Olin turned his back, Tomasino's voice turned sad. "We'll have to strike," he said with a sorrowful sigh, as a man grasping the last lifesaving straw.

The Colonel whirled around and glared at him, the anger boiling out of his eyes, his lips blue and quivering.

"You're barking up the wrong tree, you greasy little wop."

The Colonel stormed back down the street to his fortress and up the steps into the building. Without looking left or right, he marched to the back room where the linotype machines stood in rows like an armored division formed to overrun the invaders. Colonel Olin thought of it as the Great Wall of China. "Out," he shouted at the top of his pinched voice.

The room was dark. The building had stingy windows, more befitting a fortress in the frozen north. It kept the light out as well as the cannon balls. The men stopped typing. All eyes froze on Colonel Olin.

As though a kink had pinched his nervous system and vocal cords at the same time, Benjamin barked, "Every last one of you, out!"

The confused typesetters crouched, seeking protection of the machines they had worked so faithfully. Seeing the unyielding rancor in the owner's eyes, they bent over, picked up their lunch pails and moved as though their feet were too heavy to lift. They looked back bleakly, hoping he would call them back, tell them it was all a joke. After all there was a paper to get out, and they were proud to have jobs that were important. You couldn't just suddenly do without them. They weren't dispensable as soiled newsprint. They were men.

Then he repeated the action with the printers in their folded paper hats. When they had gone and Benjamin was alone with the three giant presses it took to print the *Tribune* in 1890, he thought back to Martin, Ohio, and his beginnings at the single hand-fed press. How uncomplicated things were in comparison then.

Colonel Benjamin Raines Olin barked out to the front desk, "Go down to the Central Hotel and get those men from Kansas up here!" They were standing by to fill in, glad to work in the depression for five percent less than Benjamin was offering his own men.

Outside, Arnie Sutler saw the stream of befuddled, moaning men trickle from the *Tribune* Building like rudderless dinghies in a storm. He stopped one of them to ask the meaning, and on hearing, smiled broadly. Timing was everything, he thought.

In the excitement, Arnie came inside and followed Colonel Olin into his office. When the older man sat down and saw the big smile and open face, he glared. It was Mr. Personality meeting Old Deadpan. Old Deadpan sat stoically—pumping air in low, long cadences.

Arnie Sutler smiled his aw-shucks, dumb cousin smile. "I've come to help you in your time of need."

Olin's thunderous chest pushed in Arnie's direction like Sitting Bull squaring off against General Custer.

"Young man, I don't need any help. I have gotten this far on my own mettle, and I expect I will go the rest of the distance without you."

"I don't need to tell you," Arnie said, his eyes a sparkling light wine, promising dreamy things, "our population is half what it was five years ago, and there are more newspapers than the town needs."

"The boom is over," the Colonel boomed, as though he were arguing with the lad. "We attracted too many misfits."

A wide smile cracked Arnie's face, his big frame so at home in the insignificant wood chair.

"The solution, I'm sure you realize, Colonel, is to reduce the number of papers. Then after we have fewer papers we get the population back up."

Benjamin started to move his lips, his Ohio-sized chest painfully pumping air.

Arnie raised his palm. "An idiot could tell that, you were about to say, Colonel—"

Colonel Olin gasped. He felt weary to the marrow of his bones. He looked at the young man in front of him, then at the surroundings he had built from nothing. There was something obscene, he thought, about this glorified newsboy trying to weasel into the operation. Benjamin's mouth tasted the bile of disgust; his nostrils quivered as though the air supply might dry up. He turned his face away, exasperated.

"Now wait a minute, Colonel," Arnie fought for his attention. "I control the distribution of all the papers in this town now. A little adjustment here and there, a little persuasion in the right places might make the *Tribune* the number one paper in Los Angeles."

"Why for me?" His stare gave no quarter.

"You're the biggest man in town," the tone was of unabashed flattery. "It's no secret you were instrumental in electing Hayes president. A whole potful of politicians owe their jobs to you. I thought you had the most potential."

"Potential for what?"

"For a partnership."

Benjamin's face curdled as though he had eaten something particularly disgusting. "Oh get out of here!"

"Just a minute, Colonel. You just threw your typesetters and printers out. I know labor inside and out. Can you afford to throw me out when I'm offering you the town on a platter?"

Colonel Benjamin Raines Olin exploded. It was a fury built from his gut, culminating with reddening face, bulging eyes and it worked his mouth painfully because the opening wasn't large enough to let out all that was in him.

"You little nothing," he screamed at Arnie. "Get out of here, or I'll set up my own distribution system."

Arnie smiled, that rare smile that was starting to get under the Colonel's skin. "How could you do that, Colonel?" There was that aw-shucks farm boy again, and he scratched behind an ear to prove it. "You don't know any of the subscribers."

"Out!" Benjamin screamed, pounding his palm on the desk.

The next day the southwestern route of town did not get its daily *Tribune*. Somehow the whole load wound up on the bottom of the canal.

There were numerous complaints, which the *Tribune* referred to the distributor, who apologized.

The next day it happened again.

# 24

With wonderful death-
less ditties
We build up the world's
great cities,
And out of a fabulous
story
We fashion an empire's
glory.
One man with a dream,
at pleasure,
Shall go forth and con-
quer a crown;...
But three with a new
song's measure
Can trample an empire
down.

—Arthur William Edgar
O'Shaughnessy
Member of the Zoological
Department
British Museum

Arnie Sutler sat on the lumpy bed in his spartan bedroom, with the door closed. The box from the novelty shop lay open on his lap.

Gretchen and the children were looking in on Aunt Suff to commiserate in her latest complaint.

Humped beside Arnie on the bed, thrown down as though the act would help age them, were the overalls he bought at Frankfurter's. He had rubbed in the printer's ink, then washed and sun-dried them to a fare-thee-well.

The box on his lap was opened to a full beard and mustache, and wire-framed glasses with clear lenses. Underneath was a small jar of gum adhesive which he took out and spread first on the mesh backing of the hairpiece, then on his face.

When he had completed his make-up and stood before the glass in the bedroom with the cap pulled down, he decided he could pass for a printer.

Downtown, in the shadow of a

sapote tree, Arnie felt his whiskers and pressed them against his flesh. He pulled the cap down over his eyebrows and tagged behind two men who were entering the tack room.

In the dark room, the restless men were tightly packed like stewing tomatoes coming to the boil.

The room smelled of horse sweat and leather, manure and urine, but the men felt right at home. For now, Tomasino decided, they were better off out of sight.

Dressed in basic black, the workers were milling in agitated conversation, their perspiration steaming. Tomasino tried, from his perch in the corner at the far end of the saddle rail, to bring them to order. Some who still had jobs wore their greasy aprons; all but a few wore the same black shirts and black pants—black the color of ink—and some brought the same color with them under their fingernails. Arnie took his place in a rear dark corner.

"Gentlemen!" Tomasino shouted. "Gentlemen—please...."

They had assembled there with the usual burdens of man pressing down on them a little harder because they were poor, because remedies were harder to come by when you had only ninety-three cents to your name—and they had trouble over how they would make it taking home twenty percent less.

But they also realized the alternative to twenty percent less might be one hundred percent less, and so the assembled, for the most part, were just as happy to meet in secret after their twelve-hour day, exhausted to the bone, worried about rent, about the wife's rheumatism, the child's club foot, the mother's creeping, debilitating senility, the baby's colic.

Tomasino Taravella stood on his perch, shouting over the damp bodies. "Gentlemen, please...we'll be here all night if we don't get started."

Suddenly looking at the mob of helpless men, Tomasino thought of his father and how he had laughed when he heard what Tomasino was about. "Youse boys is kiddin' ya'selves if ya tink da haves is gonna share wid da have-nots." He had spoken through an obscenely fat black cigar, under a gray fedora, over a diamond stickpin. He never let the carnation in his buttonhole wilt.

"You godda hiddem wid power...hiddem wid might," he had said in his inimitable way. "Light a few fires, throw a few bombs. The way you get a jackass's attention is hiddem between the eyes wid a sledgehammer. Bosses ain't no different."

Tomasino looked at his men and wondered if he was devoting

his life to a lost cause. As frustration piled on frustration it became harder to resist the cries for violence that so many others were employing.

He finally shouted the mob down to a low rumble.

"Olin's a snake," someone shouted from a dark corner, and a groan of assent tumbled through the tack room.

"All right, men!" Tomasino tried to put some command in his voice. "The question is what are we going to do about it?"

"Someone ought to burn down that new building of his." The man speaking was standing next to Arnie and looked straight at him as if seeking approval to overcome a dark suspicion. Arnie nodded and said, "Go get 'em."

There was scattered laughter and a halfhearted cheer. Arnie seemed to shrink into himself. His glasses were fogging from the steamy room, but he was afraid if he took them off to wipe he might be recognized.

Tomasino looked over the roomful of men.

They were watching him with intent eyes tending toward the glassy, and grunting their approval.

"Here's what the strike committee is proposing—but understand, we don't do anything without the membership approves us."

"Strike! Strike! Strike!…"

Tomasino held up his hand and nodded his head vigorously. "Yes," he said, "we strike the *Post* and we strike the *Gazette* and we strike the *Chronicle.*"

"The *Tribune*," Arnie shouted, "strike the *Tribune.*"

There was a strange, sudden silence in the room as the eyes turned to Arnie as if trying to figure who this was, and Arnie's face around the beard flushed red in a sudden panic that he would be recognized.

"The *Tribune's* locked us out, friend. We've got to take them up a separate case." Arnie breathed easier, but it took another ten minutes for his heart to stop pounding.

"Crown's *News*, the committee proposes we leave for last. Isaiah's been a friend of the workingman way back, right, Aaron?" He addressed the question to Aaron Birnbaum standing down front, with his hands in his pockets, still carrying a jovial face with a few more wrinkles in it, with a head of wavy hair gone gray. Aaron nodded.

"The hell with Crown," someone said. "We gotta get Olin."

A groan shook the saddles on their pegs.

"Gentlemen," Tomasino pleaded.

"He ain't no gentleman," the ruddy-faced man in front next to Aaron said, "he's locked us out. I say we gotta take care of him."

"All right. All right!" Tomasino shouted. "We'll hear from Aaron Birnbaum now. He's worked for both Isaiah and Benjamin Olin. Let's get his thoughts on this thing, but for God's sakes quiet down a little so's we can hear."

Aaron Birnbaum took his time stepping up on the little wood box in front of the men. His was the dignity of years of devoted labor.

"Thanks, Tommy," Aaron said, looking at Tomasino, then back at the crowd. "Benjamin Olin was with Isaiah Crown when I was, and when he took over he wanted to cut ten percent off the wages. I left so he wouldn't cut the others, and he cut them anyway. But he's not a man who wants money for anything but the power the paper makes him feel. If we offered him two million bucks to retire from the newspaper and never write another bigoted, scathing, hateful editorial, he'd laugh at us. No, the only way to bring him around is through his circulation and his advertising. With Olin, our only hope is the boycott."

The men groused and rumbled.

Aaron spoke with a simple, unaffected timbre. "We've got to organize solid—our families, our friends, our neighbors and any strangers we can get to stand still and listen. You don't buy from anyone who advertises in the *Tribune*."

In the back of the room, Arnie's eyes were glowing behind the steaming wire-rimmed glasses. The man next to him said aloud, "Somebody ought to see he has an accident."

And Arnie said, "Yeah."

Tomasino hushed the crowd again. "Please, please. Our cause is just. We aren't going to ruin it with violence.

The vote on the boycott was taken and carried with one voice against. "I say we burn 'um."

The voice was Jonathan Esty's. He was not noted for his intellect, though when he had money in his pocket he meant no harm. It was the pressures of a hungry family with five or six kids too many that stirred his blood.

Outside, Arnie stepped into Jonathan's way as he rounded the corner of the tack room.

"'Scuse me, sir," Arnie began and startled the man. "You have a minute?"

He regarded Arnie as though trying to place him. "Do I know

you?" The brow was pinched.

"No."

"You look familiar." The eyes searched beyond fairness.

"I'm not."

When they parted, Jonathan understood he had never met the big man who had been good enough to leave him a small cash down payment which he referred to as "earnest money."

The Colonel did not appreciate the ambush from the tall, gangly bushwhacker who called himself Arnie Sutler, with that country-boy, aw-shucks manner he must have thought was ingratiating. Announcing his name as if it had some importance to it, as if you should be glad to know him. The outpost was one of those tiny tables at the new Chisolm restaurant. It hardly went from one side of Benjamin to the other. Less is more, Benjamin had heard, but he didn't buy it.

The owner advertised the Chisolm as Los Angeles' quintessential French restaurant, and the decor bespoke his opinion of the French: red brocade wall hangings, cut glass chandeliers, red tablecloths, fleur-de-lis silver service and crystal water glasses. Many establishments aped the French, the Chisolm aped the apes.

The Colonel was pouting over a tabloid-sized menu separating him from his only unmarried daughter, Mary Ellen, who was waiting expectantly to hear what he would order for her. The other two girls had made reasonable matches. Mary Ellen was still at home, worked sporadically at the paper, and went to lunch with her father whenever he could part with a few of his hard-earned shekels.

It was midafternoon on a balmy Thursday, and Arnie would have preferred not to have to discuss his business in front of Benjamin's daughter. It had been his observation that men were more prone to swagger and to easy dismissing when there was in their company a female to impress.

Mary Ellen looked easy to impress. She was lean and well-dressed, with just enough ruffles up and down the long dress to seem feminine, but not so many as to seem frivolous. There was an intelligent but desperate gleam in her eye. Her features were still as awkward as when Arnie first saw her at the Fourth of July parade, but when she looked at him, her glance rested on his face momentarily, as though taking what she could quickly without seeming to pry. Arnie now found her inexplicably attractive.

Mary Ellen watched her father frowning over the prices. She knew he would be finding everything outrageously expensive, but she had been told many times he was a man who had a dollar and a half between himself and starvation at the age of fourteen, and, consequently, a man who appreciated the value of a dollar. His white mane was undulating as the muscles of his face moved in small circular motions of concentration.

Benjamin looked up, his face taut and sour as vinegar.

"You're becoming a nuisance, young man."

"Would you excuse us a moment, ma'am?" Arnie said, looking at Mary Ellen with her bosom pushing forward and puffing the white frills of her bodice.

"She's not going anywhere," Benjamin snapped.

Arnie nodded. His face might have pleased a conscientious undertaker. "I just received word of a union threat to your person, and I thought only to warn you."

"You have cheek, young man, barging into a public room like this where a man should have some sanctuary. I'm a veteran of the Civil War. A colonelcy doesn't come to cowards."

"Very good, sir," Arnie said, bowing from the waist overpolitely. He nodded to Mary Ellen and departed through the hoi polloi.

After Arnie was clear of the room, Mary Ellen smiled at her father. "You were awfully hard on that young man," she observed.

Benjamin drank, set the glass down and blotted his mustache and goatee with his white linen napkin, a bit too suddenly, Mary Ellen noted.

"He's the jackal that dumped my papers...a whole route, into the canal, to threaten me."

Outside, Arnie paused to enjoy the pink sun that was peeking through the gray clouds. He looked across the street at the horse and buckboard. The driver barely nodded his recognition and turned to trot down the street.

When Benjamin finally came out of the restaurant with Mary Ellen and stood still for a moment under the burgundy awning, it was as though he were giving a signal of his own. The medal on the left breast of his white suit gleamed in the sun.

"Thank you for the lunch, Colonel," Mary Ellen said. "It was delicious."

"It was good," he grumbled grudgingly, "but awfully dear."

Arnie quickly took a handkerchief from his pocket and wiped his forehead. Jonathan Esty moved the horse and buckboard down the dirt street toward Benjamin and Mary Ellen.

Arnie put his handkerchief slowly away and started down the

sidewalk toward the Olins.

Jonathan whipped the horse into a gallop.

Benjamin continued across the street, never looking either way, as though no one would come near a man of his importance.

Mary Ellen was distracted by Arnie Sutler coming straight at them waving frantically.

"Colonel!" Arnie shouted. "Look out!"

Colonel Olin looked at Arnie, and winced, perturbed that any-one should be shouting instructions to him in public.

It was all over so suddenly no one was sure afterwards exactly how it had happened. Jonathan vanished in the dust and excitement.

Benjamin felt a sudden thrust at his sleeve and felt himself yanked backwards. Arnie Sutler, or the horse, or both, knocked him over.

Sitting in the dry street, Benjamin dusted his white suit, touch-tested his manifold bruises, and looked up at the tall figure of Arnie Sutler who seemed to loom over him like a gloating fistfight victor.

"Are you all right?" Arnie solicited from on high.

A crowd was gathering. "I told you before, young man, I don't need your help."

Arnie nodded gravely and after backing up a few steps, tripped quietly away from the gaggle of onlookers.

With the aid of his daughter, Benjamin got unsteadily to his feet. He raised his hand to the blurred, babbling crowd and forced a slight upturn of the corner of his mouth. "Just a runaway horse."

Mary Ellen, when they were free of the gawkers, said, "You know, Colonel, I think that Sutler boy saved your life."

He grunted once until his thought processes cleared the fog in his head.

"Or tried to threaten me—"

"Funny." Her eyes perked up—her face shed some years, "I rather like that young man."

# 25

So spoke the false dis-
sembler unperceived;
For neither man nor
angel can discern
Hypocrisy—the only
evil that walks
Invisible, except to God
alone,
By his permissive will,
through Heaven and
Earth;...

—John Milton
*Paradise Lost*, Book III

On that Saturday morning toward the end of 1890, the sky could have been painted by some portrait artist in a dull gray wash to highlight and flatter his commission.

Arnie was oblivious to the weather as he made the rounds of his customers on the farms in the outskirts of Los Angeles. While bouncing on his speckled white mare, he pondered just what it was a newspaper meant to these hard-working, sparingly-educated folk.

It was a gossiping companion and angry visitor whose opinions usually provoked agreement. It was a courier of tidings, glad and ill, from the world over, putting the simplest bucolic soul in touch with the big goings on. But most of all it was a friend that spoke only when you wanted to listen.

It gave the farmers a shot at the weather, the farmers' wives a look at who was so important in society they got their names in the paper. News of happenings far off came the same day now by telegraph, news that used to take a week to come through.

And you were kept current on the marvels of commerce. You learned of miracle lotions and potions, elixirs, aids for sexual potency, figure improvement; where to borrow money or buy the greatest piano on earth, where to find the best deal on a cheap fine team of horses, a fresh young Holstein cow. On the front page you got the results of a prize fight two thousand miles away. It took Corbett only twenty-two rounds to knock out Sullivan (Sullivan had taken seventy-five bare knuckle rounds to K.O. Jake Kilrain the year before) and you knew it the next day.

Some papers puffed the politicians and world leaders, the *Tribune* puffed the advertisers, running a "Then and Now" column telling what all the advertisers of ten years before were doing now, who was still advertising, and who didn't make it. Benjamin never forgot where the money came from, and Arnie admired him for it.

Then, of course, there were the non-literary uses of the paper: bundling garbage, wrapping fish at the market, insulating cold cellars, and supplying the outhouse.

Later, Arnie developed the garbage theory of newspaper growth, viz., the growth of the newspaper from four pages or a single sheet, to twelve pages or three sheets, was the direct result of the growing influence of town over farm, and the increasing affluence of Los Angeles.

In the beginning, with the four-pager, the farm predominated, and the scraps of food were fed to the animals or used for compost. As the town grew and the ratio of people to animals increased, there was more need for garbage wrappers, so pages were added to the paper.

He came riding up now with that "How y'all" greeting and mile-wide smile, and he would tousle the towheaded kids' hair, running his hand right friendly-like across those little happy heads, and they trusted him, and wouldn't you?

And as soon as he tied his old speckled mare to the hitching post they were upon him, the kids looking for a walnut or a sweet from his pocket, or just the Dutch rub on their heads.

The shanty was up the dirt path, and as soon as he set foot on the path Arnie could see the expectant face at the door.

On the poor edge of town, the slightest commotion outside was an event.

"Afternoon, ma'am," he said, lumbering up the path, as welcome a sight as her favorite uncle. "*Chronicle* man," he sang out, and lands' sakes she always said her *Chronicle* man could easily have sung on the stage of the Merced."

"Wait," she said, "I'll get my money." Her graying hair was bunned, her head severely held. There wasn't sufficient food on the table to burden her bones with extra padding. She would take her time getting the money, to prolong the thrill of the visitor's presence.

When she returned, Arnie was poised with his pencil over his tablet like a census taker. "If I could speak to you in confidence, ma'am?" he asked, his blond eyebrows tweaking shyly.

"Confidence?" (her face in a bewildered contortion as though trying to place a strange word in a familiar context.)

"I've heard some rumors that I might pass along, that is if you swear not to repeat them."

She swore all right, for what could be juicier to a bone-weary housewife than a bit of gossip?

"Well, the *Chronicle* hasn't been too healthy lately. What with all the people going back East and the population way down from what it was in the boom, I just can't guarantee how long they'll be giving me papers to bring you, and I know your money doesn't come easy. What in life does, eh?" he said, winking deeper into her confidence. "And I don't know if they'd be in any position to give your money back."

The woman gaped at him, slack-jawed, trying to grasp his meaning. He was such a handsome man. Why, lands' sakes, she'd trust him with her life, he was so clean-looking.

"Now if you had any notion to change, I could recommend the *Gazette* and the *Tribune* as the strongest."

She wrinkled her nose.

"Course the *Tribune* has a special this week for new subscribers."

"Oh, special—what's that?"

"Half price for the first month," he said. "Sort of a get-acquainted offer."

"Well, then," she said, hoarding the coins in her purse, returning half of what she had withdrawn to the silken sanctuary where they would rest until they were traded for some beans, bread and cheese. "I guess I'll take a look at the *Tribune* for a month."

"Yes, ma'am," he said, writing on his pad, accepting the money, his cost for the paper. "I'm sure you'll be happy with it, but if you aren't we'll just switch next month."

And so, though it wasn't always that easy, especially with more educated, suspicious patrons, it was only a matter of weeks before Arnie Sutler was able to pick up from fat and frumpy Gus Unger the inventory and fixtures, as well as the name and goodwill of the Los Angeles *Chronicle*, for a song.

Gus was relieved to get out, what with the way the circulation plummeted in this recession.

Arnie sat at the supplicant's side of the Colonel's desk, his heart taking him on a bumpy ride. Benjamin was hovering over him, his big belly close to Arnie's face as Benjamin looked down his nose at him. Arnie had that smile on his face that he had downstairs when they told him Colonel Olin wished never to see him again. It was that aggravating grin that said, "Shucks, maybe I got better cards than it looks like."

Arnie had smiled his biggest bumpkin smile. "Just tell him I bring insider news of the *Chronicle's* new owner. The words rolled off his most mellifluous tongue, and in a few minutes he was ushered up the two flights of stairs.

He sat and Olin stood, and Olin had ice water in his eyes and he said, "All right, let's have it. Just what do you know about the *Chronicle?*"

"I know it was sold."

"When?"

Arnie pulled his pocket watch from his vest, popped open the silver lid with his thumb and looked at it without haste. "Within the hour," he said, and snapped the silver top shut.

Colonel Olin winced at the sight of the pocket watch, almost as though it scared him. It was aggravating to be reminded of his mother's gift to him. The one he hocked to begin his career, then lost because he was thirty cents short of redeeming it on time, and the bartender wouldn't compromise.

"Who is the buyer?"

Arnie smiled.

Benjamin glared at him, "Young man, I don't have time to fence with you. I tried to buy the *Chronicle,* on more than one occasion. Who succeeded where I failed? If you don't know, you will do me the courtesy of leaving, or else I shall have you forcibly ejected."

Benjamin started for the door. Arnie stood abruptly to block his path. For a second they just glared at each other.

"I bought it," Arnie said beaming. Benjamin studied him, and the full impact, when it landed, sent him reeling and back into the chair he never used in company.

Colonel Olin moved his jaw like a pensive cow grinding a cud.

He looked over at the grinning man, not much more than a kid really, he thought. They were like two warriors from the *Iliad*, frozen in time—the Colonel kept his shield in front of his breast, but Arnie's javelin had somehow pierced it.

The long silence depressed Benjamin, his outrage tied his tongue.

"Would you like to buy it?" Arnie asked like a child.

Benjamin's lips twitched unconsciously, but Arnie saw it and did not cover his amusement.

When he found his voice, Benjamin croaked, "You'd sell it?"

"Sure. I'd sell anything...for the right price."

"The right price?" Benjamin cocked his head at him, wary as a horse trader.

"What I paid for it..." Arnie said, "and..."

Benjamin sank back. "And what?"

"And what we discussed before," he added as a harmless afterthought. "A spot on your paper."

The tic returned to Benjamin's mouth. Arnie sat watching and smiling—smiling and watching. It was building again, but some safety valve in the Colonel's brain closed off the building steam and hissed, "Listen to the lad." His melon head slumped.

"What kind of—" Benjamin hesitated, having difficulty with the word, "spot did you have in mind?"

"Oh, something where I could be of some use. General manager, perhaps. Assistant to the publisher."

"Well, I guess I should be relieved you don't want to be publisher."

"Oh," Arnie said reassuring him with a slow crescent wave of his hand, "not yet."

Benjamin's head shot forward with a cough. Arnie pressed on. "Understand, I am not asking for a handout. If after, say a year, you feel I have not been of any use to you, we can call it quits."

"And I shall decide that question alone?"

"Yes, sir."

"You certainly are a confident young man."

"Yes, sir, and I'm confident I can do a lot for you and the paper. I think I can take the stress out of your labor problems. I can build your circulation." He smiled broadly at him again, his lips parting slightly, baring his nice, even, white teeth. "As I believe I have already demonstrated."

"All right." A thunderous clap of Benjamin's hand rocked the table between them and he jumped up. "All right," he said again. "Under one condition."

"What's that?"

"You sell me your circulation routes too."

Now Arnie's smile broke into a gentle laugh which grew slowly into a thunderous body-shaking guffaw, like a rolling riptide pulling him from shore. Benjamin glared at him. Arnie's huge body heaved under the exertion of his recovery before he spoke.

"Well, Colonel, perhaps I was foolish coming here again. I thought I might be of some use to you. But I don't see any reason I shouldn't start up the *Chronicle* again. I did get it dirt-cheap. Maybe this town does need the *Chronicle* after all."

"The devil!" Benjamin said to himself. "It's what he is: the devil incarnate and I'd never be able to trust him. Clever and shifty," his brain valves shifted again, "but when all is said and done, you want that kind of devil on your side rather than against you."

A neat arrangement was made with cash paid for the *Chronicle*. A one-year mortgage was given in consideration of his employment by the *Tribune*, at a reasonable salary. Arnie kept his circulation routes. If there was any similarity to Benjamin's own start with Isaiah Crown, he preferred not to acknowledge it.

After Arnie left, Colonel Benjamin Olin sat staring into space. His hand slowly rubbed his thigh. The kid was smart, he thought, and resourceful. You had to hand it to him, he had a good head for business on those broad shoulders. Yes, Benjamin thought, maybe it would work out after all. He only wished he could get rid of the feeling he had been outwitted.

On his way out of the *Tribune* building, Arnie Sutler could barely keep from whistling. When he hit the outside steps, he saw coming toward him the slim, tall figure in the sunbonnet with frilly lace trim and the soft earthy hair around the edges, and the long white dress scuffing the walkway beneath. Mary Ellen Olin was laden with packages, and Arnie stopped to open the door for her. It all passed between them in the merest instant, that look of hers resting on his boyish face, that smile of his cutting straight to her heart.

"Why, Mr. Sutler," she said, her dark eyes gentle, "fancy meeting you here. Have you spoken again to my father?"

To his grin he added the barest nod.

She lifted her brows. "Did you get what you came for?"

His smile broadened to take in the whole outdoors. She hurried into the building so he wouldn't see her blush.

# 26

1894

No one was happier with the parade than Matilda Olin.

The brass bands and floats, the uniformed marchers were all so thrilling to watch. She felt as though they were marching just for her.

But if she were to admit it to any living soul, she would say it wasn't the parade that thrilled her, it was her name on all the invitations, right up there with the cream of Los Angeles society—not only the cream, but *la creme de la creme*. Everyone knew speaking French was class, even a few phrases.

Social acceptance was sweet all right, but it had not come easily. Tooth and nail, they fought, she was fond of reminding her husband, but they made it to the top. No one would deny that after today.

She sat in the grandstand erected for the occasion, between her stoical husband and fidgeting daughter, Mary Ellen.

It was her name on the invitations

that went out for the first La Fiesta de Los Angeles Carnival and
Ball. She was listed near the top, as a patroness with Avery, Childs,
Ducommun, Griffith, Hazzard (the Ball that evening was being held
at Hazzard's pavilion), Howell, Hughes, Hunt, Van Nuys, Vail, Wid-
ney—and even a countess.

And an *Olin*: Mrs. Benjamin Raines Olin.

Of course protocol demanded they list three men as chairmen
of the committee, but there wasn't any doubt that the real credit
went to the patronesses.

The growing appetite for recognition laid society at the mercy of
the press. The Olins grabbed that brass ring and rode their golden
hobbyhorses to social glory.

Arnie and Gretchen Sutler had watched the parade, standing on
the corner of Seventh and Main, but something sent them home
early—Gretchen crying, and Arnie on her heels trying to find out
what was bothering her.

Gretchen's straw bonnet shaded her alert eyes when the queen's
float went by. Arnie lifted his derby and wiped the perspiration from
his forehead with a handkerchief.

"My," Gretchen said wistfully. "Isn't her dress elegant? Just look,
it's all embroidered, and a velvet train, why it must be ten feet long."

Arnie, who liked his beauty a little younger and slimmer, said,
"That's nothing next to how you're going to look tonight in your new
dress." He reached over and pinched her lightly on the cheek. "My
little pumpkin," he whispered in her ear.

And a gasp came from Gretchen like someone had pulled the
stopper out of one of those newfangled bathing tubs, and the water
poured out of her eyes.

It wasn't until they were home and Gretchen dissolved, sobbing,
in the old horsehair chair that she told him. Told him how she
couldn't bring herself to go to that fancy shop where all those fancy
ladies would look down their fancy noses at her. How she had walked
past it for three days, but each day instead of working up courage, it
became more difficult, and finally she just gave up and went to the
dry goods store, bought the fabric and made the dress herself.

"Gretchen," he said, taking her hands tightly in his, "this is
probably the most important night of my career. Colonel Olin has
invited us to his house to the biggest event of the year. I think he's
been pleased with what I've done for his paper, but social acceptance
is *it* in this town. Now I wish you'd forget this nonsense about not
being good enough. You are so beautiful, you'll be the prettiest

woman there."

The air in their parlor was hot and languid, the kind of motionless heat that made you faint on an empty stomach.

"But—I'm so—*scared*," she murmured, a light tremor shaking her vulnerable body.

He was impatient with her self-abnegation. He remembered when he found it charming; now it sickened him. Now he realized it was not a pose—she really felt inferior, and for good reason.

She was even afraid of the butcher.

But, Lord, she was always slavering for his attention. Now, when he gave it to her, it was like she didn't want it.

He realized he should have taken her by the hand and marched her down to the dressmaker. But if you don't make them stand on their own feet, there's no end to what you'd be called upon to do.

Before Gretchen could catch her breath for another sob, Arnie was gone, next door, as a fly disappearing from trouble, to return with the dreaded concoction he himself would never touch.

"What is it?" she asked fearfully, feeling ridiculous in her rumpled dress.

"It's nerve medicine," he said, taking it to her.

Her nose wrinkled at the odor. "Nerve medicine," she said gasping, a hand at her throat. "It's whiskey."

"It will calm your nerves," he said.

It warmed her, that bitter-tasting hot metal, and her eyes opened wide. She felt as never before the entire course of the liquid over her lips and tongue, down her throat until her stomach exploded.

Her chest was heaving like the bellows of the old pump organ at church, but her mind was not on heavenly things. Funny, the hot whiskey did seem to calm her anxiety. A little more would probably make her forget it completely.

"But we mustn't have too much," Arnie said.

"No, no, no, not too much," she protested, her cheeks puffed up expectantly like bursting overripe peaches.

Arnie poured her another.

In certain circles in the United States at that time, the tone of a house was set by the presence of a portrait of a Civil War soldier, usually over the mantle. If it was an officer with medals dangling from his breast, it was high-toned; an enlisted man was not as high-toned, but better than nothing.

Colonel and Mrs. Benjamin Raines Olin had not only the portrait of a colonel, they had the soldier himself strutting in full regalia to greet his guests.

No one joked about his wearing the uniform with the shiny medals draped heroically on his barrel chest. Colonel Olin was not a joking man.

Benjamin was at one with the overdone room, and the environment seemed like a stage setting whose sole function was to heighten his presence. His uniform had a high-priest-like collar, stiff and formal. Somehow, calling him "Colonel" seemed too familiar.

When Arnie and Gretchen came into the room, she hanging on his arm to steady her uncertain legs, Benjamin advanced toward them in forced friendliness. He was in command, all right, but his efforts at cordiality were cold as a dead salmon.

Arnie slumped next to his petite pumpkin, Gretchen. Their cheeks twitched in unison.

He saw the eyes of the august guests sweep as one over his wife's cotton frock, rumpled as a bowl of dry cereal.

Arnie was in the height of fashion with his new tuxedo. Why didn't these snobs look at his brand-spanking-new tuxedo pants with the sword-like creases sharp enough to cut butter? His white shirt was starched, his black bow tie *de rigueur*.

Gretchen tittered when she curtsied to her host and hostess, who stood gawking before her.

Gretchen giggled. "I forgot you were so short."

Arnie felt the room freeze. Matilda tried to rescue the girl in the awful cotton frock, so inappropriate for this grand occasion. "Oh," Matilda said with a shy smile and relaxed wave of her hand, "I don't mind being short."

Arnie squeezed Gretchen's hand to stop her forming contradiction. "Dear God," he prayed silently, "please see us through this all-important evening without incident."

Matilda Olin, at this juncture of her life, looked like nothing so much as another piece of furniture in her baroque living room. Short and lumpy and underneath worse for wear, but freshly slip-covered with new, busy fabric, dust ruffles and outsized tassels brushing the floor. She was what she seemed: rugged, sturdy, serviceable and uninspiring. Weathered by the storms of life but not yet bent, she was loyal to the man she married at the cost of alienating her family.

Mrs. Olin hovered over her guest like a matriarchal bird, making no effort to minimize her turkey breast. She was imperial with the servants, her orders were crisp and clear and devoid of any *déclassé* familiarity.

"Oh, your house is just lovely, Mrs. Olin," Arnie said.

"Why, thank you," Matilda said, her sparse lips striving for a smile.

Arnie surveyed the room he had just complimented. On the fleur-de-lis-patterned wallpaper was a baroque gilt-edged landscape, dark and dreary greens and browns, as if in the shadows of life; the corner cabinet was crammed with porcelain figurines. There was Venus supporting a rose-filled vase on her back. The patterns on the rugs seemed to fight with the patterns on the wall. Heavy valances dropped golden tassels over the ponderous velvet drapes, the ensemble acting like a bulwark against the outside, where cattle trod the streets and an occasional cow stood patient while being milked.

The upright piano against the far wall promised a culture that never took. Beside it a kentia palm grew from a polished brass spitoon.

Gretchen looked around with Arnie and her eyes jumped from all the clashing patterns.

"Why can't we decorate like this?" Arnie's high-pitched voice was praising his hostess rhetorically.

"Because you don't want to spend any money," Gretchen said, and followed it with another reedy, musical laugh.

Colonel Olin pulled the bottom edge of his military jacket over his mounding belly and cleared his throat.

His wife came to the rescue again. "Oh, doesn't she have a wonderful sense of humor, Colonel?"

"Wonderful," he said as though he had bitten a sour apple and was called upon to praise it. He moved to safer ground, as a mechanical soldier with a tightly-wound spring releasing meshing gears in perfect rhythms.

It was a select group that sat down at the Olin's pre-fiesta party.

Colonel Olin was seated next to Gretchen Sutler, though he had whispered a request to his wife that a change be made. Matilda responded that it was quite out of the question since the place cards his head pressman had printed for the occasion were already in place and seen by several people.

Arnie was usually as jovial as a big bear drunk on berries and beer—the kind of man who would sneak up behind you and pound you on your back, sloshing your drink or sending that piece of ham gristle you were secreting between your tongue and lower teeth down your windpipe, causing an embarrassing fusillade of coughing.

But tonight Arnie's dinnner companion, Mary Ellen Olin, told him he seemed distressed.

Arnie denied it, and forced a smile to prove he was just as happy as the next fellow. But the smile disintegrated, and Mary Ellen's attempts to draw Arnie Sutler into conversation were met with monosyllabic utterances.

"Your wife is very pretty," she said as the butler was serving the cream of mushroom soup.

Arnie winced. Her beauty was not the quality on his mind at the moment.

"You must be terribly proud of her," she said, glancing at him through misty, teasing eyes.

Anxious to shift the attention from Gretchen, who seemed to be weaving erratically in her seat next to the beribboned Colonel, Arnie said, "Your escort tonight is quite handsome too, Miss Olin."

Her face wrinkled, the cheeks eroding like an over-watered hillside. "I suppose if you only look at him. Charles barely speaks the language." She waved her hand in the sublime indifference of wealth and position. "My mother arranged it."

Arnie started to speak, but Mary Ellen wasn't finished. "Not nearly so handsome," she said dropping her eyelids, "as you, Mr. Sutler."

Arnie blushed and put the white linen napkin to his mouth to cover his embarrassment. Mary Ellen's lips extended in a pout. "Too bad," she said, "I'm not so pretty as your wife."

Arnie gasped.

"For I should make a terrible play for you," she said.

Good God, he thought, she couldn't expect him to argue with that. Mary Ellen Olin was heavy in the haunches and unfashionably bright for a girl in her day. She was the kind of woman he should have married for these important social situations. He wouldn't have to dread every moment what would come out of *her* mouth. She had a *most* pleasing personality. Why, after you talked to her for a few minutes you got the idea she *was* pretty.

"Oh, you needn't answer, Mr. Sutler," Mary Ellen said. "I shouldn't be fishing with such a long pole." Her eyelashes flapped briefly.

"Daddy thinks a lot of you, you know," she went on, the soup spoon poised over the bowl of mushroom cream like a bird hovering over its prey.

Arnie shifted his big legs under the table.

"And he's been eager to make your wife's acquaintance. He thinks women are so important to their men." She paused, looking over at Gretchen and her father. "Funny, I heard she was rather shy, but I certainly don't see any evidence of it."

Arnie followed her eyes to his wife. Gretchen had her long fingers on the great man's chest and appeared to be toying with his medals.

A sudden hush came over the room as all heads turned toward the pretty woman who seemed to be igniting Colonel Dynamite.

"They are so shiny, Colonel. How do you keep them so shiny?" She was giggling. The nerve medicine had worked too well, Arnie feared. "Do you polish them, Colonel?"

There was a quiet gasp from the crowd.

"Does it make you feel good to dress up like a soldier?" she asked.

"Madam," he answered with his icy gaze, "I *am* a soldier."

She tittered, showing her pretty teeth to everybody. Arnie tried to sink in his chair when he overheard the whispered comments: "She's an idiot," from the banker's wife, and, "They used to lock her kind in the attic," from the steel manufacturer.

"Arnie always slouches around you," Gretchen said, "to make you feel taller." She glanced at Arnie and waved her pink, blemishless hand at him.

"Oh, dear," Mary Ellen said at his side in a most commiserating tone. "She seems a bit tipsy. If I didn't know we don't serve alcohol, I would have suspicions."

Arnie sat up straight.

"Mrs. Olin," Arnie said in a voice too loud for the silence that pervaded the baroque atmosphere, like a hiccup at the wake of a beloved aunt, "the cream of mushroom soup is a sheer delight."

Gretchen looked over at her husband as though he were a stranger reciting Greek poetry in a saloon. She waved her hand, the little finger mocking him. "Wonderful soup," she started to say—but suddenly felt strange and out of place with all the fancy people around her. Her skin was wet and she felt as though she had been soaked in scalding soapy water and dashed against the river rocks like yesterday's wash.

All the fears she felt before the nerve medicine were converging on her stomach along with Matilda Olin's cream of mushroom soup, and it kicked on her insides like one of those runaway horses going hell-for-leather.

It all came up like the eruption of Vesuvius, with a particularly powerful stench, and it sprayed unsparingly across the shiny medals festooning the breast of Colonel Benjamin Raines Olin.

Colonel Olin grabbed his napkin and shot upright like a ball from one of his cannons, rubbing at his chest, as if the mere motion of his violent arm would vacate the wretched odor.

Silence grasped the diners. The Colonel threw his head back and marched from the room, careful not to appear in too much haste.

Gretchen lay slumped on the table, her digestive tract churning as if it had come loose inside her.

Mary Ellen held the drapery gingerly in her hand as though it were a stage curtain and she was peeking out at the faces of her audience to see how she had been received. She had not lit the lamp, so Arnie could not see in, were he to show so much interest as to look up at her second-story bedroom.

Mary Ellen stood beside the curtain looking out, trying not to remember how many backs of young men she had seen walking away from her door—young men who had not returned to grace her parlor, to look upon her bone-stretched, plain face with the hair pulled severely back in the unremitting bun, to listen to her voice grating like an ill-tuned clarinet; not to hear her giggle over the stereopticon or see her flirt outrageously as a woman who felt the ebb of her youth draining her desirability.

She touched her face, her long, thin fingers gently feeling for the lines she knew would soon cut deeper.

What was he thinking, that tall, strong, married man who was walking now down the rutted road toward his wife and children, showing her only his broad, purposeful back? Did he feel anything at all for her? He seemed to, but how could she be sure? Hadn't he walked her home? And without any real coaxing on her part, Charlie having long since taken her meaning and gone home alone.

And hadn't their eyes met in a moment of intimacy when they undressed Gretchen and put her to bed with the floppy doll?

She'd coaxed him back to the ball. He protested, but she knew he wanted to go—to wipe up the spilt milk—to apologize to the Colonel.

And the Colonel had accepted, commenting offhandedly that Arnie and Mary Ellen made a handsome couple.

Arnie was startled, but she thought he was pleased.

She was twenty-nine years old now, things were different. Both her younger sisters were married and she was heavy on the trail of spinsterhood.

But Arnie Sutler was married. Surely it was foolish of her to expect....

And yet his wife was an albatross about his neck....

And divorce was becoming more common—not the stigma it once was....

As she watched him disappear around the near corner of the Crown house next door like a ghost in a dream, she made herself a silent vow. "This one is *not* getting away."

# 27

Not everyone has the
imagination for reality.

—Goethe

In the weeks that followed, the summer turned unusually hot, the sun, uninhibited by clouds, burned spitefully into the anemic dust and separated the widely-spaced gingerbread houses with glowing light that danced on the windows like breaking waves.

Gretchen Sutler sat in the old rocker in the parlor window, her long white dress dotted with tiny cabbage roses hiked a few inches in the vain hope of circulating some air underneath. No one could see her—the children were outside playing under the big old fig tree in back—but Gretchen didn't feel comfortable raising her hem more than a few inches. It didn't seem ladylike.

She sat staring out the window, across the porch with its feeble attempt at a gingerbread canopy, to the blazing diatomaceous earth, parched to powder underfoot of the occasional lazy travelers (it was too hot for the horses) who found an oasis under the sporadic shade trees in the street.

A paper fan with "Ritter Funeral Home" printed in black letters lay dead in her lap. The house was a small clapboard affair, cheap by the standards of her husband's bloating wealth.

She picked up the fan and began fanning herself with a slow, lugubrious rhythm. The fan of death did not put any life in her; the thoughts of her husband and his new girl friend were raising her temperature.

He wasn't being very discreet about it; everyone was telling her, though she preferred not to hear. Did the plumber's wife think she was doing her a favor at the Wednesday night prayer meeting with: "Well, I don't know if I should tell you this, but they always say the wife is the last to know...."

Her last well-wisher, Alice, the spinster Sunday school teacher who just might have been touched by a twinge of envy, had just left her with the news that Arnie was visiting the Olin house again and, "It don't look like paper business to me...."

Now Gretchen felt that neither heaven nor earth could move her from her rocking chair. She rocked with a rhythm that tied her to life with a tenuous thread.

Her hand glided down the front of her body, tracing the still-supple contours.

I am no longer desirable, she thought. He used to want me with such a passion it scared me. As God is surely my witness, I try so hard to please him, but the caring has gone out of him like the stuffing out of my rag doll that I loved too hard. I am inadequate to his success.

She could smell the marriage decomposing like fallen leaves rotting in the rain.

The air was steaming in her lungs as if trapped in a pressure cooker.

The back door slammed like a shot in the dark. Little Cora Sue, just turned eight and petite for her age, came tearing in like a terrier bringing with her more of the outside than Gretchen cared for, and getting it on the hooked rug. If Gretchen hadn't been so weary, she would have scolded her.

The little pink, lumpy cheeks were covered with tears. Gretchen thought her daughter would keep womanhood trapped inside her beyond its due. Junior, on the other hand, put her in mind of a boy with a man caged inside him, wary, watching and waiting to burst out full blown.

"Junior took my doll and I want her back, 'cause she's mine."

The words tumbled, punctuated by deep sobs.

It took a great effort for Gretchen to focus her eyes on the little ragamuffin.

"It's not fair," the girl whimpered.

Gretchen nodded, her lips pursed in solemn agreement. Yes, life was not fair. People took anything they wanted.

"Mommy," Cora Sue demanded petulantly, confused by her mother's alien silence, "make him give her back to me. I hate boys. They're mean and they take what doesn't belong to them and I hate them."

Gretchen stared at her as though she were a stranger with ill-timed news. She thought of protesting that all boys weren't like that, but she couldn't bring it out.

"Mommy," the child insisted, "what shall I do?"

Gretchen looked back out the window, detached from her child. "Take it back," she said.

And now she sat pondering, Cora Sue having sulked back outside, disappointed in her mother.

Oh, Arnie may have tried to fool her since that fatal night when she was so terrified in the imposing company of Colonel Olin and his pretty peers that she threw up all over his storefront uniform. But she knew Arnie was repulsed at the very sight of her.

"I'm so embarrassed," she had told him. Her voice was still light and musical, but it had developed a bittersweet flute quality. "How can I ever make it up to you, Arnie?"

"Don't be silly." He wished she would just disappear.

"But I *am* silly, Arnie—you used to tweak my cheeks and call me 'My silly.'" She frowned.

"Forget it." If only *he* could forget it.

But she knew he couldn't, and his refusal to talk about it just drove them further apart.

And a nausea terrorized her body.

She was alone except for the sound of the wood rails of the rocker pressing down on the oak wood floors in rhythmic certitude, squeaking like two old leather shoes rubbing together.

Grugh, gruk, grugh, gruk....

Somewhere in the stillness of that hot room with the hooked rugs, the crocheted antimacassars on the horsehair chair, and the unsettling absence of her husband, Gretchen felt the heart of a mother hen pound within her. She must protect her beloved brood.

She stood abruptly from the rocker, gathered the children out back, slapped the dust from their clothes and marched them to Aunt Suff, who though she was ailing with the arthritis, found an embarrassed joy in the young children.

Gretchen looked like a wilting flower taking pains to put purpose in her step as she made her way under her daisy-festooned yellow bonnet to the showdown (Aunt Suff said the sun's rays prematurely aged young women). Her long skirt slapped the dust about her heels, the hot air stifling her inside the impractical costume of the day.

She took a short cut to the Olin place because her courage was fading with every step.

Her soul smoldered in the heat. She felt more alone than when she crossed the ocean, a child with a tag around her neck, clutching a rag doll.

The white iron fence surrounding the two-story Victorian gingerbread Olin place with its turret windows and geegaw frills was like gleaming teeth, chomping down on outsiders.

As she opened the back gate and started across the rear yard, strange guttural sounds, as though from barnyard animals, stopped her.

Ahead of her there was nothing but the silent ballet of hands gentle in accommodating motions, a strange, dreamlike intimacy under the shading pepper tree. The shed gave them only partial privacy.

Arnie and Mary Ellen were standing, careless and defiant, then crumbling, as if their legs suddenly lost their starch, to the indifferent earth covered with pepperpods, rough to their oblivion.

Gretchen's generous heart was thumping in terror. Her insides felt as if alley cats were tearing each other apart.

When the ballet on the ground accelerated with legs rising and flailing in maniacal embrace, some demon inside of Gretchen cried a blood-stopping scream.

Mary Ellen shot up on an elbow, her face a peculiar mask of surprise and wry amusement. She led Arnie's glance with her eyes, then put a hand gently on his elbow and said, "Now would be a good time, Arnie."

"Come home, Arnie," Gretchen said trying to sound more possessive, with a touch of righteousness failing its target. Her limbs were numb and they tingled as though the circulation ceased and they were withering on her body.

Trying to control his rapid breathing, Arnie straightened his clothes and gave Mary Ellen Olin a solicitous hand with hers before rising. He felt shoddy and cheapened.

Arnie went with Gretchen, leaving Mary Ellen bemused and self-satisfied under the pepper tree. Gretchen was two paces ahead of Arnie, her head high. Say what they would about her, she wouldn't give them the satisfaction of seeing her crumble.

Behind her, Arnie hung his head. He couldn't find the words Mary Ellen wanted him to.

He followed his wife into the parlor, and his house felt strange —dark and claustrophobic. Even the air, cooler than outside, seemed unfamiliar, as though he had stumbled into a cold cave and his body couldn't adjust.

Suddenly he heard his voice as though it spoke from another body. "I guess you'll want to divorce me."

He dropped into the horsehair chair, his tall, lumpy body collapsing like an autumn cornstalk.

"No, Arnie, I don't want a divorce."

Arnie's head shot up, his soft face glaring in shock. "But," his high voice stammered, "but, but, you certainly would be justified."

He tried to explain it to her, how he wanted someone with the social graces who would be at home in the exclusive clubs and on the blue ribbon committees, someone with a ready wit who could hobnob with the smart set in town and hold her own with the intelligent, monied classes, go to the opera guild and committees to further the welfare of whatever cause was in favor at the moment. But it all came out wrong and he sounded like a tremendous snob, and Gretchen laughed at him.

He wanted to make her understand. "The paper is growing by leaps and bounds. We're hiring more and more people. The competition for the top is getting fierce. I intend to marry Mary Ellen."

"It certainly should give you the inside track," she said.

"I hope to tell you," he said, adding hastily, "and my success will be good for the children. Insure their future."

But she wouldn't understand. They were just words, and the heat and the passion seemed to bleed them of their meaning.

"Dear God," he prayed silently, "please let her divorce me. It will be good for the children."

"Remember before we were married," she asked him, "when you came courting on your bicycle? You made me agree we would die before we would ever divorce."

She read his thoughts in his bloodshot eyes and sagging, bloodless flesh. Mary Ellen wanted the divorce, and so did her father, and he must have it.

She stared at him so long, he twisted in the chair sending an antimacassar to the floor.

Arnie was seized by the perfect solution.

"I'll give you a thousand dollars," he said, the spittle of excitement at his brilliance sputtering from his mouth like the spray from a waterfall, "for a divorce."

Gretchen looked at her husband, her pretty face crumbling to the disappointment.

"Money, Arnie?" she said. "You think I would trade you for money? A thousand dollars? That is what you are worth?"

"I'll give you a thousand a year," he topped his offer.

"A price on us, like slaves? How much for the children, Arnie? Shall we sell them? How much shall we ask for them to get our investment back? We want a fair return, don't we?"

"I'll give you a thousand a *month*! That's more than most people make in a year."

She watched his face flushing with the hope that his words would find a home in her heart.

She shook her head and smiled at him as at some schoolboy who had just told a tall tale. "Where would you get all that money, Arnie?"

"I'll get it, don't you worry. When I marry Mary Ellen, I'll have all the money I want."

Her eyes closed to block his insensitivity. "Some things are not to be measured by money, Arnie," she sighed. "I am sorry for you that you don't know that."

"Gretchen, be reasonable."

"I married you, Arnie, for rich or for poor, in sickness and in health, 'til death do us part. I promised, and you promised."

Dear God, Arnie prayed, why is she so blasted obstinate? She isn't giving me any choice.

"'Til death do us part," Mary Ellen Olin mimicked Arnie's words when he related that evening his session with his wife, "what a quaint idea." She cocked her head like her mother had done as a girl.

Arnie studied her peculiar pose. Was she thinking what he thought she was thinking?

# 28

Oh why should the
spirit of mortal be proud,
   In this little voyage
from swaddle to shroud?

       —James Thurber
*Further Fables for Our Time*

The new *Tribune* Building was a stone fortress modeled after prominent armories, and it gave Colonel Olin the cherished feeling of a field command over his ever-growing troops, pushing one hundred minions by 1894, putting out over twelve thousand papers every day.

The rolls of newsprint were delivered twice a week by a two-horse-drawn wagon, and every week over five tons of the paper traveled through the new Hoe cylinders.

As Los Angeles adjusted to the aftermath of population upheaval, the economy settled in and a confident Benjamin Olin reduced the amount of advertising on the front page from five of seven columns, to three, then two.

There was still plenty of it on the back pages, but the first page was increasingly devoted to news of the whole world, with a growing use of drawings. Graphics, once limited to cuts of pigs and geese to call attention to advertisements, branched out to show the figure of Gentleman Jim Corbett, the prize fighter, in full body profile, fists clenched, ready to strike an unseen adversary.

There were maps of the area, cartoons, bird's eye views of the Chicago World Exposition, Uncle Sam, the Republican elephant waving a flag and broom for a clean sweep, and in the midwinter issue, flattering views of the town, of nymphs strumming mandolins in idyllic rose-festooned settings.

When the roof was finished on the new *Tribune* Building, a huge bronze eagle was hoisted up and bolted in place overseeing the entrance. The eagle, a predatory bird whose strength, prowess and intelligence have been greatly exaggerated, symbolized for Colonel Olin royal power rather than the fairly efficient exterminator of rats it was.

Congress had designated the eagle the national bird in 1782, and that was good enough for the Colonel. Years later, Nazi Germany would also find the bird useful.

Head high, the bronze eagle sat on the roof directly above Colonel Olin, who always kept *his* head high. The new building had marked the disappearance of the publisher, and his glass-cased gun collection, from his ground-floor accessibility, spiriting him away to a large third-floor corner office where he could keep his eye on city hall, the county court house and the police station.

In the next office, Arnie Sutler sat with his head bowed, one hand propping it up, the other pensively rubbing his forehead with slow, troubled strokes.

Life had not been easy for him since he decided to kill his wife.

His elbows rested on the piles of newspapers, the bills and invoices he approved, the circulation charts and advertising statistics. The labor boycott of the *Tribune* advertisers had put a dent in their lead, but they were still on top. Colonel Olin had a way of making Arnie responsible for keeping them there.

Sutler's eyes were bleary from lack of sleep, his belly hanging over his pants tops from nervous eating.

Arnie turned to look at the sampler cushion on the chair in the corner behind him. He didn't hear the door open as he stood and bent over to pick it up.

The letters were royal blue on a white background and the stitches were small. It was something Gretchen had worked on while the *Tribune* Building was being built. "Something to remind you of us," was all she said when he asked her what she was stitching so long. Holding it now, he remembered how pleased she was to give it to him. The letters stood boldly in the center of the cushion. He couldn't get over the feeling that they were taunting him.

YOUR FAMILY
LOVES YOU

it said, and she had even stitched figures representing herself and Arnie Junior and Cora Sue, standing on their front porch with out-landish smiles on their yellow faces, greeting a God-like figure of a man striding across the green lawn.

After weighing the pillow in his hands with a light, absent-minded bouncing motion, Arnie set it back down, this time burying the letters in the seat of the chair, and turned to be startled by Mary Ellen standing at the door, her special conspirator's smile crinkling her skin.

"If it bothers you," she said, "why don't you burn it?"

"Mary Ellen, please, I have a lot on my mind."

"Are you making progress?" She had closed the door and walked toward him. He quickly stood behind the desk to put a barri-er between them, for in the past she was not at all inhibited about kissing and hugging and rubbing him right there, scaring him to death that someone might see them.

"I hope they do," she would say, "I have nothing to be ashamed of."

"I don't have time to talk now," he said. "Your father is turning the heat on me. There's a Pullman strike and I'm supposed to calm down our own typographers who are on the warpath again with union talk. We're preparing another booster campaign. The Mer-chants' Association's got to stick on the labor thing. Isaiah Crown isn't fading away peacefully—but how he or anyone else can stand the wrath of your father is beyond me. We lost a little competition in the hard times in the eighties, but what's left is just stronger. He's asked me to quietly bury Crown and his *News*, but he's never been stronger. I can't do everything at once."

She looked at him like his mother used to, back on the farm when he was a boy and she was displeased. "You've done nothing?"

Arnie slumped down into his chair and sat hunched as though compressed by a stronger force. He made desultory protestations, his dissipated eyes unfocused, about morality, risk, opportunity, with-out mentioning his main concern that Mary Ellen would have an untenable blackmail weapon.

She waved her lace-framed hand in a gesture of easy dismissal.

"What is all that next to the future of a brilliant man—a man who deserves to be at the top?" She smiled her accusative smile and said, "I'll keep an eye on the pillow. When it's gone I'll be back."

She turned and walked out, almost getting knocked over by her father storming in, his face the color of a ripe tomato. In his hand was the morning edition of Isaiah Crown's Los Angeles *News*, and it was shaking like petticoats in a gale.

He slammed the paper on Arnie's desk and pointed a finger, commanding his subordinate to read.

### TO BE FAIR (OR NOT TO BE, THAT IS THE QUESTION)

Benjamin Raines Olin, that malevolent publisher of a rival newspaper, who prefers to be called Colonel, has been hurling some less than warm encomiums at this publisher, among them "flea brain," "a lily-livered, wart-faced turncoat," and numerous others we are inhibited from publishing for want of space.

Though many may remember we gave him his start in this town, our Colonel seems to be on his high horse because our opinions occasionally differ from his. But we wonder if his opinions are so tenuous that he must react in violent fear to anyone who dares disagree. Is freedom of speech only sauce for you, my goose?

What has sent our Corporal on the warpath, his thick, corpulent flesh trembling like some gelatin dessert in the hand of a nervous waiter?

Labor.

The gallant men and women who, by the sweat of their brows, have devoted their lives to the welfare and profit of owners like Benjamin Raines Olin.

Now what do these men and women want?

To take over ownership?

No. To replace management? No. To dictate policy? No. To run the business into the ground and thereby do themselves out of employment?

Certainly not. What they want is a feeling of belonging, a feeling they can count for more than a dray-horse. And they want security—the kind they may get by banding together in common interest.

Not at all unlike the Merchants' Association Olin is so fond of. Yes, we know the argument "Where would labor be without capital provided by the owners?"

But turn the coin over and ask where would capital be without the men and women who make it work. You may replace them with others more complaisant, but you will never do without them.

If we could make a recommendation to you, Benjamin Olin: calm down. Your hurling scurrilous epithets at people who don't agree with you robs your beliefs of credibility. Be strong. This town is big enough to hold more than one opinion.

While Arnie read the editorial, Colonel Olin positioned himself like a rock in front of Arnie's desk. When Arnie looked up, Olin glowered down at him and said, "Well?"

"We have said some stronger things about him."

"Yes, but for good reason," Olin sputtered, spit flying across the desk, a spray landing on Arnie's face, requiring all his willpower to keep from wiping it off.

"A month ago I told you I wanted him taken care of. What have you done about it?"

"I've been trying to find the right angle."

The Colonel's eyes pinched in accusation, reminding Arnie of Mary Ellen a few moments earlier. The whole family seemed to be manipulating him.

"In other words, nothing?"

"Well, I...." He felt emasculated. A nausea was swelling inside him.

"Don't stammer around me, young man. Can you handle the job, or shall I give it to Henderson?"

Arnie flinched at the mention of the new man Benjamin had taken to praising in his presence, hinting now and again how Henderson might even do for Mary Ellen's husband should Arnie fail the task.

"I'll do it," Arnie said, closing his eyes and wondering how.

"We've got to keep labor from taking over this town. It's the only advantage we have on San Francisco, and by God I mean to pass that snotty town, and pass them good."

Colonel Olin put his palms down on Arnie's desk, bent over and fixed his eyes on the younger man. "I want Crown closed. Preferably bankrupt and ruined. But I will buy the business from him if I must. If he refuses, you go to the advertisers. They know if L.A. goes union we might as well fold."

He straightened up and added, "You have two weeks, Sutler, then I'll try Henderson—he's a very capable man and this just might be the time to test his mettle."

The door slammed when he left.

Arnie took painful steps down the stairs with their shiny oak banisters and onto the marble floor of the ground level of the *Tribune* fortress and out past the ornate bar that served as a reception and ad-taking counter with three men behind it, shirt sleeves pulled up to puffs by arm bands.

Out in the street there were wires everywhere—telephone, telegraph, electric for the new electric cars. The tracks cut through the cobblestones, slicing the street in two, and when the car came down the street the carriages and pedestrians scurried out of its way.

The two-story buildings of brick and masonry with lettered windows proclaimed medicine, dentistry, quackery, merchandise of every description, palmistry, elixirs, grocery, butchers, blacksmiths, book shops, newsstands, bakeries, perfumes and fine jewelry, title insurance and trust, banks, hotels and liveries.

The town wasn't sleepy anymore. There was a constant buzz of activity, men in toppers and bowlers, spats and canes, weaving in and out, the warp and woof of each block distinctive and yet the same. Women with bustles and bonnets, or without bustles, spotted the streets less frequently than the men, for the woman's place was in the home, and except for the unfortunate working girls and occasional shoppers, the streets belonged to the men of commerce, the professionals and the merchants. Even the laborers had a way of remaining hidden at their tasks in the shank of the day.

As he made his way down the street and crossed under a maze of wires at a corner—a tangled web of threads that looked like a large spider had run amuck—Arnie thought there wasn't a man in town that could succeed with this assignment, and he suspected Olin realized it.

Crown's *News* had grown like an adolescent boy, right out of his britches, but Crown had not bothered to move or build a memorial edifice, but rather tacked shack after shack on his original hovel, and when Arnie walked through the door, he thought he might have stumbled into a blacksmith's shop.

Isaiah Crown was standing hunched over a table in the corner of the room looking over some copy. He took for himself none of the trappings of his station, preferring to mingle with the men than to be cooped in a cubicle like a show dog.

The *News* looked like nothing more than a trash dump, but the tone of the place went through Arnie like the exciting band music on Sunday when Gretchen and the kids dragged him to the park. There was none of the *sotto voce* grumbling he felt at the *Tribune*. The men here seemed happy at their tasks, not pressured or beleaguered. As soon as he walked in, he knew the reason the *News* was still open when a quarter-dozen papers had closed after the population dropped by half—was Isaiah Crown and the dedication of his men to him.

Isaiah had passed forty with the grace of a gazelle and looked upon the younger thirty-year-old as a second-generation Olin. He had heard the rumors and thought it would be just a matter of time until the young opportunist would marry the old opportunist's daughter. The Olins and the Sutlers, as far as he could see, deserved each other.

After Isaiah waved a hand at a chair and Arnie slid into it, he said in his smooth, fatherly tone, "Good to see you, Arnie."

"I guess you know why I'm here," Arnie responded, in his hail-fellow-well-met salesman's voice.

"I suspect you're looking for a job," Crown smiled.

Arnie shifted his body in the wooden chair, "Not exactly."

"No?" Crown smiled. "I don't suppose you'd want to join the union."

Arnie didn't crack his face with a smile. He was thinking, not listening. "You ever consider selling?" he asked.

Isaiah brought his feet atop his desk, resting them on piles of copy. "No, but I'll bet Olin's considered buying."

"Well, I suppose there are less graceful ways to leave town—"

"Oh, my—" he rubbed his chin, frowning, "a threat."

"It's no threat," Arnie said, his high voice becalming itself, "I just thought if things got too rough—you know, too hard to handle—it might be nice to know you could get a good price for your efforts. More than enough to start up someplace else. Lots of areas growing around here could use a good newspaper. Wouldn't have near the competition you have here."

"Oh, I don't mind the competition, Arnie—I suppose it's all right to call you Arnie?—or does the Colonel call you 'Corporal'?"

There was a sudden spasm at the corner of Arnie's mouth.

Crown laced his fingers behind his head and swallowed a yawn. "You know, Arnie, your boss told me a story back in the days he used to work for me at the *Tribune*—it was an inspiring story about how he stood up to a bunch of hoodlums who were trying to silence the opinions of the paper. He ever tell you that story?"

Arnie nodded once, his eyes closing.

"Considered himself quite the hero for it—in that little bantam rooster cock-of-the-walk way of his. Funny, now he's getting so fat, he can't brook any differing opinions."

"The labor thing," Arnie tried to explain—"is very big to him."

"Yes, and why? Is there some sin in sharing some of your advantage with the men who made it possible?"

"Well, that's a generous view of the matter; his is different. He says he was the one who built the business, and because of him these men have jobs to feed their families, and he doesn't want those he pays to tell him how to run his business, how much pay, how many hours they can work, and so forth. He is perfectly willing to let them go to better jobs if they can find them."

Isaiah scratched behind his ear. "Well of course that's his privilege, and I'm not over there trying to close him up because I don't agree with him. Why, I used to know everybody's family here, but we've grown so big it's hard for me to remember everybody's first name. I don't kid myself I could put this paper out alone. I want them to feel part of it—we get a better newspaper that way. I'm making enough money. A union makes them feel fairly treated—'s okay with me as long as I have it to give, I'll give it to them."

"Well, that's easy for you to say maybe," Arnie said, "because you don't have any children to pass your estate to."

Arnie watched the blast go to Isaiah's heart and work its way through his bloodstream until his face turned the color of cold liver.

Arnie stood up—"Well," he said, putting his straw hat on his head and gingerly patting it into place, like a salesman who knows he has made a sale without even asking for the order. "If you change your mind we'd like to hear about it soon—the property won't be worth as much if the circulation and advertising drop—" and he turned and strode out, his long strides resounding confidence he didn't feel.

Isaiah Crown did not get up, but looked after the broad, self-confident back as it pushed so easily out of the big, sprawling shack, and he thought, "Sutler and Olin, Olin and Sutler, they deserve each other."

But Isaiah Crown was no match for them. The same week the Merchants' Association turned on him and withdrew their advertising because, as Benjamin Olin told them, it would bring chaos to the business community if Crown had his way and they were all unionized.

The *Tribune* cut its price to two cents at the office counter and three cents on streets and trains and all news agencies, bolstered by its advertising. The unions called a boycott on all merchants who advertised in the *Tribune*, but that left the union families very few merchants from whom to buy. The boycott concentrated on Frankfurter's Department Store, but fizzled as Frankfurter increased his advertising in the *Tribune*, luring defenseless customers with enticing sales.

The defeat of Isaiah Crown was not as sweet for Benjamin as he had hoped. Instead of selling out to the *Tribune*, or simply folding, Isaiah sold to Robert Lawrence Quint, a wealthy San Franciscan who was buying up papers all over the country and who, curiously enough, espoused a pro-labor philosophy.

Isaiah packed his profit and his childless wife, Clara, off to San Diego where he bought the San Diego *Courier*.

# 29

He that increaseth knowl-
edge increaseth sorrow, and
in much wisdom is much
grief.

—Ecclesiastes

When he left the house that morning, Arnie's wife and children hugged
him in a passionate desperation that
frightened him. As he lifted and planted
his long legs, he tried to sort the clutter
of his family and Mary Ellen Olin in his
mind. He thought back to his beginnings in cold, inhospitable Vermont by
friendless Lake Champlain. His mother
and father slaved all their lives and
ended no better than they began, thinking everything was God's will and their
every move had been planned before
they were born.

Arnie tried to use predestination to
his advantage, like when his school
marks were less than perfect and his
father questioned him.

Arnie shrugged and said, "Maybe
it's preordained." And his father boxed
his ears for his impertinence.

Arnie was gone from his home now,
but he never forgot where he came
from and what God had ordained for
them all. His father's skull had been

crushed when a frisky horse he bought at a bargain threw him ("I fear neither man nor beast," were his last words) and kicked him in the head.

His mother was painfully crippled with "the rheumatism." It was God's portion to her. Her letters to Arnie spoke unfailingly of "God's merciful goodness and love." She would live another progressively tormenting four and a half years, and, without telling anyone, wish she hadn't.

Brother Peter, the parent-pleaser, was ordained to teach mentally deficient children in Worcester, Massachusetts, and to marry a serpent whose glorious body began to disintegrate on his first beholding of it uncluttered. Peter suspected she had spun some sorcery with her garments. From the time she said "I do" at the altar, Peter had not drawn a peaceful breath.

Arnie shook his fist at the heavens. "By God," he thundered, "you are going to ordain a better lot for me, or I'll just take it myself."

One of the things he decided to take was the boss's daughter.

The doctrine of predestination was a comfortable faith. It helped him rationalize marrying Mary Ellen. Getting free of Gretchen was more difficult.

After four brilliant years at the *Tribune* Arnie understood one thing: the real power and prestige of the paper would elude him until he became part of the family.

Though Colonel Olin only wore his uniform to formal balls and on holidays celebrating some glorious war, Arnie Sutler was rarely in his presence when he did not visualize him all decked out in the epaulets, medals, medallions, ribbon and gold braid.

Isaiah Crown was not far off: Arnie, more than once, felt like a corporal and often longed for...well, a captaincy at least. It would be so nice to be spoken to as an equal.

Benjamin stood behind his chest-high desk and Arnie was invited to sit, which invitation Arnie recognized as a command from his superior officer. Benjamin still wanted people looking up to him, especially difficult for Arnie since he was eight inches taller than the Colonel.

In case anyone missed the implication in Benjamin's bearing, his office soon brought them back to reality. The Stars and Stripes were in one corner, the Union Jack in another behind his standing desk. On the side wall to the left was a glass and mahogany case, ornate even for the nineties, with muskets, swords and miscellaneous weaponry from the glorious Civil War. In a separate small case beside it—a case you might find in a candy store or bakery—was a jar with a bullet in it, a piece of lead ball that was dug from Benjamin's hard, defiant body on the battlefield at Antietam. There were numerous photographs of the Civil War, including one Benjamin staged of his leading his troops up a hill in a sword-drawn charge.

An oil portrait, more dramatic than the one in the Olin's living room, hung on the back wall between the flags. It had a brass plate on the frame:

Colonel Benjamin Raines Olin
Union Army 1861-1865

In it he looked, full-figured, over the room he called his "head-quarters" with the most splendid uniform ever to ooze off an artist's brush. His purposeful stance, with one foot in front of the other and his head tilted upward, suggested a man of bold action, with a vision to match.

Arnie always suspected the artist had taken generous liberties with the actual uniform, and the result made the Colonel look like a drum major at a convention of military band leaders on some poignant anniversary after the war.

Whenever the two men met, there was the electricity of combat in the air.

Sitting there under the heavy belly of the older man, Arnie's toes pressed against the bottoms of his shoes, tightening one at a time the muscles of his dense body.

Benjamin got to the point. "I'm disappointed that you failed."

Arnie's teeth ground like wheat-mashing stones. His lips pressed hard together, his toes working in the worn-out shoes.

"I guess you are the only one in town big enough to succeed with Isaiah Crown."

"Hmph," the Colonel grunted, his swelling body listing forward. "He wouldn't speak to me."

"You expecting union trouble from the new owner?" Arnie asked.

Benjamin turned his head in disgust, his nostrils flailing like an angry bull. "Crown had a socialistic conviction about it. Quint panders to labor purely to sell papers. That's far more dangerous."

Benjamin was making pen marks on newspaper copy on the

writing stand in front of his chest. He dropped his pen and stared down at his subordinate as if to penetrate an armor Arnie had thrown up about him.

"Sutler, I'm not getting any younger."

Arnie shifted his weight in his chair and raised his chin from his chest, "None of us are, sir."

"No, don't disagree with me. It is time for prudence, and I have had discussions with my lawyer, Louis Talbot, about the shape and content of my will, with the main object in mind being the orderly continuation of this considerable newspaper enterprise I have built."

Arnie swallowed quietly. Benjamin began pacing the floor, his hands clasped behind him, his sound chest tilting him forward, his eyes alternating between the floor, and Arnie, whose eyes were on him like a hypnotized sports spectator's.

"As you know, I have no sons, and it is unthinkable to let a daughter operate a newspaper. I've always thought you a clever and resourceful fellow and among the most likely to succeed me."

"That's kind of you, sir."

Benjamin ignored the response. "It's no secret your wife has not met my expectations for you, but important as that is to a man's career, and as ineffectual as you seem to have been in solving the problem, that is something I can't help you with."

He was at parade rest in front of the guns in the cabinet now, and Arnie shifted to see them behind Colonel Olin, outlining him like an obedient infantry.

"Talbot says I can best achieve my aims by having you marry my daughter." He gave a dry chuckle, deathless and lifeless at the same time. "But barring that, he suggests I put the shares in trust for my daughters so that the paper will stay in the family and they cannot fritter it away on amusements. Then name you as administrator of the will, giving Mary Ellen the controlling interest in the voting but dividing the capital assets three ways."

"What would my duties be in this connection?" Arnie asked softly, without moving.

"You would see to it that all the provisions of the will were carried out. It would be my wish, of course, that you become the *Tribune*'s publisher, but that decision would be left up to Mary Ellen."

"I see," Arnie muttered.

"Oh, by the way, Sutler, I'm having a small party at the house on Saturday night and we would be pleased to have you join us."

"Thank you."

"I hope you will forgive us for not including your wife. The list includes only pillars of our community, and we wouldn't want any further embarrassments. My daughter, Mary Ellen, will, of course, be in attendance, should you require an escort."

Arnie stood, without noticing Benjamin's surprise. He had not been bidden to rise. He looked down on his mentor. "My wife has caused some embarrassment for which I have apologized. But she is my wife."

The Colonel nodded curtly, uncomfortable looking into Arnie's chest.

"What can I do?" the tall man asked with a pathetic helplessness on his sagging, splotchy crimson face. "Gretchen won't give me a divorce."

Did Benjamin really glance over at the muskets, before he said, "You are a resourceful man"?

Arnie wandered out of the Colonel's office experiencing vertigo. In his own room he moved as a brooding fish in a murky tank, aware of predators, with nowhere to hide.

Mary Ellen was just down the hall on the pretense of filing an article on the burgeoning number of women in responsible jobs. She had seen to it he was aware of her presence, but neither spoke.

After twenty minutes, Arnie stopped at his desk and scrawled a note:

Miss Olin:

Please see me about the article we discussed

A. Sutler

He gave it to his secretary for delivery.

# 30

Then said my Lady to
me: 'Do not damp
    the flame of thy desire,
but let it soar
    Well making manifest
the inward stamp;
    Not that thy words may
make    our    knowledge
more,
    But that thou mayst
acquire the habitude
    to tell thy thirst that we
for thee may pour.'

            —Dante
    *Paradiso* Canto XVII
            *Comedy*

It had been cold when she started
out on the electric car with the "Mount
Lowe" painted in gold on the front. She
wore the baby-blue dress her mother
had referred to as "Fetching," and it
covered her in the fashion of the day
from head to toe.

By the time she reached the end of
the line and the neat wood planks laid
side by side underfoot, the sun was hot
and she was suffocating in the ruffles
and flourishes of her dress.

Mary Ellen waited in the shade of
the lone sycamore tree for the electric
trolley that would carry her up Echo
Mountain. She stood sedately with the
small valise in her hand, looking like a
young woman on a holiday trying to
hide her excitement.

Thadeus Lowe, a Civil War com-
rade of Mary Ellen's father, built the
electric trolley up the sheer slope. It
was the world's first incline railway.

The ride up the mountain was
sometimes supported by nothing but

timber trellises; she found it exhilarating; and the view of the broad flat floor that was Los Angeles, awesome.

She checked into the Alpine Tavern Hotel at the top of the mountain, went to her room and waited for Arnie.

The room smelled fresh and piney. The window was open on the mountain air but it wasn't cool enough to keep her from perspiring. Or was it, she wondered, the memory of that other room that brought the droplets to her temples at the fringes of her wispy, mouse-colored hair, carefully pulled back to let the scant air caress her pale skin?

It had been forty-eight hours of her life, all told, the first twenty-four, the most glorious emotions that ever touched her. The next twenty-four were a nightmare of escalating depression where she lay staring at the mottled ceiling in dogged determination to make something that never would be: to will the dream from the dust.

It hadn't been easy, those bittersweet years ago, getting him there to that musty hideaway, whose only appeal was the anonymity it offered, with a reputation for sporting a desk clerk who asked no questions.

The evil winds of Santa Ana were blowing, and it was too stifling for the birds to chirp or the dogs to bark. It was a day much like this one, but she lay in the bed naked then, and now she sat dressed on the cushiony chair. On that day, had she sat in the threadbare chair she would have seen shacks and a woodpile, garbage cans and three mangy dogs hazily indifferent to the plague of insects buzzing hungrily for their sweat. But he had told her "Stay right there. Don't stir your beautiful body. I will be right back."

So she lay in the seedy boarding house that smelled of dirty socks and lye soap, softly moaning for her "Warren, Warren, Warren"; staring at the mottled ceiling, seeing bits and pieces of her Warren everywhere.

And she'd had to beg him to take her there and she did everything he wanted, so he wouldn't be sorry. She thought it was the only thing she had that he wanted, but he took the bait and escaped the trap, and as she lay there oblivious to her fervid, sticky body, she was sure he would be back. He had said such sweet things to her.

She would wear white to the wedding, she didn't care about the custom. She was sure she was pregnant. She felt different and didn't she know how it was done, for Lord's sakes? And if you gave yourself to a man he was duty-bound to marry you. No one could fool her about that. She had read a lot of books and she wouldn't be fooled.

The next eight hours she dozed intermittently and recalled her childhood and resented all the things she had done to please her parents.

She never thought she was pretty, and when she looked in her glass she saw a frontier face long set in the wind, ruddy, freckled, hardy-looking— not soft and beautiful.

She knew only a smattering about men and their lust and misunderstood most of it. Enough to offer the bait but not enough to spring the trap.

He'd had an animal fanaticism about him, her Warren, which in her inexperience she confused with devotion.

Maybe her mistake was pressing marriage—but surely he was an honorable man. He pleaded an emergency, some personal matter vague enough in the telling to provide her the darkly deceptive, reassuring straw for grasping.

And then, she didn't remember when, some internal clock ran down, the spring snapping perhaps, she realized she could not lie there forever staring at the lath-exposed ceiling in that dreary room starting to smell now like moldy cheese.

If she were a plant that decomposed in nature in the time it had taken to grow, her time was up. And so she bestirred herself, feeling almost overcome with the hunger of her soul and stomach; wavering, steadying herself on the brass bedpost, dressing as though she were detached from herself, a stranger in an unfamiliar place on her way to nowhere.

No one had missed her. Her parents were on a train returning from San Francisco and it seemed there was no one else who cared she existed.

Sometime, somehow, she came to some conclusions:

1. She was not pregnant.

2. Warren's other girl, as she would always refer to Sally, was prettier than she.

3. Warren was the sort of man who found it important to be in the company of pretty women. He thrived on the admiration of other men for "his woman." He was too dumb to know that they merely lusted, just as he did, and that lust was unrelated to him. He gloried in the envy he imagined they had of him, but they wanted her, not him.

4. Warren had a secure place in his father's bank. Mary Ellen's position and financial security didn't interest him.

And the last conclusion she came to was that the sonnets of William Shakespeare made wonderful reading.

An hour later Arnie Sutler repeated Mary Ellen's itinerary. Mary Ellen was watching out of her window when he climbed down from the trolley and walked as a man making a conscious effort to saunter as though he were completely without purpose.

Her being the daughter of an opinionated newspaper publisher may have put off other possible suitors, but it didn't put off Arnie Sutler. She knew what he wanted, and it didn't bother her.

She sighed in relief as she saw him mount the steps to the hotel. She knew in her heart he would come, but still....

She left the room, turning to lock the door, the numerals shiny and ornate reminding her of the number on the trolley.

Outside, the air was dry and hot and she could feel the cold perspiration under her arms. It was one of those days when the bright sun woke you up but the ninety-six degree heat made you want to stay in bed.

Birds were chirping and the early rains had made the hills, so recently parched brown, look like emerald peach fuzz on the chin of a pockmarked adolescent.

They met on the hotel porch. Butterflies danced about the occasional low bushes in the barren landscape. Their impromptu stroll would not have the relief of shade. Mary Ellen wore her bonnet, and Arnie tipped his straw boater.

"Why hello, Miss Olin," he said. "What a pleasant surprise."

"Why, Mr. Lynch, this *is* a surprise," she said, the faintest blush on her cheek. Their voices carried across the yard and into the hotel lobby, and they wore shiny faces that were satisfied they were convincing. He registered as Jeremiah Lynch, which he thought a sight more creative than Smith or Jones. She wore a thin conspiratorial smile that would fool no one.

They walked in the glare of the sun as the Santa Ana winds, gentle and hot, blew at them from across the desert, as though trying to melt their deceptive facades. One of the seven evil winds of the world, it did its duty on the conspirators. They passed a bashful couple, an excited young man and pretty, frail girl holding hands and looking into each other's eyes with self-conscious smiles.

When Arnie and Mary Ellen stood on the rim of the hill looking down at the broad, flat, endless expanse of Los Angeles, Arnie marveled at how it had grown since his arrival in town, ten-odd years before.

"Why, it's five times the size it was, at least."

He looked at Mary Ellen, hot in her blue dress, and he felt the heat trapped unmercifully inside his own frock coat. He wondered if she would take off the blue dress for him.

"Well," she said, looking him full in the face as though trying to read a map to paradise. "Have you been thinking?"

"Of course I've been thinking," he said, his high voice hoarse with a hint of aggravation.

"Ideas?"

"Some."

They discussed and discarded before they settled on their method. Looking down on Los Angeles made them feel like the world was in their hands. Arnie never doubted it for a minute, but he wished, he didn't mind telling her, there was some other way.

She smiled a smile that struck his heart with such force it left him breathless. "Perhaps, it is preordained, Mr. Lynch," she said.

# 31

Even the wisest man grows tense
With some sort of violence
Before he can accomplish fate,
Know his work or choose his mate.

—William Butler Yeats
*Under Ben Bulben*

1895

Little Arnie Junior wore his black sheriff's costume around the house for days before Halloween, and his mother had to fight to keep him from wearing it to bed—especially the big hat.

His father took the boy to bed the night before Halloween and asked him to put on his nightshirt. The room was small but neat, and he shared it with Cora Sue. She was allowed to stay up a half-hour longer than Arnie Junior. She was older.

"I want to sleep in my sheriff suit," he said, his big eyes pleading his case.

"Why?" his father asked.

"'Cause I'm gonna be a sheriff."

"Why?"

"'Cause they catch bad men, and Ma told me sheriffs were good and I should want to be good too, and I'm gonna be like my pa." Arnie Junior threw his arms around the big man's waist.

Arnie's hands were shaking when he grasped the blankets to tuck his son into bed. The boy was still wearing his costume and hat.

"How can you sleep with that big hat on?" he asked.

"It feels so good," the boy said, looking up at his father looming over his bed like a giant. "Pa?"

"Hm?" Arnie was having trouble focusing through the annoying mist in his eyes.

"I'm glad you came home again."

Arnie's head dropped suddenly. He kissed the boy on the forehead then jerked himself up and bolted from the room to sob in privacy.

"Dear God," Arnie muttered, "go easy on me."

The next night for Halloween dinner, Gretchen made Arnie's favorite meal: pot roast with the vegetables cooked to mush, and gravy thick and strong. And she made sure the children were quiet.

Arnie Junior and Cora Sue were wolfing down their food; Cora Sue in the angel costume her mother had made, pale blue with silver-tipped wings, and little Arnie Junior sitting sententiously as the strong-silent sheriff, his feet not yet touching the floor.

On the porch the jack-o'-lanterns were lit and the little army descended the steps into the gentle wind that was blowing leaves from the tree, one or two at a time.

When Gretchen and Arnie Junior begged Arnie to come along, he pleaded he had work to do. They were on their way to Aunt Suff's in the hope of finding a sweet.

Arnie stood watching his family disappear down the dark street as though being swallowed in eternity.

He looked at the stately ash tree in the front yard lit by the hanging lantern, and watched a leaf float to the ground. He thought about the annual death of the leaves and how the spring brought new ones to life. For a brief, embarrassing moment he hoped for reincarnation for Gretchen to a life where she found a man better suited to her.

When Gretchen and the children returned with glorious tales of their sweets and Gretchen pouted in mock disappointment that *she* didn't get any sweet, Arnie got his idea.

Suff was weak, she told him, but she seemed so delighted to see the children in their costumes.

"But I'm afraid she can't last long, Arnie," she said.

Suff was Gretchen's only link to the past, he thought. The only family that might stir up trouble.

"I'm sorry to hear that," he said.

The next morning Arnie went to the bake shop and bought an apple turnover and a poppyseed cake. Before entering his house he crept to the shed in the backyard and carefully inserted a small amount of the silver metallic crystals into the turnover without breaking the flaky crust. He repacked the sweets in the small paper box, and after replacing the poison walked through the sunny backyard to the street and entered the house from the front.

"Yoo hoo, Gretchen," he called.

She put her head out from behind the kitchen wall. "Why, Arnie, back so soon?"

"I brought you a sweet."

"Oh, Arnie."

"Since you didn't get your fill on Halloween. Now you sit down at the table and I'll serve you."

"Oh, Arnie, what is it?"

"You'll see. I got your favorite."

She sat at the kitchen table with the simple square cotton tablecloth, fading green, and folded her hands in her lap. Her heart was in her throat at the attention she was being paid. Did she dare hope it meant Arnie had changed his mind?

Arnie set the turnover in front of her and the poppyseed cake at his place, with plates and forks, and sat down watching her reaction.

She looked down at her turnover, then over at his poppyseed cake. Then she giggled.

Arnie's bushy brows furrowed. "What's so funny?"

"Oh, Arnie. I love you. I so hope your new attention means we can start over."

"Maybe it does," he said, a little testy. "Now eat your turnover."

She giggled again.

"Gretchen!"

Arnie grew so quickly impatient, she thought.

"Oh, Arnie love," she said smiling broadly and swallowing another fit of giggling. "You bought my favorite, all right, but you put it down in front of you." And with both hands, in one motion, she switched the plates while Arnie's eyes bulged as he felt his body tremble.

When she picked up the fork and sliced it into the poppyseed cake, Arnie's fist came crashing to the table making the little cake plates jump under their sweets.

"Why in the world do you have to be so picky about what you

eat?" he demanded in a voice of such force Gretchen jumped in her seat like the sweet. "Can't you be gracious like other women and accept my gift without criticizing me for some mistake?" He cleared embarrassment from his throat. "Poppyseed is *my* favorite. I had my heart set on it."

"I'm sorry, Arnie," she said, reaching for the poppyseed cake across the table. She stopped and frowned with her arm in mid-air. "Which one am I supposed to eat?"

"The turnover," he pointed to the pastry in front of her.

Her forehead creased. It took her some time until she realized he had switched the plates back to their original positions.

"Oh…yes," she said, bringing the fork to the apple turnover in front of her. "Thank you for bringing me the sweet, Arnie. It was very nice of you." She paused as if to consider a new thought. Then she laid down the fork. "Would it be all right if I ate it later, Arnie. I'm not very hungry."

Arnie patted her hand and smiled a smile Gretchen thought was put there by a demon. "Eat it now, Gretchen," he said calmly, "I'd like to see you enjoy it."

Gretchen studied his face. The strange smile was still frozen on his lips.

With a weariness born of repeated surrenders to the man of the house, Gretchen took up her fork, checked his face, then cut into her apple turnover.

Arnie watched with an eager expectation as Gretchen put a small amount of the apple turnover in her mouth and chewed with the pensive motion of a dumb animal, not hungry enough to eat with any relish, yet afraid of the long-term consequences of missed opportunity.

The turnover tasted bitter on her tongue. She didn't know why her marriage vows crept through her head. "For rich or for poor; in sickness and in health; 'til death do us part."

The sound of the front door opening jarred Arnie. It was Cora Sue home from school early.

Gretchen was glad to have an excuse to put off eating.

"Cora Sue," she asked, "why are you home so early?"

"Teacher got sick," she said with a blithe wave of the hand. "Too many Halloween sweets, I guess." She looked at the table. "Ooo, what's that?"

"It's an apple turnover. Daddy bought it."

"Oh, can I have some?"

"Sure, you can have it all, I'm not hungry."

"No you can't," Arnie shouted.

Both girls looked at the strange reaction. "Oh, Arnie, why not?" Gretchen asked. "I'm not hungry and she is—"

"I bought it for you, Gretchen."

"Okay, I'll just have a bite," Cora Sue said and picked up the turnover, and her little teeth chomped down on it like a monkey on a banana, before Arnie leaped out of his seat and grabbed his daughter by the throat and started throttling her.

"Spit that out," he shouted desperately.

Gretchen jumped up now and tried to intervene, but her frail body was no match for the strength of her husband.

"Oh, Arnie," she screamed, "what's wrong with you?"

Arnie choked Cora Sue until she spit out the mouthful.

"Did you swallow any?" he demanded.

Cora Sue shook her head, but Arnie wasn't sure. He dragged her to the kitchen and forced her, screaming, to drink soapy water until she threw up.

Horror and terror drained Gretchen's face as she stared at her husband.

"These kids have to be taught to obey me," he said, "I'm their father. I said don't eat it and I meant it."

Gretchen watched her husband seething violence through every pore. Arnie had lost his temper often enough and she was always quick to jump in and take the blame, but this time it was different. Arnie was possessed. Instinctively she thought his reaction was somehow her fault.

Then she began to wonder.

Gretchen and Cora Sue ran upstairs crying to their beds. Arnie gathered up the turnover, took it back to the shed, and returned disgusted to his office at the *Tribune*. "God," he said, shaking his fist at the heavens, "you let me down."

Two days later, Arnie found a dead rat in the shed. Its little tongue hung limp, the marbled eyes stared at him in mock accusation, and the maggots crawled all over the carcass.

Arnie shuddered while his head snapped away from the corpse. "I can't do it," he said to his God.

Arnie Sutler and Mary Ellen Olin walked like two conspirators on the beach beneath the stately Redondo Beach Hotel which loomed above them on the gray January afternoon like a haunted castle boding evil.

The hotel seemed to go on forever, like one of those mansions that was continually added to in the belief that unceasing construction would ward off the Grim Reaper. There were endless gables, a dozen chimneys, the obligatory round turrets on each corner, cupolas, an observation tower which rose above the third-floor attic servant's quarters, and looked out obliquely on Catalina Island on clearer days.

The wide lane down to the beach was lined with citrus trees, azaleas and nondescript shrubbery.

Arnie's coat collar was pulled up over his high starched shirt collar. Mary Ellen's scarf was flapping in the wind. They were not encountering many strollers as they walked on the wet sand at the ocean's edge, while Arnie made his excuses for not carrying out his mission and told Mary Ellen of the traumatic scene with the turnover and poppyseed cake. There always seemed some hindrance: the death of Aunt Suff, Thanksgiving, Christmas; it wasn't so easy.

The ocean was restless, and impatient waves broke and rushed toward their feet. Mary Ellen had seemed irritable since their meeting in the lobby of the two hundred and twenty-five room hotel, which on this winter Monday was like an endless empty cave.

She had taken a room without telling him. They had feigned surprise again at their coincidental meeting, but no one was watching. The clerk wasn't even at the desk, which was hidden by the pillars and potted palms anyway.

"I love you, Mary Ellen," he said, his hands plunged deep in his pants pockets, "and I want you to be my wife. But this takes time."

"Yes, but how much time?" she said. "You haven't even given the first dose yet so word can get around she is sick, and winter is the best time—more sickness."

Her cheeks were red from the cold, her nose pointed straight ahead, a blunt blade in the wind.

"It looks like sugar, doesn't it?" she said. She had a plan, she said, "…even you can carry out, Arnie."

He looked at her in peculiar admiration. She was good at this.

They went up to her room. She had told him she would not give herself to him again until the deed was done, but when he took her in his arms and she felt his hovering, quaking body against hers, diminishing her, and saw his red face and heard his panting moans muffling his outpourings of endearments, she gave in.

Men are such animals, she thought.

Arnie sat bleary-eyed at the breakfast table across from Gretchen in her simple house-dress. It always annoyed him that she wouldn't dress more elegantly for him. He had put a lot of thought into his own clothes and was proud to be well-dressed.

He watched her heap four spoonfuls of sugar into her coffee and he felt a tightness in his chest as he watched her drink it.

When Arnie Junior came trundling down the steps dragging his square frayed yellow quilt with him, Arnie panicked. When Arnie Junior climbed into a chair silently to await his breakfast, Arnie Senior tensed, and when the boy's hand came up over the tabletop and seemed to be moving in the direction of the sugar bowl, Arnie's arm shot out and knocked the sugar bowl over, requiring a second action to spill all the contents.

"Oh," he exclaimed, "sorry."

The boy wet his finger with his tongue and was about to dip into the pile of white sugar when his father arrested him. "Don't eat that, it's dirty. "I'll get you some more," and he brushed the spilt sugar into his hand and took it out the back door.

Arnie did not return to the house. After the children left for school Gretchen felt nauseous and a bit faint, and she lay down, something she rarely did in the daytime. There was a lot of ague going around.

Three weeks later Mary Ellen stopped at Arnie's office to tell him she was pregnant.

# 32

Arnie felt like he had been run through one of the *Tribune*'s new giant presses with its tons of pressure crushing the life out of him, and every day the pressure seemed to build. He stood hunched with the weight of his woe on his back looking at Friday's paper with the peculiar article he felt must have been placed there to devil him.

He had received Mary Ellen's dreadful news standing over the same desk, in roughly the same cluttered disarray it now held. She had returned to the paper doing some dreadful little articles on household hints from the woman's view, something she had decided there was great need for, but something she knew very little about. He'd remembered she'd been curt and businesslike, as though she were asking him for the latest circulation figures.

She'd had the sickness, she said, and it was her folk's idea she was with child, not hers, and her father made her tell him. "If it were up to me," she had

said looking straight at his astonished face, "I wouldn't have told you
...all the hurry you seem to be in about marrying me."

He slumped into the chair and she turned her back on him and
walked out.

Now he looked at the article in the paper on the desk and
thought again of the awful disgrace, and how powerless he was.

The day after he'd received the news, he showed up for the editorial meeting he'd always attended and found no one there. On
inquiring to Colonel Olin's secretary, a tall, thin young man with dis-
dainful whiskers, Arnie was told the meeting had already been held
and his services would not be required at future meetings until further notice.

That afternoon, Arnie was passing the Colonel's office and heard
unusual raucous laughter from the new editor, Lester Henderson,
and Colonel Olin. Arnie was sure they were laughing at him. He'd
never heard Colonel Olin laugh like that before.

On Friday he watched in sullen silence as Colonel Olin and
Lester Henderson went out to their weekly luncheon without him.

And here was this article staring him in the face. The last straw
in a wagonload of insults.

He was well aware of the Colonel's penchant for inserting articles
made up out of the whole cloth and by-lining them Chicago, or some
other far-off, unverifiable source—articles usually tailored to
increase advertising either by flattering an advertiser or threatening
him.

This article was inserted in the "One Day" column, and read in
part:

> From Chicago—A man set out to poison his wife and
> got cold feet. She discovered the ruse and turned the
> tables and gave him a dose of his own poison. The services
> held yesterday were ill-attended, a tribute to the man's
> worth.

That night in desperation, Arnie gave his wife, Gretchen, another dose of arsenic. He'd thought of almost nothing else for the past
week, and after fervent supplication to God had come to the grateful
conclusion that what with Mary Ellen pregnant and all, it was preordained.

Why did she look so much like the Madonna in bed, Arnie wondered as he stood looking down into her beatific face that made him

suddenly think of a deathmask.

Her eyes were gently closed and her face was a bluish color—like the sky on a day untroubled by clouds. The steam from the hot tea in his burly hands warmed his face. The rag doll lay beside her in Arnie's place, helpless.

"Do you want a drink of tea, Gretchen?" he asked in a quiet, solicitous voice.

She opened her eyes a crack, her blue lips forming a strange knowing smile.

"Oh, I do not think so," she answered weakly, "thank you."

He couldn't blame her. He'd overdone the tea last night, he'd put too much of the powder in it and she'd spit it out, saying it tasted awful. This morning he could have sworn she saw him tampering with the sugar, and she seemed to taste her tea very carefully. Since then it had been cat and mouse.

"It's time for a little more medicine," he said.

She opened her eyes again. "Must I?"

"You must, if you want to get well."

She stared at him without guile. "I'm not going to get well, Arnie," she said.

It was black outside and the little kerosene lamp on the night table next to her did little to break the darkness. There was a chill in the room that no amount of stoking of the stove below seemed able to keep out.

"Don't say that," he said.

Her eyes were unwavering, looking deep into his. She understood, she said, and Arnie's hands trembled on the cup.

"Doctor Becker is optimistic."

"Doctor Becker," she sighed. "He is so old and blind and deaf he does not know you from me."

"He used to be the best," Arnie offered weakly.

"He used to be the only. I ask for young Dr. Simmons, but you would not have him."

"I don't trust these inexperienced men...."

"At least he can see," she said. "And he is been to university."

"Here. Drink some tea. It will warm you."

"I am enough warm."

They looked at each other deeply. "Then you don't mind if I take a sip?" Arnie said. "I'm cold," and he drank half the cup.

She smiled. "Very smart, Arnie, maybe I have the rest," she said. He helped prop her up on the pillows, and she drank.

He turned away from her. He couldn't stand that knowing stare any more. She knew, he was sure of it now.

"I'll get more tea," he said with his back to her, "for the medicine...."

When he returned with the steaming cup in his hands watching the surface of the pale amber liquid so it wouldn't spill, she was still propped up and she said, "You do not give up, do you, Arnie?"

"I won't give up trying to make you well."

Cat and mouse.

He brought a little paper packet from his pocket. "Now take your medicine," he said, "like a good girl."

Her blue lips moved out as if pouting in consideration. "It is in the medicine, Arnie?"

"It? What's in the medicine?"

There was a long silence in the cold blackish room. Arnie's patience was exhausted and his arm was tiring from holding the little folded paper packet in front of her and trying to keep his hand from trembling.

He was not proud of his thoughts about Mary Ellen. If Gretchen cooperated and died tonight, the best he could hope for, decency demanded a minimum mourning period of a year and his child would be three months old by then. Even if he pushed it to six months, Mary Ellen would be as pregnant as an elephant at the altar and the disgrace would ruin him.

What had become of him, he wondered, since he was a little boy with feelings for his fellow creatures. Tears stood in his eyes as he remembered his pet lamb in the jaws of the wolf. He leaned over the bed and took Gretchen's hand in his, the packet falling limp in his other hand.

"Gretchen," he said, putting a plea in his voice. "We've had some good times, haven't we?"

She looked up at him, her weakening eyes flashing open for a moment. She seemed about to speak, but the eyes closed.

"I've tried to be good to you and the kids—I guess I'm just not very good at it."

He waited for an argument that never came. He pressed her hand to his bosom.

There was a sudden, almost lackadaisical knock at the door. Arnie sat back with a start and dropped Gretchen's hand.

"Who could that be?" he said, hoisting himself with a wince of annoyance.

Downstairs, he opened the door on the wizened Dr. Becker who was clutching his black satchel under his arm as if to squeeze the life out of it. His face sagged like an overcooked custard and the rheumy eyes looked at Arnie through fat lenses.

"Evening, Mr. Rothenberg," said the doctor with a low voice that crackled like a sputtering fire. "Sorry I'm late—came as quick as I could."

Arnie smiled and stood aside, while Dr. Becker marched through the room.

Arnie grabbed the doctor by his upper arm to keep him from colliding with the armchair that was well out of the path to the stairs.

"Doctor," he said, using a higher decibel count, funneling it into the old man's ear canal.

"Hm?"

"My wife doesn't want to take her medicine." He held up the packet and waved it in front of Becker's thick glasses. "Will you get her to take it?"

Dr. Becker sucked some air though his stumpy teeth to give a stout resolution to his short nod.

Arnie led Dr. Becker upstairs to his wife's bedside.

"Now see here, Mrs. Rothenberg," he said, wagging the packet at Gretchen, "why aren't you taking your medicine like a good girl?"

"Arnie," she said, drained of even her gentlest emotions, "get this poor blind quack out of here."

"Take your medicine, young lady," Dr. Becker insisted, brandishing the packet of medicine at no discernible target.

Gretchen startled him by reaching her weak, shaking hand for it.

She laid the folded paper with the medicine inside on her shriveling breast and crossed her hands over it, then closed her eyes. The chill black air seemed to shroud her in contentment.

Arnie gagged. He had a terrifying suspicion she was giving him a preview of her final coffin pose. He may have relished getting the better of his fellow man, but he wasn't cut out for this.

He fought to hold his body in check. "Please God, let her help me," he prayed. If she took it without any more fight, he thought, he would be halfway home. He'd put enough in the medicine to lay out an elephant. The dosage had not been as gradual as he'd hoped, but she had been sick for some time and in bed now just under a week, but what with the pressures of the pregnancy, of the not-so-subtle ploys at the paper, Arnie's patience was wearing paper-thin.

Arnie took Dr. Becker downstairs and the old gent bumped into the banister *en route*, waking the children. After letting the old man out, Arnie returned to the dimly-lit bedroom.

Aroused by a strangeness in the air, the children tiptoed with a foreboding of fear to the dark hallway outside their mother's bedroom.

Inside the chamber Arnie had found Gretchen muttering to herself, and he bent his head to her lips.

She spoke with effort, short starting intakes of breath setting off her words. "I could not ever divorce. It would mean you did not like me and you were only one in my life who ever like me. I would not live without you."

"Gretchen—don't," the reeds in his voice seemed to split.

"Well maybe my *Mutter* and *Vater* like me all right, but they die before I remember. Aunt Suff did not want me. I remember you courting. I could not believe someone liked me."

"Oh God, Gretchen," his voice choked and he slumped to the bed beside her, putting his hand on her hands, she knew not if to stay their task or hasten them.

His voice was weak, his spirit broken. "She's pregnant," he croaked, as if to explain everything.

"Oh, Arnie," she looked sorrowfully into his eyes. "That is oldest game."

If only—could he dare hope?

"You are so much more smart, Arnie, you must not be made a fool."

"But—but—Mary Ellen wouldn't lie to me." He looked stricken at the idea, as though he had never considered it. "You know, if she weren't pregnant, I would want to stay married to you. You must know that. Don't you see the trap I'm in?" He spoke in abject desperation.

Gretchen wanted to believe him. "Maybe she will be better than I," she sighed, reaching a hand out to grasp his.

"I—" The floodgates broke and stentorian sobs heaved Arnie's huge body like an empty wine bottle tossed on a churning sea.

Outside the room Cora Sue looked at Arnie Junior. Neither of them had ever seen their father cry before, and neither could fully understand what they were seeing.

"Forgive me, Gretchen," he quaked.

Her blue lips were struggling to form the words. Speech was becoming harder for her. "I forgive," she said.

His body was wracked with a coughing spasm now and he felt so foolish, unable to control himself.

"Take good care of my children, Arnie. I love them so." She opened her eyes and turned her head to the side to look at his huddled, sobbing body.

"Do not to make me out too bad in their little minds. They will scarce remember me more than I do my *Mutter*...."

The eyes in the blue flesh had turned the color of the ashes in the old stove that niggardly croaked heat through the small house: the heat that was always sufficient for Arnie's well-padded skeleton, but never took the chill off Gretchen's bones.

For Arnie each battle had to be won, Gretchen knew, each foe vanquished. She was worn out from the struggle; she was a pacifist at heart. She would be happy with a cease-fire, or even a surrender, but she knew Arnie would not compromise on total victory.

A terminal weariness overtook her. She tried to open the folded medicine packet with her fingers, but they fumbled ineptly. Arnie reached for the packet. "Here, let me do it."

"No, I do myself," she said, and, forcing her will on her feeble fingers, she unfolded the paper. "I do," she said again, as Arnie watched her with undisguised expectation.

"I do it for you, Arnie, I do." She gave a tiny, hollow laugh as though she knew she had not the strength to sustain it. "In our wedding I say 'I do.' I do 'til death do us apart. I do for you. I have been bad wife. Unhappy for you."

Her tongue crawled over her drying lips as if to oil the machinery for one last journey. She lifted the packet to the plane between their eyes.

"I do because is only thing I can do to make you happy. I do to help your ambitionness.

"I do."

Arnie didn't look at her; he felt a few crystals touch her tongue as though an electric impulse shot the message through his body.

"I will drink tea now," she said.

He handed her the teacup and looked with a heavy heart into her face as she poured the rest of the crystals on her tongue, then shuddered as she washed them down her throat with Arnie's tea.

Suddenly her body heaved, a convulsion that rattled the rickety bed, startling the children. They came running.

"Daddy," Cora Sue cried. "What's wrong with Mommy?"

Arnie was in control of himself now. He could cope with death.

It was the tedious dying that annoyed him.

Death was final, the uncertainties resolved, the aggravation removed. All that was left was the fear it would be misunderstood. He might be blamed.

But Arnie was strong. He could cope with fear ever since he held his dying Lammy Sammy in his arms and let the warm blood of the lamb just ooze all over him.

After all, who was he to interfere with God's plan?

"Mommy's dead," Arnie said, his eyes flat.

"How do you know?" Cora Sue demanded and shook her mother's body, gently at first, then with a frightening vigor for one so small. But her mommy ignored her pleas to "Wake up."

Arnie Junior stood behind, watching intently, but not understanding.

Arnie Senior looked down at Gretchen's face and saw the beauty that had ignited his passion. There in undemanding repose lay the singular, unsurpassed, skin-deep loveliness.

It was not the beauty that failed him. It was because the simple soul, flown now from beneath this serene deathmask, was not complicated enough for the complex universe of Arnie Sutler, prospective son-in-law to the publisher of the Los Angeles *Tribune*.

His first wife simply could not keep pace with his ambition.

"Shouldn't you do something?" Cora Sue gasped, her matchstick arms fighting the air like windmills. She stared at her mother, lying cold on the bed, then fell on her like a suttee on the funeral pyre.

Arnie put his hands on his daughter to lift her from the body.

"It's too late," he said.

# 33

Mourn no more, children.
Those to whom
The night of earth gives
Benediction
Should not be mourned.

—Sophocles

1898

The afternoon before Gretchen Sutler died, Mary Ellen Olin saw red. Her first reaction was relief, then confusion, then depression. How would Arnie ever believe her after this?

When she weighed all the pros and cons of telling him, she decided against it. She finally feared her blood would spare Gretchen's, and she was to the point where she would rather be dead herself than live without Arnie.

She waited until Gretchen's funeral to tell him, thinking it would cheer him up, but he reacted so strangely, just staring at her as though she had tricked him.

He was embarrassingly emotional during the services, and she realized, finally, her good news only made him suspicious.

She tried to reassure him, telling him they could wait a year now if he thought that best, but the small children needed a mother and everyone would understand if he wanted to marry sooner.

But he was so strange.

There had been talk of an investigation into the mysterious, sudden illness of a woman as young and strong as Gretchen, but Dr. Becker had signed the death certificate he couldn't see, ascribing the cause to consumption. The police chief, who owed his job to Colonel Olin and the *Tribune*, asked his benefactor awkwardly if he thought it was his duty at least to perform a cursory investigation. "I've had some calls for it," he said sheepishly, standing uncomfortable in his uniform, at Olin's desk.

"I'll vouch for him," the Colonel said in dismissal of the matter and the Chief.

"That's good enough for me," the Chief said, saluting Benjamin and vanishing like an obsolete spirit.

Benjamin had been solicitous of Arnie. "Take all the time you need to recover," he had said with an eerie lack of emotion. "Perhaps it is for the best."

He was not comfortable with Arnie's display of emotion. True soldiers didn't cry. It wasn't manly.

But with Gretchen out of the way and the path cleared for Arnie's marriage to his daughter, Colonel Olin became a new person, cordial, almost friendly. Arnie was included in all the meetings and was promptly promoted to assistant publisher and assistant general manager. He was left in no doubt that he would as quickly be stripped of his titles if he didn't marry Mary Ellen, and he realized that with his help the *Tribune* had become so large and well-known that he would be hard-pressed to put it under with circulation shenanigans.

They waited six months before the open courtship and another five months for the marriage.

In those early years she made every effort to be the wife he wanted. He was never ashamed of her in society.

Arnie had even eased his conscience about Gretchen, considering she had welcomed death, almost like a suicide, really, taking the poison so obligingly. It was not long before Arnie wiped out of his mind any personal connection to her death.

As happy as the marriage was for Arnie, it was miserable for his children. Cora Sue had not spoken to her new mother, and showed no sign of weakening. Arnie Junior's communication was limited to monosyllabic mutterings.

By the time Mary Ellen was *enceinte* with her second child, she told Arnie it was time they should be thinking of boarding school for

Cora Sue and Arnie Junior. Arnie put her off.

It wasn't long after the marriage to Mary Ellen that Arnie slipped into the comfortable routine of the home in his heart, the newspaper.

Arnie stood on the edge of the cavernous roomful of reporters, just outside his office. He rubbed his palms together, stole a draught of air, and decided the time was right to fraternize with his troops.

The hard-bitten crew could, it was said, scribble their articles in the midst of a three-alarm fire without ever looking up. But when Arnie Sutler, the assistant publisher, strode by, it was as though the undertow of a new current carried the message through the room.

The reporters were spread around the large area, manning evenly-spaced desks. They looked like sailors in rowboats without an oar, in a sea without a shore.

But Arnie thought of them as miners who mined as if their only fear was if they stopped, the lode would vanish. But as long as they kept digging, something would turn up.

On the wall behind the proofreader, a calendar with the dates in one-inch squares wore X's on each December date but the thirty-first.

The calendar was a gift of the Columbia Press Company. On the top half was a picture of their largest state-of-the-art Hoe cylinder press. The copy underneath lauded the improvement of their presses in speed and capacity to keep up with the increasing growth of the nation's newspapers.

Arnie thought it should remind these writers, who sometimes acted like prima donnas, that their precious words were nothing without a press to press them onto paper so someone could read them.

"Mr. Sutler," a young reporter named Chick Rafferty had the courage (or naivete, as some of his fellows would have it) to hail his boss in the workplace.

But Arnie was in an expansive mood and welcomed the attention. He always felt it was good politics to appear to be one of the boys to his employees, but he realized he lacked the talent for it. He was more at ease with big money men. So he was content to make an occasional pass at what passed for camaraderie. It was like making mud pies without getting your hands dirty.

"Mr. Sutler," Rafferty spoke with a quavering voice and a flush of color in his face that bespoke the fear he tried to swallow. "What do you think of the first picture in our paper?"

Arnie grinned and winked. "Wave of the future," he said.

"You don't think it's too hard to tell what it is?" Rafferty asked.

Arnie picked up the paper on the lad's desk and squinted at the black blob with the caption under it. "It'll improve," he said. "In the meantime we'd better write damn clear captions."

Now the laughter was not self-conscious.

Chick Rafferty was frowning. "Do you think when the quality of the pictures improve, they will take over half the paper and half of us reporters will lose our jobs?"

Arnie put a reassuring hand on the lad's shoulder. He didn't know his name. There were just too many of them.

"Son," he said, "by then, the paper will be twice the size and you'll have to find something else to worry about."

No sooner had Arnie returned to his office and sat at his desk, than Colonel Olin came bounding in waving a letter and hollering like a jackal. It was unusual enough to see the great man enter his office, but to see him display this kind of emotion was unheard of.

The Colonel laid the letter with a ceremonious flourish on Arnie's desk. Arnie looked down at it and saw the signature of William McKinley, President, United States of America. His eye was scanning the part about reporting to the Philippines when the Colonel let out a battle cry.

"You may call me General now," he said, as though he were bestowing a favor.

Arnie forced a smile. "I'm so pleased," he said.

## 1899

The boy and girl sat in the railroad car in the Los Angeles station, sweltering in the August heat...four months before the 1800's petered out. The girl would turn thirteen on the trip, and she sat stoically like a little mother while her eleven-year-old brother cried his eyes out and rubbed them red with the ball of his fist. The train windows were all open but it didn't seem to help. Arnie had just left his two children in the car when the black conductor yelled, "All ah-boh-duh—all ashore that's goin' ashore."

Arnie Junior was wearing his big cowboy hat, the ten-gallon job that had been such comfort to him since his mother died.

Cora Sue made a halfhearted attempt at being a mother to Junior, but was not very good at it. "Oh hush, Arnie," she lamented. There were no tears in her eyes.

Arnie left the train, dragging his paunchy frame down the aisle, looking like not so much the fox Mary Ellen fancied him in the beginning as a lame oxen stumbling through a narrow slaughter-house chute.

Since the death of his first wife, Gretchen, Arnie's personal habits had deteriorated steadily.

Word began to spread that it was a touching bereavement for his loss. Arnie heard the rumor, liked the rationale it provided him, and cultivated it.

He no longer showed any interest in the sartorial splendor he once championed so eloquently with his tuxedo and butter-cutting trouser creases.

He never shined his shoes, except to rub them occasionally on the back of his trousers, and he usually needed a haircut two weeks before he got it. Often, his neckties didn't match his suit, and the pants he wore to take his children to the train were so baggy in the knees, he could have carried a watermelon in each leg.

Mary Ellen had tried to spruce him up on numerous occasions, but he seemed so preoccupied with his deals, she gave up.

Though she only admitted it in the locked "Remembrances" she kept in her bureau drawer, her diary that no one saw, Mary Ellen wondered if Arnie didn't have such immaculate grooming while Gretchen was his wife in order to compete with her stunning beauty. Since she was gone and her replacement was plain-looking, he no longer had to compete.

Arnie Junior looked out the train window. Cora Sue did not. Their father was waving a half-raised hand, but he looked like a man unavoidably detained. He was fidgeting as though he couldn't wait for the train to pull out, his long legs pawing the platform, his unwaving hand rubbing his face as though to keep awake.

Mary Ellen had convinced him of the necessity for this exile. One of the things she had not convinced him of was the inferiority of "that woman's" children. She was deaf to his reminders that the children were half his.

After the birth of Katherine in '97 and Louisa in '98, the first son, Warren, was born. Mary Ellen came alive at the birth of the boy. Arnie was so busy at the time, he was only slightly annoyed to hear she had selected for their first son the name of her first love, but Mary Ellen assured him it was only the sound of the name she liked.

Mary Ellen had blossomed into a new woman with the birth of Warren. It was as though in having an heir to the throne she had finally fulfilled her destiny. She could brook no competition for her new son, and while Arnie Junior was being banished, there was no sense keeping that pouty little girl around either.

Arnie's brother, Peter, was childless and had a new position teaching in a boarding school in Massachusetts. He could use the extra money and the bargain was struck. Mary Ellen didn't think the fact that Arnie didn't like Peter was relevant.

Arnie Junior was looking at his father through his tears, the out-sized hat pulled as far down over his eyes as it would go. Arnie Senior was consulting his pocket watch again.

Suddenly a whistle blew and the powerful black engine gave a lurch that pulled the cars behind it a short distance and then seemed to push them back in place as though it were all a mistake.

The sudden motion of the train scared Arnie Junior. His eyes darted forward and his hands shot to the back of the seat in front of him to brace himself, and when he was thrown back in his seat he began to cry again.

"Oh, hush," Cora Sue hissed at him. "You aren't going to be a big baby for this whole trip, are you?"

"Hush yourself," he sobbed and looked out the window as if seeking sympathy from his father. But his father had turned his back and was lumbering away down the platform.

He probably had something more important to do, Arnie Junior thought. He always did.

# 34

I feel as vultures feel,
   They are no birds when
eagles are abroad.

—John Keats

1899

With the General gone to war in the Philippines, Arnie was feeling his oats.

One of Benjamin Olin's fellow publishers, Robert Lawrence Quint, had rattled the saber and hounded the servants of the public trust to go after the Spaniards wherever they might be on our peaceful planet.

And we went and made our hostile gestures and found out again how peace-loving those Spaniards were, and have pretty much left them alone since then.

Arnie was in clover. The burden of the Great One looking over his shoulder was lifted, and it was a monumental relief not to have to consider his every move in light of the old man's reaction.

And Arnie took the opportunity of his freedom to do what his late, first wife, Gretchen, used to call "scheming and conniving."

Arnie kept the Benton boys waiting outside his office over an hour. He knew what they wanted and figured the longer they waited, the more they would want it.

It was the piece of land he had bought after Benjamin Olin demurred.

Sitting in his office, his feet on the beaten roll-top, Arnie remembered how he had approached Los Angeles' finest business leaders with the proposition. The land was smack in-between downtown Los Angeles and the proposed deep water port that Olin and the *Tribune* were fighting for. Tooth and nail they were fighting Henry Huntington and his Southern Pacific Railroad who wanted the port in Santa Monica where they controlled the land.

"What does the Colonel think?" they asked, before he went off to war a General. "Is he in on it?" When they found he was not, they declined with a tone that left Arnie feeling like a rejected suitor.

But he would show them. He would not live his life as Olin's messenger boy.

Well, he thought, time to let the Bentons in. He didn't want them to leave, after all, and his uncanny instinct told him he had stretched the wait as long as he could. Besides, there was the troublesome letter on his desk from his son, Arnie Junior, along with pieces of a letter from his daughter, Cora Sue, which Arnie Junior had mailed to him. Cora Sue had written it, then torn it to bits, and he had to piece it together like a jigsaw puzzle. He wanted to put off his response as long as possible.

Apparently they didn't like his brother Peter any more then he did, and wanted to come home. Arnie was sorry for them, but he was just too busy to have them underfoot in Los Angeles now. Maybe later.

"Mr. Simpson," he called to his secretary, a gawky young man with a prominent Adam's apple. "Send in the Bentons."

Arnie rose to greet them. The boys were striking and darkly handsome, he thought, and he could see the resentment flashing in their eyes while the lips tried to smile ingratiatingly.

"Forgive me for keeping you waiting," Arnie said without explanation. Their faces showed they knew why they waited. "Please sit down."

They sat almost in unison on two chairs facing the publisher pro tem. Their bodies they held erect—on guard.

"What can I do for you?" Arnie asked, interlacing his fingers on the desk in front of him.

Silas Benton Junior looked quickly at his brother, Wayne, then as quickly away. The boys were agents of their father, Silas Benton Senior, a land baron and cattle merchant who had branched out into railroads, and Arnie looked down on them as superfluous appendages of the father.

The boys in their turn considered Arnie the lackey of General Olin, and a man who had gained prestige and prominence by marrying the boss's daughter. They were never entirely convinced of that dubious story about the timely and convenient death of his first wife. Silas Junior wished there were some way to use it in their negotiations today, but Wayne convinced him it would be self-defeating.

Silas was the spokesman. A squat man with broad shoulders and a nose that flared at the sides like a spread-eagle Indian. He spoke in deep droning tones that made Arnie sleepy.

Wayne looked very much like his brother but wore a full beard to disguise it. He watched his brother speak, and occasionally punctuated the rambling sentences with a glance shot at Arnie, who for the most part studied his interlaced fingers.

"Mr. Sutler, it has come to our attention you own a piece of land smack in the middle of a section we thought we had a legal option to purchase, out in San Pedro. Our attorneys indicate they are prepared to proceed on the option which we came to find out, when we went to exercise it, why, you had a title to it. Our father is a man of gentleness, and he don't want no court battles, so he send us with an offer to buy."

Arnie looked up from his fingers and into Silas's eye. "What's your offer?"

"Ten thousand—"

Arnie bared his regulation white teeth.

Silas shifted in his chair, a man ill at ease. "It's a sight more than you paid for it, and way more than our option price."

"Yes, and so much less than it's worth."

"Worth, now, is a matter of who and when."

"And why," Arnie added, unlacing the gangling fingers and laying them palms down on the table.

He opened the drawer in the center of his desk, just over his thighs, and pulled out a few sheets of paper. Silas and Wayne glanced over at the sheets and saw lines and mathematical calculations.

Arnie studied the papers as though he didn't have the contents memorized.

"Well then," Silas broke the silence, "what is your idea of a fair price?"

Arnie kept the brothers Benton waiting again until he could feel without looking the droplets of perspiration pushing out on their foreheads. Finally, he put his fingertips on top of one of the papers, and with a twist of his hand turned it to face the Benton boys.

They looked at a crudely-drawn map of the section with a solid line going through the center of a box, roughly in the middle of the page. Another broken line skirted the edge of the box.

"Now that straight line is your proposed railroad line," Arnie said dispassionately, "and the broken line is your option of going around my property." He looked them full in the face now. "My preliminary conservative calculations indicate it will cost you over a hundred thousand to take the road around my land." He stopped as though in mid-sentence, gathered the papers and dropped them back in the drawer and snapped it shut. He rose as if to dismiss them.

Silas stood but Wayne kept his seat. "You want a hundred thousand for that land?" Silas said, blood vessels standing out on his neck like blue straws. "Why you only paid six."

"I didn't say I wanted to sell the land. You came in with an offer to buy, remember?"

"Yes, but," Silas fumbled, "you would sell it for a hundred thousand certainly, you'd be a fool not to. Mind you I don't have the authority to go that high, that would have to come from Silas Senior himself, you understand."

"Thank you for coming, boys," Arnie said with a thinly-drawn smile on his lips. "My regards to Silas Senior." He extended his hand to Wayne, gesturing him from his seat.

"Ah, just a moment please," Silas Junior said. "What may we tell him?"

"Tell him? Why, nothing."

"But, but—but, but," Silas said, spraying spittle. "I've been instructed to return with your best counteroffer."

Arnie just stared at him with the crooked smile of the horse trader.

"You...you wouldn't sell for a hundred thousand?" The air left Silas Junior as though it had been punched out of his bloated body.

Arnie pivoted his head, once.

"What?" Silas couldn't believe it. Wayne was staring too, with his mouth open. "What do you want, man? That land without the railroad will only be worth six thousand."

Arnie watched him sink within himself as a man drowning in his own saliva.

"Tell Silas Senior I don't want to sell."

"You what?"

"I'm willing to hold it for the future."

"Oh."

"If I did sell, it would be a strip down the center for the railroad right of way. I might consider that at a hundred thousand."

"What, that's crazy. He'll never go for that."

"Then there is no use for me to go on."

"Go on? There's more?"

"No, no. Just forget it."

Wayne nudged Silas Junior. Silas closed his eyes. "What else?" he muttered.

"A percentage."

"A percentage?" The eyes were bulging now. Blue blood capillaries could be seen popping in the white background. The spread nostrils were flaring.

"Something modest, just enough to keep me posted, say five-ten percent."

"He'll never go for it, not in a million years," Silas said as he was ushered out.

But Arnie knew better.

# 35

It is not only the wonderful warm winters that attract throngs to our fair city, but the summer is desirous as well for its balmy evenings where a cool breeze ever prevails.

—1901 Midwinter Edition
Los Angeles *Tribune*

1901

Arnie's desk at the *Tribune* was piled high with dispatches from General Olin in the Philippines, extolling the glories of battle and the heroism of his comrades in arms.

Long and deadly boring dispatches, crying out for stringent editing.

Arnie would, of course, run them without deleting a word. And they would spill all over the back pages after beginning, of course, on page one.

Though most of the skirmishing centered around the swatting of mosquitoes, General Olin was able to scare up enough real fighting to make it sound like a bona fide war.

The publisher pro tem fervently prayed to his generous and forgiving God, to have the old man stop a well-placed bullet. It would have been, for Arnie, the sweetest predestination, if only God could find it in His heart.

But, it was not to be.

General Benjamin Raines Olin managed to keep his distance from the bullets and the mosquitoes, and returned home, safe and sound, to a welcoming parade and memorial service for the handful that gave their lives for the news story of the year—most to malaria.

Another cluster of ribbons was added to the uniform that he wore so proudly to all the commemorative ceremonies.

While Benjamin was gone Arnie was in command of the Los Angeles outpost, and when the General returned, he seemed pleased with its growth. Arnie had not attempted to wrest the paper from him as Olin had from Isaiah Crown some nineteen years earlier. And why should he? He was part of the family now, and it was only a matter of time, and the approaching Grim Reaper, before he had control.

One of the responsibilities Olin passed to Arnie was the overseeing of the midwinter issue of the *Tribune*, which had evolved over the years into a bulky puff piece extolling the charms of Los Angeles. The blatant promotion to entice those east of heaven to move west became known as boosterism, because it was meant to boost the population, thereby boosting the subscribers to the paper, boosting the demand for goods and services (and consequently newspaper advertising revenue) and increasing the pool of cheap, captive, non-union labor.

The paper landed in the frozen North in the depth of winter, and it proclaimed the warm, hospitable land in a sunny light that seemed to melt the icicles on those Northern roofs.

And the people came. Came like locusts swarming the land in the Eighties, only to discover too many people had the same idea, and Olin learned you could promote growth but you couldn't force the economy to be hospitable. And what's more, too many of the lame and halt came for the hinted-at miracle cures for all ailments, and too many of the lame and halt could be a nuisance. After the boom and depression of the Eighties, Benjamin Olin put out the word via the midwinter that only the able-bodied need apply, and the lamp of liberty would be extinguished for grifters, no-accounts and the disabled. "Get ye back to your teeming shores, our sun-lit golden shores are yearning to breathe free."

And so the extravagant claims were soft-pedaled for a time, until Arnie was eased to the helm and they decided Los Angeles could take another shot at overtaking San Francisco, sell a few more papers, jack up the ad rates and add to the pool of scab labor.

One of the fringe benefits Arnie bestowed on his brother, Peter, when he took his children was the midwinter edition of the Los Angeles *Tribune*, and strict and authoritarian as Peter was, he saw no reason to prohibit the children from seeing this remote link to their father.

By the time the second midwinter edition of the *Tribune* arrived in Worcester, Massachusetts, Arnie Junior and Cora Sue were secretly committed to escaping the repressive care of Uncle Peter and Aunt Helen, and returning to the land of sunshine.

At thirteen, Arnie Junior had an innate economic sense. He quickly figured how much money he would need to take his sister back home. How to get it without Uncle Peter knowing, was more difficult.

Obviously, he had to work at night. He made the rounds of the saloons, and no one wanted a thirteen-year-old boy.

But he didn't give up. His trail of nighttime employments led to Pauline's Pleasure Palace on the outskirts of town. Pauline found Arnie Junior and his cowboy hat simply adorable. She hired him as sort of a mascot and janitor.

He so charmed the gentlemen callers (as well as the girls who rented their bodies to them) with superfluous courtesies, that he picked up extra tips by the bushel.

The girls began calling him "Yank," because he wasn't a Yankee. He wanted to be called "Tex," but the name never took. The patrons picked up the name from the girls and it stuck; before you knew it, Arnie Sutler Junior was referring to himself as "Yank."

The down side of the job was he fell asleep in school and the teacher told Uncle Peter, and strongly suggested medical attention.

Against his better judgement, Uncle Peter packed Arnie Junior off to Dr. Keplish in downtown Worcester.

The doctor and boy recognized each other immediately from Pauline's Pleasure Palace. Under protest from Uncle Peter (who, never fear, wouldn't have been caught dead in Pauline's), Dr. Keplish "examined" Yank alone.

Together they formulated the secret plan. Yank would come daily to Dr. Keplish for expensive "treatments" which would entail his sleeping in the back room so he might stay awake in school. Dr. Keplish would put his fee in what he called the Escape Fund.

Uncle Peter did not like the smell of it, but Dr. Keplish left him no choice—he threatened to call the lad's father and hint at illtreatment from Uncle Peter.

Peter easily got the "treatment" money from his brother, Arnie, skimming just a modest "handling charge" off the top for the extra aggravation and deprivation of the boy's services around the house.

Arnie financed his children's surprise trip home without knowing it.

Arnie's secretary, wispy-thin Thurmond Simpson, debated making the call to his employer about the surprise, realizing that's where his allegiance should be. But his emotions were with the kids who had run away from their foster home and finagled their way across the country. So he went about his business as though nothing had happened.

As it happened, Arnie Sutler could not have been reached in the bosom of his hearth and home. He was at an outlying hotel in the bosom of a waitress named Belle Pasternak, who never seemed to tire of talking marriage. Lately Arnie was finding her tiresome.

Belle, however disappointed, was a woman of her word, and for the modest financial consideration, said goodbye, making no further fuss.

Before Arnie had left home for his farewell tryst with Belle Pasternak, he had discussed with his wife the possibility of Arnie Junior and Cora Sue spending part of the next summer vacation with them.

She wouldn't hear of it. He was too cheap to get her help around the house and she had her hands full with four demanding kids and a fifth on the way.

Arnie sometimes thought of getting help for Mary Ellen, but he liked to keep her busy. It took her mind from his other women.

The boy had written he was henceforth to be called "Yank." The boys at the boarding school called him that to be contrary, he said. He wore his Western cowboy hat and wanted to be called "Tex." So they called him "Yank."

That was his story. He decided the true origin of the name from the girls at Pauline's Pleasure Palace might not set too well with his dad.

Arnie breezed into his office without glancing at his secretary, Thurmond Simpson, who got up eagerly and followed him to catch his reaction.

The kids were fossils in stone. All the anxiety in their young minds through the exhaustion of the escape was focused on this one reaction from their father.

Neither child breathed until they saw him blink twice, stare blankly, and then blink again. His jaw dropped, "Oh my God," he said, and spread his arms. Cora Sue and Yank leaped simultaneously to the nearest arm. Cora Sue buried her face in his side and Yank took it like a man—standing up.

Arnie's secretary finally understood his boss's icy glare, wiped the smile from his face, and backed out of the room. The poor man would lose his job.

Thurmond couldn't know that Arnie had been considering hiring a young woman who could help him forget Belle Pasternak—a lot of men were starting to use female secretaries, and it was an idea he rather liked. There was a young girl in the typing pool who had a prominent set of breasts that were impossible to hide, and they were always set apart by the rather large crucifix she wore around her neck. It was a tantalizing test of predestination.

But what to do about these kids, the one burrowing her head into him like a mole, the other fighting back tears. There were important meetings all day. He was doing a little arm-twisting, and he couldn't look like a babysitter to the chief of police and half the city council.

He stood back, disengaging Cora Sue while Yank let go as if out of loyalty to his sister. Looking at them, Arnie broke into a big smile. "Well I'll be darn," he said.

"Are you glad to see us, Poppa?" Cora Sue asked with wide, expectant eyes.

"Of course I'm glad to see you, but you can't blame me for being a little shocked, I hope."

Cora Sue giggled.

"We're not going back," Yank said.

"How in the world did you get here?" Arnie asked, tilting Yank's cowboy hat to look into his eyes.

He realized he did not have to reach as far as before he left. The boy had grown inches while he was away.

Cora Sue had become a pretty young woman, but Yank was a gangling boy who didn't seem to know how to carry his arms.

"Yank worked," Cora Sue answered, her eyes pulsing from tight white sockets. She put her hand to her mouth to cover a titter, "At a bawdy house."

"What!" Arnie's head jerked in her direction.

Yank hung his head so the brim of his big hat cut his face off from Arnie's view. "It was the only job I could get at night—after Uncle Peter was asleep."

Arnie nodded. He wondered why Uncle Peter didn't bother to tell him his children were missing. Dr. Keplish let Peter in on the surprise after the children were beyond retrieving. Peter decided the best thing would be to write Arnie a self-serving explanation of the incorrigible kids' repeated disobediences. The letter arrived three days after the children.

What the hell, Arnie decided, I am the man of the house and these are my children. "Bring your bags," he said. "We're going home."

Hand-in-hand they went down the back stairs.

It was raining lightly when they started out for "home." By the time they arrived at the simple clapboard house, the little band of intruders was forced to take shelter on the front porch, where Mary Ellen was sweeping, a strand of her falling hair hanging in her eye. Arnie thought she looked like a scrub woman.

"No, no, no," she shouted, reddening as the poor waifs looked up at her in her thickening majesty. Excessive motherhood was taking its toll. "A hundred times, NO." The raspberry jowls trembled. "You leave them here, you'll be sorry you did."

Arnie flushed. "These are *my* children, Mary Ellen."

Yank looked at the unfriendly eyes of his half-sisters, who had now congregated on the porch around their mother's skirts. It was your team against our team, he thought. Cora Sue was looking off the porch, away from the enemy.

She drew within herself like a frightened snail. Her tight, white skin grew tighter and whiter. Her eyes were like a blind child's suddenly startled. She felt there was a fist in her throat.

Mary Ellen turned her back on "their team" and went into her house. Arnie took his children down the porch steps to the street, now turning to mud from the rain. He suddenly wished his first wife, Gretchen, were still alive. Up the mushy street they trod, their feet sticking with every step, adding to their burdens, this silent army, grim but determined.

Arnie had no idea what to do with his two waifs, now suffering the extra weariness of thwarted hopes.

It disconcerted him to realize that after living in the amenable town of Los Angeles for almost twenty years, he did not know anyone that he could ask to keep his children for a few days.

He asked Frankenfield, the city editor, whose wife had been unable to bear children, but was told she was now bedridden with a debilitating disease that had mystified the doctors.

He considered and rejected a printer and a linotyper, thinking their influence might be too—well—uneducated.

It was one of the ad salesmen who told him about Minnie Ritter.

# 36

Life can only be under-
stood backward, but we
must live it forward.

—Soren Kirkegaard

It was no time for a man with
Yank's burdens to be falling in love.

But when he stood before the desk
of his father's new secretary his heart
was pounding just as hard and fast as a
frightened bullfrog.

Things had not gone as smoothly as
Yank expected since he returned home
eight months before, and he was here to
thrash it out with his father, like a man.

There were only two private offices
on the floor: General Olin's and Arnie
Sutler's. Everybody else was spread
across the room that, when it was unoc-
cupied, looked like a warehouse of
office furniture.

Theresa Lavendowsky had replaced
Mr. Simpson as Arnie's secretary. She
was young and slender, and was stationed outside her boss's door, in the
warehouse. She was a serene and com-
posed angel among bustling, raucous,
temporal beings.

On her desk sat a new typewriting
machine, and a stack of letters she had

put through the machine as blank pages only to have them come out with lightning-like efficiency with words all over them.

She looked like the freshest pink rose, all dewy in the morning sun. She was not much older than Cora Sue, Yank thought, but she would think herself way too old for him. He pulled down his ten-gallon hat.

Between her prominent breasts that were only partially camouflaged by the fabric, hung a heavy crucifix.

With her long black skirt and high-collar, frilly-white blouse, she looked to Yank like a soft hourglass—one of those sand and glass contraptions.

Theresa was smiling at him with the most inviting lips and gleaming teeth. She radiated robust health, glowing like vibrant sunshine through a wispy cloud. She smiled at his hat, too tight on his head. It was dusty and sweat-stained and looked like he slept in it.

He supposed he looked like a fool staring at her. "Ooo, you must be Yank." She gushed, "I've heard *all* about you."

He swallowed hard. He wanted to say something clever but could barely manage to ask to see his father. She told him he wasn't there.

"May I wait?" he gulped.

"Why sure," she said laughing like a child singing a happy song. Yank hoped she wasn't making fun of him.

To Theresa, Yank was a serious little man. It was as though childhood had passed him by.

Theresa gave Yank a piece of chocolate candy and he took off the wrapper, put the sweet in his mouth and methodically chewed it without taking his eyes off her.

"How old are you, Yank?" she asked.

"Almost fifteen," he said.

"I'm almost seventeen," she said with a twinkle in her eye. Was she encouraging or discouraging him? He wished he knew more about girls.

He blushed, looking at her, wondering if she knew he had exaggerated his age. He would be fifteen in ten months—and she would be seventeen in a few weeks.

Theresa was the most huggable-looking girl he had ever seen. He only wished he could be more grown-up and slow the pounding of his heart.

When his father came breezing into the office with his retinue of sycophants, Theresa had to call Mr. Sutler's attention to his son.

"Oh, hi, Yank," Arnie said, trying to force a cordiality he didn't feel. He threw a pile of papers on Theresa's desk. "Look," he said to Yank, half apologetically, his face flushing, "I'm awfully busy—it's always best to check first…" And the landing party washed into his office on a riptide, leaving Yank beached on a remote island.

Yank settled back to watch Theresa typing from the papers his father had thrown on her desk. Those new machines sure made a lot of racket, Yank thought. Handwriting was a lot quieter.

In ten minutes a flurry of men exited the office like a flock of quail frightened from hiding. Arnie yelled, "Come on, Yank," with an edge of impatience, as though the boy should have known he was expected.

Yank slipped into the chair that faced Arnie's desk. At last his feet touched the floor, but he still seemed lost in the chair, like being shriveled up in a dressy suit, many sizes too large.

"What's on your mind?" Arnie asked his son, his eyes blinking up from the papers on his desk just long enough to frown at Yank's cowboy hat.

"Cora Sue," Yank said without fanfare.

Arnie's breath retreated for regrouping. His shoulders sagged.

Outside, the wind was roaring and rattling the windows, punctuating their speeches, as if to remind the siblings of their insignificance.

Arnie did not sit on an elevated platform as General Olin did. His presence was imposing enough to dominate the modest-sized room, not only with his height and broadening girth but with his overbearing manner, frequently disguised in some not inconsiderable charm. But the charm was reserved for hard cases: recalcitrant advertisers, union-smitten workmen, too-independent reporters, stubborn politicians. This was only his son, and blood required no charm.

Arnie was not one for decoration or material aggrandizement. It wasn't his nature, and he realized if it had been, General Olin would have found a way to stop him. The two oak file cases behind his desk were said to contain the personal data on anyone who could be useful to Arnie and the *Tribune*, and they stood majestically, offering a tacit threat to those who sat in audience.

It was queer how that rumor got around. Arnie never referred to it as a source of blackmail—the most he ever admitted to was a newspaper's need to be current on any personal information of anyone who might make the news.

And so they sat, father and son, in that sparse room that emanated such mysterious power and terror. There was no file on Yank. Sometimes Arnie wished there were no Yank. Like today.

When you came to see him he swiveled his chair away from his roll-top to study you, the desk behind him adding heft and thrust to everything he said. And beside the desk, of course, were the "personal" files.

"Now, what is this nonsense?" Arnie asked, looking down on his first-born son like some biblical father considering sacrificing him to an insatiable God. There was the old thrust in his tone that he used when he considered charm useless.

Yank sank back from the blast. He didn't feel he was in the presence of his father, but rather some remote, rather nasty, authority figure.

"Cora Sue met a man," the boy said, his voice subdued. Yank was tired and hungry. He had waited a long time for his father and he knew he would not be given much time.

"He is a bad man," despair crowded Yank's changing voice that vacillated between reedy highs and cough-like lows. "Cora Sue needs a father."

Arnie plunged both hands on the desk and shot himself upright like a launching rocket gaining more height on the boy. The man who humbled giants felt precariously defensive in the presence of his fourteen-year-old son.

"I'm sick and tired of hearing about your Cora Sue. Listen," he bent over his son, in strictest confidence, "I was never so humiliated in my entire life as when that sissified school principal came in here with his psychology crap." Arnie stood straight and marched away from Yank. When he turned to face his son, he was an armada training its guns on the enemy. "You realize she's been going to school in that nightgown."

"Yes," Yank murmured, digging his fingernails into the warts on his hand as if trying to crawl back inside himself.

"Well, what the hell's the matter with her?" Arnie asked, as if speaking to a large and unfriendly audience.

"That sissy principal wanted me to come to the school to talk to him. Said it was sensitive. I told him in no uncertain terms I was too busy and he got all touchy." Aggravation seeped from Arnie's pores. "It finally got through to him who was more important and he came here and whispered all the time. But," Arnie said jutting out his jaw, "I made him wait over an hour." He grudgingly parceled a smile at the memory... "The pantywaist was standing to leave when I had him come in. His wrists got even limper." Yank's feet were twisting listlessly under the chair. His eyes held a dull sheen. So, his father made people wait until they got nervous?

"Psychological help," the word twisting Arnie's tongue with its sour taste. "He says she needs sigh-koh-loh-gee-cal help!" This time Arnie drew it out to ridicule the principal.

Arnie hauled his ponderous body around the tight room. "First she wouldn't go to school at all. Then when I told her I would force her to go at gunpoint, if necessary, she went in that nightgown." He turned to face Yank. "Do you understand it?"

Yank's argument stuck in his throat. "Maybe she just," his voice trailed off, "wants something to remember her mother with."

"Oh," Arnie threw his head to the side, a man drowning in frustration. "I wish I had never let her have it. It seemed a harmless remembrance at the time." He shoved his chair under his desk. "I had no idea that tattered nightgown would become an obsession. I bought her new clothes," Arnie protested, "why doesn't she wear those?"

"They weren't new, Father," Yank said. "They were hand-me-downs from girls who are younger and smaller than Cora Sue." Yank sank back in the chair. "She burned them."

"Well, I'm fed up with her. I don't know what you expect me to do." Arnie brightened with a solution. "Do you want me to give you five dollars to buy her a new dress?"

Yank shook his head. "She wouldn't wear it. I think if *you* took her to buy a dress, she would wear it."

Arnie waved his hand to show Yank how little he thought of that enterprise. "Men don't buy dresses—perhaps Mary Ellen would go with her."

"*No*," Yank suddenly blurted.

Arnie shuffled back to his desk, pulled the chair back out and sat. His spongy hands pulled at the flesh of his cheeks. "Why is she trying to embarrass me like this?"

Suddenly, Yank felt his father's anguish. And just as suddenly he gave him the answer neither of them wanted. "She thinks you killed Mother."

Arnie dropped his hands as though off a hot stove.

"She was at the door when Mother died. I was there too."

Yank watched the peculiar twist of his father's face, as it turned the color of old horseradish.

"She says she will never forget the words 'I forgive you'…" Yank stared at his father, accusing yet timid, hoping for a convincing denial. "For poisoning her." A fearful tremor quaked the wispy young body. His hands went lifeless in his lap.

"That's utterly ridiculous," Arnie yelled, a pale fuchsia color rushing to his face.

Yank didn't take his eyes off his father. "And that you got an old doctor who didn't know anything, and you were dating Mary Ellen Olin before Mom died." The words were flowing from Yank without consciousness. "And the nightgown she wore to rags is the one mother was wearing when…" Yank paused, as if considering the impact of different words, then settling for "…she died."

Arnie's elbow dropped to the desk, his head fell into the upraised palm and his head swiveled slowly, pathetic in that palm. Then he snapped his head up and faced Yank.

"You tell her I won't take any more of this. If she doesn't stop disgracing me and my family, I will have her locked up."

Why couldn't Yank understand how things were? Gretchen was dead, and with her that phase of his life died. Yank and Cora Sue were outsiders. Arnie, at last, was an insider. He wasn't interested in kids. The Olins and their paper were his family now.

Yank got up and looked into his desperate father's eyes once more, trying to understand. His father turned away from him and opened the center drawer of his roll-top desk. For a moment Yank thought he might be looking for a gun to shoot him.

"Well, hi there, Yank," Theresa sang cheerfully when Yank came to the outer room. "You had a nice long visit with your father."

Yank came magically alive in her presence. She melted his heart from the ice block that froze inside him while he talked to his father. Theresa was so sweet and radiantly lovely, he could forget anything when he was with her.

There was a popping sound from somewhere on the floor and Theresa jumped as if to escape her skin.

It was one of the reporters on the end of the floor having a bit of fun blowing up and popping a paper bag. To Theresa, it was a reminder of death.

While Yank stood at Theresa's desk, dragging out his leaving the beautiful girl, a short, heavy man with a white beard came out of the next office.

"Who's the boy?" he asked Theresa.

"That's Arnie Sutler Junior, General Olin," she said to him, with the same guileless smile she gave the office boys.

Olin frowned down at the child, as though he were looking for something to say—then he decided, no, better not, and moved on. Gruff and unpleasant, Yank thought, a sorrowful man.

General Olin was struck by the boy's resemblance to Arnie Sutler. He didn't have to ask who he was, he would have known him anywhere: the tight smile, high forehead and that inner push, not seen but felt as surely as you could touch it. And just as Benjamin Olin had seen himself as a young man in Sutler, he saw himself as a child in Sutler's child. Yank wasn't the only one who was intimidated by the brief meeting.

Yank and Cora Sue's room was on the second floor at the side of the house looking down on some scrawny, drought-ravaged shrubs (Minnie Ritter's thumb was not green). Their room was next to the upstairs bath shared with Minnie's other boarders, ranging in number from three to seven, depending on the season, the efficacy of the *Tribune's* latest booster campaign, and the price of a railroad ticket from the nation's heartland. At this particular time, there were four other boarders besides Cora Sue and Yank at Minnie's—three of them had been moved to seek their fortune in the land of perpetual sunshine by the glowing prose in the *Tribune's* midwinter issue. The walls of the bathroom being what they were, Yank and Cora Sue became familiar with the bathroom habits of all the boarders.

Cora Sue was sleeping on the bed. Yank wanted to talk to her but didn't want to wake her. He realized he should sleep when she did if he was going to be her protector, but he didn't seem able to. His mind was alive with heart-softening thoughts of the lovely Theresa, as he sat in the lone chair watching Cora Sue at peace. When she awoke, he confronted her gently.

"You might get hurt," he said. That was all he cared about. She could go off and walk across the United States, long as she didn't get hurt. And he knew about men and the things they did to girls, and it just seemed to him that, well, struttin' round like that with her growin' up an' all, is asking for trouble.

"Maybe trouble an' me belong together," she said.

"Oh la," he said, "nobody wants trouble—sure not that kind."

She stretched her lithe body out on the bed like an eagle exhausted from flight, her hair hung listlessly to her shoulders, and she looked away from Yank out the window, as if trying to avoid facing something.

The gray night was creeping in, sending a chilling pall over the young pair.

"What is it?" he asked.

"Nothing," she said.

Yank jumped up from the chair where he kept his vigil, and put his hands out over her, pressing them to her shoulders then shaking her.

"Talk to me," he shouted.

She trembled under his throbbing hands, but stayed silent.

"I know you," he spoke in argument, with a lifeless opponent, "you think nobody cares about you. Well *I* care—and I don't want anything to happen to you—and if you care about me, you will stop this dumb stuff right now!"

He released her and stood back to look at her. She was like a rag doll, serene and vacant.

When he at last settled in bed beside his sister, Yank took his pillows in his arms and nested his head into its soft folds. He murmured softly, "I love you, Theresa."

"Hm?" Cora Sue asked, half-asleep.

Yank touched her forehead gently with his fingertips. "I love you, Cora Sue," he said.

# 37

Come away, O human
child!
 To the waters and the
wild
 With a faery, hand in
hand,
 For the world's more
full of weeping than you
can understand.

—William Butler Yeats
*The Stolen Child*

It was sultry hot late in August
when she got away from him. He just
couldn't keep his eyes open.

Cora Sue was perspiring under the
death-gray flannel nightdress that had
belonged to her dead mother. She had
been thinking about the gingham dress
for almost three months. She had been
back often in the daytime after school to
look wistfully in the window—that window where she first met her man.

She couldn't understand why she
found his smell exciting, why it raced
her blood and made her tingly all over.
She didn't think it was a particularly
nice smell, but it had a memory for her:
a memory of someone who seemed to
like her.

Tall and gangling, with a shirt that
looked to Cora Sue like a screen door
with fly specks on it, the lad's name was
Barnard. Some referred to him, behind
his back, as Barnyard. The one person
he overheard sustained a fair amount of
butchering.

It was hot and lonely tending cows all day. And he had never gotten used to the smell. Los Angeles was growing—the population had reached 128,000 in 1902, but it still had the flavor of a cow town, even if the cows were being pushed farther out. Some said the terrible tic Barnard had on the left side of his face was related to watching his cows chew their cud all day. But Barnard's tic was more sudden. The whole left side of his face would spasm, his eye closed in a wink, and rumor had it the last person to comment on that went to an early grave.

Barnard was changing bars when he noticed Cora Sue. They hadn't been too friendly at the Blue Moon, and he was crossing the street to the Silver Dollar when he saw this waif with the blossoming body in the dirty nightdress. His first thought was that she was some old loony, but on closer look he noticed how young she was. Young and nubile. Clear, soft-looking skin, and she was looking in the window of Hester Hinkle's Dress Emporium at some fancy dresses.

The first thing Cora Sue noticed about him was his black cowboy hat with the sweat marks like low ripples around the crown. It reminded her of Yank, and she smiled that she had fooled her brother again. The stranger thought she was smiling at him. He took off the hat in a ridiculous motion.

"Pleased to make your acquaintance, ma'am," he said, his tall body following the hat in a sweeping bow. "My name's Barnard," he said, appraising the goods with a critical eye, a startled smile and an awesome spasm of his left cheek. "What's yourn?"

Cora Sue thought she should walk away without answering him. He smelled something awful, and he didn't really look too nice, but he was staring at her so, she was a little afraid to make him angry. "Cora Sue," she muttered.

"Nice name," he said, grateful for the confidence. "You sure are a pretty thing," he said, following her eye to the window. "You like them there dresses?"

She nodded.

"Want me to buy you that there bustly one with the big red bow in back?"

Cora Sue's hands slid down her flannel nightgown and for a moment she realized she was as dirty-looking as he.

She shook her head.

"No?" he looked at her, his eyes askew, and laughed. "The joint ain't open anyways. How about giving me the pleasure of your acquaintance in the Silver Dollar. Buy you a beer?"

Barnard caught her hesitation. "You old enough, ain't you?" he asked.

"Oh sure," she said, drawing herself up. "I'm almost twenty-two."

Barnard smiled. Gaps and black spots abounded in halitosis haven.

He bought her a beer at the Silver Dollar—she insisted she was old enough and no bartender ever argued with Barnard.

Yank woke up in time to break that meeting up, but he was sufficiently alarmed to go to his father.

His father was too busy.

This time Barnard sneaked up behind Cora Sue at Hester Hinkle's dress store window, his gap-toothed grin in place, his fly-speckled-screen-door flannel shirt that had soaked up his body juices from the beginning of time, sticking to his back like a molting skin.

"Still looking at that ol' dress," he said, spanking her playfully on her pubescent bottom.

She looked up, startled, and turned her head abruptly so he wouldn't see the blood of her embarrassment rush to her face. He took her arm and turned her toward him. The left side of his face twitched. "You want to have it?" he asked her.

Her eyes grew tall. He smiled, showing all the rotten teeth, and her heart began pounding.

He took her by the hand and went in the door. A large-bosomed matron known in the trade as Polly, looked him up and down with a sour purse to her lips, like the drawn string of a miser's money pouch. Her eyes slid over the ridge of her bony nose in terrible disdain.

"Somethin' wrong?" Barnard asked the woman, whose monocle hung on a silver cord around her thick neck, and down over her mountainous bosom.

"May I help you?" she said in that haughty accent that Barnard had despised all his life, ever since his first grade teacher punished him by setting him off from his peers as an undesirable element, using that very accent. "We want that thing in the window."

The matron looked at Cora Sue and her nose curled. "For this girl?" she asked in that infuriating tone.

"That's right," Barnard said, adding a snarl to his voice.

"Well, I'm afraid we'd have to insist she take a bath before she tried it on."

Barnard swooped down on the woman, grabbing the silver cord

with the monocle and twisting it, bringing her head within inches of his, and blowing in her face the beer, the onion and the bean. He imitated her lah-dee-dah voice while his cheek twitched, "Well, she ain't a gonna take no bath, she's gonna try on the dress."

He gave the saleswoman a shove backwards and stripped the dress off the mannequin and thrust it at Cora Sue, who looked at it as though it were something strange and delicate, something contagious perhaps, something beyond her comprehension.

"Put it on," he said.

The woman spoke. "If you have any intention of stealing that dress, I warn you I shall go to the authorities. You can't intimidate me."

Barnard's face twitched and he began laughing, a loud, raucous laugh that grated on the woman. "Lady, I can scare the bejesus out of you, and you know it. You think I can't pay?" He took a roll of bills from his pocket and waved them menacingly in her face. "Don't you worry you' fat tits 'bout me payin'."

Cora Sue put on the dress in the dressing room, over her nightdress, and ran her hands down the sides incredulously. She looked in the big mirror, and the matron, with a mixture of fear and the sense of an easy sale, began rhapsodizing on what it did for the girl. But she didn't have to exaggerate. Cora Sue was stunning in the dress. And everyone there was gripped with an overwhelming silence while the fact sunk in.

"Fits her very nicely. Amazing," said Polly Bloomgarden, our matron.

"Like it a little tighter in the tits," Barnard allowed. "You do that for me, we'll take it. I want to pick it up tonight."

Polly opened her mouth and sucked in some air to protest, but seeing his cheek twitch, thought better of it. "That will be eight dollars," she said, expecting him to balk at the price. She knew he had to work a long time to earn eight dollars, but he peeled four bills off and stuffed them in her hand.

"Give you the rest tonight." When they were outside, he told Cora Sue he lived in the house in the field before you got to the big Conklin farmhouse on Figueroa. He would be waiting with the dress.

Cora Sue went right home and tried to sleep, but she couldn't. She sat on their bed and smiled at Yank. It was the first time since they came back to Los Angeles he could remember seeing her smile.

"Yank," she said, "I'm going to grow up now."

Yank threw his arms around her and wept. Her tears followed his, and when they finally pulled themselves apart, she said she would take a bath.

The night was warm and the path was dark as she hurried toward the farm on Figueroa. Yank had not slept as soundly in months, so reassuring was his sister's new attitude. She hadn't meant to trick him, but she could think of nothing but the dress and how she felt like a grown woman wearing it.

Inside the shack on the Conklin farm, Barnard was busily setting things in order, his nervous hands twitching with every rearrangement of his simple belongings. The gray and white gingham dress with the red bow in back hung over the ramshackle door to his closet, and every once in a while Barnard would touch it longingly and sigh with that rising feeling of lust in his soul. The girl looked like a lost waif in that nightgown, but in the dress she was a princess.

It had been a long time since his last woman. He couldn't remember exactly when or who, but he wasn't going to admit to anyone that this was his first amateur. And he didn't consider buying the dress as paying for the woman, either.

Barnard had made an attempt at washing himself, and now he decided he should try to comb his hair. He stood before the broken piece of mirror he had picked up in the Conklins' trash and tried to brush the recalcitrant hairs into some semblance of order. It was a hopeless task, and he finally slammed the brush down. Barnard had a very low threshold of frustration and it had been exceeded.

He looked at himself in the glass again, and decided he might look better in his other shirt. Hastily, his thin fingers fumbled with the buttons. One of them caught on the wrong side of a torn buttonhole and he ripped the shirt off, with stubborn buttons popping here and there. The decision was now made for him. It was the other shirt or nothing.

He picked up the green witch hazel bottle and poured from it liberally into his open palm, spilling it off the sides of his hand before he could wash his face, neck and armpits with it. Then he put on his last shirt.

Outside, Cora Sue paused on the path leading from Figueroa Street, and looked at the shack and wondered if what she was about was not a rather poor idea. She had pictured something nicer than this weather-beaten tool shed. The path was silent and dark and her stomach didn't feel good. But the dress was so beautiful.

Suddenly her heart pounded like it was going to burst from her chest and her stomach turned queasy. She whirled to run away.

She heard a door opening at her back. "Cora Sue? Is that you?" She turned with slow uncertainty to see him peering out in the darkness at her, the light from his kerosene lamp throwing a darkish-yellow glow behind him. His hair was slicked down with some kind of grease, and she could smell the witch hazel from across the scary black sky.

Then there were footsteps on the path behind her. She started quickly away. "Cora Sue, where you goin'?"

She stopped. "I...I don't think I should be out here."

"You don't wanna see the dress?"

"It's late...and dark," she said without facing him. He laughed, with a rapid sucking of air, like he was afraid of something.

"So come on in where it's not so dark. The dress is so pretty. I want to see it on you."

"Well," she said hesitantly, "maybe just for a minute."

He started to laugh again, he was sucking in barrels of air now. "Yeah," he said, "just for a minute," and he took her by the hand and led her into his home.

Inside, Cora Sue's eyes traveled over the decor: the washbasin, the broken mirror, the packing crates that held his hairbrush, and another larger one that served as a couch with a dirty blanket thrown over it.

Barnard was shifting from one foot to the other, his hands torturing one another in front of his crotch.

Then Cora Sue saw the dress hanging in all its majesty on the slanting closet door, and her heart bounced in her chest and her hands went from her throat down the sides of her body to feel again the tattered nightgown that Yank called her security blanket. Barnard was smiling at her.

"Well, ain't you gonna try it on?"

"Oh," she said. "Oh."

His long, bony fingers caressed the dress sensuously before he took it from its resting place. He bared his black teeth like a cheetah eyeing a snack. "It ain't gonna do me no good you don't wear it."

Cora Sue looked at the dress, her eyes watering with joy. "Oh," she said. "Oh, I don't know...."

Barnard held it in front of her now and cocked his head in appraisal. "Looks mighty purty," he said, teasing her with his fluttery hands and dancing feet. "Come on, take off them rags you wearin' an put on this here 'spensive cloth. You gonna look mighty swell. Paid 'nuf for it," he said, showing all the teeth he had left.

"Well," she said, her thin white arms slowly encircling the dress as though she were taking it for a dancing partner, "maybe just to try it on."

Barnard's lips tightened, his eyes held fast on her arms about the dress. In slow motion he let her have sole possession of it.

"Where can I put it on?" she asked, her thin body trembling against the sudden chill she felt.

"Right here," he grinned, sucking some more air.

"Oh," she giggled while her eyes twitched, "I think I should go in the other room."

He sucked in some more air and let it out, grating on Cora Sue like running her fingernails over slate. "There ain't no other room," he wheezed. "'Sides, I wanna see what I bought."

The leer on his face did not reassure Cora Sue, and she looked behind the door to see a small closet. "In here then," she said, opening the rickety door and disappearing behind it.

As soon as she was inside, Barnard went over to the door and put his eye to the knothole, a self-satisfied grin covering his face, his hands itching at his side, rubbing his trousers for relief.

In the darkness of the tiny closet, Cora Sue could hardly move and Barnard could barely see her pale body between the removal of the old nightshirt and the donning of the dress, but what he saw sent flames through him and for a moment he didn't think he would be able to breathe again.

When she stepped out of the closet they both froze. He was staring at her loveliness, and she was watching the impression she had made reflected in his doughy face. Barnard's jaw dropped and his eyes bulged. She felt for the first time like a grown woman.

Suddenly he thrust out his arms to embrace her, a little rougher than he had intended, and Cora Sue drew back with such suddenness, she hit her head against the wall. The blow and the leer on his face and the salivating of his mouth, with trickles of its juices oozing down from the corners, frightened her, and she let out a little yell.

"Wassamatter?" he said, tightening his grip on her wrists, "you ain't scared o' me, is you?" He leaned forward and tried to kiss her on her lips, but she turned her head away. He burrowed in, kissing her on her cheek and turning his head to find her lips.

He felt cold and wet to her, unpleasant. She wanted to run, but couldn't loosen his grip. "Barnard," she pleaded. "Please let me go."

All her hopes and expectations drained from her with the menace of his face next to hers. The thrill she felt in the dress, the dreams she had, all evaporated in the night. Barnard was not letting her go. He was closing in for the payoff.

"Come on, baby, just one little kiss for the dress." His breathing quickened and the air was taken in sharply in short gulps without any laughter.

"No, please, no." Tears filled her cracking voice. Barnard was losing his patience and his hands were working now, working their way to the back of the dress and down her legs and back up again.

The cold, bony hand on her warm bottom sent Cora Sue into a panic and without thinking she brought her knee up to hit him in the groin. He reeled back and yelped but did not let go.

He hit her across the face with a stinging blow. Her innocent mouth gasped at the air that stung her lungs with the smell of sweat and witch hazel. He hit her again, a long flat hand against the pink cheek, and then again and again. Her head swung from side to side with the blows which she took like a numb rag doll, and when he felt he had made his point he threw her on the floor and straddled her with his sharp-boned body as he tore open her dress.

"Ain't no woman treat Barnard like that an' gets away with it." His hands kneaded her young budding breasts, while she shrank from the pain. Why was he...what did he?...

"Ungrateful bitch."

Cora Sue sobbed and thrashed her body. "Lie still, bitch!" Barnard yelped, and when she didn't oblige him, he had no choice but to apply some pressure with his hands to her white throat.

Upstairs in Minny's Boarding House, a boarder who had imbibed more than was his quota at the Silver Dollar Saloon, thinking he had completed his climb, tripped on the top step and made such a commotion going down and getting up that it woke Yank from his soundest sleep in months. Yank turned over to pat his sister on the shoulder, a gesture of his gratitude for the reassurance she had given him of the new life she was going to lead. But his hand fell in the air.

He leaped out of bed, threw on some pants and tore out of the house and into town. He cased all the bars but found nothing. At the Silver Dollar, he got from the barkeep the approximate location of Barnard's lodgings and ran from the saloon, down Figueroa Street into the outlying country, and didn't stop until he found the Conklin place.

He raced up the path to the door, his breath heaving his body. He heard no sound within. He knocked a short, tentative knock.

There was no answer. He knocked again, this time opening the door.

She was on the floor only a few steps from him. The beautiful new dress was in pieces and hanging from her body like shredded rags. Her tongue lay on the corner of her mouth, and her pretty face was battered and smashed and a blue maze of burst blood vessels.

Yank screamed her name and fell on her, his fear crazing him to terrible silence.

There was no breath left in her body.

"Barnard," he screamed. "Barnard!"

He jumped up and tore into the only door in the room. Finding the closet empty except for the old nightshirt of his mother's, he ran outside, circling the shed, terror and revenge in his eyes, but no man in sight.

Yank went back inside to his sister, and fell down, laying his head gently to Cora Sue's still, blue breast. Then he surrendered his manfulness and burst into quaking sobs that shook his young body like a milkweed in a whirlwind.

# 38

Morals are not made for
sovereigns.

—Machiavelli

Yank had no idea how long he lay
on the floor of the shack with his sister,
Cora Sue, before an inner voice arrested
him.

Yank felt dead himself. His body
was not a part of him. "Him" was the
shard of remaining consciousness, that
acted like a subliminal guidance system.
It wasn't anything to do with thinking
that moved him to his father's office and
made him feel worse because he had nowhere else to turn.

The *Tribune* Building was deserted
except for a night watchman downstairs
and his father and Theresa upstairs.

The watchman recognized him,
spoke a few words. "Little late for a little
fella to be out." But Yank didn't have
enough of his auditory response system
left to handle the message.

Everything was hazy; everything
happened in slow motion, yet was over so
fast it was like it hadn't happened at all.

The vast convoy of desks on the
third floor was deserted.

The new incandescent lamp over Theresa's desk gave the players a strange whitish glow that made them look like ghosts.

Yank's receiving systems took in his father, who seemed naked without his jacket. But why shouldn't he relax? General Olin was long gone to bed. It was less clear why he should be bent over Theresa with his bare shirt-sleeve arms over her shoulders, his hands gently pointing the way to the newspaper on her desk.

Theresa was red when she saw Yank. Arnie drew back, straight as a soldier. He thought his son was staring blankly to judge him with his pale, deep eyes an inch under the cowboy hat.

Their voices came at him like two bands playing different tunes at once: Theresa's low and hollow reed "Hi, there," and Arnie's accusative brass "What are you doing here at this hour?"

"Cora Sue is dead," Yank said.

Theresa saw his body tremble and reached out to circle him in her arms. "Oh, Yank," she gasped, pulling his head to her breast.

The crucifix felt cold to his forehead as the gory details poured from Yank, between sobs and gasps. "The police. We must get the police."

His father's face disappeared. That flaccid face that looked so jovial sometimes, now just blanked from Yank's vision.

"Come along," the voice came from somewhere in Arnie's body. Theresa watched them trudge on home to get the horse and buggy.

While Arnie hitched the horse, Yank watched his father's face go in and out of focus.

They rode in silence, Yank's insides churning like the jarring wheels of the buggy. They approached Barnard's shack and Arnie pulled the horse to a halt. Without a word he went inside. Yank followed. After a quick look around, Arnie nodded to Yank and they lifted the body to the buggy outside. They placed her gently in the back with Barnard's blanket over her, as though she were still alive. Touching the dead body of his sister wrenched Yank's little heart, and his thin body gave way to wracking sobs.

Arnie hoisted himself back onto the driver's seat, feeling drained, but not at the loss of his daughter. Death was convenient in its finality. The display of living emotion was a nuisance. It made him impatient to return to normalcy—where people were placid and orderly, and he could control them.

He had never had the time to develop interpersonal skills to deal with emotions.

They woke up the undertaker, a heavyset man whom Arnie

called "Hayword." The man had a grim, pale face, thick lips which he pursed sympathetically, and stubby hands which he wrung to prove his sincerity.

"You should have got me to go for the body," Hayword said, wringing his hands, as they moved Cora Sue into his preparation room.

"Didn't want to bother you this time of night," Arnie said. The place had the pervading odor of formaldehyde, and Yank felt like he was going to vomit.

"What happened to the poor girl?" Hayword asked. Yank started to answer but his father put his hand on his arm and squeezed it.

"An accident," Arnie said. "We'd appreciate your cooperation in the matter."

Hayword looked at the girl's face. "Looks like foul play," he said. "The foulest," on second thought.

Yank started to speak to his father, but the older man shook his head. "Hayword," he said, reaching for his wallet and extracting a large number of bills, "I came to you because I trust your discretion. You will remember when you asked me for the same courtesy."

"But we'll have to fill out the papers. I have to know her name."

"No you don't. Were there any papers on those accidents you had?"

Perspiration oozed from the undertaker's pores, so big they could have been made by bullets; he wrung his hands. Hayword nodded, under a heavy burden. "I'll take care of it."

As soon as they were out of the workroom and free of the smell of formaldehyde, Yank said, "You mean we aren't going to have a service for Cora Sue? Just hide her away in the ground where nobody knows?"

"What can we do? The man who did it is long gone. He won't be found. Even if he were, we have no proof. It would be a long court case dragging me and the paper in the mud."

"You?" Yank asked. "What about Cora Sue? It's okay for her just to disappear?"

"We have to weigh other considerations."

"How do you know that undertaker isn't going to tell everybody?"

Arnie prayed silently, "Dear God, I don't need this." Then he spoke mechanically. "He supplements his income getting rid of unwanted pregnancies. Now and then he loses a patient. It's good money when it works. When it doesn't, we don't publish it."

Yank turned in silence. In his own unsophisticated way he understood his father. And he despised him. As they rode on, Yank made another attempt to get him to go to the police, but Arnie shook his head.

"They owe us some favors. We might keep it quiet, but I don't think I have to use our chips on this."

Yank felt what was left of his last meal slap at his stomach.

As they rode into the barn behind Arnie's house and unhitched the horse, the gears of Arnie's mind were grinding. There was one facet he knew he had to contend with and that was the most elusive.

Yank.

Oh, he felt some for the girl, Cora Sue, but she was gone. Arnie was nothing if not pragmatic. He thought it might have been different, but it must have been preordained. His convenient belief salved his conscience.

Then he had an idea. "Yank," he said, putting his hand on the boy's shoulder. "Would you like to stay here for the rest of the night?"

"Mrs. Sutler wouldn't like that," the boy said, his head dropping.

"Mrs. Sutler will understand under these circumstances," the father said. "Come on, there's something I have to talk over with you." Perhaps he could atone for the loss of his daughter by salvaging his son.

As they walked up the steps, Arnie's arm was still around his son's shoulders. "How would you like to work for the paper?"

Yank's jaw dropped as he looked up into his father's face. "Do you mean it?" he asked.

The wagon creaked through the night with a lugubrious whine. Holding the reins was undertaker Hayword, a black derby on his head. Behind him, on the weatherbeaten wood-plank seat, were Yank with his disreputable cowboy hat, and Theresa in her long black coat. She was holding his hand.

It was a macabre midnight march to the burial ground. The undertaker had a new motor hearse but Arnie told him not to use it. It might attract attention.

Behind Yank and Theresa, the coffin swayed with the shifting flanks of the aging horse, as though marking time.

With the jarring of the wagon in the rutted roads, Yank could hear the body of his sister striking the sides of the unlined pine box.

Arnie's instructions to the undertaker had been clear: no fuss, no frills, and expedite.

Hayword took the back way to the cemetery. Unpaved, unpeopled roads, and sometimes they just rode over fields, causing Cora Sue's body to rumble more in the coffin.

Lightning slashed across the sky at the cemetery. Yank had seen lightning when he lived with Uncle Peter, but never in California.

The gravediggers were still working when they arrived at the cemetery on Spring Street near Temple. The undertaker had arranged everything and an extra tip to the diggers discouraged their questions.

Yank helped Theresa down from the cart and the smile of gratitude she gave him melted his heart.

The undertaker motioned to the gravedigger. "Give me a hand with this, will you?"

Yank blurted, "I'll do that."

The undertaker gulped a breath of sustaining air. "It's heavy," he said, shuddering.

"I can do it," Yank insisted.

The coffin was rectangular. There had been no time to make Cora Sue the fancier shape that flared from the feet to the heart then back slightly to the head. The lumber was rough knotty pine.

The undertaker took the foot end and slid it out for Yank to take hold of the head end. It felt light and lifeless as he carried it over to the grave. The heaviest weight was on his soul.

A great bolt of amber lightning flashed down through the sky, striking the horizon with a frightening force that sent Yank deeper into Theresa's arms. With the cracking thunder that followed it was like the heavens were splitting apart at the seams.

Yank thought his father must be so powerful that he controlled the weather and sent the lightning and thunder to scare him into his place. He tried to control his quaking body. He couldn't revenge Cora Sue's death if he died.

The three mourners stood by the open grave, silhouetted from time to time with the yellow-orange tearing of the sky, flashing a macabre orange across their faces.

The undertaker asked Yank if he wanted to say a few words about his sister.

Staring at the coffin lowered in the grave, the next of kin's hand was in Theresa's—and beside him the heavy, fidgeting undertaker whose face hung slack as a bulldog's. Undertaker Hayword wore the appropriate mourning face for all his funerals, but the only time he got sad inside was at the burial of a child.

It was cold but he was perspiring. He was short and moved in nervous jerking motions. He did not want to be caught at the *sub rosa* service, and every noise of the night made him flinch.

Standing off to the side, the gravedigger was wracked with coughs and spit every few minutes. With these maudlin auditors Yank spoke, his voice cracking:

"Cora Sue and I were more than brother and sister—we were friends. We had the same hopes and dreams. But I guess sometimes you can dream so hard they don't work out. Cora Sue and I were always in the way. We were in the way here so my father sent us to his brother's, and we were in the way there. Nobody wanted us, but we couldn't believe our father didn't want us. So we struggled and ran away. And when we came back and found out we were *still* in the way, it was too much for poor Cora Sue to take. So I guess she didn't have much choice but to die. But I think if she had a real home, she would still be alive."

Theresa squeezed his hand, and he again became aware that there were others at the open grave. He bent over and took a handful of the dirt piled at the head of the grave and sprinkled it in the hole, around the head of the pine box, taking care not to hit the box directly. That would be another affront to his sister's dignity.

It was the custom of the gravedigger to wait until the mourners had left the cemetery to fill in the hole. Arnie had instructed the undertaker not to leave the site until all of the dirt had been replaced. The digger argued with him, coughed and spat, and said it was rude and uncouth and insensitive to the feelings of the bereaved, and he refused to do it.

Theresa led Yank across the dark graveyard, out of sight while the undertaker took the shovel and, in his black mourning suit, filled in the grave.

There, behind an ancient oak tree, gnarled by stingy rainfall, Yank flinched at the sound of each thudding shovelful of earth—a process unnecessarily protracted by the poor physical condition of the shoveler, with the interval between thuds lengthening with each shovelful.

Theresa felt the muscles of Yank's body jerk with each pounding of earth. She squeezed his hand, then put her arms around him and held his head to the crucifix of her Lord between her breasts.

The rain fell lightly, steadily.

"You must be strong, Yank," she whispered. "There is no one

but yourself for your grief. Your father couldn't help you. I can't help you. We are alone in this world, alone to get through as best we can."

Oh God, oh God, she prayed, help me to help him.

While Yank cried, she rocked him gently in her arms and hummed softly.

# 39

Parting is all we know
of heaven,
    And all we need of hell.

    —Emily Dickinson

The thunderstorm had ended, but the dull amber light from the kerosene lamp on the table in Theresa's living room seemed like the afterglow of the lightning.

Standing shivering where he could touch all the furniture in the room without taking a step, Yank looked like a bare white birch tree after a heavy rain: thin, wet and defenseless.

There used to be life and personality in the room, but it went out when the father of the family blew up in the basement of the *Tribune* Building.

The walls were festooned with samplers with *au courant* sentiments of the day, like" "Life Through Prayer" and "God is Love." Since Mrs. Lavendowsky was bedridden, it gave her pleasure to create these reminders of the many blessings of God.

Yank fidgeted, as though he weren't quite sure how to negotiate the transfer from his wet, clinging clothing to the dry ones Theresa had put on the table by the lamp.

Reluctant as he was to remove it, he realized the sopping wet felt cowboy hat had to come off first. It was like an amulet, and he thought taking it off would signify some irreverence toward Cora Sue.

He had listened for the rolling of her bones behind him in the coffin on the rattling trek home from the graveyard. It was only when he didn't hear them that he realized his sister was forever gone.

When Theresa came out in her oyster-white robe with her crucifix outside it, she saw Yank on the couch in the dry gray work clothes and wet hat, and she giggled.

"You look like a balloon with the air leaking out."

Yank blushed. "They are a little big. Where did you get them?"

"They were my father's."

"Doesn't he wear them?"

"He died," she said with a far-off look, as though she might see him in the distance if she looked hard enough. "In an accident at the paper."

"What?" Yank sat up.

"Mom makes us keep everything," Theresa said. "Oh, she never looks at anything, she just feels safer with something of Dad's around."

Theresa dropped her eyes. "I almost forgot," she said, focusing back on Yank, "I have a present for you."

When she returned with the big box, Yank was wiping his eyes with his sleeve.

She settled in beside him on the couch and handed him the box.

There was a curly gold ribbon on top of the box. The label said "Kaufman Haberdashery" and Yank was embarrassed that he didn't know what it meant.

A sheepish smile lifted Yank's lips. His wet hat pinched his head and he raised it a moment.

His thin, white fingers tugged tentatively at the gold bow, as though he were afraid of hurting it. When the slow process was completed, he lifted the lid and looked down into the open box. There sat the most handsome gray ten-gallon hat he had ever seen.

He took it out of the box, and caressed the wide brim with his fingers.

"Well, aren't you going to try it on?" Theresa prodded him, taking the old, dirty, sweat-stained hat off his head.

He put the new hat on carefully. It was not tight like his old hat and it felt good snuggled down to his ears.

Theresa turned him to look at his face. "Oh, Yank, you are so handsome!" Her hands circled the brim to turn it up all around.

The color flushed his face and his gratitude stuck in his throat. He leaned over and kissed her cheek.

"What happened to your father?" Yank asked, settling back.

"He liked to smoke cigars. I can hardly picture him without a cigar. And," she tittered lightly, "I loved the smell—I guess because I loved him."

Yank nestled his head on her shoulder.

"He was a pressman at the *Tribune*. Mom says he was the best one and he could fix things when they broke. The presses were in the basement and there was an underground room where he went to fix something and there were gas pipes—some of them leaked and Daddy's cigar caused a big explosion."

"Oh, Theresa," Yank said, "I'm sorry."

Theresa shifted under his weight. She had a burden that needed lifting.

"He was trying to get a union into the company. He worried about workers being fired. The company was death on unions, so naturally," she stopped abruptly.

"The company got rid of him." Yank helped her.

Light tears were trickling from her eyes at the memory.

"Some of the union men claimed the company knew of the gas leaks and didn't want to spend the money to fix them because they were going to build a new building anyway, but some of the real hotheads said the company shouldn't have sent Daddy in that room with a lit cigar."

"Did my father send him in there?"

Theresa watched Yank's eyes harden.

"Listen, Yank, your father has been *so* good to us. He gets my mother doctors and medicine and he pays for this house so we didn't have to move, and he gave me the job as his secretary. I wouldn't have gotten a job anywhere near as good being so young."

"Would you trade your father for your job?"

"Yank!" Anger flashed across her face. "How can you be so cruel?"

"You don't think *he* was cruel to Cora Sue?"

"I don't think he ever meant to be—he is an important man, Yank, and very busy. I say he is *the* most important man in town—why, everybody comes in at all hours. The General is more interested in the paper. Mr. Sutler cares about the whole world of business. Why, he has not only the mayor and chief of police come to pay court to him but even the governor. And just yesterday all the bankers were in." She gave a little unconscious laugh.

"Mother lives for the stories I bring home. 'Who was in today?' she'll ask, and, 'What did he get from them?' I swear her spirits are so much better since I got this job. Why, Yank, everybody bows and scrapes to him, and I mean *everybody*," she said, and gave him a long hug.

Yank bristled, "If my father *is* so powerful, maybe he had Cora Sue killed to stop embarrassing him. He doesn't want any investigation—and maybe he had your father killed because he didn't want any union."

"No, Yank, your father is not that kind of man."

Yank gave her opinion fair consideration. "Why do you think he doesn't want to catch Cora Sue's murderer?"

"Gosh, Yank, I don't know. He must have his reasons."

"I'm going to do it myself, then."

She hugged him so hard her breasts swallowed her crucifix. She didn't want to dispel his childish fantasy.

It was dawn before the two forlorn creatures on the couch disengaged, Theresa to go to work and Yank to go, with his heart pounding from the little kiss on his cheek Theresa gave him, back to Minnie's boarding house, dreading the memories of Cora Sue.

Before he left Theresa, Yank dropped his dirty old hat in the wastebasket.

"I won't need it anymore," he said, running a finger around the brim of his new gray.

"You could have *two* hats," Theresa said.

"I'd only wear the one from you anyway."

After he left, Theresa took the hat out of the wastebasket. She would keep it in her room as a reminder of the dear, sweet boy. Maybe she would wash it, and maybe she would just let it be.

Minnie greeted Yank in his balloony clothes at the door. "Well, young fella," she said, with her fists on her hefty hips, "I thought you ran away from home—gave your room to a new boarder, stored your stuff in the back room upstairs—nice and warm over the kitchen."

When he awoke that afternoon, Yank started out for the Conklin place looking for Barnard.

Yank couldn't get Barnard out of his mind. Hunting him down became an obsession, as if retribution for his sister's death were his only salvation from the pain of her absence.

Yank had vivid visions of a showdown gun battle with Barnard ...or just shooting him straight out.

Yank was watching Barnard's shack from behind a clump of brush, when suddenly he heard a noise behind him. He swung around like a gunslinger getting the drop on an ambush, but it was only an old man.

"Help you, young fella?" Mr. Conklin asked, pushing back the lock of gray hair that continually fell over his forehead.

"Looking for Barnard," Yank mumbled.

"Me too. Just left the other night with the wind, I guess. Nary a word. He was strange, that one—say, what be your business with Barnard?"

"Just looking for him, is all," Yank said.

The next morning Yank presented himself in Arnie's office at the *Tribune* to begin his job.

He brought with him a single yellow rose, which Minnie's neighbor told him he could have when she saw the bleary focus of his admiring eyes as he stood before the flower.

"This is for you, Theresa." His hand was trembling like the end of a breeze-blown branch.

"Ooh," she exclaimed, that warm smile taking over. "For me? Why, how awfully nice of you, Yank. I'll set it right here on my desk where I can look at it always." She winked at him. "I like your hat."

"I do too," he blushed. "Thanks."

"Would you like a piece of candy?" Theresa asked, opening the cut crystal candy jar she kept on her desk and passing it to Yank. He selected a piece and ate it thoughtfully.

When his father came in, he looked first at Theresa, then at the rose, and then at Yank. He went over to Yank and put his hand on his shoulder. "How are you, son?" he asked, and Yank felt a flow of genuine concern.

"I'm ready to start working," Yank said.

"Good," Arnie said, turning to Theresa. "Could you find something for him to do this morning?"

"Oh, yes," Theresa said. "Do you like my rose, Mr. Sutler?"

Arnie looked at the flower and thought it looked a bit forlorn on the neat desk. "Well...yes."

"Yank brought it to me. Wasn't that nice of him?" She looked at Yank, love and pride filling her eyes.

"I'll need the Mexico file," Arnie said, and disappeared into his room.

That morning Theresa found messenger chores for Yank and introduced him to Lormer in the mailroom for whom he would be working. Yank was so excited he thought he would ask his father not to make him go to school when it started again in September.

At his lunch break, Yank stole around the corner to a Main Street shop. He pushed open the door and a bell clanged and frightened him.

He stood at the glass case off to the side and stared down at the wares. The sunlight through the high windows made the metal gleam.

The man was watching him from the back of the shop, as if waiting for a signal. When Yank just continued to stare at the display of handguns for sale, the man moseyed up to him, facing him from the other side of the counter.

"Help you, son?"

"How much is the cheapest gun?" Yank asked, still transfixed with the merchandise.

"Well, son," the smile on the man's face, understanding, "you bring your dad in with you and we'll talk about it."

That afternoon two dozen long-stemmed American Beauty roses were delivered to Theresa with a card that read:

Dearest Theresa,

Not even roses can express my appreciation for the way you took over and handled my young son, Arnie Junior, in the time of his grief.

Love and admiration,
Arnie Sutler, Assistant General Manager.

That afternoon Yank came to deliver the afternoon mail to Arnie Sutler, assistant general manager of the Los Angeles *Tribune*. When he stopped at the desk of Theresa Lavendowsky, Yank saw the gargantuan floral bouquet dwarfing his lone, forlorn rose.

The speech froze in his mouth.

Theresa glanced up at him through her eyebrows and her eyes closed gently. Both their hearts beat faster.

The next morning Yank's rose was the only one on Theresa's desk. When Arnie Sutler came in, he said, "Miss L., what happened to the roses?"

"Oh, I took them home to Mother, they were so beautiful," she said, smiling broadly at Arnie, "it was *so* nice of you."

The damage creased the big man's face. "Oh, Mr. Sutler," Theresa said, "Yank needs encouragement so much, and the twenty-four flowers so overpowered his little gift. I knew you would understand."

Arnie's lips worked as if tasting the juice of a lemon. "Get me the file on the phone book printing contracts." He started for his room, then turned back to glance again at Yank's rose. "Oh, and Miss L., tell my son I'd like to see him in my office."

"Yes, sir."

Yank stood before his father, ill at ease as always in the presence of the great man. "Sit down, Yank," his father said. Yank took the chair at the far end of the room and faced his father, who sat with one arm on his roll-top desk.

"Yank, if you're going to work here," he said, "there are certain things you have to understand. One is you are my son, and you have certain responsibilities that the ordinary employee doesn't have. Your first responsibility is not to fraternize with the other employees."

"I shouldn't talk to anybody?" Yank protested.

"Let me finish. Some people will try to take advantage of your friendship. And," he said, looking at the floor, "some of the young women may consider you an advantageous catch."

"You aren't talking about Theresa, are you?"

"I'm talking about everyone," Arnie said, hair rising on the back of his neck, above his starched white collar. "I asked her to help you with the funeral and she did it conscientiously, but it wouldn't do for you to become too involved with her."

Yank stared at his father, trying to fathom that passive, heavy face.

"Dad," he pleaded, "the only thing that got me through Cora Sue's death was Theresa's kindness. To ask me to turn my back on her now is...well, I can't do it. Without her I think I would have lost my mind." And without waiting for an answer, he stood and left the room.

That afternoon another two dozen long-stemmed American Beauty roses were delivered and placed on Theresa's desk. The card read:

> Dearest Theresa,
>
> I would like to see these roses complement your beauty on your desk as a reminder to me of my gratitude for all your help.
>
> Warmest regards,
> Arnie Sutler, Senior.

The note frightened Theresa. Her boss had never used "Senior" behind his name before. It was as though now he were afraid she would think Yank had somehow magically been able to afford two dozen roses.

That day when Yank delivered the mail to General Olin, his secretary was away from his desk and he heard no sound from the inner office.

Yank tiptoed to the door and found it slightly ajar. He looked in and pushed it slowly open.

He looked behind him, and when he was sure no one was watching, he went inside to the gun case and tried to open the glass door. It was locked.

He was wondering if the General kept the key in his desk, when he heard the footsteps.

He spun around to face the man all his fellow employees feared, the General himself.

"What are you doing in my office, boy?" was the gruff question.

"I was just looking at the guns."

"You don't come in here without being asked, you understand?"

"Yes, sir," Yank said, hurrying past the barrel chest.

When Yank got to Theresa's desk and saw the funereal floral display, he looked from the roses to Theresa's eyes and saw her close them gently.

"Do you own a flower shop?"

They both had a good laugh, until Arnie put his head outside his door and said, "Please, I'm trying to concentrate," looked at Yank with a withering glare and went back inside. Yank looked at Theresa; she smiled at him. He whispered, "Theresa, could we go on a picnic on Sunday?"

"Ooh," she said, "what a nice idea. I'll make the lunch."

Yank went to the Conklin place every morning before work and every evening after work. There was no sign of Barnard. At night he went from saloon to saloon, trying to catch a glimpse of him by peeking in the door when it opened. No one seemed to know anything about him.

That Sunday, the sun returned to shine on Los Angeles after three days of hiding, making everything look bright and cheerful. When Theresa said "Hi, there," in that endearing singsong, Yank's heart fluttered as a hummingbird in flight. Theresa looked so fresh and clean carrying the big wicker basket covered with the checkered cloth she would spread on the grass for a tablecloth. She had made

chicken sandwiches and fruit salad and cookies with nuts and oat-
meal in them, and to drink there was a nice fruit juice mixture all her
own. They ate on the lawn of City Park with other young couples
around them. Excited children romped around while Yank and
Theresa looked silently into each other's eyes and felt warm and
serene.

"Theresa?"

"Hm?"

The young boy hesitated.

"Come on, Yank," she teased, "out with it."

"I'm afraid to admit how good you make me feel."

She smiled and cocked her head. "But why, Yank?"

"Because if you think I'm over my mourning for Cora Sue," he
blurted out, "you might not want to have anymore to do with me."

"Oh, Yank." She dissolved with her head cradled in his lap.

On the way home they passed a shop that stood across the street
from City Park. The little shop specialized in appealing to the fantasies of young girls. There were dresses and pinafores in the window, along with children's furniture, a highchair, and a small bed. On
top of the bed was propped a china-faced doll.

"Ooh, look at that darling doll," Theresa said, absently touching
the crucifix on her chest. "Wouldn't you just love to have one of
those?"

"No," Yank laughed, "I don't play with dolls."

They laughed.

"Well, gee," she said, "you don't have to *play* with them. You can
just look at it and see how pretty it is." Yank had never seen her eyes
so big. "Someday I'm going to have a baby girl, just like that doll."

She got home late to make her mother's supper. Yank stood at
the front door nervous and out of sorts, looking into her eyes. Theresa
seemed a little strange herself. Yank's heart was pounding as she took
both his hands in hers. As he leaned forward to kiss her, his nerve
failed him and he drew back an inch, but Theresa stemmed the
retreat and their lips met in a delicious mingling of tingling souls.

On his way home, Yank's feet did not touch the street.

On Monday morning Yank appeared at his father's roll-top desk,
and the big man looked up at him with no mask on his impatience.
"Father," Yank said, "I wonder if I could have an advance on my
salary?"

"Oh, why is that?"

"Well, it's to buy something for someone."

"What? For who?"

Yank was embarrassed and he looked at the floor while his heart pounded for Theresa. "It's a doll," he said bashfully, "for Theresa."

There was a long silence. Arnie nodded his head, feeling frustration in his throat. "Where did you see this doll?"

Yank looked surprised. "Does that matter?"

"I'll take a look at it. I don't want you overcharged."

Hope worked through Yank's veins, and he gave him the details.

The next morning the doll was perched in Theresa's chair with a big red ribbon tied around its neck. When Yank came in early that morning and saw the doll and the happy expression on Theresa's face, his heart sank.

"I didn't mean for you to buy it for me, silly," she said. Tears came to Yank's eyes.

When his father came in, Yank barged into his office.

"Why did you do it?" Yank demanded, tears still standing in his eyes.

Arnie shrugged his shoulders. "You said she wanted the doll, and when I saw it would have taken more than a week of your pay, I bought it." He waved his flaccid hand to minimize the importance of the decision. "I didn't put a card on it, so I'm sure she thought it was from you."

Yank stared at his father. He began stuttering. His father held up his hand. "Wait a minute, Yank," his voice shot out, harsh with anger. "I told you before and I'll tell you again, I don't want you fraternizing with the employees. That includes Theresa!"

"But," Yank sputtered, "it's all right for you to?"

Rage gripped Arnie's face. "Get out of here," he barked, "and don't come back."

# 40

Ignorance more fre-
quently begets confidence
than does knowledge...

—Charles Darwin
Introduction to
*The Descent of Man*

Unemployed, Yank spent hours with
a penknife whittling a simple oak slab
he had bought at the lumberyard. He
carved Cora Sue's name, her birthday,
and the date of her death. A softer wood
would have gone faster, but Mr. Hayword, the undertaker, told him hard
wood would last longer.

His father would not approve, so he
did not tell him. When he had finished
and placed the marker on his sister's grave,
his idleness grew into painful remorse.

He pulled himself out of his self-
pitying brass bed, and headed for the
police department.

The nice man at the desk, with the
sleepy eyes and the shocking red hair,
listened to his story. He twirled his artistic mustache that curled up on the ends,
while he listened. Then, when he heard
who the boy belonged to, he opened
those sleepy eyes wide and took him in
the back to see the Chief.

Chief Delaney was a man who never
thought much of physical activity, pre-

ferring to limit his to the hoisting of a full glass of beer now and again at the Mercantile Club over on Second Street. And today he couldn't keep his eyes off the clock and the thermometer. He would take as early a lunch as possible, because it was an hour before noon and the thermometer had already crossed ninety and was still climbing. And he didn't mind telling you he didn't care for these stinking hot blues in the summer.

The red head passed Yank over to the Chief with a raised eyebrow. At the big man's request, Yank repeated the story.

The Chief's fingers entwined over his sack-of-beans belly, and after Yank finished his story he watched the mound move up and down.

The Chief turned his round red face to the wall. Then back to look deep into the boy's eyes. He was sincere, all right. No blarney there.

"Hmmm," he said. "Yes." The words fell like a lace handkerchief at a politician's funeral.

Yank fidgeted in his chair. The old chief had smiled friendly to him. Offered him a cigar, which he politely declined. He seemed sympathetic, but now that Yank was finished, he didn't say anything.

Of course Yank didn't know the chief's history, or he might have understood.

It all started when General Olin came storming into Arnie's office with a newspaper flapping on the wind behind him. He spun it around like a sail in a hurricane and his son-in-law jumped as it landed on the desk in front of his nose.

"Damnation, Sutler, look at this story will you. Here's a sweet murder: a young man in his twenties shoots his estranged wife and a young man who walked her home from a dance, and we only hear about it when we read it in the *News*. I'm sick and tired of playing second fiddle to the *News* in the crime department. How do they do it?"

A few days later Arnie returned with the answer.

"The Chief was picked by Quint at the *News*. It was their reward for supporting the mayor in the last election...."

"Well, find out what support they gave and double it," General Olin said with a frown. "No, wait. There's bound to be some scandal in the police department. Something you can trace to the Chief."

And it worked. Relatives on the payroll, a little graft here, a little corruption there.

STENCH OF CORRUPTION<br>
IN POLICE DEPARTMENT

sold a lot of papers, and the mayor was in General Olin's office at the end of the first week of stories, hat in hand.

"What do you want, General?"

And the General told him. In exchange for the support of the *Tribune*, he would pick the chief of police, someone who wouldn't embarrass the department. "We'll run an editorial supporting you for your courage in dismissing Chief Williams—an old friend gone wrong. I'll make a hero of you."

"Thank you, General."

On days like today the chief wished he'd stayed a patrolman.

"Do you know Barnard, sir?" Yank asked, finally breaking the dead silence.

"What?" The Chief seemed startled. "Oh, Barnard. Yesss...."

"Do you know where he is?"

"Ah, no. He seems to have disappeared. Not surprising, after what you told me."

"Do you think you can find him?"

"Ah, that might be difficult...."

"Could you try?" Ah, ha. There it was. On the table. The simple question. On the other hand....

Chief Delaney stood up, his face pained reluctance, put on his blue jacket and said, "Come on, my lad, I think we should talk this thing over with your father. Get his slant on it."

Yank shook his head, terrified. "Oh, no, sir. He would be very mad if he knew I talked to you."

"Yes, you said," the Chief smiled at the boy and patted his hair. "But I know Arnie Sutler from way back. He *was* the girl's father after all. My duty.... We need a complaint from him in any case."

"But what if you have a complaint from me?"

"Well, that's all well and good, lad, but you are still a minor and I'm afraid the law still operates for the adults of the world. Now come along."

When Arnie saw the police chief with his son Yank, he knew what had happened. He cleared his office of the staff. The unusual courtliness of his father gave Yank a sudden burst of hope.

"Chief," Arnie said, extending his hand, "it's good to see you. Come in, come in. Sit down."

The Chief felt the band of his hat as his fingers circled around it as though touching an amulet to ward off the evil spirits. Yank looked up past the belly into the red face and thought he saw fear pasted there on top of the blue uniform with the gold stripes and the black neckband.

The Chief sat, nodding his gratitude.

"Boy here come to me with a story about his sister," he said, still working the gold hatband.

Arnie took over, sensing the Chief's discomfort, and not wishing to relinquish any control.

"Yes," he said, waving his hand to dismiss a bothersome fly. Yank expected him to say "Hmmm" and "Yesss" a few more times, but his father was never indecisive. "I didn't want to bother you with it, Chief. It all seemed so hopeless. A drifter seduces a young girl. And then there was the consideration of course of the scandalmongering that would go on, and I just didn't see the benefit to anyone. I'm sure the culprit will be gunned down any day in a saloon brawl and save the taxpayers the expense."

"Yes, I..." the Chief made an attempt to speak.

Arnie waved him down again. "I don't think Yank realizes all the implications here. And I don't fault him for that. At his age, I wouldn't have either."

"I expect that's true," Chief Delaney said, his tongue gliding over the dry cracks in his lips.

Arnie made a pretense of checking his calendar. "Tell you what, Chief, I've got a clear lunch hour and I'd be honored if you'd join me for lunch at the Mercantile. Might even buy you a beer. Sound good?"

"Sounds good to me," the Chief said.

"Good," Arnie said, rising. "If you'll excuse me for a minute, Chief, I've a few things to attend to first. I'll be with you in a minute."

"Certainly, Mr. Sutler," he said and bowed his head, backed up a step and turned to go. Yank stood up to follow him, but his father turned his palm toward Yank to stop him.

When the door closed behind Chief Delaney, Arnie fixed his son with a terrible glare. "You broke your word with me, young man. Don't let it ever happen again." He slammed his fist on his desk with a suddenness that made Yank jump. "Now I'm going to have to waste a perfectly good lunch hour with that idiot."

Yank looked into his father's reddening eyes. "I didn't want you to have to bother with it. But Cora Sue was important to me." His head dropped as he mumbled, "I couldn't just do *noth*ing."

Arnie sighed. "I know," he said, shaking his head. "It's not an easy thing...."

He towered over his son. "Tell Miss L. to cancel my lunch with Frankfurter. I'll stop over and see him after lunch." And he was gone as though a wind had blown through the office taking him on its wing.

Yank went back to the Conklin place and found a new hand in Barnard's shack.

Barnard was not seen or heard from again in Los Angeles and, though it was easy to speculate that he came to a sudden and violent end, no one knew for sure.

In September, Yank went back to school, a sadder and wiser young man.

# 41

Contrary to what the
Methodists tell us, money
and success are good for
the soul.

   —Lord Jersey

1904

Arnie Sutler could look at a piece of ground like no other man. He could look at that ground, brownish diatomaceous, grayish graphite, or maybe parched black adobe, and see into its future and his. It was dirt not only in the path of progress, it *was* the path of progress.

His biggest scheme, the one he would be most remembered by, was one that didn't have his name on the documents.

It was the secret, massive land grab in the San Fernando Valley and the *Tribune*-promoted drive to bring water from the Owens Valley, some four hundred miles to the north.

When he invited General Olin into the scheme, the General balked at having Arnie in it. Arnie protested that it was his idea. He had done the work.

The General shuffled the massive documents. "This is an awful lot of money. Do you have this kind of money?"

"I can get it," Arnie assured him.

But he hadn't reckoned with the old man's power. A few phone calls and Arnie discovered no bank would lend him what he needed.

He turned in desperation to a long time friend who bought Arnie's share in his name.

And so the syndicate to buy the San Fernando Valley to annex it to Los Angeles was set up by Arnie Sutler but without his name on the documents as a partner, and as far as he knew nobody but Elijah Samson knew he had a financial stake in it.

At the next editorial board meeting, Oscar Lattimer, the aggressive City Editor, asked General Olin a question.

"Is it true that the aqueduct will deliver eight times the water we need now, and four times the water we would need if the city was solidly developed to its borders? And is it true that this surplus would be enough to irrigate one hundred thirty-five thousand acres and that would be double the needs of the Owens Valley? And if it is true, how do we handle it?"

Oscar Lattimer had spoken, it seemed, almost without breath and looked up tentatively and saw General Olin turning pale beneath that facial hair so neatly trimmed. The old man was gleaming white now in the afternoon sunlight that filtered through the window. Arnie wondered if he could be having a stroke.

"I mean, I understand it isn't even under consideration, letting the Owens Valley have enough of their water—the water we are taking from them—to keep them from expiring?"

No one was surprised that Oscar Lattimer didn't work at the *Tribune* after that.

## 1909

There was a theory among devotees of fox hunting that the best hound for the job was not necessarily the one with the best developed sense of smell, though it helped. No, the sense that made the difference in the kill was the sense of hate.

Arnie Sutler never went fox hunting. He thought it was a pretentious and ridiculous sport. But the killer instinct never left him. By 1909, and his forty-sixth year, Arnie had already laid the groundwork for his participation in land up and down the West Coast and as far east as Phoenix, Arizona. He had partnerships in banks, railroads, oil drilling equipment, ranching, retailing and manufacturing industries.

But it was not enough. It would never be enough for insatiable Arnie. He would prove himself again and again as though each new conquest added a burden to his expectations, a burden which could only be lifted by adding another burden.

Being assistant publisher of the Los Angeles *Tribune* put Arnie in contact with the money men of Southern California, and he soon became known as the man to turn to with that surplus cash you wanted in a sure-fire investment. By 1906, word of his involvement in, and the scope of the water deal leaked out. And people brought him deals; all day long he considered deals, always including General Olin so there could be no thought of conflict of interest.

Word had reached Arnie through a San Diego banker that President Diaz of Mexico was friendly to foreign capital, to help build his impoverished country. He had devised a scheme to get national lands into the hands of his compatriots, which in turn could be sold to foreigners. The scheme was supposed to help stabilize and enrich his poor country.

President Diaz had run a taut ship and Arnie thought the circumstances warranted an investigation, so he went south.

Southern California and Baja California, Mexico, were deserts, and the only hope to do anything with a desert was, of course, water.

The Colorado River started with a trickle near Denver on the Continental Divide, and with the snow and ice melts built into a mighty river that cut its way deep into the Grand Canyon's red rock and wound through Searchlight, Arizona, Bullhead City, between Erp and Parker, forming Lake Mead at Las Vegas, Nevada (now Hoover Dam stemming its flow). For about two hundred miles it forms the eastern border of Southern California, then through the Chocolate Mountains, passing El Doctor and spewing into the Gulf of California at La Bomba just before El Golfo de Santa Clara (a vertical fall on its run of over twelve thousand feet), where it empties its water at the crotch between Baja California and Mexico, finally making its way to the Pacific Ocean.

Arnie put three thousand dollars down for a three-year option on the land and started buying up on the United States side of the border too, until he finally had over eight hundred and fifty thousand acres of land. He immediately went to work getting estimates on expenses for irrigation canals, cattle raising, alfalfa, cotton, and went home to look for investors.

Three years later, Arnie had raised the money and was ready to move in with his equipment and men as soon as the title transferred.

The syndicate had paid just under sixty cents an acre for the land. His partners were Olin, Elijah Samson, Emmit Bergstroms, president of Columbia Title and Trust Company who would insure the title for a tidy sum, with the customary disclaimer about intervention or nationalization by foreign powers.

One of the first things Arnie did on taking the option was to begin a systematic program of articles in the *Tribune* about the glories of Mexico, promoting tourism and friendship with the country which had enjoyed benevolent and stable leadership for over a decade. News features ran on how the interests of one country were really synonymous with the interests of the other.

Arnie had taken to inviting his secretary, Theresa Lavendowsky, to dinner with him when his days were especially hectic and she stayed to work late. Usually it was nothing fancy, a quick sandwich, perhaps, at a local lunch counter.

That night he surprised her and took her to the posh French restaurant, *Fleur de Lis*.

The candlelight flickered fleeting shadows across their faces—Arnie's, round and fleshy, Theresa's, smooth and translucent.

It made her head spin—all the finery, the fancy clothes and horse-choking jewels. And Arnie speaking so softly—in low, considerate tones, not like a boss at all, but more like, well, yes, like an equal.

Telling about his secret deals—his foray into Mexican land—all exotic and mysterious-sounding; and about his disappointing marriage.

"Mary Ellen and I have grown so far apart," he said. It was a line that usually raised at least one eyebrow of hope in the young women Arnie set his sights on. Theresa rather responded with pity and sorrow—and encouragement.

"I'm sure if you make a little effort, Mr. Sutler, you will be able to get closer together."

He shook his head dolefully, as if he had tried so often and he was exhausted from the effort.

"When two people are incompatible there is nothing to be done."

He looked so forlorn and unhappy to Theresa, she wanted to reach out and pat his hand, to comfort him—like she did to Yank. Arnie seemed as young and vulnerable as his son.

Arnie was stirred by Theresa's tender, transparent beauty and unspoiled loveliness.

Theresa was warmed by the soft light and the sparkling symmetry of the china, crystal and heavy sterling silverware on the soft white tablecloth. It made her glow inside, sending forth the light of a radiant star in the night.

To Arnie she was a prize to be pursued and won. To Theresa he was an important and generous man, generous not only in his attentions toward her, but also to her mother.

Arnie sat back after he had devoured his rare roast beef with the subtlety of a lion feasting on a vanquished prey, his swelling belly rising to the forefront, his hands resting on it in a lazy caress.

"You ever been to Mexico?" he asked casually.

Theresa tittered. He knew she had never been out of Los Angeles. She put her right forefinger to her temple and scrunched her eyes.

"Gee, Mexico," she pondered. "I've been so many places, Mr. Sutler," she said in mock seriousness, "it's hard to remember which is which."

"Would you like to go?"

Her eyes were balloons. "To Mexico? Me?" Her glee was of the child who does not allow herself to get too excited at a prospect she knows is too good to be true.

He nodded, gravely now. "I'm going to need a lot of help. There will be contracts to draw, leases, purchases, letters to write." He could see some doubt written on her face. He frowned, "Of course, I will contract for a chaperone."

Theresa laughed and clapped her hands. "Why, Mr. Sutler, you're old enough to be my father."

Mr. Sutler laughed too.

Yank and Theresa were in the park. The light in her eyes shone like sunlight, and she moved with a quicker grace.

"I've a secret," she sang to him when he called for her for their Sunday picnic at City Park—the outing they both looked forward to all week long, every week for almost seven years. Yank was working hard and saving money so he would have enough to ask her to marry him.

"What is it?" Yank asked, taking his cowboy hat off to wipe his brow with his arm, as though it would stimulate his brain to crack the mystery.

The more she teased, the more curious he became.

Finally when the sandwiches and punch were laid out on the

blanket she could contain her excitement no longer.

"I'm going to Mexico," she blurted.

"What?" Yank's jaw fell.

She nodded vigorously, excitement welling in her breast. She didn't see Yank's forehead creasing anxiously under his ten-gallon hat.

"Your father asked me to go."

"My father?"

She nodded joyously. "He needs a secretary. There is a lot of business he has there."

"Who else is going?" he asked, the words forming slowly on his tortured lips.

"Who else?" she asked perplexed, her finger touching her sensuous lips. "Why would he need anyone else?"

"No—chaperone?"

She laughed. "Oh, you silly. He's your father. He's old enough to be my father."

"Do you know anything of his reputation—with women?" Yank asked. His heart was pushing the blood through him like a fire hose.

"Oh, you silly boy," she said, touching the tip of his nose with her forefinger. "He's offered to get a chaperone but I said it was silly."

"Well," he stood up from the blanket and looked down across the bridge of his nose to the fertile flower of womanhood at his feet. "I forbid you to go." His chest was out—it was all he knew to give the weight of authority to his order.

She laughed. But when she looked up and saw the pain on his face, she stood up and tried to take his hand. He withdrew it.

"Please," she said, into his sad eyes. "I want us to be such good friends—always. I don't like it when you get mad at me."

"Good friends," he mumbled. He wanted to be more than "good friends."

There wasn't any doubt in anyone's mind that the elderly woman who got on the train to Yuma, Arizona, carrying her own carpetbag, thank you, was a chaperone—it was written all over from her sunbonnet to her wrinkled face, and spare, no-superfluous-foods figure, to her high-button shoes.

Arnie had not flinched when Theresa asked if he would consider a chaperone.

What only Arnie and the chaperone knew was she was leaving them in Yuma.

If anyone had known the hardships of Mexican travel, they could have seen at a glance that this old woman would never survive it.

Arnie arranged for the woman to take her meals in the compartment she shared with Theresa, while he and Theresa sat in the dining car and discussed business.

It quite excited Theresa, her boss's courtly manners and his avid interest in her feelings and opinions about things. It was a head-lightening experience to be in the sole company of this important man. They were on their way to Mexico where he owned more land than was in most cities.

Each time she left Arnie to return to her compartment and chaperone she thought more about Arnie and less about Yank.

When the chaperone got off the train with them in Yuma and said her curt, dry-skinned goodbye, Theresa was relieved to see her go—she always seemed in the way.

Arnie muttered something about getting a replacement for the next leg of the journey which would be by stagecoach, then horses, but Theresa gave him no cause to think she required it, and the subject just fell of its own weight.

# 42

they speak whatever's
on their mind
    they do whatever's in
their pants
    the boys I mean are
not refined
    they shake the moun-
tains when they dance

                —e e cummings

They traveled as father and daughter to raised eyebrows and slanty-eyed
looks. After they left the Southern
Pacific Railroad in Yuma, Arizona, there
was a leg on a stage, then on horseback
across the land, his land, the Mexican
part of his 850,000 acres.

Mile after mile of flaming sun and
dust in their throats, Arnie and Theresa
plodded on. Arnie admired Theresa's
youth and enthusiasm. Nothing seemed
to get her down, not missed connec-
tions, not delays, not the frustrations of
primitive travel and accommodations,
not the broiling daytime sun, nor the
cold nights. Always there was that
expectant sparkle in her eye, and the
smile on her lips, and the soul-tingling
sheen on her hair. And, wherever she
went, the crucifix of her Jesus lay heavy
on her heart.

They rode over low hills, barren
plains, valleys of chaparral and an occasional tree; an oak, perhaps, or an iron-
wood; a torote in a pile of rock. Or the

cacti: cardon, hedgehog, velvet, barrel, teddy bear cholla, and the bizzare cirio that looked like a telephone pole that had sprouted stubble up the sides, and at the top put out a half-dozen or so branches reaching straight up with little shoots growing here and there from the tips.

Theresa loved these strange plants. They reminded her of the exotic Chinese children back home: unusual, uncommunicative and irresistible. She became fond of her horse named Calico, because he seemed to be able to navigate any sort of terrain, from the cactus fields to the beds of rock, the soft and shifting sand to the steep hills. There was a bond between them. He was proficient; she was grateful.

Arnie had been circumspect. More than once he had wanted to reach out and embrace Theresa, but something held him back.

Only once, as they sat by a campfire after having eaten their evening meal of beef, hardtack biscuits, beans and coffee, did he speak on a personal level, as he had in the restaurant before they left Los Angeles.

The air was still as a placid pond. The stars were bright pin-points in the sky.

Theresa felt strangely secure in Arnie's presence. He looked so commanding and strong.

The only sounds they heard were the crickets and the crackle of the dry branches burning.

The orange glow of the flames threw flickering shadows like the tongue of a friendly dog lapping at their faces.

Arnie, as if fulfilling a conversational duty, asked Theresa, "What was the best experience of your life?"

"Oh, this trip," she answered so cheerfully, he was wary of believing her.

"And the worst?"

Theresa frowned in thought. It was not because she didn't know her worst experience, there wasn't any doubt. She just didn't know if she should tell him.

"Well?" he prodded her.

"I guess when my father died," she said, looking into the fire.

He watched her and felt his stomach sting. "Yes," he said so quietly his soft high voice barely reached her over the crackling flames.

"My mother was devastated. She couldn't move. You know, sometimes I think she fell on purpose so she wouldn't have to face anything. I was fourteen, and I went to the morgue to identify him.

I'll never forget it as long as I live. He looked happy—like even death couldn't get him down. I tried to tell Mother, but she didn't want to know anything about it. It was just too hard for her."

"You're a strong woman, Theresa," he said.

"No—you just do what you have to do."

The fire crackled.

"What was your best experience, Mr. Sutler?"

"Oh, this trip," he said, and they both laughed.

"But seriously," he said, "you mean a lot to me, Theresa. You are probably the most remarkable woman I know."

"Oh pshaw, Mr. Sutler," she blushed. "I'm just a child, really."

Air rushed out of Arnie's body.

"And your worst experience?" she asked.

He dropped his head to stare beneath his upraised knees.

"I'm not sure," he began cautiously, "I think maybe marrying Mary Ellen."

"Mr. Sutler!" she reprimanded him.

"She is a good woman in many ways," he explained. "When I met her I was crazy about her. She seemed so bright and clever. Very quick on the uptake. But now," he hung his head in his hands. He drew in a gallon of air. "Now I think she just wanted a trophy—someone to give her children to perpetuate the newspaper—make a dynasty out of it. I don't think she was ever interested in me as a person."

"Mr. Sutler!" Theresa responded, as though she were scolding a child for using bad language.

He put up his palm to calm her. "You don't know," he said. "She named our first son after her true love—the man who used her, then left her for a younger, prettier woman."

Theresa blushed. "Why didn't you suggest another name?"

Arnie shrugged his broad hunched shoulders. "I never thought naming children was my responsibility, I guess. I did register some surprise—but she was so adamant, I let it drop. Once when I was mad at her for something, I don't even remember what, I said we should name the next girl Gretchen—after my first wife."

Arnie couldn't take his eyes off Theresa's crucifix. Or was he, she wondered, looking at her breasts?

"You're a handsome, successful man," Theresa said, "you could have had any woman you wanted."

"No," he said, shaking his head, "I couldn't have you, for instance."

The color, that seemed to come and go like the waves in the

ocean, returned to her face.

"Well, Mr. Sutler. I mean if you weren't married."

"Oh."

"I don't go after married men, you know. I'm a simple Catholic girl." She said it with such a melancholy melody in her voice that he thought she might be encouraging him.

When they finally arrived at the ranch headquarters, Theresa marveled at Arnie's hail greetings to all his Mexican contacts, the smiles of gratitude on their faces when they talked to this tall, flashy gringo who was flooding their parched plains with Yanqui money and God's own water.

Arnie had sealed the contracts for the 850,000 acres: the planting, the fencing where necessary to hem in his cattle, the political expediencies and local bribes. And Theresa had been a part of it all, manipulating her borrowed typewriter until the metal was warm to the touch and her fingers ached.

It was well past dark when they stopped on their way back at a one-room cabin that was so ramshackle Theresa wondered if it would stand through the night. She considered sleeping outdoors, but the wind was blowing so cold over the bare hills, she barely heard Arnie apologize for the accommodations.

He built a fire in the cracked adobe fireplace and he threw his bedding in front of it. Arnie saw Theresa pause with her bedding pressed against the crucifix on her breast. "Would you like me to move mine?" he asked her.

Without responding she threw her blanket in front of the fire, next to his. Then she looked around for a place to undress. Arnie watched her then said, "I'm going outside to gather some more wood for the fire. Will you be all right?"

She nodded, and he walked out the crooked door and felt her eyes on his back.

When he returned with an armload of wood, she was under her blanket, her back to his bedroll. He put the wood down quietly, fed another pair of logs to the fire, took off his shoes, and settled in under his blanket.

He was dog-tired from the long journey but he couldn't go to sleep. He could tell from her breathing that she was not asleep either.

Arnie turned toward her, and gently stroked her silken hair. She did not resist, but turned to bury her face in his shoulder.

Theresa felt a voluminous blanket of flesh warm her. Arnie Sutler was a powerful man. He felt so strong and shielding. Nothing could harm her now. She could sleep peacefully in his loving, fatherly arms.

When Theresa was a child her father read to her on the couch, lighthearted articles from the newspaper he so proudly printed.

He always put his arm around her. His arms were strong and warm and caring. She felt secure and comforted. It was a lifelong, lingering memory of love. She missed it.

Better. Arnie felt much better than a father. Suddenly she thought of Yank. She had never been this intimate with Yank. She saw the boy with his loose arms and shy sincerity, then his image quavered and faded.

"You feel nice," she said and nestled closer to his body.

"That's good," he said. "You feel nice too."

"Hmmm."

"You are so soft and beautiful."

And he was so hard and handsome. A mystical feeling made her tremble. She gulped for breath.

"There, there," he said.

"Oh.... Oh, ahhh."

"Yes?"

"Yes.... Oh, yes."

"Ahh, you are the most beautiful woman alive."

"We're going home," she gave a little cry.

"No."

"Ooooookey."

"Better?"

"Better."

A rustling of bodies barely disturbed the air. The fire was dim. The wind was whistling through the wide spaces between the boards of the shack, but neither of them heard it.

"I love you, Theresa."

"I know," she said and sighed.

"Are you glad?"

She didn't speak, but she felt her lips caress his earlobe, causing a sensation in him that raced his heart so he thought it would burst his chest. Her thin soft fingers made tiny circles on his breast as though to calm a leaping beast within.

"Hmmm?" he held her gently to him. The crucifix pressed into his chest, startling him.

"I am glad," she admitted, not understanding and not wanting to.

"You are so good," he said, his voice choking on the air, forgetting the crucifix.

"Oh....Oh, that feels so good."

"OOhh. Yes. Yes?"

"Yes, oh yes. Oh, oh.....Oh, it's so beautiful. Soooooo beautiful."

"Oh my love...."

"Oh....ahhh.....oooooo....Oh, mmmmmm."

"Oh, Theresa, you feel so nice. Oh...I love you so much."

"And I love you."

"Oh."

"Ahhh"

"OOOoooo."

"Mmmmmmmm."

He could not be blamed for preferring the young, silky pink skin of youth to the rapidly fading liver-spotting flesh of his older wife—old enough to be the girl's mother. His pleasure came first. It was all planned before he was born. "Oh, God," he prayed, "don't let me lose her."

Theresa, for her part, was smothered in guilt, feeling at once comfortable in the arms of the most important man in Los Angeles, feeling tingly and excited and in love, and beautiful and important herself, and at the same time a wretched biblical adulteress engulfed by the fires of hell.

When they returned to civilization in Yuma, Theresa sought out the first church she came to and asked for special confession, which she made to a kindly old priest who assigned her a number of "Our Fathers" and "Hail Marys" and called her "My Child" and suggested she cleanse her soul and spirit and walk a straighter path in the future. In his voice the sadness of a lifetime of forgiving the sins of the vulnerable, constitutionally unfit to live up to the admonitions of his church.

She promised him, she promised herself, and she promised God.

Then she boarded the train for Los Angeles with Arnie Sutler, her boss and her lover. She made no sign of surprise or protest when she discovered they shared the same compartment.

While Theresa was in Mexico, Yank had taken to looking in on her mother, in the little clapboard house behind the shiny yellow one on Hope Street.

The little house was dark. There were no picture windows or sliding patio doors. They built their houses like they did where they came from back East—to keep out the elements. The roofs were pitched, the doors solid, the windowpanes in small checkerboard squares.

Yank had come to like the old woman and admire the dignity she maintained in her infirmity.

In Mrs. Lavendowsky, lying in her bed as though it was more fight to get up than she had left in her, Yank saw a touch of his Theresa. They had the same stature, the same shape to the face, though the mother's flesh had drawn into itself like a fallen cheese souffle.

About the time Arnie and Theresa were due back in Los Angeles, Yank began dropping in on Mrs. Lavendowsky twice a day. He would ask with all the nonchalance he could muster, "Have you heard from Theresa?" And she would tell him she hadn't. And every time she did, her heart twisted a little harder.

It was late one bright Wednesday afternoon that the automobile taxi pulled up in front of the yellow house and discharged its passenger.

On seeing Theresa in her long gray travelling dress alight from the cab, Yank's heart shot to his throat and he ran out the screen door, letting it slam like a shot, sailing down the driveway to take her in his arms and give her a fierce hug.

"Hi there, Yank," she said as she always had, but the music was gone from her voice. Yank instantly understood, and his heart dropped two stories inside him, and hit sharp and deep in his body.

Stunned, he stood back to look into her eyes. She seemed older to him, with a strange worldliness about her features, and her eyes were looking at him but seeing someone else.

They stood there with her suitcase at her feet, like two estranged lovers.

"What's wrong, Theresa?" he asked, his eyes boring into hers.

"Nothing," she said wearily.

Theresa reached for the suitcase, but Yank grabbed the handle. He trudged after her up the walkway, the weight of the suitcase tugging at his arm, the weight of the world pressing on his back.

At her door she turned to look into his dolorous eyes, reached out for the suitcase and said, "Please don't make it hard for me, Yank—I want to be your friend."

Yank stared at the pretty face and released his grip.

She took up her suitcase and put her hand on the door handle.

"May I come in?" he asked, the life and hope ebbing from his tense body.

"I'm tired," she smiled weakly. "Maybe later in the week. Maybe...."

Yank watched the door close behind her. She hadn't looked back.

Yank couldn't remember how long it took him to get back to his little room or how he got there. He couldn't remember anything but the pain.

# 43

For your life adhere to
me,
    (I may have to be per-
suaded many times
    before I consent to
give myself
    to you, but what of
that?
    Must not Nature be
persuaded many times?)

—Walt Whitman
*Starting from Paumanok*

1910

Arnie bought Theresa a farm in the
Eagle Rock Valley, but put the deed in
his name. They filled the cottage with
soft-cushioned chairs—lots of china
dolls and a four-poster bed. Theresa
hung a dark wooden crucifix on the wall
over the center of the headboard so her
blessed Lord's mercy would flow to both
of them equally.

Yank monitored her movements
like a detective. His heart rose when she
moved out of the Eagle Rock farmhouse,
after she caught Arnie with another
woman, and sank to pitiful depths when
she moved back in.

Yank had begun a real estate business in Hollywood. First he worked for
Harry Franklin, an old broker, who
started him out with the admonition to
"Always remember one thing, Yank.
Nobody wants to pay a commission, and
that includes you and me."

After dazzling Harry with the number of people who seemed happy to pay
Yank commissions, he went out on his

own. He was a tireless worker, good at giving people what they wanted, and he decided the time was right to buy some land and build a few houses.

It was midsummer and *lilium longiflorum,* the Easter lily, was blooming. The flower of the resurrection covered the corner of City Park with fragrant, abundant blossoms.

The flowers symbolized life, death and rebirth to the Christians of the day, and nobody wanted to be a better Christian now than Theresa, as she trod with reluctant step into the park to meet Yank.

It was their first Sunday in the park since Theresa came back from Mexico. The sun was bright and high in the sky, but her spirits were low.

Yank was an hour early, pacing the one-block-square park like a soldier waiting in a jail yard for the firing squad.

There among the lilies and the cypress, Yank and Theresa talked on a park bench, with wooden slats and gracefully curving iron arm-rests. There was no lunch, no cozy blanket on the ground, just two strangers on a park bench: a young man with earnest eyebrows and furrowed forehead under a comical broad-brimmed hat, and a young woman looking like she couldn't keep enough food down to hold any color in her cheeks. She did not seem to want to talk to the young stranger by her side, and yet the weight on her shoulders inhibited her from leaving.

The sun lit them from the front, like players in a melodrama, Dickens, perhaps, or Henrik Ibsen.

"If this is what he's doing to you, Theresa," Yank implored, elbows flying in excited gestures, like a male bird trying to attract the attention of an indifferent female, "I say you should leave him."

Theresa's silence tried Yank's patience.

"That's not as easy as it sounds," she gurgled from a constricted throat.

"Why not?" There was no silence from Yank.

Her hands were twisting each other in her lap like two cobras in a death struggle. Her eyes were on that struggle.

Between them the air was charged with opposing electrons.

"Theresa, I've never seen you like this. What is it?" Yank pleaded. "Tell me."

He remembered pleading with Cora Sue just before she died, and the thought of it compressed his heart.

"Theresa," he said, softly now as though the strident tones of his excitement spun themselves dizzily out. "Are you?..." he couldn't finish the question. It stuck in his throat like a piece of meat clogging his windpipe.

Her eyes turned up to meet his for only an instant, falling again to her twisting hands.

What was it in that look, so sad, so desperate, yet in a way encouraging him to complete his thought, hoping he would, yet fearing it with all her being?

"Are you," he tried again, muttering, mumbling, afraid to give to his tongue the words, and yet the suspicion grew like a tumor.

"With child?" he spoke in the softest voice, yet her head snapped like he had slapped her.

Yank got up and whirled around Theresa to face her from the other side of the bench. She turned away again. He went back and put his hands on her shoulders.

"Theresa, look at me!"

Tears coursed down her soft skin. Her head dropped. Anguish swelled within her.

"Yes, yes, *yes!*" she shouted. "Now leave me alone."

Yank sank down beside her on the bench, taking her hands in his. The gentle scent of the lily brushed his brain. Death and rebirth.

"Oh, Theresa, oh, my poor Theresa," he said singsong, like an old black slave, lamenting his earthly woes.

"I'm ruined," she sobbed. "I'm so stupid." She was hoarse and desolate, but without bitterness. "I deserve it."

"Oh, Theresa no—no, no, no." Yank tried to comfort her. "Does he know?"

She shook her head.

"Does anyone?"

She shook her head again, the sobs wracking her body and catching in her throat like the backfiring automobiles that passed in the street.

Theresa dropped her head to Yank's shoulder and rested it there under his broad-brimmed hat.

"You must tell him, Theresa," he said, holding her to him.

"I can't," she said.

"Do you want him to marry you?"

"Only if he wants to—not because of…this." Her body trembled in his arms. "Nobody will marry me now," she cried.

There was between them a silence that reached far down into each soul.

Yank sat up, shifting her weight on him.

"I'll marry you, Theresa," he said gently, not moving a muscle. "If you'll have me."

"Oh, Yank," Theresa cried with joy. She felt so unworthy. "How could you? I'm not...clean...."

"Theresa, you could never be anything but pure to me."

Her body tortured with sobs, Yank held her tightly to his breast.

They were hour-long minutes, until her quaking subsided. Then Yank told her what she had to do.

The sun and attendant hazy clouds seemed hastily assembled by a weather god with more important things on his mind. The sky was as bleak as it was on the darkest days and it was gloomily tepid, yet Theresa had never felt so cold.

She looked at the brass eagle in the center of the front door. The wings were folded, the bird was at rest. Now all she had to do was pick it up and bang it, once, maybe twice, and the door would open and she could say, "Mrs. Sutler, I'm Theresa. Arnie wants to marry me."

Yank said it would be so simple.

She looked back at the eagle. The eyes seemed to be looking askance at her, mocking, taunting, daring her to do what she came to do.

She put out her hand and grabbed the eagle door knocker with a firm, tight grip, squeezing it until her knuckles turned white.

A wave of nausea swept over her, making her forget the cold. The situation had changed, suddenly and irreversibly. She could no longer afford the luxury of time. The days would press on each other. A child was waiting to escape her dark womb. And before she realized it, she would start to show.

She looked at that eagle door knocker. The menacing beak and the frightening talons. Three short raps of brass on brass, and Theresa stood back and cleared her throat, as though she were about to address some intimidating senate. She worked a brave, painful smile to her lips.

"Mrs. Sutler, I'm Theresa Lavendowsky." The simple, straight-forward introduction went through her mind again and again, but the door was opened by a ten-year-old boy.

Warren Sutler looked up at her with sweet, enquiring eyes. "Yes, ma'am?" he said.

Theresa's jaw fell slack. She felt as though she were suddenly confronted with a fatherless child.

"Ma'am?" Warren questioned, looking gently up into her eyes. "Ma'am, do you want to see my mother?"

Theresa touched her hat as though it were about to blow off her head, though the air was quite still.

"Um, why um, yes. Could I please?" she said.

"Do you want to come in?" the boy asked.

"Um, I guess I better wait here."

"All right," he said. And he turned, leaving her feeling alone and friendless.

When the eagle knocker had sounded, sending the dull, metallic clang through the house, Mary Ellen Olin was upstairs in her bedroom writing in her book. She called it "Remembrances," for she didn't like the sound of "Diary," or the clandestine connotations it held for her.

Now the pen in her hand was raised from the paper, horizontal, with the suggested thrust of an arrow in flight. Her eyes were down on the page reading the still damp, black ink:

> "I miss going to the *Tribune* offices. Arnie has asked me not to come. My presence embarrasses him, he says. Like I might be telling him how to run the paper in front of General Olin and all the others. But I know better. He doesn't want me around to see him and his young secretary carrying on.
>
> Are wives ever as ill-informed as their husbands hope? Perhaps when you have been the "other woman" yourself it is harder to be fooled.
>
> All the same, I think if I were to see that young hussy alone I might strangle her."

She couldn't imagine who was knocking at this hour of the day. She didn't feel like leaving her "Remembrances" just now.

But Warren came up the stairs to get her.

It was only a moment before Mary Ellen Sutler appeared at the door. She was large and strong with heavy, complacent bones, dwarfing the slim figure on her doorstep, looking ill-at-ease in her calling hat and ruffled white "company" blouse with the high collar and puffy sleeves. And, Mary Ellen noticed, that terribly large crucifix.

"Hello," Theresa stuttered, "I'm...."

"Yes, I know who you are," Mary Ellen said, her voice tired and resigned. "Would you like to come in?"

"Well, I...."

"Oh, come in," Mary Ellen said and turned on her heels, leading the way to the parlor.

The gray dress on Arnie's wife seemed to be outlandishly padded at the bust and bustle, until Theresa realized that misshapen padding was Mary Ellen herself. She carried it like a burden she would like to unstrap and walk away from at the end of the day.

Theresa found the parlor simply furnished, with worn stuffed chairs similar to those in a workingman's home. The oriental rug on the floor had been a gift from Mary Ellen's mother and covered all but the edges of the oak floor. Mary Ellen would have furnished it differently, but Arnie always argued the General would resent any competition. And when she had, in the early years, turned to her father for extra spending money, the General had frowned and told her the man of the house had the say, and gave her to understand he was not about to undercut that authority. And so, Mary Ellen was left to cope with the modest means of, as she liked to say, one of Arnie's pressmen.

When Theresa saw the surroundings, she swallowed. How strange it was to see for the first time the home of the man who said he wanted to marry her. As her eyes traveled the room, she realized instantly that the house Arnie had bought for her was furnished more generously than this one.

"Sit down, sit down," Mary Ellen said to her, waving at a chair across from her. This was her enemy's domain, Theresa thought, watching Mary Ellen sit.

Mary Ellen clapped her hands, "Katherine?" she said sharply. A young girl, perhaps thirteen, appeared at her side. She seemed tall for her age, had dark blonde hair braided tightly on the back of her head. Her eyes on Theresa were biting and haughty beyond her years.

"Yes, ma'am?" she said.

"We'd like some tea," Mary Ellen said.

The girl looked quickly at Theresa, then her haughty eyes returned to her mother, then fell to the floor. "I won't serve her," she said, and scurried out of the room, her head aloof from the sinner.

Mary Ellen looked at Theresa and then to the doorway through which the girl had disappeared. "Katherine!" she shouted with angry authority. In a moment the young boy who had opened the front door for Theresa, appeared.

"May I help you, Mother?" he said.

"Get Katherine in here this minute," she said.

"Katherine went out," he said, looking at Theresa. "I'll bring the tea."

"Oh, all right," his mother said. "Theresa," she said, "this is my son, Warren."

"How do you do, Warren?" Theresa said. "That's very nice of you."

Warren nodded to Theresa, "Thank you, ma'am," he said, and left the room.

When Warren had gone, Mary Ellen said, "My daughter is a headstrong girl. She has been a great help to me, but sometimes I think her usefulness has gone to her head, and she seems at times to lack common courtesy."

Mary Ellen seemed to settle back and relax. Theresa was still sitting at the edge of her chair, her posture upright, her hands planted firmly on her knees.

"Now," Mary Ellen said, looking out the window at one of those new horseless carriages that was going by, making the putt-putting sound that irritated many of those who did not own them.

Theresa felt the perspiration dripping under her arms, her hands felt clammy, her heart was constricted as though the old eagle from the front door had gripped it in its talons and squeezed, diverting that adulterous heart once and for all from its path of wickedness.

Theresa was sorry she came, but she was glad she had worn too much scent. The aroma of it had begun to bother her, but now, mixed with her perspiration, it seemed to offer a reassuring fragrance not unlike the ether at the hospital. "I," she began, the talons tightening on her heart. She cleared her throat. "That is, Arnie and I want to get married."

Mary Ellen looked at her as though at some woman speaking a foreign language and trying to decipher the meaning of the words through her facial expression. Then suddenly Mary Ellen burst out laughing, her trussed body trembling.

A frown creased Theresa's forehead. Her fingers worked her kneecaps, probing her sharp bones.

"My dear child," Mary Ellen said, her laughter subsiding. "What an absurd notion. Mr. Sutler is already married, as I assume you must acknowledge by your presence here."

"But, but he wants to marry me," came the anguished response.

In the hallway leading from the kitchen to the parlor the ten-

year-old boy with the kindly eyes and the tray of tea, froze in his
tracks. So this is why Katherine would not serve this woman. This is
what his second sister, Louisa, meant when she counseled him
against going in there. Warren knew he could not go in the room
now and serve the tea, and he was afraid that if he turned around
and returned to the kitchen the noise would alert them.

Theresa squirmed, "But he *wants* to marry me."

The older woman smiled to herself, and kept her eyes fixed on
Theresa. "I know you have been carrying on with him," she said,
"and I'm not surprised that he told you that he wanted to marry
you."

"But...."

Mary Ellen waved her hand. "Oh please," she said, "you must
understand he's told I don't know how many women the same thing."

"But, but...this is different."

"No, my dear," Mary Ellen said, "my husband has many good
qualities. The consideration of others, especially women, is not high
among them. Arnie is married to the newspaper. I have his name,
but he has the paper. It's a power and a position he would never
sacrifice, not for all the women in the world. Don't you see that?
After all you're his secretary, you should know what that power does
to him."

Theresa looked out the window, swallowed hard. "But he loves
me," she said weakly.

Mary Ellen smiled and sighed, "I'm sure he does, and you're not
the first, either. And I know you don't want to believe it, but you
won't be the last. Arnie is acquisitive, he has to acquire everything he
sees. It's a passion with him, a disease almost. But his talent is in the
acquiring. It's like the money: he can make it, but he can't spend it.
And once he has a woman in love with him he doesn't know what to
do. The challenge is over. The journey is all-important. The arrival
leaves him floundering, itching to start the next journey."

The small space that separated them in the parlor was like a
chasm of frightening depth. And while a mere few feet separated
them, the women were worlds apart.

Mary Ellen thought back to the beginning of her marriage to
Arnie Sutler. They were criminals, she thought, criminals never
caught, but never to be pardoned. Was it worth it? she wondered.
She had wanted a man so much and she had gotten him. He had
wanted the paper so much and he had gotten it. But, did they really
want each other?

Out in the hallway Warren stood still, afraid that his trembling body would throw the tea to the floor. He sensed the lull in the conversation and brought the tea in, making his footsteps as heavy as he could to alert the two women that he was coming. The boy had impeccable manners. He bowed and offered to pour for Theresa, who thanked him and watched his every move thinking, that's *her* son, he's all right, but *my* son will be special.

The women sat drinking in silence. When Warren left the room Theresa said, "Nice boy."

"Yes," his mother said, "he really is a sweet child. Maybe it's all the smothering affection he's had all of these years from his sisters."

The atmosphere had become almost friendly, as though the women who started out as adversaries had shared something. Not only the tea, but the same man.

"How old are you, my dear?" Mary Ellen asked.

"I am going to be twenty-five," Theresa said, as though the reality presented itself with ponderous finality.

"My dear," Mary Ellen said, "you're so young."

Theresa couldn't explain why it happened. Whether it was the tone of voice, that sympathetic, motherly, almost envious tone, or whether it was her tension welling up within her and bursting forth in the torrent of tears that now cascaded down her pretty cheeks.

"What's wrong, child?" Mary Ellen asked, standing up and crossing that impassable chasm, putting her arms tenderly about the sobbing Theresa and wondering if her life would have been changed had Arnie's first wife, Gretchen Sutler, had a confrontation with Mary Ellen and put her arms about *her.*

"He must, he must," Theresa sobbed. "He has to."

"He has to what?"

"He has to marry me," she sobbed, her body trembling in Mary Ellen's arms.

"There, there, dear. Arnie Sutler is not a man who *has* to do anything."

"But you don't understand."

"Understand what?"

"You don't understand. I have his baby inside me."

Slowly, without conscious effort, Mary Ellen removed her arms from the pretty young woman. She looked over her head as though searching for an answer from a higher being.

"Oh dear," she said finally, "oh dear, dear, dear."

Theresa said, "I'm sorry."

"Does he know?" Mary Ellen asked.

Theresa shook her head.

"Well," Mary Ellen said, "perhaps the first step has got to be you must tell him, and then you must do something about it."

"Do something?"

"Of course, child, you can't have his baby."

"I can't?" she laughed a nervous, uncomfortable laugh, "I can't? But I am. I wish I couldn't, but I must. How can I stop it?" And as she asked the question and saw Mary Ellen's glance she knew what Mary Ellen meant. "Oh no, but no no, I...no."

Mary Ellen nodded short, curt, resolute, "There's no alternative, your life would be ruined. You couldn't work for him, you couldn't work for anyone else, you're young, you're beautiful, there's no end to what you can accomplish. Saddled with a bastard child," she said choking out the words as though the very idea was too offensive to talk about, "you would be worse than nothing. You would be an outcast."

Theresa jumped up, her fists clenched against her sides, "Oh, oh you," she said, starting toward her and then turning abruptly and running out the door. As the front door closed, another door closed simultaneously in the kitchen where Warren stepped back, his body still with shock.

Arnie did not get the news from Theresa that she was with child. It came from his wife, Mary Ellen, instead. When he angrily confronted Theresa she turned sullen and said, "So what, you're going to marry me and everything will be all right."

She didn't seem to understand that he really wanted to marry her but he just couldn't. Her whole attitude toward him seemed to change and Arnie couldn't understand why. He'd insisted that they'd have the baby taken care of and she'd refused. She was, after all, a good Catholic and saw no justification for murdering a human being because of their indiscretion. Arnie was firm. Los Angeles was a provincial town, a bastard child would not be accepted in his social circle and he was not going to permit her to have it.

Theresa looked at him and mocked him with her smile. "Arnie," she said, "I've already been ruined. You ruined me when we went to Mexico. But you will not kill my baby," she sighed a gasp of hopeless resolution, "without killing me."

Arnie wished he could make her realize how unreasonable she was being. She was beginning to remind him of his stubborn first wife, Gretchen. He was not accustomed to having people balk at his wishes. For days he was beside himself trying to find a solution.

And then it came, from the most unlikely source.

# 44

Many sins may be for-
given such a dynasty.

—Will Durant
on the de Medici dynasty
*The Renaissance*
from *The Story of Civilization*.

Labor was rearing its tiresome head again, and a strike was threatened by the non-union employees who wanted union representation. Tomasino Taravella was garnering a growing following. There was a Socialist candidate running for mayor. He had surprised everyone, including himself, amassing the highest vote in the primaries—and Olin and Sutler were not the only ones who were convinced his election would send Los Angeles to hell in a handbasket. They could kiss goodbye forever Olin's cherished goal of passing San Francisco in population and influence.

Then an opportunity presented itself from the strangest quarter.

Tomasino Taravella from the union of linotypers and pressmen paid Arnie Sutler a visit.

The union had harassed *Tribune* advertisers: stink bombs in the Merced Theater, paint sprayed on Frankfurter's merchandise. Violence was on the rise, Taravella's non-violent influence on the wane.

Bombing the *Tribune* was next on the agenda. Tomasino wanted no part of killing. He told Arnie he could remove the bombs after they had been set, or evacuate the building.

After Taravella left, Arnie thought of a third option.

On October third, the Olins left town, leaving Arnie in charge of the paper. Three days later Arnie was at his desk, watching the street out the window. Two men approached with black bags. Arnie looked down on them thinking they looked not so much like angels of death, but two dry goods salesmen, perhaps, or simple pressmen without their paper hats, coming to do an ordinary day's work for an ordinary day's pay.

In the outer office Theresa was humming quietly to herself. It was warm for October and Theresa was wearing a lightweight full skirt of dark brown poplin that set her hair off like shiny milk choco-late. Her blouse was buttoned up to the neck. The crucifix lay between her breasts as though engulfed by a hedonistic world.

In a minute Arnie got the expected visit from handsome Herb Dixon from the desk in the main lobby.

"Two guys from the building department to make an inspection are downstairs," Herb said, tightening his fists and causing a rippling muscular reflex up his arms while searching Arnie's preoccupied face.

Arnie nodded as though short of time. Herb wouldn't have said anything had Arnie not looked up with a faint flicker of a question in the corner of his eye, which was actually no question at all, but a hint of irritation at Herb Dixon for not leaving the office.

"They are both carrying black bags," he said. "Does that strike you as funny?"

Arnie looked at him, feigning insouciance. "Oh, I suppose these busybodies bring tools so they can poke around where they are not wanted."

Herb nodded slowly as though accepting the possibility without being completely convinced.

When Herb left, Arnie followed him out to Theresa's desk. Theresa was still humming to herself as she typed.

"Let's take a break," he said.

Theresa looked up and then back at the letter in the typewriter and said, "Oh, I think I'd better finish this while I'm at it."

"No, not now," Arnie said ominously. "Let's take a break, I want to talk to you."

Theresa looked up, shrugged her shoulders, and sighed. She stood up, picked up her purse and followed him through the newsroom and down the stairs out into the dark street. It was a few minutes after ten o'clock in the evening.

Arnie took her to a cafe two blocks from the *Tribune* Building instead of the one across the street where they usually went.

"Why are we going so far?" she said.

"Oh, I just feel like a change," he said, fidgeting as though charged with energy. "Do you mind walking?"

"No," she said. Theresa was walking a little heavier now, but she knew it was good for the baby. The doctor had told her to keep strong and fit.

"Nice night," he said, his voice constrained like a bassoon on the lips of a beginner.

"Hmm."

They entered the cafe and took a table in the corner, finding themselves virtually alone. The night waitress with curly hair that matched her greasy apron took their order, writing it on the pad after she had wiped her hand on her apron. Theresa ordered milk, Arnie coffee.

After they had been served, Arnie took an envelope out of his jacket pocket and placed it on the table. After running his fingers along the edges, he pushed it toward Theresa.

"What's this?" she said.

"Look at it," he said.

She opened the envelope and saw it stuffed with large bills and a note.

"Money, again?" she said. "I told you I wouldn't do it."

Arnie searched her face, the creases of his own flaccid, aging face tightening. "I know it," he said, "this is money to take you to Mexico so you can have the child. There is a contact inside. You'll be well taken care of."

"Then what?" she asked.

He looked at her, his head cocking in question.

"Then what after I have the baby?"

"That will all be taken care of," he said. "The baby will be easily adopted in Mexico."

"No," she laughed artificially while her soul was being wrenched with the crushing force of his insistence. "I'm sorry, Arnie, I know how you feel about it, but it's my baby too, and I'm going to keep it."

Arnie sighed and threw his head to the side. "All right," he said looking back at her finally, "but go, before you are shamed out of town."

"Me?" she said. "What about you?"

He took a sip of his coffee, set it down, surveyed the room afraid someone might hear them, then said softly, "I can always deny it. You can't."

She laughed softly, showing Arnie again the guileless acceptance of her fate he so loved and so feared because he couldn't understand it. She looked down across the crucifix at her growing womb and said, "I suppose you're right."

"You'll go then?" he said.

"Oh no, I'm staying here," she said, "this is my home."

"What?" he exclaimed, "you still don't have any conception what this will do to you, do you?"

"I know," she said. "As soon as I finish those letters I'm leaving."

"You're what?" he said.

"I'm leaving," she said, "this is my last day."

"But, but what will you do?"

She pushed the money back in the envelope and moved it across the table back to Arnie. She looked at him and smiled, "Yank has asked me to marry him," she said.

Arnie felt the jolt wrack his body. His own son, no—impossible. "You haven't accepted?" he said, anxiety choking him.

"No, but I'm about to."

"Theresa, how could you?"

She smiled and shrugged her charming shoulders. "I don't know," she said, "he loves me. I tried to talk him out of it."

"Do you share the feeling?" Arnie asked.

"I think I do," she said.

"But, but how can you?"

"How can I? How could I let you work me in between your real estate deals and your politicians? The question should be why did I let myself be a convenient little sideline for you?"

"Theresa!" Arnie protested. In that moment he felt as low as he had ever felt in his life. "We are lovers," he croaked, hoarse from his anguish.

She smiled at him. She had never seen Arnie so flustered. She pitied him and his selfishness.

"But how will you live? What will you do? No one will hire you."

"Yank is doing all right."

Arnie's thighs clashed, his body shook. "You can't," he said, "you just can't."

"Why not? I'm not ashamed. If you are, I can't help it. But I'm not going to hide. Not to please you."

Arnie stared at her as at a blank wall. He took some of the money out of the envelope and left it on the table to pay the bill along with a five cent tip, then stood up.

As he walked out with her he was touched again by her beauty. She seemed to have special radiance with his child inside her. He for a moment weakened. "Theresa," he said, "perhaps you should go home and get some rest."

"No," she said, "I'm going to finish. And I hope you'll find someone tomorrow who can do everything you want."

They walked the two blocks back to the *Tribune* in silence, he stopped across the street at the corner and took a long look at the building. She started to cross the street and realized she was walking without him. Her face turned in a question. "Aren't you coming?" she said.

"No, I think I'll stay out a while, I need to think."

Strange, she thought, he had never needed to think anywhere but at his desk before. But, she decided, he had been acting rather strangely and this was just part of it. "All right," she said. "Mail my check to my mother's, and—" she paused, tilting her head in that endearing manner against which Arnie had no defense whatsoever. "Thanks for everything," she said, and turned to cross the sidewalk and climb the steps into the fortress.

Just before Theresa Lavendowsky disappeared into the doorway, she turned and waved a happy, contented wave at Arnie, her smile a guileless smile of one whose soul Arnie would never be able to touch or understand. He lifted his hand as if to reach out to her. His dry mouth opened to call her name, but she had turned and disappeared inside.

It was after he had circled the block six times, his mind in torment, that he decided he should really go inside and make Theresa leave. But he looked at his watch and was afraid if he did he would be trapped. For the two "building inspectors" had made a special inspection of Arnie's own office and wired one of their bombs under his desk. The same evening a bomb would tear a hole through General Olin's house the size of a barn door, but the house would be empty.

Arnie walked around the block again, trying to overcome his fears. The spies were well-paid—and yet he would not be the first victim of a double-cross. It was just as he was turning the last corner that brought the building into view that he saw the terrible flash and heard the thunderous roar. The stone wall trembled and a cloud of dust answered the roaring thunder, shooting rubble everywhere, and in a moment, badly-torn people poured from between the blazing, shattered stone walls.

Arnie looked for Theresa, half hoping he would see her. He had seen the brightest blast come from the third-floor window where day after day he sat, directing the fortunes of the *Tribune*, and Los Angeles. And now across the street, smoke pouring out of windows demolished to slivers of glass, he saw a man carrying another—a broken body with his arm hanging by a thread.

Arnie gasped, the enormity of the event tearing his body with sobs. Then, little by little, he regained control of himself. He would be needed across the street. He was the leader.

He couldn't be sure the last bomb had not exploded, so he hesitated about crossing the street.

Frank Ratner, a union man to the core, came limping toward Arnie, a six-inch slice in his cheek, his hands trembling, his legs unsteadily carrying him to some impossible fate.

"Mr. Sutler," he said. "This time, they've gone too far."

Arnie nodded, a curt acceptance of the tribute, and looked up at the third-story window as though there was some salvation there. He closed his eyes quickly and tried to blot out the vision he had, a vision of Theresa waving and smiling at him. On her lips were the words, "I forgive you, Mr. Sutler. I forgive you."

> From *A History of the Tribune:*
>
> Only a quirk of fate saved Arnie Sutler from the bomb that had been planted under his desk. Sutler had an unexpected appointment and was out of the building for the first time in months at that hour. Theresa Lavendowsky, his secretary, whose desk was next to his was killed instantly where she sat.
>
> Arnie Sutler, miraculously alive because of his absence from his office, joined the others in the street, but all were helpless to aid their dying comrades inside.
>
> Almost instinctively, the entire staff began preparing to put out an emergency edition. It appeared impossible but in a few minutes preparations were under way.
>
> Could the paper be put out?
>
> One thing amid all the horror and turmoil made it seem possible. General Olin, who was out of town at the moment of the explosion and was on his way home from Mexico, had prepared for such a possibility only a few weeks before by equipping an auxiliary plant down the street. And the little bandaged crew, heads wrapped, arms in slings, braved their despair and went to work.

# 45

UNIONIST BOMBS
DESTROY TRIBUNE
BUILDING SCORES
DEAD AND INJURED

—Headline from
October 7, 1910 edition
Los Angeles *Tribune*
printed in auxiliary plant
at Los Angeles *Post*

No one seemed to question the rapid verdict, arrived at in some two hours, about the origin of the bomb. No one, that is, except Arnie's son, Yank, who got the news the following morning from a newsboy shouting, "Extra, extra, read all about *Tribune* bombing, eighteen dead."

The *Tribune* was already on the streets taking earliest advantage of the drama, and playing the anti-unionist sentiment to the hilt.

"Theresa?" Yank muttered, hushed, afraid.

He bought the paper and stared at it in his trembling hands.

His father was alive.

Theresa was not.

The only other deaths were pressmen and linotypers—all working a good distance from Theresa's desk.

Yank dropped the paper like a hot stone and ran the five blocks to the *Tribune*. One image of Theresa after the other tumbled in his vision.

Was this her God who took her from him after eight-years of impossible obstacles, after he had finally won her?

He thought of her crucifix. It had not protected her, and wasn't that what it was for?

Was it still hanging, ineffectively, around her neck? Or had it come off in the blast?

Yank felt like he was in the eye of a hurricane. He was not prepared for this reality.

When he arrived at the bombed out *Tribune*, he saw the wires of the electric trolley strung from a building across the street. They seemed to be holding up what was left of the once proud *Tribune* fortress: about half of the structure on the corner was blackened and gutted, but the exterior walls were still standing. The rest of the building was demolished, with only a pile of rubble crushing down on twisted presses as a reminder of what stood there before.

Atop the wall still standing at the corner, not far from Theresa's desk, the bronze eagle remained, unharmed by the explosion.

In the crowd of men milling around the disaster scene, Yank found a workman shoveling stone fragments. He wanted to ask him if he had seen a crucifix, but his nerve failed him. He decided it would still be on his dear Theresa, or melted beyond recognition, and he didn't want to know. The man directed him to the temporary *Tribune* quarters around the corner.

The one room looked like the first *Tribune* print shop.

Yank was struck by the neat stacking of supplies, the careful placement of tables and chairs through the room for reporters and editors.

It didn't look like a spur-of-the-moment setup to him.

Three linotypers in the background were pounding their metallic sounds on tomorrow's edition, the excited din of emergency work trying the walls of the room.

Standing over the shoulder of a linotyper was eleven-year-old Warren Sutler, who had brought a lunch pail to his father because he would be "Working straight through this mess." Warren was fascinated with typesetting and loved to see it turned into print.

A boy was bringing bars of metal to feed the machines.

Warren wanted to help; it was exciting just being there—but he was afraid he would be in the way.

He was sorry so many workers had died in the blast. Those union men were terrible people—and now everyone was joining together in the common cause of getting their paper out.

The *Tribune* was being produced in this temporary quarters and would be printed on the *Post* presses, General Olin's most recent fortuitous purchase.

Yank found his father conferring with a small coterie of men and shot through them like an arrow from a steel bow.

He grabbed his father's lapels—the lapels of the ill-fitting-shiny-pants seersucker suit he wore to a fare-thee-well, his impeccable dressing having fallen by the wayside with his first wife Gretchen's death.

"You killed her, you killed her!" Yank yelled, shaking the hulking giant in the shiny seersucker.

"It was an accident," Arnie shouted, raising his arms to fend off the dull mechanical blows from his son in the cowboy hat.

"Nothing you do is an accident," Yank said, pushing his father's overgrown body into a linotyper next to Warren.

"I didn't do this," Arnie insisted with a sputtering sound like a locomotive stalled in its tracks. "The union—" he tried again but Yank cut him off.

"No!—how could you know so soon—unless you knew before?"

"Threats—they made threats, you idiot...."

Everyone who pulled Yank from his father was not sure he was doing the right thing; some did not act as quickly as they might have.

"You killed them all—murdered my mother, my sister and *Theresa!*"

"You are mad. If you don't get out of here I'll have you locked up."

"With *your* police force."

It was the final exchange of glances, the eye-to-eye lock, that said Yank would not rest in his grave until this final wrong was remedied.

Long after they dragged Yank from the newspaper's temporary room, Arnie felt those pale blue eyes burning into his.

That afternoon, while Yank was on his bed, unable to make progress controlling his body's tormenting sobs, a workman at the demolished *Tribune* Building was shoveling debris onto a flatbed truck.

He didn't look like enough man, in his dusty grays, to lift the shovel.

He always got the stinkin' jobs, being a janitor for the *Trib* in normal times.

Well, this was one he didn't want, he could tell you. Shoveling rubble with the dust swirling up and playing hell with his sinuses, not too good in the best of conditions.

Wasn't that why he left Pennsylvania in the first place, jackassing across this endless land of ourn, to get away from that blasted coal dust?

He had mixed feelings about all this, that's for sure. A damn fool thing blowing people up like this. *Working* people. He could have been one of them. Yet the *Trib* was awful jackass stubborn about labor. A union wouldn't kill them. They certainly weren't hurting for money.

Here he was breaking his back in this goldurn dust when wouldn't you know it, his shovel pings on a piece of metal, and he's got to bend over and pick it up, because they told him to look for any signs of anything the police investigators might have missed. Anything that might help the investigation.

Well by damn, if it wasn't a crucifix—a little charred and scratched, but there was Jesus hanging on the cross for the sinners. He looked at it, turned it over, held it up as though he might see something new that way. Then he threw it over his shoulder into the flatbed truck with the rest of the debris.

He spat some of the dust from his lungs. Leastways, he didn't hold no truck with the papists.

Arnie cried at Theresa's funeral. Yank did not. He barely took his eyes off his father through the service in the Catholic church, the smell of incense strong in his nostrils, or at the graveside in the Catholic cemetery, on top of Mount Washington, smelling of freshly overturned earth.

The priest had wanted to deny Theresa burial in the holy ground on some rumor that she had been impregnated without benefit of clerical dispensation, but Arnie had quietly set him straight through the bishop, a more reasonable man, who knew it was more blessed to have the press for you than against you.

The mass funeral had to await the return of General Olin from Mexico.

Benjamin Raines Olin wore his general's uniform, complete with medals over his left breast, covering that large, generous heart that agreed without flinching to pick up the tab for the victims of this treacherous bombing.

Hundreds attended the ceremony. The local press and national wire services were there in full force. Photographers from every paper within a hundred miles. Seventeen coffins lined the stage of Orchestra Hall, the only building in town large enough to hold the multitude of mourners.

Some of the families had preferred individual burials, and Arnie Sutler, who was in charge of the arrangements, sympathized with them and said certainly he would respect their wishes but let them know that the *Tribune* would be happy to pay the costs of the mass affair, but regrettably, if they wanted the more expensive single funeral, they would be on their own. When Theresa's friends discovered she was not among the seventeen coffins, one of them had the nerve to ask Arnie Sutler what happened to Theresa.

Arnie looked the young woman in the eye and said, "Her mother preferred a private interment, she is in frail health, and it was held a few days ago."

Yank had written a letter to the *Post*, under the name Seymore Battle, asking some hard questions about the *Tribune* bombing. One of them concerned the rumor that management of the *Tribune* had been warned that their gas piping was old, so old it was porous and leaked gas underneath the pressroom, and that the bombs were intended only to scare the anti-union *Tribune* and not to cost any lives. He intimated that had the pipes been replaced as had been recommended, the bombs would have had much less effect.

As for the bomb that had been wired to Arnie's desk, he noted that Mr. Sutler was conveniently away from his desk and asked if there could have been any possibility that Arnie had some warning, or prior knowledge, that kept him away from his desk at the height of activity, and at a time when the publisher of the paper was out of town, leaving Arnie responsible for the entire paper.

The letter was never printed because Arnie controlled the *Post* for its secret owner, General Olin, intelligence that had not been shared with Yank.

The mourners were in the audience, the families of the deceased in the front rows, the bigwigs of the *Tribune* and all the individuals' clergymen were on the stage with the departed pressmen and linotypers.

General Olin stood in full military uniform, his eyes straight ahead, as though he had spotted an enemy in the back row, and his soul had been shorn of its moorings. His dignity had been assaulted but he was keeping his chin up.

If you hadn't seen him for a year or so you would say "My how he's aged." His flesh was slack, his face pasty, kneaded dough before the oven would give rise to it.

Arnie stood with a mournful slump, his shiny black bereavement suit tailored for someone smaller. He glanced at his father-in-law furtively from time to time, fearful that the General would lapse into one of his senile periods and make some remark or launch into incoherent speech that might implicate them in the tragedy.

But the General held his peace. The Philippine battle hat sat on his head like a troop ship riding the waves of a stubborn sea. Arnie wanted to tell him he should bare his head in respect for the dead, but he feared a scene.

The men were buried amid pomp, circumstance and florid rhetoric, offered up by Arnie Sutler, who shook his fists at the heavens and said, "This evil will not be forgotten. This outrage will be revenged not in kind but through purity and decency, hard work, freedom, and individuality, and freedom for workers everywhere to choose their own destiny. And no one, no matter how brutal, how terrible, will intimidate those who are pure of heart, those who are resolved to do right as they see the right."

When Arnie finished, he glanced at the General, who still stood at attention, his eyes straight ahead. He thought for a moment that he saw a flicker of approval there, but then he turned away.

The Los Angeles Band was on hand. They played an arrangement of the Chopin *Funeral March*. And the crowd stayed until each coffin was removed from the stage. Then they climbed aboard special trolleys and were spirited to graveside at the Inglewood Park Cemetery.

Two weeks after the mass burial, which Matilda Olin attended two paces behind her husband, she took to her bed and remained there for six long months until she died. She never spoke to her husband about the suspicions she had concerning the bombing, but she had had a soft spot in her heart for the socialist candidate for mayor who was the favorite after his primary election triumph.

When Matilda's father died he had left all his money to establish an orphanage for white boys. Matilda was never to have a dime's worth of her own money. It was money appropriated from her husband under false pretenses that she gave to the socialist's campaign. It was the only way she knew to compete with her husband.

In the early days she had written poetry for the newspaper, but though the paper had grown many times the size of the early paper, her husband could no longer find the column inch or two needed for poetry.

Matilda was a better writer than Benjamin was, more creative, more restrained, more literate, and even more intelligent. She suspected her literary career was doomed when he finally understood that.

Matilda was simply worn out. She had given up her will to live and when death finally came, she felt a kind of sweet repose sweep over her. Her head twitched and her eyes opened for the first time in twenty-four hours and she said to her daughter, Phoebe, sitting alone by her bedside, "It was worth waiting for," and she closed her eyes and passed on, to what she was sure would be a better world.

In an editorial, General Benjamin Raines Olin, mourning the loss of his wife, played heavily on her poetic contributions to the newspaper and suggested that her death was a direct result of the bombing of the *Tribune* Building, since she had taken to her bed immediately thereafter and never gotten up again.

Arnie Sutler dated the precipitous decline of General Olin from the death of his wife. It appeared in some strange way that the General was dependent for his strength and sustenance on a woman with whom he barely communicated. His moments of irrational senility increased. It became a challenge to his relatives to keep him away from the paper. There was an understanding among the staff that though Benjamin continued to come in, and though his name remained on the masthead as publisher, Arnie had the last word.

At the General's command, the raised platform and throne from his private office were moved to the end of the newsroom. From time to time the General would appear as though out of a cloud, stalk across the room, and, finally, being too tired to stand, sit on his high-backed throne and bark out, "Boy, bring me the wire releases." He still wore his Philippine hat, and when he could find no excuse to wear his military uniform, he wore his medals on the left breast of his civilian jacket.

Many of the *Tribune* men made fun of him, though they realized that without him there would have been no *Tribune*. With any other man at the helm the *Tribune* would have gone the way of every other paper in the town. But with his tenacious leadership, his instinct for the jugular, his resilience, the General had not only made the *Tribune*, he had saved it. They realized that the newspaper was the child of General Olin: born, suckled, nurtured, reared and educated by the man they now ridiculed sitting on his throne, making clownish pronouncements, giving meaningless orders that were never followed.

And when the last note had sounded from the last bugle, General Benjamin Raines Olin lay alone on the battlefield of his own bivouac, in the mansion he had erected on Wilshire Boulevard.

No one had expected he would ever die.

# 46

The soul, doubtless, is
immortal—
    where a soul can be dis-
cerned.

    —Robert Browning
    *A Toccata of Galuppi's*

1919

Shortly after Christmas, with its
panoply of colored lights, and evergreen
trees cut from their roots and brought in
from the cold world, the General slipped
peaceably away in his sleep; but not
before he had written his self-serving
manifesto full of platitudes, guiding the
replacement troops in their steering the
helm of the good ship *Tribune*, and not
ignoring the opportunity for self-
congratulatory bravura, crediting himself
with foresight, vision, the patience of Job,
the fortitude of Jupiter.

It was soon after the execution of the
trust that the General began to decline.
His daily uniform became that of the
Philippine cavalry. In his riding britches,
with his crop held firmly in his right hand,
he would parade up and down floors of
the new *Tribune* Building slapping the
side of his calf with the crop, barking
unintelligible commands to the troops.
Outside he would wander in the streets
without finding his destination.

He reverted to his childhood and

tried to make up for all the things he didn't have as a child. He gorged himself on sweets, and didn't like the taste of them, played with his toy soldiers, and watched for hours the children playing baseball on the school ground near his home. Once the children let him join the game, but he was unable to play because he had never learned how.

The cloud layer had forced itself down to the ground in Los Angeles for the funeral of Benjamin Raines Olin at the Armory in Exposition Park.

Winter funerals were better than summer ones. You could wear your solid black without perspiring by the gallon and making unsightly rings around your armpits.

They were spilling over the lawn of Exposition Park, paying their last respects. This overblown crowd of black-suited men with long faces and their women in solid mourning black, spoke in hushed tones as in the public lending library.

It was not so much deciding what to say about Benjamin Olin as how to make it sound sincere.

You had to gauge to whom you were speaking. Arnie Sutler would require only perfunctory remarks, he probably wouldn't hear you anyway. All he would care about was seeing you there, doing your duty.

Mary Ellen Sutler, the General's oldest daughter, would expect some obeisance, and she would look in your face for sincerity.

Mary Ellen's sisters, Phoebe and Delia, could be taken care of with a drop of the head and some sympathy card cliché.

The grandchildren were a different kettle of fish. Warren was a brick. You could just throw your arm around his shoulder and give it a squeeze and he'd smile that boyish smile that would make you wonder how this lamb came out of that barracuda.

That other son—what was his name?—he wouldn't take much, he was young and never seemed to make much of an impression —Paul—was that it?

Of course the girls were bitches. There simply wasn't a nicer word for them. They would be the real challenge. The oldest, Katherine—you wouldn't forget her—would make you feel like a copper penny while you stammered to say the right thing. You'd be damn lucky if she said "Thank you," or acknowledged your sympathy with so much as a nod—like as not, she would simply look away from you, like you just weren't worth her precious time.

Arnie looked over the crowd and saw in the front row his son Warren, home from Stanford for the funeral. Beside him, that cute little round-faced girl, Duffy Durham, whose father had a dry goods store out

in Santa Monica. There were disconsolate tears in Duffy's eyes. Next to
Warren and Duffy were Arnie's daughters. There were no tears in their
eyes. This day marked the beginning of their share in the trust. They
were looking out of the sides of their frowning eyes at Duffy Durham.
They had already decided that Duffy wasn't good enough for the Sutlers.

Benjamin Raines Olin was being buried in his uniform with a passel of medals on his breast, his sword, gilt gold, lay beside him.

When Arnie got up to deliver the eulogy, he looked to his left and
to his right, at the governor, the mayor, the state's two senators. The
president should have been there, he thought, but these politicians were
giving him their rapt attention. Many had said that without the *Tribune*
none of these people would be in office. Whenever confronted with that
theory, Arnie would scoff and say it was a great exaggeration.

After the ceremony Arnie Sutler accepted many compliments on
his speech. Senator Brewster pleaded a prior commitment, and asked
to be excused from attending the graveside ceremony. Arnie looked him
in the eye and said,

"Senator, I think it would be best if you attended."

They were milling around the General's house like swans in a
crowded pond. Everyone was trying to be relaxed and friendly and yet
show a touch of reverence for the dear departed. Queues of mourners
advanced to the food tables, took their fill and moved on to form cliques.
Occasionally one or two would mention some memory of the departed
General, some great deed he had done, some anecdote to make him
seem like a regular guy.

The upstairs hall was lined with a lifetime of pictures and memen-
tos of General Benjamin Raines Olin, beginning with his first job as a
printer's apprentice back in Ohio.

Of all the General's children and grandchildren the one most like
him was his granddaughter, Katherine, Arnie and Mary Ellen's oldest
daughter. She stood now in the upstairs gallery, the montage of historical
excitement swirling about her.

Katherine was a tall, angular woman in her mid-twenties who bore
herself with a straight spine and always seemed years older than she was.
She was a right-is-right sort of person who saw no grays and very few
whites. All her life she had doted on her young brother, Warren, and
though she had made a proper marriage, something seeped out of her
when Warren trumped off to Stanford. Many said her marriage at
Christmas time of Warren's freshman year was her reaction to that loss.

Warren came out of the bathroom now and was startled to see

Katherine standing there.

"Oh, hi, Sis," he said in his friendly, devil-may-care voice.

"I've got to talk to you, Warren," she said, the somber genes of General Olin pounding in her throat.

"Sure, Sis, what's up?"

"Warren," she said staring, her eyes getting to the point before her words, "I've got to know what your intentions are about this girl you brought down for the funeral."

"Intentions, Sis?"

"Yes, don't you think it is a little peculiar to bring a stranger to your grandfather's funeral?"

"Gosh, Sis, no, I didn't. Was it the wrong thing to do?"

"Well, I suppose it depends on *who* you bring."

"Oh?"

"Warren, I have to know is this just some plaything that you've picked up, or is this someone you have some serious intentions toward?"

Warren threw back his head and laughed. "Oh, Katherine," he said. "Did you think I would marry her in the middle of the memorial service at the Armory? It might have saved a lot of money, we had the audience all there, right down to the senators and the governor."

Katherine looked at him, stern creases in her dimples. "Don't be flip, Warren, the girl simply isn't cut from the cloth that is going to fit into this family."

"Oh? Maybe I'm not cut from the cloth that will fit into her family."

"Warren, don't be ridiculous."

"Ridiculous, Katherine? Who is being ridiculous? Here is a perfectly acceptable young woman, Stanford student, family successful, hardworking business people, what exactly is the problem?"

"Oh, Hon, can't you see it? She is just not our type, some small-town huckster's daughter. I mean, Warren, there just isn't any class in that."

Warren nodded, trying to understand. "So you mean that your marriage to the son of the president of the First Los Angeles Bank and Trust Company was a marriage of class, and my bringing a girl whose father only owns a dry goods store out in Santa Monica, is not class. Have I got that right, Katherine?"

"Warren, please don't be patronizing, you know perfectly well what I mean, the girl barely knows which fork to pick up."

Warren nodded, frowning again. "Of course little qualities like compatibility, sense of humor, ambition, sensitivity, conscientiousness, a pretty face, a nice figure and all those things I guess are secondary. Tell you what, Katherine."

"What!" Katherine was losing patience with her younger brother.

"Maybe if we worked real hard, oh, maybe for three or four months, maybe a mite longer, we could teach her which fork to pick up."

He patted his sister on the head and descended the stairs amidst the photos and memorabilia of his famous departed grandfather. When he saw Duffy talking to Yank, he broke into a broad smile. Duffy was so pretty, with her shallow dimples and a winsome smile. She had been queen of something at Stanford, but she looked uneasy in company, as though she were worried she was not as good as everyone else. Her shy, almost frightened demeanor was so engaging, it made Warren want to hug her. He took Duffy by the arm and stepped a few steps away from Yank, gave her a hug, and whispered into her ear.

"Duffy, why don't we get out of here and get married?"

Duffy's eyes fluttered when she looked at him. She stood clutching her purse in front of her crotch and running her fingers nervously back and forth across the top edge of the blue suede bag. The corner of her mouth twitched. She burst out laughing. "Oh Warren," she said "that is the nicest thing anyone has said to me all day." She twisted her purse straps and laughed again.

She thought he was kidding.

# BOOK III

# THE POWER OF COMPASSION

Duffy Durham Sutler

# THE COMMONER

> "My lady liege, through all the world," said he, "women desire to have the sovereignty over their husbands, or of such as love them, and ever live in mastery above them."
>
> —Geoffrey Chaucer
> *The Wife of Bath's Tale*
> *Canterbury Tales*

# 47

1920

At the moment that Los Angeles passed San Francisco in population, with 576,000 souls, Duffy Durham of Los Angeles was looking out a window near San Francisco. Her knees were trembling and bumping each other. She tried to control them, but couldn't.

She stood in the bedroom that was assigned her just down the hall from the one they gave Warren. She tried to sit down, but she couldn't sit still, so she was on her feet again. The room was large, the furniture was ornate, the walls were decorated with pink cabbage roses; swirling velvet draperies bordered the window, burgundy velvet like the blood of so many revolutionists. The room looked like it had fallen under the spell of one of the late Louis decorators.

Duffy's dress was satin and it fell gently below her knees like clear water cascading off polished stones. It was the palest shade of blue—so pale if you didn't look closely you would have taken it for white.

Duffy looked out the window at the

large oak, which had been carefully pruned and pruned again to keep it alive, with metal rods screwed into its large branches to keep the limbs from splitting. Behind the tree in the distance was a border of flaming red bougainvillea in full and splendid bracts.

The house, in Hillsboro, had been provided by a friend and classmate whose parents found the idea of a simple wedding in their backyard quite exciting. It stood on five acres and was built to resemble one of those musty chateaux on the Continent and to satisfy the aspirations of those of wealth who rightfully belong in the dwarfing rooms, under tall windows wrapped in fulsome draperies.

Duffy turned from the upstairs window and fretted her way to the mirror gilded with gold fluted leaves above the rosewood dresser. She checked to see if she could ascertain what handsome Warren Sutler could possibly see in her. In the mirror she saw a reflection of the impressionist painting of a young woman from the wall behind her. She studied it a moment then looked back to her own face in the mirror.

If one of those impressionist painters had painted me all fuzzy and furry, she wondered, what would I look like? Would my eyes be brown, or a shimmering gold?

Her hair was short, falling well above the shoulders in a round, almost helmet-like fashion. Duffy was convinced Warren would not marry her if he really looked at that hair.

Yes, oh yes, that was where the artist could help her. Paint the hair long flowing and full, blowing into thick rich tresses to frame her face and make her look beautiful. Tears started to form in her eyes; she wiped them lightly with her knuckles. She was an easy crier, she would have to get a grip on that, Warren's sisters would never approve.

As happy as she was to be getting married, she was sad that her father wouldn't be here to see it. She had wanted to invite him but Warren talked her out of it. "No family," he said, "just you and me." It was Warren's way of saving her the unpleasantness of his sisters.

She studied the mirror, Duffy Durham fading to an image painted by an impressionist artist. Her soft red lips, and filmy blue eyes, the flowing gold hair. Once again, she was a child, sitting beside her father in his horse and buggy.

They were a happy family, striving together to achieve a better place in the world. It was what the Sutler girls referred to as "the immigrant mentality," though Levi was not an immigrant. General Olin was not an immigrant but he had the mentality.

Levi's mother, Rachel, had named him. Levi's father, Robert, who did not share Rachel's Jewish faith, had a tinge of remorse when he heard Rachel wanted to name the boy after her father. He had secretly hoped that the boy, only half-Jewish, would not have to bear the travails that he feared were in store for him. For Levi shared not only the name with his grandfather but the sharp features: the hawk-like nose, the sleek black hair, and the deep-set eyes burning like coals in the night.

When Duffy was a young girl she was called Doris Fay, half after her mother, Doris Jane. Levi went from door to door in his horse and buggy selling pots and pans, cloth, dry goods, and some canned goods.

To Doris Fay, it was the most exciting thing in her life to go with her father door to door. She looked up at him while he spoke to the women and her heart brimmed with love. Her older brother, Dale, two years her senior, had not been so interested in the dry goods business, and so Doris Fay's bond with her father was special.

Dale was high-spirited and fun-loving, but not too attentive to the directions of his mother who had repeatedly warned him about those bothersome new horseless carriages.

The driver had been young, drunk and inexperienced, and the machine had simply gone out of control, and so, as Doris Durham was to lament for the rest of her life, her only son was taken from her and crushed and mangled beyond anything she could bring herself to recognize.

After they buried him, shortly before his ninth birthday, and came home from the funeral, Doris retreated to her room and closed the door on Levi. She had refused to have the traditional gathering at her home.

Sitting in her room on her bed with the door open, little Doris Fay Durham could hear the conversation in the next room. She was seven years old and the words took some time to etch themselves on her subconscious. Her brother was gone and would never come back, but Doris Fay was still alive and she wanted to love her mommy. Doris Fay could take his place.

Levi gathered his courage. "Doris," he said, "this is no good for you. Grief is natural, suffering is part of life; God knows we have had our share, but suffering is only valuable for the lesson we learn from it. We must pick up the pieces, Doris, and move on."

Doris was staring at him from the bed, her eyes glassy, as though she could see him but could not hear him. She turned away from her husband, setting a barrier between them that would never again be lifted. "My son is gone," Doris said to the wall, "he will never come back."

"But you have a fine daughter," Levi said to his wife's back.

"Daughter?" Doris said. "Ha," she tried to chuckle with a mirthless

derision. "Women are only put on this earth to be slaves," she said.
"Doris!"

"Slaves to man's desires," she said, "his stomach and his lust."

Levi came into Doris Fay's room and sat beside her on her bed. He took her in his arms and felt her sobs against his chest.

"Daughter, don't you pay any attention. Your mother is distressed, she didn't mean that you could never do anything but be a slave to a man. Just remember that you can do anything."

When she returned to school after her mourning she began writing her name D. Fay Durham. She never used Doris again. It wasn't long until her peers picked up on her signature and began calling her Duh Fay, which quickly degenerated to Duffy, which was fine with her.

She also started singing in the school choir and found it was a marvelous way to take her mind off her tormented mother.

Levi went on to parlay his horse and buggy to horseless carriages, to a warehouse to house his trucks, and then began selling his goods at the site. The warehouse grew into a flourishing dry goods store.

Duffy was angry with herself for her lack of self-confidence. She had never before felt herself inferior. She was loved by her father, did well in school, went to Stanford, was a cheerleader and May queen. Yet Warren's sisters didn't think she was good enough for their brother. She secretly feared they had found out she was one-quarter Jewish. She so admired them their self-confidence, their total Aryan blood.

There was a knock on the door. She turned with a snap of her body. She could tell it was someone who came to tell her Warren had decided against marrying her.

The door opened and Rebecca Wilson came in. "Oh, Duffy, you're so beautiful. You're the most beautiful bride in the world."

Duffy froze. Her hands clutched the faint blue dress as she saw Rebecca, her college friend who was going to act as her maid of honor.

"Oh Becky," Duffy said, a weak smile working its way around her lips. "Is…" she asked, her voice stumbling. "Is Warren ready?"

Becky laughed. "Oh, silly, do you still think he's going to change his mind at the last minute?"

Becky paused to examine the bride. A wide smile crossed her face. "Come on, Warren can't wait."

# 48

For myself, I do not know what truth is, what beauty is, what love is, what hope is. I do not believe anyone absolutely. I think people are both evil and well-intentioned.

—Theodore Dreiser

1921

The circulation department of the Los Angeles *Tribune* was near the noise of the presses, on the ground floor, so the employees got the feel of the place where the product they pushed was produced.

Reporters and editors had to think, so they were two floors up from the pounding of the presses.

The isolation of the circulation department from the editorial department was not related to any lip service that the two should be independent of each other. Indeed, the idea would have been laughed at in that day.

The presses were pounding longer than ever before, printing more, larger, newspapers, telephone books for the increasing number of telephone users, and the *Tribune* still did outside printing jobs.

Wilson's war was history, and the little town that not long before was a sleepy Spanish settlement was creeping up to a million folks, crowding the sidewalks, shoulder to shoulder.

It was a postwar boom, and it was

stretching the town as never before, but the *Tribune* had seen to it that Los Angeles was eminently stretchable.

Warren Sutler, grown to manhood, looked much like Warren the boy. His face was smooth and remarkably symmetrical, like an idealized marble of one of those Spartan athletes.

Some of his co-workers might have felt better about the boss's kid had he had some blemish on that perfect face—a mole, a wart perhaps, a childhood scar—but there was nothing.

Warren's hair was sandy blond and always fluffed up like it had just had a good shampooing.

He smoked cigarettes and took to social drinking because everyone else was doing it and he didn't want to stand out.

He wore collars rounded at the tips and a tie that looked like it took the colorful pattern from the fancy oil-washed end papers of a rare book.

He did not cut a figure of swash like his father had, but rather of boyish gentility. Those who knew them both couldn't see them cut from the same bolt of cloth. Looking at Warren you wouldn't think he had the motor skills to haul himself up the handful of steps to the circulation department.

But when he walked, so easy, so unassuming, he was like a lad set out across a dance floor, a young man who knows the right girl is waiting for him on the other side. And the other girls at the dance would like to fall over dead as he went by.

Jack Ellsberg, head of the circulation department, called Warren into his office. He waved his hand at an empty chair for Warren to sit down. Jack was a tall man, with the jowls of a man twice his age. He wore a bow tie and sucked continually on an unlit pipe.

"Warren," he said, looking at some papers on the desk in front of him, "I'm in an awkward spot here."

Warren noticed the ponderous man shuffling his fingers uneasily over the reports on his desk. "I had high hopes for you," he said, his broad hand coming up to stroke his dewlaps. "But the numbers…" he paused, looking over Warren's head, "the numbers seem to be slipping."

"Numbers, sir?" Warren answered, scrunching his eyebrows, "I'm not aware of anything slipping."

"Yes," Jack's voice rumbled ominously, his fingers still working his dewlaps, as though the rhythmic stroking would make this bad dream go away. "It was no secret that I wasn't keen on having you in my department," he said candidly. "In the first place your father was mad as all get out you got married and dropped out of college. So I didn't take it as a compliment, him dumping you off on me. I guess no one really wants the boss's son looking over his shoulder."

"Oh, Mr. Ellsberg," Warren said, "I never looked over your shoulder."

Jack Ellsberg waved his hand silently, "No, of course not, but I didn't know you then, and I've come to like you. But I'm on the spot. I gave you the downtown vendors, the railroad. I felt there was more business there than we were getting and you were a better man for the job than Lem Sax. And you know he's not happy about you being here—let alone getting the best route he had. And Skip, his supervisor, is mad that I usurped his prerogative in assigning you the best route." He sat back and let out a sigh. "And soon you'll be off to another department, and they will still be here." He shook his head. "Now it appears I was wrong."

"Wrong, sir?" Warren's clear eyes asked the question.

"The figures," Jack said, turning, with his pyramided hand, the papers toward Warren. "The numbers have been slipping steadily for six weeks."

"But, but that can't be," Warren said. "My sales have been increasing. I've been getting the best position, stand after stand. Are these my reports?" He picked one page up and studied it, then moved on to the next until he had gone through the pile of the half-dozen reports. He nodded his head with fatalistic cadence. "So that's it," he murmured.

"That's what?" Jack looked at him with tightened eyes.

"Those aren't my numbers," Warren said. "Somebody altered them."

"You've sold more than that?"

"Many more."

"But the totals check out," Jack said.

"Then someone sold less than their totals indicate."

Warren looked Jack Ellsberg in the eye and Jack nodded slowly, his massaging hand freezing on the dewlap.

When Warren went home that evening to the one-room apartment on Westmoreland just north of Wilshire, Duffy was waiting for him. She opened the door before he could and threw her arms around him.

"Warren," she said, "I've been waiting all day to give you a hug."

Warren's hug was perfunctory and Duffy looked into his eyes. "What's the matter, Warren?" she asked; and he told her.

They sat on the brand new couch inside the small living room, and Duffy consoled him. The couch was upholstered in pink roses. It was the only new item of furniture in the apartment. Besides the couch, on the bare wooden floor that Duffy had polished to a fare-thee-well, there was a card table and four chairs loaned to them by Warren's sister, Louisa. The bed came out of the wall on creaking springs that shot through the whole building when the bed was raised or lowered.

"Maybe I should look for another job—somewhere where I'm not the boss's son."

The next morning Duffy called her father-in-law and asked if she might see him for a few minutes. Arnie Sutler was surprised to find the suggestion exciting to him. He offered to take her to lunch.

They ate at a new restaurant with a French name and French chairs to match, white tablecloths, and silver crystal glasses. "Vive la différence," Duffy blurted aloud and giggled. When Arnie pressed her for an explanation she said, "I was only thinking of the difference between the entertainments at the top and the bottom of the *Tribune*." Her eyes swept the room, her smile engaged her companion.

The veal had been tender as had Arnie's attentions, but Duffy was beginning to sense by the time the creme caramel came for dessert, that Arnie was becoming restless to know the meaning of her visit.

When she told him, he said "Thanks" as though pushed by some surprising force. It was not so much the event that surprised him; what shocked him was that Warren's wife, his distaff, spouse, the little woman, was bringing him the news. In all his years, with all his wives and women, Arnie had never included them in his business decisions.

Arnie stared at Duffy for a long moment. Then his hard eyes turned soft. Understanding gripped him as he searched out the crinkling eyes and round face, the guileless lips, turned in a warm smile. Arnie realized that he could never smile like that, his smiles were thinner and more grudging, hers were so simple, so defenseless, so open. He could understand why Warren was willing to confide so much in her. But, understanding it or not, he still considered it a great weakness.

"Duffy," he said, "you're a brave girl coming to me with that tale. I'm going to look into it."

"Thank you," she said.

Later, in Arnie's corner office, Warren stood, fists clenched at his sides. Arnie waved Warren to a chair, and said, "Warren, I need your help. I know you are very close to your wife and one of my employees' wives just called me to complain about his treatment by his superior. This interest by a wife is new to me; I don't know how to handle it. What would you recommend?"

Warren searched his father's face, as if for the missing piece in the story. "What specifically was the complaint?" he asked.

"I'd rather not get into that."

"Well, did it seem justified or not?"

"Oh," Arnie said scratching his neck, "probably so."

"Well, I don't understand the problem then. Is the problem that you heard it from his wife instead of from him?"

"Yes, I suppose that's it."

"It was Duffy, wasn't it?"

His father nodded, gravely.

"Well, I'm sorry if she disturbed you," Warren said.

"Oh, Warren," he said, staring at his son as if trying hard to understand. "You know, your grandfather used to wonder if you could handle it, and now I'm beginning to wonder too."

"Handle what? I'm doing my job. I'm doing it better than it's been done before. Jealousy is a natural thing. Their changing the figures—I didn't see any reason to bother you with it. I've told my boss. I don't need instant recognition. I don't want to run this company if I'm not capable of it."

"Yes, yes, but there's a family tradition," Arnie said, almost impatiently, "not to mention the benefits of family control under the trust."

"Listen, isn't the important thing a good paper? Who makes it good is secondary. Why, it's even conceivable that some day a woman might be running it."

"Oh, Warren," Arnie said, "let's not be ridiculous. If you want to get anywhere here at the *Tribune*, or anywhere at all, you're going to have to start wearing the pants in the family."

# 49

Well hast thou motioned,
well thy thoughts employed,
   How we might best fulfill
the work which here
   God hath assigned us, nor
of me shalt pass unpraised;
   For nothing lovelier can
be found in woman than to
study household good,
   And good works in her
husband to promote.

          —John Milton
          *Paradise Lost*

1925

"Pasadena, Yank," Duffy Sutler said through the telephone, her voice betraying an excitement, mingled with a slight nervousness.

The classified section of the *Tribune* was spread out where she sat on the floor. It was turned to the "Homes for Sale" section. "What do you have in Pasadena?"

"Snobs," he said. All the Yankee Realty ads were for homes in Hollywood.

Duffy laughed and when Duffy laughed you laughed with her. Duffy's laugh was infectious, uninhibited and as big as all outdoors.

And they made the appointment for Yank to show Duffy houses in Pasadena.

It was maybe twenty-five to fifty thousand years ago when an angry Earth coughed out the Sierra Madre range. Nothing more than barren rock. But fifty thousand years is time enough for rain, wind, fire and sun to wear down granite and spread it out over the lowlands until there is enough soil to bear vegetation. Seeds came, no one knew from where. Vegetation colored the hillsides, and it wasn't until 1770 that white man first set eyes on this marvel that took so long to produce. Not much more than two hundred years ago. A dot on the time line of evolution.

The Indians had it first. The chaparral was always greener in the arroyo; and the water, it came up from springs in the base, up the valley and it was sweeter. Funny how the Indians always pointed the way to the sweetest water and the greenest grass long before the white man came with his education and his craftiness, his factories and his smog.

No, the Indians didn't clear out by choice, they never did. But, they might look back on the days of the green chaparral and the sweet water and sunshine and clear air, and decide that the way it turned out, it was better they evacuated.

The Pasadenans have all but forgotten the Indians except for the occasional name of a street or movie theater.

Pasadena to Duffy was heaven on earth. It was the home of the young intellectuals who cared about the finer things in life. "Culture vultures," Warren called them. All of Warren's sisters lived in Pasadena and if it was the last thing Duffy would do, she would win over Warren's sisters. Her children would go to the same schools as their children. Her children would ride the same ponies, and before you knew it, the artificial barriers would break down, and Duffy would be one of them.

Duffy rarely paused to think why it was so important to her to gain the acceptance of Warren's sisters. She certainly didn't like them as people. But they did represent the society to which every young woman in her place aspired. And they were pure Anglo-Saxons, and Duffy could still feel the slights of her youth because her father looked so Jewish and had a Jewish name.

Yank found a house for her that she simply fell in love with; of course it was more than she could afford to pay but she refused to worry. It was a modest stucco box with a red tile roof, on the east end of town not far from houses with more pretentious character and only a little further from the Henry Huntington estate. It had a nice yard for the children, white picket fence, a massive oak tree for shade, and it had three bedrooms so each of the children could have their own room. Of course, it was in terrible shape, but she would fix it up.

No matter what time Warren came home, Duffy was waiting for

him with a martini. Occasionally after a trying day with the children, Duffy would taste the martini without waiting for her husband. She really had no taste for alcohol but it did soothe her throat and calm her down, and she began to look forward to her evening drink.

Two weeks before the open house, she was having her drink by the fire in the living room of their new home, sitting on their love seat.

After Warren sat down next to her, she blurted out, "Warren, I haven't heard from any of your sisters yet about the party."

Warren looked at her, sympathy in his eyes strained from a day of reading reports, columns of figures, marketing surveys and projections, and he said, "Duffy, it's a stone wall, why do you want to keep hitting your head against it?"

Duffy fixed him with one of her resolute stares, where the eyes seem to leave the round face. "It isn't right, Warren," she said, "it isn't right for families not to speak to each other, and I'm not going to put up with it."

Warren sighed and put his arm around her, patting her shoulder, resting his head on her other shoulder. "I love you, Duffy," he said.

Back in the office the next day, Warren called Katherine, the ringleader of his sisters, so feared and admired by his wife.

Warren asked about her husband and kids. She knew through the small talk why he was calling.

"Duffy is a little sad she hasn't heard from you and Louisa and Amy about her party."

Silence. It was Katherine's most potent weapon.

"Would it really hurt you so much to be civil to her?"

A throat clearing on the other end.

"Katherine, are you there?"

"I'm here." The voice was low, withdrawn.

"Will you just do it for me. Try to be civil. It means so much to her and would cost you so little."

The plea in his voice was almost pathetic, Katherine thought. "Well, if it means that much to you," she said, leaving no doubt for whom she was being obliging, "maybe this once."

Secretly, of course, Katherine wouldn't have missed the party for the world. She wanted to criticize it. Now they would owe her a favor, rather than she being obligated to reciprocate the invitation.

Duffy worked twenty-seven hours on the preparation of the food for her open house. The party was on a Sunday afternoon. Duffy and Warren stood alone in the kitchen before the first guests arrived. Warren surveyed the magnificence of his wife's handiwork.

There was food everywhere, artfully prepared and designed— reds, greens and yellows of vegetables; greens of dips; tawny brown petit fours. There were chicken legs and meatballs, salads of greens, macaroni, pickled beets, seven kinds of dessert, and more.

Extravagant foodstuffs were avoided, but all the less expensive viands were artistically cut, arranged and displayed.

"People eat with their eyes," Duffy confided to Warren.

He looked at her with a mist in his eyes and said, "Duffy, you're a wonder."

Duffy beamed, "Well," she said, "at least they'll never be able to say that I didn't try." Warren understood "they" meant his sisters.

The doorbell rang. Duffy's heart leapt to her throat. Her eyes twinkled with expectation. "Maybe it's one of your sisters," she said, full of hope and fear at the same time. But Bob Franks and his wife Connie came first—Bob, the affable, round-faced man with the loving cup ears, and his wife in her stylish black velvet hat with jaundiced feathers. And then it seemed like the room filled with people from the office, neighbors, friends, so fast and furiously that Duffy barely saw the Sutler sisters arrive.

She was standing in the corner talking to her father-in-law, Arnie Sutler, who patted her on the shoulder with encouragement and said how nice everything looked, what a wonderful job she'd done with the house, how beautiful the food was.

"It's pretty as a picture," he said, "and so are you."

There was a din in the room: the buzz of voices, the clanking of forks on plates, ladles on bowls, ice on glasses, glasses on teeth. It flashed by Duffy so fast it seemed like a surrealistic painting. She'd had so many compliments she was feeling lightheaded.

She saw the Sutler sisters across the room. When her eyes met theirs they looked away. They were congregated in the far corner as though members of a disapproving religious sect.

Duffy took a deep breath, and made her way across the room. As she got closer to the sisters she began to feel perspiration beading at her temples; her lips seemed a little parched, her palate dry. The long olive green skirt she wore was suffocating her legs. She wished she had sacrificed her high-neck blouse for the open neckline that hung lonely in her closet. Katherine had on a cool sleeveless dress, her arms and neck fleshy. She was matronized twenty years before her time, but her boundless self-assurance intimidated Duffy.

There were three smiles on the Sutler girls as Duffy approached. Katherine's smile was tight, and frankly disapproving. Louisa's lips were turned up in wry amusement. The only trace of warmth was on the youngest, Amy's, lips.

Duffy stood before the trio, smiling her own inimitable smile: open, friendly and begging for approval. Then on feeling a chill from her in-laws, her smile faded until it became a mere line between her nose and chin. The edges of that thin line trembled.

"Thank you for coming," Duffy said. "Warren and I are so happy in our new home and we're just so glad you could come." She nodded her head slightly in a quasi bow, humbling herself before the gods.

The three smiles focused slightly over Duffy's head as though Duffy were just some maid, who should be treated with civility certainly, but who was not worthy of any real social effort.

Katherine spoke first, "Warren wanted us to come," she said. "Personally, I find open houses a bit tiresome."

"Oh, I'm sorry," Duffy said quickly. She backed off and was halfway across the small room before she turned her face from the intimidating trio.

Later the three sisters were seated on the couch facing the fire. The party had begun to thin out. Duffy was passing a tray of petit fours, approaching them from the rear, when she was stopped to hear Katherine saying:

"It's so tacky."

Amy made a meek defense. "Oh, Katherine, she means well."

"Oh, what does that mean?" Katherine snapped. "This place looks like an underfunded bordello."

"And the lovely oak floors," Louisa said, "they're completely covered. Have you ever seen anything like it in your life? Carpet all over the floor? In Pasadena?"

"If you ask me," Katherine said, "the one with the tackiest taste is our brother, Warren." And they all laughed.

Duffy backed away, the tray trembling in her hands. She saw Warren at her side. She put the tray in his hands without a word and stumbled off to the bathroom.

Warren followed her with his eyes and set the tray on the table and went to the bathroom where he found her dissolved in tears, leaning a hand on the sink for support.

"Duffy, why are you crying? Your party is a smashing success. Everybody is raving about what you've done to the house. Everybody is ecstatic over the food. What's the matter?"

Duffy only shook her head. When she caught her breath, she said, "Oh, I don't know Warren, I guess it's just the tension. I'm sorry." She dried her eyes with the handkerchief he handed her. She laughed a quiet, apologetic laugh and said, "I'll be all right, Warren. I'm ready to go back to the battlefield, as Grandpa Benjamin would have said." And she went back to the living room where several people were looking for her to say goodbye.

When Warren's sisters decided to leave with their husbands, Duffy extended her hand graciously and said again as though she had heard nothing, "Thank you for coming." None of the girls said "Thank you" for having them, or "I enjoyed it," but Louisa said, "Yes."

"We'll have to get together for lunch sometime," Duffy said, the corners of her mouth twitching, her fingers playing at the seam of her skirt.

"Oh," Katherine said, "I'm so frightfully busy at lunchtime, but I tell you what, the very next free moment I have, I'll give you a call."

"I'd like that," Duffy said.

When the last guests had gone, Warren put his arm around Duffy and said:

"Duffy, that's the best party I've ever been to in my life." And he couldn't understand why she started crying again.

# 50

Almost all absurdity of
conduct arises from the
imitation of those we cannot resemble.

—Dr. Samuel Johnson

1932

Duffy was slumped over on the
couch with the print of little pink roses.
It was as though she couldn't decide if
she were going to sit up or lie down.

"I'm a thorn among roses," she tittered to herself. She was quite alone, as
usual, thank you, and, no, it wasn't very
much fun, thank you. And she was getting mighty tired of saying "thank you"
all the time when there wasn't anything
to say thank you for, thank you. She giggled again.

The living room was changed. Only
the wall-to-wall carpet and the couch
with the tiny pink roses remained from
the open house seven years before. New
furniture and Venetian blinds had been
added to the room that was smaller than
the kitchen in General Olin's mansion.

But it was too large for Duffy. It
would have been just right for two, but
so seldom were there two lately.

The children were in bed. The children were her life—her charges. Now
they were asleep.

Her husband was at work. He always was.

Duffy wanted Warren to be as large a part of her life as the children were. But she discovered the paradox more years ago than she could remember: the higher he rose at the *Tribune*, the longer and harder he worked; and he promised her with each promotion he would spend more time at home, as soon as he got the hang of the new department.

Instead of a fuzzily colorful young girl in an impressionist painting, Duffy was taking on the cherubic clarity of a Rubens woman. There was a surfeit of stuffing between the hard bones of her frame and the soft fabric of her flesh. After eight hard years of wear and tear, the rose-covered couch had less padding than she did.

The hands on the brass clock on the mantle were poking their way past one forty-five. It was getting late even for Warren.

Her own hands were poking around the glass martini pitcher. Surprised in her haze at not feeling any leak in the pitcher, she peered over the edge of the couch and ran her hand in small circles on the floor to see if she had spilled any.

She squinted at the brass clock and thought she'd better get up to make some more martinis for Warren. She pushed herself forward but just didn't have the strength to go all the way.

Warren found her asleep on the couch when he arrived home an hour later.

The moment he touched her gently on her shoulder her eyes popped open as though they were on springs activated by his touch.

"Oh Warren," she said, making an unsteady effort to sit up. "I'll make you a martini...."

His hand held her shoulder to keep her in place. His eyes searched her pink puffy face. "What's wrong, Duffy?"

"Warren," she said, her eyebrows knitting to bring forth her memorized speech, "your sister Katherine had a party, and I wasn't invited."

"Oh Duffy, don't worry about them." He sat beside her and took her head to his shoulder.

"I've had her to *so* many parties." She started to cry.

He kissed her cheek, held her close and felt her sobbing body, smelled the heavy gin breath and vowed to himself to spend more time with her, a vow he knew he couldn't keep because he was the boss's son and the boss's son had to prove his mettle.

Warren held his wife in his arms on the fading sofa and looked around the room, debris strewn everywhere, the martini pitcher on the floor, beaded with perspiration from overwork. On the table next to the sofa, a half-eaten pork chop sat as though Duffy had battled to take some food, and lost the struggle. A napkin with lipstick was balled up on the floor at her feet.

"I must do something," he thought. But while he was trying to think what, she was fighting to hold her eyes open.

"Tomorrow," Duffy mumbled, "I'm going to take the children riding. Horses scare me and I'm so afraid the children will get hurt, but it seems to be the only thing I can do with your sisters."

In a moment she was sleeping. Warren carried her into the bedroom, gently undressed her and covered her with the blanket. He kissed her forehead and stood back to look at her, remembering the petite college girl he had married.

Sunday Duffy was up bright and early with Carrie and little Olin. Now it was her turn to look at her sleeping husband, so peaceful and untroubled.

She clapped her hands. "Children, get in the car."

The black Ford was four years old and Duffy loved the wind on her face and the dust on her clothes and the sun, the beautiful sun on her hair, warming it, like a loving parent. When the children piled on to their favorite rumble seat, Duffy had second thoughts about leaving her husband on this beautiful morning.

"Mom," little Olin said, "do we have to go?"

"Oh, you'll love it, horseback riding is loads of fun." Her foot slipped from the brake to the accelerator, and down the road they went to Pasadena's finest stables, to be with Pasadena's finest people.

The stables were at the bottom of the arroyo, a long row of buildings nestled at the bottom of the sloping chaparral; next to the long stables, a riding ring, fenced in white.

When Duffy saw her son Olin sitting astride the giant horse, her heart went out to him. He looked so frail and uncomfortable.

She was on the outside of the fence looking into the ring. She wanted to be in there, to pat his head and tell him he was every bit as good as his cousins. She looked across the ring and saw her sister-in-law, Louisa, talking to her sister-in-law, Amy. They had so much self-confidence, Duffy thought. She just could not take one more step toward them. That did not prevent her from glancing at them every few seconds for the smallest sign of friendship.

Olin was listening to the instructor, a young girl with riding britches and cap, who liked to caress the crop she held in her hand, and like an old cavalry captain, punctuated her pronouncements by slapping the crop to her palm. Little Olin watched the girl as she spoke but his mother could feel his discomfort.

The sun was sliding down across the chaparral, making long shadows in the clear morning air. Olin nodded at his teacher and kicked his little heels into the horse's ribs and the horse began walking about the ring.

Duffy noticed Olin's cousins, Harriet, Sally and Pete, cantering their horses and felt the smug satisfaction of her sisters-in-law watching their superior horsemanship.

Olin's sister, Carrie, was still at the stables, her horse not yet saddled. Duffy looked over to see what was taking so long when she heard the thundering noise. Looking back to the ring, with a start, she saw the three cousins racing at full gallop. It was the apocalypse as they passed little Olin, enveloping him in a cloud of dust.

The little guy rubbed his eyes with the back of his fists and started to cry. Duffy wanted to reprimand the rude children. She wanted to go across the ring and speak to their parents, but she knew Warren would not want her to and her anger boiled.

Before she had time to gather her thoughts, the horsemen thundered around again, this time catching poor Olin's horse in the spirit of the chase, and as Pete cut dangerously close to Olin's horse, the animal carried away the little child at a gallop of his own. Olin, frozen in terror, stiff and helpless, was crowded against the fence, his leg caught between the fence rail and the horse, wrenching him from the saddle and dropping him to the ground with the most terrorizing thud.

Duffy squeezed herself between the rails and rushed toward him. She leaned over the unconscious body and cried, "Oh, my God." She scooped him up in her arms and started towards the gate that was now opening to admit Carrie on her horse.

The sisters watched the tableau and Katherine commented on what a dowdy dresser Duffy was.

Duffy cried, "Carrie, come with me. Open the car door."

And she laid her only son on the front seat and got behind the wheel while Carrie scurried into the narrow back seat and said, "Mom, is he dead?"

Louisa and Amy appeared at the car, "What's happened?" Louisa asked.

Duffy fixed her with an icy, withering stare, threw the car into gear and drove off. Louisa looked at Amy and said, "I guess she doesn't want any help."

The car flew over the rutted roads to the emergency entrance of the Good Samaritan Hospital with Duffy blowing the horn and screaming like a mad woman. Less than two blocks from the hospital, Duffy felt Olin suddenly stiffen beside her. Sitting up in the back seat, Carrie said, "Mom, why did Olin jump like that?"

Cold panic swept Duffy's body when she felt the arresting of her own heart and pulse. It was as though the blood had frozen in her veins, and so blowing the horn and screaming at the hospital emergency entrance offered scant release to her unbearable tension. The young intern in the white smock came to the car and said, "What's all the racket, lady?"

"My boy, my boy, he's had a fall. Take him in."

The young intern, blond, with the cool, impassive face, looked at the boy, put his hand on his wrist and the other hand in front of his nose and mouth and said, with chilling dispassion, "Your son is dead."

Duffy hated the intern, a cold, venomous hate that shot through her body like death. Again the car flew into gear, "He's not dead," she screamed, and accelerated, almost taking the intern's head along while she drove off to the next hospital.

She pounded the lifeless Olin on his little chest, and said, "Don't die, you can't die, you're not dead, I won't let you die, they won't take you from me, they can't, they mustn't, they won't."

The little car threw more dirt than the herd of horses that had thundered down on poor little Olin. It was a Thomas Hart Benton lithograph, black and white, its tragedy comical, its heartbreak, heartwarming: his stoic mother, and the still, rigid child, and in back a frightened, forgotten girl. Sleeping at home in his bliss, the father of the family.

The rock hard tires pounded the ruts in the rough street.

The dirt behind the little black car swelled with her frantic quest to find a doctor to share her impossible dream.

The white adobe hospital, the Sacred Heart, loomed large on her right, like a cloud of the heavenly host, opening its welcoming heart to her; the screaming and the blowing of the horn repeated automatically. This time two nurses and an intern met the car and then the boy was placed in a stretcher and carried into that warm-hearted, loving cloud, where he disappeared.

Mother and daughter kept a silent vigil while Duffy's mind raced over prayers she didn't realize she knew, calling out to God for mercy, for justice, for compassion, a God she felt had been a stranger to her, an estrangement she earnestly sought now to rectify.

Sister Carrie, cold with terror, looked up at her mother, her eyes wide with imponderable fear, "Is he dead, Mother?" she asked in a flat, morbid tone.

Duffy pulled herself up as though she drew strength from the floor beneath her feet. "He's not dead, Carrie," she said, her eyes malfocused, as though her indomitable spirit made it so.

Duffy tried to get in to see her son but a kindly old nun said, "Mrs. Sutler, it's best to let the doctors concentrate and do their work."

The wait was interminable, it became intolerable. Duffy paced the floor like a frightened hen, biting her lips, balling her fists, speaking vacant words of hope to her daughter who sat on the chair at the wall paging through magazines she didn't look at.

When finally the doctor came toward her, she knew her judgement had been vindicated. The man would not carry a smile like that on his lips if he were bringing bad tidings.

# 51

Of course all life is a
process of breaking down.

—F. Scott Fitzgerald

1934

The air was cold and cloudy, the
rain had fallen steadily all night. In the
early hours of New Year's Day, 1934,
waiting for the Rose Parade to begin,
Duffy felt a lightheaded loneliness,
though her beloved Olin was on one
side of her, Carrie on the other. They
were huddled in raincoats and boots
under a man's umbrella that kept them
damp instead of soaked. Her husband
had promised to join them later.

They were sitting on the sidewalk
at the foot of the reserved bleachers,
where the people who could spare two
dollars a seat were able to come in luxury just minutes before the parade
began.

To get the prize place on the curb
they had to come out the night before.
The children brought sleeping bags and
considered it the best time of their lives.

Throughout their nightlong vigil
Duffy tried to hug her son to her bosom.
He always pulled away. He was embar-
rassed by his mother's overt affections.

Duffy hugged Carrie too, but both children could sense it was not with the same intensity.

She had never rushed Carrie unconscious to the hospital to have a doctor tell her her daughter was dead.

Duffy had fortified herself through the cold night with a thermos full of gin that kept her warm, and gave her courage and strength to go on. Though lately it was taking more to do less.

By eight-thirty in the morning the Pasadena sidewalk was thick with people, though the parade was still an hour away. Down the street on the five-mile route, the crowd thinned with each succeeding mile. Everybody wanted to be at the start of the parade to see the flowers when they were the freshest, to hear the bands when they were the most alive, and see the horses at their spunkiest.

Duffy heard a familiar voice saying, "Excuse us, excuse us, excuse us," and she thought for a moment Warren had arrived. She turned around to see her brother-in-law, Paul Sutler, dragging his two children by the hand, pushing his way through the crowd to angry looks and grumbles, while his wife Natalie followed in their wake.

"There you are, Duffy," he said, "I've been looking all over for you." He spoke as though Duffy had been hiding from him. "Can we squeeze in here? Have you got some room saved for us?"

Duffy's jaw went slack, the added flab of her dewlaps seemed to joggle. She wanted to say: "Paul, we sat here all night long. I don't want your kids standing in front of mine." But something caught her tongue.

Paul moved his two daughters right in front of Olin and Carrie, who had to scrunch up their knees to make room for their cousins. Paul and Natalie nestled close on either side where Duffy sat on her folding chair. Both of them eyed the chair as though Duffy should give it up to them.

Paul was dressed in tweed pants, an open-neck golfing shirt and a tam-o'-shanter tweed hat that almost matched his tweed pants. He was a slightly built young man, with soft, pasty features, like unrisen dough; he had the look of a man who was waiting for the world to fall at his doorstep.

Though Paul's wife, Natalie, was his same height, she wore shoes that made her seem to tower over him.

Natalie had a sensuous behind. Warren told Duffy so, and, ever since, Duffy couldn't look at her sister-in-law without noting the tight packaging and undulant rhythms of Natalie's derriere. Her shape was so exquisite it made Duffy physically ill to be so close that everyone could compare them.

Paul turned around after searching the stands. "It gripes me," he said to Duffy, "to see Katherine and Louisa up there in the two dollar seats when we've got to stand down here with the peons."

Natalie turned her sharp nose to Duffy and said, "Duffy, you aren't very communicative this morning," and she sniffed the air with the superior attitude she was always so adept at conveying.

"Well, I guess I'm a little tired," Duffy said. "We've been here all night. I'm only thinking of my children."

"Well, of all the selfish…." Natalie said.

Paul looked at his wife, "Oh, Natalie," he said, "lay off her, she did give us the places."

"Well," she said, "don't you get tired of her preoccupation with her fair-haired son, Olin? I mean he's not nine years old and she's grooming him to be the next publisher of the *Tribune*." She gave a short, dry laugh.

Paul stiffened. Natalie was a proud woman of some Russian ancestry with an abrasive, competitive edge that cut through the fog like the Potemkin.

Paul's beginning at the paper had caused Duffy no end of grief. She had become, in Warren's words, absolutely paranoid about the matter. It would be over her dead body that anyone would take from her son his rightful position at the head of the paper.

"Paul, were you at the paper last night?" Duffy asked.

"On New Year's Eve, are you kidding?" he said. "That kind of joy-killing is for your husband, I was at a party."

"Oh," Duffy said, "I thought there was a lot of work on New Year's Eve."

"Well, I did my work, I don't give them anything extra. They don't do anything extra for me."

The parade began with the pulsing of drums and blaring trumpets, and Duffy could feel the arms and the elbows of Paul and Natalie pressing her flesh as the crowd jostled for better views. Duffy stood up.

Warren had arrived at the parade scene but stood at the back edge of the crowd. He saw the space Duffy had tried to keep for him was occupied.

The floats seemed to swirl before Duffy's eyes like a whirlpool of roses and carnations, gladioli and mums all mixing together, the colors washing as though they were water-colored paint, swirling and

streaking. One moment she thought the displays were more resplendent than ever before, the next her eyes could barely focus.

Then it started to rain again, a light but persistent shower to
dampen Duffy's terror. The bands played on, but it was a wash of
sound. The drum and bugle corps went by and the pounding of the
drums stretched the walls of her head beyond their capacity to contain her nightmares. The trumpets cut her eardrums, shattering her
defenses, the wet air seemed to become scarce. Several times Duffy
gasped for air. Now she felt Paul looming over her like a viper intent
on tearing out her entrails.

Paul Sutler had graduated from Stanford; Warren, his older
brother, and Duffy dropped out to get married, and in every conversation Duffy had with Natalie, that seemed to take paramount, if
unspoken, importance.

Another float went by, girls waving and smiling, teeth and
hands, happy girls, happy-go-lucky girls without a care in the world;
without in-laws. There were some waving branches on the float but
to Duffy they turned suddenly into eels and those eels swam toward
her and started swarming in her hair, then crawling in her ears where
they tangled into one another, turning into roaches, some of them
coming out of her nose and her mouth; and in the back of her brain,
swordfish were fencing and making a scratching and grating noise.

She put the thermos to her lips again and then again. She
thought last night that it was crazy to bring so much gin for so short a
time, and now she cursed herself for having brought so little. The
bottle was empty. She dropped it on the street. It made a mocking
metallic sound.

Another float went by with more girls waving and laughing at
her. Why were they laughing at her? Natalie was saying something to
her but she couldn't hear what. Paul was talking in the other ear but
it was a jumble of noise. Then Natalie seemed to talk to Paul, and
Paul to Natalie, but she couldn't hear a word. The air seemed to dry
up. There wasn't enough to breathe.

A nightmare rushed to her head for just a second as she gasped
to keep from suffocating. Paul was walking very slowly on the beach;
he bent over to pick up a book on the sand. It seemed to float in the
air. Holding the book upside down and scratching his head, Paul
dropped the book and lay down on the sand with his feet up. Duffy's
father-in-law, Arnie, floated toward Paul with the *Tribune* Building
on his back. When he got to Paul, lying on the sand, Arnie took the
building off his back and handed it to Paul, who said: "Set it down

over there, I don't want it yet." Arnie sank into the sand as though it were quicksand, and disappeared. Little Olin came scurrying down the sand, with a toy sand pail and shovel, saw the building and tried to pick it up but he wasn't strong enough.

She reached down for her thermos of gin but her hand circled Paul's ankle. He gave her a light kick.

Suddenly a troop of six horses, laden with heavy silver saddles, ridden by broad-brim-sombreroed riders broad in the beam, came toward them.

Duffy could see plain as day Paul and Natalie pulling those invisible strings about the horses, straight for her little son Olin. They were trying to kill Olin.

She reached out to hug him to her protective bosom, but he rebuffed her with whip-like arms. The horses turned their heads and bared their teeth as though they were going to tear him limb from limb. Duffy screamed. One of the horses reared and flailed the air with his forelegs, trying to get at Olin with his iron hooves, the rider looking every bit like Natalie with her tight, perfect buttocks clutching the saddle. And the saddle was beginning to look like Warren. Duffy screamed again and again and though the horses were well down the street, she continued to see them trampling Olin, whose pale, wet face was now looking at his mother saying, "Mother, shh... Mother, what's the matter?" But Duffy couldn't stop. There was a rustle in the crowd and Warren was by her side, holding her and stroking her and the crowd parted while he helped her out of the suffocating multitude, and there in the back of all the people she collapsed in hysteria, muttering, "Did they get him? Did they get my Olin? Did they get him?"

From the authorized version of the Sutler family biography:

"Feeling inferior to the Sutler family, Duffy Durham Sutler checked herself into a Pasadena sanitarium, early in 1934, as a result of the breakdown, caused by her excessive worry."

# 52

The essential feminine machine is no better than the essential masculine machine; both are monuments to the maladroitness of a much over-praised Creator.

—H. L. Mencken

The ambulance tires squished, slipped and spun in the muddy ruts of the Shadyside Sanitarium road.

There was water everywhere, for Southern California in the thirties could not cope with the record rainfall, and the streets became rivers. Though they were astonishingly adept at bringing water to Los Angeles, they were hopelessly inept at getting it out.

In the back of the ambulance, beside his prostrate, whimpering wife strapped on her stretcher, Warren Sutler thought it was an insidious plot perpetrated by the *Tribune* and its boosterism allies to see that there were no storm drains in a dream climate town with such rare rainfall. As though a drainage system would give lie to their claims.

But God couldn't hold His water forever. He was, after all, only human in that regard. So the rains fell and the water collected and flowed downhill until there was no more downhill there, and the rivers turned to lakes.

From the rear of the ambulance Warren heard the driver curse his luck. He kept playing with the accelerator and the gears, rocking the vehicle back and forth until it lurched forward, often only a few feet before he had to repeat the process.

Warren's empty stomach heaved with the lurching of the ambulance.

"You think they got someone to take her in? I know she's feeling poorly and all, but I didn't sign on to get soaked to the skin. I got another half a shift and I don't figure spending it getting pneumonia."

The sanitarium was hidden in the trees behind the two squat stone pillars that marked the entrance to the main road.

The low buildings were shaded on the sunniest days but today were plunged into macabre darkness. It was a time in Southern California's brief history when mental illness was kept in the dark.

"This place better be open," the driver muttered as he slid to a stop at the first door he came to, taking advantage of a slight downhill turn to the left.

Warren pressed two dollars into the driver's hand, and they carried Duffy on her stretcher through the sticky black mud and pounding rain, up the back steps which led into the kitchen of the sanitarium. The driver put his end down in the middle of the kitchen floor, and Warren obliged him.

"I've got to get back," the driver announced.

There were only three small windows in the room to let the outside darkness in. The others were blocked with kitchen equipment.

There were three actors on this stage that smelled of boiling cabbage. Three generations of indomitable yet despairing Middle Americans washed west in a tide of hope.

The balance wheel of the family was a young woman with a round face and cascading mocha hair. She had a well-proportioned body that did not seem to belong to her.

She was methodically taking raw potatoes out of a five-gallon kettle of water and slicing them into scallop-sized bits which she pushed to a mountain of potato slices at the end of the table. She wore a white kitchen helper's uniform. On it a badge proclaiming her Nora Yates.

Across the table was her mother, in a sack of a black dress that looked like it had seen happier winters. The woman had seen happier winters too, but so long ago she couldn't remember them.

The old woman seemed little more than a dried head and a

dress—there was no sense of any body beneath it. And that was just the way she wanted it.

Her hands were in her lap, and she was working up the energy to help with the potatoes.

A large knife lay on the table in front of her.

On the floor was a towheaded two-year-old boy playing with a raw potato. He moved over to check Duffy—then held the potato up to her mouth in a peace offering.

Warren said: "Hello—I'm Warren Sutler," in his disarmingly friendly tone, as though he were at a cocktail party.

It sent a bolt of lightning through the room.

The old woman grabbed the knife in front of her and the young mother in white shot her mother a reproving glare while tightening her grip on her own knife.

Warren looked at them both, his jaw tensing. He felt a deadly current. "Is there a doctor here?" he asked too easily. No one answered him. He suspected these women were disturbed patients.

Duffy began to groan on the floor and then let out a scream that brought the room back to an earthly orbit.

The young woman was about to speak when a middle-aged woman in white, prematurely gray, entered, followed by two orderlies.

Warren felt the stares of the women hot on his back as he left the room with Dr. Genevieve Banks, while the orderlies carried Duffy's stretcher.

Warren's heart sank when he saw the padded cell where they put his wife. It seemed like cold storage to him.

He looked back at her as Dr. Banks put her hand on his arm and said, "Come—" Then Duffy shrieked: "Don't leave me alone!"

Warren begged the doctor to let him stay but she tightened her grip on his arm and shot him an unmistakable order.

Duffy's hands opened in the straps across her chest, then closed involuntarily. Her screams filled the hallway.

In the barren room with a blank desk and file cabinet, Warren sat across the desk from Dr. Banks and wondered if she were quite old enough to be his mother.

Her gray hair was serious and severely tied in a bun in back, and she resented the time it took her to do that. Hers was not a job to keep hair light and bouncy.

She sat with a quiet air of exhaustion, her back to the lone window. On the sill was a dish of birdseed.

When it wasn't raining the window was open during her sessions with patients so she would have an escape route should a patient signal violence. She had never had to use the open window for anything but feeding birds. It seemed impossible to be hostile to her.

"You are the doctor?" he asked.

She smiled, showing sturdy teeth. "Surprised?" she asked.

"Well, a woman…" he faltered.

"You sound like my father. He said, 'So marry a doctor, okay, but for heaven's sakes don't *be* one.'" She laughed again, easily.

Dr. Banks laid her glasses on the desk and leaned over to tell Warren they would do everything they could for Duffy. She was surprisingly comforting when she told Warren that only about ten percent die in her sanitarium from acute alcoholism, but less than half fully recover.

"We're in for three to five very rough days. I will keep you posted by telephone."

Warren begged to stay. She told him it was no use—he couldn't see Duffy for days. Warren declined a ride back and walked the three miles in bone-drenching rain.

"Oh, what have I done to you, Duffy?" he wailed over and over.

Tomorrow he would submit his resignation at the paper. He would take any job that allowed him to spend more time with Duffy.

There was no electricity in the room above the garage, except that which existed between the parties, for here was a strange undercurrent that now and again sent sparks flying through the silences. Mother and daughter sat in silence at the table. Nora's hands on top, palms down, fingers splayed, her mother's gnarled fists clenched together in her lap. The baby was sleeping fitfully on the mattress.

The rains were still pounding outside, and the wind was working the water angrily through the leaking roof, dripping into pans at a half-dozen locations. The lugubrious sound of water on metal gave an eerie, staccato beat.

In the far corner of the room, beyond the sleeping child and the drip pans, a stack of *Tribune* newspapers were growing earth brown in the fetid air. At first glance they seemed a random collection, but each of them had an article about, and/or picture of, someone whose name was Sutler or Olin.

The room smelled of the closeness of bodies and the dampness of the rain.

The mother spoke first, dredging up all the twisted fates of the past, the smoldering agonies, the wretched wrongs.

The woman didn't alter her gaze into the vacant space ahead but her eyes seemed to harden, her body tensed.

"You'll have to kill her," she said.

The father sat with exaggerated casualness, the son, stolid and dejected, his mind far off from the newspaper office in downtown Los Angeles.

The office was a far cry from Arnie's old modest room with the roll top. He could sit now in splendor with a desk of battleship proportions between him and his visitors. Arnie didn't see any compelling reason to underplay his importance. General Olin had been dead fifteen years, and Arnie was feeling that he had taken his long, dark shadow with him at last.

But now it seemed as soon as the pressures of one generation were removed, they were being applied by another.

Warren, the son, sat glum, his hands in his lap, as he might have in church during a particularly boring sermon.

The father listened to the son's resignation speech, and then said: "Well, you won't need to leave for a while—not while she's at the...ah...sanitarium. What's the point of being precipitous? I was just ready to make you assistant to the publisher. At least think about it."

"I was going to take care of the kids, Dad," Warren said.

Arnie got up and circled his sprawling desk to lay his arm on his son's shoulders.

"That's a fine instinct, Son—but that's women's work. We'll hire you a maid. It would be a shocking waste of your talent. I'm sure Duffy would agree. When she comes home you can quit as an assistant publisher. It will look better on your resume."

Warren had never heard his father allude to any "talent" before.

"My advice is let her be," Arnie said exhaling a ton of air as if to clear his system of a poisonous conversation. He turned back to question his son.

"What would you do?"

"Anything—an eight to six job anywhere. "I'm sure Duffy's father would hire me."

"To do what?"

"I don't know—sell furniture, anything."

"Ladies' shoes?"

Sparks of their darting eyes stung the air between them.

"Take two weeks off," Arnie said, "see how you feel."

Warren looked at his father as though he were speaking a foreign language.

"Duffy needs me, Dad," he said. He dropped his head to his hands to hide his tears. "She's tried so hard to make friends—to be accepted in this high and mighty family. But your daughters have been absolute bitches to her."

"What can I do about that? You have any idea the things I've had to endure?"

"You're a man, Dad. It's a lot different."

Arnie slammed his palm on his desk and dropped his feet. "Dammit will you stop toadying to women? It's the *men* who count. And don't you forget it."

Warren stood up, looked silently at his father, put on his hat, touched it into place and left.

# 53

Many a man would rather you heard his story than granted his request.

—Lord Chesterfield

Screams rent the air of the Shadyside Sanitarium like mortar shells bursting anonymous hearts.

The smell of Lysol was in the air.

Outside Duffy's room, Warren leaned against the pendulous pine, his face drawn.

And Duffy screamed, and screamed, and screamed, and Warren imagined he could tell Duffy's screams from all the rest. But screams were indistinguishable, primal sounds, without nuance.

There were so many screams, like sirens wailing shattering cries, and finally he admitted he couldn't tell them apart.

As the days dragged on into weeks, the screams turned to groans, then to moans, then to whimpers.

In the early days of Duffy's confinement, Warren stole a look through the tiny barred opening in her door. There he saw his beloved, once lovely wife looking as haggard as an old harridan: white, gaunt, sunken cheeks, with hair a wiry old dry mop and spittle trickling from the corners of her mouth. The weight she quietly dreaded had fallen from her like melting chocolate, and her bones were beginning to show where her arms and legs poked through the floppy white hospital gown.

Warren's sisters invited him to parties, now that they no longer had Duffy to contend with, even offering him "suitable" escorts, but he declined.

He did, once, have dinner with his brother Paul, and Paul's wife, Natalie. Natalie had wrapped her buttocks snugly in scalloping silk and wiggled the ensemble in front of Warren at every opportunity.

Natalie had a genius for draping her exquisite curves to maximum advantage, making the ultimate use of light and shadow, undulation and repose.

For, contrary to popular delusion, clothing was never devised for warmth. It was rather instituted to allure members of the complementing sex, to set one off from his fellows.

When Natalie slithered in next to Warren on the maroon and gray striped couch, she snaked her body slowly, and it seemed the last part to settle in was her sensuous behind that jiggled with a fluid, snuggling motion.

"Comfortable?" she asked, smoothing the tight silk skirt on her legs.

"Hm?" his mind was not on her now. "Oh, yes, thank you."

"You miss having…a woman's touch?" she asked touching his shoulder lightly with her index finger.

"I miss Duffy," he nodded. "I sure do."

"Could *I* do anything to help?" she said, her eyes sparkling generosity. "*Any*thing?"

"Oh, no thanks," he said. "I'll work it out."

Paul made his entry with the tray of drinks.

Warren stared at his as though fascinated by a strange aquatic creature in the bottom of the glass.

"Something wrong with your drink, Warren?" Natalie asked.

"I was just thinking of Duffy."

"Oh, you shouldn't…."

"Why not?" he snapped suddenly, splashing a wave of the amber over the side of the glass. It trickled down his hand.

"Well," she drew back, "I mean you shouldn't feel you have to give up the pleasure of an occasional drink because of…of what happened to her."

When dinner was served he felt nauseous and couldn't eat.

He watched instead, in morose fascination, his brother and sister-in-law in hasty mastication of hearty, yet tasteless food. It was as though he were watching mimes working hard to make sure the audience understood what they were doing.

And, all the while, he thought of Duffy.

Thirty-six people died in that New Year's storm. Almost as many were injured in the record thirteen-inch rainfall.

Then the rain subsided and a glorious Southern California February sun fell on the land. The rains returned, and the wind, and the fog and mist with the overcast dull clouds, before Duffy was quite herself again. She had lots of visitors: Warren and her father came every day, Yank came to see her, and Arnie Sutler. She didn't want her children to see her in this condition.

In the beginning when her father came, Duffy turned her head from him in silence. When Warren came she stared straight at him but didn't speak. The first words to her husband were five weeks into her confinement when she said, "Warren, I'm so ashamed." For the thirty-minute visiting period he held her tightly in his arms, and neither spoke again.

One day Duffy was sitting outside in the sun on a bench overlooking the wide lawn that separated the buildings. On the far end of the lawn a stand of trees marked the sharp edge of freedom. Duffy looked up to a clanging sound and saw Nora Yates come toward her with a bucket and mop.

"I'm on barf control patrol," she said with a wrinkled nose. "I'll never worry about unemployment."

Duffy laughed. It felt good to laugh. She couldn't remember how long it had been since she last laughed.

The women sat side by side, Duffy in her thirties, Nora not yet twenty. The younger girl, uneducated, a simple menial, yet Duffy looked to her for strength and support.

Duffy talked in excited animation, when suddenly she stopped, blushed and turned to Nora. "I'm sorry to carry on so," Duffy said, "tell me something about yourself."

Nora said, "Well, I'm not going to kill you."

Duffy threw back her head and laughed her unguarded laugh. After she recovered she looked at Nora's face and saw Nora wasn't laughing. Duffy furrowed her brow and said, "There was a time I would have considered killing me a favor. But why would you want to kill me?"

Nora looked away, across the field of newmown, rain-cleansed grass. There was a cool breeze blowing between the buildings that seemed to separate the women, forming islands of their own, and yet the more Nora spoke, the closer Duffy was drawn to her.

"We came from a small town in Kansas. My father was a big man, strong. He loved his family, worked hard; he repaired farm machinery and he traveled all over the county fixing threshers, plows, cultivators, anything. You name it, he could do it. The weather was kind of harsh back there. In the summer we'd get these terrible dust storms, and no matter how tight we closed that little house we lived in, putting rags along the bottoms of the doors, plugging the keyhole even with cotton, that dust would get inside everything in the house and even inside the sugar bowl. And the winters of snow and ice sometimes made it impossible to move.

"It was not an easy life but we were happy, happy because we knew no better, I suppose."

The sun was on the treetops across the way at the freedom line. It gave them the warm, vibrant glow of brilliantly faceted emeralds.

"For more years than I can remember, Mommy and Daddy got the midwinter issue of the Los Angeles *Tribune* and used to read about what a paradise it was here, how the sun was out all the time, the flowers grew all year long, and the good life was available just for the taking.

"When everything went sour and all Daddy's customers lost their farms, Daddy couldn't pay the bank for our little house; and just when everything seemed to be blackest, the midwinter issue of the *Tribune* came to town and Daddy said, 'Now's the time for us to taste of the land of milk and honey, firsthand.'

"I remember my daddy repeating the silly rhythm, 'Califony, Califony, we're going to Califony.' I never saw such hope, after such despair. I was fifteen years old and on my way to perpetual sunshine, work for all the able-bodied, and Daddy sure was a hard worker."

Nora's eyes swept to the right, possessed by her memories. She glanced at Duffy and saw her hanging on every word. "We loaded that old truck that my daddy used to drive from farm to farm, making his machinery whole again. We loaded that truck so high, with our belongings we just couldn't bear to leave behind, it was like to fall over; and we set out for the unknown, full of dreams and scared.

"Well, I can't tell you how many flat tires we had. How many times we had to be pushed by strangers who soon became friends, because we had that bond, that common bond of searching for the

Holy Land. One of the times we were pushed, in a little town in Texas, just there at the Panhandle, I met a girl my own age, Sally Burgstresser, and we became friends and we traveled the rest of the way together.

"And no matter what the hardship, Daddy would always say: 'Isn't this great, girls? California is going to be so great.' He always called Mom and me 'girls.' Now he was including Sally 'cause we were just like sisters." Nora shook her head at the irony. "California," she said, the word's bitterness sinking to the roots of her teeth.

"Well, when we got there, you wouldn't believe what we saw. There were people camped out at the border, as far as you could see. Some living in cardboard boxes, and all along the border were men with guns to keep us out. You had to prove at the border that you had the money to get yourself started. And all those people were waiting for some miracle, a notice of jobs that would let them through. I remember when my friend Sally went through the line of soldiers and crossed the border and we waved at each other. I tried hard not to cry 'cause I knew how it would affect my daddy, but I just couldn't help it and he saw me, and I saw him snap his head like he had been shot."

Nora's thumbs caressed her fingers in the lap of her starched white uniform. Her eyes were straight ahead.

"By this time, my mother was screaming at my father to do something. But none of us knew what. Then, after being rejected the third time at the border, and after giving the guards a piece of his mind about the Los Angeles *Tribune* and how they lied and got all these poor people out here and then wouldn't let them in, we turned back; back to where, we didn't know. But my father, from that day on, was a beaten man. He just completely lost his self-respect."

"Oh, my dear," Duffy said, "you poor, poor dear."

"Somehow we got home, I don't know how. Our house was still empty. We hadn't paid the mortgage, but we just moved back in as though nothing happened. I was lucky to get a job in the hotel, downtown, changing beds, cleaning toilets, 'cause the owner knew my mother and felt sorry for us. I barely made enough for us to eat, and my father just sat in his chair, staring out the window as if some miracle might pass.

"A few months after I started at the hotel, a traveling man came to town, dressed like a dandy. I swear he was the handsomest man I ever saw in my life. And oh, did he know how to have fun. Said the sweetest things to me I ever heard in my life. I was sixteen years old, now mind you, I wasn't what you call experienced. But I grew up real fast."

Duffy's eyes were watering.

"He had a wife, and of course he loved me more. He was going to leave her. 'Til I told him about the baby. Then he was just as sweet as he could be, he was so sorry, he really wanted to marry me but his wife wouldn't give him a divorce. He gave me a hundred dollars, all the money he had in the world, and the name of a man in Wichita who could help me.

"I couldn't tell my mommy and my daddy, I just couldn't, until one day I fainted right on the kitchen floor, and when I came to, I saw Ma looking at me in that funny way, and she like to have never gotten over the disgrace." Tears were staining Nora's cheeks, and Duffy's eyes were not dry either.

"My father died a few days later. Mother says of a broken heart, and I believe her. Well, instead of spending that hundred dollars killing my baby, we buried Pa and came to California, and this time with what was left of the hundred dollars we got in."

She took a deep breath, then let it out as though reluctant to part with it. "My ma thinks this wouldn't have happened if it hadn't been for that old newspaper of yours, and I don't know if I can rightly disagree."

"Oh, you poor child," Duffy said. "You must understand I have nothing to do with the paper. My husband has a small job. He's paid a salary like everybody else."

"Oh, I know that's all neat and logical, but my ma wants something."

"An eye for an eye, you mean?" Duffy said.

Nora looked away. "I don't know," she said.

Duffy had had many sessions with Doctor Banks; fruitless, frustrating interviews in the doctor's simple office, with the window open and the dish of birdseed on the windowsill.

Then one day there was a light drizzle outside and the sky was gray and hopeless. Duffy surrendered her guard.

Doctor Banks wore the simple smocked dress that she wore most of the time. There was a tremble in Duffy's voice as she spoke with her soft country twang. "I'm just so embarrassed and humiliated," Duffy began, "at all the pain I've caused."

Doctor Banks said, "Have you ever considered the pain others have caused you?"

Duffy stared at the birdseed and her brow creased as though she were counting the seeds. "My husband's relatives have a very low opinion of me."

"And what is your opinion of your husband's relatives?"

"Well," an involuntary laugh leaped from her throat, "they're *established* people; *important* people."

"Important to whom?"

"Oh, Doctor, the *Tribune*, the paper, the Sutler family."

"And what do those people have to do with the paper?"

"Do?" Duffy asked perplexed. "What do you mean, do?"

"Well, what specifically are their accomplishments that make them so awesome?"

Duffy turned the word accomplishments over in her mind, three, four times, and her eyes seemed to travel inward as though searching inside her own skull. Doctor Banks noticed a kind of gentle repose take over her features.

"Now, let's try to find out what it is you think about yourself that doesn't measure up to what *you* want to be. Of what significance is it what someone else wants you to be? After all there are hundreds of millions of people in the world and if they all met you they might all have different ideas what they wanted you to be. So what does that leave us? You can either try to tailor yourself for every person you will ever meet, or you can try to be yourself and get the most out of what you have."

As the sky mellowed later in the afternoon, Duffy went for a walk. There were white, wispy clouds in the luminous blue sky. It was as though a giant comb was pulled through them stretching fine strands of soft white in random patterns across the blue.

Duffy walked along the path to the freedom trees and pondered what Doctor Banks had said, she looked at the tall trees and envied them. She envied their self-sufficiency, she envied their steadfast position, immovable, unconquered by opinions, never trying to be what they were not.

And in that moment with the pale sun and hairy clouds in the sky, Duffy made up her mind to be like those trees.

# 54

To lift a load so des-
perate
Would need your cour-
age, Sisyphus!
Though keen the soul
that burns in us,
Yet art is long, and time
grows late.

—Charles Baudelaire
*Unlucky*

The heavy rains greened the trees
and the grass and washed the pine needles off the roofs, blessing the Shadyside
Sanitarium with pristine freshness.

Duffy had started to eat better, the
woolly feeling inside her mouth subsiding, but she felt restless and guilty for
abandoning her children.

Warren had been trying to get
Duffy to come home for a weekend.

Duffy protested she wasn't ready.

"Then I guess I can't tell you my
surprise," Warren frowned.

"Oh, Warren," she lit up, "I love
surprises. What is it?"

"When you come home I'll tell you."

It was a crisp day, and the tall black
trees were waving gently in the soft
breeze that put so much life into the air.
The pine cones shook majestically, but
hung tenaciously to their branches like
children on their mother's skirt.

When Warren arrived to pick up his
wife he was brimming with excitement.

When he saw her his jaw dropped.

She was still wearing her white baggy robe and was lying in her bed staring at the ceiling.

"Oh, Warren," she said, "not today. I'm so sorry, but I just can't do it today. Maybe next week."

Warren sat next to her on her bed—kissed her lightly and did not press the visit. He ached with disappointment.

The sky was overcast and the air cool for Duffy's big first trip home. In the car Duffy felt the dashboard with her fingers, tentatively, as though experiencing a new sensation. Warren was happy, Duffy was scared. "Warren," she said.

"Yes, dear."

"What kind of mother do people think I am? Abandoning my children...."

"Duffy, everybody we care about thinks well of you. This didn't happen to you by choice, and now you are going to lick it with your courage and we're all going to be better people for it."

Duffy surveyed life outside the car window. There were people on the streets walking freely. Stores open for business. It was as though she had been removed from reality for four months and was surprised to see that all these people had been going about their business with no thought of Duffy, and Duffy with no thought of them.

"But what will they think," she said at last, "if I come home and don't see my children?"

"If you want to see them, Duffy, I'll get them for you."

"Oh," she paused. "I...I don't know if I'm ready."

"Then there is nothing to worry about. I haven't put it in the newspaper that you're coming home, you know."

When the laughter died, it was almost as though it had been a mistake, that the situation was too serious to laugh about. Warren put his hand on hers, squeezed it and said, "Duffy, I love you."

Duffy smiled at him, a weak, thin, unconvinced smile.

When they got to the door, Duffy stood back as though trying to place her home in her memory.

Inside they collapsed in each other's arms.

In a moment they were on the couch. Duffy, dazed by a strange sense of freedom, yielded tenuously at first, then feeling a tenderness, a throbbing passion fired by urgent need, the two became fused as one current in the stream of time, feeling the ebb and flow of the tides; touching, caring, loving: one current flowing in one glowing light.

"Oh, Warren," she cried softly, "I missed you."

"Duffy, I need you."

Then they sat at the small kitchen table with the flower print oil-cloth cover, an unopened *Tribune* lay between them. Duffy looked out the window at the backyard. Some azaleas were blooming, greener from the record-breaking rains of the winter.

She was exhausted with an eerie contentment. She felt a creeping depression, as though drawn back to her history, piled so high with unutterable sadness.

Across the table, Warren watched as Duffy seemed to melt like a candle in heat too strong. Pouches formed under her eyes, the twitching corners of the mouth turned down, jowls sagged. Warren touched her hand.

She was paying with remorseful dividends for the joy she had experienced but felt was not her due. She felt as an idle spear carrier on the stage of life. The stars of the show were carrying on in front of her while she stood silently behind, holding her spear, turning left, turning right, walking off the stage, coming back on, her participation offering very little to the opera.

"Warren," she braved a smile.

"Yes, dear?"

"When are you going to tell me your secret?"

A mischievous, elfish grin came to his lips. "Now'd be a good time," he said and fell silent, still smiling.

"Well, come on then," she said, jumping up and setting herself on his lap, feeling coquettish. "Well?" She put her index finger on the tip of his nose.

"It's good to have you home, Duffy," he said, circling her with his arms.

"The secret, Warren," she said sternly.

"Don't rush me. I'm getting to it." He tightened his hug and kissed her cheek. "I missed you so."

"I miss you too, Warren."

"I've felt so responsible for what's happened."

"Oh no, no!" she said.

"Yes, yes. I was working too hard—trying to prove myself to my father, I guess. Stupid. I left you with all the family burdens."

"Now I've left you with all the burdens."

He shook his head. "No, you had it much rougher. You saved little Olin's life. What a strain that must have been! How many mothers would have gone on after a doctor told them their child was dead?" He beamed in amazement. "Only you, Duffy."

She smiled. She couldn't pretend she wasn't pleased with his compliment. She shook her head. "You've no idea how many times I dreamed of that doctor telling me Olin was dead. And I would just scream, and scream, and scream." She sighed to wash away the memory. "I'm so glad you weren't there to hear me." She looked around the little breakfast area. "But, where's the surprise?"

"My surprise is, I'm not going to ignore you and *your* needs again. On New Year's Day in that ambulance I realized nothing in my life is more important than you. The thought of losing you shattered me."

"That's sweet, Warren," she said and kissed his chin—a quick motion, and then she dropped her head back to look at him curiously.

"So I can spend more time with you," Warren explained almost apologetically, "I have quit my job at the paper."

Duffy stiffened with a suddenness that startled her husband. She turned cold.

"Oh, Warren, you can't," she frowned, her eyes holding a new terror, "you *can't* mean it."

"I do."

"But the future, Warren...." Her eyes were clouding—her throat was dry. "My dreams," she muttered.

"My future is with you—nothing else matters to me—"

"You can't, Warren—"

"Yes I can."

"But think of *Olin's* future. Someday he's going to be publisher of the *Tribune*."

"That's okay with me. But I'm not. I'm going to be *your* husband, not married to a newspaper."

Duffy had turned pale, her face a blood-drained contortion of anguish. She grabbed him desperately.

"Promise me you won't quit, Warren," she spoke in rapid desperation. "It's easy for you to give it up—but it wouldn't be easy for me or little Olin. Paul would get in there, Warren—you have to stay to keep him from taking over."

He laughed. "Duffy, there is room for both if they want it. I want you."

She argued. Pulled all the stops—the sisters' ridicule, Paul over Olin, but her arguments were not hitting home.

Demons were clawing inside of her. She had to open her body somewhere, *anywhere*, to let the demons out.

She felt helpless to the familiar overpowering thirst that now parched her mouth. Her tongue was shriveling in dehydration. The water faucets were only a few feet from her but water would not slake this thirst. Duffy's resourceful mind raced over the possibilities. Her tongue made several passes over her lips trying to moisten them.

"Warren," she said sliding off his lap, "do you think you could bring the children, just for a few minutes?"

Warren looked deep into her eyes and tried to understand the sudden change. He smiled, encouraged. Was she on the long road back?

"Certainly, Duffy, if you're up to it."

Duffy's tongue again went around her lips, pausing at the corners, working first the upper lips then the lower, then the lips themselves made contact as the tongue disappeared. Still they felt dry, she needed something, and she needed it badly.

"How long," she said, "would it take you?"

"Well I don't know," he said, "I…I could probably be back in half an hour. Wouldn't you like to come with me?"

"Oh no," she answered too quickly, "I've got to stay here and rest."

Warren looked at her. He wanted to believe, he wanted to trust so badly that he buried his instinct that told him something was wrong.

She didn't hear Warren make the phone call. But he came back into the kitchen and said: "They'll be so glad to see you. Are you sure you'll be all right?"

"Oh yes, I'll be fine."

She stood at the front window, watching the car disappear down the road. Duffy crossed the lawn and knocked on the neighbor's door.

A teenage girl came to the door and Duffy said: "Hi, I'm Duffy Sutler and we live next door." Duffy was smiling like no one else. "Is Mrs. Bronson in?"

"No, she's not," she said, "I'm the baby-sitter."

"Oh," Duffy said, "gracious, I have just come to borrow a bottle of gin for a cocktail party I'm having."

"Gee, I don't know," the girl said, "she didn't say anything."

"That's all right," Duffy said, marching into the house, brushing the girl aside, "I'll get it myself. Duffy went straight to the pantry, took the bottle off the shelf, looked at it and deciding that it was not full enough, put her hand out and took a bottle of bourbon too.

"I'll just borrow these two," she said, "and I'll replace them as soon as my husband comes back."

The girl stood aside and said, "Gee, I…I really don't know if I should…."

"Oh, that's all right, Millie knows me, we do it all the time." And with the pronouncing of her employer's name the girl felt reassured.

The burning liquid felt so good going down Duffy's throat. It had been too long and she couldn't get enough of it and couldn't seem to drink it fast enough, so by the time Warren returned with the children, Duffy was unconscious on the kitchen floor.

The children stood on either side of their father, each holding a hand.

Carrie was eleven and her small features turned in helplessness. She wished she were grown-up and knew how to help her mother.

Nine-year-old Olin stood, tall for his age, staring down at his mother, with pinched, brooding eyebrows. While Carrie was sympathetic, Olin was embarrassed. Too many kids on the block had seen his mother drunk.

And if Olin heard one more time that it was because some doctor told her he was dead when he obviously wasn't, he would scream. Olin turned his brooding eyes on his father. "Why is she on the kitchen floor?"

"Well, she is just so exhausted," he said, "she just fell asleep."

Olin's sister looked at the oilcloth covered table. There was an empty whisky bottle beside the rolled morning *Tribune*. She picked up the bottle, looked at it and looked at her mother and shook her head.

Olin said, "Dad, she's drunk."

Warren stared at his wife, took the children and turned them toward the living room. "I guess," he said, "we'd better go back, it's very hard for your mother, very hard, and we've got to give her another chance."

"Why waste your time, Dad," Olin said, snorting disgust from his flaring nostrils, "she's just a drunk."

Warren's hand swept up and grabbed the *Tribune* from the table and cracked the boy across the face. It was the only time Warren had ever struck his son.

Olin's head snapped back with the blow. His hand started up to his face to subdue the sting, then froze midway before he dropped it.

Instead of comforting himself, nine-year-old Olin decided to stare defiantly at his father.

It was a hateful glare, and one Warren declined to meet.

# 55

The depressing smell of Lysol reached up to the little space over the garage where the two women and the towheaded boy were picking over the evening meal Nora just brought from the sanitarium kitchen.

Nora had tried to eat but her mother's accusative stares inhibited her.

Nora slammed down her fork. "All right, Mother, what is it?"

The shrunken woman fixed her daughter with a stare from withering eyes set deep in her craggy skin.

"When...are...you..." each word shot out like the lunge of a stiletto, "going...to...kill...her?"

Nora pounded her fist once on the table, rattling the dishes like skeletons on a tin roof. She jumped to her feet.

"Dammit Mother, we're *not* going to kill her," Nora screamed, and the towheaded boy cried. Nora stopped short, then slunk back to a chair in the corner of the room, next to the pile of *Tribunes* mentioning the Family, and sank into it like a rejected animal.

"Then I'll do it myself. I'm not afraid of the electric chair," her mother hissed. "I'll pay your debts, slut!"

"Oh Mother," Nora yelled, her face red with rage, "don't talk crazy."

Duffy sat on the bench at the edge of the grass with the freedom trees across the way. She wasn't looking at them now.

Turgid tears of despair rimmed her lower eyelids. She had failed again. There were so many failures. Wouldn't everyone be better off if she were just dead? she wondered.

Her mind grazed over modes of suicide, and she decided a lot of sleeping pills would be best all around. She would not leave any maudlin notes, maybe they would think it was an accident.

She looked up at the trees and a fatalistic smile teased her lips. She realized she could just get up and walk out of the Shadyside Sanitarium, but she had no desire to go anywhere. She had disgraced herself once too often with her family, and she had no one else.

Duffy closed her eyes and decided the best thing would be for her to find where the sleeping medication was kept, and steal it. It wouldn't be quick or easy, but she had plenty of time.

She did not hear the old woman approach from behind. The broad-blade butcher knife was concealed in the front folds of the shapeless black sack Nora's mother wore.

If Duffy had seen her, this black avenging angel, if she'd had time to talk it over with her, things might have worked to their mutual satisfaction.

As it was, the woman stood unnoticed behind the bench within easy striking distance of Duffy. She drew the knife with a dramatic rustle of fabric as though she wanted Duffy to see her, as if she didn't want to be robbed of her dramatic due.

The knife froze in her hand, upraised and posed to strike, when she had a sudden paralyzing thought. Was it, she wondered, cowardly to strike the helpless woman from behind? Wouldn't it be more proper to strike her in the front where she could look at her?

The sound of the swishing fabric made Duffy turn around, and she threw her arm up to deflect the butcher knife. The sudden blow knocked the frail old woman off balance and she pitched forward, like a falling tree.

The knife lodged between the back of the bench and the old woman's slight abdomen. Blood oozed with a relentless certainty down the black robe and the woman collapsed over the back of the bench like a half-empty sack of potatoes.

Duffy screamed, and screamed and screamed.

It took a good load of sedatives to calm her down. But it wasn't enough to kill her.

When Duffy came out of the sedation her mind was fogged and her first thought was she had tried to kill herself and failed. The sanitarium looked to Duffy like the reverse side of a tapestry, all knobby with the colors running together.

When it all came into focus for Duffy, she was confused that something within her should fight to stay alive. Duffy decided it was an omen—a message that she really wanted to live. She began to take charge of herself.

The first person she asked Warren to bring to see her was his father, Arnie Sutler.

To Warren's surprise his father was delighted at the prospect of going out to see Duffy. But then, Warren didn't realize his father had another girl friend, named Hilda, in Pasadena and it gave him a humane excuse for seeing her.

The visiting room was simple with its threadbare blue chintz couch and two Bentwood chairs with cane seats that were held together by faith. The men sat on the couch and Duffy on the Bentwood chair that appeared to have the best chance of seeing her through the meeting.

After an opening pleasantry, she told them the story of Nora Yates. Her eyes rarely left Arnie Sutler's as she unfolded the tale. Arnie drummed his fingers on the couch as though that might hasten Duffy's conclusion.

Arnie's eyesight had slipped and he had taken to wearing steel-rimmed glasses. He had some time before lost interest in food, and anything else that got in the way of making money. His lackadaisical dress, by now legend in Los Angeles, some considered further demonstration that he was above every convention. Others had to dress to be accepted. Arnie Sutler needed to impress no man.

Warren spoke first, "That's a moving story, Duffy," he said, then he turned to his father, "don't you think so, Dad?" Arnie paused, his mind reluctantly leaving his last memory of the comfortable Hilda.

"Very moving," Arnie said without enthusiasm.

Duffy looked at her father-in-law with a sudden sense of hopelessness.

"Did you ever think," she said, "that you might be so big and so powerful that you could lose sight of what you did to people like Nora Yates?"

Arnie's eyes rolled toward the ceiling. He looked at his son as if to say, "I told you about wearing the pants in the family," and turned back to his daughter-in-law. "Duffy," he said, "you must understand that the boosterism campaigns we run through our midwinter issue have been responsible for building this town, for surpassing San Francisco in the West, and in the future I predict we'll be third or fourth in the country. Now this kind of progress has its price. Certainly people are going to get hurt in the process; but consider the hundreds of thousands, yes even millions of people we've given a new life to. You don't eat chicken without wringing the chicken's neck."

Duffy started to speak but Arnie held up his hand, "No, no, just a minute," he said, "let me finish. It's a wonderful thing to love your fellow man in the abstract, but you don't want a town full of dead-beats, do you? You don't want the streets lined with starving beggars, like they are in India. That's why those people were kept out of Los Angeles. We oversold, I'll admit it. We oversold to the wrong sort of people, people who had nothing. There weren't enough jobs to go around here as it was. What would you have done, Duffy? Open the floodgates to everyone?"

Duffy seemed flustered. "Well," she said, "couldn't you have made that clear?"

"If you'll read the papers," he said, "we tried to make it clear. Unfortunately," he said, his eyes drifting from Duffy's face, until he stared out the window, aimlessly, "unfortunately, no one sees himself as a deadbeat or a grifter. But the depression brought tens of thousands of them, Duffy. We had no room, we hadn't the employment for them and we're very sorry it happened. It was a miscalculation."

Duffy looked at him, her eyes tight with resolution. "Well," she demanded, "what are we going to do to rectify the situation?"

Arnie snapped his head at her use of "we." Warren jumped in:

"Duffy's taking to using the plural, Dad. She doesn't mean anything by it."

Duffy eyed her husband as if to silence him from some embarrassing mistake.

"When I say 'we,'" Duffy said, "I mean *we*. We are all Sutlers now and we're *all* responsible for what happens in the Sutler paper. A woman just tried to kill me because I was a Sutler, and from now on I intend to say 'we.'"

Arnie closed his eyes hoping the apparition would die in the darkness. He took a deep breath, and he thought of Hilda waiting. He opened his eyes and looked at Duffy. "Duffy, what exactly do you want?"

"Nora and her mother worked here like slaves for room and board," she said. "Now her mother is gone. Give her a job."

Arnie closed his eyes again and nodded his head slowly trying to absorb the impact of this skirt, and he wondered what he would have done if his wife had ever talked to him like this. His wife, who actually *worked* on the paper. And now here he was listening to what seemed to him like an ultimatum from his son's wife in the visitor's room of this loony bin. He opened his eyes.

"You know, Duffy, I'm laying off people, times are a little hard now, we don't really have room for unskilled labor. There're many people we owe things to we aren't using, I don't see how...."

Duffy cut in impatiently, "Oh, you can get her some small job, anything."

Arnie gritted his teeth. He turned to his son Warren, "Can you use her?" he asked.

Warren looked at Duffy and then to his father, "I think we can find a space for her."

Duffy jumped up and clapped her hands and said, "Oh, thank you." And before he knew it Arnie felt he had been dismissed by a woman. It made him uneasy.

Duffy ran to find Nora in the kitchen to tell her her good news. But Nora took the breath away from her with her stare. "Aren't you pleased?" Duffy asked.

Nora wiped her hands on the tea towel and turned from the sink and the dishes she was washing. She put her hand on Duffy's hand and locked her eyes on Duffy's eyes.

"I could never work for them. You must understand, it's not that I don't appreciate what you've done, but I would starve to death before I would take a nickel from a Sutler."

"Over my dead body," Katherine had said when Warren told her Duffy would like to see the sisters at the sanitarium.

"Do it for me, Katherine," he pleaded.

"Sorry Warren, not this time," she had said.

Warren was forced to turn wily, and wily Warren turned to his father.

"Dad," he said, "Duffy is close to being cured."

"Glad to hear it," the patriarch of the *Tribune* said in his office.

"Duffy's doctor thinks it would help Duffy cope with her release if she could see your daughters at the sanitarium. I've asked. They refused me."

"They're impossible," Arnie agreed, shaking his head.

"Impossible for me," Warren agreed, "but not for you."

"Ah, I can't do a thing with them."

Warren looked impassively into his father's evading eyes.

"Well, Dad, I guess if we can't do this little bit for Duffy I'm going to have to devote all my energies to her cure. I'll have to resign, of course, but I don't doubt Katherine might like the job."

Arnie looked at his son, and his face fell into a grudging smile.

"Blackmail," he said nodding his approval. "We may make something of you yet."

He picked up the phone and got Katherine through the operator.

"Katherine, it's your old dad. Katherine, I want you to take Louisa and Amy out to the Shadyside Sanitarium to see your sister-in-law."

"Dad, we'd rather not."

"I've been to see her a dozen times. Everyone's been to see her but you."

"It's a free country, isn't it?"

The kid was getting too damn big for her britches, Arnie thought, reddening. "Listen, Katherine, listen to me good. You get your ass out there tomorrow, and take your sisters with you if you don't want to be cut off without a sou!"

He slammed down the phone, exhausted. The sound sent a pinging, ringing vibration through the room like the aftershock of an earthquake.

Katherine, Louisa and Amy sat in a row on Duffy's bed in the sanitarium, like pigeons in a shooting gallery. The wall behind them was pale green and as blank as their faces.

The sisters on the bed looked like they had been dressed by the same nanny. They all wore formfitting felt hats and breezy dresses of polka dots (Katherine), horizontal stripes (Louisa) and spreadwinged eagles (Amy).

There were fatty deposits on their bodies here and there, but not where you might hope to find them.

Their clothes were stylish; the girls were frumpy.

Their hemlines all fell to the same spot below the knees, but sitting on the bed forced them up over the knees. Katherine cleared her throat and pulled hers down. Amy left hers up. The air felt good on her thighs. Louisa tried to cross her legs to look casual, but she only sank further into the soft mattress and had to awkwardly abandon the maneuver.

Each sister seemed to dress for the approval of the other, careful not to be too provocative or too staid, too modern or too dated.

Duffy looked at Warren's sisters crimping their necks to look up at her, looking for the first time more frightened than she. Perhaps they thought she was a madwoman who would suddenly assault them, and they were keeping their defenses ready.

She thought of her sessions with Dr. Banks, that patient, loving, sympathetic ear, the repository for all her anxieties.

"WASP envy," the doctor called it, "though with only one Jewish grandmother you are really reaching for a stigma."

Doctor Banks had said so many revealing things, like: "But why do you rush to subscribe to the erroneous hypothesis that Jews are inferior, when all our studies show the opposite? And mixing the races produces more intelligent offspring."

Duffy had said that may well be so, but Dr. Banks didn't have to suffer the slurs of her schoolmates.

Dr. Banks sighed, shook her head and said, "If it weren't for the fuss that paperhanging corporal is kicking up in Germany, the one with the comic mustache, we might have forgotten about the Jews."

Duffy decided, with a twinge of amusement on her remarkably calm lips, that she would, in dealing with the terrible three, tell herself she was *all* Jewish, and so far superior she was doing them a favor bothering with them.

Duffy Durham Sutler, on the verge of release from a sanitarium for the mentally unstable, looked each of the fearsome WASPy sisters in the eye, as though she were training a bullet on each brain. She watched them fidget and take on a new insignificance.

"It was nice of you to come," Duffy began. "I know you don't want to be here." She chuckled, her mouth twitching. "But believe it or not, I didn't want to be here either." From her angle, close and above, Duffy saw only their heads shielding their comfortable matronly bodies.

"Warren thinks my problems stemmed from my fear of you three women. But I've come to a comforting conclusion that the trouble was not that you didn't approve of me, no…" she said, waving off the beginnings of a mild protest from Amy, who was trying to make her face and posture unthreatening. "No, the problem was mine. I thought for some reason I had to win your approval. I now realize what I think of people is more important than what they think of me."

"Well that's just wonderful, Duffy," Katherine said with an ungainly smile. Louisa cleared her throat and Amy elbowed her older sister into silence.

Duffy smiled down at her. She looked again into the eyes of the three sisters on the asylum bed, the close air in the small room compromising their dignities.

"I'm going to live my own life now. Warren will be the only member of your family I will defer to. I hope we can be civil. It will be up to you. If you can't," she said, leveling her confident staring eyes at her audience of three, "just stay out of my way."

The next day, Duffy Durham Sutler left the Shadyside Sanitarium for good.

# 56

Ford we are twelve; oh
make us one,
Like drops within the
Social River;
Oh, make us now
together run
As swiftly as thy shin-
ing Flivver.

—Aldous Huxley
*Brave New World*

1935

The April sun was high in the Hollywood sky as Yank Sutler strode down
Hollywood Boulevard from his office at
the corner of Highland to the Hotel
Taft.

Arnie "Yank" Sutler Junior was tall,
tan and tightly muscled and could have
played lady-killing roles in the pastiche
motion picture theaters he built along
Hollywood Boulevard. "Yank's mon-
strosities" he called his pagodas and
temples. "It's a crazy business so you
show the product in crazy palaces."

It was a teetotaling couple named
Wilcox, out of prohibitionist Kansas
City, who plunked down 18,000 hard-
earned American dollars, and bought
themselves 120 acres of sheep pasture
at the foot of the Cahuenga mountains,
and they named it for a ritzy Chicago
suburb.

Hollywood would, from that day
on, be considered derivative.

In 1903, when Hollywood was incor-
porated, Holy Harvey Wilcox banned

liquor, and saloons slammed shut as suddenly as coyote traps. An ordinance was adopted to forbid the driving of more than two thousand sheep down Prospect Street, the main street, now called Hollywood Boulevard.

It was moral rectitude that Harvey Wilcox brought with him when he bought that tract of land. They named a street after Holy Harvey, and Wilcox Avenue ran right through the center of town, slicing it in two like the sword of Deuteronomy, bringing terror and destruction to both the young man and the virgin....

In 1910, Hollywood was annexed to Los Angeles to be blessed by The Queen of Angels with the fecund waters of the Owens River. Los Angeles had become, thanks to General Olin and Arnie Sutler, the sole distributor thereof.

In 1911, Yank remodeled a defunct saloon at Sunset and Gower for a New York glove peddler to make movies.

There were 4,000 souls in Hollywood in 1911, but by 1930 the movies had increased the population sixty-fold to 235,000.

One was hard-pressed to find a person among them without aspirations to stardom.

In the early part of the century, Hollywood was just a quiet, moralistic town where Yank was housing the homeless. As the Industry grew, he built movie studios and movie theaters, banks, and later the audacious Hollywood Amphitheater.

Yank made so much money he had to create his own bank to protect it.

In 1921, the Hollywood Chamber of Commerce sent out a flier showing a mass of people, extending beyond the frame of the picture, with a caption, "Thousands have bucked the line on every call issued for a few movie extras." The bold headlines said:

DON'T TRY TO BREAK INTO THE MOVIES
IN HOLLYWOOD UNTIL YOU HAVE OBTAINED FULL FRANK
AND DEPENDABLE INFORMATION FROM THE
HOLLYWOOD CHAMBER OF COMMERCE
(HOLLYWOOD'S GREAT COMMUNITY ORGANIZATION)
(IT MAY SAVE DISAPPOINTMENTS)
OUT OF ONE HUNDRED THOUSAND PERSONS WHO STARTED
AT THE BOTTOM OF THE SCREEN'S LADDER OF FAME
ONLY FIVE REACH THE TOP

The antibooster campaign didn't work, the people kept coming like locusts on a plagued land. They came: the stage moms and their cute children with dimples a mile deep, star struck teenagers vowing to do *any*thing to make it, families with all their belongings on top of the flivver. The black plague couldn't keep them away.

Outsiders could sneer and call it "Tinsel Town," because the Christmas trees were tinfoil and there was scarcely any holly and precious little wood. It was the land of plastic smiles and porcelain teeth. But by 1935, the depths of the Depression, Hollywood had become a boom town with the film and its related industries.

One of Yank's monuments along Hollywood Boulevard was the Hotel Taft, twelve stories looming high in the sky, tallest building in town. He breezed now into the grand ballroom where the Rotary Club met each Thursday at noon. At the head of the rows of tables was the Rotary flag, the gold helm on the white silk, with the motto, "Service Above Self." The club had been organized a few years before by Yank and Jud Crown, publisher of the Hollywood *Breeze*.

Jud's father, Isaiah Crown, now eighty-four years old, tall, stately-looking, spare, white-haired, a sartorial gentleman, had come to hear his son speak.

After the pot roast, gravy, mashed potatoes, and canned peas, Yank rose from the head table to introduce the speaker.

Jud Crown stood up, a frail youth of thirty-seven, and smiled to acknowledge the applause of his fellow Rotarians. He made the obligatory opening remarks ("Mr. Chairman…"), and then said, "I would like to share a little story with you. It is about my father and me. He and my mother—may God truly rest her soul—lost seven children to miscarriage, stillbirth and infant death. After he was convinced they could not have children of their own, he came to visit the orphanage I called home.

"Our fondest dream there was to be adopted into a loving home. We thought we could tell, from the way they looked us over, the loving parents from the bums. Sometimes we were wrong—but everyone agreed Mr. Isaiah Crown was the catch of a lifetime. And we weren't wrong."

The crystal chandeliers overhead tinkled with the loud applause.

"We could *always* tell who the shoppers would pick among us. Always, until that day. For you see, I was a scrawny, sickly runt, and I had long since my first dozen or so rejections, given up hope. I still remember when our super came and told me Mr. Crown wanted me, I thought it was a bad joke on me. But then the super told me he tried to talk him out of it, saying I was sickly and the orphanage couldn't give out any guarantee how long I would live—and Mr.

Crown said, 'That's just what I want. We will love him and make him strong. He will be our own.'"

Jud turned to his father at the end of the head table.

"I just want to say, Dad, you've been the best father anyone could ever have—and I hope I will someday be worthy of your goodness."

Isaiah Crown took out his handkerchief and blew his nose, though that was not where the trouble was.

"Today, unemployment is well over twenty percent. People still find a few pennies for a newspaper, it's cheap entertainment. But they don't have the money to buy the advertisers' products, so advertisers have less money to spend in newspaper advertising; and the price of the paper barely pays for the newsprint without any printing on it."

Jud was no great orator. Though he had gone through Yale his voice was still as unaffected as the country boy he was.

"For the first time in over forty years, the *Tribune* has lost its circulation leadership to the *News*."

"As for me and my little Hollywood *Breeze*, I guess we aren't going to bring any of the giants to their knees. But we're happy doing what we like best: printing articles about our friends and neighbors, their birthday parties, their achievements, hopes and aspirations, and catering to the local merchants.

"For as the scrawny runt said as he was being picked on by the muscular bully. 'Why be biggest when you can be best?'"

Applause cut through thick cigar smoke.

The Rotarians routinely displayed their manhood by lighting up fat black cigars during speeches.

Afterwards, Yank and the Crowns stopped in the lounge and sat at a small table in the corner where they ordered ginger ales.

"Good speech, Jud," Yank said, "very nice indeed."

"Thanks Yank. But most of all, thanks for sending me that Nora Yates. She's the best secretary I've ever had. Easily the best thing you ever did for me."

"Duffy Sutler gets the credit," Yank conceded. "When the new Duffy wants something she doesn't give up until she has it."

"That's just the way Nora is."

While he attacked the bowl of peanuts in the center of the table, throwing them into his mouth one at a time, Yank said, "You ever regret giving up the *Tribune*, Mr. Crown?"

Isaiah Crown laughed an introspective laugh. "As I remember

it," he said, "I didn't so much give it up as have it taken away. I didn't think there was any way in the world Corporal Olin could raise that money that fast, but he did it, and it was way more than the paper was worth. I started another paper and had a lot left over. Now we have seven papers and they have one. The circulation of our seven is more than their one. Just barely, I'll admit," he smiled. "But that's something. We have more money than we could spend. Who could ask for anything more?"

Yank threw another peanut in his mouth, chewed it pensively and said, "I could."

"You could?" Jud said, surprised. "I thought you'd weathered the depression fairly well."

"Oh yes, I suppose I have. But that's not what I mean. I'm talking about the *Tribune*, and the hold my relatives have on it and on Southern California. I want you to help me take it away from them."

The two Crowns looked at him like at a good friend who was going to put the touch on you for a donation you didn't want to make.

Jud stared at Yank while Isaiah shook his head gently.

"I am afraid," Isaiah said, "that your dream is far beyond reach."

"Why so?"

"Because they've built an empire of such fantastic wealth. If everybody in Los Angeles County combined their wealth against them at this moment, everybody else might come out second-best."

"But times are tough," Yank said, "the paper is slipping. Their advertising is down. They've just spread themselves fairly thin with that new building which they had to scale down."

"Yes, but that's the paper," Jud said. "Arnie Sutler is still the richest man in Southern California. The paper is almost an insignificant part of his wealth."

"All I want is the paper."

Jud whistled softly through his thin lips and shook his head, "So," he said, "how would you go about this takeover?"

It was Yank's turn to laugh. "Well, certainly not alone," he said, "but there are many angles. One is to compete with the paper or other papers. To drive it down to the point that they have to sell it. Lord knows they've done that enough in their time." He turned to Isaiah Crown, "What do you think?" he said.

Isaiah turned his head once to each side. "As your immortal friend, Sam Goldwyn, says, in two words: Im possible."

"Why?"

"Oh, momentum for one. It's hard to stop a stone that big rolling downhill. Arnie's limitless wealth—his pride."

Yank frowned, "Okay," he said, "momentum can mean many things. You can be in an unstoppable plunge. Second, I know my father is a proud man, but I also know his passion to pile up more dollars than anyone else. He isn't going to sit by and watch his pile of dollars dwindle just to prop up the family paper. Third, there are existing papers that have fallen on harder times than the *Tribune*. I'm sure one or two of those could be picked up very reasonably. Seven papers may be a lucky number, but think about eight or nine. Another one or two in downtown Los Angeles. And I'm offering to put up the lion's share of the money. All I'm asking you for is the expertise."

Isaiah's eyes wandered over the smoke-filled room with the padded leather chairs with brass buttons running up and down the back edge. He heard the hum of the last Rotarians drifting back to reality.

Jud looked at his father and he saw a tired man taking great care to form his words.

"I never went into an area just to spite someone, or just to add a few dollars to my bank account. If I couldn't offer something positive, or fill a void, I stayed away. I'm afraid, Yank, I wouldn't be interested in your proposition."

Yank turned pale, "I'm sorry," he said. "It was just a crazy idea."

The memory exhausted Isaiah. His roaming eyes came back to settle on Yank's face, drawn with disappointment. "You know," he said, "you might have a surprising friend in Franklin. That great friend of the unwashed, may have, with his new tax laws, done you a tremendous service without knowing it."

"Oh?" Yank lifted his eyebrows.

"He's raised the top tax rate to seventy-five percent, he's added income tax to inheritance on top of the estate taxes, he's made it extremely difficult to pass wealth from one generation to another. We know, we've got the problem, and we are looking into ways around it. One of the ways, of course, is to go public, and if you go public the general public has a chance to buy shares in your company. And theoretically take it over."

"Are you going to go public?" Yank asked.

"I think we can get by another generation," he said. "We aren't that big yet. The *Tribune*, however, is just about there. Of course tax lawyers can come up with all kinds of gimmicks, and they may find a way to save the *Tribune* from Franklin D. Roosevelt's clutches."

Yank said, "Isn't he the one who said, 'Now I hate the income tax like we all hate the income tax, but if elected I promise to keep the income tax at the bah-rest minimum.'" Yank was using his broadest Harvard accent.

"That's the one," Isaiah laughed. "But while we can make fun of him, I don't think we can beat him. My suggestion to you, Yank, is to forget the wrongs your father has done you. He has diminished *his* soul, not yours. Give up the idea of taking the *Tribune* from the family."

"That's the one thing I can't do."

# 57

Skepticism is the chastity
of the intellect, and it is
shameful to surrender it too
soon or to the first comer.

—Santayana

Duffy was in her faded peach
quilted bathrobe, assembling the school
lunch at the kitchen sink in their small
home. Olin, her son, was growing like
Topsy and now at ten years, was almost
as tall as she was.

The bloom was back in Duffy's
cheeks. Her flesh had firmed and her
back had stiffened. Her head was at a
slight pixyish angle and she looked like a
woman who had survived adversity. But
it had left her with a scar on her psyche
that still tugged at the corners of her
mouth so she appeared everlastingly
touched with uncertainty.

The events put in Olin the gait of a
man five times his years, and built in his
physique sublime confidence. His face
with its broad cheeks, high forehead
and thin parsimonious lips looked more
confounded.

His sister, Carrie, sat across the
table from him picking at her cereal.
She was a pleasantly constructed child.
At twelve years old she already had the

pride of the Sutlers in her bones.

"What are you doing?" Olin snapped at his mother.

"I'm making your lunch."

"I told you I don't want you to make lunch."

"But you said lunch at school is terrible."

Carrie looked up. "Olin makes believe he doesn't have a mother," she said, "and if he brings a lunch, the other kids will think he does."

"Shut up, Carrie," Olin lashed out at her with his arm, she ducking the blow.

Duffy sighed, wiped her hands on the tea towel that was lumped on the counter, moved to her small desk, opened her purse and gave the boy ten cents for his lunch. Olin took the money without looking at his mother, thrust it in his pocket, stood up from the table and said, "Come on, Carrie, we'll be late."

Carrie got up, put her hand on her mother's arm and said, "I'll take the lunch."

Duffy handed her the paper bag while her memories tugged at the corners of her mouth. "Be good, children," and she followed them out the front door where she picked up the Los Angeles *Tribune*, bringing it inside to her kitchen desk.

There on the front page she saw the picture of Dad Sutler and her Warren. She didn't know how long she'd stared at that picture, pride creeping through her body like a plant burgeoning with blooms.

She felt Warren's warm lips on her cheek and his arms around her waist, before she heard him. "Ooo!" she said. "Congratulations."

Warren looked at the banner headline:

TRIBUNE OPENS MOST MODERN NEWS PLANT IN US

and underneath the picture, the caption:

Arnie Sutler Publisher and Warren Sutler General
Manager open doors to Tribune's new Headquarters

The picture is of father and son standing before the ornate brass doors of the new building. Arnie's face is thinner and drawing close to his teeth. His steel-rimmed glasses seem outsized on the shrinking skull.

Arnie's pants are baggy, Warren's cuffs break just perfectly over the shoe. The part on Warren's hair is creeping toward the middle of his head, and the hair is pasted to the skull with some manly smelling tonic.

Warren's hand is on the door. The letters above the handle spell "PUSH," but Warren's expression says it is going to be a long pull for the *Tribune*.

"General manager!" Duffy enthused. "I'm so proud of you."

"You get a lot of the credit, Duffy," he said. "It was you talked me into keeping the job."

Warren sat at the table. Duffy brought him his cornflakes and coffee, kissed him on the cheek, and then went to her desk to use the telephone.

Warren said, "Who are you calling, Duffy?"

"I'm gonna make my quota for the day," she said smiling. "Five more subscriptions before lunch."

Warren laughed. "There was a time," he said, "when you couldn't take your eyes off me until I left the house."

"Well, Los Angeles needs some culture," she explained. "It's good for the town, it's good for the paper. The paper ought to support the Symphony more."

"We'll look into it, Duffy," he said, blotting his mouth with a napkin.

Katherine was on the phone to her sister Louisa. "Have you seen the paper?"

"Yes, I was just about to call you."

"Duffy must have just wet her pants."

Louise tittered. "Paul could have been in it," she said.

"It's the monarch and the first-born male child."

Yank Sutler sat in his office on the third floor overlooking Hollywood Boulevard in the building he had constructed for his savings bank, Hollywood Savings and Loan Association. The building was six stories high but an insurance company paid a premium for the top floors. Yank took the cheaper space.

In the corner a Bentwood hat rack held his ten-gallon hat. The wall behind him was filled with pictures of himself at ribbon cutting ceremonies for his numerous housing tracts, motion picture theaters, office buildings, the Taft Hotel. Pictures of him with celebrities, movie stars, Hollywood producer Sam Goldwyn, politicians; citations loaded with whereases, and every tacky testimonial plaque devised by the mind of man.

Yank was not a man who needed these reminders to boost his ego, but he didn't want to hurt the feelings of anyone associated with any of these awards who might come to his office.

"Hello," he said. His secretary had told him Duffy was on the phone. He listened to her spiel.

"Oh Duffy, you are a wonderful saleswoman, but the Symphony? I just don't know. I fall asleep at those things."

"That's all right. We have a whole section of sleepers," she said. "Do you snore?"

"I don't think so."

"Good. I can get you closer then."

"Oh Duffy, you want people who will listen."

"Sure," she said, "but that's two rows, and I want a full house. I'll put you down for six so you can take five guests."

Yank sighed, "All right, Duffy, anything you say. You know, I was just about to call you."

They met for lunch at the Florentine Palace, halfway between Pasadena and Hollywood. Yank loved Italian food. The tablecloths were red, wine bottles hung from the ceiling in their rush baskets, sawdust was on the floor. The hostess was a fat Italian woman with dark hair and laughing eyes. They sat in a booth against the wall and Yank dropped his hat beside him. He ordered linguini with clam sauce for himself, and ravioli for Duffy.

Duffy said, setting down the menu, "I put you down for a thousand dollars, Yank. I hope you feel that is sufficient for your first contribution."

Yank whistled softly.

"Because if it isn't, I can easily raise it. I don't want to be presumptuous," she said, "but I don't want to minimize your ability to help."

"Well, Duffy," Yank said, "you sure are a persuasive woman. May I put off my answer until we've eaten? There're some things I'd like to ask you."

Duffy's eyes held a deep question.

"I'm curious about the ownership of the *Tribune*," he said.

"Well, General Olin put it in trust to his blood relatives. As each dies it moves down his direct line. The General controls the paper forever from the grave."

"How are the shares proportioned?"

"Well," Duffy said, "General Olin had three daughters. Each has one-third ownership. The publisher gets a share for every two years he serves—your dad now has ten percent. At his death or retirement his shares go back to the family and the new publisher starts over. Until he gets to ten percent."

"My father could be outvoted by his wife's sisters?"

"Oh sure. But they need each other and they know it."

"Is there a chance of your getting any of that stock?"

"The only way is if Warren dies before me."

Yank was chewing thoughtfully on a roll, nodding, trying to make all the pieces fit in his mind. "Can anybody," he paused, "sell his share?"

"Only to family shareholders," she said. "And if the family refuses to buy, then there is no sale."

Yank chomped on the roll and nodded his head. "Pretty clever," he said, "the old man was pretty clever."

"I don't think anyone ever disputed that," Duffy laughed. "Say Yank, what's all this about?"

"You see how he keeps them hopping," he rushed in, ignoring her question. "If they don't keep that paper going, their shares are worth nothing. Papers fold all the time, at least ten have closed up since the *Tribune* started, but the *Tribune* will always endure."

The entrées came and they ate in silence, broken only by Duffy's occasional small talk. While they were sipping coffee, Yank asked, "You have any idea what the percentages are now?"

"Why are you asking all this?"

Yank smiled, a smile that almost competed with Duffy's most open, what-me-devious? smile. "Just a trade: information, shall we say, for donation."

The conspiratorial wink put Duffy right at ease. She smiled back. "If it's big enough," she said.

"The General's daughters have thirty percent each; Phoebe has no children, Delia has two. When Delia dies, her children will each get a half of her share; when Phoebe dies, her shares go to her sisters; and when Mary Ellen dies, her children will divide Mary Ellen's shares."

"What are Delia's children like?" he asked.

"Well, the boy, Clyde," she said, "doesn't have any thought in the world of working, and the sister, Hilde, some say," Duffy shook her head sadly, "doesn't play with a full deck."

"So what happens in a case like that?"

"She votes her share," Duffy said, "unless they have to commit her. Then her shares revert to the others."

"Does anybody want to commit her?"

"Oh, maybe Paul, but I suspect in time he will understand the wisdom of letting Warren—and then Olin—be publisher."

"Duffy, you're an incorrigible optimist."

Duffy smiled, "Shall we make it two thousand?" she said. Yank laughed and wrote her the check.

Yank climbed the stairs of the brick boarding house on the corner of Wilcox and Yucca. Yank had not built it. He suspected roaches had. If not, they must have taken it over awfully cheaply.

The stairs were soft from dry rot and they groaned under Yank's feet in the darkness.

The door was open, and inside a mountainous man was parked behind a littered desk that the Salvation Army would reject. He had on a gravy-stained shirt that early in its career might have been white. Yank looked down at him from his six feet and tried to imagine what the man's features would look like if they had not been rendered indistinct by the fatty tissue. Intelligent, he decided. The man would look intelligent and sensitive. But now he just looked fat.

"Pardon me for not getting up," Max said. "My caloric intake has been recently curtailed, and it saps the bejesus out of my energy. You are?" he asked as though Yank had intruded on the sanctity of his thoughts.

"Yank Sutler. I spoke to you on the phone." He made no move to take off his hat.

"Oh yes," Max answered airily, "oh yes." He shifted his bulk in the chair like a man trying to squirm out of trouble. "What can I do for you?" he said, as if he didn't mean it.

Yank looked around the room, a dingy space, out of touch with order. The only concession to life enhancement were some faded color prints of birds on the floor leaning against the wall as though he had just moved in and didn't have time to hang them. "You've been recommended," Yank said and trailed off, as though there had to be some gross mistake.

A small smile curved one corner of Max's mouth.

"Honest, they said," Yank muttered, "reliable, competent, discreet, reticent."

"Hard to believe isn't it?" Max said, waving his hands at the decor.

"Low overhead, I guess."

"The lowest."

"Would you mind if I ask a few questions about your background?"

Max waved him into a chair with a broken back, across the desk.

Yank sat and the two men stared at each other in silence for a moment. "Education?" Yank asked.

"Undergraduate work at Yale. A Ph.D. in psychology from Harvard."

Yank's jaw tilted out of alignment. "What are you doing in this line of work?"

He let a ton of air escape his recumbent frame. "Backed into it, actually. I was working at one of the studios, and one of the owners asked me to do a little research on his partner, and his partner found out. He was a big-time embezzler, but overnight I became unemployable. Then I discovered that research into peoples' backgrounds was up my alley. I enjoyed it. The partner had a friend who wanted his wife followed. Another friend suspected his business partner of cooking the books. One thing led to another," Max shrugged his shoulders.

"I should call you Doctor," Yank said.

"I think that would be nice," Max purred, his bulbous cheeks relaxing in a grin.

"Can you be discreet?"

Max waved his hand at the room again and said, "I don't go to the papers and they don't come to me. How do you want me to help you?"

"Two things," Yank said. "One is a person named Hilde Sutler Bascomb, who has some sort of, shall we say, psychological deficiency. I would like to find out about her." Yank saw the fat man looking impassively at him over the desk and said, "Aren't you going to write this down?"

Max waved a hand at him, "You want secrecy you don't write things down."

Yank nodded.

"And second?"

"This one is perhaps a little more off the beaten path," Yank murmured.

Yank looked at Max's impatient frown. Yank had checked him as thoroughly as anyone could be checked. He had not come up with a wrong note. And yet, though he had been warned not to expect anything fancy, the seediness of this man went beyond anything Yank had imagined.

"Come now," Max pressed. "Surely there is some reason you are here instead of at the Pinkertons. Out with it man, my time is valuable."

Yank found something engaging in the man, so strange he was, but not devious, bizarre, but not deceptive. "All right," Yank said looking him in the eye, "you are familiar with the Los Angeles *Tribune*?"

The mountain shook with laughter as though in seismic disturbance.

"Yes of course, I'm sorry. I should like you to place someone there, or to buy someone who has access to news breaks, financial conditions, programs to increase advertising and circulation. Inside information. The reason for this—"

Max waved his arm hastily, "Silence," he cut in, "I don't want your reasons."

Doctor Max Underwood settled back in his chair like a collapsing circus tent. "What you are asking will not come cheap," he murmured, causing Yank to strain to hear him.

"I can pay," Yank said.

The deal was struck. Looking at Yank's hat, Max said, "I've never done business with a cowboy before."

As Yank walked back down the creaking, rotting staircase, he decided the fees of Doctor Max Underwood were reasonable. He did not realize that the good doctor added a twenty percent surcharge, for it was another old adage in this town that if there was one person you didn't mess with, it was Arnie Sutler.

# 58

1936

The fist fell on the desk like a
sledge hammer. The papers, paper clips
and paperweights on top took a frightful
jump.

Publisher Sutler's temper, never
too tempered, was deteriorating. While
General Olin was alive, he controlled it.
But the General had been dead for seventeen years.

"Don't tell me Mary Ellen's sisters
put you up to this," he shouted at his
son Paul as though Paul were standing
at the end of the noisy linotype room,
instead of right across Arnie's new
mahogany desk, watching the blood rise
in his father's neck. "I see the fine hand
of my do-nothing children here."

"No, Dad," Paul protested. "Aunt
Delia and Aunt Phoebe hold sixty percent of the stock. Can't you at least talk
to them?"

"No, dammit," Arnie kicked the
wastebasket under his desk, "they want to
use their stock to throw me out—let them
put you in charge. That's their option."

Arnie heard no more about it. The sisters were intimidated, but still curious about their drastically dwindling dividends.

To stem this sliding fortune, Warren Sutler tried a myriad of tricks to increase the advertising revenues for the Los Angeles *Tribune*. In the depth of the Depression he sent his advertising salesmen door to door to suggest homeowners take in boarders to help alleviate their financial strain. And hinting also ads in the *Tribune* might be the ideal vehicle to attract prospects. In cases where the people could not afford the cost of the advertising, for a higher fee the *Tribune* would wait for payment until the room was rented.

Warren dusted off one of Arnie's old techniques, streamlined and modernized it. He signed advertisers to exclusive contracts whereby if they ran ads in the *Tribune* without advertising in other local papers, the rate would be considerably lower and credit would be extended. As the merchants took advantage of the extension of credit, they would get deeper in debt to the *Tribune* and could not jeopardize their favorable rate by advertising in another paper.

In some cases it worked, but in many cases it only provided advertisers with free advertising, and the *Tribune* with a long list of uncollectible debts.

Robert Lawrence Quint's Los Angeles *News* was forging further ahead. The dividends to the Sutler family disappeared by mid-1936.

Then, only four days after Arnie's confrontation with his son Paul, Warren brought his father news which knocked him back in his chair, as though he had suddenly been hit by a Pierce Arrow sedan.

Phoebe Olin Fennel had died suddenly in her sleep. Since Phoebe was childless, Delia Olin Bascomb now had forty-five percent of the paper and Mary Ellen had forty-five percent.

The numbers were all right since Arnie and his wife had fifty-five percent control, but Mary Ellen was in failing health and Arnie suddenly found himself praying for her speedy recovery. It was easy to see one of his five children stirring up Delia to vote against him and that's all it would take. And he would not put it past Paul. Nor would he be surprised if one of his daughters turned on him.

He looked out the window, grabbed his gray felt fedora from the hat rack in the corner of his office and slammed it on his head, hurried out his door and startled his secretary by saying:

"I'm going home."

He stormed into his house, threw his hat down on the table in the parlor and stalked upstairs to the bedroom where his wife lay abed, looking ashen and gaunt, with her eyes closed. Seated at bedside was her nursemaid, the thin, severe spinster who always looked sour to Arnie, as though she disapproved of him.

Arnie dismissed her with a perfunctory wave, and suddenly all the women in his life seemed sour and disapproving.

He took the chair vacated by the nurse, leaned over, putting his flat hand on his knee, and tried to inculcate his voice with a gentleness that he didn't particularly feel at the moment.

"Mary Ellen," he said.

Her eyes half opened and looked at him as if to say, "What in the world are you doing here?"

Arnie looked down at his wife's wasted face. The chalky look of death was upon her. It repulsed him.

Arnie didn't realize it, but he looked like an old man himself. He wore a gold chain across his vest from pocket to buttonhole. There was a gold watch in his pocket. He had started wearing it as soon as General Olin was buried.

He had begun to look like a kindly old college professor with an Elk's tooth, rather than the shifty, used-car salesman of his earlier years.

"How are you?" he asked, faking feeling to cover frustration.

Her eyes seemed alive and alert as they searched his face for something that eluded her. Here was her husband in what appeared to be the middle of the day, it was still light outside, she could tell that, and he was asking her something. She sank back, thinking he was simply here for another signature for one of his deals.

"Did you ask how I was?" she said, her voice stronger than her body.

"Yes, dear," he said.

She smiled at his high-pitched voice, trying to sound matter-of-fact like he might speak to a dispensable subordinate.

"Well, I suppose I'm dying," Mary Ellen said in a low, unemotional voice, looking away from his face and out the window as though searching for some more auspicious solution.

"You can't die," he said.

Her frail body shook to the light, painful laughter.

"I very much fear," she said at last, "that my death is one thing that will not wait upon your convenience."

"Agh," he said, stomping to his feet and pacing the room in frustration and bitterness.

His wife watched him bemused; today she actually seemed to gain strength from his anger.

"You realize of course," he said, "the implications of your death?"

"Well," she said, pondering the question, "I suppose it's another job for the undertaker. I suppose it will cause you some inconvenience at the office as you may have to miss an hour or two for the funeral, not to mention another day perhaps for appearances. Other than that I can't imagine it would cause much more than a ripple in the flow of your exciting life."

She watched him go around her bed. The room was really quite small, smaller than General Olin's last bathroom. Arnie's peripatetic pacing had to be done in a confined space in the shape of an L around the side and the foot of the bed. Now he came to a halt at her headboard and looked down at her and said:

"Phoebe died, you know, a very untimely death. She might have been more thoughtful about it, for now half the stock less my meager portion is in your hands and the other half in Delia's hands. She'd never say 'no' to anyone; not a robber, not a rapist, should she be so fortunate."

"Arnie," Mary Ellen said from her bed, "please be charitable."

"You don't know what they're putting me through," he said. "Your children are sitting around like ghouls, just waiting for you to drop off to permanent dreamland so they can swoop down and pick up their shares and throw their weight around. I've half a mind to resign," he said. "Let them sink or swim."

"Why don't you?" she asked.

"Agh," he said, "you don't know what you're talking about."

She looked up at him. "How much money have you made, Arnie?"

His face twisted. "I don't know."

"You don't know?"

"No one that's made real money knows how much they have."

"You're seventy-three years old now, maybe you're entitled to stop killing yourself, see if there isn't something besides making money and knocking heads together that would give you some pleasure—before you wind up in my shoes."

He looked at her as though she had lost her senses. "What in the world are you talking about?"

"Well, what's it to you if the paper flounders? Maybe the best thing could happen would be to sell it to someone, divvy up the proceeds and let the kids spend it any way they want."

"I'm not a quitter."

Her eyes wandered from him and a smile settled on her lips.

"What are you smiling at, dammit?" he asked.

"Oh, I was just thinking my life was so meaningless to you, and now on the brink of death here you are begging for me to live."

"Very funny," he said.

"You know, I was thinking too about how this all began. Our life together was built on the death of your first wife. You weren't begging her to live, you were begging her to die and she obliged."

Arnie looked at her genuinely perplexed. She looked back and realized he had forgotten the arsenic and everything.

"This damn thing is going to give me an ulcer," he said. "It's eating me alive."

"Well," she sighed, looking around the small blandly-furnished room, her attention focusing now on a fly buzzing around the foot of the bed. She felt good talking to her husband this way. She was gaunt but she felt feisty and she never had had a docile bone in her body.

"You know what?" he interrupted, "I don't think you want to live."

"I suppose," she said, "there were times when I did want to die. One of them was when that pretty young secretary of yours came to me to tell me she was carrying your child. I don't know if you ever really understood the depth of that hurt."

"Oh, that's ancient history," he said, waving his hand.

Arnie's shoulders sagged and his head tilted downward as though the starch had softened in his spine.

"Listen," Arnie pleaded for her sympathy, as though their situations were reversed. "I earned ten percent of the shares in twenty years of work. When Delia dies, the forty-five percent pass to a queer musician and a girl not playing with a full deck. Your forty-five percent, when you die, pass *over* me and go directly to our children. Now sit back for a minute and consider what kind of newspaper we'd have if Delia's daughter and Paul and some of your hoity-toity daughters were pulling the strings.

"Let's face it, Mary Ellen, the only one of the litter who will ever amount to anything is Warren, and Warren is no killer. If they wanted to vote Warren out tomorrow, he'd smile and say, 'Fine, fine, anything you want.'

"You don't understand, Mary Ellen, how the paper is sinking. Strange things are happening—it's almost as though we were being sabotaged from within. Scoops that we get are lost to other papers almost the moment we get them. We searched the staff to see who's vulnerable to blackmail, but we haven't come up with anything."

Mary Ellen looked at him, her eyes half closed, "Vulnerable to blackmail?" she said. "Look no further than yourself."

"That's not funny, Mary Ellen. Our circulation is slipping, our advertising is down. We are losing money. I'm telling you if your children, who will outvote me four to one, take over this paper, it will be sudden death."

Arnie sat at the foot of her bed, dropped his face in his hands, and all his depressing prospects engulfed him. He cried like a baby, stirring his wife's deathbed.

Mary Ellen's eyes fluttered. She seemed to be weakening.

"You *can't* die," he pleaded, sobbing into his hands. "Don't *do* this to me!"

She closed her eyes. "Well, Arnie," she said, "what's done is done. But you know if I were able to live forever, if I had the choice, I don't think I'd take it."

She cast off burdensome breath, then suddenly her body quaked and Arnie heard the rattle, and Mary Ellen Olin Sutler passed to her eternal reward.

Arnie watched her die, then his sobbing stopped. He stood up and moved over to where her head lay lifeless on the pillow, a strange upward turn of self-satisfaction to her cold lips.

He put his hand in front of her quiet nostrils to make sure her breath had ceased.

He sucked in a quick bite of air as if to assure himself of his own mortality.

His lips tightened and he turned to the writing desk that had been her sole personal refuge in the waning years of their marriage.

The drawer was locked. He knew it would be. He couldn't be bothered to look for the key, it would be a sign of weakness. Wives didn't lock their husbands out of *any*place.

He brought up his shoe and crashed it into the drawer. The lock gave up without a fight. Arnie was pleased with himself, not so much at his strength as at the wisdom he had displayed in buying cheap furniture.

The leather-covered diary was inside. He chuckled at the lock that held its pages closed. He knew he could bite it open with his teeth.

Instead he used the letter opener he found in the broken drawer and lifted the lock.

So there it was in Mary Ellen's almost artistic hand—the title page:

Remembrances
by
Mary Ellen Olin Sutler

Arnie read only three and a half pages of Mary Ellen's opinionated prose. It was all he needed to confirm his suspicion that he was not presented in the most endearing light.

He took the book downstairs without looking back on his late wife.

He burned the pages one by one in the fireplace. After the orange glow died from the last page, he called the undertaker.

# 59

"Dirt's a funny thing,"
the boss said. "Come to
think of it, there ain't a
thing but dirt on this
green God's globe except
what's under water, and
that's dirt too. It's dirt
makes the grass grow. A
diamond ain't a thing in
the world but a piece of
dirt that got awful hot.
And God-a-mighty picked
up a handful of dirt and
blew on it and made you
and me and George Wash-
ington and mankind
blessed in faculty and
apprehension. It all
depends on what you do
with the dirt."

—Robert Penn Warren
*All the King's Men*

1939

He looked like one of those leading
men in a Hollywood spectacular, sitting
at his desk with memorabilia of his life
and character alive on the wall behind
him.

Yank was hunched over the work
like a long-distance athlete crouched for
the starting gun. He looked fit and lean
with his undisciplined hair, the color of
wet sand, misdirected on his tanned
head, the clear sky-blue eyes set like a
man who had the fate of nations on his
shoulders.

And why not? At fifty-one it was his
town, Hollywood. He had practically
built it with his bare hands, and had
become so wealthy he could afford to
devote the rest of his life and resources
to his lifelong goal.

On the top of his desk, next to the
pile of Sutler family dossiers, was a
bright yellow chart. It was a Sutler family tree, with the percentage ownership
of each heir to General Olin's *Tribune*
estate.

He had paid, in the last three and a half years, almost $100,000 to Max Underwood for his services and he never considered it anything but money well spent.

It had been twenty-nine years since the bomb exploded at the *Tribune*, killing Theresa and almost a score of other innocents.

When his father took her from him the brightest flame in his life was snuffed out.

In his imagination, she never left him. She lived in his house, had her own special chair at his table and in his living room. When they were alone, he consulted her about everything—"What do you think, Theresa?" "What would you do?" She rode with him in his car, accompanied him to dinner. It caused him a few embarrassing moments. Once he took her out to lunch at a sidewalk cafe on Sunset Boulevard. He sat at a table for two. She sat across from him. Three people came to use the next table and asked him if they could use the extra chair.

Though Yank had taken only a few bites of his sandwich, he rose with a courtly bow, pulling his chair out from under himself and setting it at their table.

In response to their curious glances he said, "I'm finished." And he paid the check and left.

With Theresa by his side.

Yank took a deep breath and winked at the empty chair across his desk.

The door opened, and his secretary stepped gingerly in.

Miss Henrietta Tober was an affable woman in her early enough thirties with a delightful nature and crooked teeth who never found a husband due to the male penchant for looks in preference to nature. She lived alone in an unkempt, inexpensive apartment building on Orange Avenue. It was walking distance to work.

On Saturday after work, she walked to C.C. Browns, which she called Buster Browns after the shoe, and had a hot fudge sundae —her weekly treat, with rich, snow-white ice cream, roasted almonds, a sliced banana and dark chocolate syrup served in a tiny warm pitcher. At night she wrote in the diary she never read. Sunday she spent in church and reading; she liked movies but rarely went.

She devoted her life to Yank and often thought how nice it might be to be married to him—but he never gave her an opening and she would not have dreamed of being so forward as to make the first move.

Yank looked up and said, "Yes, Miss Tober?"

"Mr. Sutler," she said, "the insurance company is on the line, you remember that thirty-five dollar claim I didn't want you to submit?"

"Yes."

"I told you they were going to cancel. Well they did."

Yank was looking at the biography on his desk of Amy Sutler Volkes subtitled by the capricious Max, "Or how to live beyond your income. Birds of a feather may flock together but they don't have to like each other."

Yank's eyes traveled to the line referring to Mr. Volkes. "He sells insurance, but not nearly enough to keep them in style. He would dearly love the *Tribune* account, but so far it has eluded him, largely, I suppose, because Arnie can't stand him. And after a cursory meeting with Mr. Volkes myself, I can't say I blame him."

"I think I'll pay a visit to Elbert and Amy. We'll get our insurance."

Yank fished on his table for the other biography. "Oh yes," he said, "Mr. Randaulph Parker Hines the Third, husband of Katherine Sutler Hines, nine percent," a smile crossed his lips, "is a banker. Make a luncheon date. The country club should appeal."

That year an insidious cancer struck Arnie Sutler, forcing him to turn the *Tribune* over to his son, Warren.

With it went his ten percent ownership. Warren would earn one-half of one percent for each year he served as publisher to a maximum of ten percent.

White pain flashed across the top of Arnie's head and seared his eye sockets. He prayed to the God he had not called upon in years, prayed fervently for relief.

He sat in his living room chair, threadbare now, Arnie the widower having no aptitude for housekeeping. He was wearing his gray overcoat and felt fedora. He had been on his way to the *Tribune*—a few steps out the door—when another of those dirty street ragamuffins handed him another letter. It hung loose now in his palsied right hand, down below the arm of his chair as it always did when he read one of these hateful notes. The pain shot up his trembling arm like a fast-burning fuse, to suddenly explode in his brain.

Arnie's hair was white and thinning, his once robust body was emaciated; his suits hung on him like Salvation Army hand-me-downs. The area around his graying lips was sunken to fill the void left when he lost his teeth, and the fake ones he had made at a discount were ill-fitting and hurt too much for him to wear.

He prayed again to a God he didn't believe in for a quick death in preference to the suffering—and the humiliation of these anonymous notes. This one read, "Murderer: The blood of innocents is on your hands. It will haunt you to your grave."

The others had been similar. After the fifth or sixth one, Arnie had put on his long wool overcoat and followed the young urchin who delivered it. He lead him only to a shack on Los Angeles Street, and when Arnie grabbed his arm the pain seared the old man's fingers and coursed through his body like a flame.

"Who gave you that note?"

"A stranger," the boy said.

Arnie's angry sunken eyes grasped for a hold on the boy when his hand failed him.

The boy spat on the old man's shoes and ran away laughing.

Bombs were being selectively detonated at Arnie's home.

One went off in the garage, opening a respectable hole in the south wall; another blew the lid off his garbage can right onto his neighbor's back porch. They were all carefully set and timed not to hurt anyone. But now Arnie was wishing he could step on one of the bombs as it went off. It would end his misery suddenly, and maybe make a martyr out of him and get back at the perpetrator.

He didn't like the cowardly choice of weapons one bit—or the allusion in the notes that the bombing of the *Tribune* Building in 1910 was his doing.

It had taken Harry, Yank's gardener, slightly over six months to get all the fuchsias placed. "Your house look like fuchsia farm," he told Yank. "Too many fuchsias," he said, shaking his head.

"You'll get used to them," Yank said.

The next day Yank got the reaction he was waiting for.

Delia Sutler Bascomb (forty-five percent—and known locally as Madame Fuchsia) was failing but valiant. As soon as Yank saw the chauffeur he hired for the occasion help the frail slip of a woman out of the Packard, he knew he had miscalculated.

For Yank had not realized how fragile Delia's health was. The only hope he clung to after spending a small fortune turning his home into a fuchsia showplace was the residual good will that might accrue to her children (twenty-two and a half percent each) as a result of his flattering attentions to her.

Yank greeted Delia with a hug, his nose atop her soft gray hair, then looked to the sky. "Perfect weather for few-ksee-ahs," he said, careful to use the authentic pronunciation.

"Oh my, Yank," her eyes sparkled, "you certainly must love fuchsias as much as I do."

"Oh, yes," he said. "I only wish I had your vast knowledge of them."

"Oh," she blushed. "You flatter me."

The next day, a Tuesday, he had lunch with Randaulph Parker Hines III. Yank took him to the Los Angeles Country Club and enjoyed his mouth-watering reaction to the celebrities from the Los Angeles business world.

"Mr. Hines," as all the tellers at the bank called him, was a man of respectable girth with outstanding sparkling teeth and saucery white eyes. He always dressed impeccably with pinstripes and silk foulards of muted hues. His posture would have made General Benjamin Raines Olin, his wife's grandfather, look like a slouch.

His head was unabashedly bald with only a half muff of mousy hair over each ear. Cognizant of his best features, Randaulph was not stingy about flashing his devilish teeth and his heavenly eyes wherever he went. He walked with a solemn gait into the dining room beside Yank.

"We keep the movie stars out," Yank opened offhandedly. "Not considered desirable." He smiled, but Randaulph nodded and easily outsmiled him, obviously in league with the restrictive forces.

After the meal had been served and the small talk dispensed with, Yank slipped into the subject.

"I've been thinking of moving my accounts, a matter of getting the service you want. These bankers often hire cheap help and they get what they pay for."

Randaulph Parker Hines III nodded in somber agreement. He had barely cleared his mouth of the well-done porterhouse steak when he said, "I'd be delighted to accommodate you."

"That's good of you. I used to have my own bank—sold it. More bother than it was worth in these times. Have you gotten any business from my father, your father-in-law?"

Randaulph the Third, frowned. "That's a sore subject."

Yank raised his hand to block the unpleasantness. "I'm not surprised. A man of your background should be on the board; why God, man, you're family."

"Yes," he agreed sadly, "Katherine and I have discussed it."

"Have you ever spoken to Arnie about it?"

Randaulph frowned. "Once. And...."

"And?"

"I left there feeling like dirt."

"Well," Yank sighed, "he won't live forever. Now about my accounts, would you find it personally helpful if I moved them? I mean would you be given some kind of credit?"

Randaulph the Third looked around the room as though trying to gauge his host's worth. "What," he cleared his throat, "just to get an idea of the nature of the deposits, I mean what would be the approximate range of the dollar amounts?"

"Oh," Yank said, tilting his chair back, "our operating accounts run anywhere from five to ten thousand into the millions."

Randaulph Parker Hines the Third was all eyes and teeth.

It was simpler with Amy and Elbert Volkes. Yank took Amy a yellow Baltimore oriole for her porcelain bird collection and Elbert wrote Yank's insurance. Over thirty-five million dollars worth.

Amy had filled out her frame with surfeited flesh as was the prerogative of one of her station. Her turkey-like body amazed her husband, who kept an eye out for replicable phenomena of his wife's former self. She wore rimless glasses to keep a better eye on her husband's roving eye.

Now dwarfed by his wife, Elbert was a short, lean fellow, who in his forties still had a boyish cast to his face, freckles and all. He moved with sudden, darting motions that made him appear startled by some threatening presence.

While Elbert poured the drinks afterwards and Amy cooed over her oriole, Yank asked, "You ever get any business from Amy's father?"

Elbert frowned, "Arnie Sutler doesn't like me," he said.

It took only one trip to Arnie's house when he was out, by a resourceful protégé of Max Underwood, to swap the pills.

Dum dum for morphine.

The doctor shook his head sympathetically when Arnie screamed at him, "These pills are worthless!"

"I'm sorry, Mr. Sutler," the young doctor said, "there is nothing stronger. If the disease has spread to that stage, I'm afraid there is nothing more we can do."

And so he suffered. He couldn't sleep, and eating was an unpleasant chore he forced on himself to keep alive, though with the unremitting pain, he wondered why he bothered.

Arnie virtually crawled to and from home. In the evening he ate a bite of soft cheese and bread, a glass of warm, often sour milk and dropped into his easy chair with his coat on in the hope that he would fall asleep, a hope that was seldom realized.

He grew short-tempered and unreasonable and alienated himself from his employees and children. The only regular visitor he had was Duffy.

She came twice a week to bring food and tidy up and care for him as a child, as she had been cared for at the sanitarium. He liked it when she called him "Dad." It was his last vestige of usefulness.

Dad had deteriorated into an androgynous being with his high voice crackling squeakier than before, and his long gray overcoat, like the security blanket of his childhood, hanging like a Victorian skirt about his calves.

He thought often of Lammy Sammy, his pet lamb who was taken from him by vicious fangs of the wolf, and how that was the last wolf he allowed to take advantage of him.

At first Arnie resented Duffy. She was a woman meddling in a man's world. She sat with him and tried to take his mind from his pain. She made him put in his teeth and eat the food she brought.

They spoke of the *Tribune* and Arnie's manifold investments. It was all he was interested in. Arnie thought his son Yank was behind the hate mail he was getting, but Duffy assured him Yank was not at all capable of such a thing.

"But some of those things I get," he croaked through his sore, cracking lips, the tender flesh burning as he spoke, "he's the only one who knew those things," he paused and looked out the window, "imagined them, I mean."

"No, Dad," she insisted, "there is never only one person who's heard rumors. Why, I heard every one of those things myself."

"You did?"

"I did. Now would you like me to get Yank here to reassure you?"

"Ah. He wouldn't come."

"I think he would."

Arnie's graying eyes clouded grayer, as though he were trying to conjure up an image from the elusive past.

"All right, but say it in such a way that I won't be begging. I won't beg."

# 60

...the bodily powers for laborious life are on the decline. He cannot bear the same quantity of fatigue as at an earlier period. He begins to earn less, and is less capable of enduring wind and weather; and in those more retired employments where much sight is required, he fails apace, and sees himself, like an old horse, beginning to be turned adrift.

—Thomas Paine
*The Rights of Man*

It angered Arnie to see Yank stride into this house for the first time in his life as though he owned it. And he always insisted on wearing that goddamned cowboy hat that Theresa gave him. He did it just to spite him, Arnie was sure.

"Hi, Dad."

The tightly-pursed lips, drawn inward in pain, did not move. With a curt nod Arnie Sutler indicated a chair across the barren room from him.

The living room smelled of decaying cheese rind that Duffy picked up on her visits. But picking them up did not cure the odor that had been absorbed by the furniture and carpet.

It felt closed-in, like some summer home being opened after a long, damp winter.

The old man sat with a blanket on his legs, and his hands trembled. The room was warm, but Arnie was cold.

The pile of threatening notes was in his lap, like a year's supply of soiled napkins. He wore his long oxford gray overcoat, which had soaked up spilled food and drink to saturation.

Some attributed Arnie's constant wearing of the coat to senility, but it was, rather, vanity. He wanted to look hale and robust, so he had to cover the cancer-ravaged flesh that sagged on his bones.

"It's been a long time." Yank tried again to thaw the chill in the dark chamber of his father's heart. Yank sat leaning back, his hands in his pockets.

Arnie resented his son's success and salubrious good looks. He spoke, the rasping tone of a mummified oracle.

"What do you want?" The white lips grew whiter, the knuckles on his bony hands flushed their color.

"Never were one to waste words, Dad."

"Don't call me Dad."

"Oh?" Yank raised his eyebrows. "Mother?"

Arnie flinched, as a child hiding his feelings.

They sat, father and son, squaring off, frightful adversaries in mute testimony to the hopelessness of expectations.

Speech should have been superfluous, the stares spoke.

"What do you want?" Arnie demanded, the thin fingers touching the edges of the letters in his lap.

"Oh, I want many things," Yank said, making himself comfortable in the chair, leaning way back and recrossing his legs. Arnie watched him through rheumy eyes. "I want my mother back, and my sister, and..." he paused, having more trouble delivering the name, "Theresa."

"I can't bring back the dead."

"No, you are better working it the other way around."

Arnie lurched forward, then gripped in a vise of pain, dropped back, "You...." he choked.

"No need to get worked up, Dad," he used the noun again with a special satisfaction. "Just remember, you asked me to come here."

"Yes." Arnie thrust the pile of letters at him and asked the question as he had rehearsed it. "Are you responsible for these?"

Yank had to stand and take two steps toward him, then reach out and take the papers. He returned to his chair and sat leisurely, paging through them with exaggerated interest.

"Well?" his father demanded.

Yank took his time and perused the stack again, "I can't say I don't share some of these sentiments, but that's not my writing."

"Oh, don't play coy with me. The fantasies in there are yours, and yours alone. Admit it."

"Why?"

"Clear your conscience."

Yank burst out laughing, "*My* conscience?" he said, "oh, my..."

"*What* do you want?" There it was again, the question, like a recapitulation in a Mahler death symphony.

Yank glared at his father, only a painful whisper of the feared and hated man he once was, and a twinge of sympathy nudged him. Their stares didn't waver.

"My wants are simple," Yank said, rising to full height to drop the stack of notes back in his father's lap. He returned to his chair and sank in with an elaborate slouch. "I want you to relinquish control of the *Tribune*."

A strangled groan escaped Arnie's gut, "I have, don't you read the papers?"

"No, I mean *sell* the paper, *give* it away, atone for all the crimes you committed to keep the paper, by giving it up."

"Stupidity," Arnie muttered, turning his face to avert his son's eyes. And then sucking in air to tighten the reins on his temper he said, "You don't know anything about it. This depressed economy has taken its toll. I've sunk a lot of my own money into it, money I have no hope of seeing in my lifetime. Another million and a half is due next year. I don't know where it's coming from."

Yank let him wind down, and when he was sure his father had finished he said, "Save it, Dad. Let's not kid ourselves about a debt of a million or two. I know what you have. The airline, the banks, the miles and miles of land from here to Mexico to Arizona and back, the title company, the mines—gold, copper and silver—the forests and hotels. I could go on all day. You might not live to the end of the recitation of your holdings. How many boards of directors are you on? We lost count around sixteen. The water coming to town alone made you over twenty million. What's it all add up to, Dad? Eighty, a hundred million? So you have a million and a half due. It isn't exactly going to bring it all down on you."

"That's nothing to do with the paper." The father looked in disdain at his estranged son. "You were talking about the paper."

"All right, let's talk about the paper. So you slipped to second place, and so there is a depression. I know your advertising rates, and I can count."

Arnie turned his face in disgust and tried to wave him away with his hand, as though with the gesture that pained him physically he could block some of the mental anguish. "Did you also count the hundreds of people who haven't paid for their ads?"

Yank paused and began again slowly, *sotto voce*: "Then, if things are as bad as you say, no one should mind your giving up the paper."

"Oh, don't talk so foolish. Where would we find a buyer in this economy?"

"I'll buy it," Yank said blankly, yet with a certain force that pounded the words into his father's heart.

Without thinking Arnie said, "Now why would you do...?" then suddenly he understood, and he stopped short, the words catching in his throat like some surprising bone. "Oh," he said. "Oh."

"Sell, Dad. Relieve your conscience," Yank offered in a quiet voice.

Arnie balled his bony fists. "The fanciful acts you accuse me of, with no proof whatever, are so far in the past that I can't even remember them. The statutes have run."

"There's no statute of limitation on murder."

"What do you know of murder?" Arnie snapped suddenly like a man in ruddy health. "Have you ever held the fate of thousands of people in your hands? Workers, investors, managers, pressmen, linotypers, reporters, editors? You speak of an isolated life or two. I held in my hands the fate of thousands. I still do. You are harping on ancient history. You have carried your hate over a generation. Whatever deeds I may have done inadvertently, are long in the forgotten past. It is you who perpetuate evil with your senseless, irrational hate."

"Very nicely done, Dad, but a little off the path. I have the goods on you. Protest all you will, I will have the paper."

Arnie groaned. "The *Tribune* is in the blood. You can no more separate the Olins and Sutlers from the paper than you can fly to the moon."

"I *am* a Sutler."

"Yes, and I don't deny in many ways more suited than your brothers for the job. But you have no issue, and you're not an Olin. The *Tribune* is a family institution that must live, my father-in-law saw to that. I resented it, but now in my dotage I appreciate it, *and* the Olins."

"And the blood is on your hands."

Arnie fixed him with his weak, anemic eyes, "You've shown your hand," he said, "I'm grateful for that. You know," he said, patting the pile of letters on his lap, "two can play this game as well as one."

"Ah." Yank stood and leaned over his wizened father and fixed his eyes on those colorless eyes. "Just try something, and I may be able to pick up the paper real cheap."

"Get out of here," Arnie shouted, a high, painful croak.

Yank straightened, snapped his hat brim in a curt nod. "As you wish, Dad."

"And *don't* call me Dad."

# 61

After Yank left, Arnie reached for
the phone and called Warren.

"Warren," he croaked, the phone
trembling in his hand.

"Yes, Dad."

"I want you to get him."

"Get who, Dad?"

"Dammit," he exploded, didn't
Warren know who he had just spent the
most unpleasant hour in his life with?
Duffy had arranged it for God's sakes.
"Yank!"

"Yank?"

"I want you to get him and good so
we won't have any more trouble. Do
you understand?"

"Not really," Warren said to the
dead phone. His father wasn't used to
waiting for answers. His word had always
been law.

But Arnie hadn't reckoned with the
new generation. Warren thought he
must have wanted Yank for some project. "Get" to Warren did not connote
"kill."

Yank, too, used the phone when he got back to his office.

"Max," he said, to the detective who had been serving him exclusively for almost four years, "he didn't tumble, we are blown. Turn to plan B if you please."

Arnie sat in his chair with the filthy blanket over his frail legs and thought, long and hard, before he got up and felt the pain shoot from his feet right up his spine where it crashed through his skull.

He went to the telephone and called Stephen O'Shaunessy, his personal attorney from O'Shaunessy and Maxwell.

The lawyer cancelled three appointments and left another client in his office and drove immediately to Arnie Sutler's simple home in a fading area of Los Angeles.

Arnie waved him briskly to a seat, did not thank him for coming so promptly, and told him what he wanted done.

O'Shaunessy smiled. The telephone would have sufficed but Arnie hadn't changed, he still liked personal attention.

Stephen O'Shaunessy was a tall, spare man, not unlike Arnie's last visitor, and the annoying resemblance to Yank grated on Arnie. The lawyer's hair was more ruly, he didn't wear that ridiculous hat, but his eyes were just as pale blue—and of course he was just as tenacious. That's what he liked about O'Shaunessy. It was comforting to have the tenacity on his side this time.

Grandfather O'Shaunessy had been a prospector in the gold rush, a man who did well enough to drink it up along with the best of them. Depending on whether or not you liked O'Shaunessy, his grandmother was a dance hall hostess or a prostitute.

Stephen's father was a man of many trades, who began the practice of law in his fortieth year. By the time he was fifty, he was on his own and his son Stephen joined him in practice in Los Angeles. A lot of barroom brawl clients to begin, a few pickpockets, a smattering of injury work.

Now they were lawyers to the rich and famous. Stephen O'Shaunessy had a knack for turning up where the money was. And he was a semi-gracious bluff; a wonderful warm combination of obsequiousness and camaraderie that greased the skids to high society.

"I don't like lawyers," Arnie said every time they met, as though he expected preferential treatment because he was condescending to associate with a lawyer. "You know America has too damn many lawyers. No other country in the world has anywhere near the per capita lawyers we have."

"I wonder why that is?" O'Shaunessy mused.

"Because we have a society that's built on paranoia."

"And how did we become that way, from reading the newspapers?"

Arnie was not amused. He was scarcely ever amused anymore. "You come here to do business or to run up my bill while you talk stupid? I need a Will, I'm dying."

"Oh, you're going to be around to gripe for years to come, Sutler, getting on everyone's nerves. You may look like the devil, but I don't think God is ready to take you on just yet. After all He's not a young man anymore."

"Oh," Arnie Sutler said waving his palsied hand at him, "I don't want any of your insincere sympathy." O'Shaunessy allowed a tight smile.

"Can it be done?" Arnie asked, after he told the lawyer what he wanted to accomplish.

"Suppose you get up a trust of your own, the income of which shall be used for the benefit of the *Tribune* Corporation just so long as the conditions you set down prevail. You can keep it in the right side of the family forever."

"Unless some communist Supreme Court says otherwise...."

"Always that chance, I suppose. Then if the company ever goes public you can stipulate in that event to divide a predetermined portion of your income to buying shares. So, if, as you say, your black sheep son Yank is planning a buyout, you could practically be assured of forestalling him from any meaningful inroads due to the size of your assets as compared to his."

"But he could get other investors. He wouldn't have to do it alone."

"That's true," O'Shaunessy agreed, "but I have a fair idea of your holdings, and I don't think you should worry too much, Arnie. You could," he added, "go public now. You may be at the point of no return, where your heirs can't raise enough cash to satisfy His Majesty's tax gatherers."

"Could I provide for that?"

"Yes, by stipulating which assets are to be sold to pay the taxes." O'Shaunessy sighed. "However, the value of your personal assets are increasing at a rate that far outstrips the cash available to pay the income and inheritance tax on your demise."

Suddenly Arnie seemed to go soft before O'Shaunessy's eyes. "You think there will be any tears at my funeral?"

O'Shaunessy, surprised at first, considered the question. "Oh, I don't suppose a hell of a lot. Mary Ellen probably would have come through, but she's gone."

Arnie nodded his agreement. "Quite a few happy to be rid of me I suppose."

"I suppose," O'Shaunessy nodded. "I'll be thinking about my fee, of course."

"Well, that's one thing I should take comfort in, O'Shaunessy."

"What?"

"You never have pulled any punches with me."

"What good would it do?"

"Not much. Well...draw it up and make it airtight, and don't dawdle. I'm not feeling long for this world."

It was a strange wind that blew through the City of the Angels that morning of all mornings that Arnie Sutler picked to be taken to the office.

The wind had a bite to it. The temperature was forty degrees, bitter cold for Southern Californians, and the wind played havoc with the women's skirts, flopping them hither and yon, immodestly.

Arnie had seen the hemlines rise in his lifetime. But, he was discovering while the hems rose with his age, his capacity for appreciation fell.

Duffy picked up Arnie.

She laughed as she eased the car in gear. "I wish you would let me buy you a new overcoat," she said.

"Why? This coat is perfectly good. In fact I'm thinking about leaving it to Warren."

The trip was painful. Arnie's inflamed joints cut him with every step. He eased the pain by leaning on Duffy as they walked across the round reception area into the elevator.

When he got to the office, he was surprised to see Paul and Natalie waiting there, as well as Katherine, Louisa and Amy. None of them seemed too comfortable; all were trying their best not to appear as vultures, hungry to pick the bones clean of Arnie's undernourished meat.

The sparse room was a tomb, devoid of any personality, just as his home was. Arnie took inventory of his issue.

He decided the best-looking of the girls were married to his sons. Natalie was a stunner. Arnie would have gone for her in his day. And Duffy, though hardly sexy, with the new bloom in her cheeks easily surpassed her sisters-in-law who suffered from the pallid com-

plexions of those who felt a birthright to superiority. Duffy was solid-
ifying in a nice way.

Paul's lean face had an expectant pucker about it as though he
had secret knowledge of a pot of gold behind some rainbow.

Warren was the only one in the room at ease with himself and
his relatives.

Paul looked like a dapper clothing salesman who could have
been at home in Bullocks Wilshire. Warren might have been the
head librarian at the main downtown branch. The two architectural
monuments had much in common. Bullocks Wilshire had the taller,
more flighty spire, while the library's tower was squat and more
down-to-earth.

Both Sutlers were lean, handsome men of unthreatening intellects. You wouldn't call on them to recommend a good book or to
solve a mind-wrenching dilemma—but you might solicit their opinion
on the guest list for a social function or the favorite in a football game.

Paul spoke up, his left cheek twitching. "Everybody was so
happy you were coming in, they wanted to be here to see you."

"That's a load of crap!" the old man grumbled. "It's the smell of
death puts that glimmer in your eye."

"Dad!" his daughters protested.

"We thought," Paul broke the awkward silence, "you might want
to talk to us all, give us some directives for the future."

"Oh," Arnie grunted, "a farewell admonition to the troops like
that pompous ass, General Olin. Well you won't get any of that self-
serving claptrap from me. The business is yours, you run it."

And here he did the "Dance of the Marionette," as he called it,
painfully strutting about like the peacock he considered the General,
his predecessor to be. He paused mid-goose-step as a thought hit him.
"I saw a reporter refer to him as crusty! It's very flattering. Use it."

Paul cleared his throat. "How shall we refer to you?"

Arnie thought a moment. "Oh, 'dynamic' would be good." He
frowned. "They will probably say I was ruthless." He paused to struggle for breath. "I am ashamed to admit I have been giving my
mortality some thought. That's why I'm here."

Arnie took a key from his pocket. Fighting to control the key in
his shaking, bony fingers he unlocked his desk drawers. "I've come to
clean out my desk." He was looking quickly through the accordion
file pockets in his drawers, "Don't want these falling into the wrong
hands."

"Oh, Dad, we'd see to that," Duffy said. He looked over at her, not able to mask his admiration for her guts or his resentment at her "butting in."

"I'll feel better seeing to it myself." He called in his secretary and asked for a number of files by name, and at the sound of familiar names, the sisters and brothers looked at each other: "Mayor Shaw, the Richmond bombing, Chief Davis, Owens Valley."

Even Arnie's secretary bespoke the decline of his powers. After an unrelieved string of buxom young women, "Miss Pruneface," as Paul called her, was not a woman to cause a wife a moment's pause.

When the secretary retreated to bring the files, Arnie looked at the gathered clan over his thick steel-rimmed glasses. "You come for advice? Let me give you some. Don't ever allow any biographies or exposés. Don't cooperate with any reporters who want to do a story about you or the paper. No histories. The predators will crucify you." He allowed himself a dry, deathless chuckle. "I should know."

When the secretary returned with the pile of files, Arnie undid the elastic band that held each one closed, peered inside, rifled the papers; then, laying it aside he repeated the process with the next one. When he was finished he said, "Warren, help me carry these to the incinerator."

"We can do that for you, Dad," Paul offered too eagerly.

Arnie shook his head once, a curt, deadly cutting action. "Some things you don't delegate."

O'Shaunessy had said there were many ornery years left in Arnie Sutler. Three and a half to be exact. And Arnie's death was not to be quiet in his sleep, but a prolonged searing pain that tore through his body like terrifying lightning that struck his nervous system and clung to him with an intensity that rendered him insensitive to everything but the pain.

As the end came like a silent enemy bearing coveted gifts, the last live cell of Arnie's brain took him back to his childhood in Vermont.

He remembered the cool night when he stole from his bed to have a romp with his pet lamb.

"Lammy Sammy," he croaked aloud, and smiled his last smile.

"I'm satisfied," he thought, "satisfied I sided with the wolves."

Perhaps it was all preordained.

In one of Arnie's last lucid moments, between bouts of all-consuming pain, he thought of one of the petty deceptions of his career. Inexplicably, it was when a reporter was doing a profile of him for the house organ, the news magazine for *Tribune* employees, others called it a puff piece. The reporter asked Arnie what he would have dreamed of being other than a newspaper man, and he had answered, almost without thinking, "A statesman. A man who would bring a business acumen to the business of government where too often we are handed lawyers and college professors and petty politicians made good, none of whom know the first thing about running the nation's biggest business."

"A teacher too," Arnie had said. He had allowed as though he might be a teacher, to pass his wisdom on to other generations, the image of the benign and patient man, altruistic to the marrow of his bones. This was even more outlandish than his first canard.

Arnie had lied, and why should it plague him now when the claws of the beast were tightening on his brittle bones and the fires of hell were searing his flesh? For now in his torment and terror he had a glimpse of his secret desire, and the comely young women were lying in long rows waiting for his examination. There were seventeen of them. He had forgotten a few, and he could no longer remember all their names. But he could still picture them all, in the examining room of Doctor Arnie Sutler, gynecologist.

# 62

But we shall always find it hard to love the man who darkened the human soul with the most absurd and blasphemous conception of God in all the long and honored history of nonsense.

—Will Durant on
John Calvin
*The Reformation*

1943

"Arnie Sutler is Dead" was the page one heading in the Los Angeles *Tribune*. Just as winter was surrendering to spring, Arnie surrendered gratefully to the Reaper.

And when he was gone he was scantily mourned by the working press, the people who set and printed his obituary: the printers, the compositors, the linotypers. For it was never said that the ink of the printer ran in his veins.

Ice water, perhaps; not ink.

He had lived too long to have many cronies pass his casket, and there weren't many discernible tears. Duffy shed a few, but her husband always said Duffy could be counted on to cry anywhere, even at a football game.

Arnie's daughters devoted the funeral ceremony to a calculating of the worth of their inheritance.

His grandchildren were bored.

Paul and Natalie were mentally conniving to wedge Paul into the publisher's chair between Warren and his son Olin.

Olin was speculating on the relative merits of two surfboards, and how much he could get the vendor down in his price.

Attorney O'Shaunessy, as he promised, was thinking about his fee.

And Yank was speculating on the wisest approach to bring it all down.

After his father's funeral, Yank drove up to Max Underwood's cottage in the foothills of Santa Monica. When no one answered the door, he walked around the house and let himself into the cage in back. It was swarming with parakeets, parrots, canaries, cockatoos, and numerous other species Yank couldn't name.

Max was holding a parakeet and inspecting the underside of its wing, another greenish bird was on his shoulder pecking at his Ralph Waldo Emerson beard.

"Birds, birds, birds," Yank groaned, waving his arms about in an effort to keep them from roosting on his shoulders. "How do you ever have time to do your work?"

"Oh, I'm always working," Max said. "Out here with the birds I'm thinking. I talk to them; some of them talk back, though I don't claim they say anything profound, at least they're a presence. And when all is said and done, when people converse, how much listening is going on? Here there is no pretense of listening."

Max took his time about abandoning his preening of the birds, while Yank shifted his weight from one foot to the other.

"Are we closer?" Yank asked.

Max set the last bird on a bush limb and looked Yank in the eye. Yank saw the eyes were like a beagle's, drooping and filmy.

Max shook his head. "I'm afraid," he sighed, with a loss of air that made him seem, momentarily, a thin man, "we've lost quite a bit of ground."

Yank's cheeks twitched.

Max wiped his hands on the side of his pants and gestured toward the house with his head.

Inside, the room looked like it had been transferred intact from his ratty apartment.

"Have a seat," Max said, pointing to a badly-stained, off-yellow wing chair with a pattern of cabbage roses. The item, Yank knew, was one of the few pieces that Max's former wife left behind when she picked the place clean. It elevated Yank's opinion of her taste.

Yank sat in the chair stiffly as if to avoid contact with some contagious disease.

Max disappeared into the kitchen, and returned with a plate of cheese, crackers, fruit and cold meats which he put on the coffee table in front of a blue crushed velvet couch which survived several wars, with honorable scars.

"Want some?" Max said with a mouth full of beef tongue.

Yank waved him off. Max ate like a vacuum cleaner, while Yank fidgeted.

"What did you find out?" Yank pressed.

Max waved a cracker piled with Cheddar at him. "Plenty," he said, swallowing. "Ain't good."

Max sank back in the crushed velvet couch while Yank sat forward on the cabbage roses. "Arnie couldn't buy control of the paper for his heirs—General Olin's trust saw to that. So when times got rough, he loaned the Trib millions to keep it floating. That attorney, O'Shaunessy, set up a trust around those loans, with Arnie's kids the beneficiaries."

"That still doesn't give them ownership."

"Right you are. However, suppose they default? Would anyone object to giving ownership shares for forgiving loans? If the option is closing the paper? After all, Olin said they could sell within the family."

Yank groaned softly.

"It was O'Shaunessy's idea to increase the hold Arnie's descendants had on the paper. It would give them more financial clout, especially if the paper had trouble paying the loans off, which Arnie, at the time of his death, had every right to expect it would."

Yank sank back in the greasy chair. Why should he be frightened of a little disease when the black plague was upon him?

"What now?"

"Ironically," Max said, popping a hunk of bologna in his mouth, "you should pray that Warren becomes so successful and makes the *Tribune* so big that they have to go public. At this point I don't see another hope."


"It's a slap in the face," Paul Sutler said to his wife Natalie. "A real slap in the face—that's what it is."

It was barely past three in the afternoon, and he usually left work at the stroke of five, but as he told Natalie at her apricot-colored dressing table, he couldn't stay there another minute, it was all too humiliating.

Natalie was winning the tacit battle with Duffy for the most grandiose home. Paul had learned the magic of mortgaging, exaggerating his responsibilities at the *Tribune.*

For her part, Duffy thought it unpatriotic to spend on personal luxuries during the war, so Paul and Natalie forged ahead without serious opposition.

Natalie examined her nails—the flashy red polish gleaming at her as the bloody nails of some preeminent jungle predator. It was not that she didn't share his anger, it was just that at the moment her fingernails seemed more important.

At thirty-four, Natalie Sutler, nee Popovich, was a handsome woman with dark, mysterious eyes and sensuous hair. Of Eastern European extraction, she would be as far as anyone in the family would get from White Anglo-Saxon Protestantism.

Her body was tightly compacted through diet and exercise, and it was a point of pride with her that she could still fit into her high school dresses (though she would never wear anything that old).

Paul was pacing and pouting.

"'I've been doing so much for the paper,' Duffy says, without a *trace* of modesty, 'that Dad and I decided I might as well go on the payroll and move into the office next to his.' Well," Paul fumed, "I was supposed to have that office. It was all agreed. And Arnie not cold in his grave yet, it's a perfect disgrace. He couldn't stand the meddling bitch."

"As who can?" Natalie made her first contribution, the blood-colored fingernails having passed muster. "So what are you going to do about it?" she asked with that unmasked sarcasm that drove him crazy.

"Do about it? I've screamed bloody murder."

"Was it effective?" Her eyebrows raised a millimeter.

"Dammit, Natalie, don't take that ridiculing tone with me." He looked down at the table full of bottles of lotions and potions, creams and polishes, all serving to gloss over reality.

"Well, what did he say?"

"You know Warren, his Duffy can do no wrong. Ever since she got out of the nut house he's been a pussycat to her. He took me aside and said I was still second in command and she was only executive assistant to the publisher and the office next to his wasn't symbolic at all, it was only a convenience since they would be working so close."

"Hmm," she said looking over the vast rows of jars and settling on one, the contents of which she applied to her hands, rubbing them thoughtfully. "You know what I think?"

"What?"

"I think we are in big trouble."

Paul stalked about his wife's dressing area like a caged lion frustrated at his inability to strike back.

"And, I didn't tell you the clincher."

Natalie looked at herself in the mirror, "Oh, what's that?"

"She's got them to rig up an apartment right there in the building so she can stand twenty-four hour guard. Oh, she says it's to save gas for the war effort, but I don't swallow that for a minute. She wants to know everything that goes on. People are already saying she is the real brains of the outfit, and the one who runs the paper anyway, might just as well *be* there, they say."

"Well, we're going to see them tonight," she said. "Maybe I'll talk to Warren."

"Oh my gosh," Paul said, "I completely forgot," he frowned, "I don't think I want to face them, thank you. I may stay home."

Ordinarily, Warren and Duffy were not in the same social circles as Paul and his sisters. Warren had helped form the International Affairs Club downtown and Duffy had her Symphony events, and was not a bridge player or ladies' luncheon enthusiast. When she went to lunch with someone it was to raise money; and Warren's only social interest was in aiding the paper. Cocktail parties struck him as frivolous.

But tonight was a *Tribune* testimonial cocktail party honoring the boys in uniform, and no one would miss it.

They were driving in their Buick on gasoline rationing stamps Paul bought on the black market. Paul was glum. "I need this like a hole in the head," he said.

"Oh," Natalie tried to reassure him, "a little flag-waving never hurt anyone."

"Yeah, but I get so sick of listening to those sanctimonious bitches like Duffy drool over the boys in uniform."

"Well, try not to be so sensitive about not being in uniform."

When Adolf Schicklgruber, a.k.a. Hitler, a former paperhanger and corporal in the Bavarian Army, started to roll his Krupp tanks all over the place to secure *Lebensraum* for his master race; and after Hirohito, Tojo and their comrades bombed the bejesus out of Pearl Harbor so we wouldn't meddle with their economic imperialism, Warren was the first to line up at the induction center. (The *Tribune* cameraman, camera in hand, was second.) But Warren was soon (some thought too easily) convinced his contribution to the war effort would be much more effective as the head of one of the nation's leading newspapers.

He was, after all, over forty, and it had been a longstanding tenet of war that the young should fight it.

When Natalie and Paul arrived, the party was well underway. Paul cringed as he saw Duffy sashay toward them. There was an oversized banner on the far wall that said "The Tribune loves its servicemen." It would appear in the paper the following morning with a soldier, sailor, a marine, Duffy, all smiles, and an unsmiling young lad in an army uniform that no one seemed to know. Max Underwood had sent him; the lad had a remarkable memory.

While Duffy was greeting them, Natalie looked over her shoulder to find Warren, and Paul tried to get away. "It's so nice to see you," Duffy said, as though the party were more hers than it was his.

A waiter passed and Paul grabbed a drink off his tray without looking to see what it was.

A few drinks later he inexplicably found himself back in Duffy's company. He saw her playing the obliging nobility to a group of young peasants in uniform.

Natalie was across the room talking to Warren. She seemed to have him cornered, and he couldn't understand the unusual sweetness about her. Could she actually be flirting?

"It was nice of you to have this party for us, Mrs. Sutler," one of the earnest young men in an army uniform was saying to Duffy. He had been a copy boy before the war.

"Well, we're just so glad to be able to do a little something for our boys who are sacrificing so much to rid the world of the horrible menace of the Germans and Japanese."

"I don't know how much credit we all can take for that, ma'am," said Private First Class Karl Gibbs, a classified ad salesman and defender of democracy, "none of us here been out the country yet."

"But never mind," Duffy waved magnanimously, "you all volunteered to go and do your parts. A lot of people could have gone who didn't."

Paul felt the slam. "You mean like your husband," he answered too quickly, having mistaken her innocent small talk.

But once threatened, the animal puts her back up and defends with a thrust of her own. "He was over the maximum age," she said, fixing her eyes on her brother-in-law in unmistakable spite. "And what is your excuse?"

"Flat feet," he said, and realized as the words came out the ridiculous ring they had to them. He heard a tittering from the boys in uniform which Duffy belatedly joined; and Paul took his drink to his lips and drained it in one swift, defiant motion, turned on his heels as smartly as any boot camp dogface and made a beeline for his wife Natalie, across the room.

Warren was relieved to see him coming.

Natalie was annoyed.

Warren smiled a big brother smile at Paul, and was anticipating an opportunity to escape when he saw his little brother's straining face.

"Natalie," Paul said. "Let's go."

"Oh, why, dear?" she said. "We just got here."

"Is something the matter?" Warren asked in party solicitude.

"I can't stand the bitch," Paul murmured, but not quite quietly enough for Warren to miss. "No offense, Warren," he said full voice, "come on, Natalie."

"Oh, Paul," she said, pert petulance playing with her lips, "I'm having such a good time. Warren, could you take me home?"

"Well, I...." Warren faltered.

"Oh, I'd appreciate it so much. It isn't out of your way too much, and it will save ever so much gas for the war effort."

Paul stalked off.

When the party was over past midnight, Duffy said she was just too tired to go home, she was going to "just drop in my new bed upstairs."

When they were settled in his Chevrolet, two years older than Paul's Buick, Natalie used her softest feminine tones, "I'm sorry about Paul," she purred.

"I understand," Warren said. "He had a bit of a blow today. I didn't realize that particular office was so important to him."

"Of course you didn't," she answered without pause. "You aren't as status conscious as he is. But then you have it."

Warren seemed to be thinking that over when she broke the silence with, "Warren, did anyone ever tell you, you are a handsome man?"

He laughed, his fingers strangling the steering wheel. "Not lately," he said.

"Well, it's true," she said. "Everyone admires you, you know. You and your ambitious wife," she added with an edge.

"Well it gives her something to do," he explained, half apologizing. "She is rather restless and it keeps her out of trouble."

"Do you ever get in trouble?" she asked with a husky, sensuous voice.

"Well, I hope not," he laughed uncomfortably, gripping the wheel tighter, as if it might save him from drowning.

Natalie looked right through him. He was a pigeon, she thought; a babe in the woods. That awkward wife of his couldn't possibly give him what he wanted.

"Would you like to stop off at your house before you take me home?..." She seemed to speak through her dark, fluttering eyelashes.

"Why would we do that?"

"For a nightcap?" She wondered at his naiveté.

"I'm pretty tired," he said. "If you don't mind, I'll just take you home."

When the Chevy pulled to the curb at her house, she darted across the seat and planted a kiss on his startled lips. When his reaction went no further than surprise, she withdrew and said, "Thanks for the ride. I'll see myself to the door."

When she closed the car door she leaned inside the window and blew him a kiss. "I'll take a rain check," she said, and turned to the house.

The street lamp's glow spilled over on the shining satin, highlighting the bulges of Natalie's high-toned gluteus muscles, so provocatively wrapped. Warren gulped like a frustrated fish, whipped his head forward and threw the gearshift to low.

Natalie smiled as she turned to watch the car drive off, and said to herself, "You'll take a rain check, too."

When she got into bed, she discovered that Paul had not been able to sleep.

When he attempted to reassert mastery of his hearth and home with clumsy amorousness, Natalie told him about her excruciating headache.

# 63

Get up, get up, my
hardy sons,
From this time forth
we are
No longer men, but
pikes and guns
In God's advancing
war.

—Stephen Vincent Benét
*John Brown's Body*

1951

Rich and poor alike were called upon to serve their country in a non-aggressive police action in Korea. The rich were given deferments while they attended college, but after they got out, by golly, if the "war" was still on, in they went. And so it was with Olin Sutler.

But duty assignments were more of a mystery. It seemed as though there was a benevolent invisible hand guiding the big names away from the front lines. In war the anonymous are treated anonymously.

When Olin Sutler sat at his Fort Ord, California, desk as duty officer in personnel, it was as though the desk were an insignificant part of him—two legs that never developed right. The army desk makers never reckoned with boys with such commanding torsos.

Olin saw his buddies shipped overseas, one by one, and he knew the dates of their departure before they did; and so he knew how much time they had to wind up their affairs stateside: write their Wills, tell their loved ones, and sell their cars.

In the same mail with their shipping orders, the soldiers got a tasteful notice that Lieutenant Olin Sutler would be happy to relieve them of the bother of selling their cars, and he would pay cash. Since the nearest used-car dealer had a reputation for mean-spirited, close dealing, it was a rare army man who would not first consult his comrade-in-arms about the disposition of his wheels.

All business was tastefully transacted at his residence, a one-bedroom Quonset hut on the edge of the base where he and his wife Nell resided.

Nell, one of Olin's army buddies commented, was the size of one of Olin's arms.

She was dark and beautiful, like Olin's Aunt Natalie, and she was a stranger to deprivation. Their corrugated metal home was furnished with large, dispensable pieces, but the portable accessories were anachronisms of startling quality. Nell liked nice things, and Olin wanted her to be happy.

Much of the china, silverware, glassware, satin bedding and plush towels were the products of a large, socially elite wedding. But the porcelain figurines, the little bronze sculptures, the paintings, the ornate clocks and priceless oriental rugs were her own doing. "Things we can just throw in the car and move," was the way she put it. The junk would stay behind.

Olin flashed a smile at her. She was reading something to him from the Los Angeles *Tribune* that Olin's mother sent them.

Olin never read it. He wasn't interested in reading or newspapers. He had just graduated from Stanford, and he had more than his fill of reading there. His only contact with newspapers was his ads in the classified section of the local paper.

Nell stopped reading. It was some war news, he thought; he didn't pay that much attention when she read to him. She didn't seem to expect any response to her reading aloud. One-sided communication satisfied her.

He flashed a smile for his end of the conversation.

He could flash a smile one instant, and just as suddenly it was gone like a spark from an electrical short circuit.

From the front, his nose didn't seem large enough to feed enough oxygen to his washtub-sized lungs. The nose was a paring knife on edge, sharp and squat, cutting the center of his husky face. It was the only part of him that didn't develop to gargantuan proportions.

Outside were parked two Chevies and a Ford. Olin didn't own a car of his own, he drove his inventory. He had one, way back, but someone made him an offer—someone who thought Olin's personal car would naturally be better than the clunkers he was pushing. So Olin let the guy put one over on him. Of course the poor soul was wrong, and he needed a valve job and a transmission in short order, and when he came screaming at Olin, the lieutenant could shrug and say, "I tried to sell you the other one, and it's running just fine."

That is not to say Olin was always that lucky. He bought some cars that cost him more to get running than he got for them, but he learned to cover himself.

He would drive the inventory, he said, so he got the feel of the car himself. And he could pass on firsthand information.

Olin advertised his cars in the base paper and the local paper, and occasionally sold to dealers in town for a twenty-five to fifty dollar markup—just to keep things moving, sometimes to teach a lesson to a procrastinating buyer. "Nope, that one's gone," he could say, and sell the second choice rather rapidly.

"Oh God, not another one?" Olin's wife, Nell, said when she heard the knock at the door. Olin had promised to take her to the movies, and now he would have another excuse not to.

Nell Bergstroms was a wispy, dark-haired Stanford girl with a good pedigree for Los Angeles. Her grandfather was in the Valley land deal with Olin's grandfather and great-grandfather. And her father was in the International Affairs Club that Warren Sutler, Olin's father, had begun—it being a high-class Rotary Club where members of the hoi polloi would meet for lunch, pretend to listen to some high-blown speech on foreign affairs—later broadened to include any affairs at all—and after lunch do business with one another. It was an elite group and provided many advantageous pairings for the Sutler children.

Nell was ambitious. She wanted the best of the world's goods, and she wasn't particularly patient about getting them. She almost admitted in a moment of combined candor and anger that she had really expected that Olin's parents would have done more for them financially. God knows they were rich enough.

But there were no dollars from the home front for Olin—all his capital came from his meager salary. He started small and built, and when he was finished he was still small, turning over cars from nothing to five hundred dollars profit.

He was stymied in feeding the expectations of his wife, who could hardly be blamed for expecting some of the perquisites of great wealth to trickle down to the least of these my brethren, but it was not in the cards. The Sutlers worked for theirs—there was no contingency fund for familial charity.

Nell liked nice things, and the proceeds of Olin's car dealings went to procure nice things.

Olin didn't have anything against nice things, but he was hoping to save enough money so when he got out of the army he would have a nest egg so he might (1) take a vacation and (2) take his time deciding on his life's work.

At the door the young boy stood with the notice in his hand that went out with the orders of transfer.

"Is it a buyer or a seller?" Nell asked from the bedroom where she was getting dressed to go to the movies. She was admiring the new quilted bedspread she had bought with the profit of the last three car sales. "They're the only visitors we get," she muttered. "I hope it's a buyer. They don't scream so much."

"Less pressure," Olin said going to the door.

It was a young, blond private named Gus Miller. He was ill-at-ease.

"Hello, sir," he fumbled, saluting even though Olin did not have his uniform on.

"That's okay, soldier," Olin said, "what you got?"

"I got my orders—I'm a little shook up, I didn't expect to go so soon." Olin watched as Pfc. Miller glanced at the letter Olin had mailed him. "Says here you buy cars."

"Sure do."

"Well I got this Plymouth here," he said waving over his shoulder at a well-worn red vehicle.

Olin nodded, "Mind if I take a look?"

"Oh, no, sir," the boy gasped. "Please do, sir."

"Look, Gus," he said reading the lad's nameplate, "this is not official business, so why don't you just call me Olie like my friends do."

"Sure, sir—Olie, sir, anything's fine with me, sir—"

Olin smiled and gave up. "Can we go for a spin?" The lad turned pale. Olin could see his knees trembling.

Being rather short, Pfc. Miller had the double front seat pulled forward as far as it would go. Olin could barely get himself into the car, and when he did, his knees touched the steering wheel. He tried to move the seat back, but it was frozen in place.

After he started the car, Olin understood why the lad was so nervous. The engine had a very unfriendly knock to it. As they pulled away from the curb, Olin felt the mushiness in the steering wheel and he said nothing. The lad was perspiring, and when they crossed the railroad tracks all parties to the transaction felt the woeful want of shock absorbers.

Olin drove back home, letting some air escape through his teeth. When he pulled up to the curb in front of the house, behind one of the Chevrolets, he said, "What do you want for it, soldier?"

"Well, I only had it little over two months, like I says I didn't expect to ship out so soon. I'd take a hundred less than I paid for it."

"What did you pay for it?"

"Nine hundred ninety-five."

Olin whistled again. He did a quick calculation of the amount of repairs it needed.

"I'd like to help you," Olin said, his big hands drumming easily on the steering wheel, "but I don't think we can come to terms."

"Wait a minute," Pfc. Gus Miller said, getting hot under the collar and waving the come-on letter he still clutched in his hand. "This says you will buy any car."

"So it does, soldier," he said, "so it does. I'll give you a hundred for it."

The burning desire to excel, to make a lot of money, was never far from the surface of Lieutenant Olin Sutler, but outwardly he appeared rather casual, and for most of his transactions he looked like a sleepy poker player about to throw in his cards.

"A hundred?" Gus was aghast. "A hundred dollars?" he repeated, as if to clarify some ridiculous thought in his own mind. "The tires are worth that."

"I don't buy tires," Olin said. Then the features of his large, angular face softened. "You must understand the car needs about six hundred in work for openers. I don't see getting a dime over seven-fifty for the risk. I'll probably lose. It could cost seven hundred to repair, and I could sell it for six-fifty—"

"If I have it fixed will you give me seven hundred?"

Olin flashed his short circuit smile, "You are all right, Gus," he paused and nodded. "You fix it the way I want it, and I'll give you six-fifty. Why don't you price the repairs?"

Gus already had—six hundred on the nose. He was bluffing.

"Ah, I don't have time."

"Hey—why don't you take it to the dealer you bought it from. He ought to give you more."

"To Omaha, Nebraska?"

"Oh—well I'm sorry. Run it into town. It might go that far. You might get an extra fifty or a hundred. They can repair wholesale."

"Thanks, Lieutenant. I'll do that."

Gus left, and when Olin got back in the house Nell said, "Well, we missed the movie—I hope you made a good deal."

Olin grinned, "I hope not," he said, and picked her up like a barbell and pressed her to the ceiling.

"Olie, let me down this minute—ooo Olie—"

The next day Gus Miller was back.

"Is the offer still good?"

"Oh, I suppose—what did I offer you?"

Olin knew—there was always the outside chance the private forgot and would ask for less.

"A hundred," Gus said dolefully. "That's nine hundred bucks for two month's driving."

"Cars are rough," Olin said. And he peeled off three fifty dollar bills and handed them to Gus, who looked at them without knowing what to say. He looked up at Olin, "This is a hundred and *fifty*," he said.

"I'm a pushover for a sad story—just don't breathe a word of this to a soul or my reputation as the lionhearted lieutenant will go down the tubes." Olin showed his politic smile. "Now just don't tell me I've been had again—you probably picked up the heap in a wrecking yard for seventy-five."

"No, I swear."

The pink ownership slip was passed and Olin wished him luck.

Pfc. Gus Miller was killed in action eight days after he arrived in Korea.

Olin spent two hundred and forty-seven dollars sprucing up the car, and sold it for seven ninety-five.

Then he took Nell to the movie, but he didn't like the film.

Nell Sutler had hair that always seemed just the wrong length. She was already restless as a homemaker and wanted children to keep her occupied. Olin thought it was too soon—the life of a serviceman too uncertain. But Nell won—nature being what it is.

While Olie was at Fort Ord, his mom bombarded him with letters. They were all addressed to him alone:

> Dear Olin:
>     Your father and I were so thrilled with the news that you had a son. And to have the first-born be a boy is unprecedented in the direct line of accession. We have big plans for you at the paper when you return, very exciting. Your father simply won't hear of your doing anything else,

so you get that notion out of your head. You must understand, the *Tribune* needs you—your father does not look
on it either as your birthright, or a charity—you will be
doing us a favor.

We are both glad to have Nell's letters, but let us hear
from you once in a while.

Love,
Your Mother

Olin had no interest in working for his family's newspaper. He
didn't know what he wanted to do, he just wanted to be independent.

Though Olin had somewhat outgrown most of his resentment of
his mother, he had still not come completely to terms with her. It
was an embarrassment to have his mother meddling at the paper. He
was sure if he worked there she would be bossing him around. None
of his friends' mothers worked, and he never heard of the head of
any company who had his wife in the next office, making suggestions—some said telling him what to do.

Nell saw herself as the *Tribune* publisher's wife. She had from
the moment she engineered their first date. So whenever Olin
expressed his distaste for the paper, she would say, "Oh, it might not
be so terrible. But whatever you want, Olie, I'm behind you a hundred percent." She always spoke as though she were in a committee
meeting.

The news of Nell's second pregnancy, in 1952, coincided with
Olin's mustering out, and inhibited his flexibility somewhat.

When they arrived home for what Olin thought was going to be
a vacation visit, his father handed him, with a gleeful smile, a list of
departments in the paper, along with a length of time behind each.

Olin read: Circulation, six months; Production, six months;
Classified, three months; Editorial, three months; Marketing, six
months; and on through the list.

"What's this for?" he asked a touch naively.

"That's your training program."

"Oh—well—gee—you mean at the paper?"

"Of course the paper, dear," Duffy enthused.

"Well, I thought we'd have a little rest. I'll sure give it some
thought."

"Rest?" Warren asked perplexed. Then he smiled, "We don't
rest in this family. Resting is very expensive—how much money have

you got?"

"Well—not a lot—you mean we can't have a little vacation here?"

Warren shook his head. It was his sad duty to set a loved one straight.

"Maybe we can stay with Nell's folks."

"With the baby?" Nell said. "Are you kidding?"

Ah, Olin thought. She is in on it. She's not opposed to me going right into harness. He looked at the list again—well—it might be interesting for a year or so. You never know, he might even like it.

"Okay," he said. "I'll give it a go."

Duffy and Warren cheered.

"For a couple of months, anyway," then he added as an after-thought, "I suppose I'll be paid."

"Well, of course you'll be paid," Duffy said.

"Oh, don't you think he should pay us?" Warren said. "After all we are giving him priceless training."

"No, we'll have to pay—he has all these mouths to feed."

"I had nothing to do with that," Warren said. "Oh, I suppose we'll give him enough to cover room and board and some small change to buy toothpaste in the beginning. Then we'll see."

# 64

Not half so dear were
Clytaemnestra's Charms,
    when first her bloom-
ing beauties
    bless'd my arms.

                    —Homer
                *The Iliad*

1952

Where do you think you're going?"
Warren demanded.

"I don't *think* I'm going," Duffy
retorted in a huff, "I'm *going*."

She was bundling up a smattering
of clothing and heading for the guest
bedroom down the hall from the master
bedroom in their two-story, palatial
Hancock Park home that they moved
into in the summer of 1951. Warren was
indifferent to moving, but Duffy said a
man of his stature needed a house to
match his importance.

Now Warren was wondering if he
hadn't given in to his wife once too often.
"Duffy," Warren protested, "you're being
ridiculous."

"Well, you may think so, Warren,
but I'm leaving your bed until you come
to your senses and endorse General
Eisenhower."

"Duffy!"

"Don't you 'Duffy' me." She was
riding on euphoria. The television station that had been her idea was turning

the corner, and there was an offer to buy the *Tribune* share for a five million profit, which Duffy said was not enough. Thanks to Warren, she had been accepted in the councils of management at the paper and she was becoming more open about her contributions.

Warren had even started an afternoon paper to help soak up some of his wife's florescent energies. They called it the Los Angeles *Standard*, and he let her run it pretty much as she pleased.

The *Standard* endorsed Ike.

"Senator Taft is a dinosaur," she said. "He has no personality, and no one will ever vote for him."

"Duffy, he's brilliant."

"Nobody cares."

She left the room, then came back for a second load. "You know what I'm thinking?" she said, her arms full of underwear and cosmetics.

"What?"

"Grandpa Benjamin Olin fought tooth and nail against Lincoln." She smiled her condescending smile. "You probably inherited your political wrongheadedness from him." Sashaying too broadly out the door, she said, "When you come to your senses, I'll be back."

"Well, maybe I won't want you back," he muttered, but softly enough so she didn't hear him.

Two weeks later, on a Saturday in late June, Paul and Natalie Sutler had a party to raise money for Senator Taft's campaign for the Republican nomination for President. All the family were there, except Duffy.

Natalie and Paul's house had a colonial facade right out of the antebellum South. After the film of "Gone with the Wind" swept the country, their friends started calling it "Tara." The other three sides were plain stucco, but adequate trees were planted to camouflage that.

Inside, the taste reflected the same period, and Natalie was an aggressive decorator. The walls were thick with horsey prints, and water colors and oils of the Wild West. The fulsome furniture was museum quality antique. Someone once said if you spent ten minutes in each chair in the house it would take a year to hit them all. Of course that was a wild exaggeration, but so was the decor.

The house was crammed with Taft supporters. It was one of those parties where you had to sidle like a crab to get anywhere.

They were just a sea of anonymous faces to Warren, who from the moment he arrived sought an excuse for an early, gracious exit.

He knew Duffy had blabbed her "Lysistrata" ploy all over town, and Warren hoped for nothing so much as avoiding the confrontation he saw leering in those supercilious eyes. He puffed on a cigarette, taking the smoke deep into his lungs with unusual urgency.

Natalie and Warren drifted together in a corner. Warren was a social drinker, but tonight he was being more social than usual. He could, he explained to Natalie, take all the tasteless jokes about his manhood, and he might even stomach Duffy moving out temporarily. After all, they had been married thirty-some years. What he didn't care for was the way she felt she had to broadcast it.

"She's made an impossible situation for me," Warren said, his glass tilted in his hand. "If I stick to my principles, I lose her favors. If I please her, I've caved in my integrity."

"You poor man." Natalie was the soul of sympathy.

Warren puffed his cigarette, then took another swallow of his drink. "The paper's been Republican since the beginning," he said as though to excuse his position. "Eisenhower hasn't voted in decades. I don't think he's even a Republican."

Natalie and Warren talked on. Natalie, with a twinkle in her dark eyes said, "We agree on everything, don't we, Warren?"

"Yes, I suppose," he muttered thoughtfully, taking another sip.

"If you want to know what I think," Natalie said, pressing her lips close to his ear in a whisper, "I think you have been too good to her, and now she's trying to see how far she can push you."

Warren put out the stump of his cigarette in the ashtray on the colonial window sill, then lit another.

Natalie dropped back a few inches. "I mean, how many husbands would give their wives offices next to theirs? And listen to them too—as virtual partners? And start newspapers for them?" she asked through an arched eyebrow. "Do you think," she was ladling up the *coup de grace*, "Duffy appreciates you?"

Warren took another sip and did not answer.

She drew closer to his ear. "I wonder, Warren, have you ever experienced what real appreciation is?"

"I don't know," he muttered.

"Would you like to have lunch?"

"I don't know."

"Tomorrow?"

His eyes scanned the room as if the answer were out there somewhere. "All right," he said.

"We'll do it here," she whispered. "It's private."

Before Warren could lodge the mild protest that touched his mind, Paul approached them with his patented smirk. With heavy sarcasm he said:

"Well, Warren old boy, be sure and tell Duffy how much we all missed her."

"How much is that?" Warren asked, leveling his eyes on his brother.

"Why, a whole bunch," Paul said. Then he added, "And don't forget to remind her of what a fine president our last war hero made: Ulysses S. Grant. Yes sir, just what we need is another one of those."

"I've used it," Warren said. "She counters with George Washington."

"Say, you aren't going soft, are you? She hasn't got your horns growing already, has she?"

"What?" Warren's mind was on Duffy. "Oh no," he said absently. "No."

"After all," Paul poked a sharp elbow into his brother's ribs and winked too broadly, "it's only been a couple of weeks."

Natalie saw Warren to the door. He had avoided his sisters Katherine, Louisa and Amy. She squeezed his hand surreptitiously, "'Til tomorrow," she said.

"What?" Warren said, distracted, a dying cigarette clinging to his lower lip. It was the first time Natalie could remember seeing Warren talk with a cigarette in his mouth.

"Our lunch," she whispered with a husky voice. "Here," she pointed at the floor, "—about noon."

Warren's eyes glazed over, and Natalie thought she caught him nodding.

His car was parked around the corner. He had been one of the last to arrive and one of the first to leave. When he slid behind the wheel he felt nauseous and he couldn't move for fear he would vomit. He lit another cigarette, but it tasted like dirt and he meant to put it out, but he didn't seem to get around to it until he felt the heat of the ash on his lips. He sat there another twenty minutes until the familiar longing for Duffy took hold of him.

He drove home, left the car outside and took the stairs two at a time, expecting to find Duffy working in her home office where he left her. He opened the door on what used to be his study before the decorator and Duffy made it look so pink and flowery feminine he took the smaller room, which they had decorated with brown leather chairs and dark mahogany wainscoting.

Warren closed the door and walked quietly to the guest room, where he found his wife in her separate bed.

"Duffy?" he whispered. "Duffy?" Louder.

She didn't answer. She smiled to herself under the covers. "He's weakening," she thought. "It's against the whole family, and he's coming around."

The next morning Duffy seemed slow in getting up, so Warren, who had suffered a rather sleepless night, dawdled in the kitchen over the *Tribune* and its competitor, the *Inquirer*.

When Warren heard her footsteps on the stairs, he jumped to his feet and went out to greet her.

Duffy's loose, flowing, blue silk robe was flowing a little wider lately, her face was puffy and her limbs were thickening. But at that moment Warren thought she was still the most beautiful girl at Stanford.

"Good morning, Duffy," Warren said, looking ridiculous standing at the foot of the stairs watching the queen descend for some royal ceremony.

He reached out for her hand, she withdrew from his grasp. "Have you changed your mind?"

"Duffy," he pleaded with his eyes, "you're the only one that wants Ike."

She swept by him as some doyen past a pariah.

"You may come to my bed only when you've changed your mind," she said, with her back to him.

It was a warm and sunny day in Los Angeles, but not anywhere near as warm as Warren felt.

When Natalie opened the door, he realized he had not misunderstood the invitation.

She stood before him in a shiny black silk dress that just seemed to gently touch and tumble from all the right places. She was a striking woman framed here in the white doorway, her freshly-washed black hair glimmering in the bright sunlight that slanted through a side window and back-lighted her, setting her silhouette ablaze and emphasizing for him how sheer her dress really was.

"Oh, Warren," she purred, "I'm so glad you came."

"Well, I am too." He managed to complete the phrase without swallowing. She certainly was a gorgeous woman, he thought, so beautifully made.

"Come in, come in," she said rapidly, and so musically, he felt his heartbeat quicken beneath the plain maroon silk tie that he had chosen especially to go with his gray pinstriped suit.

The air was sweet with her perfume—a light scent of some flower that just seemed to tickle Warren's nostrils as though he had never been conscious of perfume before. It had always been something in the back ward of his subconscious, like classified ads in his paper in categories foreign to his interest.

As he stepped across the threshold, his heart slammed the blood through his tingling body. She smiled at him, and dammit, even her teeth were better than Duffy's.

After she closed the door against intrusion, an awkward silence enveloped the room. It was as though they were two strangers in a foreign airport, attracted to each other but each afraid to speak for fear it would be in a language unknown to the other.

Natalie had planned her every move, but now she was unable to move.

"Drink?" she said at last. They were still standing, foolishly facing each other.

"Sometimes," he said.

Her dark eyes blinked. "Now?" she asked.

"Why not?"

"Have a seat," she said. She turned to the kitchen, her tightly wrapped buttocks gyrating with a sensuality that squeezed Warren's heart.

When she returned with the martini pitcher she smiled at him sitting on the Early American print couch. He looked so ill-at-ease. She handed him a glass and filled it with the chilled stimulant.

They drank in silence, side by side on the couch.

"Um," he said. It seemed like years later. "How did you know this was my favorite?" The alcohol had warmed his veins and freed his tongue.

"You had quite a few of them last night," she said.

He laughed. She loved his laugh. It was so free and pure. They drank some more, and Warren couldn't say no to a refill.

They felt warmth pass between their shoulders touching on the couch.

At some point she said, "Hungry?" and he responded with a vague, "Hmm."

She reached for his hand, he took hers, and she led him to the dining room where he sat at the dark, shiny table with Williamsburg place mats while she vaporized into the kitchen, floating on her undulating hips, and reappeared with the chicken salad.

A bottle of wine materialized from somewhere, and the hostess's chair moved closer to her guest. She poured his wine without getting up and without taking her eyes off him.

"I think it's a dirty shame what Duffy is doing to you," she said, wine-relaxed.

"What?" Warren asked in his haze. "Oh, that." He paused to clear his head to receive the thought. "Yes."

Natalie parted her lips to bare her teeth as she inserted a forkful of chicken salad. Warren's lips barely parted for his fork.

"Of course," she said offhandedly, "Paul wouldn't care if I did that to him."

"He wouldn't?"

Natalie shook her head. She had a drop of chicken salad on her chin and Warren reached up to pick it off with his finger, and Natalie misunderstood the gesture and took his hand and kissed the tips of his fingers.

She smiled foolishly at him, then took his fingers, one by one, into her mouth.

"Do you like that?" she purred, a Cheshire cat.

"Well, oh, I...Yes."

"Hmmm."

She had not made any dessert, and there didn't seem to be any call for it.

She stood up from the table and took his hand. He watched the black silk shimmering in the sunlight with all the shadowy recesses and highlighted protuberances. The lithe and artistic undulations sent his heart racing all over again.

The bed was a four-poster with a chintz canopy. It startled him.

The next thing he knew he was on his back and he felt cold fingers on his buttons and warm lips on his mouth. His eyes were focusing on the chintz canopy cover. It seemed so ludicrous to him—like a child's bed. He wondered how his brother could sleep in this bed. The excitement he had felt seemed to vanish from his body, and though his mind tried to call it back, there was no response.

Then suddenly he saw Natalie was naked. The contrast to Duffy was startling. Where his wife drooped and sagged, Natalie was round and pointed, firm and supple. Where Duffy bulged, Natalie had curves of such gentle perfection, dimples of delight.

Duffy had nerve to bargain with such inferior collateral. She *was* taking him for granted.

What would his wife say if she could see Natalie and him now? He looked out the window, and kept listening for her car to drive up.

In Natalie's warmth his hands found pockets of paradise. They kissed as though untouched by experience. His heart was racing —her breathing was labored. Warren's blood boiled wildly while he tried to suffocate in her flesh. She was doing things to him he had only dreamed of. He drew back to look and couldn't believe his eyes.

When it came time for the final transaction, the merger—the incorporating of the two corporal entities, the negotiable instrument flagged, and in the final thrust of the takeover, the stock offering failed to float.

They eased apart, only their feet were touching, and he apologized.

"Don't apologize," she said, a soft purring from her gleaming lips, "maybe you weren't sure."

He was grateful to her, and he listened patiently as she artfully turned the conversation to Paul.

And Warren said he saw no reason why Paul shouldn't have a crack at the top spot. Olin was still very new to the company and unproven.

"No," Duffy said firmly when he returned home that night, "you're not crawling into my bed until you endorse General Eisenhower."

"But every last one of my partners is for Taft," he lamented.

"But," she said, fixing him with her country eyes, gone city, "you are the *publisher*. *You* make the decision."

Senator Robert A. Taft (someone had saddled him with rather unfortunate initials) had a meeting of high-level press officials in Chicago, and Warren went. Olin took him to the airport after Duffy refused.

They were in the massive Palmer House Hotel in the shadow of the elevated train, and after Senator Taft had relieved himself of his prepared remarks, he spoke individually to the press lords from all over the nation, some supporting his candidacy, some not.

The senator was a dour-faced man with an augmented belly, who always looked as if he'd rather be someplace else.

When it was Warren Sutler's turn, Senator Taft greeted him with outstretched hand. Warren introduced himself, "Warren Sutler, Los Angeles *Tribune*," he said.

"Glad you could come."

"My pleasure, Senator." Warren felt a heady euphoria in the presence of such a famous man.

At that moment a press photographer pushed his camera in their faces and prepared to shoot a picture, when Senator Taft raised his hand and said, "No pictures." The photographer lowered the camera, smiled wryly, and left.

Senator Taft continued the conversation as though nothing had happened, but Warren was disturbed.

Later, he wasn't exactly sure just how harsh Senator Taft had been. He was a fairly staid, stolid, sometimes gruff man, but the incident unnerved Warren—here Taft was playing host to the leaders of the nation's press and he had the nerve to reject a photographer of the working press. Warren chose to remember it as an unfriendly act.

Perhaps his detractors were right and Taft lacked the common touch.

At any rate it seemed a good excuse. The following day the *Tribune* came out for General Eisenhower, citing the pragmatism inherent in winning politics. "And as highly as we esteem Senator Taft, we must lend our support to that great American General, Dwight David Eisenhower, because we think his mass appeal gives him the best chance of winning in November."

Duffy waited to see the editorial in the morning edition before she moved back into the master bedroom.

# 65

Nevertheless, some men turn every quality or art into a means of getting wealth; this they conceive to be the end, and to the promotion of the end they think all things must contribute.

—Aristotle
*Politics*

1958

The sisters were furious. They wanted something done about the losses.

As always, Paul took up the gauntlet for them and waved it under his brother's nose.

The women sat in a row in the *Tribune* meeting room at the long mahogany table.

To Duffy, who sat self-effacingly back in the corner, the Sutler sisters looked like three overstuffed toys sitting on the shelf in a shooting gallery: feathers preened and fluffy, helpless against being knocked over by a pot shot.

Duffy eschewed the limelight today. The bone of contention was her baby, and her sisters-in-law had that well-I-declare huffiness about them that Duffy would just as soon avoid.

For a time it had seemed as if everything Warren and Duffy touched turned to gold. And then they started the afternoon paper and named it the Los Angeles *Standard*, to compete with Robert Lawrence Quint's Los Angeles

*News* and the newer, liberal Los Angeles *Bugle*.

Paul Sutler had been vehemently against the project as he had been against so many others—but now, ten years after it began, it looked as if Paul was right.

Papers were going under everywhere, victims of the great electronic eye that fed you all the news and sports you ever could want without ever having to get off your duff—except for an occasional trip to the fridge for a beer. And it was free. No hassling with change, no delivery boy to tip to find out how the home team did.

The three afternoon papers in Los Angeles were pegged to the working stiff. But even though the tabloid articles were in big type and were short—television was shorter.

Circulation was down and drastically. The *Standard* had come on the market in '48, and undersold the competition by two cents a copy. The afternoon market was bad enough without that.

It wasn't long before that Duffy was saying, "If we could only kill the *Evening Bugle,* we could make a go of the *Standard*." So Warren brought home the bacon for $400,000.

Money just kept disappearing into the black hole of the enterprise, and now, just short of ten years after it began, Paul was publicly demanding, "Close it down."

Paul was seated at the chairman's end of the table at the meeting he had called. His sisters were on one side, their husbands absent, attending to their own affairs. Warren was standing across from his sisters.

"It was ill-advised in the first place, but there is no reason to drain our resources like this indefinitely." Paul was gesturing energetically. "Each and every one of our family has lost a million dollars cash this year with this debacle—how long do you expect us to sit still for it?" He was directing his question to Duffy, in the far corner.

She deferred to Warren for a response.

"First," Warren said, looking across the table at his sisters Katherine, Louisa and Amy and then focusing on Paul's narrow eyes at the head of the group, "we have to admit the afternoon paper has not lived up to our expectations. We thought our buy-out of the *Bugle* would strengthen our position, and if it helped anyone it was Quint. It was a miscalculation. We are sorry about it, but I suppose that doesn't cut any ice with anybody."

"I think we're entitled to expect to cut a loss like this before it takes us all under," Paul said.

"Well, there are other aspects here," Warren said, again addressing himself to Paul. "First there is the tax advantage. If you will consider that, you are looking at a much smaller personal loss than you stated."

"I don't understand," Amy said. "What does it mean?"

"Well," Warren smiled at her, "if we had not had this loss on the *Standard* this year—assume we broke even—each of us would have had a tax bill of around nine hundred thousand more than we did—that's the result of the loss, the depreciation and being in the highest tax bracket. So instead of the million or so loss to each, it is actually more like a hundred thousand each."

"Nothing to brag about," Paul muttered.

"No, certainly not," Warren agreed. "And yet I hope you will put this loss in context with our other gains. No one can operate a business as diverse as ours has become, and not expect losses now and then. Sometimes these losses, as in this case, shelter other gains. We get to buy an asset which can be sold later at a profit—sometimes eradicating the loss."

"Have you looked for a buyer?" Paul asked. "I shouldn't imagine they would be standing in line."

"We have not looked for a buyer."

"I move we do look for a buyer for the *Standard*," Paul said.

"I second that motion," Katherine said.

"Me too," Louisa chimed in, her face a mask of serious concern for financial details out of her ken.

"Just a minute," Warren put up his hand angrily as if to stop the steamroller. "We've been working our tails off to make a go of this thing—and not only of the *Standard* but the whole operation. What were your shares of the profit last year? Over three million each?" He looked around the room. "Does anyone want to complain about that?"

Not a sound disturbed the growing tension in the *Tribune* meeting room.

"You know," Warren plowed on, "our father did a lot of business for his own account—no one criticized him—no one interfered. We could have done that too—but all our efforts have been in your behalf."

"And yours," Paul said.

"Yes, certainly," Warren snapped,"—but it could have been our personal enterprises."

"You didn't have the funds," Paul said.

"We could have gotten them," Warren cut in. "If you don't like what we've done for you, I'll make you a proposition—Duffy and I will buy the *Standard*, but along with it we will buy the profitable ventures we have acquired. You may all keep the *Tribune*. If you will recall, that was all you inherited directly—and that from your grandfather. You share in the profits of your father's trust, but you can't get your hands on the principal. What we have done," he looked at Paul, "has made you fabulously wealthy."

Amy spoke first after the uncomfortable silence. "May I ask a question?"

"Certainly," Warren said.

"What do you think we should do with the *Standard*? Does it look like it will ever make it?"

"Well, frankly, Amy, and I hope you will not let this get out of this room," Warren said, "our best studies show that the chances of it becoming profitable are virtually nonexistent at this time."

Paul let out a hiss of victory.

"What to do may not be so simple." Warren went on. "There are our tax considerations number one; number two it is not an easy thing to throw that many people out of work. On the one hand we are still making millions, and on the other we have the poor working stiff who gets from a hundred to two hundred bucks a week—and so do we really have to have another hundred thousand each at their expense?"

"Poppycock," Paul said. "Capitalism isn't based on charity—it's based on the profit system."

"Yes, all right," Warren said. "Amy asked for my advice. My advice is to hang on—because while we do, we keep circulation from our arch-rival. We help our long-range cause by forcing him to spend. The name of the game is dominating the market, and if we ever achieve that, the rewards will be incalculable. To achieve that dominance Duffy and I have a plan we hope will turn a lemon into a golden apple."

"What's the plan?" Paul wanted to know.

Warren lifted his palm. "Sorry, we can't divulge that at this time."

"Wait a minute," Paul demanded. "Are you saying you can't trust us?" Paul waved a hand at his sisters.

"I'm saying," Warren said firmly, "that we aren't going to take any chances."

Paul grumbled.

"And by the way—we never voted on Duffy and me buying you

out of all the extraneous enterprises including the *Standard,* leaving you all with the *Tribune*—still a handsome property, and millions in cash. All in favor raise your hands."

Paul smirked, but no hands went up.

After they all left, Duffy rolled her eyes. "Now that that's over shall we see if we can unload this turkey and take control of this town once and for all?"

"But the Justice Department will never allow it," Max was saying to Yank in his Santa Monica aviary.

"But that's the beauty of it," Yank said, flailing his arms to keep the birds at bay. "There's nothing to allow. It's a swap. They both go out of business and they make this beautiful exchange—on the surface mutually beneficial—but deep down outrageously advantageous to the *Tribune.*"

Getting the secret plan was, Yank thought, one of Max's more brilliant coups.

Warren and Duffy had kept the plan from Warren's brother and sisters. It was a wily female operative of Max Underwood's who wheedled the story out of one of the *Tribune*'s law firm's young lawyers who was researching the project. The coup was made during an adulterous relationship in *flagrante delicto.*

"Well, if they bring it off," Max said, pondering, "it will be a stroke of genius; victory from the jaws of disastrous defeat. Say, you don't think this was their idea from the start?"

"No, but I've got to prevent it."

"How you going to manage that one?"

"I'm going to see Quint first."

"If he'll see you first."

"Oh, I expect he will." Yank frowned. A bird landed on his shoulder. "Max!" he pleaded.

Max took the bird from Yank's shoulder.

"Max, we got to meet somewhere else. I'm getting bird fever."

Max chuckled.

Yank groaned. "Don't you think it's about time you consider getting a new office?"

"Who do I have to impress? You're my only client."

Yank reached the press lord by phone in New York where he had his flagship paper and asked for an appointment the next time he was in California.

"I'll be out at Yandro after the first of the year to see your brother," Quint said. "Why don't we make it after that?"

"Could we do it before?"

Yank's emphasis was not lost on Quint. There was a pause before he answered.

"What's this about? You in the market for my junk again?"

"Maybe."

"I might be in a better humor after I've seen Warren."

"And you might not."

# 66

Wine tastes like gaso-
line.

—Colonel Harland Saunders

1959

Quint and Yank sat facing each
other before a roaring fire in the baro-
nial library of a castle built after many
years of planning and changing of plans
by Robert Lawrence Quint. The castle
sat three miles up the mountain and
looked over the Pacific Ocean. It
feigned the look of a mission, with a bell
tower and another half tower that
looked like Quint had changed his mind
halfway through the construction and
told the masons to stop, which was
exactly what he had done.

The California missions were pur-
portedly spaced a day's walk apart so the
faithful would have an overnight stop
anywhere from Mexico to San Francisco; but Quint's mission, which he
called "Yandro," was not walking distance from anything, nor were its
visitors religious supplicants, but rather
business people connected with his
nineteen-paper Newspaper Empire,
and an endless battering of Hollywood
celebrities whose acquaintanceship with

things theological was remote. Quint lived and worked here off and on through the years with his mistress, Dotty Bookman, and from this West Coast headquarters dispatched his pungent, some said vitriolic, front page editorials, as well as directions for the day-to-day operation of all his papers.

He was an ambling, rangy man well over six and a half feet tall. His bearish frame, slouched in the chair by the fire, looked like it was lightly packed with goose feathers. His sleepy eyes made his face look like a bulldog's.

For a man who made his mark on the world as an outspoken, and even nasty, editor, Quint spoke with a surprisingly high, squeaky voice and he looked shy, diffident and lacking in self-confidence.

He made his fortune in the days of silent movies and before. If he had been an actor he would have lost his job when the talkies came in. As it was, his financial decline began roughly with the advent of the talking pictures, and the stock market crash in 1929.

He had a wife somewhere: a good Catholic wife who chose to remain Mrs. Robert Lawrence Quint, retaining the name if not the man. Quint did not press it, divorce being somewhat difficult to obtain without two consenting parties.

Yank waited a half an hour to see Quint, who had been busily dictating editorials on some crisis of the day, long since forgotten. Quint was looking at the fire, and he mused in his high voice, "Did you ever consider the miracle of fire, Yank, and how it disposes of the unwanted in life? It is truly one of life's miracles," he sighed. "You know one of life's biggest dilemmas is always what to do with the unwanted, and fire solved the problem. History tells us there was a time before fire was discovered, but it had to always be there, like water and air."

Quint ran his big hands along the arms of the chair and said, "Well, I've got some unwanted properties that are draining me dry, I got some properties that aren't really saleable. I suspect your brother is in the same boat.

"So, I expect he's going to offer a trade: my Los Angeles morning paper for his afternoon paper. He's got leadership in the morning, I've got it in the afternoon."

"Yes, but," Yank broke in, "you would be giving up far more than he."

"Well, that may be. But it isn't unusual in negotiations for someone to give a little more than he gets. You know if it weren't for your father, I would no longer own Yandro. He made me a loan when I was in pretty dire straits, put a mortgage on it, and I've never forgotten it. I never did get along with him. I'm sure he hated me as much as I hated him. It was still an act of kindness that I'll never forget."

Quint paused and looked into the fire then looked back at Yank Sutler sitting across from him. "So what's your interest in this, Yank?"

"Would you like me to buy your *News*?"

Quint sank back in his chair as though the removal of the mystery of the visit lifted a burden from him. "Well, I'd certainly consider an offer, but I'm not sure it would solve my problem in Los Angeles. You see, there we're up against a one-family operation, in most other markets we're against chains, other people who've spread themselves ungodly thin as I have. But here, one-nineteenth of my energies and resources are going against a hundred percent of the Sutlers' journalistic resources. Kind of long odds, don't you agree?"

"Well in a way, yes," Yank nodded reluctantly. "But on the other hand, have you considered what a monopoly would do to the town? And your agreeing to close your morning paper would make the biggest journalistic monopoly in the country for the Sutler *Tribune*. What would you be left with? An afternoon paper that's struggling at best? And even should you gain all the circulation from the defunct *Standard*, you might still have a time making a go of it."

Quint nodded. "Yes, Yank, your point is well taken, but sometimes in life it's a matter of alternatives and the lesser of the evils. Sure, I'd rather have your brother concede me the morning market, but what do you think the chances of him doing that are?"

"Nil."

"Exactly. Then of course the anti-trust boys would never let us sell to each other, so what better solution is there than the swap? In a way it's beautiful, foolproof from the anti-trust standpoint, and what Warren does with the Los Angeles morning market is his business. I size Warren up as a pretty decent chap, and I suppose Los Angeles could do a lot worse."

Yank shook his head dolefully. "Look," he said, "if it's a matter of money and you don't want to sell the paper, I might be interested in some more art purchases. You probably have three or four warehouses left."

Quint laughed, "It is a matter of money," he conceded, "but not the kind of money we're talking about. This is money that drains out of the coffers with annoying regularity. Sure, I could make another big sale to you and keep the wolf from the door for another six months, but what good would that do me? They'd just keep eating away at us. Times are not like they used to be for the newspaper business. But tell me, I'm curious, don't you get along with your brother?"

"I'll make a deal with you," Yank said. "You don't make any commitment to my brother this afternoon and I'll return after he's gone and make a clean breast of it and you can decide whose side you are on."

Quint raised his eyebrows, "It may be a long time, I've invited him to dinner and to stay overnight."

Yank's jaw tightened. "I'll wait," he said.

The Los Angeles *Standard* was from the start considered Duffy's baby. The paper took a more liberal tone than the *Tribune*, though it was careful to maintain a firm anti-communist stance, and while the object was to compete with Quint's lurid and sensational afternoon paper, the *News*, more or less on its own level, Warren had given strict instructions that it should be a paper that no one would be ashamed to take into his home.

But while Duffy was the guiding force of the paper and was instrumental in arranging the secret meeting with Robert Lawrence Quint for their mutual salvation, Quint was not too liberal in his policy toward women in any position higher than gossip columnist. And when Warren called to propose a meeting of Quint with Duffy and himself, Quint said:

"Well, I'll be happy to see you, Warren, anytime, if we could do it without your lovely wife, Duffy."

"Well," Warren said, "I suppose we could, but Duffy's really a big part of the paper."

"I'm sure she is, Warren, and I hope you will forgive my hopelessly old-fashioned chauvinistic attitudes, but I could never be comfortable dealing with women on a business basis."

And so it was arranged that Duffy would stay at the little motel at the foot of the hill and wait his summons to dinner.

"You never know," Warren was speaking in the same chair Yank had occupied a few hours before. Warren was shorter, Quint thought, not as intelligent perhaps, not a master of the language, but an engaging and unthreatening man who was immediately likable. Quint wondered about the rumors that their success was his wife's doing and decided to reject it as sour grapes. It was impossible for Quint to imagine a woman contributing anything to business.

"You never really know about the future," Warren was saying, "but it just seems to me from the present indications, that Los Angeles will not be able to support four major papers anymore than it has in the last few years." He spoke haltingly, pausing as though groping for the next thought.

Quint cut in, "Of course there was one less until ten years ago when you decided to compete with my *News*."

"Now what I'm recommending," Warren said, ignoring the amiable needling, "is a mutual agreement to close down our two losers and concentrate our resources on our profitable items."

Quint nodded with silent gravity.

"What would you think?" Warren pressed.

"I suspect that what I think is I might be interested in retaining the morning market, but I doubt if you would be too keen on keeping that god-awful *Standard* you put out."

"No, uh, I...."

"You should have come to me for advice, Warren," Quint said with a fatherly smile. "I could have told you how to run a tabloid. What in the world were you after with that thing? You don't go half lurid if you want to sell papers, you go all the way."

Warren hung his head and interlaced his fingers between his knees, "We failed," he admitted, "we don't have your genius for it."

Quint smiled at the transparency, but he couldn't help liking Warren. Maybe his daddy was wrong when he said nice guys finished last. Wasn't Warren living proof that a nice guy could do quite nicely on a mere hundred million or so?

"I suppose you realize," Quint said, "that the anti-trust boys will be breathing down our necks if we attempted anything like this."

"But we're not selling our papers to strengthen someone's position, we're closing them."

Quint nodded, "But it has the same effect."

"But how can they force us to stay open if we both decide, you know, unilaterally to close?"

"Oh, is that what you're proposing?"

Warren shrugged, "Well, uh, sort of."

"And without that you're prepared to continue with that god-awful *Standard* until you run it right into the ground?"

Warren shrugged, "Maybe it will get better."

Quint smiled, "I'm sure if you thought there was any chance at all that it would get better, you wouldn't be here now."

Warren squirmed; he did not like the direction the conversation was taking. That nice old fuzzy-looking, soft-hearted bear sitting opposite him with the hair in his eyes, was really a pillar of granite.

"Well, let me think about it, Warren," Quint said. "My first reaction is that the morning market is going to be the best market. Now if we could come to some agreement whereby you brought out your *Tribune* in the afternoon, I might be amenable."

"Well, gosh," Warren said, "we'd never considered such a move."

Quint nodded, "Perhaps it's something you want to consider now. In the meantime," Quint stood up, "I've got some more editorials to write, some more hell to raise, and I shall be looking forward to having dinner with you and your charming wife."

Warren stood up with a courtly bow, hoping that his disappointment didn't show.

On their way back up the hill to dinner Duffy said to Warren in the car, "You'll never guess who I saw at the motel."

"President Eisenhower," he said.

"No, silly. Yank."

Warren frowned, "Now what in the world would he be doing here?"

"Well, I suspect," Duffy said, "he was here to buy some more art."

"Did he tell you that?"

She hesitated. "In a way...." she said.

Warren dismissed his suspicion. Yank wouldn't want to buy newspapers at this stage in his life.

The dinner was a quiet affair at Quint's Yandro. There were eight couples seated at the long, regal table in the high-ceilinged room that comfortably sat two hundred diners.

All through the dinner Warren had heartburn. The food he ate seemed to assault his stomach like a charging troop of cavalry. Across the table he saw Duffy chatting in amiable animation with the Chicago newspaper bear. She wasn't worried about Yank. She didn't seem to worry about anything anymore.

When Warren shook hands with his host in farewell he said, "I understand my brother Yank's been to see you."

Quint said only, "Yes, yes he was. Fine man Yank, one of my favorites," and passed on to the next guest.

# 67

My candle burns at
both ends;
  It will not last the night;
  But ah, my foes, and
oh, my friends—
  It gives a lovely light!

—Edna St. Vincent Millay
*First Fig*

When he arrived back at the castle
the following day, Yank was met at the
door by Quint.

"Nice to see you, Yank," he said as
though he were speaking to a stranger
whom he thought might do him some
service. "Let's walk in the garden."

The two tall men bounded at a
quick pace through the yard that was
starting to show neglect from reducing
the gardening staff from six to two.

"How was your meeting with Warren?" Yank asked, as they passed the
circular fountain with the statue that
looked like a de Milo girl with chubby
arms.

Quint smiled, and Yank was becoming accustomed to that enigmatic
smile, and a little afraid of it.

"Look at that statue," Quint said.
"You see anything with your artist's eye
that seems just a little off?"

"Well, the arms are a little hefty."

"Exactly," Quint said, not too surprised at Yank's perception. "Now look

at the rest of her—what does she remind you of?"

"Venus—de Milo?"

"Go to the head of the class. I have this theory—that something like this could have been the origin of the great Venus—the artist could have been frustrated at not achieving his vision, or just plain angry at the way the arms turned out, and he could have just whacked them off and inadvertently created a masterpiece." Quint paused to stare at the statue. "What do you think?" he said.

"It's a nice analogy," Yank said, pondering the fat-armed woman, "I suppose it happens in art—the accidental masterpiece, but I wouldn't count on it working with newspapers."

"Well," Quint said, resuming the walk, "I like your brother. He's a gentleman, not at all pushy or power-hungry like your father was. Warren makes his point and backs off to let you consider what his idea will do for you." Quint showed a smile again.

"Not exactly what I came to hear," Yank muttered.

"Your brother came to offer me the proposition we thought he would"—Quint's voice faded as they approached the stables where two horses remained out of fourteen.

Yank took a deep breath. "How do you feel about revenge?"

Quint nodded thoughtfully as if understanding everything. "Revenge," he said. "Some of my greatest moments can be attributed to revenge."

Yank unfolded his story and Quint listened intently. Both men had stopped at the paint-flaking fenced riding ring, and following his host's lead, Yank had raised one foot to the middle rail.

"That's quite a load," Quint sighed when Yank had finished. "Of course it matters little to you that the perpetrator of the crimes is dead and gone?"

"It matters not at all," Yank said.

Quint nodded. "Well, I'd be happy to help you, Yank, if I saw any way I could. I confess, much as I like your brother, you and I have much more in common."

"You'll sell me the paper?"

"No, Yank. I like you too much. I've made some calls since talking to you both, got some numbers that only reinforced what I already knew. Warren can outlast me and that's just what he would do. I wonder now if he only started the *Standard* as a bargaining chip to get me to close my morning *Inquirer*. But I don't credit him with that much foresight." He paused, pondering something. "What about that wife of his—would she be capable?"

"I really couldn't say. But I'm sure you could go broke underestimating the capabilities of that woman."

"That's what I thought," Quint said. "I wasn't fooled by that countrified manner. Tell you the truth, I wouldn't let him bring her. I was scared to death to deal with her."

Yank smiled at the candor.

"No, Yank. You couldn't make a go of it. Television is taking over the tabloids. The numbers just aren't there anymore. I know it, Warren knows it. So we become a burlesque—two heavyweights knocking each other senseless in a match that can only produce two losers. And what's worse, there is probably not enough market for *one* successful afternoon paper."

"You sure?"

"Of course no one can be sure of anything, but let me tell you this: I'm as sure as I can be. I'm afraid my only hope is to combine both papers—the features, the best writers. Salvage what circulation I can, and take his deal."

"Why won't selling me the morning *Inquirer* be better for you?"

"Because we'd still have four papers in a market that will be generous if it provides for two. There are only so many readers. You could do two things if I sold to you: one, you could make a success of it. What would that do for me? It would hurt the hell out of me is what. Second, you could flunk out, strengthening not me, but Warren Sutler and his boring *Tribune*."

"But wouldn't I be hurting the Sutlers more?"

"No. I sell a viewpoint. If you want to be dull and staid, Warren's already got it in spades. If you want to be sensational I do it better than you ever could. How could you win?"

"A bargaining chip?"

"For what?"

"To get a foothold in the *Tribune*. Let *me* make the deal with him."

The big foot of Robert Lawrence Quint came down off the railing and he lumbered on down the path, past the guesthouse—a five-bedroom manse—to the main house. Yank followed. Quint stopped at the front door, he did not invite Yank in.

"I'm sorry, Yank," he said, "there is nothing I'd rather do than bring down the *Tribune*, but it's not in the cards." There was true sympathy in his voice. "They are way too big. We have their numbers—they are still privately held, but we know."

Yank looked surprised.

"We know a lot of things, Yank—we know you are the source of those leaks and we do appreciate it—but scoops have lost their luster in the electronic age. Wham! they're out there with a camera before we can turn the press, let alone distribute the papers."

He put his hand on Yank's shoulder. "It's a dying game, Yank. The country is headed for a series of one-paper towns. The big metropolises might manage two, but only if everything works right. I just can't help you. It's not in my interest. Your family had the wisdom to keep the unions out. I've mortgaged my soul to them. They may be the end of me."

"So why did you let the unions in?"

Robert Lawrence Quint stood tall and his eyes scanned the horizon for a placebo. He shrugged his bulky shoulders and said, "I had newspapers that championed the cause of the working man. I thought if I gave them some say, some feeling that we would listen to them, they would act in good faith. I should have realized what would happen: that people would rise to the top who were only simple working men—with little intellectual capacity really—and their only understanding would be power, and the employment of that power would become more important to them than preserving the institutions that gave their constituents jobs. Everyone has within his grasp enough rope to hang himself."

"Are you saying one of the reasons you want to close the *Inquirer* is to teach the unions a lesson?"

Robert Lawrence Quint seemed to slump a bit, and for a moment before he turned his back on Yank to open his door, Yank caught a glimpse of Robert Lawrence Quint's very own super-enigmatic smile.

Warren Sutler loved Sun Valley, Idaho, from the moment he saw it in the early-Fifties. He went back every winter and marveled at the changelessness of it. It was like a movie set, even the trees seemed not to grow. It was a fairyland where Warren felt free and fresh.

Duffy did not share his enthusiasm for the snow and cold. She used to say that the only person who gained anything from her trips to Sun Valley was the owner of the phone company. She called the paper four or five times a day with suggestions and questions, while Warren called perhaps twice a week.

The weather had turned unusually warm when Warren fell on one of his ski treks and a strange virus attacked him. His temperature climbed to an alarming degree and Duffy was frantic. The doctors at the Sun Valley Hospital were baffled, and she had him helicoptered to Boise.

Warren was turning pale and gaunt before her eyes. From a ruddy, robust man with well-toned muscles and a husky timbre in his voice to one whose bones draped tenuously with flaccid flesh, his voice a raw-throated rasp.

Duffy was terrified she was going to lose him. She tried to appear as though she hadn't a care in the world, but he saw through her.

The doctors in Boise were not much help. Specialists were called in, but no one seemed to know what Warren had, and none of the treatments were effective.

And all that time at his bedside and on the phone, all she could think of was if anything happened to Warren, Paul would take over the paper. Paul and not Olin. And with Paul in control, the next successor would be Paul's youngest child, and only son, Alfred—who already had a few seasons at the paper and had shown more aptitude for it than Paul himself.

Then just as mysteriously as the virus had struck, it lifted, and Warren's temperature, after a few wild and inexplicable gyrations, returned to normal, and he and Duffy flew home with the unencouraging valedictory from the doctor that Warren would have to be very careful and would have to be watched all the time because since they didn't know what he had, it could happen again—just as suddenly.

Her first question to Warren on the plane was, "How do you feel?"

"I'm much better," he said.

"But do you feel normal?"

"Well, maybe not quite, a little weak, but I'm all right."

Her next question was, "How far do you think Olin is from taking over?"

Warren took the question in good grace. He understood his wife. After all here was the woman (not a man mind you—the men had tried and failed) who was single-handedly going to produce a center for the arts for Los Angeles. And so he thought seriously about the question for a while.

"Far," he answered.

"Why?" Duffy asked as though Warren had been derelict in his duty.

"He hasn't moved into any management spots yet."

"Let's find him one," she said.

Warren smiled at his wife. "Okay, Duffy," he said sheepishly—
"but I feel fine. If worst came to worst, Paul could get by."

"No!" she snapped. "That would be the worst thing that could
happen to us." She looked out the small window of the plane. "What
was the name of those business consultants we had do the feasibility
study for closing the *Standard*?" she asked almost absently.

"Kittner and Grambsch, why?"

"Get them back." The muscles on her neck stood out. "And that
young man who tried so hard to please—request him. I want him to
study succession at the company and make some recommendations—
only I want to talk to him first."

Her muscles relaxed. "You are going to take it easy for a while."
She smiled and patted his hand in a gesture that was meant to be
reassuring but wasn't. "Now what kind of opening do we have in
management for Olin?"

"We don't have any openings right now."

"Well, we'll have to make one," she said. "What's his strong
suit?" she asked.

He thought for a long while, rejecting in his mind department
after department that Olin had served competently enough but without any fireworks going off.

"Athletics is his strong suit."

"The sports department?"

"He's no writer."

"He's competitive."

"Yes."

"Let's try him in marketing."

"What am I going to do with Zack Bates?"

"Find another spot for him. Let Olin apprentice for a few weeks
until he gets the hang of it then kick Zack upstairs."

Warren's brow furrowed. "It's going to take more than a couple
weeks."

"It better not," she said ominously to herself. "We might not
have the time."


Olin Sutler believed a healthy body was a prerequisite for a
healthy mind.

By the mid-Fifties there had been three additions to the
Depression-built *Tribune* headquarters.

One of them was over the loading docks where the fleet of blue
*Tribune* trucks took their papers to the far-flung customers strewn all

over the Southland.

During the third remodel, in 1955, Olin got his mother and father to give him some basement space to supervise the installation of exercise equipment in a gym room.

Duffy thought it would be good for employee morale. There was no union making demands on them, and they felt good when they could do something for the employees, unsolicited.

It was a well-equipped room with barbells, rowing machine, stationary bicycles, wall weights, sit-up and chin-up bars, a couple showers and a sauna.

Of course Olin was the employee who used the gym most, there being very little general interest in physical fitness.

But the locker room (men only) was a good place to gather for gossip and a smoke.

When he worked out, Olin could feel the vibrations of the giant state-of-the-art presses the *Tribune* had recently purchased that drove newsprint between the massive rollers with such incredible speed.

Olin often thought, as he was pressing weights in the basement gymnasium, how marvelously mysterious it was that presses of their size, speed and power could draw through their complicated machinery material as flimsy as newsprint without pulverizing it.

Olin had just come from his shower after pressing four hundred pounds, one hundred and twenty sit-ups in two minutes, and thirty chin-ups.

He was a remarkably-built, outsized man who seemed bent on broadening a chest that was already the size of two men's.

Olin *was* Southern California. He *was* the *Tribune*.

Simon Gottlieb was shooting off his mouth in the locker room while Olin worked out. He was an East Coast, irascible intellect who would have been happier with the intellectual challenge of The New York *Times* or the artistic freedom of the late lamented New York *Herald-Tribune*.

Simon Gottlieb wished the *Tribune* library upstairs was as well-equipped as the gym. He thought it kooky to be obsessed with bodily fitness in an enterprise devoted, however obliquely, to the mind.

He was often asked after one of his anti-*Tribune* tirades why he didn't find another job, and he would respond with a startled, "What? You don't escape from a velvet prison. You're locked in for life with salary and benefits like no union stiff ever had. You got to say this for the Sutlers, you go along they make it nice and cushy for you."

A group of five boondogglers was in the locker room as Olin Sutler came from his shower.

Simon Gottlieb was the loudest among them. A tough, squat, cigar-smoking man with a restless, inquiring mind, he was known to his intimates as Attila the Hun.

Simon was restless. He drew on his cigar with rapid, staccato puffs, each demi-explosion of smoke signaling a new thought.

The reporter always thought it was peculiar, the way they named the lad after both families in the dynasty. Didn't even allow the poor kid the luxury of a middle name, as though they feared he might use it and shirk his responsibility to his heritage. Sometimes Simon felt sorry for Olin Sutler. Like the way he clawed his way through all the departments, desperately trying to prove himself—but to whom, and why? The people he had to impress were pre-sold. And his immediate superiors in each department resented him. Simon used to say you could tell the character of a department head by how he went about disguising his resentment for Olin. Some were overly polite, some servile, some cold, some overcompensated by being more doctrinaire and overbearing than they ordinarily were. Only one thing was certain: no one was comfortable. It was like having an enemy spy in the ranks. And he was going to pass you up no matter how good you were.

"The big problem here, lads," Simon said, his trombone voice booming as though he hoped the cavernous walls would echo the sentiments to the executive suites five floors above, "is we are so big and so successful we have lost our way."

"How's that?" Hank Gross groaned quietly, having just come off an assignment with Olin himself.

"There's no integrity here. There's no biting investigative reporting—everytime I suggest something they cut me down. 'We're not that kind of paper,' they say. 'We don't rock the boat, we keep it floating.'"

"Well, I guess there is something to be said for that," Hank Gross said.

"Ah, read the paper," Simon boomed. "There isn't an ounce of excitement or intellectual content in it. We've just been voted by our esteemed colleagues for the umpteenth time in a row the worst paper in the nation."

Olin was seething. He could have left the locker room, but he wanted to hear this loudmouth out. What did he know about running a newspaper? There was a lot more to it than writing some fancy article in such high-blown prose that no one would read it. A newspaper reflected the people who read it. It was the thermometer not the fever. My God, Simon had a job, didn't he? Did he think that came out of some smart aleck investigative reporter? Did he ever meet a payroll? Ever try to sell an ad to someone who had been offended by something in the paper? These bellyachers didn't know a damn thing about running a paper—

"I mean, what's it all about?" Simon Gottlieb was still declaiming, his back to the awkward lad who was heir to the throne. "Doesn't a newspaper have a responsibility to the community it serves? A responsibility to probe and report fearlessly on its institutions and leaders, to challenge people's prejudices, to stimulate their curiosity for knowledge, to challenge their intellects?"

The small group of men froze as they heard Olin's locker slam shut. He strode over to them with a controlled casualness. He was the sleepy poker player of his Fort Ord days. He stopped, facing Simon Gottlieb.

"Gentlemen," he said, his voice thick with commitment, "the reason a newspaper is in existence is to make money." Then he walked away.

Charles Soames stood before Duffy's desk in her office at the *Tribune*. Duffy sat behind it. For some reason she neglected to ask him to sit down.

Soames was in his thirties, wore rimless glasses, had a smooth, narrow face and servile posture. He was extremely grateful to the Sutlers for giving him this break with his new venture, Charles Soames Associates—he had worked so well with Duffy when he was with Kittner and Grambsch. She had hinted the time might be opportune to strike out on his own.

Duffy was subtle but clear. The fee would be generous, enough to float Charles Soames Associates for several years should the findings please her. And it didn't take a genius to figure out what succession plan she had in mind. His job was to legitimize it with some high-sounding, sound-business-practice rationale.

How long will it take you?" Duffy asked.

"Well," Soames cleared his throat. "I'll have to collect the data, sort it, analyze it. So, depending on availability of data and accessibility of executives for interviewing, I should be able to get the time frame between three and four months."

He could tell from her stare that he had not pleased her.

"Mr. Soames," she said through a plastic smile, "the fee we agreed on is not based on your stamina or longevity. *Time* is the essence here." She leaned forward, elbows on her desk top. "Is there any way you could complete the project in two weeks, for, say a ten thousand bonus, without compromising your professional standards?"

"Well," he cleared his throat again. "I could do my best—"

"My husband's grandfather—who started all this—said, 'It's not the effort we care about, it's the results.'" She sank back and smiled and watched young Soames fidget. He wanted so much to please. "He started this paper on a shoestring and look at it now. With the right clients, you can do the same."

She got no argument. "Actually," she said leaning forward in confidence again, "if you swear not to let this leave this room, one of the reasons I'm in such a hurry is we are in the preliminary stages of talk on taking the *Tribune* public. We will need some heavy management consulting on that. This fee would pale by comparison."

Soames swallowed hard.

"Well, get to it," she said. "We've wasted enough time already."

A few days later, Paul Sutler came storming into Duffy's office. "Who is the snot-nosed kid who's come poking around my office asking me for my job description and how old I am? Says you sent him."

Duffy could see Paul fuming. "Oh, it's nothing, Paul—humor him. He's from the management consultants who did that dirty work for us on the *Standard*."

"Why the hell wasn't I told you were bringing in an efficiency snoop? I'm supposed to be the number two man around here and I'm sick and tired of not knowing what's going on half the time."

She smiled at him, that disarming, engaging, aw-shucks smile. It didn't appease him.

# BOOK IV

## THE POWER OF COMPETITION

# OLIN SUTLER

# THE AGGRANDIZER

> He loves glory, but he
> does not know what a
> weight glory is.
>
> —Erasmus

# 68

Everything is true except the facts.

—Malcolm Muggeridge

1960

After Duffy read the "Management Report On Orderly Succession of Los Angeles Tribune Executives" submitted by management consultants Charles Soames Associates, she threw her arms around Mr. Soames and called him "Charlie."

The report said for the good of the Tribune Company, and to make the proposed public offering more palpable, the publisher should offer at least fifteen years of continuous leadership before mandatory retirement at sixty-five.

Paul was fifty-three years old.

It was a ridiculous notion on the face of it, but the "independent" management consultant elevated it to legitimacy.

Charlie earned his bonus, and Duffy happily paid it and put him back to work on a feasibility study on going public.

Paul and his sisters were opposed to the offering of *Tribune* shares to the public, and to paying hefty fees to Charles

Soames Associates to study it.

Each day filled Duffy with the dread that her husband would suddenly drop dead without her son in his place.

"Lord," Warren would say, "Olin's not near ready yet. He hasn't any real management experience—besides, I feel fine—I'm going to be around awhile."

"I know you will, Warren," Duffy would smile that maternal smile that said, "I will humor you, but Mamma knows best."

Olin in the meanwhile was doing his stint as manager of marketing where his competitive spirit came to the fore, and he was not afraid of rocking the boat with changes; he was bent on out-producing his predecessor and Quint's morning *Inquirer*.

His style was to get ambitious people and to turn them loose, and gently but relentlessly egg them on. He was an administrator. He didn't have a lot of ideas himself, but there were plenty of people with ideas and he was good at recognizing mistakes, but he never rode them into the ground. He wasn't ashamed to cut his losses. And so under his leadership the star of marketing rose and gently eclipsed his Uncle Paul, who was a good man to attend minor ceremonies, excelling at handshaking and posturing.

The press was called to the ballroom in the Statler Hotel, with the teaser "A message of great importance."

No one except Warren and Duffy knew what the announcement was about. When Paul got wind of it he insisted on knowing.

"Come and find out," Warren said jovially.

It was an April morning, sunny, clear, warm enough for Los Angeles, and the weather had most of the crowd in good spirits. No one was expecting to go away with a message of earthshaking importance, nor were they looking forward to the *Tribune's* "reception," for these events were notorious for tepid coffee and cardboard cookies.

Seated at the table on the risers were Warren and Olin on one side, Duffy, in her finest innocent blue suit, on the other next to Paul, who was on the end. No one asked Paul to sit there—he moved his chair up. He may have been in the dark about the press conference but he wasn't going to look like they left him out of things.

Olin had only been told to prepare a short speech on what he saw in the future of the company. He was wearing a gray suit, white shirt and solid red tie. He was looking forward to cutting out on the meeting as soon as it was over for a morning of surfing in Malibu.

Warren stood and greeted his fellow journalists, radio and television commentators.

Simon Gottlieb was covering for the *Tribune*. He was seated near the rear of the room with his girlfriend, Amanda Racine. Simon was making untoward comments throughout Warren's history of the paper, so he barely heard the publisher say:

"And so effective as of this minute, I hereby appoint as publisher, Olin Sutler."

The general din that pervaded the room during his recitation of unexciting statistics about the paper's growth ceased as though everyone had stopped breathing.

When he had rehearsed the speech in his mind, Warren had always imagined enthusiastic applause at the end. Well, he thought as he stood at the rostrum awaiting some reaction, perhaps the stunned silence means they are too overcome with emotion to react.

While Olin stood up in response to his father's beckoning hand, Amanda broke the silence. "Good God in heaven," she whispered a question to Simon Gottlieb that was heard around the room, "what are his qualifications?"

"Sh," Simon said to her, "you don't ask about qualifications in a monarchy. Now with the kid in place they can go public. It's a cinch no board of directors would ever have picked him."

At the end of the dais, the blood had drained from Paul's face.

There was still no applause as the thirty-four-year-old publisher of the largest newspaper west of the Mississippi stood in his place at the table, his massive chest anchoring the ship of state to his family, while Paul looked like a drowning man ignored by the captain.

Olin flashed his boyish smile, and just as suddenly it disappeared. He felt like he had at Stanford when he had thrown the hammer farther than any living soul. It was a giddy, lightheaded, victorious feeling.

"Gosh," he said.

It was a word that some said set the intellectual tone for his reign at the *Tribune*.

He read the speech he had prepared without realizing what it was for. He read it without the excitement he felt, for while his eyes were rolling over the words on the paper, and while his vocal mechanisms were engaged in forming the sounds, his mind was tumbling over the meaning of this surprise. The power and prestige it would bring him. The wealth.

He caught sight of his wife, Nell, beaming in the front row of spectators. He couldn't ever remember seeing her look as happy.

The minute Olin had delivered himself of his prepared text,

bogged down with platitudes, the meeting broke up. The coffee and cardboard went begging. Paul rose out of his chair like a fast-growing plant.

"Goddammit, Duffy," he stood over her, glaring down. "This is outrageous. What gives you the almighty authority to make these unilateral decisions?"

"Oh, we had a management firm recommend it," she smiled sweetly. "I'll show you the report when you get back to the office," she stopped a moment. Her eyes twinkled. "—If you are *going* back."

"Bitch."

Warren Sutler stood with a long face in front of the employees of the *Standard* in the newsroom where they had assembled on an hour's notice.

"I stand before you today," Warren began. He was no orator, not even a passable speechmaker, the short pressman in the front thought as he stood with his eyes fixed on his boss, a man he had never seen before.

The pressman was Alex Birnbaum, grandson of Aaron Birnbaum, who had walked out on General Benjamin Raines Olin when the General was still a colonel. Alex had heard the story many times and still couldn't understand what drew him to the Sutler empire. He had a wife and five kids and was in no position to play Russian roulette, and yet here he was in his little newspaper cap, worn at a jauntier angle than his colleagues, and his eyes never left Warren Sutler, grandson of Benjamin Raines Olin.

"I stand before you today," Warren repeated, in an effort to get the group quiet.

Alex Birnbaum mused at the want of originality in the opening salvo, and the lack of creativity in simply repeating the same canned phrase. "Just like the Sutler papers," he thought.

Warren raised his voice and a semblance of order was settling over the crowd. "I stand before you today, a humble and despondent man." He was choking on his suppressed tears. "This is the saddest thing I have ever had to do in my life. As you probably know, the *Standard* has been for these twelve or thirteen years a pet project of mine.... But we have been unable to make it profitable. We did everything we knew how to save it. Finally, we called in management consultants. Six months, and tens of thousands of dollars later, they concluded there was just no way to make the *Standard* break even.

Our losses have been staggering, and so it is with deep personal regret that I announce effective with this afternoon's edition we are ceasing operation of the *Standard*. We will try to hire as many as we can at the *Tribune* and others will be given severance pay, based on length of employment."

Birnbaum reached up and took off his paper hat.

Later that day when word spread through the *Standard* Building that Quint was closing his morning paper at the same time, there was some grousing among the ranks that if they had had a union it wouldn't have happened.

"Listen, the way papers are dying' all around us," Alex Birnbaum said, "we'll be lucky to get jobs. Union or not."

# 69

LOS ANGELES
TRIBUNE
GOING PUBLIC?

—Headline, March 7,
1961 *Wall Street Journal*

Yank's house was a sprawling mirage of ranchy stucco that was thrown up by an overworked contractor in a long-past building boom to appeal to the wealthy man who had neither the time nor the taste to seek something better.

Unfortunately, when Yank completed the house with its ten thousand square feet and views of the world from its perch on the Hollywood Hills, he couldn't interest anyone in paying his price. He decided it was not quite schlocky enough for the plebeian *nouveau riche*, so he moved in himself.

Immediately he began stuffing the place with art, so now it looked like the home of a Texas oil millionaire turned over to a museum *in situ* with the stipulation that everything stay just as it was in the original.

Max rang the bell.

Yank answered.

Seventy-three years old he was, and with each sliding year he took on more dignity. He seemed to forestall all the benchmarks of the aging process twenty years. His bearing was benign, his joints agile, his hair held its color remarkably under the cowboy hat with only a smattering of gray in the sandy blond. He had lived in the sprawling house so long he became part of it, like the favorite chair you looked for each time you visited. The favorite chair you wouldn't realize was Theresa's chair.

Yank greeted Max like a welcome friend.

Max would never change. The fat under his skin kept it smooth. The pancake-sized dandruff on his dark blazer seemed larger than usual, his hair was grayer, but he was otherwise the same old Max.

Jud Crown and Nora Yates were seated on the white couch in the sunken living room with the great expanse of glass that overlooked Hollywood and Los Angeles.

"Congratulations are in order," Yank said, waving his glass at Jud and Nora.

"Congratulations," Max said mechanically. "What are they in order for?"

"Nuptials, my friend," Yank said. "The blessed state."

"Wasn't so blessed for me," Max grumbled. "And how would you know, you never tried it?"

Nora Yates still had the engaging, guileless smile. It reminded Yank of Theresa's smile, though Nora was older than Theresa would ever be. Seated with the gray and gaunt Jud Crown, Nora looked like his happy, healthy, middle-aged daughter.

Jud looked distracted. He had just completed a messy divorce from his tyrannical wife to whom he paid forty million to disappear into the woodwork. He had discovered sometime after the divorce that he couldn't live without Nora, who had served him so well as his secretary for over twenty years.

Jud looked like a man exhausted from a long-distance run, short of breath, with all the energy sweated out of him. He didn't know it yet, but his body was host to nascent cancer cells.

Yank's living room was two stories tall. The second story was surrounded by a balcony lined with books, with a sliding ladder to reach the top shelves.

The ground floor was the museum.

A reclining nude in black marble by Matisse was on the glass coffee table between Max and Yank. Yank had bought it from Robert Lawrence Quint.

The walls were laden with impressionist paintings—with a

heavy tilt in this room and the corridor toward Monet.

"Well, the big news is the *Tribune*," Yank said cutting off the small talk. "It looks like they are finally going public."

"I'm not so sure," Max said, sitting forward in the off-white chair. "The sisters and Paul fear a takeover. The business consultants Duffy hired told them they would probably be safe with just twenty-five percent of the common stock; they don't believe it."

"Well, assuming it goes through," Yank said, looking at Jud, "would you be game for a little raiding party?"

Jud seemed to turn paler on the white couch next to Nora. He shook his head in amazement. "I don't see how you can keep it up all these years."

"I can," Yank assured him. He looked at Nora. She said nothing. Yank turned to Max. "The statistics please, Max."

"Talk is," Max began, "they would issue about six million shares, at around twenty bucks a share. That would be one hundred and twenty million—of which the family would hang on to forty-two to forty-eight millions' worth. To take over we figure we would need forty to forty-five million to be safe, less if we could crack the family."

"Those are big numbers," Jud mused.

"Of course," Max said, "there is the problem of getting control *sub rosa*. It is, thanks to J. P. Morgan, Diamond Jim Brady and their cronies, now strictly illegal to take a position of any consequence in a stock without reporting it to the Securities and Exchange Commission."

"How do you propose to do it then?" Nora asked, patting Jud's hand as if to reassure him she was just being sociable.

"That's why we are soliciting help," Yank said. "Outright purchase is only part of it. I hope to call in some markers from the sisters. I've bought a lot of insurance from that hack Volkes, and I've put a lot of gelt in Hines the Third's bank. The cousins, of course, are the enigma. They have the real shares."

"One's a fruity musician," Max offered, "and the girl's a religious nut. The musician dotes on Duffy. She's got him believing she's going to get him a performance with her Symphony. And the girl's a tossup."

"What does that mean?" Nora asked politely, the sparkle in her eye betraying her eagerness for the scheme.

"She goes along with the family—that is with the movers and shakers—Warren and Duffy. And the minute she wavers, they'll commit her—it only takes a signature, and no one could deny it was legitimate. Those two loonies control forty-five percent of the family's stock—and you can just write them off."

"That leaves the Sutlers—my half brothers and sisters," Yank said. Each family has nine percent—but isn't it the irony of old man Olin's genius that a piano player and a religious nut each have more shares than the publisher?"

"I suppose it could help us," Nora said. Jud looked at her suddenly and caught the gleam in her eye on the word "us."

"No chance," Max countered quickly. "With their friends and well-wishers—who cannot be underestimated—we would have to pull around thirty-five to forty percent ourselves to do any real damage."

"Is there another angle?" Nora asked.

"Well," Yank said, "we were thinking of stock swaps for mergers and buyouts. Say we own a lumber mill and we sell out to them. They are delighted to give stock instead of cash.... So if we buy those things, or have them, like newspapers," he said eying Jud, "we might make some inroads."

"Too rich for my blood, I'm afraid," Jud said wearily.

"Ah, but what you may be missing is the economic potential," Yank said. "Even if we fail, the cost of buying us out to prevent another attempt at takeover—which is very costly for a company to resist—is high—usually we get substantially more for our shares than we paid, and more than the market price."

Jud excused himself. He wasn't feeling up to snuff, he said.

On the way out Nora winked at Yank and said, "We'll think about it."

# 70

...and she set there, very impatient and excited and handsome, but looking kind of happy and eased up, like a person that's had a tooth pulled out.

—Mark Twain
*Huckleberry Finn*

Duffy and Warren sat in the glass-enclosed breakfast nook that looked out on their colorful Hancock Park garden. Duffy hired a landscape architect, who was a *Tribune* "Woman of the Year," to renovate the garden after they bought the house. "Give me color all year," Duffy said, and she had: with azaleas, bougainvillea, begonias, fuchsias, impatiens, daisies and a host of annuals and flowering trees. The renovation was still going on and two gardeners were planting annuals along the path to the swimming pool.

Warren was reading the morning *Tribune*. "Olin's doing all right," he said, shaking his head and clucking his tongue. "To look at him you wouldn't expect he had more on his mind than bench-pressing a couple hundred pounds and riding his motorcycle, but he's doing all right."

Duffy beamed. She never said, "I told you so," to Warren.

"He's got the Sunday circulation

over a million. Quite an achievement."

Duffy reached across the table and laid her hands on her husband's hands. "But you must take some of the credit, dear. You laid the foundation."

Warren wet his lips and turned his head. "He gets the laurels. He's the boss now—over four thousand employees—thanks to you."

Warren had no bitterness in his voice. Not even remorse. Duffy would swear to that. He was just as proud of their son as she was.

The paper sold for five cents in the 1880's, and except for some price wars to drive competitors out of business, stayed at a nickel for over sixty years. After World War II it shot up to seven cents and now in 1961, it was a dime.

The format was eight columns wide and they ran large attention-getting pictures above the fold on the front page. And, they might run three columns of pictures of an automobile accident right down the middle.

In appearance the Los Angeles *Tribune* was somewhere between the New York *Times* and an afternoon tabloid.

And, there was always a profusion of ads:

Out in Reseda you could buy a real home, "Not a box," for $7700, or $41.20 a month, and for $2.79 a month more they would throw in an eight-foot G.E. Hotpoint refrigerator, Westwood chrome range and Bendix washer.

You could catch a burlesque at the Colony Club at Western and 149th.

You could have two prime rib dinners ("All you can eat") at Rand's Roundup for $2.79, or two steak dinners for the price of one at the Pink Pussycat on Santa Monica Boulevard, while you watched the world-famous show with students of the Pink Pussycat College of Striptease.

Duffy lowered the coffee cup from her lips. "I'm missing something," she said.

"What are you missing, Duffy?" Warren asked, setting down the morning *Tribune* he was reading.

Warren always dressed for breakfast in the three-piece suit and tie he wore to work, but he had a harder time getting started in the morning than Duffy. She wore her blue robe and was usually bright and cheery.

The early rhythms of a morning newspaper crept into the marrow of Warren's bones and set him throbbing in march time late at night—quickening at deadline when he put the paper to bed. In the morning the pulse was more adagio—waltz time.

He had been off the late night routine for many years now, but he still felt the nightly ups and morning downs.

Warren was looking older than he had before his mysterious illness. His skin was chalky and it hung loose from his sharp jawbone. Yet he was more at ease being the chairman of a conglomerate, buying and selling companies, than he had been as publisher. He liked being a gentle buccaneer.

Duffy had more protective fat, though with her corsets she hardly looked overweight. At breakfast Duffy reminded Warren of a squirrel darting here and there to find sustenance, then scurrying back to salt it away, repeating the process endlessly.

But today Duffy seemed out of sorts.

She sat in her silk bathrobe that was as blue as the heart of a low fire, holding her coffee cup below her mouth with her elbow propped on the table. It was as though her mind had taken hold of some disturbing thought that demanded a solution before she could do another thing.

Warren lit a cigarette while he watched her impassive face and waited for her response.

In the late-1940's, a group of downtown businessmen, including the *Tribune's* Warren Sutler, put up the money to buy some land in the Bunker Hill area, an area of low-cost housing, not to say slums. The land was not too expensive, and the men had in mind the creation of perhaps an opera house to ward off jeers of outsiders who always ridiculed Los Angeles for having no culture.

It was time to counteract the many slurs on the city, from the innocuous: "Dozens of communities in search of a city," to the worst: "If you gave the country an enema the operation would take place in Los Angeles."

They would take it no more. Los Angeles would get off the defensive once and for all. They were going after culture hot and heavy, and nothing spelled culture like opera. And it didn't matter to the men involved that none of them knew anything about opera; very few of them had ever heard one. It was these great institutions that survived. Why, look at Virginia City, Nevada, the ghost town—isn't the opera house still standing from the gold rush? It was no use suggesting that might have been a different kind of opera.

Three times the matter was submitted to the voters for their approval, and three times the bond issues failed. Perhaps the critics were right. Los Angeles was still a hick town that wanted no part of *haute* culture; not if it was going to cost anything.

The business committee didn't give up. Duffy wouldn't let them. The downtown auditorium her Symphony was using doubled as a Baptist church, with a neon sign on the roof that said "JESUS SAVES." It was depressing.

As she had pointed out before they bought the land, the merchants were not doing much business with the denizens of the old clapboard houses on Bunker Hill. This would be the beginning of a revitalization of the squalid downtown area to compete with the fancy new shopping centers going up all over Southern California. Every place else was growing. Downtown was dying. The *Tribune* was downtown and the Sutlers owned land downtown. They certainly didn't want to die with it.

A complex loan agreement was made with the city and county pension funds with the assurance that private fund-raising of donations would at least equal their loan. Duffy pledged to raise four million.

She did her damnedest with the old guard friends of the paper, and she did well—but the well was running dry and only a little over half had been collected.

"So, what are you missing, Duffy?" Warren prodded gently.

"I have a feeling I've only scratched the surface. I've stayed with the old stand-bys. They're all Establishment and WASPs. Oh, the Cardinal gave me twenty-five thousand and I've a handful of other Catholics, but you know what's missing—the Jews. I don't have a single Jew. And Hollywood. There must be money in Hollywood—the studios. A theater and arts center should be a natural for them."

"Now you are talking tightrope time," Warren said, putting his fork down next to his scrambled eggs.

"What?"

"You court those people, you're going to have to answer a lot of questions: about our clubs, which don't take them as members—or even as guests—and the paper whose political philosophy is diametrically opposed to theirs. They will blame you for all of it."

"Well," she said, "it wouldn't hurt to listen to them. Who do you think I should talk to first? Someone who knows the ins and outs of the Democrats, Jews and Hollywood."

"Sadie and Herman Marks."

"The Democratic councilwoman?"

He nodded. "And he is a big Hollywood lawyer, and the Democrats' biggest fund-raiser. And they belong to the Hillcrest

Country Club."

"Well, that's a real find, Warren."

He picked up his fork. "But don't think you are going to have an easy time of it. They hate our guts."

"Nothing ventured, Warren, nothing gained."

Duffy Sutler, scion by marriage of the old guard Republican, WASP, Establishment Sutler and Olin clan met with Herman and Sadie Marks, *nouveau riche*, Jews, prime movers of Democratic party politics and Hollywood motion picture circles.

The meeting was over lunch at Perino's restaurant on Wilshire Boulevard.

Duffy made it a point to be fifteen minutes early so she would be seated when they came. She wore her gray suit with the delicate burgundy stripe and under it the frilly white blouse that made her look like she had a chest full of whipped cream.

Perino's was pure. There were no food odors about the place as there were in other restaurants. The only odor at Perino's was of crisp fifty dollar bills.

When the maitre d' showed the Markses to the table, Duffy stood up to greet them.

The Markses were a short, dark couple. Both had khaki-colored skin and black, wavy hair. You wouldn't mistake them for Norsemen, Duffy noted with glee. Herman was a bespectacled, bookish-looking man with a pencil mustache, more at home in the Talmud from his looks. Sadie was compact and wiry, full of life, energy and fun.

"It was so good of you to come," Duffy said when they were seated—she in the middle of the booth, Herman on her left. Sadie, on her right, wore a pink suit and sat straight with her hands darting from caressing Perino's heavy silverware to touching the crystal that adorned the light pink tablecloths. It seemed as if there were more waiters in tails than there were customers. Old Perino knew how to put on the dog, and Duffy liked to use his unbounded opulence to make her prospects feel ashamedly rich. "The easier to part with their money, my dear," she had explained to Warren. Even the food was pretty good—and if not, you paid so much you wouldn't allow yourself to question your judgement.

"No one turns down an invitation of Duffy's *Tribune*," Herman said with a smile.

Duffy smiled back. Sadie smiled. There were a lot of uneasy smiles at the table. "I didn't ask you here to talk about the *Tribune*,"

Duffy said, "I want to talk about my music and theater arts center."

And talk she did, telling her dreams for the city, what it would mean to everyone, and especially the Hollywood crowd. How this was just the thing to bring down the social barriers in town.

Herman rotated his water glass with the stem between his thumb and forefinger while she talked. When she finished he raised his eyebrow. "But Mrs. Sutler," he began courtly.

"Oh Duffy, please."

He smiled. "Duffy, all right. Do you have any idea what it means in this town to be a Democrat and a Jew, and read your paper?"

Duffy wrinkled her cute nose, perplexed, so he told her.

"It is hell, pure hell," he said. "The *Tribune* has not drawn an objective breath since it began. Fairness is simply so far out of the question it would be naive to ask for it." He looked at her, she was listening sympathetically.

"Democrats are the lowest of the low," he went on, "and Jews are the forgotten religion, never pictured, never mentioned. You know, Duffy, it is a new world for minorities all across the country, but not in Los Angeles. A great deal of this town was built on the movie industry, and yet anyone associated with it is banned from the L.A. Country Club. I mean Jews are used to being banned from clubs, but a lot of the movie industry are Gentiles, and they aren't used to it."

"Well that's not the paper's fault," Sadie said coming to Duffy's defense.

"It's all part of the same bag," Herman said. "It's the Establishment against the rest of us. And the biggest gun in the Establishment is the *Tribune*."

Duffy nodded, "I appreciate your frankness," she said. "You've opened my eyes to some real problems I just never thought about. I'll see if we can't make some changes."

They ordered the lunch and talked some small talk with Duffy pumping them both for names of people they knew with big money to share with a worthy cause.

When dessert came, Duffy said, "I hope you will help me—I understand how you feel about the paper, but this is my project, not the *Tribune*'s. It is a charity, not a business venture. It is for the good of *all* mankind."

"Of which the *Tribune* is a very big part," Herman said.

"I am putting together a committee," Duffy said, "leaders of the elite in Los Angeles. I'd like to put you both on it."

Herman looked at her, then at his wife. "You do that, you'll lose half the others."

"I don't think so," Duffy smiled. "How would they explain it in the paper?" She blotted her mouth with the pink napkin. "Anyway, I'm willing to take that chance. Los Angeles has been a closed society way too long. My theater complex is going to be for *all* the people. But I can't broaden our base without your help."

"I'm game," Sadie the city councilwoman spoke up, not unmindful of the publicity attendant to membership on one of Duffy's blue-ribbon committees.

Herman was weighing the competition for the contribution dollars of his contacts against the publicity and goodwill his participation would engender. "And who knows," he thought, "maybe this *will* be a chance to get us outcasts in the game."

"We'll see what we can do," he said.

After she saw the Markses to the door (she had prearranged with Perino to bill her) she went back to the dining room where she had spotted two oil men having lunch. They were friendly rivals who Duffy knew loved to get the edge on each other. One was J. Karl Gittens, tall and introverted, blond, tassel-like hair resting on his gold-rimmed glasses; the other, Hugh Penza, huge and jolly, balding, always smiling, always scheming.

Karl wore a navy blazer with an irrelevant crest on the left breast, gray slacks and a solid gray tie. Hugh Penza wore a western jacket, string tie with a silver clasp on the black strings and a rumpled white shirt straining at the buttons.

"Hello, gentlemen," Duffy said.

"The Queen of the *Tribune*," Hugh Penza said. "Sit down, dear. Have a drink with us." J. Karl fidgeted. He didn't really want the company.

"Well if I'm not intruding on anything." She sat with a smile of contentment before there was any time to withdraw the invitation.

J. Karl had that devastated "she's-going-to-put-the-touch-on-us" look on his face, but Penza was ever-jovial and made believe nothing could be further from his mind.

"What'll you have?" Hugh asked her.

"Oh, nothing, thank you," she said. "I just finished a big meal with the Markses."

"Yes, we saw," Hugh said. "Get anything?"

"We'll see," she said, usually noncommittal unless she had something substantial. "I'm in a real bind, boys," she said, "and I wonder if you could help me?"

"How much is it, Duffy?" Hugh asked.

"I'm three hundred thousand short of my initial promise to the board of supervisors. They simply can't wait any longer. I've got to get it by tomorrow. You have any idea where I could get my hands on that kind of money today?"

J. Karl spoke up, "You tried the Sutlers? They're the richest people in town."

"Oh, I don't know about that, but yes I've got handsome help from the family and the paper and the corporation. I'm still short. What I need is one or two rich oil men to see me through this phase. If I do, there will be no stopping me, I'm sure."

"I'm sure too, doll," Hugh said. "I love that paper of yours, you never let me down—none of that bleeding heart liberal crap like those New York phonies. Promise to keep it the same forever, doll baby, and I'll give you a few bucks."

"Well, I don't run the paper you know."

"Not much, baby," he said and winked broadly at Karl.

"My son is publisher now," she said. "And he listens to me even less than my husband did."

"Right," Hugh said winking and nodding again, and pulling that long face of exaggerated disbelief.

"Well, do you fellas think you could help me out?"

"Not today, Duffy," J. Karl Gittens said, anxious to get her out of there. "I gave at the office."

She laughed. He seemed pleased.

"I've got to run, Hugh," he said. "You want to flip for lunch?"

"Naw, you tightwad, I'll pay it. I wouldn't want anything to happen to your first nickel you still squeeze the bejesus out of."

"It's already taken care of," Duffy said. Both men looked at her with enlarging eyes.

"Mighty white of you, Duffy," Hugh said. "Why would you do that?"

"Oh, someday I might ask you a favor."

He nodded, "Anytime."

"Like today," she pressed gently.

He grinned and took out his wallet. "How much did you say?"

"Three hundred thousand," she said, swallowing softly.

He wrote in silence. "Here's half of it," he said looking at Karl, who was blocked in his seat by Hugh on one side and Duffy on the other. He looked like he was considering crawling under the table.

Duffy was holding the check and studying it lovingly. "You didn't fill in the payee—"

"You do it, doll. Just make sure it's something deductible."

"How long do I have to cash it?"

"Why would you want to hold it?"

"I mean, you don't have to transfer funds or something?"

Hugh smiled, his hands brushed crumbs off his bloated belly. "I expect it's good now," he said. "Now as far as the other half," he said looking across at Karl, "the only other guy in town who might come close to matching the same feat is sitting in between us looking like his liver is about to collapse. Don't let that shy crap fool you, Duffy, he's rich; not rich like me maybe, he hasn't been that successful, but rich enough. But confidentially," he leaned forward and lowered his voice, "he has the reputation of being something of a nickel and dimer. He might be able to write you a check like mine if you can wait a couple days while he switches money from his interest bearing accounts to cover it. That's the sure sign of a small-timer, Duffy, when a guy has to piddle around for taxable interest. But I doubt you'll ever get him to tumble, he's so tight he squeaks when he walks."

"Go to hell, Hugh," Karl said.

"Show her what you're made of, you cheapskate. After you transfer the funds you won't even miss it—come on, give her a hundred if that's all you can spare and make her scrounge around for the other fifty. For Chrissakes, Karl, she bought you lunch!"

J. Karl Gittens looked to his left and right as if hoping one of them had vaporized so he could escape. He sighed and pulled out his checkbook and wrote a check with slow, painful strokes of his fountain pen. He tore the check from its moorings as though parting from a dear friend for the last time. He pushed the check, face down on the table, to Duffy. She nodded her grateful thanks and thought it best not to look at it until she left. She jumped up, kissed both men on the cheek and said, "God bless you, boys, and if He shouldn't, I will—" and she was off to tell the maitre d' to put their lunch on her bill with a larger than life tip.

It wasn't until she was behind the wheel of her eggshell-blue Cadillac that she had the courage to look at Karl's check. It was for one hundred and fifty thousand dollars.

It wasn't always that easy. She had made the first watermark with that miracle, but broadening her base caused her endless difficulties. As everyone had predicted, there was infighting and backbiting. Some of the old guard were aghast to see Jews on the society pages of the *Tribune*. And through it all Duffy kept her chin up, placated and cajoled (and never found it necessary to mention that her grandmother was Jewish).

She heard all the expected exchanges. "We fought a war for you so don't tell us we discriminate."

"You didn't fight for us. If it had been Hitler against only the Jews you wouldn't have been in it."

But as she went along she learned to cope with all sides, how to appease, and stall confrontations. For a million dollars she gave one savings and loan owner the naming of the buildings, then took another million from his arch-rival, Hyman Abrams, on the condition that a theater would be named for him. She would worry later about the inevitable conflict.

Few realized how many had tried and failed before her to do the very same thing. But Duffy was indomitable, and where others failed she succeeded. They could say what they wanted about her, call her a hick, a country bumpkin, Mamma's Duff; there were plenty of sour grapes on the vines. Many said she had blackmailed the rich with the bludgeon of the *Tribune*, threatening them with unwanted and untoward publicity.

It was a rumor Duffy saw no point in disabusing. If it gave her an unsolicited leverage, so be it. The cause was just. But she would never be that crude. Nor was she anxious to have anyone know that her days at the paper seemed to be numbered, that her son, Olin, on whose head she, and she alone, had placed the crown, was not as generous about listening to her advice as his father was, and every day seemed to grow more independent. Fortunately that independence seemed to play very nicely, thank you, into her hands.

And nothing pleased her more than his John Birch Society Caper.

That is not to say the power never got too heady for her. She was giving her all for her Symphony, more than any living being, and she knew she was vital to its success.

She referred to the organization as "My Symphony," and no one contradicted her. For immodest as the phrase was, it was also unarguable.

She realized the Hollywood star system spilled over to her Symphony. You sold the stars to fill the house. The big-name artists you paid through the nose for, that's what sold the tickets. It was always personalities, not the music, that brought the standing rooms. A violinist with a beatific smile, or a pianist with the touch of Venus on his fingertips, came and went. But the star who remained week after week was the conductor.

Los Angeles had had a fair share of good conductors, but they had also suffered some second-raters. The question always seemed to be, did the Los Angeles audience know the difference?

It so happened that during the excitement over the new home for the Symphony, Los Angeles was in an up phase conductor-wise in the person of a severe, tall, angular Hungarian named Zoltan Egri. But Zoltan had an ego, as most conductors had, and when he attended the reception after his first concert under protest ("I 'ave too eggs-haw-sted to make social smallness after I geeve all to ze moosek—but zis vun time seenze eet ees furst—if you inseest—but veel also be lohst.") he was outraged to find it an occasion for presenting Duffy Durham Sutler with some stupid award, and the next day she got more space in the papers than he did.

It was a shaky start. But the real furor arose over the selection of an assistant conductor. An obscure Greek trombone player named Aris was conductor of the Toronto orchestra and was signed for a guest appearance with the Los Angeles orchestra while Egri was fulfilling contract obligations in Europe.

The Greek wonder had a dark olive, sparkling skin, was twenty-four years old, and the women's committee adored him. No matter his musical gifts left the orchestra on the cold side, he was a born showman, and some of the players nicknamed him "Barnum."

Before his guest stint was over, Duffy knew she had to have him for her orchestra. Egri didn't have any sex appeal. He may have been a first-rate musician, but he wasn't moving the tickets. Duffy pronounced him too stiff for lotus land. Egri wanted an assistant—but he wanted to choose him himself. But Egri was in Vienna. Tough luck, Egri.

Duffy handled it all with a telegram:

> EXCELLENT NEWS FOR YOU STOP ARIS HONORED
> TO BE YOUR ASSISTANT CONDUCTOR STOP

Zoltan Egri expressed his thoughts on the matter on the transatlantic telephone lines, and followed with a cable, resigning.

Duffy was ecstatic. She had her *Wunderkind*, and as her music director.

There are many misconceptions about power. One is that it springs full-blown on the soul and wipes out everything that stands in its way by some premeditated drive to absolute supremacy and/or the abject defeat of one's adversary.

But it was not so with Duffy. She was not interested in power *per se*. She was interested in accomplishing things, and she was pleasantly surprised to discover that one success led to another with a gratifying steamroller effect.

# 71

Life is an effort that
deserves a better cause.

—Karl Kraus

The Sutlers were afraid. Afraid
someone would be able to get enough
stock to outvote them. It just seemed to
Paul and his sisters that going public
was not worth the risk.

The meeting was called in an effort
to stop the public offering of *Tribune*
shares before it was too late.

Olin conducted the meeting as a
courtesy to his aunts and uncles. Warren
and Duffy did not attend. Nor did the
major stockholders, Hilde and Clyde
Bascomb. They had given their proxies
to Warren.

They all had become, under Warren
and Olin's stewardship, almost obscenely
rich. They were sensitive about having
to publish just how rich, and the public
offering of the *Tribune* would force
them to reveal all.

Sitting on the couch under a buffalo head, the Sutler sisters were all
grandmothers now and carried that burden proudly.

Katherine, at sixty-four, would have

been pushing retirement age if she had had a job. A gold watch they might have given her and a farewell luncheon banquet, depending on how far she had advanced. But they wouldn't be sorry to see her go.

Louisa was sixty-three, and as self-absorbed still as an adolescent. Amy, at fifty-eight, was the most noble of the crew, if acceptance and enjoyment of her wealth and station could be termed noble.

There wasn't a real rebel among them. None of their kids were hippies. There was a strong strain of conformity in the chromosomes. The sisters were all fulfilled shopping for the finest wardrobes, traveling first class to the most exotic spots and passing the time playing bridge and lending their names and clout to charity, but not the Theater Arts Center. That was Duffy's.

They were not boat-rockers anymore, but placid passengers. Now someone else was threatening the comfort of their ride. So Paul had stirred up the sleeping tigers.

With their puffed up chicken breasts the sisters had come to cluck.

Here was young Olin in this stuffed animal museum driving his desk like the captain of the ship, and they were superfluous passengers, helpless to do anything but pick up their checks.

And Duffy had engineered the whole damn thing. Duffy, the fugitive from the funny farm.

But their biggest fear about the *Tribune* going public was that they would be taken over by someone and would see their majority share dwindle to the minority.

Olin responded to the fears.

"Then we will just have to get so big no one can touch us," he said, his pointy jaw jutting upward, daring any comer to take a poke at it. "And of course if push comes to shove, we can always buy more shares ourselves. There's nothing that says we have to roll over and play dead should someone try to take us over."

His secretary brought him a note, he glanced at it, crumpled it and dropped it in the wastebasket.

He adjourned the meeting and left the office. Paul went to the wastebasket and retrieved the note, smoothed it out in his hands and read:

High tide 3:57 p.m.—great swells. Surf should hold.

And so they went away as they came, empty-handed. For Olin had decided the only way to compete as a world-class paper was to raise enormous, unprecedented sums through a public offering of the stock.

And Olin had the votes.

Olin was driving on the freeway from his home in San Marino to the Theater Arts Center in downtown L.A. for opening night.

The Olin Sutlers made a habit of locking the car doors for their freeway trips. Because however you went on a freeway to get to downtown Los Angeles, you traveled through a poor section of town.

They called them freeways, not because you could travel freely on them for more than a couple years after they cut the ribbon, but because there were no tolls to be paid anywhere. Let's see them do *that* in the East!

And so they kept laying down the wide-ribboned cement freeways to handle the cars. They opened these futuristic roads with a ribbon-cutting ceremony, and when the cars came there were still too many. So they built more freeways. There was more than one car per person in Los Angeles, and it often seemed like all the Angelenos were on the road—each in their one-point-one cars.

And the *Tribune* had pushed for the freeways—the bonds, the gas tax—all laid in concrete, crisscrossing this great city like the wrappings on a mummy. And what if the Sutlers had some land in those golden corridors? *All* the land couldn't be in poor sections. There was no law that said you had to lose money in real estate.

So to compensate for the more expensive land where substantial houses had to be bought and torn down, the heart of a new freeway cut through the poorer sections. The land was cheaper and the state didn't have to hassle fighting fancy lawyers in three-piece suits.

And the poorer kids came out in force with big white eyes to watch them maul the earth with their fat old tractors, and strap the steel skeletons that were the bones that held the mighty roadways together.

But when the giant buckets of concrete came, dangling from cranes that looked like dinosaurs, the kids scattered. They didn't want that glop falling on their heads. They didn't want to be planted in the ole freeway, no sir!

All those freeways poured cars into downtown Los Angeles where they were building skyscrapers all over town. It wasn't as though there wasn't enough land, Los Angeles had 455 square miles of land, the largest city in the United States geographically. It was as though the Los Angeles developers thought the only way to be considered a world-class city was to have tall buildings—to have traffic snarls in a compact downtown area.

They crammed that little cow town chock-full of the future. If you stood on certain corners you could think you were on Manhattan Island.

Los Angeles would do anything to kill those enema jokes. Tall buildings could not be sneezed at—especially gratuitous tall buildings. Why, San Francisco, that two-bit tourist trap to the north, had tall buildings—and they had Kul-cha with a capital K.

It was not the first war of imitation.

In 1961, the metropolitan area of Los Angeles was almost five thousand square miles. It was a long way to deliver newspapers. Freeways were an awful big help.

Nell had not spoken on the trip to the gala opening of her mother-in-law's Theater Arts Center. It made Olin uneasy. Without thinking, he blurted: "I don't plan to live in the shadow of my mother all my life."

"Interesting," Nell said, her thoughts elsewhere.

"Your mother has been an inspiration to me," she said, tugging at the front of her low-backed black chiffon dress, hoisting it over the firm breasts. "I want to start working."

"You've got enough work at home," he said.

"Pandering to the heirs?"

Silence for the rest of trip—

Inside the great hall the mirrors were two stories high. Ah, mirrors! Could you ever get enough of them? When you spent that much to wrap your body for the Symphony you wanted people to see it, to admire your taste. But there was nothing like seeing yourself, life-size, in the polished glass of this temple of culture. Everyone looked smashing in glass of that quality.

The names of the faithful were chiseled in marble on the side walls, the letters highlighted with gold. Each name was under its unique, monetarily keyed heading. So there could be no misunderstanding just how much gelt had been forked over for this worthy cause. You couldn't touch Duffy for passing around the credit.

Olin adjusted his coat lapels and ran his hand over the dark rep tie, checking his appearance in the giant mirrors as he entered the great hall.

He had been getting a lot of public attention ever since he was named publisher of the *Tribune*. He felt like a movie star under the admiring, inquiring stares.

He checked the marble slabs for the names of the *Tribune* and his mother and father. He didn't have far to look, they were right on top.

Nell was talking to someone about one of her charity meetings. "We've got to come to a meeting of the minds," she said as Olin took her arm in his hand and the couple climbed the broad carpeted stairs to the Donor's Circle, as though they were ascending into heaven amidst all those heavenly mirrors, to sit at the right hand of God, the Mother....

It was a gala affair. After they were seated, Nell whispered to Olin, "There're enough jewels here to choke a horse."

The young Greek conductor's skin shone like a well-lotioned face long in the sun, taking the ladies' breath away.

The program was safely mired in the Classics and Romantics to keep the minds from wandering too far. And at intermission the big donors gathered in the private room dedicated to them and imbibed booze under a full-length oil portrait of Duffy Durham Sutler.

Olin was embarrassed by all the attention being heaped on his mother. Hers was the only portrait in this room. He made a mental note to take her picture off the *Tribune* wall just as soon as he found a graceful way to get rid of her.

His Uncle Yank was looking at him across the room. Olin didn't know why he was always so uncomfortable with Yank, he was affable enough. But Yank's stares always made him feel like he was being judged.

And Yank was so irreverent. It was as though nothing was serious to him. He had called the new building "Duffy's Tavern" because the saloon was such a showcase.

"That high falutin' music goes down a little better if you're half swacked," Yank had said.

Olin wished he had the guts to leave before he had to sit through another hour of that posturing Greek phony his mother was so gaga over.

Well, she had done the job, there wasn't any denying it. There were cement buildings all over the place with countless slabs for cars underground.

It was like Pharaohs' tombs with the multileveled catacombs beneath to store earthly treasures. In Los Angeles the most significant earthly treasure was the automobile.

The music critic, Jimmy Allen, had been the agricultural editor before he got culture. He was an affable man who didn't know good music from Shinola, but the ninety-eight percent of the readers who didn't either didn't care. He was a gusher and he did a job on the opening.

When Olin read the review the next day at breakfast he felt ill.

"This isn't a music review," he said to Nell, who was still in her robe, "this is a paean of praise to Mother."

"Well, hon, she deserves everything she got. Without her the Center wouldn't have been built—you want to be the last person on earth to acknowledge that?"

"Ah—she wouldn't have done it without the paper—"

"The paper didn't do much without her," she said. "Olin—why do you begrudge her a little glory—God knows she earned it."

He threw the paper across the breakfast table.

Nell was starting to get on his nerves. How could she talk so dumb? She knew the scuttlebutt going around that Olin was all his mother's doing. They gave her the credit for his dad's success, and now they were trying to give her the credit for his. Not only had she given birth to a male heir on the second try (unprecedented in the family), but she had brought Olin back from the dead—then single-handedly made him publisher through a rather outrageous management report, when he was still a child. And the more spectacular his performance, the more they seemed to credit Duffy. It was making him sick. And his wife's phony naivete wasn't helping matters.

"We're supposed to be a national newspaper—we have a music critic who talks more about how my mother is dressed and her gracious speech—'It's not little me that's important,'" he said, mimicking her with exaggerated waving of arms, "'it's the music.'"

His face tightened. "Well if the music is so goddamned important, why is he talking about her dress?"

"Oh, Olin."

He went to the phone on the white tile counter and dialed the paper.

He was put through with heartwarming deference all along the way to the arts editor, Nick Miller. "Nick, who's the best music critic in the country?"

"Matter of opinion—some like Schoenberg with the New York Times—Virgil Thompson is good but retired, and others like Will Shroyer at the New Yorker. Many find him a little acerbic for their taste."

"Okay—get me that one."

"Not so easy."

"Why not? I'll pay anything within reason. Get me someone with some integrity."

"New York, Olin—why anyone wants to live there is beyond me—but that's where they are. They look on Los Angeles as a hick town."

"We're changing that image—get one of them," and he hung up the phone.

"Who is this Shroyer person?" Duffy shrieked when she read the first review under Will Shroyer's by-line. "And what does he think he's doing to my orchestra and my conductor?"

Olin held the phone away from his ear and smiled.

"I've never seen such a terrible review."

"Was it that bad?" Olin asked, nonchalantly. "But then you've never seen anything negative in music criticism, have you?"

"Well, certainly not as unfair as that," she grumbled.

"We're no longer a small-town paper that only puffs the high school marching band. We've got a man who knows a violin from a tractor and we've told him to call a spade a spade."

"Well, Olin," she turned soft and feminine, "is there any *need* on your part to tear down the symphony I've spent my life building up?"

The nerve had been hit. Olin grimaced at his mother's perception.

"No need, Mother," he said, "just a new look to the paper—the boys in the arts section thought we needed to beef up the music criticism—seemed to think we were on the level of some rural farm journal."

"But Olin, you don't build things up by tearing them down," she said.

"I've got to run, Mother," he said. "We'll talk again—"

She started to say something, but the line went dead.

# 72

Let us return to the past; it would be progress.

—Giuseppe Verdi

1962

If it is human nature to be nervous when summoned to an audience with a new boss, Managing Editor Rodney Taylor was unexceptional.

A man of loyalty and devotion to the company he served, Taylor was on the threshold of sixty and not dreading the thought of retirement from the rat race.

An ex-Marine who had given his heart and soul to the Corps, Rod had left it all behind when he rejoined the *Tribune* after the last smoke of battle cleared his sinuses. All that was left was the crew cut he insisted on having in spite of the longer hair in fashion, and occasionally, when thinking of something else, he would whistle "The Marine's Hymn."

Rod Taylor sat in a neat gray suit and speckled blue tie in front of the stuffed polar bear Olin had bagged in the northern reaches of Canada, and made small talk about the last auto race Olin had been in. They spoke of cars and horsepower, millimeters and millisecond reaction time on the curves, the thrill of speed, the exhilaration of beating the danger.

"Rod," Olin got back on the track, "what do you think of the paper?"

It was a question for which Taylor was not prepared. He knew all the criticisms about the biases of the news columns, the monotonous support for any Republican candidate—dull features—warmed-over press releases like some small-town advertiser. But surely Olin didn't want to hear that.

"Well," he began warily, "it has its good points," he said, almost apologetically.

"What are they?" Olin loomed so large over the desk he reminded Taylor of a Marine buddy who dominated a landing barge with his whale's physique.

"Well, the sports coverage is pretty good."

"And?"

"You always know where we stand editorially—we don't pull any punches."

Olin nodded, and waited for Rod to go on. Rod was enjoying the hum of the air conditioning—and deciding that the biggest improvement during his tenure had been the air conditioning. When he started at the *Tribune* it had been as hot as blazes.

"Very successful," Rod said, as though reaching to please without being false. "More classified ads than anybody—highly profitable, I understand." Then he added as though some apology were called for, "So we must be doing something right."

"Do you think it's the best paper in the country?" Olin was boring in with narrow eyes.

Rod Taylor shifted his weight in the chair. "That might be a little strong."

"In the West?"

"Well, west of what? The Sierras? You might make a case. We're certainly most successful at making money."

Olin's stare made him uncomfortable. Rod heard the story of the locker room confrontation when Olin told Simon Gottlieb that the purpose of a newspaper was to make money, but now he had an uncertain feeling in his stomach.

"What would it take to make the *Tribune* the best paper in the country?"

Rod Taylor whistled softly. "Lot of money."

Olin nodded as though he already knew that and it was no

problem—Rod Taylor was encouraged.

"You'd have to establish a lot of foreign bureaus, beef up the Washington office—do more nationally. Get some new blood around here—we've got an awful lot of people coasting for pensions—get the best, then give them freedom—to produce—to write a story as they see it. Make the editorial page more objective. Redesign the layout. It looks boring, so people start reading with that impression. Get better features on both sides of the political spectrum. We could use another cartoonist." Taylor sank back and sighed as though it were hopeless.

"Anything else?" Olin asked.

"Not offhand," Taylor muttered, suspecting he had just talked himself out of a job.

"Do you have any idea why these things have not been done?"

Taylor looked at Olin—was he that naive? "Well," he began, pressing his hand to his collar to relieve the pressure on his throat, "the bosses haven't wanted it that way." Should he go on and explain to the big dumb kid what it means to work for a family paper when you weren't part of the family?

"I'm the boss now," Olin said. "Let's turn it around—you do what you have to to make this the best paper in the country," Olin said. Then, as if attacking the agenda item by item, he began, "Where can we get a cartoonist with some independence?"

"St. Louis's Bill Whitlaker's the best artist in the country for my money—only—"

"Only what?"

"He may be a little *too* independent. And his themes are often a little heavy-handed—and always, *always* liberal. Your family would scream bloody murder."

As if his authority were being challenged, Olin said, "Get him anyway." Olin was the boss now, and it was high time he showed it.

Rod Taylor nodded. He would, as he always had in the Corps, follow his orders, but he would prefer not to be around when Warren saw what the kid was up to.

Rod Taylor, at Olin Sutler's behest, cleaned out the news room of the dead and dying, established thirty-one international news bureaus. The cartoonist contracted, Taylor turned the editorial page over to liberal writers, as Olin Sutler demanded. Sometimes, he discovered, change for the sake of change could be, if not always indubitably good, very satisfying. It made people sit up and take notice of you.

Olin's liberal stance should have come as no surprise to anyone who knew him at the Eastern prep school he attended.

Olin Sutler went to Radnor Hall, an institution which molded the children of the rich and famous to Ivy League proportions.

The ivy-covered Gothic buildings, the quadrangle courtyards, the high-ceilinged dining room with long, dark oak tables and high-backed ladder chairs all conspired to infuse the young men with the grandeur of society's noblemen.

Young Olin Sutler was barely fifteen when he was shipped off to the Eastern boarding school with lots of warm clothes to insulate him from the brutal winters that Duffy told him to expect.

The rooms had been assigned by the administration, and when Olin went up to his room, his roommate was already there.

He was a young, handsome man who extended his hand and said, "Hi, I'm Andrew Carter," and looked up at Olin through eyes at once friendly yet uneasy.

Olin took the hand, shook it and said, "Olin Sutler." He did not even consider hiding his surprise, for he had not been prepared for Andrew Carter.

Andrew Carter was black.

It was the kind of news Olin shared with his family in his first letter home. They experienced a rush of paranoia, speculating that the school had purposely done it as a slap in the face at Westerners. The Los Angeles *Tribune* was conservative. Academia didn't like that. The important families the school administration wouldn't want to offend were Eastern. Duffy considered calling the headmaster to discuss it.

But at length Warren reasoned that *some*one would have to live with Andrew Carter, and every parent would have felt the same way. "And you know," he said, "if he can afford to go to that school, chances are good that he's not a hoodlum." And so Duffy and Warren appeased themselves with the thought that (1) no one else would have to know, and (2) it might actually be good for Olin's character.

After the initial shock, Olin found Andrew a likable chap with a delightful sense of humor, a good head on his shoulders and a strong aptitude for passing a football. And nobody liked to catch a football better than Olin.

One day in late September, Olin was sitting alone at the end of the big oak table in the dining room with its vaulted ceiling and wood plank floor, when Ray Hagan sauntered up, followed by a coterie of flabby-fleshed young men who, for reasons that Olin couldn't understand, reveled in Hagan's leadership.

Hagan was a slick-looking, smooth-talking, strongly-built young man a shade under six feet. He brought with him from Georgia dark hair and restless eyes and a know-it-all manner that irked Olin. He was a competent halfback on the football team, but no match for Olin's size and stature.

"Tell me something, Oley Baby," he said with a leer that his fans made an earnest effort to duplicate.

"Yes?" Olin said.

"Where's that jigaboo roommate of yours?"

Olin grasped the end of the table, his knuckles whitening. "Why don't you learn to speak like a gentleman?" Olin's voice rumbled, his temper preparing for takeoff.

"Okay." Hagan showed all his gleaming teeth, tossing his head back to make sure his audience was with him. "Nigger, then."

Olin pushed his chair back and stood up and glowered down at Raymond Hagan, summoning all his self-control to keep from throttling the smart aleck. "Let me tell you one thing, Hagan," he said.

"Oh, what's that?" Hagan taunted him.

"Andrew Carter is worth twenty of you."

Hagan's eye blinked and his cheek twitched. "Is that so? My, my," he shook his head in deep thought, "the thing I don't understand is how can you see him at night?"

All the boys thought that was hysterically funny, and the jelly-bellied rat pack seeped out of the dining room behind their hero.

While Olin stared at their backs, he formulated his response.

The opportunity presented itself the next day at the football team scrimmage. Olin was playing defensive end when Ray Hagan was handed the ball by the quarterback, Andrew Carter, who had, by prearrangement, called the play in which Raymond Hagan was to go off tackle on Olin's side. Olin had never felt so good in his life when he saw Hagan coming toward him, charging like a bull. Olin sidestepped in front of him and threw his shoulder under Hagan's head and hit, as in one artistic motion, his right shoulder into the lad's nose, mashing it to a bloody pulp before digging his elbow into the boy's gut, knocking the wind from him. Olin's arms circled the now-helpless Hagan. He straightened to his full height, slammed Hagan to the ground and then plowed on top of him like a shiny steel blade slicing into virgin earth. The boy's jaw was dislocated, that handsome face a bloody mess.

Andrew Carter stood by, his arms limp at his sides, his eyes flying saucers.

The coach came running on the field. "What the hell's the matter with you, Sutler?" he shouted. "This is a scrimmage, this is your own team you're murdering."

Olin got up, stepped back, looked down at the bloody, unconscious Hagan and said, "Gosh, coach, I'm sorry. I guess I got carried away."

Coach looked up at him, his brow pinched in doubt. "Yeah," he said. "You're gonna have to learn to control your power. This is not some medieval jousting match, this is a football game. A *game*, you understand."

"Yes, sir," Olin looked at the ground, humble and contrite, but he never felt better in his life.

Raymond Hagan was out for the season. The doctor said he was lucky to escape with his life. He made no more racial slurs around Olin.

It was a story that came back to Olin whenever anyone mentioned abusing his power. And today it was his father who stood before him, between the stuffed polar bear and the hanging elk's head in Olin's office.

Warren Sutler was the chief executive officer of the *Tribune* enterprises, and Olin, as publisher of the Los Angeles *Tribune*, was under him. But Olin seldom ventured to his father's office, and Warren, being the larger spirit, came to him.

"Power is a funny thing," Warren was saying. "It can be used or abused. Sometimes one of the hardest things to do is to control your power." He felt weak, his stomach was bothering him and his cheeks seemed to sting from the accumulated slaps from his son. "Are you enjoying your new job?" he asked with a quavering voice.

"Love it," Olin said curtly, looking his father in the eye.

"And how do you think the staff is reacting to you?"

"That's immaterial to me. I've got things I want done and I'm gonna do them."

"With no thought of people's feelings?"

"Not much." Olin looked behind his father at the decapitated stuffed trophy on his wall.

His father looked at him, feeling pity in his heart. "Olin," he said, "what's the purpose of a newspaper?"

Olin spoke as though a drone in his head slid unconsciously to his throat. "The purpose of a newspaper is to make money," he said with glazed eyes and a stiff back.

Warren's sharp breath burned his heart.

"But that's not enough for me. I'm going to make this the best newspaper in the country."

"By firing everybody?"

"If I have to."

"And hiring that pinko cartoonist?"

"He's the best in the country."

"I suppose he might appeal to you if you were a hard left-winger, but that's not the kind of paper we've had."

Olin bristled, "You want the same old rag you've always had?"

"What same old rag?"

"You know, the dull, provincial paper that's made us the laughingstock of the journalistic world. I'm not staying in the gutter with it, I'm gonna bring it up."

Warren caught his breath, the pain in his belly flared up. "You are going to take it from right to left, is that it? That makes a great paper? What about the people you put out on the street?"

Olin shrugged, "That's their problem."

Warren thought, "He really is a throwback to Arnie Sutler."

Warren sat down in the chair at the side of Olin's desk feeling great relief, as though he had moved from his shoulder the crushing dead weight of the world. He sighed, "You know, Olin," he began gently, "when I took over as publisher I went to my father with every question that ever concerned one soul on the staff. There were changes, sure, but we went at them gently, not with a meat ax. We didn't offend people who had given the best part of their lives to us. We didn't run a paper that rubbed our advertisers' noses in the dirt. And after a while, after my father saw that I could be trusted, he started to rebuff my questions. 'You're running the paper' he told me." Warren shook his head with a ponderous sadness. "Well you're running it now," he said.

Warren felt a wearing effort in his words, as though a little life left him with each breath.

"But I wouldn't be honest with you if I didn't tell you that I'm so uneasy with what is happening here, and it's not only me, it's my brother and sisters. Don't forget they each have as large a stake in this paper as we do, and you may not like them, but there's no way around considering their feelings. They have been extremely unhappy."

Olin shrugged his shoulders that still looked padded for football. The same shoulders that smashed the face of Ray Hagan back in prep school.

"You don't discuss anything with me," Warren said, his eyes pleading pathetically, "you don't even pay me a courtesy call now and then."

Olin ignored him, "People are saying the paper is improving," he said.

"Yes, the liberals. They should be in heaven, but that doesn't charm the advertisers."

"I'm not running an Establishment organ," thirty-seven-year-old Olin said.

Warren's face flushed. "Just remember this," he said, "the Establishment you are so superior about pays the bills around here, your salary included." He was making a good fight but his stomach was still queasy and his knees were weak. "The minorities and the poor and the lame and the halt are all noble members of the human race, but they don't buy the advertisers' stuff. When you reverse the whole orientation of the paper you aggravate the people who pay the bills."

"Something had to be done, Dad. The paper was impossible. My God, we were voted the worst paper in the country a few years ago."

"It's overkill, Olin. People are saying you're power hungry. That's unseemly in a man of thirty-seven."

The corners of Olin's tight mouth lifted. He turned and looked out the window and thought of the coach telling him to control his power back at Radnor Hall. He turned back to his father. "You watch this paper shoot off the charts while I'm in control. I'll double everything you did in spades." His finger shot out at his father, as if daring him: "Watch my smoke."

Warren mumbled, giving his son the option of not hearing, "Just don't burn the *Tribune* to the ground making your smoke."

Back in his sparsely-furnished office, Warren lay down on the couch and prayed that his sickness would pass.

# 73

It is not enough to suc-
ceed, a friend must fail.

—Duc Francois de la
Rochefoucauld

1964

"I'm enormously gratified by the
results of the public offering of the Los
Angeles *Tribune*," Olin Sutler was
quoted as saying in a *Tribune* press
release. It appeared verbatim in his
paper.

The issuing of the six million shares
of additional stock had brought the
company an additional sixty million dollars in capital, while the Sutler family
retained thirty-five percent ownership.
It was quick and easy interest-free capital for the further expansion of the
business. They would buy new presses,
build a second plant in the San Fernando Valley, buy another paper mill to
meet the needs of their burgeoning
operation, and perhaps even look at
another newspaper or two in other parts
of the country.

The public offering also lifted the
burden of the tremendous inheritance
tax that would become due upon Warren's death.

Yank had purchased, through many

corporations, around a million shares, or sixteen percent of the total shares outstanding.

He knew Nora Yates Crown still ached for her own revenge. So when Yank heard that cancer had been diagnosed in his friend Jud Crown, he was ashamed of his immediate feeling that soon he would be able to utilize, through Nora, the vast resources of the Crown chain in his battle for control of the *Tribune*.

"I don't like to be the one always complaining," Paul Sutler said, slouching before Olin's desk, "but I've inherited the position of spokesman for the disinherited part of the family."

"This damn crybaby is getting on my nerves," Olin thought, "he does nothing but bitch and moan."

"But that cartoonist is getting on everybody's nerves."

Olin nodded. "Hot damn," he thought, "something is working."

"I mean we don't mind the view from the left once in a while, especially if it is done with some subtlety or cleverness, but that guy is a sledge hammer. How can you think he's good for the paper? Our readers don't think like that."

"Well, Paul," Olin said, "as you've seen, we're opening things up to all views around here, it's not like it used to be. The cartoonist happens to have a left slant, but he wins all these prizes for us so someone must like him."

"Sure, the pinkos," he said. "You're running the paper. I just want you to know how the majority of the stockholders feel." He pulled himself up, nodded curtly.

Olin rose—"I appreciate it, Paul," he said.

Paul pursed his lips and left.

"I've got to get rid of that bastard," Olin thought, and he asked his secretary to call in Simon Gottlieb.

When he got the call summoning him to Olin Sutler's office, Simon Gottlieb had an annoying intuition that he was going to be fired for his locker room remarks. Ever since he had chided the paper for its anti-intellectualism and Olin had set him straight with his "The purpose of a newspaper is to make money" speech, Gottlieb thought his days were numbered. When Olin suddenly became publisher, Simon began considering alternative work. But after two years and the departure of a passel of old retainers, he began to relax. Now this summons set his mind rumbling over his past in search of other indelicacies he might have committed against what he liked to refer to as "The Paper Dynasty."

Olin was affable when he asked Simon to sit in the chair facing the desk. It was friendly enough, Gottlieb thought, but it would have been more friendly with both of them on the couch under the big stuffed buffalo's head. All the macho stuff around Olin's office bothered Gottlieb. It put him in mind of the cerebral content of the man at the helm and he wondered how an institution could rise above the intellectual level of its leader.

The publisher wasted no time. "What do you think of the John Birch Society?" he asked.

"It stinks," Gottlieb spoke instinctively. Immediately he thought he had been too outspoken.

"Want to do a series on it?"

Simon Gottlieb looked at him as though he feared he was being goaded into a trap. "Ah," he said, as though he understood. "I don't want my by-line prostituted."

Olin was leaning back on his huge tilting chair. "No. It will be run as you write it."

Gottlieb shuffled his feet and cast his eyes down at them.

"What's the matter now?" Olin asked. He had expected a more positive reaction.

"You know who is prominent in the John Birch Society?"

"Who?"

"Paul and Natalie Sutler—"

Olin nodded. "I expect you could do an honest piece without mentioning them—"

"Well—"

"It's up to you. You want me to put someone else on it, I will—"

"Like who?" Simon bristled.

"Oh, I don't know. Maybe Aubrey Cappleman. He's a top writer."

"But too conservative. He'd distort it."

Olin shrugged.

"I'll do it," Gottlieb said.

And he did.

So much venom had built up inside of Simon Gottlieb for so many years without anyplace to spill it that it just bubbled forth like boiling froth and spewed over on the sheath of papers on his desk in what he referred to as the Velvet Prison.

The employees of the *Tribune* quickly took up the Velvet Prison cry from Simon. They were locked in with velvet-soft working conditions, mouth-watering stock options and pensions, more pay for less work than any rival newspaper. They could take three months working on a piece, type it and turn it in and see it run the next day in its bloodcurdling, boring entirety, spilling over page after page between corset ads and get-rich-quick schemes.

The John Birch series was remarkable more for length than pungency. Looking back you might wonder what the fuss was about. But it signaled a complete turnaround for the *Tribune* from ultra-conservative to ultra-liberal, and Olin was pleased. He wasn't any sort of political animal. Political processes bored him. If Olin could have shocked and angered his family by embracing Zoroastrianism, he would have done it. There was a *new* publisher at the *Tribune* now and he was his own man. Going from Right to Left was the only way he saw of making that statement of separation, without having to share the credit with some member of his family.

But the rival press fooled him. They gave the credit to his mother, of all people.

Warren was aghast at the Birch Society series. He got so many complaints from his friends. "What is the kid, a commie?" they asked.

But the family took it hardest of all. Paul, after his initial outburst, sulked for days, then tried to get the series stopped. Katherine, Amy and Louisa all had married staunch conservatives, none of whom could believe their eyes. The switchboard at the paper lit up like Christmas Tree Lane in Pasadena. Subscriptions were canceled in record numbers.

The stock took a tumble. Yank bought one hundred thousand more shares.

But the Eastern Establishment thought it was the turning point. The New York *Times* ran an editorial headlined "The Los Angeles *Tribune* comes of age."

The only member of the family who was not displeased was Olin's mother, Duffy. It was as though she had finally delivered the *coup de grace* for the Democrats, the Jews and the liberals who were so generous to her Theater Arts Center campaign.

It outraged Olin that people actually gave Duffy the credit for the new direction of the *Tribune*, and the closest she ever came to denying it was to smile sheepishly and say, "Gosh, no, don't give me the credit—there were so many people involved."

Fred Codwell was on the line.

Fred was an old Stanford buddy of Olin's. He remembered him

as a handsome, debonair man who had a way with the women that Olin admired. What is this guy doing now? Olin wondered. He had no major, graduated perilously near the bottom of his class, but he sure had the gift of gab, and you couldn't keep the girls from him. Olin had not heard from Fred in many years and he took the call as a delightful surprise.

They renewed old times with a happy boisterousness that Olin hadn't felt since he took on the power of publisher. For it *was* lonely at the top, not because the people at the top wanted it that way, but because their old friends were intimidated.

Fred Codwell invited Olin to lunch after the New Year. Olin accepted with pleasure.

Paul stood in Olin's office. Olin, seated behind his ponderous desk, did not ask his uncle to sit, and lately Paul made it a point of pride not to sit until he was asked.

Uncle Paul, never a man of happy countenance, became sadder with each passing indignity to his person at the hands of his young nephew who was content to run the *Tribune* without his advice and counsel. The Birch articles were just the latest and most blatant in a long series of insults.

The smooth, boyish, feather-plucked face was gone from Paul. It was rough and eroded now and he looked like a man who always expected more than he got, who always counted and recounted his due because he suspected life of short-changing him.

The Uncle Paul of yore—feisty, angry, vainglorious—was gone now. In his place stood a man resigned to his lot—shadow punching for the last vestige of dignity with his nephew who had the job Paul coveted all his life—the job he thought was rightfully his.

Looking briefly up from his desk, Olin suggested if the new face of the paper was not palatable to Paul, for the good of all he should consider sacrificing his duties to the larger good of the *Tribune*. It was, after all, "highly counterproductive" to have him at odds with the publisher all the time....

"We are going to be objective," Olin said in his office, "and if you can't stand that, I don't see how you can continue to promote us in the community." (Paul's last responsibility, a thinly-disguised ticket to oblivion).

"You call that Birch series objective?"

"We're going to give our reporters their head."

"To do hatchet work?"

"If that's the way they see it."

"And all left-wingers? What's got into you, Olin? Do you know what made this paper? Do you have no sense of responsibility to your heritage?"

Olin smiled wryly to himself—considered several answers including, "None, you hare brain,"—but settled on:

"My responsibility is to make this paper great. That's a responsibility to *all* the shareholders now, not just the major ones. That's going to constitute major changes in direction and policy, and many people will find that offensive. You seem to be prominent among them." Olin spoke like an athlete with perfunctory wisdom. "I would strongly recommend to the board that top management of this company be of a like mind on these major policy decisions. You and I don't see eye to eye—I doubt we ever will."

"Olin, Olin," his Uncle Paul said, putting out his arms to embrace his thirty-nine-year-old nephew who now occupied the chair he coveted, "we don't have to be enemies...." It was a conciliatory gesture but it missed its mark.

"We didn't have to," Olin said, "but that's the way it worked out." He stood up, "Now if you'll excuse me, Paul, I have some people waiting. Give it some thought."

"What?" Paul's head snapped.

"Whether you want me to recommend the board remove you from your position or you want to resign."

Paul was stunned, but he found himself deftly escorted out of the office.

Olin closed his door with the shiny gold letters that spelled "Publisher" on Paul's back.

Paul didn't see anyone waiting for Olin.

Item eight on the *Tribune* board of directors' agenda passed without a fight.

On the new board of directors, mandated by the Security Commissions Act for publicly held companies, the *Tribune* had the head men of an airline, a college, a law firm, an oil company and a space industry. Movie moguls had been considered and ruled out because of their transient nature.

In exchange for their attendance, membership and loyalty, their industries were seldom pictured in less than favorable light on the pages of the *Tribune*.

So when item eight on the agenda came up for a vote, there was no horsing around.

Item eight:

> "The alteration of executive responsibilities...Paul
> Sutler, Executive Vice President to be retired with full
> pension benefits"

was buried in a morass of other changes transparently calculated to
strengthen Olin's hand and diminish those at odds with him.

Paul had been a member of the board for twenty-seven years.
His docile sister, Amy, would be taking his place. He attended the
meeting, heard item eight moved, seconded and passed unani-
mously, and stood up as a courtly gentleman and bowed his
acquiescence and left the room. Olin thought it was the most positive move of his uncle's career.

# 74

Education is highly desirable in achieving refinement and culture. But for making money it may be a liability.

—H.L. Hunt
Multi-billionaire

1965

The lunch with Fred Codwell lifted Olin's spirits. It was great to see Fred again—he had puffed out a bit, "Rich food and poor booze," he said with his hale 'n hearty have-you-ever-had-more-fun-in-your-life laugh.

Olin had been twenty minutes late for the meeting but Fred drove up in his silver Rolls Royce a few seconds later. He had been parked across the street awaiting the arrival of Olin in his three-year-old Oldsmobile.

As Fred moved toward him in front of Perino's, Olin thought he walked like a woman trying to make up her mind about showing her pregnancy.

He had this belly and he couldn't decide if he should straighten up at the cost of showing it or slouch to minimize it. So his posture became a combination of both.

The sun had kissed him with lascivious abandon, then jilted him, leaving him a blushing pink.

The quick pulse of his metabolic

clock burned enough calories to keep him from obesity, so he had the look of a light-heavyweight fighter lately out of training.

Fred wore a pale blue seersucker suit with a yellow shirt and pink-and-yellow-striped tie.

Olin was in his summer-weight oxford gray suit, white shirt, maroon paisley tie.

What is it about a person that transmits the signals that form our first impressions? Is it simply the face and the arrangement of the features thereon? Is it the posture, bold and assertive, or relaxed and unthreatening? Or the body, full, firm, round, soft, or tautly thin? Or is it a symphony—a playing together of all three—throwing in perhaps the cut of, and color of the hair, and the pains, or lack, taken to dress the entity for public inspection? Can you read a soul in fleshy lips or close-set eyes? In the pectoral muscles?

Olin couldn't decide about Fred. He was a hail fellow well met, and neat enough, yet there was a slovenly edge about him.

They sat in a corner booth at Perino's. Fred knew Olin's mother frequented the place but Olin never felt he could afford it. Olin looked around in the vain hope that his mother would see him.

Caesar salad for two, the rack of lamb luncheon special for Olin Sutler, and reminiscences of the good old college days.

Olin said he would have to jog an extra five miles to work off this size lunch. Fred laughed. He didn't realize Olin meant he would do it, rising an hour early the next day to get it in. For Olin set goals for himself and he stuck to them. He jogged regularly before he went to work, and he did his five miles rain or shine. If he had an earlier appointment than usual, he got up earlier. He didn't slight his regimen.

"All your old buddies are proud of you, Olin," Fred said, "running the West's biggest newspaper."

Olin waved a modest hand. "Doesn't mean much being biggest, we're going to be best."

Fred raised his glass. "I'll drink to that."

"Well, Fred, what have you been up to?"

Fred shrugged, "Oh, not much. A couple business ventures." The drawing of breath seemed an event for Fred. He was always sniffing like his nose was on the verge of dripping.

"Don't be modest, Fred," Olin said. "I saw the Rolls."

"Just rented for the day." The boyish grin broke into a broad smile, and then the guttural guffaw, winding down to a chuckle.

"I don't have a Rolls," Olin said, seeming to genuinely regret it.

"I s'pose you could," Fred Codwell said. "You're hardly on welfare."

Olin shook his head like a hound dog shaking off water. "I've got a reasonable salary, I guess, but I pay my taxes, support a wife and five kids. There isn't much left to do the things I like."

"What's that?"

Fred's eyes roamed the room. He sat with that look of a man who wants you to know he knows how to live, by God.

"Oh, I won't mind going on a big game hunting safari in Africa," Olin said, with that bleak "It'll never happen" look on his face.

"No kidding?" Fred said, slapping the table. "I don't believe it! You've just hit on my life's ambition—and damned if I wasn't looking for company—when can you get away?"

"Look, I told you, I really can't do those wild things now."

"It's on me, Olin—well worth it too, to get the company."

"You're joking."

Fred shook his head, "Never more serious in my life."

"Wow." Olin was starry-eyed. "You must have some oil well."

"Several," Fred said grinning. "I'll tell you about them in Kenya."

"Wow, I've never flown first class before," Olin said.

"Really?" Fred Codwell was surprised. "A man as big as you—height and importance—should never settle for less."

"Wow."

"Stick with me. I only go first class."

And so was their hotel on the edge of Nairobi—first class. A suite bigger than most houses on the African countryside. Olin liked the sybaritic feel of it all.

They stood on the balcony of their suite overlooking the green hills and low coffee fields beyond the hotel's immaculate landscape resplendent with birds of paradise, red hot pokers, geraniums, African violets and clivias. In the background a doum palm with its trunk divided in many "Y's" topped with green fronds like a parrot's tufts; and the tall aloe, quaintly called the kokkerboom tree, with its weeping blades like a punker's haircut.

"Isn't it beautiful?" Fred asked gazing at the horizon sparkling with sun-flecked moisture.

"Sure is," Olin said, his eyes swelling in wonder.

"Tomorrow it's the big beasts of the jungle against the little beasts of the city," Fred chuckled.

"Fred," Olin said, "you certainly know how to live."

Fred grinned. "Yep," he said, "and you should too. You know there is no sense at all having money—I mean it is absolutely worthless—unless you spend it. Then it makes all you had to do to get it worthwhile."

"Yeah," Olin sighed, without removing his eyes from the mesmerizing emerald spectacle in front of him. It was not a new idea, but Olin had never related it to himself before. He had always made money to live—people thought of him in connection with the *Tribune* and the immense wealth his father and grandfather had accumulated, but that had not trickled down to him.

"We need a station wagon," Olin said offhandedly, "to haul that brood with bottomless pits for stomachs around with all the sundry equipment, and I haven't as yet been able to see myself clear to buy one."

"Well," Fred said, "I guess that underlines my theory."

"What's that?" Olin turned to face him.

"That the only way you can make real money is to be in business for yourself."

"Well, Olin hung his head, "that lets me out."

"Not necessarily," Fred said. "Shall we get some dinner?"

"Sounds good."

In the dining room with its sparkling crystal and snow-white tablecloths, silver candelabra and high-backed cane chairs Olin felt the lift of luxury. He looked around the room that was only half full to see if his mother were there.

She had seemed surprised when he told her he was going on a safari, as though she didn't want him to have a good time away from her proscribed home ground. It gave him a grand feeling to be able to go on a trip not funded by the paper.

"What does he want?" Duffy had asked him.

"He wants *my* company," Olin said.

But Duffy had looked at him funny, and he resented the implication that no one could want his company unless he thought the *Tribune* could do something for him.

The thoughts of his mother faded from his consciousness as he sat looking at the biggest steak he had ever seen. Olin had been reluctant to order it because of its price, but Fred had encouraged him and finally insisted.

Olin had stars in his eyes. "What exactly is it you do, Fred, to be able to live like this?"

Fred Codwell laughed his jolliest from-the-gut laugh.

"Oil, my friend," he said. "And promotion. I set up oil explo-ration syndicates. We call it Earth/Craft. About half to three-quarters of every down payment is deductible in the first year, so I can hardly keep up with the bucks they throw at me—it's easier to collect the money than to find worthy projects to put it in."

"So where do you make yours?"

"A setup fee—and a piece of the action."

"Do you ever have the syndicate go sour—you know," Olin was almost embarrassed to say it, "lose money?"

"Sure," Fred nodded candidly. "It's risk-taking enterprise—but less risky than most because we pool the projects as a hedge against failure—so people who invest have a piece of many explorations, and when they hit they hit big."

"So you could have five or six losers in one project and one win-ner?"

"Exactly."

"Well, I can't say it's hurt you," Olin said, waving his hand as though the room belonged to Fred.

The great roar began in Fred Codwell's bowels and trembled through his body to spill out of him, and an earth tremor unsettled the room.

"I can't say that it has."


They drove with their guides out past the coffee plantation on the dusty, narrow road without passing another car.

But they passed eucalyptus and mimosa groves and the "upside down tree," the quaint baobab, with its fat, swollen trunk for storing water through the dry season. The fine branch work looked like the roots. It was sixty feet tall and just as wide, and there were colobus monkeys laconically hugging the branches.

It was a land where darkness is final and morning light is both eagerly anticipated and dreaded. The unknown rumbles, your fears magnify. The morning brings with it the vision to contain the fear but also the crematorium fire of the sun.

When they parked their jeep under a mimosa to catch some shade, they walked deeper into the savanna through elephant grass with deep, drought-surviving roots, cowpea, sapele, acidanthera and the prickly crown of thorns euphorbia.

They were dressed to kill, these two white hunters, in their starched khaki hunter's shirts and hunter's pants (and hunter's shoes and hunter's socks).

Their black guides, leading them to the kill, wore ragged sawed-off jeans and nothing else. Olin was disappointed. He'd expected loincloths.

"No, buddy," Fred told him. "That's only in the movies."

Hunting requires patience. Some use the time for introspection, others for small talk. Still others speculate on the nature of things.

As they sat under sparse eucalyptus trees with their rifles across their laps in a break from monotonous, silent crouching, Fred said, "What do you think, Oley? You think you can tell the makeup of a beast by its swagger—from the way they carry themselves when they come for you or try to avoid you? Are there human attributes in those glances that bounce off you like the sunlight?"

Olin shrugged his massive shoulders. "Why not?" he said. "Their physiognomy is the same as ours. All the organs are there in the same places. The brain is in the head behind the eyes, between the ears. The mouth leads to the stomach."

"And out the other end," Fred snickered. "So do you think the pleasure of the kill increases proportionately with the recognizable human characteristics of the prey?"

Olin knotted his brow. He hadn't considered it, but now that he did, he didn't have an answer.

"For me it's just the sport," he said finally. "The reflexes, the awareness, the tension, the performance. The danger, maybe."

Fred nodded, sniffing the pure air. "This air must be like it is in heaven," he said.

"Yeah," Olin admitted. "It sure beats the smog."

They had moved to a small rise on the flat land where they camouflaged themselves with their khaki poplin, using the scrubby mimosas to hide from the big cats.

The hunting was immensely exciting for Olin—man against beast—cunning intelligence, mental development and powerful weapons against agility and brute strength. But the animal has not been born that can withstand a bullet through the heart.

Fred saw the animal before they heard her, and he nudged Olin rather than taking the shot himself. And Olin reacted quickly, lifting his gun and getting off a good clean shot that struck the cat in her brain just as she was turning her head in retreat. Standing over the fallen beast, Olin immediately pictured its head placed on his wall.

The feeling of exhilaration it gave Olin was like nothing he had ever experienced. It was raw power, the conquering of nature. It was basic, fundamental, nothing intellectual about it. He had by his wits and quick reaction overcome the overwhelming, life-threatening danger of a savage beast of the jungle.

He had pitted himself against the ultimate danger and won.

It was in his blood now. He wanted to do it again.

On their way back to the hotel from the camp Olin asked how he might take part in Fred's Earth/Craft miracle.

Fred laughed good-naturedly. "You already have."

"I have?"

Fred nodded. "I've talked to you about it—you listened. I take the trip off my income tax. Entertainment of a possible client. You don't have to do anything else."

"But suppose I wanted to?"

Fred frowned out at the shiny green hills, just barely kissed by the escaping sun, the treetops glimmering like melting orange sherbet.

"Well, buddy, I never thought of you as a guy who would want to make money on the side. I mean, let's face it, I should be working for you."

"Apparently not," Olin lamented.

Fred laughed again, it was so hale and boisterous that it began to annoy Olin just a trifle.

"I don't know, Oley," Fred said, "if you want to mess with it."

"What would I have to do?"

Fred paused again. He scratched behind his ear, slowly—six times.

"I suppose I could throw you a finder's fee for getting some people into it. And if you brought in enough new blood—I could give you a piece of the action."

Fred rubbed his brow, then brought his hand down his pink face. "But I think that might be grubby work for a man of your stature—I hope you don't think I brought you out here to hustle you."

"No, no."

"That's a relief—I've just enjoyed your company, ole buddy, and I hope you'll be able to do it again sometime."

"I might be interested."

"Good—name the date."

"I mean in helping out—getting other people for your deals."

"Oh that," Fred said as though he could barely bring himself to talk business. "Well, think it over. I don't know that having another job is something your mother would be hot for."

"Why not?" Olin bristled. The nerve had been hit, dead center. Why was everyone so hung up on what his mother thought? How many forty year olds had to kowtow to their mothers? Olin Sutler was not among them. "My father had an insurance agency. All he did was curry customers. My grandfather was notorious for getting people into deals. Why not me?"

"Hm," Fred was warming to the thought, "since you put it that way…."

Olin came to consider himself a born salesman. It was so easy to sell the Earth/Craft shares to his friends—the district attorney Jonas Ryan, members of the *Tribune* board of directors, his brother-in-law, Vandenberg Clarke. The tax deductible features made it especially appealing.

And it was amazing how no one put him off or tried to evade his calls. The publisher of the Los Angeles *Tribune* always got right through.

Fred was pleased with Olin. One Friday morning before Olin went to work he found a Buick station wagon in his driveway. There was a single sheet of paper under the windshield wiper the size of a parking ticket. It said:

You're the greatest!

Fred

## 1968

Olin Sutler and Fred Codwell became good friends. Fred was grateful for the tremendous shot in the arm Olin's contacts gave his business, both financially and prestigiously, and Olin was delighted to find someone unreservedly impressed with him.

They went on two more safaris together and Olin did so well selling Earth/Craft, he was able to buy a hunting lodge in Wyoming that was twice the size of his home in Pasadena.

Fred Codwell was the only one who ever praised Olin for his work at the paper. His family was too shocked by his dramatic changes, which seemed a slap in the face to all they had built over the years; his underlings never considered he needed approval. He was the top dog after all. Who could ask for anything more? His wife was wrapped up in her own community projects, and though she adored the way the paper opened doors for her, the glitter and deference that was generated all around them, she just never thought of Olin's practical part in the thing. It was like he worked for the paper rather than the other way around.

Fred and Olin were standing at the wall-sized picture window that looked out on Wyoming flatlands to the great hump of mountain that seemed the only impediment to seeing the North Pole.

"Some place you got here, ole buddy," Fred said, with his hale and hearty smile of approbation. "Puts those puny rooms in Africa to shame."

Olin broke into his biggest grin of self-satisfaction, limited only by his tight, small mouth. "I couldn't have done it without you, Fred," he said, his words ending but the grin staying on his tanned face.

"Your mom and dad been here, Olie?"

The smile stayed in place. Olin nodded, his heart warmed with an inner secret.

"How'd they like it?" Fred asked, rolling his eyes over the enormous room with stuffed animal heads galore on the walls; the tiger they shot on their last African safari together, on the wall above the massive stone fireplace.

"I think they're jealous," Olin said, the grin disappearing for only an instant, to return again in full glory.

Olin's heart was full. He had not felt this good, secure, or appreciated since he took over as publisher of the Los Angeles *Tribune*.

# 75

The truth of things is a
supreme food for fine
intelligences, but not for
wandering wits.

—Leonardo da Vinci

1969

Olin's secretary brought a note to
the editorial meeting and placed it in
front of him at the head of the long oak
table.

He looked down at it, his eyes narrow, lips tightening.

Your brother-in-law is on the
phone—told him you couldn't be
interrupted. He got quite angry
—insisted I tell you.

Olin picked up his ball-point pen
and scrawled in his wide, open hand:

I'll call him back.

And he tuned back to the discussion of placement of stories for the next
edition.

Editor Rod Taylor was recapping
the consensus, his blond crew cut taking
on a dull glow in the fluorescent lighting
overhead.

"So there's no argument then. We
play the Sharon Tate murders in the

number one spot—a picture of her looking virginal and innocent, and we get above the fold the fact she was found in skimpy underwear."

He was referring to the newspaper practice of teasing the readers through the vending machines or on newsstands where only the top half of the paper was visible—above the fold.

"Number two spot to Nixon arriving in Long Beach for his vacation in San Clemente, and we'll fill with the legislature wrap up, Nixon's welfare reform, the school deficit and the scheduled daily feature...what is it, Jack?" he asked the features editor.

"Air controllers, our heroes."

"Oh, yes."

The meeting quickly adjourned and the movers and shakers of Los Angeles journalism moved back to their battle stations.

Back in the office, Olin thought about calling Vandenberg Clarke, his brother-in-law, but so many other things seemed more pressing. He knew what Clarke wanted—Olin had heard the rumblings of his discontent like a small tremor before an earthquake —not frightening in itself, but sinking the stomach at its portent.

Every time he heard the phone ring he thought it was Vandenberg.

And finally, six or seven calls later, it was.

Vandenberg had one of those stentorian voices that Olin hated. Since he had become publisher no one dared to use that tone with him, but Vandenberg was not at all insecure in his presence. He had come from wealth himself.

The Sutlers for generations had a genius for marrying money, and while that had distinct advantages (you were not likely to mate an out-and-out gold digger that way—and with enough money it could be useful to the enterprise and, gosh, could anyone ever get enough of the stuff?). But it also had its disadvantages, Olin was discovering. The rich tended to get uppity. To think of themselves as *equals*, for God's sakes, and even he sometimes suspected they were not above considering themselves superior.

"Olin," his voice seemed to heat the telephone wires, "I've been hearing some nasty rumors about this Earth/Craft thing. I took your advice on it and I'm trying to get some answers."

"Gosh, Van, I'm only connected as an investor like you are— Fred Codwell runs the day-to-day operation, why don't you give him a buzz?"

"Dammit, I did call him—dozens of times. He evades me, he

doesn't call me back. I talked to him once in a dozen calls; says everything is hunky-dory—those were his words, I swear. Why you ever do business with a man who uses words like that, I'll never know. But when I press him about the rumors and my suspicions of dummy corporations, illegal self-dealing and embezzlement, he turns evasive."

Vandenberg Clarke's family sold their land for freeways, for shopping centers, housing developments and way back, railroads. The U.S. Government bought their land for military bases. Vandenberg Clarke was not intimidated.

"Dammit, Van," Olin exploded. *No* one talked down to him like that. "It's not *my* company. If you have any complaints about the *Tribune* call me—but don't call me to bitch about Fred Codwell."

"Not so fast, Olin," Vandenberg said. "You were the one who pushed this shyster on me. You wouldn't have been so aggressive unless there was something in it for you."

"I don't get a penny from them," Olin was hot—"I thought the tax advantages of the deal would do you a favor."

"Not a penny, huh?" Vandenberg Clarke sneered. "Where did that station wagon come from? How many safaris to Africa you been on? I hear your office is so damned full of stuffed jungle beasts you can hardly move around."

"Look, Vandenberg," Olin was struggling to regain control —"I'm sorry if you aren't happy with Fred. He's told you from the beginning he would buy out any partner that wasn't satisfied. I suggest you take advantage of that offer."

"Oh, don't be so damn smug with me. You don't think I asked him that?"

Olin caught his breath. It was the first crack in the armor of credibility. "What did he say?"

"He said he'd have to get back to me on that."

There was a long silence while Olin considered the possibility that his friend and handsome benefactor might not be as pure as the driven white snow.

"Well if he doesn't do it," Olin offered magnanimously, trusting that Vandenberg was too much of a gentleman to take him up on the offer, "I'll buy you out."

"Good! I'll send the certificates right over."

Olin closed his eyes. He felt a touch of vertigo. When he regained his footing, he added, "I'll give you what you paid less your tax benefits."

"Fair enough."

"I'll trust you for the accounting."

When he hung up the phone he felt queasy. Should he call Fred? The wheeler-dealer had emphasized that anytime anyone was dissatisfied he would cheerfully buy them out. Was there some problem? What was Olin's responsibility to the legion of investors he'd brought into the thing? What would his father or grandfather have done?

Olin decided Fred had been far too good to him—being suspicious would not be in good taste.

"Do you have a minute for your old mother?" Duffy asked him in his doorway, and while he searched for a way to say "no" gracefully, she ensconced herself languidly on the couch, under the new water buffalo and cheetah.

"How have you been, Olin?" she inquired gently. She had on her a smile that said, "I'm-going-to-talk-to-you-as-a-loving-mother-who-has-only-your-best-interests-at-heart."

"Just fine, Mother," he said with a tense purse of his lips that always seemed too stingy for his big rangy face. At forty-four years of age he thought he had a right to expect he would be free of his mother's supervision.

"You look a little tired," she said. "Are you under a lot of strain?"

"Dammit," he flared, the back of his neck reddening. "I told you I was fine."

Duffy nodded, her lips flat and unconvinced.

"You been to a doctor lately?"

"I don't need a doctor, I'm fine."

"You should have a checkup at least once a year, you know. You don't only have a responsibility to yourself and your family now, you have the added burden of all these stockholders."

"Yes, Mother," he resorted to yessing her, his last resort. "Now, I'm awful busy, if you don't have anything else in mind I'd like to get back to work."

"Oh, but I do," she smiled benignly and didn't move another muscle.

Olin sank back in his chair as if to welcome some attack, just to get it over. His mother, he thought, was becoming a real pain.

"I'm worried about you, Olin," she furrowed her brow and looked a little blurred to Olin—it was a three-point triangle with the water buffalo, the cheetah and his mother. Was it possible Olin Sutler, pillar of strength and leader of men, could need glasses?

"When your brother-in-law, Vandenberg, couldn't reach you he called your father. Dad's not well, Olin. The drastic changes you made have seemed like a knife in the back to him. A lot of your decisions are good ones and I applaud them, they just seem, somehow —so heavy-handed."

"Well, Mother, there are so many improvements to be made around here. I could pace it more leisurely, but it would take a hundred years. I don't have that long to wait."

She stared at him as though trying to pierce with her intent eyes the hard shell of his soul. "Dad is determined not to interfere. I just pray you don't give him cause to regret our decision to give you the job."

"Dammit, Mother!" Olin slapped his big hand on the desk. "I'm getting sick and tired of this patronizing attitude. You 'gave' me the job because the paper was rotten and you knew I was the only one who could save it."

"Now stop that!" she said, falling back on the couch as if taking a blow. Catching her breath she leaned forward, "I will not have you tear down your father that way."

"Oh why is everyone so sensitive? He wasn't interested in the paper. He made potfuls of money—he was a great businessman, just not a great newspaper man."

"And what about you, Olin? Are you going to be both?"

He looked at her through squinting eyes, "Why do you ask?"

"We're concerned about Earth/Craft," she said, pursing her lips. "Vandenberg says he thinks it is a sham. Or did he say scam? Anyway, it could disgrace the paper."

"Listen," his back arched in defense, "I am making the *Tribune* one of the most respected papers in this country. Why are you looking for things to pick at me?"

"How can you say such a thing, Olin?" she pleaded. "After all we have given you."

"What?" He pounded the desk again and seemed to rise halfway out of his high-backed chair. "You *gave* me nothing! I never got an allowance, I had to earn every penny I got—delivering papers for God's sakes—my father owns the paper and I'm a newsboy for God's sakes. I never got a car like my friends did, not even a broken-down Chevy—I had to huckster cars in the army—so don't give me that—" he mimicked her, "'all we gave you,' baloney."

Duffy watched him with a curious disappointment. She took a deep breath as if trying to get cleaner air in her body.

"Olin," she fixed him with her withering, cut-through-to-the-soul stare. "Don't ever think you are so important you deny your parents. We gave you everything. I brought life back to your body after a *doctor* told me you were dead."

She looked across the big desk and up at her son and saw him suddenly as the biggest stuffed animal in the room.

"Maybe you should have taken the doctor at his word," he shrugged.

"Yes," she said. "Easy for you to say now—and sometimes I wonder if you don't have some death wish the way you race those cars and ride that terrifying motorcycle. Why do you do it?"

"I get a thrill out of it. It is man mastering machine—man at the top of his capabilities, the ultimate test of his reactions—where a millisecond lapse can mean death."

"But why?"

"Because I want to be the best."

"It's crazy to me."

"Maybe," Olin shrugged. "If it is, I come by it honestly," he said.

She stood suddenly as if jolted to her feet at the reference to her confinement.

"That was uncalled for, Olin," she said, and the force of her son's ingratitude propelled her out of his office.

"God," Olin thought, "she is really getting on my nerves. I've got to put her out to the tall grass with the rest of them."

Warren had aged so: his pallid features were sunken, making his nose sharp and eagle-like. Olin thought, on seeing him in the hospital bed, he looked like the eagle now in the lobby of the *Tribune* Building—the eagle that used to stand poised for flight, guarding the earlier *Tribune* buildings, before and after the fire.

Warren was in a hospital smock with little bows tied down the side—a tube was strapped to his arm, and the only thing about him that still seemed alive were his eyes.

Olin had put off the visit for over two weeks. His mother pushed him relentlessly. She didn't let up.

Olin had difficulty seeing his father in that condition. It reminded him too much of his own mortality. "You are next," he said to himself. Though Olin was strong and given to death-defying boldness, he buckled at the sight of physical decay.

"How are you, Dad?"

"I'm all right," he said in a voice so forceful Olin was startled. It was as though the eyes and the voice were all that were left now, and Warren was going to capitalize on them. "Thanks for coming," he added with an undetectable sarcasm.

Olin hung his head. "I should have come sooner, I've just been so darn busy."

"I understand," Warren said to his son.

And Olin was very much afraid he did.

Olin sat in the chair beside the bed, and Warren waved at the TV hanging high on the wall—"You can turn that off."

Olin found the switches built into the bedside table and silenced the electronic companion.

"You've had some tough luck," Warren said, shifting his eyes from the TV to his son beside him.

"It'll blow over," Olin said, not moving a muscle.

Warren blinked his eyes. "Everything does," he allowed. "In time," he sighed. "What are you doing about it?"

"Stonewalling, I guess," Olin said. The subject was not pleasant for him, especially not with his father. "I'm getting the story out that I didn't do anything illegal—I was just trying to help a friend and the friend turned sour."

Warren blinked again.

"I suppose all hell will break loose over it because of who I am—"

Warren said, "I suppose it will. We must always stay a couple notches above reproach."

Olin thought how much easier it was to be in the presence of his father than of his mother. The tones and inflections of his voice were not as threatening; he was simply a more relaxed person.

"How much did you make on the thing, Olin?"

Olin looked out the window on the tall palm trees wavering gently in the afternoon breeze—as if he had to calculate the figure he knew so well—"A little over two hundred," he said.

"Thousand?"

"Yes."

"Does that include the car?"

"No." The hospital smell was beginning to annoy him.

"And the shares?"

Olin snorted. "I should think the shares would be worthless."

Warren pursed his lips and Olin could tell he was not having an easy time of it.

"Here's what I want you to do," Warren said. "Pack up the

whole kit and caboodle and return it."

Olin's big head twitched. "Return it to who? To Fred?"

Warren considered it. "You could. Or you could give your commissions to the people that were duped."

"But that's all so complicated."

"I agree. The simplest thing would just be to turn it over to the Securities and Exchange Commission and let them decide."

"Only one problem," Olin said. "I don't have the money."

"You don't?" Warren's cheek twitched. "What did you do with it?"

"I spent it."

"Oh," Warren's lips contracted. How could he spend that much?

"A racing car," Olin said, "house—the hunting lodge—it went fast."

Warren groaned softly. "Well, first return the shares to Fred Codwell. That shouldn't be too hard if they're worthless," Warren said. "Then I'll have Mother give you a check which you should deposit in your account, then you write your personal check...."

"But that's such a waste—to give it to a government bureaucracy. Besides being an admission of guilt I don't feel."

"We aren't left much choice—unless you want to give a thousand or two to each one of your investors."

"Tacky."

Warren didn't disagree. The whole thing from start to finish was tacky. "The Government will decide how to distribute it. At least you've done your part."

"But why should *you* give me the money?"

"It's a loan—I want it back."

"I don't see how I can pay that back...."

"Not all at once," Warren said. "Take your time—and I won't charge you any interest. I suppose if you got anxious about it you could mortgage one of those houses it bought you, but I won't press it."

"I don't know," Olin shook his head. "It seems so—drastic."

"It's drastic all right," Warren agreed from his back—"but if you want to see how drastic it can get, just do nothing—then you'll see real drastic."

Olin started at him.

"Son, you've got to understand—you've turned the paper into an aggressive, powerful organ. You've stepped on some toes; there are legions out there that would not be unhappy to see you get yours." He smiled with difficulty. "If I weren't your father—I might be one of them."

"But I wasn't wrong," Olin said. "I didn't know it would turn out this way."

Warren closed his eyes. His flesh was so weary. Olin was momentarily relieved for the opportunity to escape the scrutiny of his father.

"You need some rest," Olin said magnanimously, rising to his full height and towering over his shrinking father.

Warren nodded without opening his eyes.

The next day Duffy came to Olin's office and laid the check for $217,500 on his desk.

Olin's eyes fell on it. It was made out to him and the line that said "For" was left blank.

He looked up at his mother and she looked at him. It was as though in that moment the fourth-generation boy had taken on the bodies and souls of all his ancestors and distilled from them the bulk of their shortcomings. Duffy smiled her judgmental smile, then turned and left.

Olin slammed his hand on the desk as if to punctuate the door closing behind his mother. It seemed the more successful he was with the paper, the smaller they made him feel.

Olin personally deposited the check in his account that afternoon, but he did not get around to passing it on to the Securities and Exchange Commission.

# 76

1972

Between bouts at the hospital,
Warren kept coming to the office and
seemed quietly intent on building an
organization of outsiders to back up his
son Olin in the event that the embarrassments of the growing Earth/Craft
scandal became too much to bear.

Warren was careful to include his
son in the decisions to hire outside people, and even, in several cases, made it
appear as though it were Olin's idea.

George Saatjian looked like a bus
driver. Portly, balding and jolly—he had
an excellent mind for figures and a nice
way about him. A comer, they all said.

He had been the token foreigner in
the prestigious law firm of O'Shaunessy
and Maxwell and they sent him to the
*Tribune* on loan to work on some buy-
out contract detail. Olin liked him,
Warren liked him. Everyone liked him.
So they hired him.

He was quiet and soft-spoken, but
he had a way of zeroing in on the heart
of the matter that complemented Olin's

zest for stomping over the competition.

For the second or third time the executive floor of the *Tribune* had to be remodeled to house all the outside executives that were layering there.

Warren and Duffy sacrificed their proximity to the publisher, and it wasn't until some weeks after the renovation and shifting of offices that Olin, who got to keep his office, realized that the shift of power seemed to be away from his corner.

George Saatjian, Executive Vice President of the *Tribune* enterprises, got off the phone and took his news jubilantly next door to Olin's office where he found Olin scowling over a letter from the Securities and Exchange Commission.

"I've just been talking to Nora Crown," George said with his round, jovial smile, "and she's willing to sell both Fresno and Riverside. And the good news," he said, arching his eyebrows, "is that she doesn't want cash, she wants stock."

Olin smiled, "That *is* good news," he said. "I thought she was having some trouble with her board."

"Apparently she's overcome that. She put those marines in their place. She had every legal right to the papers, Jud Crown had seen to that. The board just didn't think she had the guts to take over, but she sure showed them."

"What about her tax problems?"

"Well that's what baffled me," Saatjian said. "I thought she needed all this cash to get the government off her back. Old Jud should have gone public like you folks did to save all that harassment. Nora found herself in a very tight cash position, but apparently she's worked something out with the IRS, and this is only a rumor and I didn't confront her with it, but I understand that she's assigning the stock in the *Tribune* to the IRS and paying her debt with the dividends. And there's some time frame whereby if the dividends don't pay the debt the IRS may move on the stock and sell that to satisfy her claim."

Olin nodded, "Inventive," he said.

It took his mind momentarily off his letter from the Securities and Exchange Commission.

There was the tension of high excitement in the grand jury room as the twenty-three grand jurors filed into the windowless room to consider the government's case against Olin Sutler.

It was a tedious business being a grand juror, but the celebrity of the accused brought with it a spine-tingling mystique.

Sixteen was the quorum required to do business. But all twenty-three turned out to judge the publisher of the city's largest newspaper—so far ahead of the competition as to be a virtual monopoly. Nothing is juicier than a big man gone wrong.

Olin Sutler was a handsome man, impressive and imposing, seated at the table for the accused. His lawyers from O'Shaunessy and Maxwell were outside the room, forbidden to participate in the proceedings unless Olin excused himself to go out in the hall to consult them. They had all agreed to use that procedure only in a dire emergency, as it might make Olin seem he had something to hide.

Olin Sutler's posture was disciplined, his bearing military, and he had the earnest look of a friendly high school guidance counselor.

He had every reason to believe this jury of his peers would deliver a verdict favorable to him and spare him the humiliation of a public trial.

There was no audience here and that was a relief to Olin. He didn't have to suffer the additional indignity of the judgmental stare of his mother, or the pale, sad, forgiving eyes of his father, or the petulant frown of his wife.

The most aggravating thing about the interminable period between the summons and Olin's grand jury appearance was the attitude of the women in his life.

His wife, Nell, was beside herself with shame—and she ragged on him without mercy about the effect it would have on her reputation and the impediment it would be to her career which was "just beginning to take off," with her appointment by the mayor to the downtown improvement committee. He countered that she, with her insatiable thirst for material goodies, was his main motivation to make more money.

"That's right," she shouted with the snarl he had come to associate with her most hateful moods, "go ahead and blame it all on me. You never made a mistake in your life."

"Well," he said, looking straight through her as if his look could burn her up on the spot, "maybe one."

His mother's outrage took a more subtle form—little digs in conversation, oblique references to morality and ethics in high places, that maddening sidewise glance to check his reaction to her *bons mots*.

Between his wife and his mother he had had it with women. Of course that girl in marketing, that stunner, Mimi Hankins, the one who was heading up the new South Coast division, didn't seem as pushy. Ambitious, yes, effective, yes, but not so bossy. At least she didn't bug him about Earth/Craft, and she even seemed very sympathetic.

Olin told his story to the jury succinctly, and while his syntax might not have always been the best, he had about him a decent, earnest quality.

Olin seemed surprised that some of the assistant U.S. attorney's questioning of him did not seem terribly kind. Somehow the office had found out about the car he had received and the money and the free shares of stock, and they wanted to know how a man in his exalted position could countenance such shenanigans.

Olin's eyes darted to the door, behind which stood his attorneys, and he squirmed in the witness chair, only slightly shifting his massive athletic frame. Then his broad face broke into a wide smile and he said, "I've been asking myself those same questions," and his response seemed to warm the hearts of the grand jurors. In the rest of his testimony he was careful to accept culpability himself, while skillfully shifting the focus of blame to Fred Codwell, his former friend to whom, he told the jurors, he had given a "strong tongue-lashing."

He had thought about turning in the money his father gave him for that purpose, but every day that became more remote, and after he received his summons he realized it would look like he was trying to buy his way out of trouble that was not his fault.

Ironically, Fred Codwell had not yet been indicted for his role in Earth/Craft. He was currently angling for immunity from prosecution by cooperating with the U.S. Attorney's office in its case against Olin Sutler.

Olin was, under questioning, at the mercy of the air conditioning system. When the questions got especially rough, Olin tightened the muscles in his cheeks and twisted his head a quarter turn to relieve his neck from the heat and chafing of the starched white collar.

No one else seemed to think it was as warm as Olin did.

When the ordeal ended after two days in the witness chair, Olin had every reason to believe he had won over the jury. For while there might be some technical infringements on his part, he certainly hadn't meant anything evil by it.

He was, he reminded the jurors, a substantial member of the community and painted himself as a man so busy and involved in making the Los Angeles *Tribune* one of the great papers of the world, that he simply didn't have time to think of filing reports or disclosing his financial interest to the people he had attracted to the Earth/Craft scheme and to the Securities and Exchange Commission. He had learned his lesson, he was contrite and he would not repeat the offense.

And so it came as a great shock when the grand jury handed down the indictment of Olin Sutler, fourth-generation publisher of the vaunted Los Angeles *Tribune* for infringements of the Securities and Exchange Commission's law.

Olin Sutler suddenly found himself branded as a criminal.

The news of the indictment reached Olin's father and mother while they were at a luncheon in Bel Air at the home of the president of an electronics-based conglomerate.

At first when the news came Warren and Duffy refused to believe it, but a quick call to attorney O'Shaunessy confirmed their worst fears.

Duffy and Warren excused themselves from the luncheon with pained expressions and drove straight to their mansion in Hancock Park. As soon as they walked through the front door their home seemed cold and empty and oversized.

Warren went straight to bed and found himself unable to address himself to Duffy's reassurances that everything would work out all right.

"My son," he said, "a criminal."

"Well, Warren," Duffy fluttered, "it's not as bad as all that. An indiscretion perhaps, ignorance of the law, yes, but Olin's not a criminal."

Warren stared wordlessly at the ceiling, his eyes seemed to sink further into his head, his lips, pale blue, slackened. He felt a constriction in his chest and his arms began to tingle. Duffy grabbed the phone at the bedside and screamed at the operator, "Get me an ambulance, *NOW*!"

And when the ambulance came, Duffy couldn't remember having given them the address.

Warren was installed in the intensive care unit of the Queen of Angels Hospital, not far from his beloved *Tribune* Building. When Duffy called the *Tribune* to give the news to Olin, he was not available to talk to her. She called her daughter, Carrie, who came and kept Duffy company while the doctors plied their trade with tubes and machinery in the miracle of modern medicine. And two days later, through those miracles, Warren was wheeled to his private room high atop the hospital with a commanding view of the *Tribune* and city, befitting his station.

The press was amazingly circumspect in handling the matter; it was not surprising that the Los Angeles *Tribune* played it on page seventeen. The only paper that made any fuss at all was Olin's rival, the Los Angeles *Inquirer*, but even their tepid reporting could have been done by Olin himself.

In distant places Olin's Earth/Craft was picked up by the Crown chain and Nora Yates Crown had a field day with it.

Olin was furious. Here was a woman who just exchanged two newspapers for almost 800,000 shares of *Tribune* stock and she seemed to delight in biting the hand that would feed her.

Olin did not return his mother's calls, so she drove to the *Tribune*, abandoned the car to the subterranean parking lot attendant and raced up to Olin's office on the fifth floor, barging in without any more than a nod to the secretary to find him in a meeting with George Saatjian, Rod Taylor, Dr. Kelly and several other key executives. "Olin," she said, in an imperial voice as though he were a small child being scolded for tracking mud all over her carpet, "your father's in the hospital, he may be dying. I want you to come and see him, Queen of Angels, four-oh-one." She turned on her heels and left.

Olin was silent for a moment; he took a deep breath. His brain was whirling, "That's the last straw," he said to himself, "the very last straw."

When news of Olin Sutler's indictment was announced, *Tribune* shares traded ten points lower. Yank bought another sixty-five thousand shares.

# 77

Two Newarks back to back.

—Jimmy Breslin
*Definition of Los Angeles*

1979

Yank Sutler was courtly to Duffy at Warren's funeral in 1973. She seemed to appreciate it. It was the first funeral of the dynasty where there seemed to be genuine bereavement for the departed, the first in which the mourners cut across class lines, the first where condolences were couched in terms of the goodness of the man himself, not only the glitter of his accomplishments.

Yank waited a decent interval before he went to visit Duffy to talk turkey about the shares she now controlled.

After Warren's funeral Duffy decided she wanted fresh flowers in her home all the time. It was a last link to him.

There were flowers all over her Hancock Park house. A huge arrangement of fresh cut peonies, orchids, daisies and roses on the entry hall table and in the living room. Anthuriums dominated the coffee table and the piano.

The *Tribune* was on the coffee table, unopened beside the anthuriums. You could drop in on Duffy anytime and find the *Tribune* on the coffee table like an art book. It wouldn't be thrown out until the next day's paper took its place. She seldom found the time or inclination to read the paper anymore, but it was always there, the focal point of the living room.

It had all changed so after her fair-haired son, Olin, took over. It wasn't Dad's paper any more, or Warren's or hers. Olin never asked her opinion or gave her anything to do anymore, and she found it hard to keep up her interest in it.

Through the years the papers on her table told the story of Los Angeles and the world.

In May, 1973, it proclaimed the election of the first black mayor of Los Angeles. Though no credit was asked for or given, the new, broadened face of the *Tribune* deserved a large share of it. It was the fruition of Olin's (and, yes, Duffy's) breaking down the racial barriers in town that the black, ex-cop was elected mayor of the city of 2.8 million, no more than 18 percent black, with over 56 percent of the vote. The headline pointed out that Los Angeles was the largest city ever to elect a black mayor. The *Tribune* had endorsed him.

It was as though Olin Sutler had finally revenged the snub of his black prep school roommate, Andrew Carter. So the point would not be missed, Olin had the paper sent to Ray Hagan, his Radnor Hall classmate, the bigot he laid out on the football field for slurring Mr. Carter.

The paper had had a long history of electing candidates, all of them Republicans. And all of them white.

Duffy was proud of Olin, but she didn't read beyond the first page.

The paper was six columns to the page now and sometimes, when the ads were fat, it went to four hundred pages. (There were five million ads a year.) They were printing it with photocomposition now, the reporters typed on computers.

The inks for the new printing process would save the stockholders a barrel of money and come off on the readers' hands.

The high-tech production did not affect the intellectual content. But you could still buy the paper for a dime.

Daily circulation was over a million, and another twelve hundred hands were ladled onto the payroll.

A vanload of fellows used to paste up the Orange County edition while they rode the freeways. But now they did it by microwave for instantaneous transmittal.

They added over forty special advertising sections where you read an article on how wonderful a restaurant, or wine, or swimming pool, or automobile was and saw beside it an ad for the same product. There were almost five hundred different full-run and suburban sections published, making the *Tribune* a truly Southern California paper; San Diego to Santa Barbara, Olin said, would be the paper's venue, and he made good on his promise. The Japanese were creeping into our markets with a Toyota automobile advertised in the *Tribune* for $1788, full price.

Inflation soared, people waited in lines around the block for gasoline. Customers engaged in fist fights over buying the last diesel engine car on the showroom floor.

In 1974, Richard Nixon, a Californian who owed a large part of his early career to the Los Angeles *Tribune* and its unswerving support, found himself an outcast on their pages when he resigned his presidency in Shakespearean tragedy over lying about a "two-bit burglary."

The *Tribune* expanded, then expanded on the expansion. They were buying up papers all over the country, adding book publishers and magazines to its stable of companies.

And over those years the *Tribune* on Duffy's living room coffee table reported the bailing out of the Chrysler Corporation by the U.S. Government. The *Tribune* never had its hand out.

In Maryland an eight-inch metal cylinder used to replace the spine in a woman prompted Simon Gottlieb, ace reporter, to comment, "There's hope for the Trib."

Hostages taken in Iran were a field day for the media.

Inflation climbed to 13.3 percent annually.

And MIT researchers discovered the DNA molecule spiraled to the left, not the right as previously believed, causing Paul Sutler to say, "So that's what happened to the Trib."

It was all there on Duffy's coffee table unopened.

Yank kept buying shares during those years, improving his position. Nora Yates Crown, head of the Crown chain continued her pursuit of her own revenge with a swap of her Bakersfield paper for 200,000 shares of stock.

But the *Tribune* wasn't standing still, it was getting stronger and more entrenched in its position every day.

Yank waited for the optimum time to make his move—but it never seemed to come. He realized after Olin simply refused to fall on his face, that Duffy was his ace.

But Duffy wasn't so sure.

At seventy-eight, and pleasantly puffy, Duffy had become insouciant about her bathing and taken to compensating for infrequent soap and water with lots of perfume. It was a strong jasmine smell that put Yank in mind of his beloved Theresa.

"What people don't seem to realize," Duffy Durham Sutler said from her pink brocade high-back chair with wooden arms, "is that I have had control of the majority of the stock for years."

They were seated in her two-story living room with the tall Gothic windows facing the big backyard with its swimming pool, cabana and the distant eucalyptus trees. The trees were in bloom with red, puffy flowers. Duffy's investment in blooming plants had paid off handsomely. The yard was resplendent with glorious flowers along the paths as well as on the trees and shrubs.

Yank was spread casually on the couch—still limber for his ninety-one years. The gray cowboy hat was pushed back on his head. He raised an eyebrow to encourage her to continue. It didn't take much to keep Duffy talking.

"Warren's cousins have almost one-half the shares between them, and they didn't make a move without my say-so. For the last fifteen years or so I've held their proxies."

"But wasn't that slightly less than half?" Yank asked carefully.

Duffy looked at him out of eyes that had seen their fill. "Warren's share was the difference, of course."

"And you always controlled that?"

"Well, not in any sinister way. I guided him—prodded him sometimes because Warren was sometimes complacent—but I always did it with love."

"I'm sure you did, Duffy."

"Hilde and Clyde depend on me for everything. No one else in the family has any time for them. Neither one of them has the least economic sense. If I didn't shepherd their money for them I swear they'd starve to death."

"What do they do with themselves?" Yank asked.

"The boy, Clyde, plays the piano *all* the time. He's given a few recitals. I've wanted to get the Symphony to play with him, but all the directors find him too—well, peculiar, I guess you'd call it."

"And his sister?"

"Hilde—well that's another story, and we don't generally talk about it."

"I'm not 'generally,' I hope."

"I suppose not," she sighed. "Hilde is a bit of a case—she should probably have been committed long ago but no one had the heart. She's not a bad person, really, she'd never harm anyone—oh, there was some talk of the harm to our dignity, but I mean real harm."

"What's wrong with her?"

"Oh, she's got religion. But in a big way. She spends her days dressed like a bum in Pershing Square shouting at the top of her lungs about Jesus."

"And between them they have forty-five percent of the stock in the trust?"

Duffy nodded.

"And you control that as well as Warren's nine percent as his widow?"

She nodded again.

"That's fifty-four percent of the trust, Duffy," he said as though he had discovered America.

"I can add," she said.

Yank told her what he was trying to do and why. Duffy listened sympathetically. When he had finished, Duffy sighed.

"I know how you feel," she said. "Believe me, I do. I suffered plenty at the hands of that family—though I must say Warren could not have been nicer." She paused, reflecting on some troublesome thought.

"Then you'll help me?"

"Yank—you are asking me to turn on my own son—oh, I'll admit he's been a worry sometimes. It wasn't easy to smooth over the Earth/Craft thing, but we finally got the indictment quashed—well not exactly, we got them to agree not to prosecute."

She rolled her eyes to the almighty heavens.

"Well, we used up decades of goodwill on that one, I can tell you. In Grandpa Olin's day it would have been a breeze to quash an indictment. Dad Sutler would need only to snap his fingers and it would be gone. But things are different now. We've all grown too big, too impersonal. And we weren't dealing with a local government, this was the U.S. Government."

"So how did you do it?" Yank asked, not hiding his disappointment at the disadvantage he felt since the indictment was dismissed.

"There were still a few powerful people around, people we helped elect before Olin turned his back on every politician that might someday help him. And one man in the right place felt a heartwarming affinity for Warren. He knew Warren was dying, and it would be the last chance to show Warren his gratitude and respect."

She sighed—her shoulders dropped.

"We used a ton of markers on that one."

"Does Olin know it?"

Duffy twisted her lips as though she were grappling with an imponderable question. "No one knows what Olin knows. He is so insulated from the rest of the family. He's afraid someone else will get the credit for his success, so you will never get him to acknowledge help from any of us. But, I expect he knows."

Yank leaned forward and touched Duffy on the back of her hand, "So, help me, Duffy," he breathed the plea with the warm breath of his soul.

Duffy felt the warmth of his life's desire wash over her. She wanted to help.

"Oh, Yank, I don't know. Olin hasn't always been peachy to me, but the thought of turning on my own son..." she shook her head.

"Before he turns on you," Yank said.

Duffy stared at him, startled at first, then reflecting on the words and admitting to herself the possibility.

"We are what we are, Yank. We do what we have to do." She stared a moment out the big windows with the bold thick wooden frames on smallish panes—she looked back at him with a weak smile.

"If it was anything but my own son," she pleaded, "anything in the whole world."

Yank frowned. "There isn't anything else in the whole world," he muttered.

On Duffy's tip, Yank and Max took a trip to Pershing Square in the heart of downtown Los Angeles. Central Park, City Park and Fifth Street Park were the prior names of Pershing Square, a locality that mirrored the vast progress of Los Angeles. It was renamed after World War I for one of its heroes, General John J. Pershing, who fought in the Philippines with General Benjamin Raines Olin.

In the beginning, in General Olin's time, the park was a patch of grass with a few trees. In Arnie Sutler's era, the trees grew and more were planted. The lily, the flower of death and resurrection, festooned the corners. Yank and his only love, Theresa, took picnics there. In Warren Sutler's day, with the explosion of the automotive population, it was necessary to burrow beneath the surface of the park to plant tiers of automobiles under a concrete cover.

The Pershing Square of 1979 was surrounded by a fading, refurbished Biltmore Hotel, saved from disintegrating by an enterprising redeveloper—and on another side by the Temple Baptist Church (former home of the Los Angeles Philharmonic before it was rescued by Duffy) with the garish neon sign atop that proclaimed "JESUS SAVES."

On another corner a savings and loan. At certain angles you could see both the bank and the JESUS SAVES sign.

Seedy movie theaters and other candidates for urban renewal made up the rest of the immediate area.

Pershing Square was a microcosm of the sprawling city, and here collected the diverse humanity of its underbelly, from street corner evangelist to tinhorn panhandler.

Underneath were acres of parking for the ubiquitous automobiles that infested the city like lemmings in season.

It was the heart and soul of the city—hot air on a foundation of trapped automobile exhaust.

But nothing grew from the cars that seemed to just molder in their graves, and up above them, the Pershing Square Park was being worn scruffy by soap box evangelists and the happy homeless.

Yank thought the only way you could tell the one from the other was by the plane of their bodies: the evangelists were upright, the homeless were horizontal.

An ill-kempt woman was lying with her buttocks on her tightly-packed bedroll to keep them insulated from the cold concrete.

A young pretty black woman was lying on one of the few patches of trampled grass beside an old bewhiskered white man who seemed indifferent to the loving circular ministration of her fingertips to his breast.

Most of the horizontal homeless were in view of the JESUS SAVES sign atop the Temple Baptist Church. Yank decided if Jesus really did save souls, here was surely proof he did it selectively.

Cars came and went on the four streets surrounding Pershing Square. Horns blew, tempers flared and fizzled, drivers swallowed their impatience; cars burrowed into the bowels of the Square, others surfaced as though the Square had birthed them in self-defense.

Life in the new city centered around the automobile. The evangelists were atop the park blowing hot air to the heavens, the cars were diving down under, taking their hot air to hell.

With the passage of time, Max Underwood took on the flabby-fleshed look of Orson Welles near the end of his earthly portion. He had that sad and unfulfilled look, and he often felt like a man who had not, through no fault of his own, fulfilled his early promise.

He still got plenty to eat, heavy on the fats and oils, resulting in his walking like his center of gravity had gone inexplicably awry.

Yank looked like a man who was getting arthritis, but refused to acknowledge, or yield to, it.

You had to look closely to realize he was slightly bent, like the Leaning Tower of Pisa, because he walked like a patrician, with a confident but careful step, and his eyes looked more alert from without than from within.

With their neckties and pants that matched their jackets, the pair did not blend with the denizens of the Square. But, not to worry, they were only visiting.

Max's dark suit suffered some bird droppings and what could pass for cookie crumbs. The shoulders supported his prolific dandruff, and with very little effort, if he took off the necktie, he might have passed here for a native.

But Yank would never fit on Pershing Square. Not if he took off *all* his clothes, and so the regulars eyed him with suspicion. Was he a guy who might try to talk them out of their bedrolls? Or ask some atheist's questions about Jesus?

Yank and Max stood in the park near a woman they thought might be Hilde Olin Bascomb. She preached an esthetic and ascetic gospel, but showed no signs of caloric sacrifice.

Her hair was slate grayish and rangy—unruly, like a mop missing half its strands; her face bloated with red blotches. Her dress was gunnysack gray with a large ebony cross festooning a bosom worn down with neglect.

Her feet were bare and dirty brown. Passers-by looked in vain for a cigar box to drop a few coins into to help this poor woman.

People walked by her, but no one stopped to listen. She didn't seem to mind. Yank was astounded at how the strained resonance of her voice held its urgent timbre.

"...and He came to Earth to save you sinners from hellfire and damnation. He gave His life that you might have life everlasting—oh, you wretches, how can you not heed the sacred word of our Lord ah Jee-zuz Key-ryest?

"There is bounty in love, there is desperation in hate. 'Give up your sinful ways O man and come and follow me,' He said."

The short, stubby feet protruding under the ankle-length sack dress and her rhythmic rocking from side to side made her look like a penguin waddling.

"Behold, I say unto you, this day shall I see you in Paradise," the woman shouted.

Max and Yank stood off to the side near a large trash can that seemed by the surrounding rubble to be more honored in the breach. Max was listening with an ear cocked in her direction. There was new light in his eyes.

"And they mocked our Lord ah Jee-zuz saying, 'If thou be King of the Jews, cast yourself down from the mountain—come down from that cross,' but our Lord would not countenance the taunts of mere men, his guide was our heavenly Father. And you and I can do no less."

"You think she ever takes a break?" Yank whispered to Max—who was so intent on the speaker he did not respond.

But a derelict on the grass behind them—lying on his side, his head on a roll of newspapers—overheard, and answered, "Ole Hilde can go longer'n ten men—she only stops to eat and hit the john—"

Yank looked around and nodded his thanks. Unless there were two orators with the same name, this was their girl. "You know her?"

The bum retreated into his rolled newspapers. "I seen her around." Yank walked over and crouched down next to one of life's remnants.

"Talk to her?"

"Some."

"How much?"

The man on the grass shrugged his shoulders. "'Bout ev'r day."

"You listen to her?"

"Sometimes to pass the time," the down-and-outer who called himself Jake admitted, "—she's got a good spiel. More stuff than most. Don't repeat so often."

"Where does she go at the end of the day?"

"Home."

"You ever been there?"

"Naw."

"You know where she lives?"

Jake shook his head. "She takes the fifty-seven bus, all I know."

Yank nodded. "You ever talk to her about family or anything?"

"Shoot," Jake waved him away, "she tole me lotta stories, same's ever'body else—"

"Like what?"

"Rich family—trust fund keep her in style," he began laughing,

a rotted teeth rattle, "same's ever'body else here—"
   "Ever say anything about the *Tribune*, the local paper?"
   "Yah—she own dat too," and he rattled his stumpy teeth.

# 78

Living in L.A. is like living in a bowl of granola. What ain't fruits and nuts is flakes.

—Gallagher

"It's she," Yank said.

Max nodded, still watching Hilde intently. "How much you figure she's worth?" he asked.

"Maybe twenty-five million."

"Jesus!"

"That's her line," Yank smiled.

Hellfire and brimstone were raining down on Pershing Square. Hilde seemed inspired by her audience of one, now joined by a second. She was revving up for the kill.

"Give yourself to the Lord, brothers and sisters—don't shy from the hand of God. For it is written that whosoever shall love the Lord ah Jee-zuz shall find Paradise."

"Hey, Max," Yank snapped his fingers in front of his friend's mesmerized eyes. At length he succeeded in getting Max to step out of Hilde's sphere for a conference.

"How we going to get through to her?" Yank lifted his ten-gallon hat and scratched his head.

Max frowned as he looked over to take in Hilde again at full exhortation. "I don't know. She doesn't look like an easy person to get to know."

"Salesmanship," Yank muttered abstractly.

"What?"

"What does the prospect want?" Yank asked Max. "The good salesman asks himself that question. What does Hilde *want*, Max?"

"Max thought a moment and looked again at her. "To save souls, I suppose," he said.

"Exactly!" Yank said, clapping him on the back. "And she's going to save you."

"Oh no," Max backed away from Yank as though he were threatening bodily harm. "That's one job you aren't delegating. You do it."

Yank's head made a neat negative turn. "I'm too old, Max. Not believable. You she could sink her teeth into."

At that propitious moment, Hilde's last thundering exhortation crashed to the ground. It was about accepting and acknowledging ah Jee-zuz Key-ryest as your personal savior to escape the everlasting torments of hell and damnation. And lo and behold she was walking toward them with her eyes on Max.

"Excuse me, sir," she said with a touch of unexpected culture in her voice.

Max stepped back.

"I couldn't help but notice your interest in my lecture—" She was studying his face. "Would you like to declare ah Jee-zuz Key-ryest as your personal savior?"

"Well, I...." Max stammered.

"Yes he would," Yank said, pushing him forward. "What does he have to do?"

Hilde looked from Yank to Max and back again.

"Would you like to talk to him about it?" Yank offered.

Hilde looked confused. It was easy to see that in her long and arduous career as a street corner evangelist, what to do if someone said "Yes" had not occurred to her.

"Perhaps you would like to meet with my friend, Max Underwood here," Yank offered, "—in private."

Max was squirming and Yank held him by the upper arm to prevent a retreat.

"What was *your* name?" Yank asked.

"Hilde," she said, still wary.

"Well, Hilde, may we give you a lift somewhere?" Yank asked

with a courtly bow, raising his ten-gallon from his head.

Hilde considered the offer. "I wouldn't mind saving the bus fare," she announced, looking at Max. "We could talk."

"Oh, that would be wonderful," Yank said.

Hilde did not know what to make of Yank's long black Cadillac. "This is a real battleship," she said when she got in—and Yank gestured with his head for Max to follow her into the back seat.

While they drove in the direction she pointed them, Yank tried without much success to keep the conversation going.

They pulled up in front of a brick three-story apartment building on Bonnie Brae. Hilde got out.

"Can you help my friend Max here," he threw a thumb over his shoulder, "find Jesus Christ as his personal savior?"

She looked in the back seat she had just fled, the door still open, at Max who seemed to be shrinking in the corner. She pondered the proposal.

"Perhaps he should step inside for a minute," Yank suggested.

With a small move of her head she turned toward the door, up four steps from the sidewalk. Yank got out of the car and pulled Max out of the back seat. "Come on, Max," he whispered urgently, "we're coming up on pay dirt."

Hilde opened the door and they followed her down the oppressive hall, with carpet whose fleur-de-lis pattern had given up the ghost.

A shabby door led them into her apartment, and they were greeted with the squawking of a bird in a gilded cage.

"Ah Jee-zuz saves, ah Jee-zuz saves," the bird squawked with the same inflection as his mistress.

"Wow," Max said, "you got your gray-cheeked parakeet to talk. Mine only squawks."

Hilde looked at Max with awakened interest.

"What do you call the bird?" Yank asked.

"Saint Paul."

Yank nodded appreciatively. Max gagged.

The apartment was a shambles. Clothes strewn on the beige tweed furniture that looked like the "Only fifteen dollars a month per room special" from the apartment house furniture folks, as well as on the carpet that predated the fleur-de-lis in the hall. The walls seemed to have needed paint before there was such a thing.

There were pictures of Jesus everywhere, and a few of the Virgin Mary. On the TV set that must have been one of the first ever made was a picture of Jesus that looked like Charlton Heston.

Max and Yank looked at each other. Max giggled. "I thought Heston was Moses," he said. Yank silenced him with his glance, and wondered where she kept the twenty-five million.

Hilde went to her little kitchen which opened on the living room and made herself a cup of tea, and, as though she were alone, sat drinking it at the rented formica kitchen table.

"Let's get out of here," Max whispered to Yank.

"Sh," Yank said and went over and pulled the chair opposite Hilde at the table. It was covered with birdseed, a half-opened box of cereal, as though the effort had been too much for her, and a bag of sugar. On the wall, the Virgin Mary looked like Elizabeth Taylor.

"Mind if I join you?" Yank asked, and he began clearing the chair.

Hilde's round face darkened. Her eyebrows entangled their kinky hairs. "You're not the one," Hilde purred.

"Ah Jee-zuz saves, ah Jee-zuz saves," said Saint Paul.

"Pardon?" Yank wanted an explanation from Hilde, not the bird.

"The spirit of the Lord is not in you," she said, sipping her tea. She looked at Max and nodded—"I will speak to him alone."

It took some cajoling to get Max to sit in the naugahyde chair. "Jesus, it's Lizzie Taylor," he said, looking at the picture of the Virgin. "I thought she was Cleopatra."

"I'll wait outside," Yank said trying to cover Max's irreverence. He leaned down to whisper in his ear. "Don't ruin it!"

Max's eyes were those of a sheep in the last chute at the slaughterhouse.

Yank walked around the block. The neighborhood made him uneasy. When it got dark, he sat in the car and locked the doors. An hour and a half later he began to worry, and twenty minutes after that, he went back in the apartment and down the hall on the faded fleur-de-lis.

He knocked on the door. He could hear exhortations inside, but instead of the heavy hand of Pershing Square, Hilde seemed to be incanting hypnotically. Yank knocked again.

And again. Finally the door opened a crack, held by a security chain. Staring at him through the crack was hazy-eyed Max Underwood—who didn't seem to recognize him.

"Max! are you all right?" Yank asked, his hoarse whisper peppered with urgency.

"What?" Max said with a dead, flat voice.

"Max?—are you okay?" Yank's voice rose.

"What?" Max stared, his eyes blank as a Shakespeare ghost. "Oh, yes—sure," his voice trailed off, "—I'm fine...."

"You want to leave now?"

"Oh...no...I'm fine...she's got a quality about her...sort of interesting...you go on..." He seemed able to speak only in short phrases. "I'll give you a ring."

Yank tilted his head, "You sure?"

"Sure."

"Okay," Yank was not convinced. He turned to go.

"And Yank," Max called out.

Yank turned back.

"God bless you," Max said, and closed the door.

# 79

But as excess of delight is the nurse to negligence, and begetteth such an over-presuming boldness, as afterward proveth to be sauced with repentance.

—Boccaccio
*Decameron*
Fifth Day, Fourth Novel

Yank's secretary, Miss Tober, thought he was being unreasonable.

She stood before Yank in his office and tried to explain.

"I *have* been calling, sir. Every ten minutes. There's no answer at Max Underwood's, and Hilde what's-her-name has no telephone—"

"No telephone?"

"Yes, sir."

"Or just unlisted?"

"No phone," she said. She had checked with a contact at the phone company. "And I've sent telegrams to both residences."

"And?"

"Nothing. I'm still trying."

The sun was hot when Yank surfaced from burying his car under Pershing Square. This was no day for preaching. He discovered the air above-ground was barely distinguishable from that thick with exhaust fumes below.

Perspiration stood out on his upper lip, and he was grateful for the big hat to shade his face. When he felt the intense heat and the suffocating smog, he almost turned around and went below again, but he was determined to discover why Max seemed to have vanished.

He found Hilde alone at her old spot.

"If you ignore the word of the Lord, brothers and sisters, never forget that the sins of the fathers are visited upon even the third and fourth generations of them that hate our blessed Lord."

"Hilde," Yank shouted, attracting the attention of a passing couple. "Where's Max?"

"The soul of your brother," Hilde raised her voice a dozen decibels as if to drown out the sinner in front of her, "shall not be corrupted by the heathen. The Lord said, 'I say unto you, blessed is the prodigal son who returns to the fold, for we are every one of us sinners of the flesh and forgiveness is divine.'"

"What have you done with Max?" he shouted in her face.

"Blessed are the shepherds who labor in the fields, for theirs is the kingdom of heaven—" Her eyes left Yank's face and traveled to her right; Yank looked but saw nothing but a clumpy bush and a temporary structure housing some photographic exhibition.

He released Hilde's arm and followed the path. About fifty feet beyond the temporary photo exhibit that showed early Los Angeles, Yank came upon the back of a man in a long, dirty white robe. As he walked closer he heard the voice say:

"I am happy today, brothers, because I have found Jesus Christ—I have accepted him as my personal savior and I implore you to do the same. Great burdens have been lifted from my shoulders, friends, and I call upon you to join me—"

Then, before he saw his face, Yank knew—

"My God!" he burst out. "Max!"

Max flinched momentarily. Yank was standing fifteen inches from his face, looking him square in the eye.

"Max, are you nuts?"

"Purge yourself of revenge, brother," Max said, returning Yank's stare. Max hadn't shaved, and it looked like he wore under the grimy white bed sheet the same clothes he had on three days before when Yank left him with Hilde. "Your days are numbered," Max intoned ominously, "for tomorrow I shall see you in Paradise."

"Oh my God," Yank said, and then he began a laugh that grew like a torrential rain.

His head was thrown back and a few passers-by looked at him, which was more than Max or Hilde had been able to accomplish all morning.

"Max, Max," Yank said gasping for relief, "you had me fooled. You're beautiful. What a great approach." He looked back to make sure Hilde was in her place.

"Tell me," Yank leaned toward Max, "are you making any progress?"

Max stared at Yank, with a mixture of pity and confusion. "Progress?" he asked, "I've made more real progress in the last three days than I ever have in my life."

"Wonderful," Yank was excited. "Did you get her proxy?"

Max's face clouded over.

Yank searched deep in Max's eyes. Why was he acting so obtuse? "The shares of the *Tribune*, Max! Her twenty-two-and-a-half percent of the trust—will she vote them with us? Proxy, Max, *proxy*?" This last was spoken with a creeping, insidious fear.

Max seemed to wilt, as though returning from a trance, and Yank took off his ten-gallon hat and wiped his brow with his sleeve.

"Max, ole buddy," he said, replacing his hat, "you gave me quite a turn."

Max's eyes went dim again.

"It's a great ploy," Yank said, "I've got to hand it to you."

"Yank," Max said, "it's no ploy. I've found Jesus, Yank, and I recommend you do the same. I've never had such a feeling of contentment, Yank," he was urging him now, "I'm at peace with myself like never before."

"That's all very nice, Max," Yank said, "But we've got a job to do. Tonight's the recital, her brother, Clyde—remember?"

Max nodded gravely. "I'm not going, Yank," he said sadly.

"What?"

"I'm bowing out, Yank—you don't owe me a thing—go to my house—take the Renoir, sell it and keep the money. Hilde has shown me the way and light—purity of soul is more important than material things—there is no greater calling on this earth than to be a disciple of Christ. Go and sin no more, brethren." Max was gearing up to the crowd-voice, and his eyes were turning distant again.

Horns were blowing in the streets. There was the crashing sound of two autos vying for the same space.

Yank shook his head slowly with a heavy sigh.

"Preach goodness, friends," Max was yelling, "not hate. Pride goeth before a fall, and revenge is the iniquity of the devil—our Lord said forgive our debtors, *forgive* those who trespass against us—if thine enemy smite thee on the cheek, turn to him the other cheek. How many times, O Lord? Seven times? Yea, seventy times seven."

Yank turned, beginning to feel his years, a man starving on a deserted island, seeing the boat sink on its way to rescue him.

Yank went straight home, dropped into his favorite wing chair by the fireplace in the living room and sat staring at the empty fireplace, ignoring the bright sunny outdoors.

The phone rang insistently. He did not move to answer it—neither did he alter his gaze for over an hour.

At ninety-one years, Yank was fighting to hold onto his dream of retribution. But, he recognized, his grip at ninety-one was not what it was at twenty-five. The muscles were slack, the bones brittle. If you want to sink your teeth into a dream at that age, you'd better have some good strong teeth left to do the sinking.

Yank realized what he had left, after the desertion of Max, was the residual of a lifetime of planning, of hoping, of dreaming of perfect life-boosting revenge. Like the foam in the bottom of an empty beer glass.

He was still resolved, mentally and spiritually to right the wrongs the *Tribune* rolled over his life. But it was getting tougher to roll with the setbacks.

With Max's defection to Jesus, Yank realized he had put too much faith in a weaker vessel.

He was on his own. Ninety-one years old and alone against the power, might and seemingly limitless wealth of the Los Angeles *Tribune*.

"Ah, well," he thought, sinking back in the chair, "it's just as well I'm so old. If I were any younger I'd have too much sense to go on alone."

Suddenly his nostrils perked with the smell of jasmine. He looked over to Theresa's chair. "What shall I do?" he said softly.

It was the jasmine perfume that gave him his answer. He had begun buying it and putting a touch on Theresa's chair, as though with his failing eyesight and hearing he needed a new sensory stimulus to keep her vision alive.

The dainty smell of Theresa's jasmine reminded him of Duffy's heavier use of the perfume.

He had one more chance.

He hoisted himself with great effort to the phone and placed a call.

"Duffy?" he said brightly. "Would you be good enough to allow me to escort you to your nephew's recital tonight?"

There was silence for a torturous moment; then Duffy broke in cheerfully, "Why, Yank, I'd be honored."

# 80

After all, we are in the
entertainment business.

—Rupert Murdoch
Press Lord, dismissing the
fraud of the Hitler Diaries

Standing before the mirror in the
bedroom of his home straightening his
necktie, making sure every hair was in
place, Yank wondered what interpreta-
tion Duffy Sutler had put on his
invitation.

He found himself strangely titil-
lated at the thought of having a date,
and he chided himself for the tomfool-
ishness of those thoughts at his age.

Driving to Duffy's manse in Hancock Park, he felt a strange trembling in
his limbs and he tried to tell himself
how foolish it would be for him to form
any entanglements at his age. And yet,
should his lifelong ambition require
paying court to Duffy, what were his
options?

Duffy greeted him at the door and
said, "Oh, Yank, how good of you to be
so prompt."

"It's nice to see you, Duffy."

The night was warm and clear and
the lights were sparkling along Wilshire
Boulevard as he drove her the short

distance from her home to the Wilshire Ebel Theater for the recital.

The Ebel Theater was a musty old house of a bygone era with dark wood paneling and dark upholstery, but not without charm. Duffy and Yank were the first audience to arrive.

"You stay here," Duffy said, "I'm going back to see Clyde and give him my best."

Yank walked into the theater and looked at the dark, somber rococo area with the dark black shining Steinway on the stage, and he suddenly felt very warm. He couldn't understand why this dark, windowless place should be so hot. He walked down the aisle on the side and felt warm air coming out of the vents above his head. When Duffy returned Yank noticed she had taken off her fur jacket and had a light sleeveless dress underneath. "Dear me," she said. "He asked me how the house was."

"Warm, tell him, very warm."

"Oh yes," Duffy said, "that's the way he likes it. Clyde has an absolute phobia against cold."

"I wish you had told me, I could have worn my shorts," Yank said.

"I'm sorry, I didn't think."

Yank looked at his watch, then cased the empty house and said, "Do you think we'll be able to get a good seat?"

Duffy looked around and said, "Well at least there will be one more person in the audience."

"Who's that?"

"Will Shroyer, the *Tribune* music critic," she said, "and there better be some more too. I invited a hundred people to my house afterwards for the reception."

A few minutes later they began to come in. Two women came together and began fanning themselves with the programs that were on the table in the foyer, and then a man came and Duffy turned suddenly furious.

"What's the matter, Duffy?" Yank said.

"That's not Will Shroyer," she said. "They've sent some underling. It's just like Olin," she grumbled, "to shuffle this off on the second string."

Yank looked at his watch, it was eight o'clock, time for the concert to begin. He was perspiring profusely and he decided the temperature must have been around eighty-five degrees, and the heat cut right through his lightweight suit. He counted fifteen people in the audience.

Duffy read his mind and said, "It's very hard to get audiences for serious music these days." Yank nodded. In five minutes three more people had joined them in the audience and Clyde came out on the stage dressed in long, baggy woolen pants and a ski jacket with a woolen hat that had flaps over his ears, and a scarf wrapped around his neck.

At first glance, Clyde looked like a meerkat, one of those awkward furry animals with the triangular head too large for the body—standing on its hind legs in seeming defiance of gravitational principles. Large black patches about the pink eyes make them look eerily large. The arms are longer than a human's, the better to reach the piano keys.

Delia had married late and produced her issue on the brink of menopause. The resulting offspring were exceedingly bright and very strange.

Duffy handed Yank a program. The first offering was a Bach prelude and fugue in c minor from the first book of the *Well-Tempered Clavier*, and Clyde sat down at the piano and adjusted the bench.

Then he readjusted the bench.

And he adjusted some more, and it was another eight minutes before the height of the bench seemed to satisfy him and he put his hands up to play.

Yank thought the old duffer played tolerably well. He had a quality Yank found engaging.

Suddenly Yank was aware of a groaning sound coming from the direction of the stage. At first he thought it was a malfunctioning of the heating system and he prayed for a breakdown, but then his attention was directed to the stage where Clyde was working away.

Yank leaned over to Duffy and whispered, "My God, is he singing?"

Duffy nodded without taking her eyes off the performer.

Unfortunately, even Yank could tell that his singing was badly out of tune and it sounded rather like someone suffering from low abdominal pains. At the end of the piece, Clyde acknowledged the applause with a quick nod toward the audience without getting up off the seat, and Yank thought that there was something about his face that expressed resentment.

Clyde then twinkled through a Mozart sonata (B flat major) and pounded Beethoven's "Pathetique" before intermission. At intermission, Duffy glanced over the crowd and said, "Well I'm glad I talked him out of playing at the Theater Arts Center." The concert hall had been named for her, but she always modestly referred to it by its generic name. While they were waiting for Clyde to return to the stage, Yank looked around casually and said, "I don't see Olin and his wife."

Duffy's face sagged. "No," she said, "Olin wouldn't come to this."

"That's too bad," Yank said, gently feeding the fire. "I should think he might want to come just to influence your vote in the trust, if nothing else."

"Olin knows my vote is the majority. Sometimes, I guess he takes me for granted." She shook her head slowly. "He's having such problems."

"Oh?"

She nodded, "He and his wife are separated."

"I'm sorry to hear that."

"Yes, isn't it terrible? Five children. That's the first separation in our family, and I fear it will soon be the first divorce."

"Olin just isn't acting up to the tradition, is he?"

She shook her head, "No, I suppose he is a bit of a maverick."

Clyde made his re-entrance still with his ski jacket, hat and scarf. The second half opened with some schmaltz from Debussy, followed by "Aufschwung" by Robert Schumann. Short pieces by Charles Ives and Dimitri Shostakovich appeared back-to-back, Clyde's contribution to detente.

The program closed with a rousing rendition of Prokofiev's "Seventh Piano Sonata" which quite excited and exhausted Yank. Clyde stomped off the stage in a huff.

They found Clyde pacing his dressing room as though impatiently waiting for hordes of people to come bearing their plaudits.

"Oh, Clyde, you played so beautifully," Duffy enthused. Clyde looked at her with blank eyes.

Yank stepped into the breach, "I thought so too," he said, extending his hand to shake the artist's hand. Clyde looked down at it as though it were diseased and drew back.

"Oh, I'm sorry," Duffy said, "Clyde doesn't shake hands, he's afraid it passes germs."

Yank nodded as if to say, "Shucks, that's all right with me."

"Terrible house," Clyde complained.

"Well," Duffy smiled, "word will get around about how good you were. The next one will be larger."

Clyde frowned, "Next one?" he asked. "I think tonight proved the concert is dead."

"What on earth do you mean?" Duffy said.

"I could have made one recording in this time that could have been heard by millions of people. The mistakes could have been patched out, the rough spots smoothed over and I'd sound like a genius like all those people do on recordings: flawless and passionless."

"Oh, but dear, you sounded like genius tonight," Duffy said. "No one could have asked for more."

"I'll second that," Yank said.

"Now come along to the house," Duffy said. "We're going to have a little party in your honor."

"Oh, I don't know," Clyde said, "I may catch cold. You always keep your house so cold."

"Oh no, I've warmed it up for you," she said, and Yank frowned.

The party at Duffy's house was better attended than the concert. Duffy handled good-naturedly those who came to the party without coming to the concert, saying things like, "You naughty girl, you know the concert was a prerequisite for attending the party," and the old girl would smile sheepishly and offer some fair excuse and then volunteer to go home only to have Duffy pat her hand and say, "Oh dear, I wouldn't dream of it."

Yank sat next to the hero of the evening on the couch and searched valiantly for some common ground on which to open a discussion of Clyde's vast holdings in the *Tribune* trust. And after forty minutes of listening to him discourse on the evils of concerts and the relative merits of recordings, Yank made one attempt.

"Clyde," he said, "we are fellow stockholders in the *Tribune*, and I just wondered if I ever had a proposal to make that might alter the direction of the paper, would you consider listening to it?"

Clyde waved his hand peremptorily and said, "Duff handles all that for me. I'm an artist and I'm sure you'll understand," he said with a stab at graciousness, "that art and business just do not mix."

Yank nodded, "So," he said, "anything that Duffy does is all right with you?"

"Absolutely," he said, his long bony fingers swooping up on the silver tray of the gray-haired woman with the black dress and white apron as she passed, retrieving a mushroom cap stuffed with crab meat. He tossed it in his mouth and seemed to swallow it without chewing.

# 81

I know I have to make it on my own merit. My father told me the board of directors would have to approve any appointment and I have to show them my worth. I am doing a good job and getting people to like me.

—Benjamin Olin Sutler
Fifth Generation at the
Los Angeles *Tribune*

Duffy was waiting for Olin in his office when he arrived the next morning.

Olin was furious to see her there under the cheetah head, and decided then and there to stuff her too.

"Hello, Mother," he said, shuffling distractedly the letters that had been placed there for his signature. He was trying to hide his anger at his mother's intrusion into his sanctuary.

"I missed you last night," she said, in that subtly accusatory tone she was so good at.

Olin could not understand to what she was referring. "Last night?"

"Your cousin's concert."

"Oh, Mom," he said, begging for mercy. "I do my bit concert-wise—you know I don't like them, but I show my face and carry the *Tribune* flag. But Clyde?" He shook his head. "Don't you think that's asking too much?"

"No, I don't," she said stiffening. "He holds twenty-two-and-a-half percent of the trust, after all. It wouldn't take much more than that to vote you out. What do you have, Olin? Six, seven percent now?"

"What has listening to Clyde bang the piano got to do with the paper?" He straightened his tie.

"If you don't see that, Olin, you've got a terrible blind spot."

"I was busy," he ran his hand through his hair and grumbled, as if asking her forgiveness.

"Why wasn't Will Shroyer there?" She was accusing him again—

Olin looked at her sharply, exasperated.

He was sick and tired of his mother's meddling in trivial aspects of his job. He was now not only the editor-in-chief and publisher of the *Tribune*, but chief executive officer of the *Tribune* enterprises as well. And just as he competed in sports of strength and speed, Olin Sutler competed with all rivals, real and imagined. He had taken a successful company and rammed it right through the top of the charts, and every indicator known to man was blown sky-high.

Olin Sutler, the boy who said "Gosh" when his father announced he was the new publisher of the *Tribune* at thirty-four; Olin Sutler, the athlete they accused of having a muscle-bound brain; Olin Sutler, the overgrown kid who seemed more interested in surfing and speed than surviving—*that* Olin Sutler had pushed a provincial empire to national prominence, buying up, it seemed, everything in sight, making it *the* major publishing company in the world, with profits soaring like a fatal fever.

And here was his mother, invading the sanctuary of his office as though he were an adolescent with a runny nose. Why? To bitch.

"Well, Mother," Olin said, impatient for reason, "I talked about it with him and we just didn't feel it was a major musical event."

"So you sent in the second string?"

He looked at her and decided she would meddle in his business as long as she lived if he didn't do something about it. "It was reviewed," he said. "What more do you want?"

"Did you read it? You needed a microscope to see it and it was so condescending."

"What did you expect?"

"Better treatment for your father's cousin. All these years and he's never asked for a thing." Her voice was rising. "The least you could have done was treat him civilly."

"Oh," he exploded, "that's too crazy for words—you put on a thing at the old Ebel and about a dozen people show up and we should play it like the Academy Awards because he's a stockholder. I've got news for you, Mother. We have thousands of stockholders now and we aren't a little-bitty, ass-kissing family paper anymore."

"Olin!"

"Don't 'Olin' me anymore. *I'm* the publisher here now and *I* make the decisions, and my next decision is you are going to retire."

"What?" She had not considered it. "But I don't want to retire," she said.

"Then you misunderstand. I'm not giving you a choice. We are moving you out of your office—we need the space for a productive staff member. If you want to look over my shoulder, from now on you'll have to do it from your home—I'm forty-eight years old and I don't want any more of your damn interference—"

Tears filled her eyes like a cup too full of kindness. She wasn't going to say "After all I've done for you—" She just said, "But I'm on the board of directors," as though that would immunize her.

"But you are going to *resign*, Mother."

"I'm *not* going to resign," she insisted.

"Go gracefully," he said, the threat hanging on his lips.

She pouted, wiping her tears, sniffing. "What if I don't?"

"Then you'll go ungracefully."

As soon as the door to his office closed behind his mother, Olin called his secretary. "Have my mother's portrait taken from the meeting room and put in storage," he said.

Duffy drove her car home in a daze. She hoped the movers would break the picture of Olin that sat on her *Tribune* office desk.

When she got in the house she didn't know where to turn. Her husband was dead. Who would understand how callously her son had treated her?

Her head was splitting when she went to the phone and dialed Yank.

When she heard his gravelly voice she broke down.

"What is it, Duffy?" Yank asked gently.

"Olin has—fired me," she gasped, then sobbed, pulling little puffs of air through her nose.

"I'll be right over," Yank said.

Olin had refused to see him. The publisher's half-uncle had tried, on several occasions, every trick and enticement he could think of—but the answer was always the same: "Mr. Sutler is tied up in a meeting and he asks that any proposal you have be submitted to him in writing."

Olin had been freer about giving interviews than his ancestors, and he was even pictured on the cover of several magazines—racing, surfing, motorbiking, pressing weights. He was a he-man through and through. He would rhapsodize to the interviewer about the joys of sports and the strenuous life. He was much more circumspect about talking about his business ventures, and many who knew him felt he was using his upbeat athletic image to obliterate the bad taste of the Earth/Craft scandal.

And here he was in his jumpsuit at the Riverside track with his hot little Porsche and four of his sons all decked out in their pit costumes in support of old dad.

Yank arrived an hour before the race was to begin and surveyed the track and the various pits until he saw the big man and his sons.

He saw a lot of people who looked like they would attempt to keep him out of the track area, but none did. They figured with the baggy suit and ten-gallon hat and his ninety-one years he must be a wealthy, eccentric owner.

The Sutler boys were busy checking the engine timing, tire pressure, oil and fuel levels and Olin was calling instructions to them. To Yank it was a touching family scene. Almost enough to make him desist from implementing his revenge.

Almost.

He stood facing Olin now. The sun was cutting through the morning haze and hitting Yank straight in the eye—Olin could have shifted a few inches and shaded him, but he didn't.

"Olin," he said, "I'm your uncle, Arnie." After a pause he added, "Junior," as though Olin might be confused.

"I'm very busy," Olin said.

"Oh, I know you are—why, I've been trying to just talk to you for over six months now—it won't take but a minute."

"What do you want?" Olin said, cocking his head suspiciously.

"Well I didn't come to talk about car racing. Seems a damn fool thing for a man in your position—"

"You going to lecture me on the evil risk of speed, are you?"

"Nope. Never could figure it though. Man against machine, is that it?"

"Man stretched to the full limits of his capability, is what it is. The excitement, the challenge, the danger."

Yank nodded. "Looks like risky business, all right," Yank said, looking at the car with the boys crawling all over it like snakes in the grass. "I've got a proposition for you."

"I'm not interested."

"Oh, you might be—as you may know I now control more stock than you do."

Olin stared at him. Didn't this old man realize he could just inhale and blow him to paradise?

"I have eighteen percent of the stock now—and thirty-six percent of the trust, for a total of about thirty-one percent of the voting shares—you have maybe sixty-four percent of the trust, max, or twenty-two percent of the total."

Olin smiled smugly, "But the trust votes as a block. We have you two to one."

"You used to. Until you so cavalierly dismissed you mother. Now I wouldn't be so sure," Yank said, taking off his hat and wiping his brow with his sleeve.

"What do you want?"

"To save you the embarrassment of a proxy fight—to keep your family feuds out of the papers—"

"But what do you want yourself?"

"The paper."

Olin smiled derisively; he made a quick calculation in his head. "You probably control more shares of the parent company already than the *Tribune* is worth alone."

Yank nodded.

"So why?"

"Let's just say to atone for the sins of your forefathers."

"That's crazy," Olin said.

Yank's jaw tightened. This child, who could easily be his grandson, was calling him crazy? "That may be," he said, "but you can either give it up peaceably or succumb to a fight. *I* am not giving up."

Olin put on his helmet and sank down into the driver's seat of the Porsche. He looked up at Yank as though he couldn't believe this old man could be a threat to anyone.

"I'm not afraid of a fight," Olin said, a grim expression contracting his features.

Yank looked levelly down at him in the car. Olin seemed a dwarf. "I haven't contacted the other shareholders—proxy fights are so messy—but your Earth/Craft caper should be powerful medicine."

Olin started the car with the help of his boys. Revving up the engine, he drove around the track.

Yank decided to stay for the race. He found the devotion to competitive speed appalling, the risks involved foolish—and he was not surprised when Olin won the race.

# 82

1980

It was a dusty rose couch they sat on in Duffy's living room. It complemented and highlighted their pink complexions that seemed to hark back to the flesh tones of babyhood. Ashes to ashes, dust to dust, pink to pink.

Yank held Duffy's hand. She sat like a neglected Buddha in her blue silk bathrobe that Warren always liked so much.

She was not using the jasmine scent any longer, but Yank was unable to notice the difference.

Yank was, as usual, wearing his three-piece polyester blend stretch suit, and the ubiquitous ten-gallon hat.

Duffy was distracted. She was looking out on the sun setting on her garden. She could no longer see the details of the yard, but it was a green and gold mist, like looking at an impressionist painting with your eyes half closed.

"What do you think, Duffy?" Yank patted her hand and tried to gently prod her wandering thoughts in line with his.

"Hm," she said, her eyelashes snapping down twice on her eyes, her gaze going back to the green and gold mist out back.

The house was in a kindly state of disarray. Newspapers and magazines were on the coffee table, end tables, couches and floor. Unopened mail was stacked on the table in the entry hall that used to hold the spectacular floral arrangements.

She had very few visitors, being estranged from her son and his second wife, Mimi. Her daughter, Carrie, had moved to London where her husband, Vandenberg Clarke, had taken his post as U.S. Ambassador to the Court of Saint James. Duffy had outlived most of her friends, so what did it all matter anyway?

A woman came in once a week to pile up the newspapers and restock the refrigerator, an exercise in throwing out what she had brought the week before and replacing it with new nourishment that would barely be touched.

Duffy didn't want any help. She didn't want company. From time to time she would try to conjure up the meaning of her life: her place in her husband's life, her charity, her sacrifice and devotion to her son.

Now her only regular visitor was Yank and she wasn't a bit fooled. He had an ulterior motive—it wasn't her companionship he sought. Why Lord, sometimes he would come and sit and maybe try to get her to eat, and she would never take the frown off her face. And she wouldn't say a word.

Other times she would chatter on for two hours without drawing so much as a breath of air.

Way back she thought he might have romance on his mind, but she was so dead to that sort of thing, he soon realized the hopelessness of it.

It was Yank's mission with Duffy to force life and purpose into her dead tissue.

When he tried, she just looked at him and shook her head. Didn't he *know* how old they were? Why goodness gracious, they talked about people with one foot in the grave. There was hardly anything left of them *not* in the grave.

And yet, Yank did pay her the attention her son didn't. Women like attention—there was no denying they had been ignored too long. Duffy had done her bit on that score, all right. And now Yank was giving her a chance to make a difference again. Yank who came to see her three times a week. Yank who sat and watched television with her, though he could hardly see the picture, while Miss Tober insisted on waiting in the car.

Duffy would sit in the blue silk bathrobe she wore when she denied Warren her bed, and she would remember those triumphant days with pride and chagrin at her *chutzpah*. She could remember all the details of those distant years, she just couldn't remember if she had lunch.

Yank wore the suit that he got before anyone outside the trust owned a share of *Tribune* stock. Now he had so many shares he'd lost count. But he knew one thing. He didn't have enough. Not with his and Nora Yates' from the Crown Newspaper chain, not with the two point one five percent of the public he was able to stir up.

Any way you cut it, he still needed Duffy.

And Duffy felt so good being needed.

And so it had come down to this: almost a century after the tiny one-sheet, provincial Los Angeles *Tribune*'s first edition was pulled off the inked type it had grown to be one of the one hundred largest conglomerates, and the largest newspaper business, in the country. In 1980 the family trust was worth over a billion dollars.

General Olin, to preserve the enterprise from outside meddling, had set up a trust to keep the power of the press safe in his off-springs' hands. And now, almost one hundred years later, by quirks of nature, menopause babies, the whims of death and dependence—an outsider—the widow of a direct descendant to be sure, but an out-sider reviled by many of the bloodline heirs, controlled the majority of the family trust stock.

She had come a long way from the Shadyside Sanitarium.

Sometimes she thought of going back to the serenity she chose to remember there. Sometimes her in-laws thought of taking out the papers to send her there.

Oh, it was all so hazy but cozy now with Yank beside her on the couch. She *did* feel good with him there so close to her, holding her hand like no one had for more years than she could remember.

"Duffy, will you help me?"

"Yes," her eyes opened as if waking from a long, salubrious sleep, "I'll help you. What do you want?"

"To vote Warren's share and Clyde's and Hilde's with me at the meeting tomorrow."

"And what will we be voting for?"

"New management. A new board of directors, with you rein-stated. A new publisher. Olin will have to find something else to do, Duffy—do you think he can?"

"He's divorced, you know."

"I know."

"First one in the family. It's hard for a mother to take—his wife wanted a life of her own—he was always preoccupied. She wants to be an architect—being a mother isn't enough."

"I'm sorry," Yank said.

"We're old," she said. "How can you still care? Does it really make any difference who is the publisher of the *Tribune*? In the scheme of things, Yank, it is very small potatoes."

"Duffy, I've listened to that argument all my life. I have hocked all I own to buy all the *Tribune* shares I can lay my hands on. I want this as a memorial to my mother, sister and sweetie—a monument to their sacrifice. Help me, Duffy," he pleaded. "Will you help me?"

Duffy pondered and Duffy stretched her eyes in concentration. Pain creased her aging face, her skin hung loose like a deflated football. "It would not be easy for me," she said, "in spite of the way he has treated me. I *am* his mother after all. He is my *son*." Her fists clenched, veins stood out in her neck.

"I know, Duffy," Yank consoled her.

There was an eternity before she spoke. "I will help you, Yank," she said, a smile drifting across her face.

Yank leaned over and kissed her.

# 83

Yank had just saluted the portrait of *Tribune* founder, General Benjamin Raines Olin, and said, "You may have started it, you old goat, but I'm going to end it." Then he was the last stockholder to enter the auditorium.

He took a seat in the middle where he could keep his eye on Duffy across the aisle.

The auditorium was seldom used and had a fresh look about it. Pristine burgundy chairs with a serviceable carpet to match and a small stage in front where all the assembled could look up at Olin Sutler, president of the company and publisher of the Los Angeles *Tribune*.

Olin opened the meeting by flashing his instantaneous smile at the audience of some two hundred capitalists.

He was, at fifty-five, even more of a bull than he was when he became publisher twenty years earlier.

He could press two hundred and fifty pounds, and could lift his new wife at the small of her back and with one hand press her to the ceiling.

Olin was at home on the dais. He was gracious, not above handing inordinate compliments to harebrained stockholders. There was little in his speech or self-assured manner that gave any hint of the fierce competitor he was.

And Olin had moved the paper to the top of the heap. He got the same kick out of watching the numbers mount up as he got out of riding his surfboard on the crest of a mountainous wave.

People wondered what he meant when he said he was going to make the *Tribune* the best paper in the country. Did he mean more intellectual and complete than the New York *Times*? More succinct than the *Wall Street Journal*? More liberal than the Washington *Post*? More ennobling than the *Christian Science Monitor*?

They detected what he meant was the Los Angeles *Tribune* would show more profit than any newspaper in the country. And this he readily accomplished.

Everybody in the room knew that.

There simply were not many unhappy *Tribune* stockholders. Olin knew that. But he also knew there were two unhappy stockholders who became stockholders simply because they were unhappy: his uncle, Yank Sutler, and Nora Yates Crown, chief executive of the Crown Publications chain.

But two were not enough. Olin knew they couldn't do it without his mother. "Blood will tell," he reassured his supporters when they questioned his mother's loyalty.

And yet, confident as he was that his mother would vote to keep him in power, Olin couldn't help but glance furtively at her from time to time, hiding his nervousness from all but those who knew him best.

After his canned opening welcome, Olin said, "I am happy to report the decision to name this auditorium the Arnie Sutler Auditorium after the man who did so much for the Los Angeles *Tribune* and who began making us the vital and diversified company we are today."

Olin flashed his smile down at where Yank sat alone, two rows behind the closest board members and across the center aisle and behind Nora and Duffy. "As you know, Arnie Sutler was my grandfather, but he was also my mother's father-in-law, and he was so fond of her—and he was Yank Sutler's father, and we are fortunate enough to have Yank with us today—for the first time, if my memory serves."

There was a smattering of applause from the board, and Olin continued. "I am happy to hear that my Uncle Yank has apparently thought so much of the *Tribune* that he went out and bought so many of our shares."

The same board provided laughter. Yank smiled ruefully and thought the kid was getting clever, but not clever enough. If he wanted to please his mother, he should have named the auditorium for her husband and his father, Warren Sutler. But Olin didn't want any comparisons to himself that close to home.

"We are gathered here today," Olin said, reading from notes before him on the podium, "to consider a proposal by a dissident group of stockholders to elect a new board of directors. You have been given the proposed slate as well as a list of the current directors. We will vote the trust shares first. The trust represents thirty-four point eight seven percent of the outstanding shares. The vote is on the proposal to elect a new board. The yes vote will signify a vote for the new board, a no vote will maintain the same board we have now."

"I will begin with my vote of ten percent. No. Paul Sutler is here representing thirty-six percent. Paul?"

Paul stood. Gray haired now, in his seventies, his voice was resonant and clear: "Yes." He had rehearsed. He held his head up with a touch of defiance. and was successful in contrasting his last appearance before the board, where he was asked to forego his membership and he walked out head down without a word.

Olin nodded with curt acceptance.

"Duffy Durham Sutler is here representing fifty-four percent of the trust." He paused and stared at her. She met the stare. She did not feel good. "Mother?" he gently encouraged her.

Duffy kept her seat and her eyes remained fixed on her son.

Yank twisted in his chair. "Come on, Duffy," he said to himself, "do it."

Nora sat still beside her, then after the wait became too long, she patted Duffy's hand.

Perspiration was standing out on Olin's brow—his gaze was wavering—Yank thought he looked like he was going to faint.

"Mrs. Sutler," he croaked hoarsely. "Are you going to vote?" She met his gaze but said nothing. Olin thought she was deliberately making him suffer. "Mother?" he said again, but this time it had a pathetic timbre to it, like a child asking for something he desperately wants but knows he can't have.

The claw of fatalism gripped Yank's heart. Could *this* be preordained? Duffy was dragging out the suspense unmercifully. Was it on purpose? Or was she sliding again into senility? Perhaps she didn't even know she was being spoken to.

Olin's mind began to churn. Up to this moment he had not considered that his mother would vote against him. But as he watched her sit there looking so strangely at him, his absolute confidence gave way to uncertainty, then to doubt and then to defeat. He was perspiring more than after a long, hard workout in the gym downstairs.

The scandal of Earth/Craft had matured him, had made him think he could cope with anything. But it had not prepared him for his mother. The gossip. The scandal! *Mother turns on son*, staring at him from the face of his mother.

Duffy was looking at her boy through different eyes. The son the doctor told her was dead. The son who was the first disgraceful divorce in the family. The son who had been embarrassed by his mother when she came home from the sanitarium. The son who thought he was doing something big for his mother when he called her on her birthday. The son who had callously fired his own mother—the mother responsible for putting him where he was.

And yet...she faltered. She was not aware everyone was waiting for her answer. She had dimly heard the question and she thought she had been ready with her answer—Yank had certainly been more considerate of her than her own son—and yet...the boy had done a bang-up job. Oh, Yank spoke of a better paper, but Duffy wondered who wanted a better paper. Everybody spoke of how much better it was already, did anybody care if it wasn't the New York *Times*? Los Angeles wasn't New York—we were more interested in bodies, they in minds. Olin with his body beautiful was the son of the town, not the father. Perhaps the "Better paper" cry was only the cry of those who had nothing else to cry about.

Olin's perspiration turned clammy. He was chilled to the bone. He was beginning to feel nauseous. His mother was going to vote against him—"Well, all right," he thought. "Get it over with. Don't just sit there torturing me."

But she just sat and stared.

Things just seemed to jumble. Where was Warren? Everyone seemed frozen—Warren would thaw them out. Olin didn't have that warmth with people. She wanted to go up and cuddle him, to warm him. Why was he just standing there? Why didn't he say something?

Olin was sweating away, insensitive to the feelings she wore all over her worn face.

Olin gasped for breath as though he had just run a marathon. If he didn't get more oxygen he would keel over in a dead faint.

"We will adjourn for a few minutes," Olin heard himself say, as though it were coming from somewhere else, "for a private meeting between myself, Mr. Arnie Sutler Junior, Mr. Paul Sutler, Duffy Sutler and Nora Crown. I think some compromise might be reached."

Duffy heard herself say, "No." But only Nora and Yank realized it.

Duffy saw Yank standing at the end of the aisle waiting for her.

"Oh, Yank," she said. "I couldn't vote against my own son—how could any mother?" In her eyes, Yank saw the agony of her apology.

"I know, Duffy," he said, patting her arm.

"Oh, thank you, Yank."

"Now I don't think Olin knows. Shall we wait and see what his compromise is?"

Yank sat beside Duffy with her hand in his. A new thought occurred to Yank. What were the implications of the vote in the trust? It was thirty-six percent to ten percent for the new slate of directors. What did the trust say about a quorum? If less than fifty percent of the shares were voted? Could it be binding? Could he keep Duffy from tipping the scales in her son's favor if she understood the implications of her non-vote? Or *did* she understand something he didn't?

Yank knew the lawyers would be scurrying about at two hundred dollars the hour to find out, and when they had they would engage themselves in putting the best face on it.

Neither Yank nor Duffy found the gumption to get up just then. It seemed such a long way to the board room for the compromise meeting, and they seemed to be running out of steps for what was left of the road. Neither one of them had lived their lives as a compromiser. It was a new concept for the old people and they didn't seem anxious to experience it.

# 84

And while the prophets
shudder or adore
Before the flame, hop-
ing it will give ear,
If you at last must have
a word to say,
Say neither, in their
way,
"It is a deadly magic
and accursed,"
Nor, "It is blest," but
only, "It is here."

—Stephen Vincent Benet
*John Brown's Body*

Duffy and Yank were left alone in the meeting room. The principal players had gone on to the *in camera* gathering in the privacy of the board room. The minor bystanders had scattered to other employments.

Two oldsters sat alone with their memories, and with each other; he gaunt, she fleshy. On the straight chairs they looked like a Gothic painting that might have been captioned, "Father and Mother Time take a break." They were two outsiders on the inside today. The world may have been scurrying around them, but they were sitting still.

Sitting, still, on piles of money. Money, Yank thought, so important in its day, was doing so little for Duffy and not much more for him.

When it was hard to see, and hear, and taste, and remember, what difference did it make—the number of zeros on those papers the bank sent every month? If it wasn't enough to buy the *Tribune*, it wasn't enough.

Duffy was so content with Yank holding her hand. He was Warren's half-brother after all, and it was a comforting link to her beloved late husband.

Yank wondered at the bottom line of his existence, as the hotshot young men of commerce would say. The young Turks who pushed the *Tribune* enterprises to ever greater financial glory, cooking the books so every quarter was more profitable than the last.

Bottom line.

Yank's bottom line, he decided, had ample zeros. But it was nothing *but* zeros for all the difference it had made here today.

And here he was holding hands with the real power of the *Tribune*, a quasi-senile darling who by herself—without Yank and Nora Crown—could have changed the course of the paper, had she just given so much as a nod of her head.

Here they sat, two dynamos with the steam gone out of them: Mr. Hollywood and Mrs. Los Angeles.

But time passes, and passes and passes. And Yank saw for the first time that morning, time passing him. He had come close to his goal, but the clock ran out.

The clock ran out before he began, when the *Tribune* and its crackerjack family of ambitious entrepreneurs took hold of that simple opinion sheet and pumped, twisted, bent and blew it into four hundred pages and five million ads, the fattest paper from General Olin's fat land; the fattest paper in the world. And it wasn't all ads. You couldn't be that heartlessly cynical. But the ads determined the size of the edition, and they lined up to pay $25,000 the page, and they sold their scandalously overpriced designer dresses, their little purses with some designer's initials on them—to a society willing to pass their identity over to some fruitcake who decided arbitrarily where a hemline should stop on its inevitable climb toward the doors of the womb.

And the flit put his initials on everything: handbags, sport shirts (over the northern breast), jeans (on the south buttock), skirts, blouses, underwear, eye glasses and candy boxes.

And the ads swelled the bottom line like nobody's business.

Yank should have known. They just had too much of a head start on him. Nobody could catch them. Not with four generations of firecrackers blasting every horizon between here and there until it all lay at their feet. These were men who moved mountains.

Shirtsleeves to shirtsleeves in three generations? Not the Olins and not the Sutlers. And not Olin Sutler.

This paper dynasty was made of steel.

And the family coffers were larded with over a billion dollars. BILLION! And if each and every family member tried to count their share of that billion, in dollar bills, and they counted them day and night without stopping to eat or sleep or go to the bathroom, they wouldn't be able to do it. Not if they each lived to be one hundred years old.

"Oh, the family," Yank thought. "The family." He had underestimated them. The family had an astounding, tenacious genetic thread that passed through them all, tying them together against fate itself.

And there wasn't a crack in their marble facade. Not one of them married a hippie or threw it all over to follow some *persona non grata* guru to the ends of the earth in hopeless search of asylum from the heathen tax gatherers.

One after another the rival newspapers in Los Angeles folded their tents. One after another newspaper dynasties collapsed of their own weight on a rickety-kneed third-generation playboy, or sold out to megalomaniacs for megabucks they could never count.

Television, which many predicted would knock off the newspapers once and for all, did its share, but it missed the *Tribune*. And Yank grudgingly realized that it was the bone and sinew of the Sutler and Olin clan that held it together, that magical golden genetic thread that set them apart from the failures.

"Oh, they were strong, the family men who built the *Tribune*," Yank thought. They were the heartwood of the family tree.

A tree strengthens with time, it adds life rings to its trunk. But the new rings are where the sap flows.

Yank could picture a nuclear holocaust in Los Angeles with the *Tribune* coming out of a meteorite-sized hole in the ground to announce the calamity to an unpeopled earth.

The *Tribune* was on the downhill leg of the roller coaster ride. Yank could throw himself on the tracks, but he couldn't stop the train.

Yank looked at Duffy beside him. He squeezed her hand—"We'd better go on in," he said. "They'll be waiting."

Duffy's mouth darted at the corner. But she didn't move.

All her life Duffy craved acceptance. Now she had it and it had lost its enticing flavor. Yank was holding her hand. Yank needed her, she knew that.

Olin, her son, was an altogether different kettle of fish. He made it a big point not to need her. Here she was with his fate in her hands and he just walked out and couldn't care less if she got to the next room all right.

Yank cared. Yank was holding her hand.

And Yank felt disloyal, holding Duffy's hand. Seventy years after the *Tribune* bomb blew up his sweetie, Theresa Lavendowsky, Yank still felt her youth and enthusiasm beside him. And he felt a bit tawdry holding Duffy's hand, but Duffy seemed to need the reassurance.

Yank squeezed her hand again. "Duffy," he said softly, "shall we go see what compromise they'll offer?"

He looked at Duffy and saw a woman at peace. She had been torn between her pride and the golden genetic thread that ran through her husband and son. She didn't consider herself part of that family any more. Warren was dead, and her son cut her off.

A child wandered into the room clutching a yellow rubber duck. He made his way on pudgy, shaky legs straight for Yank as though he were late for a crucial appointment.

"That's Benjamin Junior," Duffy said, seeming to wake from a coma.

Yank inclined his hearing aid closer to her mumbly voice. She repeated it.

"That's Benjamin Junior," she said a mite louder. "He's the sixth generation." There was a smile of contentment on her lips—as though she felt she belonged again. "He's my great-grandson."

The boy was handing Yank the yellow rubber duck.

"He likes you," Duffy said. "He's usually very shy."

"Lord," Yank thought. "Lord, Lord, Lord." He shook his head and clucked his tongue. "They aren't trying to tell me they have the audacity to run the *Trib* with six generations, are they? And I'm nothing but a sitting duck—and a yellow one at that."

Benjamin Junior proffered the duck again. It was the legendary rubber ducky seen on the "Sesame Street" show from public television.

Olin's little grandson smiled at Yank—Yank couldn't resist. He took the ducky from its generous donor. The child dashed his eyes to the ground, then back to Yank. He was playing peek-a-boo. Yank caved in. He began playing peek-a-boo too.

The child giggled in delight, and crawled up into Yank's lap. Yank still held Duffy's hand. In his other hand he held the yellow rubber ducky by the neck, that arm wrapping around Benjamin Olin Sutler Junior to keep him from falling on the floor and perhaps shortening the reign of the Paper Dynasty.

Yank's embrace spanned four generations.

Every person comes to a point in their lives when they feel old for the first time. It might be the culmination of several agitating calamities, or it might coincide with a breakdown of the mental faculties, or a disintegration of the physical body. To many it is the result of an emotional strain that might have been bearable at an earlier age.

To Yank Sutler it happened in this room, at the climax of his failed fight to take over the newspaper that he thought had been built on his oppressive personal tragedies; here, with a yellow rubber duck and an arm wrapped around his great-great-grand-nephew, in his other hand the hand of his sister-in-law.

Yank was ninety-two years old when the hope vaporized as though it had been hit by a flash of searing sunlight which in an instant changed the course of the universe.

"Oh, there you are, Bejunior," sang a cheerful young woman with a fashion designer's name on the tight buns of her jeans. She swept through the room like an eagle with a forgotten purpose, and lifted Benjamin Junior off Yank's lap.

Her designer brassiere could be seen harnessing her significant mammary glands through a sheer white silk blouse. Through those paps had flown the juices to sustain yet another generation of Sutler men in their tenacious hold on the *Tribune*.

Mrs. Benjamin Sutler smiled at the old man. Yank squinted at her and saw a fertility goddess who was doing her part in passing on that golden genetic thread.

"I'm sorry," she said. "I hope Bejunior didn't bug you."

"Oh no," Yank said, and then his voice trailed off over the lad and the boy's mother, over Duffy by his side, and out into the streets of Los Angeles where skyscrapers were pushing out of the earth like stalagmites out of the yawning dry mouths of desert caves.

"They're waiting for you inside," the young mother said, and for a moment Yank couldn't think why.

He patted Duffy's hand. "Ready?" he asked, standing up to relieve her of the burden of answering, for he could tell by looking at her that she didn't know either, where they were going, or why.

The compromise was announced in the paper the next morning and sent to all the stockholders on *Tribune* stationery with "For Immediate Release" typed in the top right corner, as though the stockholders were newspapers themselves.

> Effective immediately, Olin Sutler will rise to the chairmanship of the board of directors of the *Tribune* companies.
> His duties as publisher of the Los Angeles *Tribune* will be assumed by Ruppert Jones, who heretofore had the title of Assistant to the Publisher. It is the first time in the 98-year history of the *Tribune* that the publisher will not be a member of the founding family.

It went on to say that several new directors had been named and some had resigned—five of the directors were Yank's—not enough for a majority, but enough to "stir up a hornet's nest," as Olin put it in the meeting.

What the release did not allude to was that an additional agreement had been signed, but not released, that Olin Sutler would step down from his chairmanship of the board of directors within five years. A time Yank would probably not live to see, but a time when Olin's son—the next in the line of bandits, cutthroats and thieves, as Yank liked to consider them—would be only thirty-four years old and hardly suitable to publish the new *Tribune*. Of course Olin had only been thirty-four when he became publisher, but that was Duffy's doing, and Duffy was out of it now. Just to be safe, Yank had the battery of company lawyers write an additional stipulation that any subsequent family member who was promoted to the rank of publisher of the *Tribune*, would have to have the vote of two-thirds of the directors—as would the addition of, or replacement of, any of the directors.

"I'm sorry," Duffy said to Yank after the meeting was over.

Walking together from the board room into the anteroom where the portraits of the Olin and Sutler *Tribune* publishers hung, a tenure spanning almost one hundred years, Duffy said, "I let you down," intoning it as a simple statement of fact, then the question for reassurance came softly on his name, "Yank?"

She watched his face. He didn't reassure her. She stumbled on, a mixture of halting explanation and apology:

"I…my own son…I gave him life, Yank…twice…I couldn't…."

Yank tipped his hat to her, then seeing the desperation on her time-torn face, the face that could never begin to show the heartbreaks it absorbed, he took her hand and intertwined it with his arm.

Nora Yates Crown strode by with a look on her cherubic face

untainted by reverence.

"Sell," she said with a wry smile, and escaped from the Velvet Prison for the last time.

Duffy looked up into Yank's eyes. "I let you down," she repeated as though each repetition might assuage her guilt.

Yank patted her arm.

"You did what you had to do, Duffy. Circumstances, your makeup, timing. We do what we must. I did what I had to do. Perhaps the fulfillment is in the journey and not the arrival." His hand went to his ten-gallon cowboy hat, unconsciously, and he touched it as though making a resolution.

"That genetic thread runs through me, too," he said. "But I couldn't weave with it on the inside—so I had to use it on the outside. But too many of those threads were intertwined on the inside. The rope was too strong. Too many foes, for too many generations. I knew them all, Duffy—no other living soul did—but it colored my thinking—warped it." His rheumy eyes cast off from Duffy. He was at sea. His breathing had the labored weight of leaden introspection. "I guess at our age, Duffy, time is our only enemy."

"If you had it to do all over, Yank," Duffy asked, "knowing it would come out this way, what would you have done differently?"

Yank looked at her as though it weren't a serious question. His hand went back to the sweat-stained hat and he twisted the brim up and down. The eyes behind the glasses that were as thick as the bottoms of Coke bottles, pinched to activate the brain. Duffy watched the whole process and was sorry she asked the question.

"Not a thing, Duffy," he said at last. "Not a damn thing."

Duffy smiled her warmest off-guard smile. Yank had alleviated her guilt, and she felt young again.

"May I give you a lift?" she asked. "I have a car waiting."

"No thanks, Duffy, Miss Tober's waiting at the curb to give me the devil."

When Duffy turned her back to start out of the room, Yank swiveled his head to take in all the portraits on the wall—the four generations of Olin and Sutler leaders, with the empty space where Olin Sutler had taken down Duffy's picture.

Yank turned again to face the portrait of the founder and putting his thumb to his nose, he waved his four fingers back and forth like a fan in hellish heat. Then, turning to face each of them, Yank repeated the gesture all around.

"That's for you," he said, and marched out behind Duffy.

He saw her to the elevator and they exchanged promises they wouldn't keep. As the elevator door closed on Duffy Durham Sutler, Yank Sutler's eye fell on the sand-filled urn that was placed outside the elevator on each level to discourage employees from throwing their cigarette butts on the elevator floor.

Yank took off his tattered hat, worn thin with the weight of time, and peered at it longingly, as though it were an old friend lately out of touch.

Then he took his old friend to his lips and kissed it, then dropped it on the urn of sand and headed for the stairway.

Two floors down, he cut through the news room where reporters' fingers were prancing on computer keyboards. They were putting out the news silently now, as though they were ashamed of it. Gone were the days of the insufferable but proud clanking of metal typewriters and linotype machines.

Yank found the side door that was used by the employees and went out into the sidewalk sunshine.

Miss Tober, his secretary, who would be waiting out front in the black Cadillac limousine, was the last person he wanted to see now. He would not be able to abide her disdain and I-told-you-so looks, and the hoity-toity, holier-than-thou lectures. He didn't need any of that today, thanks anyway. Let her wait.

Instead, he turned toward skid row. He was going to stroll his old stomping grounds.

He didn't understand why the sun felt so warm on his head. He forgot it was the first time in eighty years his head was uncovered outdoors.

As he marched down the downtown sidewalk he was the praying mantis on attack. There was a renewed purpose in those ninety-two-year-old legs.

He was leaving the city's most successful corporation, of which he was a substantial owner—and all done on his own.

If he had done nothing else, he had bought his way into his family's business.

Now the megacorporation with the mega bottom line was in the shadows behind him and he crossed the street on his way to the dregs of skid row, just down the block and around the corner. It was where he used to live with his sister, Cora Sue, in one room of Mrs. Ritter's boarding house, after his mother died, and when he fell in love with his father's secretary, Theresa Lavendowsky.

He lived there before there were paved streets and sidewalks, when the tallest building was two stories; when you could walk down the street without being accosted by a panhandler or tripping over a drunken bum or wading through life's detritus—you could cross the street without risking your life to some wild driver who drove as though every second were precious, a man (and now even the women were getting aggressive behind the wheel. It was a fringe benefit of feminism) who, the minute he got out of the car from his speedy journey was bored with the time on his hands.

And they blew their car horns at you to get you out of their way—those bleating, raucous blasts of mechanized superiority.

The cars had multiplied as fruitfully as any biblical admonition; so the politicos continued to build freeways. Now they cost $100 million or so a mile. Put in that perspective, the Sutler family would only be good for about thirteen miles of freeway. Not enough to get any of them to work in the morning.

Somehow that thought comforted Yank.

"What the heck," Yank decided as he turned the corner with a renewed spirit, then sank into the underbelly of derelict heaven, "maybe I'll do a little urban redevelopment."

His eyes behind the Coke bottles were slits. He thought it improved his vision.

"Yes…time," he said sucking in the same air that had sustained him for ninety-two years, the air now loaded with impurities. The process threw his shoulders back and his chest out. The air of his city seemed to strengthen his bones. The pulse of the auto horns, the squealing of car brakes, and the belching bus exhaust quickened his heartbeat.

"Time…yes," he said, so softly his Lucite ears at full volume couldn't pick it up amid the horns and brakes and hucksters and beggars.

"Time is our enemy, but our friend, too."